JAMES HOGG

The Private Memoirs and Confessions of a Justified Sinner

THE STIRLING / SOUTH CAROLINA RESEARCH EDITION OF
THE COLLECTED WORKS OF JAMES HOGG
GENERAL EDITORS – DOUGLAS S. MACK AND GILLIAN HUGHES

THE STIRLING / SOUTH CAROLINA RESEARCH EDITION OF

THE COLLECTED WORKS OF JAMES HOGG

GENERAL EDITORS – DOUGLAS S. MACK AND GILLIAN HUGHES

Volumes are numbered in the order of their publication in
the Stirling / South Carolina Research Edition

JAMES HOGG

The Private Memoirs
and Confessions
of a Justified Sinner

Written by Himself

With a Detail of Curious
Traditionary Facts and Other Evidence
by the Editor

Edited by
P. D. Garside

With an Afterword by Ian Campbell

EDINBURGH UNIVERSITY PRESS
2001

© Edinburgh University Press, 2001

Edinburgh University Press
22 George Square
Edinburgh
EH8 9LF

Typeset at the University of Stirling
Printed by The University Press, Cambridge

ISBN 0 7486 1414 1

A CIP record for this book is available
from the British Library

The Stirling / South Carolina Research Edition of

The Collected Works of James Hogg

The Aims of the Edition

James Hogg lived from 1770 till 1835. He was regarded by his contemporaries as one of the leading writers of the day, but the nature of his fame was influenced by the fact that, as a young man, he had been a self-educated shepherd. The third edition (1814) of his poem *The Queen's Wake* contains an 'Advertisement' which begins as follows.

> The Publisher having been favoured with letters from gentlemen in various parts of the United Kingdom respecting the Author of the *Queen's Wake,* and most of them expressing doubts of his being a Scotch Shepherd, he takes this opportunity of

assuring the public, that *The Queen's Wake* is really and truly the production of *James Hogg*, a common Shepherd, bred among the mountains of Ettrick Forest, who went to service when only seven years of age; and since that period has never received any education whatever.

The view of Hogg taken by his contemporaries is also reflected in the various early reviews of *The Private Memoirs and Confessions of a Justified Sinner*, which appeared anonymously in 1824. As Gillian Hughes has shown in the *Newsletter of the James Hogg Society* no. 1, many of these reviews identify Hogg as the author, and see the novel as presenting 'an incongruous mixture of the strongest powers with the strongest absurdities'. The Scotch Shepherd was regarded as a man of powerful and original talent, but it was felt that his lack of education caused his work to be marred by frequent failures in discretion, in expression, and in knowledge of the world. Worst of all was Hogg's lack of what was called 'delicacy', a failing which caused him to deal in his writings with subjects (such as prostitution) which were felt to be unsuitable for mention in polite literature. Hogg was regarded as a man of undoubted genius, but his genius was felt to be seriously flawed.

A posthumous collected edition of Hogg was published in the late 1830s. As was perhaps natural in the circumstances, the publishers (Blackie & Son of Glasgow) took pains to smooth away what they took to be the rough edges of Hogg's writing, and to remove his numerous 'indelicacies'. This process was taken even further in the 1860s, when the Rev. Thomas Thomson prepared a revised edition of Hogg's *Works* for publication by Blackie. These Blackie editions present a bland and lifeless version of Hogg's writings. It was in this version that Hogg was read by the Victorians. Unsurprisingly, he came to be regarded as a minor figure, of no great importance or interest.

The second half of the twentieth century has seen a substantial revival of Hogg's reputation; and he is now generally considered to be one of Scotland's major writers. This new reputation is based on a few works which have been republished in editions based on his original texts. Nevertheless, a number of Hogg's major works remain out of print. Indeed, some have been out of print for more than a century and a half, while others, still less fortunate, have never been published at all in their original, unbowdlerised condition.

Hogg is thus a major writer whose true stature was not recognised in his own lifetime because his social origins led to his being smothered in genteel condescension; and whose true stature has not been recognised since, because of a lack of adequate editions. The poet Douglas Dunn wrote of Hogg in the *Glasgow Herald* in September 1988: 'I can't help but think that in almost any other country of Europe a complete, modern edition of a comparable author would have been available long ago'. The Stirling / South Carolina Edition of James Hogg seeks to fill the gap identified by Douglas Dunn. When completed the edition will run to thirty-one volumes; and it will cover Hogg's prose, his poetry, and his plays.

General Editors' Acknowledgements

The research for the early volumes of the Stirling / South Carolina Edition of James Hogg has been sustained by funding and other support generously made available by the University of Stirling and by the University of South Carolina. Valuable grants or donations have also been received from the Carnegie Trust for the Universities of Scotland, from the Modern Humanities Research Association, from the Association for Scottish Literary Studies, and from the James Hogg Society. The work of the Edition could not have been carried on without the support of these bodies.

Volume Editor's Acknowledgements

The work for this volume could not have been completed without help from a large number of individuals and institutions. I am especially indebted to Gillian Hughes and Douglas Mack, for a continual flow of information and for wise general guidance, during the years of preparation. Richard Jackson has also selflessly pursued documentary evidence in the main Edinburgh libraries and archives. In the case of a well-known text such as the present, any editor is bound to gain from the contributions of previous editors and scholars, and in particular I have benefited from the pioneering work carried out by David Groves in Hogg criticism. Thanks are also due for particular help supplied by Anne Barbeau-Gardiner, Bill Bell, Valentina Bold, Michael Bott, Lance Butler, Peter Cahusac, Ian Campbell, Janette Currie, Penny Fielding, Michael Franklin, Hans de Groot, Robert Maccubbin, Wilma Mack, Eric Massie, Jean Moffatt, Jill Rubenstein, Patrick Scott, Christopher Skelton-Foord, and Peter Thomas. I am also grateful to the following libraries and their staff for permission to make use of and cite printed and manuscript materials in their care: the Alexander Turnbull Library,

Wellington; the Beinecke Rare Books and Manuscript Library, Yale University; the Bodleian Library, Oxford; Bristol University Library; the British Library; the Business Record Centre, University of Glasgow; the Central Library, Edinburgh; the Ettrick and Lauderdale Museums Service; the National Archives of Scotland, Edinburgh; the University of Reading Library; and the University of Stirling Library. In addition to these, I am once more especially grateful to the staff and Trustees of the National Library of Scotland for help received and for permission to quote from the Hogg manuscripts in that library. Anthony Mandal has also worked tirelessly in the Centre for Editorial and Intertextual Research (CEIR) at Cardiff University in scanning text and images, and in conducting electronic collations. Finally I would like to thank my wife, Gillian, not only for her continuing forbearance, but also for a range of practical help while researching this volume and in preparing it for publication.

Contents

Introduction

1. Genesis: Folklore and Theology

The current critical reputation and popularity of Hogg's *Private Memoirs and Confessions of a Justified Sinner* (1824) stands in marked contrast with its earlier publication history and reception. Of a relatively small first edition of 1000 copies, published by Longman & Co., less than half were sold through normal channels, the rest being disposed of at a knock-down price to the remainder specialist Thomas Tegg. A distinctly different version of the text, printed as 'The Private Memoirs and Confessions of a Fanatic' in the posthumous *Tales & Sketches by the Ettrick Shepherd* (1836–37), notwithstanding the latter's claim to include the author's 'final corrections', has all the marks of a hatchet-job, expunging challenging theological content, any hint of 'indelicacy', and the interlinking oral intrusions so vital to the original's narrative structure. Yet it was through this decimated version and its later reprintings, presented as if one of the Shepherd's less interesting tales, that the work was chiefly known until virtually the end of the nineteenth century. It was not until 1895 that an unbowdlerised version of the original 1824 text was made available, by J. Shiells & Co., under the lead title *The Suicide's Grave,* though this text on examination shows a myriad of small alterations and some egregious substantive errors. Tellingly, this edition also carried a disclaimer, in the form of a 'Publishers' Note', relaying a then current suspicion among literary historians that the book was 'not wholly written by Hogg', but that J. G. Lockhart, Walter Scott's son-in-law and biographer, 'had some part in its production'.[1] This assumption—in its roots not unlike the condescension Hogg faced in his own lifetime—was in turn hotly disputed by Mrs Garden, Hogg's daughter, who claimed to have the original holograph manuscript in her possession, 'showing no mark whatever of having been corrected or added to by Lockhart'.[2] Yet even then, T. Earle Welby, while favourably introducing another first-edition based text printed in 1924, could not quite let go of the idea '[t]hat Hogg owed something of such success to Lockhart'.[3]

The full recognition of Hogg's achievement in *Confessions* can be said to date from the Cresset Press edition in 1947, textually a derivative of the 1924 edition, but critically outstanding owing to its

Introduction by the eminent French novelist and critic, André Gide. Gide acknowledges his translator's advice about the book's special Scottish provenance, while recognising a strong theological component; but it was his focussing on the psychological intensity of the narrative that did most to ensure a secure place for Hogg in a modernist context. Subsequently John Carey's influential Oxford English Novels edition of 1969, the last until the present one to be set directly from the first edition, has done much to re-position Hogg close to the centre of British Romanticism. Interest in *Confessions* has also been buoyed up by the burgeoning field of Gothic studies, with Hogg being aligned with writers such as M. G. ('Monk') Lewis and Charles Robert Maturin, as too by post-structuralist and deconstructionist criticism, which has focussed on the text's conflicting narratives, multiple dualities, and sliding signifiers. One noticeable recent development is a growing interest in the peculiarly national elements mentioned only in passing by Gide. David Groves's assertion, in his 1991 edition in the Canongate Classics series, that '[p]erhaps no other novel presents a more balanced and multifarious picture of Scottish life', is backed up there by commentary which points sharply to divisions endemic in Scottish life both at the time of the plot and in Hogg's contemporary Scotland. Since then, Iain Crichton Smith has eloquently applauded 'a towering Scottish novel, one of the very greatest of all Scottish books'; while a poll conducted by Waterstone's bookshops in 1998, which placed *Confessions* third as readers' nominated favourite Scottish book, indicates that Hogg's once almost forgotten work now holds a secure place as one of the defining texts of Scotland in popular opinion.[4]

Whereas the re-establishment of Hogg in his original Scottish setting represents a considerable advance, the tendency to treat *Confessions* in isolation as an unexplained 'one-off' masterpiece still threatens to have an unbalancing effect. With a few notable exceptions modern critics have tended to treat this title in contexts other than the main corpus of Hogg's writing, thereby indirectly encouraging the continuing obscurity of much of his remaining output. Hopefully, the appearance of the present volume as part of a larger Collected Works edition will have (in the best sense of the word) an *equalising* effect, setting the special qualities of Hogg's novel in proper relief, while at the same time further disclosing genuine affinities with hitherto far less regarded work. A number of qualities for which the present narrative is so highly prized can be traced in almost equal vigour in a variety of other pieces, spanning Hogg's literary career: from 'A Singular Dream' (first published 1811), with its

complex interweaving of dream and reality, to the diverse supernatural effects and interpretational uncertainties of stories such as
'The Brownie of the Black Haggs' (1828) and 'The Unearthly Witness' (1830). At the same time, as the notes to the present edition
more than once indicate, our understanding of *Confessions* itself can
be enlarged through recognition of a number of intertextual
resonances in Hogg's other writings. Even *Confessions'* relative aesthetic eminence within the main *oeuvre*, which remains undeniable,
is most usefully explained in terms of circumstances directly relating to Hogg's literary career. The period of its composition not only
saw him at the height of his powers, but also settled in a relatively
stable domestic condition, and with a clear literary outlet in
Longmans available. As will be explained more fully in the third
section of this Introduction, almost exceptionally in this case Hogg
manoeuvred for himself a commanding position with regard to the
material production of the final text, thus avoiding the interventions
by printers and publishers which so badly scarred a large number
of his other works. It is also arguable that the use of the one-volume
form, at that precise moment a fashionable vehicle for new fiction,
helped concentrate materials more effectively than in his immediately preceding three-decker novels, *The Three Perils of Man* (1822)
and *The Three Perils of Woman* (1823).

Certainly no other work manages to bring together in such concentrated and dynamic form the various elements which contrib-
uted to Hogg's mature writing. Commencing in the style of an historical novel, after the fashion of Walter Scott's Waverley novels,
Hogg's complex narrative leads through a storm of political and
theological troubles to an ultimate destination in Ettrick, in the Southern Uplands of Scotland, and hence to the roots of his own imaginative and literary life. Though it had dwindled into a fairly backward
sheep-farming district, Ettrick Forest had once served as one of the
hunting-grounds of the Scottish monarchs, and remained a rich store-
house of oral tradition. A main repository of its songs and legends
was Hogg's mother, herself the daughter of Will Laidlaw, shepherd
in Phawhope, at the head of the Ettrick valley, and famed in the
region for having been the last person to have conversed with the
fairies. As Hogg's elder brother, William, recalled in 1813:

> Our mother's mind was well fortified by a good system of
> Christian religion [...] yet her mind was stored with tales and
> songs of spectres, ghosts, fairies, brownies, voices, &c. These
> had been both seen and heard in her time in the Glen of Phaup
> [...] These songs and tales which were sung and told in a

> plaintive, melancholy air, had an influence on James's mind altogether unperceived at the time, and perhaps indescribable now [...] [5]

After a rudimentary education at Ettrick Schoolhouse, interrupted prematurely through his parents' financial misfortunes, Hogg spent much of his boyhood and adolescence working as a cowherd or shepherd for a succession of local farmers, during which period he would have become fully familiar with, and adept at, the traditional art of story-telling, which provided the main form of communal entertainment in the remote and scattered farms of Ettrick and the adjacent parish of Yarrow. The input of Hogg's folk background can be sensed in a variety of forms in his imaginative writing: in multidimensional narratives, which leave much of the onus of interpretation on the auditor/reader; in a blurring of truth and fiction, enticing yet unsettling in its effect on those pursuing a literal meaning; and in a host of witches, ghosts, and other apparitions, who appear on one level to have a real physical presence, yet at the same time encourage allegorical reading, or a more sly human interpretation.

A particularly strong folkloric element can be perceived in Hogg's depiction of the devil, as made manifest in various guises in his poetry and fiction. While sharing a similar theological root, this is not so much the malicious demon of the medieval imagination, nor the grandiloquent fallen victim of pride found in Milton's *Paradise Lost*, but a more various and familiar figure, capable of causing devastation and mayhem in the natural world yet at the same time strangely bound up with quotidian human activity: Old Foxy who can lie while telling the truth and who plays on people's weaknesses and blind spots, chillingly frightening on occasions though at other points almost comically vulnerable through his own overreaching nature. In several Hogg poems he appears under the name of Gil-Moules: as an anarchic force of nature in 'A Witch's Chant', originally from 'All-Hallow Eve' in *Dramatic Tales* (1817); as a household spirit, capable of insinuating himself through keyholes, in 'The Harper's Song', in *Mador of the Moor* (1816); and as 'Gill Moullis, the shepherdis deille [devil]' in 'Jocke Taittis Expeditioune till Hell' (1830), written in Hogg's 'ancient stile', in which a loose word and thought by the shepherd protagonist leads to a whirlwind tour of the lower regions and an awakened moral awareness.[6] More than once in Hogg's tales speaking directly of the devil leads to his sudden (if not immediately recognisable) appearance, and the world of proverbial wisdom is never far removed in the narrative. In 'A Singular Dream', two such proverbs enclose a rapid and terrifying dream sequence in which a malicious backbiter in real life is transfigured into a Preacher, Satan, and finally a giant pig–the merging of the dream with the manifestation of the devil being a not uncommon feature of Hogg's writing in this vein.

Another prevalent feature is the association of the devil with religion, where 'the auld enemy' sometimes finds enlarged opportunities, not least amongst those adopting extreme positions. In 'The Witches of Traquair' (1828) Catholicism in its last brittle days of supremacy in Scotland offers 'a very convenient and profitable sort of religion' for his various pranks. Alternatively, in the 'The Barber of Duncow' (1831), it is a group of Covenanters or Cameronians (extreme Presbyterians) who are honoured by his presence, as the wife of the tinkler Will Gordon claims to have witnessed at first hand:

> ' [...] there was a great deal o' thae prayin' austere chaps, covenanters. A' the rest hatit them; an' mony a vizit the deil payed to them, sae that the hale town was keepit in a ferment [...] I hae seen him gaun to their meetings mysel wi' thir bodily een o' mine, wi' his long tail an' cloven feet, an' it was said, that some times he arguit better nor ony that was there.'[7]

The use of the folk voice as the main carrier of such insights indicates an origin in Hogg's own Ettrick community, which had attempted to maintain stability during the religious oppositions of seventeenth-century Scotland while witnessing the excesses committed by both sides.

Oral transmission would also have played a major part in the case of the other main cultural influence in Hogg's early days, that of the Bible and associated texts. Hogg's own autobiographical record in his 'Memoir of the Author's Life' indicates that he had only a minimum of training in reading and writing text in his schooling, leaving him virtually illiterate during the period of his youth: 'I neither read nor wrote; nor had I access to any book save the Bible. I was greatly taken with our version of the Psalms of David, learned the most of them by heart, and have a great partiality for them unto this day.'[8] As Ian Campbell has suggested,[9] Hogg's earliest knowledge of the Bible would have come through his family, especially his mother's instruction, leading to an unusually vivid impression of the imagery and rhetoric of the Authorised Version on his mind, and to an automatic association of its contents with the day-to-day experience of living. In mentioning 'the Psalms of David', it should be noted, Hogg in this case was not referring to the King James

Bible, but rather to the metrical version approved by the General Assembly of the Church of Scotland in 1650, and regularly sung in its churches from that point onward. Later, in 1830, Hogg vehemently defended this version against the charge that it was laden with 'the most vulgar Scotticisms, obsolete accentuation, and erroneous grammar', as argued by the linguist and poet William Tennant:

> Every peasant in Scotland had them by heart, and could repeat any part by day or by night, as suited his or her family's circumstances. [...] They are the first springs of religion in the peasant's soul [...] and to make any innovation there, would be with a reckless hand to puddle and freeze up the pure springs of religion in the hearts of the most virtuous and most devout part of our community.[10]

In particular, the metrical psalms would have featured regularly in family evening prayer, a process described by the narrator of the 'History of the Life of Duncan Campbell', first published in *The Spy* in 1811, in a passage where one might sense a strong autobiographical ingredient: 'It was my father's invariable custom to pray with the family every night before they retired to rest [...] I need not inform any of the readers of this paper that that amiable (and now too much neglected and despised) duty, consisted in singing a few stanzas of a psalm, in which all the family joined their voices with my father's'.[11] There is also strong evidence that he continued this practice in his own family, as his daughter Jessie was later to recall in a newspaper letter published in 1866:

> There was one rule of my father's which I wish every father in our land would adopt—whether noble or peasant—this was every Sabbath evening, before family worship, to assemble all in the house, including servants, when the half of the Shorter Catechism was said, ending with the Fourth Commandment the one Sabbath, and commencing with it the next. Each one repeated an answer and asked the next question. Some of us were too young to know them.[12]

The *Shorter Catechism*, which had also featured as a reading text in the 'juvenile class' at Ettrick School,[13] represents the last main ingredient in Hogg's religious upbringing. Arranged in the form of a question and answer sequence, and much used in the religious instruction of young people, it represented in its most distilled form the doctrine formulated by the Westminster Assembly in the mid-seventeenth century, which had since served as the theological linchpin of the Presbyterian Church of Scotland. Incorporating a number of key Calvinist beliefs, such as the effectual calling of the Elect (i.e. those chosen by God), it was also tempered by a strong sense of the importance of moral law, as stated in the Commandments, and of the need for good works as part of a holy life. When in *Confessions* the Wringhim family catechise, and young Robert profanely introduces his own question concerning 'Ineffectual Calling', Hogg is no doubt aware of offering a dark counter-version of his own family practice.

Hogg's entry into the world of contemporary print culture effectively began after employment as a shepherd by Mr Laidlaw of Blackhouse farm, in the Yarrow Valley, when in his early twenties, where he was able to read books from the Laidlaws' collection and teach himself to write. Gaining the local nickname of 'Jamie the Poeter', he became a published author for the first time with 'The Mistakes of a Night', a poem of rural courtship, which appeared in *The Scots Magazine* for October 1794. The then still current fashion for rustic Scots verse also helped encourage the publication of *Scottish Pastorals* (1801), which Hogg apparently had had printed while attending market in Edinburgh, though there was little to suggest at this point that its author would develop much further than a local curiosity or break free from the limiting stereotype of the 'peasant poet'. The opportunity to make contact with Walter Scott, recently appointed as Sheriff of Selkirkshire, and the editor/author of the *Minstrelsy of the Scottish Border*, whose first two volumes had just recently appeared, thus promised a considerable widening of horizons. Hogg's record of their meeting in Ettrick in late July 1802, as recollected from the distance of nearly thirty years, is remarkably fresh in its details, as if vividly remembered, but also has an emblematic quality, indicating that it had come to represent to Hogg a crucial turning point. By his own account, Hogg was working in the fields when Scott's imminent arrival, accompanied by William Laidlaw (son of Hogg's former employer), was announced by 'old Wat Shiel'. In the Hoggs' cottage, Scott then heard Mrs Hogg chant the ballad of 'Auld Maitland', the oral sanctity of which was subsequently asserted by its reciter in terms which viewed from one direction can only be taken as challenging the whole literary antiquarian endeavour as embodied in the *Minstrelsy*:

' [...] there war never ane o' my sangs prentit till ye prentit then yoursel', an' ye hae spoilt them awthegither. They were made for singing an' no for reading; but ye hae broken the charm now, an' they'll never be sung mair. An' the worst thing of a', they're nouther right spell'd nor right setten down.'[14]

The account also tracks a number of mistakes by Scott in interpreting a working agricultural community distinct from the legal world of Edinburgh and his own imagined Border associations. Having 'come into that remote district to visit a bard of Nature's own making'—Hogg's wording here is perhaps somewhat disingenuous—Scott finds himself at the Brydons' farm of Ramseycleuch having to endure interminable discussion about the relative merits of the 'long' and 'short' breeds of sheep, intervening with a supposedly condescending question, which nevertheless to its auditors at the time might have suggested a profound ignorance. A chapter of accidents also ensues on a visit next day undertaken by a party 'five in number' (including Scott's groom, 'a greater original than his master') to 'the wilds of Rankleburn', on the far bank of Ettrick Water. Scott's interest in the area lay in its connection with the aristocratic Buccleuch family, whose name supposedly derived from a hunting incident there in medieval times, and for whom Scott expressed a not entirely disinterested clan allegiance. Scott's romantic expectations of finding the family font in a ruined church are diverted for a moment by the discovery of 'an ancient consecrated helmet', but with bathetic results:

> Laidlaw, however, fell a picking and and scratching with great patience until at last he came to a layer of pitch inside, and then, with a malicious sneer, he said, 'The truth is, Mr. Scott, it's nouther mair nor less than an auld tar-pot, that some of the farmers hae been buisting [marking] their sheep out o' i' the kirk lang syne.'[15]

As a whole, the account offers the possibility of two readings. According to the first, Scott enters into a rustic community where legitimate romantic expectations are thwarted, while at the same time for Hogg a possible channel is opened up to escape the confines of orality and locality. Seen differently, Scott's narrow literary antiquarianism and a concern for family history not unconnected with his own personal advancement hit the buffers of a solid community, sure of its own values, and by no means impressed by activities which seem to them like relic-hunting. One of the most telling images left by the account is that of Scott's inappropriate mount and showy horsemanship, leading to his 'everlastingly bogging himself'.[16]

Throughout his literary career, Hogg maintained an element of detachment from official print culture, while through various strategies resisting the marginalisation of the oral as subordinate and primitive. In particular, as an autodidact, he developed an especially strong sense of the artificiality of conventionalised forms of discourse, one manifestation of which was his brilliance as a parodist, as strikingly apparent in his spoofing of contemporary poets such as Wordsworth in *The Poetic Mirror* (1816). In the present case, as Hogg's better critics have observed,[17] one should be wary of the two dominant narratives within the novel—the supposedly objective account of the 'Editor', and Robert Wringhim's more subjective 'Confessions'—not least in the first instance, where the reader might easily be lured into identifying the narrator with Hogg while at same time assuming that s/he is entering into a conventional historical novel. Hogg's editor figure is a modern, rational, North British gentleman of the 1820s who moves in the same circles as J. G. Lockhart (later named as his friend). Like Scott he has gentlemanly antiquarian tastes, and he offers to construct an account of Robert Wringhim's life (a life completely unlike his own) from sources similar to those given prominence in the Waverley Novels, 'tradition', 'some parish registers', and 'history'. An impression is given from the first sentence of legalistic impartiality, of evidence being carefully weighed, sifted, and, where necessary, qualified; though there is also a sense of remoteness, of not simply just a chronological distance from the events described. Moreover, even as the narrative attempts to stabilise evidence, new cracks and instabilities appear—in the alternative spellings of Dalcastle, then in the different versions of Colwan—so that from the onset there is a sense of underlying elements which formal written narrative is unable to hold down or fully explain. In the process, Hogg is undoubtedly also deconstructing the Scottian historical novel, with its claims to revivify the past while offering a judicious evaluation from a modern standpoint.

As events unfold, the Editor's claims to impartiality are found to be increasingly suspect, as his own establishment prejudices come closer to the surface. In the account of the marriage of George Colwan to Rabina Orde, even though the mercenary motivation of the former in making the alliance is fairly apparent, sympathies are placed squarely behind the boisterous country laird, with Rabina being made to appear frigid as well as sanctimonious, and the Editor knowing just enough about high Presbyterianism to be able mimic its language and tenets facetiously. This whole sequence at Dalcastle is told in a satirical almost burlesque style, which again one might be lured into thinking is at least partly Hogg, nudging us to empathise with the warm, human Colwans downstairs, as opposed to the priggish and hypocritical Wringhims upstairs, while missing the more essential point that a fatal division has opened up, between physical and spiritual worlds. In the Edinburgh scenes, where the rift finds political expression, the latter-day Tory prejudices of the Editor also come clearly into view. The scenes at the tennis matches again strongly invite identification with the hearty young George Colwan, rather than his 'methodistical' (p.16, l.42,[18] and a clear anachronism) younger brother, who at first sight gives an impression not dissimilar to the school sneak or outcast pestering the most popular boy at school. Another editorial blind spot emerges when George, walking towards Arthur's Seat, the high hill overlooking Edinburgh, experiences what on one level is interpretable as a vision:

> As he approached the swire at the head of the dell [...] [h]e was struck motionless at the view of the lovely vision; for it so chanced that he had never seen the same appearance before, though common at early morn. But he soon perceived the cause of the phenomenon, and that it proceeded from the rays of the sun from a pure unclouded morning sky striking upon this dense vapour which refracted them. But the better all the works of nature are understood, the more they will be ever admired. That was a scene that would have entranced the man of science with delight, but which the uninitiated and sordid man would have regarded less than the mole rearing up his hill in silence and in darkness. (p.29)

The final materialist interpretation given to the phenomenon (and supposedly in part shared by George) reflects as it unfolds the elevated stance adopted by the Editor to his material, and particularly the condescension of scientific post-Enlightenment Scotland. But the earlier 'visionary' response is not to be rejected out of hand. George can be understood to be momentarily in a state of grace, as a result of his willingness to seek reconciliation with his brother; and it is noticeable, in the immediately following sequence, that the moment he begins to think negatively the aesthetic spell is broken, a strange apparition then appearing, followed by George bumping into his brother when turning in fear in the other direction.

In the later stages, the authority of the Editor's narrative is also challenged by the intrusion of alternative voices. Whereas his own direct account offers only sparse and peripheral details concerning the assassination of George Colwan, Bell Calvert—albeit speaking from the margins of society, as fallen woman and suspected felon—offers a mesmerising account of things glimpsed at first hand, providing in this one of the sharpest manifestations of pure evil in

the whole novel. Just as telling, in their own way, are earlier remarks by Bell, when being questioned by Mrs Logan in prison:

> 'Did you know my late master?'
> 'Ay, that I did, and never for any good,' said she. 'I knew
> the old and the young spark both, and was by when the latter
> was slain.' (p.43)

The intrusive oral version invites us to re-evaluate previous events,
for instance the wedding night, where one might now suspect an
element of rape in the Laird's reclamation of his wife to the bed-
chamber. This also has the potential to throw new light on the younger
George's night out with the boys, leading to a visit to a 'bagnio'
(brothel); as well too on the cry by the mysterious figure seen by
Bell, as, through his connivance, George is stabbed ('Ah, hell has
it!')—is hearty George, no longer in grace, being consigned to Hell?
As the investigation conducted by the two now allied women increasingly occupies space and arrests the reader's attention, the
Editor is left juggling (not too successfully) with details concerning
the family relations of the wrongly suspected assassin, Thomas
Drummond, his narrative stuttering to a close with a kind of footnote detail concerning Drummond's later service in the Austrian
army and death in the Jacobite rising of 1715.

With Robert Wringhim's 'Private Memoirs and Confessions
of a Sinner', the reader meets a more subjective and rhetorically
charged form of narrative. In some respects, this follows in the mode
of spiritual autobiographies written by the Puritans in the seventeenth century, such as John Bunyan's *Grace Abounding to the Chief of
Sinners* (1666), where a number of echoes might be sensed. Some
critics have also pointed to an affinity with the *Confession [...] of Nicol
Muschet of Boghall* (1721; reprinted 1818), the last testimony of a notorious Edinburgh murderer who retrospectively interprets his associate as an emissary the devil, and ecstatically ends by asserting
himself freed from moral law through Christ's grace and forgiveness. Most of all, however, Wringhim's discourse is dependent on
biblical imagery and syntax, with a special indebtedness to the Old
Testament and the Pauline epistles in the New Testament. Like the
Editor's narrative it is thus driven by a peculiar mode of writing,
which from the opening sentences gives the impression of forcing
itself on outward events. Especially noticeable in the opening
sentences is how each word and phrase is given equal balance, with
the conjunctive 'and' soon forcing together elements which in
normative terms represent moral or experiential opposites (e.g. 'of

sorrow and of vengeance'), suggesting from the start that Wringhim's notion of his own identity and of the connection between things is badly awry. Any expectation of a deeper truth than the Editor's being made available, or one which might allow the reader to construct a more satisfying composite, are also soon dashed as the distorting effects of Robert's deceitfulness and solipsism become apparent.

As in the case of the Editor, too, Robert's text-driven account is countered by essentially oral (usually Scots-speaking) voices, the first significant such intervention coming with John Barnet, who evidently sees before him a disturbed child rather than one of the righteous. In all Robert makes a strange candidate to be declared one of the Elect, but this is what his 'father', the Rev. Wringhim, effectively offers him on his seventeenth birthday: 'That I was now a justified person, adopted among the number of God's children—my name written in the Lamb's book of life, and that no bypast transgression, nor any future act of my own [...] could be instrumental in altering the decree' (p.79). Evident here at least in superficial form are two main tenets of Calvinist belief: that God has already determined who shall be saved, and that a member of the Elect when 'justified' is freed from the confines of the old moral law. Through Robert's reaction, in some ways reminiscent of Romantic lyricism, Hogg intimates a dangerous ungrounding:

> I wept for joy to be thus assured of my freedom from all sin, and of the impossibility of my ever again falling away from my new state. [...] An exaltation of spirit lifted me, as it were, far above the earth, and the sinful creatures crawling on its surface; and I deemed myself as an eagle among the children of men, soaring on high, and looking down with pity and contempt on the grovelling creatures below. (p.80).

More especially, though coming from the other end of the cultural spectrum, there is a distinct parallelism with the Editor's earlier rationalist confidence, which had elevated him above 'sordid' men, just as Robert, likening himself to an eagle, here falls subject to a spiritual pride which from this point on will sever him from ordinary people, though warnings from that source continue to invade his narrative.

It is precisely at this point that Robert perceives the stranger who will accompany, then haunt him, for the rest of his mortal existence. Gil-Martin—the name matches the Gaelic word for the fox—drops plenty of hints that he is the devil, and at one distinct level the rest of the story is interpretable as a supernatural intervention aimed at securing Robert's damnation. Alternatively—and it is interesting how the name echoes that of M'Gill, the boy he had earlier impersonated to destroy—Robert has created his own *alter-ego*, a medium for the expression of his own repressed ideas and the suppression of remaining guilt, leading to more aggravated forms of schizophrenia as the story proceeds. As Douglas Gifford has suggested,[19] one of most ingenious features of the text is the way in which psychological and supernatural interpretations are simultaneously possible, Hogg's work representing in this respect a continuum of *double entendres*, just as its narratives are filled with doublings in characters and names. It should not be forgotten, however, that the root cause of the disturbance is the interpretation of a theological position, one moreover which Gil-Martin eagerly fastens on to, accentuating Robert's impression that he is immune from wrong-doing, while interpreting in horrifyingly literal terms the Rev. Wringhim's injunction that Robert be from henceforth the sword of the Lord. Whereas modern critical approaches have concentrated on formalist and psychological aspects of the novel, virtually from its publication there has also been a school of thought which points to an engagement primarily on a theological level, though the target has been interpreted variously as Calvinism, antinomianism (which places the Elect above moral law), or even the Kirk generally.[20]

Here one can point to two possible areas of influence, one contemporary with Hogg, the other relating roughly to the period of the novel's temporal setting. Though the Revolution Settlement of 1689/90 (followed by the Union treaty of 1707) had firmly re-established Presbyterian church government in Scotland, ratifying the Westminster *Confession of Faith* as its central doctrinal guide, it was not long before serious religious difficulties began to surface early in the eighteenth century. The Covenanting societies stayed outside the settlement, preferring to follow their own field preachers, while within the established Kirk a number of challenges were mounted by Evangelical ministers, hostile to what they took to be an increasing tendency towards rationalistic Christianity and Deism. A main expression of this was the Marrow Controversy, which occupied the Kirk authorities for five years between 1718–23, and where it is possible to point to a number of associations with Hogg. The original trigger can be traced back to a dispute concerning the proposition, requiring acceptance, put to candidates for licence or ordination by the Presbytery of Auchterarder, that 'it is not sound and orthodox to teach, that we must forsake sin in order to our coming to Christ, and instating us in covenant with God'. Behind this lay a number of basic concepts subscribed to by those considering that the Old Testament Covenant(s) of Works had been superseded by the Covenant of Grace, whereby as a result of Christ's atonement human beings might find salvation through saving faith. As a result of a complaint against the 'Auchterarder Creed' by a divinity student, William Craig, the General Assembly of the Church, evidently disturbed by its apparent negation of the importance of 'works' or good deeds to salvation, expressed its abhorrence of the proposition as 'unsound and most detestable'.

It was in the context of this 1717 Assembly that Thomas Boston, minister of Ettrick, recommended Edward Fisher's *The Marrow of Modern Divinity* (1645) to James Hog of Carnock, in Fife, another leading light amongst the Evangelical group. Consisting of a dialogue between four figures, with Evangelista representing Fisher himself, the *Marrow* sets out to negotiate a position between unsatisfactory views held by Nomista, who believes in the 'law' and salvation through good works, and Antinomista, who is against law, seeing grace as erasing all sins, past and future. Overwhelmed by the doctrine of Evangelista (who himself is not impressed by the reaction), Antinomista at one point rapturously proclaims his own success in having been 'fully pardoned all my sins, both past, present, and to come', expressing at the same time his 'pity' for 'them that are in the same slavish condition I was in'.[21] The *Marrow* in itself is evidently not an antinomian document, but it clearly represented to Hog and Boston an opportunity to reassert the 'purer' theology of the seventeenth century as an antidote to increasing establishment rationalism. Hog's Preface to his edition of the *Marrow*, published in 1718, moreover, was hardly tactful in depicting a battle between those 'burning and shining lights', who propound true Reformation principles, and their enemy, the worshippers of the Antichrist, whose 'anti-evangelical errors' are seen as gaining new strength.[22] After a brief pamphlet war, Hog and three colleagues were questioned before a Committee for the Purity of Doctrine, and on its recommendation the book was condemned in 1720 by the General Assembly on a number of counts, including its teaching that holiness was not essential to salvation and that believers were not under the Law as a rule of life.

In 1722 an unsuccessful appeal was mounted by twelve ministers, headed by Hog and Boston, whose responses to the queries put to them by the Commission are recorded in a pamphlet of that year. Especially germane to *Confessions* here appears to be Query 6

('If a Sinner, being justified, has all Things at once, that is necessary for Salvation?'), as well as the ministers' answer, which in its imagery and rhetoric (echoing Isaiah 40.31) bears some similarity to Robert Wringhim's response to his supposed 'justification':

> [...] the Path of the Just, tho' he frequently fall, will be as the shining Light that shineth more and more unto the perfect Day: Tho' he may at Times become weary and faint in his Mind; yet shall he, by waiting on the Lord, renew his Strength, and mount up as with Eagles Wings.[23]

The controversy continued to rage in print until 1723, the dominant issue being whether the *Marrow* and its exponents were antinomian in tendency or not. Principal James Hadow, who orchestrated the Commission's activities, had no doubt that both were, asserting in *The Antinomianism of the Marrow of Modern Divinity Detected* (1721) that such tenets 'tend to weaken and loose the Believer's Obligation unto Obedience, and to slacken his Diligence in the Study of Holiness and Good Works, as not necessary to Salvation'.[24] In their defence the Marrow men argued that Justification through faith rather than works does not mean that good works will not follow: on the contrary, not only are more people likely to be saved through this path, since full obedience to the law seems impossible to most sinners, but faith in Christ will also lead inevitably to the holy life. The 1722 Assembly nevertheless confirmed their earlier decision, rebuking the 'Marrow Brethren' for their erroneous doctrine, though allowing them to return to their parishes. Future preferment however was denied, with Thomas Boston remaining 'staked down in Ettrick' until his death in 1732, and a large share of the movement's supporters eventually finding a new home in the Secessionist Church.

As Louis Simpson and others have suggested,[25] there are a number of elements in the Marrow Controversy which might well have attracted Hogg's attention: among them, his shared name with James Hog of Carnock, who, though there is no evidence of any direct link, was well known in his own time as the author of more than twenty pamphlets, most of which concerned the rooting of grace in the soul. There are also a number of key images and doctrinal issues which appear to overlap. Yet one should be wary before claiming any transparent source here for the Wringhims' idea of Justification—the Marrow men, for instance, were castigated by their opponents for entertaining the possibility of a universal redemption, whereas the Rev. Wringhim propounds that salvation is only possible for the Elect. The likelihood that Hogg was satirising Marrow

theology in any direct way also diminishes when his relationship to
Thomas Boston is seen in a fuller light. More than anyone Boston
had argued against the charge of antinomianism, continuing the struggle through his notes to a later edition of the *Marrow*, published in
1726, one of which with characteristic vigour picks up on the passage in which Antinomista announces his liberation from sin: 'How
easy is the passage from Legalism to Antinomianism! Had this poor
man under his trouble and disquiet of conscience, fled to Jesus Christ
[...] he had escaped this snare of the devil'.[26] Boston's notes were
frequently reprinted with the *Marrow*, while his doctrinal writings,
notably *Human Nature in its Fourfold State* (1720), were hugely popular with the common people in Scotland throughout the century.
Oral accounts concerning his long ministry were still legion in Ettrick
in Hogg's time, and the figure of 'the far-famed and Reverend Thomas Boston, a great divine and a saintly character', features positively in a variety of Hogg's works. In 'General Anecdotes' (1827),
where 'daft' Jock Amos counters Boston's reproach for Sabbath-
breaking by demonstrating superior Bible knowledge, one might
sense an element of satire; but this is a far cry from the superficially
comparable scene in *Confessions* where the Rev. Wringhim is completely outwitted by John Barnet, and shown to lack both knowledge and understanding of the Gospels.[27] In fact, in terms of *Confessions*, one might argue that in some respects Boston is much closer to
the 'moral' preacher Rev. Blanchard, who teaches that salvation is
possible for all men and in their own hands, than to the Rev.
Wringhim who emphasises the exclusiveness of the Elect and whose
suggestion to Robert that the justified can do no wrong opens the
way for Gil-Martin.

Hogg's own position with regard to theological issues is perhaps
more profitably viewed in terms of tensions and oppositions closer
to his own period. Several critics have noted a similarity between
Confessions and Robert Burns's poem 'Holy Willie's Prayer' (written
in 1785), which directs a more obvious satirical assault on antinomian
hypocrisy. At the same time, however, there is a considerable distance between Burns's boisterous attack, launched from a broadly
humanist and theologically 'Moderate' position, and Hogg's much
darker portrayal of spiritual and psychological disintegration in his
novel. A less well-known poem of Burns's, 'The Kirk's Alarm' (1789),
written partly in defence of Dr William M'Gill, minister at Ayr—
whose surname is perhaps consciously echoed in *Confessions*—possibly takes us closer to at least one aspect of Hogg's own religious
outlook. In 1786, M'Gill had published *A Practical Essay on the Death*

of Jesus Christ, in which he attempted in open terms to describe the character and work of Christ, concentrating on his life rather than death. This however met with a series of attacks from both orthodox Presbyterians and Seceders, who suspected heresy in the shift of emphasis away from the atonement, leading ultimately to M'Gill's recantation of his own ideas in 1790. More generally, as some historians have observed,[28] the life and teaching of Christ were hardly a dominant concern for either of the two main wings of the Church of Scotland in the later eighteenth century, with the Evangelicals concentrating on Old Testament revelation, and the then dominant Moderates engaged in a rationalistic theology according to which natural order originates directly from God.

The new century nevertheless saw a number of challenges to established thinking, as well as to some of the central tenets of Calvinism. Thomas Erskine of Linlathen (1788–1870), the author of several influential theological works from 1820, rejected the idea of predestination, maintaining instead that God's love was boundless. Erskine's views in turn encouraged a number of liberal Presbyterian ministers, including John McLeod Campbell (1800–72), who was later to be deprived of his ministry at Row (or Rhu), in Dumbartonshire, for believing in a universal atonement, with Christ having died for all. As the deposition of Campbell and others indicate, there is clear evidence of a considerable hardening of attitudes at this time both in the established Church and among Dissenting groups, who themselves were seen as gaining ground at this time. Hogg's own views in this context are difficult to ascertain. A seemingly dismissive reference to 'Rowism' in his *Lay Sermons* (1834) suggests a certain discomfort with any loosening of doctrine, or furthering of schism within the Church, just as the containing essay on 'Deistical Reformers' argues against rational religion in favour of revelation. [29] A number of his imaginative writings, on the other hand, appear to point to the widest possibilities for redemption, while accentuating the importance of Christian forgiveness. Certainly there are signs that Hogg himself felt increasingly hemmed in by the resurgent Calvinism of the later 1820s: one tangible expression of which came in the form of the rejection of several of his contributions to *Blackwood's Edinburgh Magazine* by William Blackwood, on the grounds that they might offend the 'orthodox'. Hogg's assertion, apropos the first version of his 'A Sunday Pastoral' (1830), that 'the mixture of love and religion in it can only be objectionable to those who are ignorant of the pastoral life', expresses deeply held beliefs about the interrelationship of the physical and spiritual, while at the same time indicating that even the 'rustic' mode was now not immune to the age's new austerity.[30]

Hogg also had reason to feel uncomfortable about a newer kind of evangelicalism which was more invasively affecting the tone of society. A significant figure here is Lady Janet (Sinclair) Colquhoun (1781–1846), who at an early age had been strongly influenced by the evangelicalism of William Wilberforce, and who in 1799 married Major James Colquhoun, the inheritor in 1805 of the estate of Luss, in Dumbartonshire. Lady Colquhoun's difficulties in the early years of her marriage, in view of her husband's original 'prejudices against evangelical religion', are recorded in her later *Memoir* (1850); and it is not impossible that Hogg somewhat slyly introduced some elements of this situation into the more obviously mismatched alliance between George Colwan and the high-thinking Rabina in his novel. In the years immediately prior to *Confessions*, Lady Colquhoun began her career as an author of religious tracts, publishing *Despair and Hope* anonymously in 1822, followed by the more considerable *Thoughts on the Religious Profession and Defective Practice of the Higher Classes of Society* (1823). Both documents place great emphasis on saving faith, which is presented as God's gift through Christ and so beyond human volition and understanding. In *Despair and Hope*, consisting of a dialogue with a terminally ill cottager, Lady Colquhoun finally wins through with her point that blind faith offers the only escape from 'the bottomless pit': 'To receive a free salvation means, that you accept of it without respect to anything on your part; that your past life has nothing to do with it, and that even your future life can have no effect in justifying you in the sight of God [...] '.[31] Justification by faith is also a main concern in her second work, though Lady Colquhoun here makes a special effort to distinguish her own position from antinomianism, arguing that the fruits of faith will always be evident in good works. That she should make such an effort to shore up defences in this way is an indication not only that her own approach was vulnerable to accusations on this account, but also that antinomianism itself was currently very much a live issue. Another indication of its topicality is Joseph Cottle's *Strictures on the Plymouth Antinomians* (1823; 2nd edition 1824), a withering account of the preaching of Dr Robert Hawker and his son to their packed congregation, which, among other things, according to Cottle, involved people believing that they belonged to the predestined Elect only because they were told so.[32]

Ultimately, Hogg's concern in *Confessions* is not so much with the failings of Calvinism, or even antinomianism, as with the misuse of religion generally. In particular, the theological assumptions of the Wringhims can be seen to differ in a number of ways both from the teachings of Calvin and from the 'pragmatic' interpretation of predestinarianism found in the Westminster *Confession of Faith* (1647), which, with the associated *Longer* and *Shorter* Catechisms, formed the theological basis of the Church of Scotland. Above all, the Wringhims stray dangerously in making the following assumptions. i) *that an effectual calling followed by justification overrides all past sense of sin.* Calvin certainly taught that faith rather than works lead to salvation; yet, nevertheless, in writings such as his *Geneva Catechism* (1541), repentance is always closely associated with faith, as a twin Christian activity: 'the doctrine of the Gospel is comprehended in these two points, faith and repentance'.[33] The *Confession of Faith*, in a not untypical balancing act, manages to combine both components in its chapter 'Of Justification': 'Faith, thus receiving and resting on Christ, and his righteousnesse, is the alone instrument of Justification; yet it is not alone in the person justified, but is ever accompanied with all other saving graces, and is no dead faith, but worketh by love.'[34] Not only does Robert (who owns at least four Commandments broken prior to his 'saving') fail to come to terms with earlier sins, at no point does he manifest any sense of faith in Christ. ii) *that the assurance of election can be given by another person, and as an act of will.* The question of how someone might gain the conviction or persuasion that he/she was one of the Elect was one of the most burning issues in Calvinism, and quite clearly in personal terms led to a good deal of anxiety and doubt. For Calvin assurance comes through the direct act of faith, though some later Calvinists added an element of voluntarism to this. Westminster theology, while to some degree separating faith and assurance, and pointing to the need for continuing active virtues, more than once stresses that the calling comes through God's spirit working in the individual alone: 'God did, from all eternity, decree to justifie all the Elect [...] neverthelesse, they are not justified, *untill the holy Spirit doth in due time actually apply Christ unto them.*'[35] Nowhere in the *Confession of Faith* is it said that the assurance can be given through another human being, but it is no less than this that the Rev. Wringhim claims, through having profanely wrestled with God, to be able to offer Robert. iii) *that salvation is only available to an exclusive group.* The idea that Christ died for only the Elect is more obviously present in followers of Calvin than in Calvin himself, whose own position was that Christ died for all men yet all are not saved.[36] The Westminster *Confession* itself, though clearly subscribing to the idea of a predetermined Elect, nevertheless avoids giving any discouraging sense of limitation, while from its start warning that 'this high Mystery of Predestination is to be handled with special prudence and care'.[37] The Rev. Wringhim by contrast knows all about predestination, and relishes being in a narrow spiritually-privileged group, while having little pity for those who might be excluded. iv) *that it is impossible to sin or fall from grace once justified.* Robert Wringhim's behaviour after his supposed justification (which leads to his breaking all ten Commandments) offers the most obvious proof that he is not truly saved. Furthermore, though Calvin did argue that election cannot be taken away from a person, and that grace overrides the old moral law, nowhere in his writings is it suggested that the Elect were free to sin. On the contrary, faith will actively encourage good works, being 'the root from which they are produced'.[38] According to the Westminster *Confession*, while those justified can never entirely fall from a state of grace, it is still possible to 'fall under Gods fatherly displeasure', leading to the need for fresh repentance.[39] It is noticeable that virtually all the further errors cultivated in Robert's mind by Gil-Martin, such as the idea that one should anticipate God's judgement by cutting off the reprobate (non-Elect) in this world, develop through the 'logical' extension of the above false tenets.

Another sign of the fallibility of the Wringhims is their misunderstanding and misapplication of biblical text. It is only possible to indicate here briefly some of the main categories of error, though numerous examples will be found in the Notes to the present edition. A strong pointer is the almost total absence of reference to the main New Testament Gospels, with the Rev. Wringhim cultivating a specially unwholesome mixture out of Old Testament savagery and exclusivist spirituality selected from the Pauline epistles. His capacity for misunderstanding is apparent in the early interlude with John Barnet, where he inappropriately selects the title 'Apostle of the Gentiles' (adopted by Paul for inclusive reasons, his mission of allowing non-Jews to be Christians), and fails to see that Barnet's likening of him to 'the just Pharisee' in Christ's parable satirically points to his spiritual pride and likely abasement, it being 'the poor publican' who is most justified. With such tutelage it is not surprising that Robert Wringhim makes numerous errors, compounded at first by his own petulance, and then aggravated by Gil-Martin's corrupting influence. The fuller meaning of passages alluded to sometimes rebounds on Robert himself, as when he appropriates Balaam's violent words to his donkey ('if I had a sword into mine hand, I would even kill him' (p.105)), evidently oblivious to the full circumstances of the incident, in which the donkey sees a warning from an angel which his master cannot see (just as Robert has already failed to recognise several visionary warnings). One noticeable feature of Gil-Martin is his use of some of the darkest imagery in the Old Testament, especially when inciting Robert to violence. He also garbles text maliciously, and delights in double or unfixed meanings, sometimes providing thereby glimpses of his true nature and of Robert's probable fate. From his first appearance on Lady Day,[40] he has too a tendency to offer dark inversions of Christianity, especially the parables: whether dismissing Blanchard's life as no more valuable than that of a lamb, recommending that it is better that one should fall rather than a thousand souls perish, or imploring Robert to 'go and do likewise'. In distinct contrast it is invariably in the mouths of the folk or social outcasts, through various incursions into the dominating narratives, that the Christian message of charity and forgiveness is most strongly felt. Robert Ruthven, the 'auld carl' in the Auchtermuchy story who alone sees the devil's cloven hoof, noticeably combines folk wisdom (having reportedly been with the fairies as a child) and a religious belief that transcends denominational difference (his crossing himself at one point suggests a Catholic descent). Lucky Shaw, though reputedly a witch, is likewise the vehicle through which Robert hears of the Golden Rule, which has the potential to save him. Even Penpunt's '*Man mind yoursel* is the first commandment' (p.134), at first sight on a par with Gil-Martin's inversions, can be seen not only to reflect a healthy pragmatism but also to be not so far from the actual commandment to honour only God, since God can be construed as existing in man. Most revealingly of all, the Bible as introduced by such oral voices is an integral part of daily living, rather than an extraneous text applied externally.

Conversely, it is in the Edinburgh printing house in which his pamphlet 'Memoirs' is being prepared that Robert Wringhim returns for a while to his most arrogantly confident, glorifying in the prospective multiplication of his 'works [...] among mankind' (p.153). It is here too that the devil makes one of his more spectacular appearances, a manifestation which partly plays on the term 'printer's devil' (as used to describe an apprentice in the trade), but which more broadly reflects an association of print culture with diabolical activity that is pervasive in Hogg's writing. The diary entries which follow suggest a movement away from more public forms of discourse, just as a process of social deconstruction is suggested by the kinds of shelter Wringhim receives in fleeing southward, first with a yeoman farmer, then with the publican of an inn, and finally with a poor widowed hind, close to the border with England (with whom he feels safest). Though the biblical passages echoed now come chiefly from the book of Job and the Psalms, and one feels greater sympathy for his vulnerability, Robert still cannot escape from mental entrapment and self-conceit. Just as he 'misse[s] the manger' in confusion at Ellanshaws, and by implication the support of Christianity, so in the inn at Ancrum Robert inappropriately waxes eloquent in conducting family prayers.

Robert's last diary entry is headed 'Ault-Righ', and goes on to describe his arrival at this final destination, where he sleeps first in the farmhouse and then among the cows in the byre. This intensely subjective account is then followed by Hogg's own letter from *Blackwood's Edinburgh Magazine*, which thus positioned implicitly matches Wringhim with the suicide who, by oral report, worked briefly at A/Eltrive farm as a cowherd (the 'worst and lowest' employment in the district, according to Hogg's *Memoir*[41]). While it is tempting to identify this location with Altrive Lake, the small tenancy in Yarrow granted to Hogg by the Duke of Buccleuch in 1815, what is really being described is the much larger and older Eltrive farm to the immediate south-west, from which Altrive Lake had been sectioned off fairly recently. Since the sixteenth century the Anderson family had been tenants of Eltrive, and the Mr (David) Anderson who gives Wringhim shelter in the story, and resists at first superstitious prejudices, relates to actual tenants whose names are recorded in Ettrick kirkyard and whom Hogg knew about through descendants still living. More particularly, the James Anderson who as boy accompanies the Sinner in Eltrive Hope on his last day of existence is clearly based on James Anderson, sometime tenant in Eltrive, who in 1738 had married Alison, the daughter of the Rev. Thomas Boston.[42] Though their responses are filtered through three different narrative accounts in all, the Eltrive Andersons and their men provide one of the most stable elements in the final stages of the story, combining in their attitude to Wringhim both sympathy and wariness (qualities divided between the weaver and his wife in an earlier scene), while acting expeditiously as fearful Christians when the disgrace of suicide occurs close to their hearthstone.

The district then experiences one final invasion before the novel's close, in the shape of the arrival of the Editor and his party to investigate the reported grave. As Douglas Mack has suggested,[43] this whole incident, ending in the exhumation of the body, parallels in several ways Walter Scott's arrival in Ettrick in the summer of

1802. At Thirlestane market, the Editor's misunderstanding of *paulies*, meaning young ailing lambs and not a species of stock, indicates a remoteness from Scottish rural life equivalent to that shown by Scott at Ramseycleuch; just as Hogg's refusal within the story to engage in 'houk[ing] up hunder-year-auld banes' (p.170), at market time, has the air of a rerun of his resistance on similar grounds of Scott's more recent proposal that he attend George IV's coronation.[44] As in the case of the expedition to Rankleburn, five men proceed to the site of the grave (itself on the near side of Ettrick Water), the party being guided by another 'great original' in 'W—m B—e', and once again including William Laidlaw, as well as this time Scott's son-in-law in J. G. Lockhart. Whereas Scott in 1802 had seen an ancient helmet in a tar-pot, 'Mr Sc—t'[45] here retrieves a clasp knife and passes it on to an important neighbour. While, as the next section will finally argue, there is at least one other dimension at work here, more closely associating events with the Edinburgh of *Blackwood's Magazine*, the similarities with Scott's visit of 1802 are striking, as Hogg takes us back to the main starting-point in his literary involvement, while bringing to view once more a community capable of resisting the cultural condescension of both Sinner and Editor.

2. Edinburgh and the Blackwoodian Context

Notwithstanding initial intimations of a Glaswegian provenance, and the narrative's final grounding in Ettrick, *Confessions of a Justified Sinner* is unmistakably a work with strong Edinburgh associations. It can also be seen as reflecting some of Hogg's most ambivalent feelings about the moral and intellectual attitudes of the then self-styled 'Athens of the North', and, more particularly, his increasingly perplexing experiences as a participant in *Blackwood's Edinburgh Magazine*, the monthly periodical which he had helped found in 1817.

While most of Hogg's earlier works from *Scottish Pastorals* (1801) onwards could be claimed as products of the Edinburgh book trade, it was not until relatively late in life that he was to commit himself fully as an author to a metropolitan context. Even with the pecuniary success of *The Mountain Bard* (1807) and *The Shepherd's Guide* (1807), both published by Archibald Constable, his instinct was to return to the agricultural world as a tenant farmer in Nithsdale. It was only in the wake of his failure in this sphere, and after it had become clear reintegration into the Ettrick community was not an option, that early in 1810 Hogg migrated to Edinburgh in an attempt to establish himself as a professional literary man. In view

of his low social status, lack of funding, and limited literary patron-
age, the survival of his own weekly periodical, *The Spy*, for as long
as a year represents something of a triumph of resilience in personal terms. During its short run, from September 1810 to August
1811, Hogg survived the buffeting of early objections against the
paper's indelicacy (though such perhaps were later to prove fatal)
and honed a variety of voices and techniques for addressing an urban audience, while remaining inherently true to his own cultural
roots. He also developed a literary circle of his own in attracting
subscribers and occasional contributors. Through his friendship with
James Gray, a Classics master at the Edinburgh High School, it is
likely that he established contact with Whig political circles in Edinburgh, though ostensibly Hogg remained a Tory throughout his life.
Membership of the Forum debating club, which drew large audiences in the early 1810s, and where Hogg was a frequent speaker
and for a while Secretary of the society, would also have led to a
variety of contacts amongst up-and-coming professional and literary men in the city's burgeoning life, themselves eager to break the
mould of older institutional forms.[46]

With the runaway success of his narrative poem *The Queen's Wake*
(1813), Hogg seemed for a while to stand on an equivalent level to
Scott and Byron, the two foremost poets of the age. But even at the
height of its success, lionisation came on strictly limited terms. Hogg,
that is, was acceptable as a shepherd poet, whose effusions came
primarily as untutored inspiration, but as a poet with philosophical
aspirations or as a novelist claiming consideration alongside the
author of *Waverley* he was soon to meet resistance. Doors closed just
as suddenly as they had opened, with John Murray, the fashionable
London publisher, distancing himself from Hogg's next poem, *The
Pilgrims of the Sun* (1815), and effectively turning his back on *The
Brownie of Bodsbeck; and Other Tales* (1818), though again Murray's
name was on the imprint along with its Edinburgh publisher, William
Blackwood. In the 1821 version of his 'Memoir of the Author's
Life', Hogg complains bitterly of two elements that had made him
feel 'an intruder in the paths of literature': the disapproval of the
'blue-stockings', by which term he appears sometimes to conflate
the decorousness of literary ladies in Edinburgh with the increasing
primness of public taste generally; and, secondly, the control
exercised by a 'powerful aristocracy' in intellectual and literary life,
faceless in its activities, but in Hogg's innermost thoughts almost
certainly not unconnected with Walter Scott and his circle.[47] Karl
Miller perceptively refers to 'an Edinburgh ruled by piety and by

aristocracy, and by a literary élite or elect for whom [...] Hogg was illiterate'.[48]

When William Blackwood started up his *Edinburgh Monthly Magazine* in April 1817, in opposition to Constable's *Scots Magazine*, it must have seemed as if a more suitable and secure outlet was now suddenly available. Hogg's later claim in his 'Memoir' (1821) to have been 'the beginner, and almost sole instigator'[49] was later treated with derision within the Magazine itself, and has also been viewed with scepticism by some modern commentators. But it is not unlikely that Blackwood would have turned initially for advice to Hogg, with whom he was currently on good terms, especially considering Hogg's track record as an editor himself, his contributions to other journals, and contacts with suitable contributors. Hogg nowhere describes himself as actively editing the Magazine, which would have been virtually impossible owing to his settlement at Altrive Lake; and there is no special reason to doubt his claim that he was instrumental in helping form Blackwood's association with Thomas Pringle, one of the two original editors. Hogg also provided hard support in the form of contributions, most noticeably through the series of 'Tales and Anecdotes of the Pastoral Life', which provided a valuable backbone in the first three issues of an otherwise lacklustre miscellany.

Hogg also cultivated valuable new contributors, among them John Wilson (1785–1854), recently qualified as an advocate and in literary terms then a relatively unknown poet, with whom he had become friendly in 1813. 'Wilsons papers', Blackwood was advised, 'have a masterly cast about them; a little custom would make him the best periodical writer of the age keep hold of him'.[50] It is not impossible that he also helped steer the even younger J. G. Lockhart in the same direction, after the latter's return from a visit to Germany in the summer of 1817. When Blackwood broke with the original editors, after poor sales, and both immediately went over instead to Constable, Hogg threw his weight fully behind Blackwood, sending him the foundations of the satirical 'Chaldee Manuscript', representing in a prophetic biblical style the rivalry of the Tory publisher (as 'Ebony') with Constable ('the Crafty') and his Whig supporters. Even Hogg's origination of Chaldee, which appeared in the first issue of the revamped *Blackwood's Edinburgh Magazine*, in October 1817, and caused an outcry in Edinburgh, was later disputed, though in this case he had managed to hold on to undeniable proof. Certainly it was much revised and expanded –'interlarded', in his own words, with a good deal of 'deevilry'[51]–most probably by

Lockhart and Wilson. But it was still Hogg who had provided the original imaginative impetus, and who, as a result, might legitimately claim to have set *Blackwood's Edinburgh Magazine* on course towards becoming the most innovative and vital new Tory magazine of the 1820s, with an extensive audience both in Scotland and England.

One of Hogg's earlier contributions to the new *Blackwood's*, 'A Letter to Charles Kirkpatrick Sharpe, Esq. on his Original Mode of Editing Church History', offers an illustration of the potential of this medium for Hogg in developing a special voice of his own. Sharpe's 1817 edition of James Kirkton's *Secret and True History of the Church of Scotland*, though at first sight a purely esoteric antiquarian publication, was actually born in the fire of ideological opposition in contemporary Edinburgh. Kirkton's original History provides an eye-witness account from a Whig-Presbyterian vantage point of events during the Royalist 'persecutions' in seventeenth-century Scotland, largely concentrating on the period from the restoration of Charles II in 1660, when Episcopal church government was reintroduced in place of Presbyterianism, up to the defeat of armed insurrection at the battle of Bothwell Bridge in 1679. The publication of Walter Scott's *Old Mortality* (1816), at the end of the preceding year, had triggered an intense debate over this period, with Thomas McCrie in the *Edinburgh Christian Instructor* attempting to vindicate the Presbyterian Covenanters against Scott's allegedly demeaning portrayal, and Scott himself through anonymous self-reviewal in the Tory *Quarterly Review* countering with fresh documentary evidence. Aware that McCrie might be contemplating an edition of Kirkton, from a manuscript in the Advocates' Library, Scott set out to pre-empt the situation by encouraging his friend Sharpe to undertake the work himself.

The result was a colonisation of the past that is patently evident in the organisation of the completed edition, where material derived chiefly from anti-Covenanting sources tends to encase and stifle Kirkton's 'worm's-eye view' account. The juxtaposition of entirely different ideologies and discourses can be sensed in the opening remarks of editor and then author. Sharpe's prefatory 'Biographical Notice', assuming an air of impersonal reportage, immediately sets out to reduce Kirkton's credibility by noting an absence of any recorded social 'pedigree'. Kirkton, whose priorities are theological rather than social, and whose imagery is primarily biblical, in contrast proceeds in a hesitant first-person manner, conscious of his burden in describing the 'defection' from true principles that he has personally witnessed: 'Therefore, having my self been a sad spectator of the lamentable revolutions in the Church of Scotland, I con-

ceive it dutie at least to preserve some memorial of what I hade
heard and seen, if happily it might be of any use.'[52] It is difficult
not to sense some resemblance between this and the juxtaposition
within *Confessions* of the editorial 'objective' viewpoint, written from
a modern North British standpoint, and the first-person, biblically-
charged (yet vulnerable) voice which drives on Robert Wringhim's
'Memoirs'.

Aware that he was operating in dangerous ideological waters,
Hogg steers a subtle course in his review article, while leaving enough
markers for an astute reader to recognise where his true sympathies might lie. One obvious target is Sharpe's practice of annota-
tion, which serves to undermine and denigrate rather than to illuminate Kirkton, and which physically at times overwhelms the original text, itself sometimes reduced to a single line at the top of the
page. For example, in responding to mention of a 'godly lady' at
one point, Sharpe not only offers an identification, but also quotes
extensively from an account of the same lady praying in bed, alone
and in company (this incident possibly worked its way later into
Confessions, as part of the Editor's facetious account of the pious
Rabina's early days at Dalcastle).[53] Hogg's own view on this front is
made fairly explicit:

> There we have all along the upper part of the page, the manly
> narrative of honest Kirkton, speaking of his suffering friends
> with compassion, but of his enemies as became a man and a
> Christian. And below that, such a medley of base ribaldry,
> profane stuff, and blasphemous inuendos [*sic*], as at one view
> exhibits the character of both parties.

Rather than confining himself to outright attack, however, Hogg
adopts an ironical manner, positing that the editor of Kirkton must
secretly be a Presbyterian, perhaps even a Cameronian, since his
outward approach is so egregiously flawed: 'I can never be induced
to believe you capable of taking such a foolish and boyish method to
accomplish a purpose in itself so absurd.' In the process Hogg offers
his own defence of seventeenth-century Presbyterianism, one that
carefully eschews the extreme positions taken in the current po-
lemical debate. While the Covenanters were sometimes misled by
'enthusiasm', and as a result have since become vulnerable to the
condescension of 'this moral and philosophical age', their belief in
an overriding providence provided 'the compass and star to which
they looked throughout such a storm of adversity'.[54] In this way
Hogg stands up for an ideology (or rather its underlying human

aspirations) quite distinct from that prevalent in post-Enlightenment Edinburgh, while recognising the fallibility of both polarities as self-contained belief systems.

It was not long before Hogg was experiencing his own vulnerability in the face of intrusive editorship. In the following years, he was to feel increasingly edged out from the Magazine, disregarded by the Oxford-educated and socially superior Wilson and Lockhart, who effectively assumed editorial control under Blackwood. Before long he was convinced that Wilson had a policy of rejecting his contributions, especially prose pieces, and suspected too that Lockhart was intent on keeping him in a state of perplexity—though, at the same time, wishing that this was not true or part of game in which he himself might eventually hold his own. '[A]s for the two devils,' he wrote to Blackwood on 21 July 1818, 'the thing is implanted in their very natures and I must bear it though I believe they have banished me their too much loved society it may make me angry for an hour or two at a time but shall never make me admire or love them the less'.[55] Further confusion was caused by the signing of pieces not by Hogg as his, and the intermingling of these with genuine contributions. Wishing to open up a rift, other journals took up Hogg's cause, thus associating him with politically-motivated squabbles which at this time were becoming dangerously nasty. 'It is confoundedly hard that I should be made a tennis ball between contending parties', he protested to Blackwood on 20 November 1820, employing an image which now immediately brings to mind the tennis-playing incidents in *Confessions*.[56]

A tendency to mollify Hogg with high-sounding praise, just as a rift threatened, and then later to qualify or withdraw that praise, is also apparent in *Blackwood's* from an early stage. In his set-piece essay on 'Burns and the Ettrick Shepherd', in the number for February 1819, Wilson apparently places the two writers on an equal footing, even celebrating Hogg's superior visionary qualities in declaring him finally 'the poet laureate of the Court of Faëry'.[57] This could hardly have been better calculated to appeal to Hogg, who felt himself to be Burns's natural successor, though more careful reading indicates that Wilson actually leaves the earlier poet in a commanding position. In the case of Hogg's fiction the Magazine was noticeably less charitable. No room was found for a review of *The Brownie of Bodsbeck*, though Blackwood was its publisher, and that of *Winter Evening Tales* (1820), as rushed off probably by Wilson, has a routine feel to it. Such praise as is sprinkled about there is confined to qualities such as naturalness; the usual health warning is held out about 'coarseness', which was

clearly deemed especially inappropriate in the 'polite' mode of fiction; and the article only really comes to life when turning to Hogg's
own person, and, more particularly, his recent marriage, though the
tone used is both patronising and irritatingly familiar.[58] This in turn
can be seen as part of a larger process, in evidence several years
before the March 1822 commencement of the 'Noctes Ambrosianae'
series, of creating a gargoyle-like 'Hogg' persona: one that is physical,
rambunctious, instinctual, and above all non-intellectual. Much of the
resultant comedy hinges on the disparity between the singer and the
song: this accentuating, on one level, the idea of a non-corporeal 'inspiration' in Hogg, while on another surreptitiously questioning the
validity of the very qualities claimed on that account. In Lockhart's
contemporary *Peter's Letters to his Kinsfolk* (1819) the dividing off of Hogg
can be palpably felt in the depiction of Lockhart and Wilson as unusually promising and cerebral in character, while Hogg appears more in
the guise of a skipping and sensualist Bacchanalian. To Hogg in his
worst moments it must have seemed that once again, albeit in dazzling fashion, he was being led back to his stall in Ettrick.

Notwithstanding these warning signals, Hogg can hardly have
been prepared for the all-out assault that came in the form of John
Wilson's letter-review in the August 1821 number of his 'Memoir
of the Author's Life', as prefixed to the third edition of *The Mountain
Bard* (1821). While some of this might be seen as part of a habit of
mutual 'flyting', whereby one exaggerated insult is countered by another, it is hard not read this review as a quite deliberate, at times
almost manically driven, attempt to dismantle the literary identity
that Hogg had so carefully (and, in his own eyes, honestly) constructed and accounted for. One of the most recurrent of Wilson's
points is that Hogg simply does not belong in the polite literary
world, where he is apt to appear 'liker a swineherd in the Canongate,
than a shepherd in Ettrick Forest'. (The succession of porcine metaphors that follows is actually based on a misapprehension of the
meaning in Scots of 'hogg', which denotes a young sheep.) Just as in
the world of 'printed paper', 'a Life of James Hogg, by himself' simply has no place, so Hogg's claims to have made himself fully liter-
ate are risible: 'Let Hogg publish a fac-simile of his hand-writing,
and the world will be thunderstruck at the utter helplessness of his
hand.' The parallel between Hogg and Burns offered earlier in the
Magazine is withdrawn with a casual sleight of hand, which would
have seemed all the more dismissive once it was realised that the
praiser and detractor was the same person. But it is the *Memoir*'s
positioning of its subject in the literary and intellectual life of

Edinburgh that comes most persistently under attack. The account mocks in turn Hogg's offering of his ballads 'to all the booksellers in Edinburgh'; the venture with *The Spy* ('truly a sickening concern'); his participation in the Forum, whose membership is described in atrociously snobbish terms; and the (often fraught) account of dealings with publishers ('who the devil cares a jot for Mr Hogg's negociation [...] with Constable, and Miller, and Murray, and Goldie, and Blackwood?'). Hogg's inception of the Chaldee Manuscript is likewise held up as a ridiculous idea, as too his claim—actually never made in such terms—of having refused the editorship of *Blackwood's Magazine*: 'This happened the same year that he declined the offer of the governor-generalship of India, and a seat in the cabinet.'[59]

Even though in an end-note to the same article an attempt is made to lessen the severity of the assault by representing it as a form of 'deevilrie' likely to be understood and even appreciated by 'the Shepherd', there can be little doubt from Hogg's letters in the wake of the incident of his deep hurt and sense of outrage. As he wrote to Blackwood on 4 September 1821, prior to the discovery of the author: 'If you really had it in your power to have repressed this piece of beastly depravity and did not do it I must consider you as worse than the worst assassin out of hell'.[60] More than once in his correspondence Hogg in frustration had already likened the publishers, reviewers, and readers who constituted the print culture of Edinburgh to denizens of Hell, but the shift here from playful 'deevilrie' to a more Satanic form of diabolism is especially noticeable, and one suspects Hogg's confidence about his participation in the literary world—as well as his own sense of personal identity—had never been more severely shaken. Once Wilson was revealed, Hogg's whole perception of his erstwhile friend (one in whom, as he told Blackwood, he had never suspected 'any malice or evil attempt') appears to have undergone a transformation: 'highly as I before esteemed him I will never forgive him, especially for not at once acknowledging it to me'.[61] At later points Hogg would again be drawn into expressing admiration for Wilson, but always with reservation and sometimes an element of fear, with Wilson himself representing an ambivalent figure possessing supernatural-seeming powers. As he wrote to Blackwood, only months after the publication of *Confessions*: 'I have a strange indefinable sensation with regard to him, made up of a mixture of terror admiration and jealousy just such a sentiment as one deil might be supposed to have of another.'[62] While it would clearly be a gross simplification to suggest that Gil-Martin is a representation of Wilson, it is by no means impossible that some of the intense and conflicting feelings generated by this incident worked their way out through the novel, say in the form of Robert Wringhim's insecurities and vulnerability, just as the last incidents more obviously embody an attempt to offer a riposte to some of the metropolitan condescensions of *Blackwood's*.

It is possible that only Hogg's financial entanglement with Blackwood, at a time when he was under intense pressure having taken on the tenancy of Mount Benger farm, prevented a total rupture at this point. Yet there were other elements which continued to draw him to the Magazine. Part of the underlying grievance appears to be not so much that he had become the object of satire himself but that he was being excluded from the larger satirical interchange. It is perhaps significant that the same number that included Wilson's excoriating review also featured a burlesque account of a Coronation dinner in Edinburgh, now identified as Hogg's, which employs a number of techniques in the Blackwoodian manner, including incomplete names such as 'Sir W— S—', 'Mr C— N—', and (self-referentially) 'the E— S—', though overall the satire is gentler than that currently being handed out by Wilson.[63] Hogg's correspondence frequently records his relish for the Magazine and its contents, with instances being found even during periods of apparent alienation.[64] Amongst other things, its monthly numbers were a major source of ideas and fresh knowledge. At an early point, for instance, Hogg almost certainly would have seen Wilson's account of 'Marlow's Tragical History of the Life and Death of Doctor Faustus', which in addition to applauding Marlowe for 'not drawing Faustus as a monster of guilt and iniquity, so as to destroy all sympathy with his sufferings and fate', also quotes at length the final soliloquy immediately prior to his eternal damnation, several of whose words and images are echoed in Robert Wringhim's last desperate journal entries.[65] Reviews of Mary Shelley's *Frankenstein* (1818) and C. R. Maturin's *Melmoth the Wanderer* (1820), in March 1818 and November 1820 respectively, the first by Scott, would have helped keep him in touch with the new wave of intellectual Gothic developing at this time. The Magazine in turn became the receptacle for a shorter form of terror tale, often describing a horrifying ordeal from a first-person position, as in John Galt's 'The Buried Alive' (October 1821) and William Maginn's 'The Man in the Bell' (November 1821).[66]

More broadly, *Blackwood's Edinburgh Magazine* in the early 1820s became intimately connected with the output of mainstream fiction, at a time when the form was burgeoning. John Galt's *Ayrshire Legatees*

(1820–21) was the first of a number of novels to be initially serialised in the Magazine; while, at the same time, Blackwood himself became a major producer of new titles. Of fifteen novels with Blackwood imprints belonging to the years 1821–23 almost all were on Scottish subjects, the majority of these being written (anonymously) by Galt, J. G. Lockhart, or John Wilson. More than half were in single-volume form, some in the prestigious octavo (8vo) format, and exploited the smaller sharper print style then in fashion to provide almost full-length fictions at less than half the cost of a conventional three-decker novel. The Magazine was used to the full to promote these new wares, in the form of advance notices, inset advertisements, plugs in the 'Noctes Ambrosianae', and, above all, reviews. Older style contributors, notably Henry Mackenzie, who was liable to hand out praise and blame in equal measure, were edged out to make way for a new effusive ('puffing') reviewing style. Volume 11 of *Blackwood's*, covering from January to June 1822, carried no less than eight reviews (compared with only one in the preceding volume), including an article on Lockhart's *Adam Blair* (1822), by Wilson, and another on Wilson's *Lights and Shadows of Scottish Life* (1822), by Lockhart. One clear priority was to stake a claim for an autonomous new school of Scottish fiction, distinct from Scott's Waverley novels. According to Wilson, apropos *Adam Blair*, 'Every page of it is Scottish—yet there is not in it all one page that seems to have been suggested by any picture or representation in the great Novels'. Lockhart, for his part, having noticed the new supremacy of prose fiction over verse ('the writing of verses is at present an unpopular and unprofitable exercise'), reciprocated by declaring Wilson's *Lights and Shadows* 'a MASTERPIECE': 'Every page overflows with images of the most pure and beautiful tenderness.'[67]

Hogg watched this new phenomenon both as an insider and outsider. While there was no question of him being invited to provide a review, Blackwood appears to have supplied advance copies of a fair number of his titles,[68] and Hogg duly repaid him by offering his personal critiques. Clearly it was necessary to pick his words carefully, not least in Wilson's case after their supposed rapprochement, yet the qualifications made indicate a full awareness of the deleterious effect of the latter's florid sentimentalism, which in several ways foreshadows the worst aspects of the 'Kailyard' school of Scottish fiction. In *Lights and Shadows*, as he told Blackwood on 14 June 1822, 'there is a great deal of very powerful effect purity of sentiment and fine writing but with very little of real nature as it exists in the walks of Scottish life'. Wilson's *Trials of Margaret Lyndsay* (1823), in not so dissimilar terms, was found to be 'a charming work pure, elegant, and perfect; all save two or three trivial misnomers regarding the character of Scottish peasantry'. As for Lockhart's novel of that year, *Reginald Dalton* (1823), whose young hero goes to Oxford, Hogg complained of the affectation of 'inserting short classical and French quotations without end', and also felt the work too long and weak in some aspects of plotting. Here especially one can sense Hogg speculating what *he* might be capable of as a Blackwood novelist, though such a channel since *The Brownie of Bodsbeck* had been closed. 'I will never write such a book [...] but if I had such materials before me Lord how much more impressive an issue I could have made!'[69]

In Spring 1823 Hogg entered again vigorously into the pages of *Blackwood's,* resuming his 'Shepherd's Calendar' series with two of his most brilliant prose contributions, 'Rob Dodds' (March 1823) and 'Mr Adamson of Laverhope' (June 1823). Noticeably, both stories resist one-dimensional interpretation, belying their supposedly naive rustic framework, and are cunningly constructed so as to unsettle the certainties of the 'enlightened' literati of Edinburgh. The second story particularly, in a way which anticipates *Confessions* itself, juxtaposes a conventional rationalist account of startling events with the more powerful supernatural interpretations offered by the local country people, while the whole multi-textured narrative remains uncertain in meaning to the very end. In a letter of 29 March 1823, Blackwood welcomed Hogg back into the fold, praising 'Rob Dodds' as 'excellent' and inviting him to 'go on' with more—but the terms offered were strictly conditional. The same letter also asked Hogg not to take offence against his appearance in the latest 'Noctes' (no. 7, March 1823), and in particular at the 'quizzing' there about the title of his *Three Perils of Man,* which 'has made every body talk about the book, and will be worth fifty advertisements'.[70] Reference to this 'Noctes' (by Lockhart) give a somewhat different picture, with the vernacular-speaking 'Hogg' protesting that his novel has received no review in the Magazine ('Ye've never reviewed my "Three Perils of Man" yet'), only to provide a spur to the wit of the other main occupants of Ambrose's Tavern, who tumble out a variety of comic triadic alternatives for Hogg's sub-title.[71] After this number Hogg was to appear regularly as a caricature figure in the 'Noctes', under his own surname in numbers 7–9 (March-June 1823), then as 'the Shepherd' in numbers 12–14 (beginning October 1823, by Wilson and others), with alternations between the two from there on. Even as he was writing *Confessions* Hogg knew to his cost what it was like to have a double, one whose presentation as inherently rustic and instinctual contrasts strikingly with the sophistication of the pieces that he himself was actually contributing.

Hogg's irritation at the situation, to be enunciated more openly at later dates, can be sensed in the containing frame of his 'A Scots Mummy' article in the August 1823 issue of *Blackwood's*, reporting the discovery of a suicide's body found close to his home at Altrive Lake, the main part of which was later incorporated within *Confessions*. Originally in the form of a letter addressed to Sir Christopher North (Wilson's pseudonym), its preamble reads almost as a continuation from the 'Noctes', with Hogg responding tetchily to North's suggestion that his contributions should deal with the boundlessness of nature—which, decoded, means effectively that Hogg should resume his station as the unrobed laureate of 'fairy' poetry. 'You should look less at lambs and rams, and he-goats, Hogg, and more at the grand phenomena of nature.' In an interjection half way through the account—again omitted in the novel, yet adumbrating in several ways the role of 'the Editor' there—Hogg rounds in exasperation on 'Sir Christy', who is presumed to be on the point of cutting, having seen so far only an 'ugly traditional tale': 'Stop just a wee bit, ye auld crusty, crippled, crabbit, editor body, an' I'll let ye see that the grand *phenomena of Nature's* a' to come to yet.'[72] As a whole the piece matches the 'Shepherd's Calendar' contributions of that year, combining the tangible and mysterious, the chronologically specific and indeterminate, and leaving the 'sophisticated' urban reader uncertain about the absolute veracity of what is recorded.

That Hogg's reintegration into the Blackwoodian circle had limits was brutally confirmed by Wilson's stinging review of his *Three Perils of Woman* in the October 1823 issue, which at points deliberately invokes the 1821 review of his 'Memoir'. Hogg here is told in no uncertain terms that his 'coarse daubings' are unsuitable for the portrayal of female manners, and that effectively he has no future as a novelist. Letters from Blackwood to Wilson, then at his summer home at Elleray, in the Lake District, indicate that efforts were made to have the article softened down, though it is also evident how much the publisher was complicit at a private level in accepting the notion of Hogg's 'beastliness': 'When I first read your terrible scrapings of the beast I enjoyed it excessively, but on seeing it in types, I began to feel for the poor monster'.[73] It was Blackwood who arranged for a cross-reference to the 'Noctes' (no. 12) in the same number to be prefixed to the review, presumably on the grounds that this provided a compensatory viewpoint. Certainly this exceptionally rich 'Noctes' (also by Wilson) allows Hogg as 'the Shep-

herd' a leading role, creating a remarkable double act by introducing him alongside Thomas de Quincey (as 'the English Opium-
Eater'), with Hogg's earthiness, even in trance-like states, contrasting with the English author's immateriality and evident inability to
construct a simple sentence. Reference is also made to a recent visit–
almost certainly imaginary–by Christopher North to the Shepherd
in Yarrow, where North has allegedly witnessed enormous floods,
while eating copiously with Hogg, who, for his part, is made to acknowledge the benefits of entertaining such a guest: 'through a' your
deevilry there ran sic a vein o' unendurable funniness, that, had
you been the foul Fiend himself, I maun hae made you welcome to
everything in the house'. Just as surely, Hogg *as an author* is also
brought to heel. 'I wish, my dear Shepherd', North comments, 'you
would follow Mr Wordsworth's example, and confine yourself to
poetry. Oh! for another Queen's Wake!' Later Hogg is handed 'a
critique on the Three Perils' by Timothy Tickler, which leads in
turn to his abject acknowledgement of the value of the advice given.
'They lauch far ower muckle at me in their Magazine; but I canna
deny, I proudly declare't, that none o' a' the critics o' this age hae
had sic an insight into my poetical genius; or roused me wi' sic fear-
some eloquence.'[74] Yet very probably by this stage Hogg had already embarked on his most resiliently independent and defiant
novel.

　　The account in the 'Noctes' of Hogg's meeting with De Quincey,
as a now celebrated author, is not only fictional but also implies
strongly that in life there could be no serious connection between
the two. Yet in actuality the two writers had known each other for
nearly ten years, first meeting in September 1814 during Hogg's
visit to the Lake District as a guest of Wilson, and then possibly
renewing their acquaintance when De Quincey came to Edinburgh
later that same year. Early in December 1820 De Quincey returned
to Edinburgh, leaving his new home at Fox Ghyll in Westmoreland,
and staying for six weeks, with the evident aim of becoming a major
contributor to *Blackwood's*. Again he appears to have mixed widely
in literary and intellectual circles; and while, as in the case of the
previous visit, there is no direct evidence of a meeting with Hogg,
an overlap at this point seems more than likely. Despite letters of
promise to Blackwood, including mention of an 'Opium Article', De
Quincey left having made only one contribution. His semi-autobio-
graphical *Confessions of an English Opium-Eater* was then serialised in
the *London Magazine* in September and October 1821, before being
published in book form in August 1822, with a second edition being

called for within a year.[75] When using 'Confessions' in his own title Hogg can only have been aware of this well-known predecessor, as well as of the likelihood that the two works would be seen in tandem by contemporary readers. The De Quinceyan model would also have brought to mind the new secular post-Rousseauist connotations of the term itself, with its underlying sense of a supposedly autonomous self, though in De Quincey's representation that self is found more often than not to be splintered and fragmented.[76]

It is in Robert Wringhim's first-person narrative, which moves from apparent confidence to disintegration, that parallels between the two texts are most strongly felt. Just as De Quincey's persona awaits the arrival of his release from school with his 'seventeenth birthday' and (shortly later) gives his actual birth date, so with similar-seeming exactitude Robert recounts his first meeting with Gil-Martin 'on the 25th day of March 1704, when I had just entered the eighteenth year of my age' (p.82). Equally the two protagonists' experience of time can collapse into confusion and amnesia: Robert apparently failing to recollect a long passage of time at Dalcastle, the Opium-Eater, in his summary, confessing how 'I sometimes seemed to have lived for 70 or 100 years in one night'. Robert's complaint of stomach qualms while at Dalcastle could likewise be seen as echoing the 'most appalling irritation of the stomach' recorded by the Opium-Eater at an important juncture, though in Hogg's version this is defused (if only momentarily) by Penpunt's's malapropism: 'Are ye gaun to take the calm o' the stamock again?' (p.140). In escaping from Edinburgh, Robert poignantly wishes for 'the wings of a dove' (p.154), a clear biblical allusion, but one which also finds a (reverse) parallel in De Quincey, whose protagonist looks longingly *northward* from London: 'if I had the wings of a dove, *that* way I would fly for comfort'.[77] There are also interesting similarities between De Quincey's 'specimens' of dreams, given late in his account, as indications of the mental deterioration caused by opium—one with a dated heading, the other culminating in a nightmarish descent into Hell—and Wringhim's last frantic diary entries: just as structurally one might sense an equivalence between De Quincey's relatively conventional rounding off of his narrative, and the final closure provided by Hogg's Editor after the Sinner's narrative.

Even if he had not directly read *Confessions of an English Opium-Eater*, Hogg can hardly have avoided knowing about the work and its main contents, given its high profile presence in the Edinburgh literary scene during 1823. One possible link is suggested by a review of the second edition which appeared early that year in the *New Edin-*

burgh Review, a periodical which appears to have had a close affinity with Hogg, and whose printer was later to work on his own *Confessions of a Justified Sinner*. According to the anonymous reviewer, one of the key incidents in De Quincey's work, when the Opium-Eater is visited in his cottage by a mysterious Malay, to whom he gives a life-threatening dose, was 'little more than a parody' of a similar incident, involving vitriol and a whisky-drinking Highlander, in Hogg's 'The Adventures of Basil Lee' from his *Winter Evening Tales*.[78] Viewed impartially now the claim of any serious indebtedness seems at best stretched, with De Quincey's rendition appearing considerably more complex, the reader being left uncertain as to whether the incident is delusory or not. The figure of the Malay moreover continues to reverberate in the Opium-Eater's consciousness, as when recorded under the heading '*May*, 1818': 'The Malay has been a fearful enemy for months.'[79] The review comment, nevertheless, might just offer an insight into the gestation of Gil-Martin in Hogg's mind, with De Quincey providing an immediate creative trigger, though with Hogg (a possible source of the counter claim) sensing a deeper origin still in his own work. Hogg would also have been reminded of De Quincey's work, and its potential for new creation, through a number of parodies current at this time, of which the most interesting is 'The Confessions of an English Glutton', which appeared in *Blackwood's Edinburgh Magazine* for January 1823. This begins by noting the supremacy of the confessional mode: 'This is confessedly the age of confession,–the era of individuality–the triumphant reign of the first person singular'. Much of the satire that follows is in the coarser mode of the 'Noctes', with the protagonist obsessively consuming vast amounts of food, with a decided preference for pork, and being subject to a variety of associated delusions. In the closing stages however the account takes on a new dimension, when, visiting a celebrated fat man called Lambert at an exhibition, the glutton sees his double. 'The very instant I saw him, the notion struck me that I had become his second-self–his ditto–his palpable echo–his substantial shadow'. As if suffering an 'electric shock', he rushes towards the river, 'endeavouring in vain to shake off the horrid phantasm that had seized upon my mind' and all the way 'fighting against the foul fiend'.[80]

The motif of the double was given a fuller airing in Edinburgh through the publication under Blackwood's imprint of Robert Pearse Gillies's *The Devil's Elixir* (1824), a translation of E. T. A. Hoffmann's *Die Elixiere des Teufels* (1815–16). Hoffmann's novel itself was strongly influenced by M. G. Lewis's *The Monk* (1796), the most notorious as well as one of the most seminal of English Gothic fictions. Both Lewis and Hoffmann made significant advances in opening up the Gothic for a 'psychological' focussing on the operations of the subconscious. In Lewis's work, Ambrosio, the eponymous Monk of the title, is tempted from a position of elevated 'purity' into sexual depravity and murder, ultimately signs a pact with the devil to escape the Inquisition, and is then thrown into a chasm to perish as a prelude to eternal damnation in Hell. These events are interpretable in both psychological and supernatural terms, either as an overtaking of the Freudian ego by the id, or as part of a more deliberate plot by the devil to ensnare Ambrosio: in fact, especially after a first reading, the novel can be read simultaneously on both levels. Hoffmann, while more than once bowing in Lewis's direction, offers a more convoluted narrative mix. His own Monk, Medardus, having drunk a mysterious elixir–said earlier to have been resisted by St Anthony in a contest with the devil–is haunted by a double (*doppelgänger*), who seems to represent another side of his character, though ultimately this figure is explained in natural terms as being his half-brother. The representation of the situation, and indeed some of the specific language employed, strongly encourages a reading of the text as an illustration of the effects of a split personality, evoking especially a sense of schizophrenia under the pressure of guilt and repression. The effect on the reader is also more complex and disturbing than anything in Lewis, since not only is it uncertain whether the mad monk who haunts Medardus is imaginary or not, but also there is a sensation of slippage between the two 'doubles', so that it is not clear whether the first-person narrator is one or the other. In the words of one modern critic, Hoffmann shows 'the self continuously persecuted by and continuously fleeing from the self, a horrifying struggle which shatters any sense of being or even wanting to be a unified whole'.[81] As other commentators have noted, too, there are a number of incidents in the German novel, either in its original form or in Gillies's slightly reduced version, which appear to be directly echoed in Hogg's *Confessions*. Especially notable here is the episode in Hoffmann where Medardus inadvertently pushes Count Victor (his double/half-brother) over a precipice–itself a rewriting of Ambrosio's fall into a chasm–which shows a number of parallels with Hogg's account of the confrontation between George and Robert on Arthur's Seat.[82]

The proximity of publication dates–both Gillies's translation and Hogg's novel first appeared in June 1824–has nevertheless largely discouraged commentators from claiming anything more than affinities in motifs and techniques, or a mutual source in the Gothic tradition. A more dynamic relationship, however, becomes a real possibility when the closeness of Gillies and Hogg as friends and collaborators is considered. As early as 1814 Hogg had proposed Gillies (1788–1858), recently qualified as an advocate but far more interested in literary pursuits, as the most suitable editor for a periodical 'poetical repository' in Edinburgh along with Wilson and himself, and the two socialised together as leading members of the Edinburgh Right and Wrong Club. Later, on 30 November 1819, Hogg was to compliment Blackwood on employing 'Honest Gillies' as a regular translator in his Magazine: 'He is the very man for it a good scholar, a fine taste, and a polished mind but one who never gives himself the time or trouble to hunt for many original ideas'.[83] The result from that month was the long-running series of 'Horae Germanicae', mostly prepared in collaboration with J. G. Lockhart, which served as a spearhead for the revival of interest in German literature in the 1820s. In spite of differences in rank—Gillies had inherited a landed estate, and then lost his fortune—one senses little of the social condescension that was to mar Hogg's relationship with Wilson and Lockhart. Hogg's doubts about his friend's capacity for originality can be matched by Gillies's questioning, in his own *Memoirs of a Literary Veteran*, of Hogg's relish for books; but the rivalry was friendly and it would seem mutually beneficial. On returning from Germany to Edinburgh in May 1822, as the same *Memoirs* record, Gillies was first welcomed by Lockhart, 'with whom I dined the next day to meet my good old collaborator the Ettrick Shepherd'.[84]

Collaboration, at least in terms of working in conjunction on parallel projects, was still evidently an option. In the postscript of a letter to Hogg, dated only 'Tuesday' from Blackwood's shop, Gillies goes out of his way to compliment Hogg on 'your third vol. of the "Perils"'—most likely the *Three Perils of Woman*, with its biting account of the last days of the 1745-46 Jacobite rising—and then adds: 'I gave Blackwood tother day an unreadable tale, which I think you would make a good one.'[85] Whether or not the unreadable tale is Hoffmann's is a moot point, but in any case there is every chance that Hogg was apprised of Gillies's project, had heard from him the ins-and-outs of the source narrative, and was in part conscious of writing his own tale in a spirit of emulation. Whereas Lockhart in his review of *The Devil's Elixir* in *Blackwood's* was to observe how German writers such as Hoffmann 'have made more of what their country-people's old tales gave them than any of our writers have',[86] Hogg might be said

to have made a vital move in re-grounding the Gothic in the indig-
enous, stretching the possibilities in this respect much further than
Maturin's *Melmoth*, oblivious though the Blackwoodians remained
to his achievement. As several historians of the Gothic have observed, Hogg takes the motif of the *doppelgänger* into a new dimension, creating a work where the reader is left in a continual state of
uncertainty as to whether Gil-Martin is in fact an external presence
or the product of Robert Wringhim's psychosis, yet where ultimately
both levels of interpretation might relate to aspects of a single incomprehensible truth. Structurally, too, Hogg makes considerable
strides. In the Hoffmann original an 'editorial' presence is felt briefly
in an opening retrospective frame, a mid-way interjection introduces
an inserted memoir, itself for some time interrupting the main first-
person account, and the narrative ends with an appendix by Father
Spiridion, outlining somewhat distantly Medardus's dying moments
and probable salvation.[87] In contrast Hogg radically sandwiches his
own Sinner's account between two ostensibly more objective editorial frames, which in operation actually compound the difficulties of
interpretation, revealing at the same time in themselves divisions
potentially as alarming as any in the core narrative.

When considering what is now viewed as the 'psychological' dimension in Hogg's *Confessions*, it is also important to bear in mind
contemporary activities in behavioural sciences in post-Enlightenment Edinburgh. Here it is possible to point to two strands, one
now completely discredited, the other showing some of the elements
of modern psychoanalytical method. According R. P. Gillies, most
of the 'learned and wise of our modern Athens' in the early 1820s
'leaned to Craniology',[88] that is, looked favourably on the would-be
science, also called Phrenology, which claimed that a person's character and likely behavioural patterns could be determined from the
shape of their skull. After the visit of the German craniologist
Spurzheim in 1815, the doctrine was espoused by a number of people in Edinburgh, notably by George Combe (1788–1858), who
was influential in the founding of the Phrenological Society there on
22 February 1820. The years 1823–24 especially saw a rash of
associated publications, all widely advertised in the Edinburgh newspapers, with the first number of the quarterly *Phrenological Journal*,
Combe's influential *Elements of Phrenology*, and the official *Transactions
of the Phrenological Society* all being issued in close proximity.
Combe also gave lectures on Phrenology from 1822, the series for
1823–24 running from November to March, with two sessions
weekly. The cult at the same time became an object of satire in

Blackwood's Edinburgh Magazine, most fully in the 'Noctes Ambrosianæ'
(by Wilson) which served as the lead article in the April 1824 issue.
Here Hogg as 'the Shepherd' offers an uncompromisingly dismissive view: 'A fool and a phrenologist is a' ae thing, Mr Tickler.'[89] In
much the same spirit, in his *Peter's Letters to his Kinsfolk* (1819), J. G.
Lockhart had earlier given a humorous account of Hogg's reaction
to having his head examined by Spurzheim: '"My dear fellow," quoth
the Shepherd, "if a few knots and swells make a skull of genius, I've
seen many a saft chield get a swapping organisation in five minutes
at Selkirk tryst."'[90] While *Blackwood's* appears to have adopted a
fairly hostile stance to phrenology, running two sceptical 'Anti-
Phrenologia' articles in January and February 1823, one also senses
a certain fascination with the subject in several more skittish accounts
there. *Peter's Letters* itself contains key descriptions of Wilson and
Lockhart which seem to be heavily nuanced in such a way, when
dwelling on the size and shape of the brow: 'His forehead is finely,
but strangely shaped [...] the organ of observation having projected
the *sinus frontalis* to a degree that is altogether uncommon' (Mr J–
W—n, at a Burns dinner); 'his forehead is well advanced, and largest, I think, in the region of observation and perception' (Mr L—,
self-referentially, at Gillies's country residence).[91]

But it was the bumps and protuberances on the skulls of well-
known criminals–rather than those sported by budding geniuses–
which above all attracted the attention of the leading practitioners of
phrenology. One of the earliest demonstrations by George Combe
is found, somewhat eerily by modern standards, in *The Life of David
Haggart [...] Written by Himself* (1821), the main part of which is the
first-person confessional of a notorious criminal, hanged in Edinburgh on 18 July 1821. This publication interestingly has a facsimile
of Haggart's handwriting as a frontispiece, while a sizeable Appendix consists of Combe's account of his examination of Haggart's
skull in jail, a written diagnosis by Combe, and Haggart's own response to Combe's observations. A famous English murderer, John
Thurtell, was the subject of a long analysis sent from London and
published in the second number of the *Phrenological Journal*, and it
was the writer's discovery of a capacity for Benevolence, alongside
other propensities such as Combativeness, that provided the main
butt for satire in the 'Noctes' of April 1824 mentioned above.[92] A
year earlier Scottish phrenology had been able to offer a similar (if
less generous) diagnosis of Mary M'Kinnon, who was hanged in
Edinburgh before a huge crowd estimated at 20,000 on 16 April
1823, having been convicted of the murder of a young client, William

Howat, in her tavern-brothel late at night on Saturday, 8 February. Accounts by witnesses varied considerably: the women in the brothel claiming that Howat and his companion had behaved violently towards them, Henry Kerr, the main witness for the prosecution claiming that a row had broken out through the girls resisting them leaving, with M'Kinnon intervening violently in returning to her tavern. The case against M'Kinnon, who was not singled out until some time later, was flimsy even by then current standards, and its contradictory nature was pointed out at the trial (14–15 March) by Francis Jeffrey, chief counsel for the defence, who also pleaded for consideration for one 'thrown into her situation rather by misfortune than misconduct'. The extent to which the masculine establishment of Edinburgh had determined on a sacrificial victim can be sensed in the Lord Justice Clerk's summing-up, which advised the Jury to ignore the evidence of the women in favour of that of the men. A majority verdict of guilty was delivered, with a recommendation for mercy, the latter being ignored by the presiding judges, with Lord Meadowbank stating that 'nothing surprised him so much as the recommendation of the Jury, as he could not discover the slightest grounds for it'. The date of the execution was then announced, with the direction that the body be publicly dissected by Dr Alexander Monro, Professor of Anatomy at Edinburgh University.[93]

A cast of the head of Mary M'Kinnon taken after her execution by the artist to the Phrenological Society, and put on exhibition in Edinburgh, subsequently became the subject of a 'very entertaining' report read to the society by George Combe on 1 May 1823. Combe duly discovered what might be expected in the case of a violent criminal, the organs of combativeness and destructiveness being unusually large, 'giving to the back part of the head, as in those of all murderers from sudden impulse examined by phrenologists, a round cannon-bullet form'.[94] In the closing stages of *Confessions*, with the discovery of the suicide's skull, the Editor claims to be 'no phrenologist', but nevertheless manages to sound like one in describing 'a smooth, almost perfect rotundity, with only a little protuberance above the vent of the ear' (p.172). More broadly, it is hard not feel the presence of Mary M'Kinnon underlying the character of Bell Calvert in the story, forced into prostitution through ill-luck and betrayal, just as apologists for M'Kinnon claimed that as a child and young woman she had been neglected and debauched. The connection is most palpably felt in Bell's imagining herself 'hung up, a spectacle to a gazing, gaping multitude', a death which has 'something peculiarly revolting in it to a female mind' (p.42). Noticeably in the trial of Calvert it is two women, Mrs Logan and her feisty maid, who thwart the prosecutor and the Judge by securing a release, though the means justified by this end involve withholding and bending the truth. Parallels can also be found in the events leading up to the death of George Colwan. Just as Colwan and his young Tory companions leave the Black Bull after heavy drinking to visit a 'bagnio' (brothel) in one of the wynds running north from the High Street, so William Howat and his young professional friends had passed the best-known Black Bull of their day (off Leith Street) in heading towards lodgings in Bristo, stopping with fatal consequences at M'Kinnon's licensed tavern at 82 South Bridge. It is at such points in the Editor's narrative that the apparent distinction between past and present Edinburgh collapses, and the strife-ridden, partisan, ideologically-fragmented society of Scotland in its last days of independence offers a direct mirror image of the supposedly more civilised establishment world of North Britain. Hogg's reaction to the M'Kinnon case is not directly on record, but it seems reasonable to assume that he saw there a pernicious compound of some of the worst elements of the *soi-disant* Athens of the North: the prim moralism of its 'bluestockings', the callous high Toryism of Charles Kirkpatrick Sharpe (who wrote a heartless lampoon), and a scientific materialism which in the hands of the phrenologists was teetering dangerously close to treating all criminals (as well as other races) as a sub-species.[95]

More positive attitudes towards mental disorder certainly were to be found in Edinburgh at this time. Hogg knew several medical men with advanced ideas, notably Dr Andrew Duncan (1744–1828), President of the Edinburgh College of Physicians and Professor of Physiology at the University, who was on the Board of Charity superintending the finances of the Forum debating society for the session 1812–13, when Hogg was Secretary. Duncan had agitated long and hard for the establishment of a public lunatic asylum in Edinburgh, to replace the old City Bedlam, and the Edinburgh Asylum finally opened in 1813. While much medical writing on mental illness was still rudimentary, case histories were broadly reported and discussed in learned institutions. On 18 February 1822 the Royal Society of Edinburgh heard a report based on information received from Dr Dyce of Aberdeen, concerning a sixteen-year old girl who assumed different personalities in a somnambulist state. The presenter of the report, Dr Dewar, displays an interesting range of terminology in introducing 'a phenomenon which is sometimes called double consciousness, but is more properly a *divided consciousness*, or *double personality*; exhibiting in some measure two separate and independent trains of thought, and two independent mental capabilities, in the same individual; each train of thought, and each capability, being wholly dissevered from the other, and the two states in which they respectively predominate subject to frequent interchanges and alternations'. Dewar's mention of another instance of 'double consciousness' must relate, as Barbara Bloedé has suggested, to the more complicated and widely reported case of Mary Reynolds, in Pennsylvania, who showed new talents and a much higher degree of extroversion when apparently entering into a different personality state. In their diagnoses however Drs Dyce and Dewar both dwell almost entirely on the physiological, the former shaving and bleeding his patient, the latter in his summation turning to physical causes such as inhaled gasses as an analogous explanation, likening such to 'the influence of opium, and still more familiarly that of inebriating liquors'.[96] Certainly if one accepts to some degree that Robert Wringhim's disturbance in *Confessions* has a psychological origin, Hogg can be seen as offering an analysis of schizophrenia or multiple personality disorder considerably in advance of current medical theory, emphasising the familial and cultural divisions in Wringhim's upbringing, while placing the main locus in the workings of the mind rather than the empty skull of the phrenologists.

It is nevertheless an empty skull and (to him) unintelligible scroll that Hogg's Editor is left with at the end of the novel. In the final sequence describing his journey to Ettrick and the grave, Hogg offers not only a rerun of Walter Scott's 1802 visit, but also a withering critique of the Blackwoodian claim to represent a new and coherent Scottish culture. At Abbotsford, where Lockhart is found, a horse is asked for but only a pony provided, undermining any full claim to cultural parity with the Great Unknown. More so than in his opening and larger sequence, the Editor here appears completely nonplussed in offering any interpretation of metaphysical and psychological issues which seem completely alien to him. In the brutal reopening of the grave (see p.172), the focus is entirely on material objects, several of them fragmented ('part of a skeleton', 'part of the scalp'), with the Editor obsessively concerned with measurable physical detail ('cow's dung, about one-eighth of an inch thick, and in the hollow of the sole fully one fourth of an inch'). In this way the Editor and his party might be said to end by digging a hole for themselves, while Hogg in the encompassing text has brilliantly shaped a true Scottish novel, the ideal Blackwood novel which notwithstanding could not be published from Edinburgh.

3. Composition, Printing, and Publication

Little direct information relating to the composition of *Confessions* is now available, though most probably it was written and printed between Autumn 1823 and Spring 1824. The first clear glimpse of the project is found in Hogg's article on 'A Scots Mummy', published in *Blackwood's Edinburgh Magazine* for August 1823, the greater part of which (as we have seen) was later incorporated within the novel. End-dated 1 August 1823, this was apparently sent with a letter of Hogg's to William Blackwood, headed 7 August: 'I send you in for Maga the particulars of a curious incident that has excited great interest here'.[97] Whether or not the article already formed part of a larger design in Hogg's mind is a debatable issue. Certain chronological adjustments there—particularly the addition through folk report of 'six or seven years' more to the fixing of the suicide 'one hundred and five years next month' (see pp.167–68)—might be taken as part of a manoeuvring of events to mesh with the larger temporal patterning of the novel-to-be. On the other hand, it could be argued that other details (for instance, the corpse's 'fine yellow hair') would have been avoided or presented otherwise if Hogg had already developed a plan—granted, that is, that a trail of discrepancies was not being laid from the start.[98]

Whatever the true circumstances, the contribution was made just at a time when Hogg was eagerly anticipating publication of his *Three Perils of Woman* (1823), and when the possibility of a new work of fiction was most likely to be in mind.[99] Moreover, any pre-existing resolve can only have been sharpened by the enthusiastic, yet slightly suspicious, response to the article shown by the inner Blackwoodian circle, as evident in their letters to William Blackwood. The fullest of these comes from David Macbeth Moir: 'Hogg is perfectly characteristic. It is curious that all these *French phenomenons* should occur about Selkirk and Yarrow, and no where else in the civilized world. I will be happy to see your fragment of the enchanted waistcoat first time I have the pleasure of calling.'[100] Here especially one might sense the germ of the expedition to Ettrick—whether in actuality, or in Hogg's imagination alone—to verify the existence of the suicide's grave, as undertaken by a Wilson-like Editor and a thinly-veiled Lockhart in the immediate wake of the article within the novel.

Basic information concerning the commissioning of the work can be gathered from the Longman Letter Books, which include copies of outgoing letters from the publishers in London to Hogg, though none of Hogg's letters in reply have apparently survived. The project is first mentioned, almost in passing, in a letter from Owen Rees, on 25 October 1823: 'We will with pleasure undertake the publication of "Memoirs of a Suiside [*sic*]" on the same plan as we have done your other works.' Rees, a senior partner and personally well disposed towards Hogg, was back from Edinburgh, the firm having earlier (11 August) signalled his intention to travel there, and his letter of 25 October expresses surprise that the two had missed each other, in spite of a search through all the main booksellers' shops.[101] Hogg had also been attempting to negotiate terms for an edition of his Scottish prose tales, a project on which Rees in his October letter now cast doubt, clearly much preferring Hogg's other project. Possibly Rees's interest had been stimulated by the topicality of suicide as a subject, and it is perhaps significant that Longmans had just recently brought out G. R. Gleig's novel *The Stranger's Grave* (1823), where suicide is a palpable issue.[102]

Both of Hogg's previous works of fiction, *The Three Perils of Man* (1822) and *The Three Perils of Woman* (1823), had been published by Longmans, one of the largest and most respected of London wholesale publishing concerns. With a steady output of new novels, representing about 10 per cent of national output, the firm at this time dealt mostly with middle-market romance titles, much of it by regular female authors, such as Amelia Opie and the Porter sisters, though they had also acted as London managers of Walter Scott's earliest Waverley novels. Longmans' dealings with Hogg generally show a mixture of fairness and firmness, tinged with personal leniency. While for both *Perils* titles they had initially insisted on a system of 'half profits'—whereby the author waited for payment at intervals after publication, dividing any surplus from the sale with the publisher—in the event, Hogg's requests for advance lump sums had been granted in each instance, with Longmans effectively purchasing the edition. On the other hand, though the prospect of anonymity clearly held a number of attractions for Hogg, the firm up to this point were adamant that his name should be used ('we would wish to have your name in the Title').[103] In fact, the kind of 'James Hogg' Longmans had in mind is apparent in the inclusion of the poem *The Queen's Wake*, his one unquestionable literary success, as one of the works 'by the author' on both of these earlier title-pages. How a position was arrived at whereby the *Confessions* could appear anonymously—whether through a joint acknowledgement that the 'Memoirs' structure necessitated such, or as the result of more delicate manoeuvrings by Hogg himself—remains unclear.[104] It is just possible, however, that Hogg's failure to meet with Rees in Autumn was more than accidental, but rather part of a strategy designed to avoid his being tied down by preconditions.

There was one particular aspect of Longmans' dealings capable of working in Hogg's favour. With their Scottish authors at this period, as their Letter Books show, the firm was not averse to an Edinburgh printer being directly employed, this facilitating delivery of the manuscript for setting and any exchange of proofs between author and printer. In the case of *The Three Perils of Man*, Hogg had been given the go-ahead to use John Moir, while with its successor the commission had gone to James Ballantyne & Co., the printer of nearly all Scott's poems and novels (and in secret largely owned by Scott). From an early stage in his career, Hogg was attracted by the idea of by-passing Edinburgh publishers, with their (in his eyes) inflated sense of public propriety, evident willingness to mangle his texts, and mystifying accounting methods, by forging instead direct links with printers, a social group with whom he almost certainly felt at greater ease. An early instance of this latter possibility occurs with his periodical *The Spy* (1810–11), during the production of which Hogg as editor/author was intimately involved with the mechanics of production—in the earliest issues associating closely with printers in the Edinburgh Cowgate.[105]

In the case of *Confessions*, it appears that Hogg targeted from an early point the printer James Clarke, a now relatively obscure figure, whose printing works in 1823 were in Merchant Court, off the Cowgate. Longmans however were insistent that James Ballantyne & Co. be again employed. This is apparent from two letters giving instructions about printing, both dated 12 December 1823, one to Hogg and one directly to James Ballantyne himself. Ballantyne, in a letter personally signed by Owen Rees, was left in no doubt that he was to be the printer: 'Mr Hogg [...] will let you have a Tale to print on post 8vo on a page a line longer & an *n* or an *m* wider than that for Reginald Dalton &c. The paper has been sent down marked J C'. The letter to Hogg (this time from the firm) instructed him 'to deliver the MS to Ballantyne to print', while giving similar instructions about layout, though the model offered here is Scott's *Quentin Durward* (1823). It also adds as a postscript, somewhat abruptly, 'You will inform Mr Clark of the change of printer'.[106]

What happened then is uncertain. One possibility is that Ballantyne's presses, then heavily committed to printing Scott's *Redgauntlet* (1824), were under pressure, and that, with the commission to print Hogg's next poem, *Queen Hynde* (1824), following soon after, the seemingly lesser job was offloaded back in Clarke's direction. Another possibility is that Hogg went out of his way to forestall a potentially disastrous situation. The head of a then highly prestigious firm, James Ballantyne had a reputation as an interventionist printer, and his concern for public propriety could lead him into excising the slightest reference to female anatomy even in Scott's novels. His compositors and copy editors were also unusually proactive, in regularising style and grammar, as well as in making more substantive changes. A clear-cut illustration of the dangers that might lie in waiting for someone like Hogg is provided by the manuscript of *Queen Hynde*, where deletions almost certainly made by Ballantyne and/or his copy editor(s) show a willingness to censor virtually anything likely to be found objectionable in the increasingly prim atmosphere of the 1820s.[107] With the manuscript and proofs passing through Ballantyne's office, moreover, there was always the possibility of an intervention by Scott himself, and Hogg was still smarting over interventions so forced on him with his *Three Perils of Man*.[108] Furthermore, with a delicately complex text to deliver—where, for instance, 'mistakes' can be deliberate, and names shadow each other while remaining distinct—Hogg had especial reason to feel anxious. Noticeably Longmans still appear to have been under the impression Ballantyne was the printer as late as 3 May ('Be so good as to request Ballantyne will send us the account of printing the Confessions'[109]), though almost certainly by this stage the work was nearing completion by Clarke. Of its ending up where Hogg originally intended there can be little doubt. Both the printer's mark on the verso of the title-page of the first edition and the colophon at the foot of the last page of text describe the work as printed by 'James Clarke & Co., Edinburgh, 1824'.

Who was James Clarke? In the early 1820s he appears to have been working in close association with Andrew Balfour, another printer, whose work premises are also given in the Edinburgh Directories as at Merchant Court off the Cowgate.[110] It is tempting to speculate whether either had been among those lean and hungry printers with whom Hogg socialised in 1810, when *The Spy* was first being printed.[111] The first firm point of connection, however, occurs with William Francis Napier's *A Treatise on Practical Store-Farming* (Edinburgh, 1822). In his *Blackwood's* article reviewing this work, in February 1823, Hogg drew attention to its exhibition of 'Messrs Balfour and Clark's best style of printing'.[112] Napier's *Treatise* is indeed a finely printed work, with a fold-out map and a number of engraved illustrations, and bears the legend 'Printed by Balfour and Clarke, Edinburgh' both on the verso of its title-page and in the colophon. Hogg's considerable input into this text both as an author and informant is manifest, and in the circumstances it seems more than likely that he was instrumental in at least guiding his aristocratic neighbour Napier towards a suitable printer. Between 1818 and 1822 Balfour and Clarke were involved together in at least thirty other Edinburgh publications, among them John Laing's *A Voyage to Spitzbergen* (2nd edn, 1818; 4th edn, 1822), *The Edinburgh Monthly Review* (from its first issue in Janurary 1819 to its demise, as the *New Edinburgh Review*, in 1823), and J. G. Lockhart's pamphlet *Postscript to the third edition of Peter's Letters* (1819). In the 1823–24 Edinburgh Post Office Directory Balfour and Clarke are given together as printers in Merchant Court; but in 1824–25 'Clarke, James and Co. printers' are listed as at Old Stamp Office Close, 221 High Street–at which address this firm continued to be listed until 1844.[113]

Old Stamp Office Close (whose name originates from the Government Stamp Office, which moved to Waterloo Place in 1821) still survives, and is found on the north side of the High Street some fifty yards down from St Giles Cathedral, slightly above the entry to the present Cockburn Street. Granting that the *Confessions* was actually printed in Clarke's new premises, it becomes possible to point to a close correlation between the main action in the Edinburgh scenes in the novel and the site of its typographical construction. Only a few steps down the High Street from Old Stamp Office Close is the entrance to Fleshmarket Close, the home of a Black Bull Inn in the nineteenth century. And slightly further down the street was the entrance to Bull Close, before its obliteration through the building of Cockburn Street in 1859. Here the old Bull or Union Tavern stood, in the cellar of which according to tradition statesmen in favour of the Union of 1707 met and once hid from an angry mob. A short distance up the High Street from Old Stamp Office Close was Craig's Close, once the headquarters of James Watson,[114] the leading Edinburgh printer of his day, in whose printing house in the novel Robert Wringhim endeavours to print his own 'Memoirs'. Indeed, one suspects more than a touch of self-referentiality in Hogg's account of the processes which are gone through to manufacture this work:

> I put my work to the press, and wrote early and late; and encouraging my companion to work at odd hours, and on Sundays, before the press-work of the second sheet was begun, we had the work all in types, corrected, and a clean copy

> thrown off for farther revisal. The first sheet was wrought off; and I never shall forget how my heart exulted when at the printing house this day, I saw what numbers of my works were to go abroad among mankind, and I determined with myself that I would not put the Border name of Elliot, which I had assumed, to the work. (p.153; see also note on 153(a)).

No specific evidence has been discovered about the preparation or delivery of the holograph manuscript, though Longmans' letter of 12 December 1823 directing Hogg to 'deliver the MS to Ballantyne to print' could be taken as indicating that copy was ready by that point.[115] There are a number of reasons, albeit all circumstantial, for believing that Hogg produced good copy for printing, among which might be included Mrs Garden's claim in 1895 to have the manuscript in her possession 'clearly and neatly written in my father's hand'.[116] Certainly, this description accords with what is known of Hogg's practices from the 1820s, when he was increasingly operating as a semi-professional writer. Surviving contemporary manuscripts indicate not only that his work often went through several drafts, but also that considerable care was taken in preparing the final copy text, to the extent that the latter can sometimes have the appearance of scriptorial equivalents of the desired printed object.[117] Furthermore, Hogg's correspondence at this time indicates every effort was made to check proofs, whenever possible: failing that, for his nephew Robert to oversee them. Hogg was in Edinburgh in mid-November, and then again at least twice in Spring (late March and early May), when proofs are most likely to have been available.[118] The absence of press figures in the first edition suggests that the 1000 copies were printed on a single press, while the sharpness of the print points to the use of up-to-date equipment. It is not hard to imagine Hogg himself, whose concern for printing standards is a matter of record, personally taking an interest in the operation.

Without a manuscript, it is not possible to comment with any certainty on the process of transmission into printed text. One possible guideline, however, is found in the materials incorporated from the *Blackwood's* 'Scots Mummy' article, which most likely were taken directly from the article itself, perhaps after some marking up by Hogg. Comparison with the first edition reveals only a modicum of changes, most of them practical in nature as well as efficient in execution. Whereas in a normal transference into print one might expect a further accretion of punctuation, the first edition removes slightly more commas than it adds, generally freeing up the semi-automatic 'grammatical' points sprinkled about by the compositors of *Blackwood's*. The first sentence to be carried over, in its two states, is illustrative of this:

> On the top of a wild height, called Cowanscroft, where the lands of three proprietors meet all at one point, there has been, for long and many years, the grave of a suicide, marked out by a stone standing at the head, and another at the feet.
> (*Blackwood's*)

> On the top of a wild height called Cowanscroft, where the lands of three proprietors meet all at one point, there has been for long and many years the grave of a suicide marked out by a stone standing at the head, and another at the feet.
> (First edition)

Among a handful of local verbal changes, the first edition omits 'a boy then about ten years of age', information ('then a boy ten years of age') that is supplied more appositely later. The substitution of 'phenomena' for 'phenomenons' also seems valid in view of several other 'phenomena' elsewhere in the article (albeit in parts not carried over). At the same time the first edition faithfully preserves a number of idiomatic expressions of Hogg's, such as 'at the side of one of Eldinhope hay-ricks' and 'very near run of cash', which a standardising printer might easily have ironed out. Three proper names are altered (Eltrive for Eltrieve, Drummelzier for Drumelezier, and Shiel for Sheil), but otherwise the original orthography is allowed to stand. The one sizeable addition (that of the parenthesised etymology 'Ault-Righ, *the King's burn*,') has the marks of an authorial addition, either by means of prior marking up or at proof stage.

The overall impression given of a faithful and intelligent copying of text is reflected in the novel at large, where a number of Hogg-like anomalies appear to have been retained, but where one also senses a scrupulous attention to matters such as presentation. One noticeable feature of the first edition is the apparently unscathed nature of Hogg's original Scots, which in other hands could have been severely mangled. Another is the unusual consistency in representing characters' names, all the more essential (as suggested) in a text of this nature. Basic typographical errors are few and far between: a slipped stop after 'Mr', the occasional omitted or redundant quotation mark; a homonymous 'their' for 'there' (for a fuller account, see 'Note on the Text', pp.197–98). Among other things, these qualities suggest unusually close proof reading.

Thanks to the researches of David Groves, it is also possible to pinpoint a particular moment in the production of *Confessions*, one that offers a snapshot view of printer and author operating in tandem. In his *Autobiographical Notes* (1892), William Bell Scott recalls a meeting between Hogg and his father, the engraver Robert Scott, in the latter's studio overlooking Parliament Square in Edinburgh:

> I was getting my Latin exercise overhauled [...] one day when a publisher, one of my father's clients, brought in a short stoutish countryman in a light-coloured suit, who wanted an imitation of the writing of 1700 made as a frontispiece to a book.[119]

The passage from Robert Wringhim's diary chosen for engraving occurs in the penultimate full gathering of the first edition of *Confessions* (1st edn, pp.366–67; present edition, pp.164–65), so it is not unlikely that the order was placed during the last stages of preparation. Close to the end of the novel, the Editor/Hogg actually mentions its commissioning: 'I have ordered the printer to procure a facsimile of it, to be bound in with the volume.'[120] Groves in his 1991 Canongate edition of *Confessions* suggests that the disparity between the facsimile and the printed text is part of Hogg's larger ongoing satire against 'editors'.[121] However, comparison between the two reveals only four minor variants: the italicisation of 'September' and 'Amen' (matching other entries), and the addition of two fairly routine commas. This begs the question of what kind of copy text was used by the engraver. Was Robert Scott working from printed copy, a special transcription made by Hogg, or even from the now missing original manuscript? One tantalising feature of the facsimile could be taken to encourage the last of these possibilities. Especially noticeable is the visibly displayed alteration of 'creature' to 'created' to produce (as in the printed text) 'created energy', in close proximity to 'living creature' in the following sentence. Such alterations, made to avoid repetition, are not uncommon in holograph literary manuscripts, including Hogg's own. If the holograph was indeed used, then it offers yet another indication of the kind of changes that might have been made in preparing the printed version.

One of the last activities in producing the first edition would have been the setting and printing of the title-page, which normally came last in the production process at this period.[122] As previously noted, the working title in October 1823, at least as understood by Owen Rees, was 'Memoirs of a Suicide'. Later on, however, Hogg appears to have opted for a new title, possibly 'Confessions of a Self-Justified Sinner'. This can be gathered from Longmans' letter of 12

February 1824: 'With respect to the title of your work, we have no objection to the alteration, but we do not like the term "self justified sinner" perhaps you can give us some other wordes [*sic*] for these'. Hogg at this point, it would seem, countered with an irresistible answer. In their letter of 26 February Longmans conceded that the new title must stand, at least in truncated form: 'The printing having proceeded, we must now let it remain "confessions of a *Sinner*" & we shall advertise accordingly.'[123] The left-hand running headlines of the first nine octavo (16-page) gatherings (signatures B–K) in the first edition read 'Confessions of a Sinner', with 'The Editor's Narrative' appearing on the facing right-hand pages. Changing these would have meant taking down the formes containing type, and, if the early sheets had already been printed, an expensive loss of paper. In both Longmans' Impression Book and Divide Ledger the work is described as 'Confessions of a Sinner', and there is little to suggest that Longmans ever thought of it otherwise again.

Further evidence that main components of the title were in Hogg's mind at a relatively early stage is found in the additional title-page, introducing Robert Wringhim's Memoirs, which reads 'Private Memoirs and Confessions of a Sinner. Written by Himself'. Collation of leaves show that this is printed on the last leaf of gathering K, and so forms an integral part of the text (there are no signs of a cancel). The first sentence of this is then repeated in the drop-head title at the start of Robert's narrative, on the first page of a new gathering (L). Rather ingeniously, it is then reproduced in the headlines by moving 'Confessions of a Sinner' to the right hand and the introduction of 'Private Memoirs and' on the left-hand pages. This process continues until the end of Wringhim's narrative (p.368 in the first edition, and the end of gathering 2A), at which point 'Confessions of a Sinner' returns to the left side and 'The Editor's Narrative' resumes as a running headline on the right-hand pages. Finally in the last short gathering of the work (2C, consisting of three leaves, probably itself printed on the same sheet with the preliminaries), Hogg describes the title-page as found on the printed pamphlet recovered from the grave:

THE PRIVATE MEMOIRS
AND CONFESSIONS
OF A JUSTIFIED SINNER:

WRITTEN BY HIMSELF.

FIDELI CERTA MERCES.

And, alongst the head, it is the same as given in the present
edition of the work. I altered the title to *A Self-justified Sinner*,
but my booksellers did not approve of it; and there being a
curse pronounced by the writer on him that should dare to
alter or amend, I have let it stand as it is. Should it be thought
to attach discredit to any received principle of our church, I
am blameless. (1st edn, p.388; present edn, p.174)

Evidently Hogg is involved here in writing the final portion of a
text whose earlier parts have already been printed, and in the process he again draws attention to the material conditions of its production, fictionalising here his dealings with Longmans. Two possible
interpretations can be offered for these final manoeuvrings. One is
that Hogg for a while was genuinely attracted to the idea of adding
'self-justified' to the title. The term appears once within the text,
pejoratively, in the mouth of Arabella Logan when calling the elder
Robert Wringhim a 'self-justified bigot' (1st edn, p.119; present edn,
p.55); it also features in De Quincey's *Confessions of an English Opium-
Eater*, where at a key moment the solipsistic narrator refers to 'my
own self-justification'.[124] If adopted by Hogg, however, it would have
conveyed within the novel a more limiting idea of *self*-delusion (albeit favourable in some respects to psychological readings), compared with the sheer daring of 'Justified', with its theological sense
of justification through grace, of a making just *in spite* of sin. It is not
impossible, then, that 'self-justified' when mooted was something of
a red herring, one which allowed Hogg to give the impression of
acceding to Longmans' veto, while allowing leeway for the introduction of the contentious term that truly interested him by a sleight
of hand at the end.

Printing of the 1000 copies of the first edition was completed by
early June, when the bulk of the impression was shipped to Longmans
in London, with a smaller portion (probably 100 or 125 copies)
going to Adam Black, their bookselling agent in Edinburgh.[125] A
breakdown of cost totalling £150 is given in the Longman Impression book, with Clarke & Co's basic printing bill of £39 12s. 0d.
and paper costs of £64 2s. 6d. representing the main items, a further £36 1s. 0d. being itemised for advertising. Indicative of the
special care taken in producing the edition are two particular charges:
£3 19s. 6d. for alterations, and £2 7s. 6d. for paper used for proofs.
(The cost of engraving and printing the facsimile is given as £2 18s.
0d.)[126] For this, Longmans received what is undoubtedly an unusually fine example of a single-volume novel for its time, stretching to
390 pages, virtually free of typographical error, and a genuine ex-

ample of the prestigious post octavo format currently in fashion. There is no evidence, however, of Longmans re-employing Clarke & Co. as a printer, or for that matter that Clarke was ever again associated with adult fiction. From this point, his firm's main activity appears to have been the production of children's chapbook stories, usually retailing at 'Twopence each'.[127]

The novel was first announced in the London newspapers in mid-July, approximately a month after shipment. The earliest instance discovered is in *The Star* for Monday, 12 July 1824, where it is advertised on the front page as 'This day [...] published', at the premium price of 10s. 6d. boards, the rest of the notice consisting effectively of a transcript of the title-page. Similar adverts are found in *The Morning Post* and *Morning Chronicle* on 13 and 14 July respectively. Promotion in Edinburgh seems to have lagged behind, the same notice appearing in the *Edinburgh Weekly Journal* on 15 September, and in the *Edinburgh Evening Courant* on 20 September, with again only Longmans being mentioned as publishers. Another phase of advertising occurred in the London papers early in November, this time with the addition of a favourable extract from a review in the *Monthly Critical Gazette*.[128] The record in the Longman Divide Ledger reveals that Longmans had sold 326 copies of their stock by June 1825, a fairly unspectacular number for the first year of a novel's life. After this, sales virtually ground to a halt: between June 1825 and June 1826 the Divide Ledger records only five further copies sold, with 521 left in stock. Attempts to calculate profits, for a division, led to sums so small that is was evidently considered not worth paying Hogg, who so far had received nothing, his request on 3 May 1824 for an advance prior to publication having met a refusal.[129]

While it was not unusual for a novel to lose impetus once the flush of novelty had gone, the decline in this case is striking, and leads one to speculate whether Longmans had decided to disassociate themselves from a work they had discovered (say through the reviews) contained unsuitable materials.[130] Certainly the *Confessions* sits oddly with Longmans' main output of fiction at this period, which was becoming increasingly evangelical in emphasis, with tales such as George Wilkins's *Body and Soul* (1822; and in its 4th edition in 1824) setting the new tone. As the Divide Ledger indicates, with sales having virtually ground to a halt, Longmans effectively cleared the title from their backlist by selling their remaining stock to Thomas Tegg, at a knock-down price of 9d. a copy. Eventually, in June 1828, they finalised the account, with half profits of £16 1s. 2d. apparently going to 'W. Blackwood' (the 'Author' having been crossed out). This tends to corroborate Hogg's statement, made later in his own 'Memoir', that he could 'not remember ever receiving any thing for it'.[131]

4. Early Reception and Later Editions

When the novel first appeared, in June 1824, Hogg was fully occupied in Yarrow, arranging the re-housing of his parents-in-law, dealing with pressing agricultural matters, and also endeavouring to finish his long poem, *Queen Hynde* (published in December later that year). These pressures can be felt in a letter to William Blackwood of 28 June, which asks for Blackwood's help in superintending his 'unfinished poem' ('the printers and I are both in one page'), in conjunction with his trusted nephew, Robert Hogg. Even so, in spite of evident haste, Hogg still found time to canvass Blackwood's help in promoting the *Confessions*:

> There is one hint I beseech you to remember to give and which I have been too long in mentioning I see by the *Noctes*. It is that as some one of our friends are likely to be the first efficient noticers of *The Confessions* they will not notice them at all as *mine* but as written by *a Glasgow man* by all means and allude to the dedication to the lord provost there. This will give excellent and delightful scope and freedom.[132]

Hogg by this time must have seen the 'Noctes Ambrosianae' in the June 1824 issue of *Blackwood's Edinburgh Magazine*, where there are two brief references to his new work. At one point near the beginning, Timothy Tickler, in response to mention of verses in one of Hogg's 'recent masterpieces', makes a brief aside to ODoherty ('Is this in the "Confessions of the Justified Sinner," which I see advertised?'), only to be told that the work in question is the *Three Perils of Man*. The new novel is then again glimpsed fleetingly at a later point, as a result of a statement by 'Hogg' (appearing under his name here rather than as 'The Shepherd') that he will be 'buried beside Yarrow'. 'And dug up, no doubt,' ODoherty facetiously responds, 'quite fresh and lovely, like this new hero of yours, one hundred summers hence.'[133]

In the intervening sequence discussion involves commentary on a number of other recently-issued novels, including Scott's *Redgauntlet* and R. P. Gillies's *The Devil's Elixir*. Yet even more galling for Hogg than being thus cast in the shade, one suspects, would have been the all too predictable association of his anonymous work with the comic persona of the 'Noctes' Shepherd/Hogg. Publicity in the 'Noctes' was as always a mixed blessing, on the one hand severely threatening Hogg's claim to be treated seriously as a literary figure, yet at the same time offering personal publicity on a scale that could not be found elsewhere. Hogg's obvious strategy for avoiding the downside in this equation, through the cultivation of a possible Glaswegian provenance for his story, however, met with only a token response in the following July number. This came through an end note to its leading article, itself signed from 'Eltrive Lake, July 4th, 1824', by M. ODoherty—normally William Maginn's pseudonym, though the article has since been ascribed to J. G. Lockhart:

> Hogg is in great heart. By the way, I find I was quite wrong in supposing the "CONFESSIONS OF A SINNER" to be a work of his. It is, as it professes to be, the performance of a Glasgow Literateur, who properly dedicates to the Lord Provost of The West Country.—His name I have not heard. The Book ought to be reviewed by yourself in Maga in your best manner. It is full of talent—the pictures of the rude puritanic manners of the seventeenth century, betray, in every line, the hand of a master [...] [134]

The suggestion that John Wilson write a full review was not taken up, and apart from the above interventions, all facetious-sounding and (in one way or another) implicating 'Hogg', the novel was effectively ignored by *Blackwood's Edinburgh Magazine*, not even featuring in its routine monthly lists of new publications.[135]

As a whole, however, the *Confessions* received a reasonably broad amount of critical attention in the early months of its circulation. In all, ten journals have been identified which carry reviews on the work, all evidently English publications.[136] In extent, responses vary between small notices in niche magazines, such as *The Ladies' Monthly Museum*, to fairly ample statements in mainstream journals. In the latter category can be counted a full (13-page) review in the High Anglican *British Critic* (July 1824), as well as the lead article in the weekly *Literary Gazette* (Saturday, 17 July, 1824), the most high-profile of promotional 'puffing' magazines. *Confessions* likewise is the solitary item found under 'Literary Notices' in Leigh Hunt's radical *Examiner*, on Sunday 1 August, 1824, where effectively a full intellectual critique is provided; it was also one of the first novels to be reviewed in the liberal Utilitarian *Westminster Review* (October 1824). One doubts however whether so much attention would have been given if Hogg had not been rapidly exposed as the author. Six of the journals explicitly name him,[137] usually at an early point, and once the identification is made the overriding tendency is to characterise the novel's literary qualities accordingly. *The Literary Gazette*, whose early identification must have been crucial, almost immediately begins to extrapolate the outlandish and uncouth on this basis:

> This is almost as strange a book as it has been our lot to peruse. Mystical and extravagant (and, what we dislike still more, allegorical;) it is, nevertheless, curious and interesting; a work of irregular genius, such as we might have expected from Mr. Hogg, the Ettrick Shepherd, whose it is.[138]

Others proceeding in this way inclined towards either irregularity or genius mainly according to preconceptions. The Latin-punning reviewer in the *British Critic* immediately perceives 'a diseased and itching peculiarity of style, a *scabies et porrigo Porci*, which, under every disguise, is always sure to betray Mr. Hogg. We had not read twenty pages of this most uncouth and unpleasant volume, before we satisfied ourselves of its parentage'. On the other hand, the anonymous reviewer in the *Examiner* clearly senses something of a fellow mental spirit in detecting 'the strong hand of Mr. Hogg': 'a surprising lack of probability, or even possibility, is accompanied with a portion of mental force and powerful delineation, which denote the conception and the hand of a master.' Any degree of unqualified praise is hard to find, however, the general tendency being to see native talent marred by 'extravagance', inelegance, and eccentricity. 'Put no confidence in Title-pages', the *Ladies' Monthly Museum* warned the author, a succinct enough illustration of how difficult Hogg found it to slough off the skin of his public identity, and why for once he might have wished to do so.[139]

In view of prevailing modern critical approaches, it is somewhat surprising to see the theological aspect of the novel drawing most attention in the search for an underlying 'moral'. The *Monthly Critical Gazette*, whose praise of the author's 'thorough knowledge of the human heart' helped bolster Longmans' autumn advertising campaign, even places its review under the heading of 'Theology'. In this reviewer's eyes the narrative quite rightly (and pertinently) satirises the perversions of high Calvinist doctrine:

> Should any 'serious Christian' be offended at the bitter tone of sarcasm which this author employs, and think it occasionally approaches to irreverence towards subjects, which, we feel certain, he would be the last man living to deride; let them

observe the dreadful fact, that our mad-houses are peopled with individuals whom the doctrines which this gentleman has so ably exposed have driven to insanity.[140]

Elsewhere there is a fairly widespread recognition that the belief in salvation through faith rather than works is under fire: 'Mr Hogg's grand object seems to be to ridicule the Calvinistical tenet of faith without works'; 'The main object of his book [...] seems to be to satirize the excess of that Calvinical [sic] or Cameronian doctrine, which rests the salvation of mankind on *faith* without good works'.[141] Several reviewers, especially those identifying Hogg, question the writer's capacity to tangle with such matters. *The Examiner* offers by far the most informed summary of the doctrine of Justification ('the notions of election, reprobation, and faith independent of works'), but then proceeds to berate Hogg on Godwinian philosophical grounds for an incapacity to comprehend 'the impregnable doctrine of necessity itself'. The *New Monthly Magazine* felt that Hogg had created an invalid *reductio ad absurdum*, in 'attacking the religious prejudices of numbers, who, notwithstanding their speculative opinions, are in no danger of becoming either parricides or fratricides': a response echoed in the *Westminster Review*, which questioned whether a belief in 'saving faith' ever leads to a denial of morality.[142] All but one of the reviews, itself an extremely short notice, respond to the *Confessions* at least partly in a theological light, the opinions offered to a large degree reflecting particular ideological stances. A fairly pervasive feeling nevertheless is found that Hogg/the author cannot fully comprehend the issues, and should not have strayed on religious ground.

It is on an aesthetic level that the reviewers are especially hesitant or begrudging, and by modern standards most lacking in perception. One barrier seems to have been a current perception that the market was glutted with sub-Scottian Scottish novels (the same year had seen the publication of Sarah Green's lampooning novel, *Scotch Novel Reading; or, Modern Quackery*). The reviewer in *News of Literature and Fashion* in this way immediately identifies Hogg's offering as one of those 'little novels which are every day fluttering about, constructed somewhat after the fashion of the Great Novelist'.[143] Several reviews implied an element of derivativeness: two noting a strong similarity to the recently translated *Devil's Elixir*, another a marked resemblance to J. G. Lockhart's *History of Matthew Wald* (1824). Nor did Hogg's devil, when discovered, manage to impress. Compared with Hogg's 'mere vulgar devil', according the *Examiner*, Goethe's 'unrivalled demon [...] is a shadowy personification of the evil tendencies of our nature'—the reviewer thus effectively denying to Gil-Martin those very psychological aspects which later so excited André Gide.[144]

The double narrative, when mentioned, is usually seen in terms of inconsistency, as a sign of an author not in control, or even one engaged in padding. Ambiguities which are now seen as crucial can only be grasped as a fault: 'whether the numerous crimes that are perpetrated are perpetrated by the *hero*, or by the *demon*, Mr. Hogg himself does not appear to know' (*La Belle Assemblée*). The *Westminster* reviewer, while acknowledging the existence of two possible levels of explanation, soon backs off into the safety of an either/or literalism: 'one of two obvious courses must be consistently adhered to. The phantoms of that superstition must either have a real, external being; or they must exist solely in the diseased imagination of the supposed writer. [...] the author must make his election, and adhere to it.'[145] None of the above reviewers managed to convey any sense of enjoyment in reading the work, and several indicated feelings of disgust. As one concluded, 'the impression which the volume has left on our mind is so unpleasant, that we wish we had not read it'.[146]

Hogg appears to have sensed that sales were disappointing by late Autumn. Certainly a dissatisfaction with the performance of Adam Black, Longmans' book-selling agent in Scotland, seems to have been a factor in his efforts to arrange with the London firm a quarter share of both *Confessions* and *Queen Hynde* for William Blackwood. 'I have not the least doubt that we will both be ultimately the profiters by giving Blackwood an interest [...] he will at least sell two fron [*sic*] Mr Black's one.'[147] In the event, it appears Blackwood took only a share in the poem, which when published carried his name with Longmans on the imprint. In December he went even further by buying out Hogg's half share in profits for a sum of £150, this effectively giving him the largest interest in *Queen Hynde*, though Longmans retained the management. On hearing early in the following year that Hogg had already received an advance payment of £100 from Longmans on *Queen Hynde*, Blackwood's response was to consider him his debtor for the same amount; Hogg, at the same time, was encouraged to write to London for 'a statement of your Justified Sinner'.[148] The idea that profits generated by the novel would help cover the sum soon proved to be over-optimistic, however, as too did Blackwood's confident projections for *Queen Hynde*. On 1 September 1825 Hogg professed himself 'very sorry and not a little surprised that the two works have not had a quick sale', reassuring Blackwood nevertheless 'that they both deserved to have it and [...] will ultimately do us all credit'.[149]

Even this residual confidence must have been shaken a year later, when, after another Edinburgh visit by Owen Rees, Hogg learned through one of Blackwood's letters the true state of the account: 'With regard to the Justified Sinner I fear it will not relieve us much, for when Mr Rees was here he gave me the Accts by which it appeared that the whole profits that are now due you on account of it are only about £2.'[150] By 30 January 1828, when Longmans were asked for a further account, Blackwood had evidently taken over Hogg's interest in the novel: 'At your convenience you will be so good as send me the statement of Mr Hogg's acct for the Queen Hynde, and Justified Sinner'.[151] Hogg for his part was effectively left writing for Blackwood to pay off a debt which in his letters he claims more than once not to understand.[152]

In the summer of 1828 Hogg's confidence nevertheless received an unexpected boost through the visit to Scotland of Mrs Hughes, an avowed admirer of his work, and her husband Dr Thomas Hughes, Canon Residentiary of St Paul's in London. Hogg heard of their imminent arrival at Leith from Blackwood, and in a letter of 15 July offered through him an enthusiastic invitation to the Hugheses to stay with him at his farm Mount Benger; but, in the event, Hogg's only contact during the visit seems have to been at Abbotsford. Walter Scott, in a letter of 4 August to Lockhart, gives an unflattering picture of his attendance there: 'Here are Dr and Mrs Hughes [...] little leisure therefore for any thing but Hogg who roars or grunts in a good natured stile keeps Mother Hughes in play'.[153] Mrs Hughes herself later offered a noticeably less patronising account: 'We found Mr. Hogg and Mr. Laidlaw arrived. Hogg is a very simple-man-nered, pleasant person, much less rough in exterior than I expected, and has an open, good humoured face which must prepossess every one in his favour'.[154] Mrs Hughes's assessment of the *Confessions*, which (unlike most reviewers) appears to have recognised its Gothic power, was immediately relayed to Blackwood on Hogg's return: 'Mrs Hughes insists on the Confessions of a Sinner being repub-lished with my name as she says it is positively the best story of that frightful kind that was ever written. I think you must buy up the remaining copies as cheap as you can and make an edition of them for a trial.'[155]

Hogg's suggestion for a relaunch offers perhaps the best single explanation for an apparent reissue of the novel in 1828 under the title *The Suicide's Grave*, which until fairly recently represented some-thing of a bibliographical mystery. Almost certainly this was issued independently of Longmans, who by this stage had most probably sold off their own remaining stock to Thomas Tegg, and whose records show no sign of any further involvement. Examination of a rare (possibly unique) copy held by the Ettrick and Lauderdale Museums Service, Selkirk, reveals that all the gatherings match exactly the first edition: a number of pages too are covered with printer's ink marks, suggesting this copy was fabricated from materials left over from the original print run. This copy lacks the original dedication, which was previously conjugate with the 1824 title-page, and a cancel title-page has been inserted. The full new title is *The Suicide's Grave; or, Memoirs and Confessions of a Sinner*; and the work is described as 'Edited by J. Hogg', while the imprint at the foot of the title-page reads 'Edinburgh: Printed by James Clarke and Co. 1828'.[156] In between the attribution and the imprint is a four-line epigraph identifiable as from a poem by William Cowper, the morbid register of which matches the shift of focus suggested by the changed title.[157] No comparable copy has been discovered, though the University of South Carolina Library holds a copy of the first edition, with a similar 1828 title-page added by a later collector. Neither has evidence apparently survived of prior announcement by the book trade, nor of a commercial sale. In the absence of such factors, it seems most probable that the 'reissue' represents either an attempt by Clarke to clear a small number of surviving sheets, or, more probably, a mock-up manufactured at Hogg's request with a fuller relaunch in mind.

The idea for a new edition never entirely left Hogg's thoughts, primarily as a result of plans late in his life for a collected set of his prose tales. First proposed to Blackwood in the late 1820s, this scheme almost came to fruition in the form of *Altrive Tales*, launched by the London publisher James Cochrane on 31 March 1832, and planned as a monthly publication to be completed in twelve volumes. On 19 March 1832, shortly before leaving London for home, Hogg sent a plan for the first seven volumes, assigning the sixth to 'The Confessions of a Sinner', with a make-weight from another source if required.[158] Cochrane's financial failure meant that the project went no further than the first volume, but Hogg persisted in trying to find an alternative channel, finally reaching an agreement in 1833 with the Glasgow publishers Blackie & Son. In November that year Hogg sent a corrected text of his *The Brownie of Bodsbeck* for the first volume of the set, presumably in the form of a marked up copy of the first edition, with a letter which seems to indicate a willingness for the publishers to make further alterations if required: 'It is as well corrected as I can manage to do it but I never will confine

THE

SUICIDE'S GRAVE;

OR,

MEMOIRS

AND

CONFESSIONS OF A SINNER.

Edited by

J. HOGG.

Sad waste! for which no after thrift atone's—
The grave admits no cure for guilt or sin;
Dewdrops may deck the turf that hides the bones,
But tears of godly grief ne'er flow within.

EDINBURGH:

PRINTED BY JAMES CLARKE AND CO.

1828.

publishers who have such a stake on a work to any expression of mine who am notorious as a careless writer. I therefore give your corrector of the press whom I know to be a man of genious [*sic*] and good taste the power and charge to alter what he pleases.'[159] Progress, however, was slow, and in the following Spring Hogg was still sending material for the first volume, whereas Blackies appear to have proceeded no further than providing a sample page.[160] No other firm evidence of Hogg being involved in the planning or preparation of the work, prior to his death in November 1835, can be found. The work was eventually first issued between 1836 and 1837 as *Tales & Sketches by the Ettrick Shepherd*, in 6 volumes, with Hogg's *Confessions* appearing in the fifth volume, under the new title of 'The Private Memoirs and Confessions of a Fanatic'. As other commentators have noted, this version is radically different in several ways from the text Hogg had originally produced.

A full comparison between the 1824 first edition text and the 1837 'Confessions of a Fanatic' reveals approximately 680 variants, nearly a third of which involve substantive verbal alterations. Amongst some 475 changes in accidentals, the single most common feature is the removal of stops after titles such as 'Mrs.', a routine shift dictated by house style which occurs in some 150 instances, but without full uniformity being achieved. In punctuation if anything there is a lessening of marks (60 commas are removed, compared with 18 added), though the overall effect is to accentuate the grammatical structure of sentences, compared with the more indicative punctuation found in the first edition, with its fuller suggestion of the inflections of language as spoken and heard. The 1837 text also removes much of the italicisation signifying emphasis from the first edition. In the case of orthography, where there are over 40 changes, the general tendency is towards 'modernisation' (e.g., 'choose' is preferred to 'chuse', and 'control' replaces 'controul'), with the loss possibly in the process of some of Hogg's own idiosyncratic forms. The 1837 text is nevertheless technically correct in changing 'acquiline' to 'aquiline'; but then makes egregious errors of its own, such as 'stripped' rather than 'striped'—to produce a fairly risible 'stripped serge' at p.172, l.38. Notwithstanding the involvement of some of the latest advances in printing technology, including the use of stereotype plates, the 1837 text is noticeably more accident-prone than the first edition, with a significantly larger number of typographical errors. It also shows a tendency towards anglicisation, with only one word being transferred to a Scots form, compared with ten in the other direction. It should be added here, however, that the overall loss of Scots is much greater, mainly through the removal of two large areas of text where it is found most densely, the bulk of the interchanges involving John Barnet and the question of Robert Wringhim's paternity (p.69, l.31–p.74, l.13), and the whole of Lucky Shaw's story about the devil's assault on the community of Auchtermuchty (p.136, l.39–p.140, l.19).

The over 200 verbal alterations found vary between large excisions such as that of the Auchermuchty incident and minute adjustments involving single words. Only a handful of changes—some twelve, all small—are insertions, and none give any indication of authorial embellishment. The overall impression one gains is of some person or persons intent on making cuts, perhaps with a reduction in size as one goal, but also with the four following priorities in view.

i) *Grammatical and stylistic 'improvement'.* Up to 75 changes fall into this category. Most are such as might be expected at this period from a house reader, or even a compositor, though hardly any can be deemed necessary, and a good few have a deleterious effect. Little understanding is shown of Hogg's idiomatic expressions, nor of several older usages, so that 'had held' (p.7, l.18) becomes 'had *been* held', 'posted' (p.145, l.4) dissipates into 'passed', and 'the name *of* Bell Calvert' (p.55, l.25: in speech) is flattened to 'the name Bell Calvert'. A tendency towards over-literalness is evident in the correction of Hogg's arithmetic at p.10, l.31, where twelve (representing the 'devil's dozen', i.e. twelve plus one) becomes thirteen; while lack of attention to the larger context can only have allowed the pluralising to 'ghosts' at p.163, l.29, when it has previously been reported that only one ghost haunts A/Eltrive farmhouse. The changes show little sensitivity at points to the allusiveness underlying Hogg's expressions: a better awareness of Burns's 'Holy Willie', for example, might have prevented the removal of the second indefinite article in 'a burning and a shining light' (see p.67, l.11; and note on 67(b)).

ii) *Bowdlerisation.* The most noticeable manifestation of this in sexual terms is the substitution of 'another tavern' for 'a bagnio' (p.36, l.38), when quite clearly by the latter Hogg meant a brothel, of the kind that abounded in Edinburgh both at the time of the novel's setting and in Hogg's day. One effect of this is the obliteration of the image of George Colwan rising 'from the side of one of them [i.e. the resident 'ladies of notable distinction']' at p.37, l.28, as well as (presumably since it has lost its context) of the consequent pulpit warnings to youth 'to beware of such haunts of vice and depravity, the nurses of all that is precipitate, immoral, and base, among man-kind' (see p.39, ll.21–22). As a result the idea of George's moral slippage immediately before his death, and possible consignment to Hell, is seriously diminished. In the same category can be counted some fifty cases where references to the devil and God are removed, these occurring most frequently when found in the mouths of Gil-Martin or the fully 'fanatical' Robert Wringhim. Also victim of such censorship are a number of exclamatory oaths. Found especially amongst Hogg's 'ordinary' characters, these include equally the West-Country weaver's astonished 'So help me God!' (p.150, l.20), Linton's teasing 'God bless your buttons!' (p.151, l.42), and the 'the L–d A—y' element in the instinctual appeal uttered by Robert's stable-loft companion at p.155, l.41.

iii) *Removal of theological content*. While sometimes overlapping with the above category, these revisions are specifically targeted at those areas of the text where the theology of predestination, justification, and election is most in evidence. Some 55 interventions can be so defined, a large number of these involving sizeable cuts, and lead-ing as a whole to the loss of several thousand words. An early indi-cation of what is in store (as well as corroboration that the title change to 'Confessions of a Fanatic' is far from casual) is found in the Edi-tor's Narrative, where the elder George Colwan's bitter words 'about justification by faith alone, and absolute and eternal predestination' (p.40, ll.25–26) are reduced to a more innocuous complaint 'about fanaticism'. In the Sinner's 'Memoirs' the revisions cut deeply and regularly into the heart of the narrative. One striking loss is the key passage where Robert learns from the Rev. Wringhim that 'I was now a justified person [...] sealed and sure' (p.79, ll.30–42). The same policy also involves the removal of the implicit counter-argu-ments which are built into the text. Casualties here include several passages where Robert begins to have doubts about his own immu-nity through justification (see, e.g., p.101, ll.21–31); and also the Rev. Blanchard's views in favour of morality as reported scathingly by Robert (see p.93, ll.23–31). It could also be argued that the two largest cuts in the text–the Barnet interlude, where basic morality stands up to high election, and the Auchtermuchty inset story–were themselves motivated by such considerations, rather than just being the result of a more general pruning of 'extraneous' narrative.

iv) *Structural changes*. Apart from the large cuts made to the Barnet and Auchtermuchty incidents, mentioned above, the most signifi-cant interventions in this category are found in the final sections concerning the suicide and exhumation of the body, where a number of seeming disparities are ironed out. Most importantly, all mention of the author within the text is removed. The *Blackwood's* article is now referred to as coming from 'Ebony', and Hogg is no longer found *in situ* at Thirlestane market. The last significant change occurs with the removal of the whole passage where the Editor/Hogg describes the title-page of the discovered memoirs, his unfulfilled aim to alter 'Justified' to 'Self-justified', and the warning from the Sinner not to 'alter or amend'. The most obvious motivation for these changes is that *Confessions* was now appearing as an authorially-acknowledged work; and, more particularly, the changed title. In the process, however, this part of the novel loses much of its multi-textured quality, and some of the more pernickety interventions smack of the over-literalness that had governed changes in other categories.

Opinions have differed on the issue of whether Hogg himself was involved in the above alterations. Edith Batho and Douglas Gifford are inclined to believe that revisions are his, with Gifford seeing this as indicative of a general decline in Hogg's published work in later life, whereas John Carey and Douglas Mack are more sceptical, suspecting the involvement of other hands.[161] Of course, it is not impossible that some changes are Hogg's and others the work of Blackie's copy editor. This certainly appears to have been the case with *The Brownie of Bodsbeck*, where material almost certainly authorial, such as an additional song, is found alongside fussy interventions such as the removal of swearing.[162] But the cases are not directly comparable, since there is no direct evidence of Hogg working on *Confessions* for the Blackie set,[163] nor are there any additions there that seem authorial. The case of 'The Siege of Roxburgh', the version of *Three Perils of Man* which appeared in the sixth volume of *Tales & Sketches*, is sometimes mentioned in support of the idea that Hogg was prepared to downsize material to match new restrictions. However, while there are strong indications that Hogg had already planned a similar cut-down version for his *Altrive Tales* series in 1832, under the same new title, there is no suggestion that any such alteration was intended (or needed) there for 'Confessions of a Sinner'; and, furthermore, the removal of the supernatural sub-plot and its stories from the more extensive 1822 novel, which itself Hogg had come to believe was flawed, represents a quite different form of exercise.[164]

In terms of the internal evidence in view, any argument ultimately is bound to centre on the removal of 'theological' content, which, as already suggested, so severely disturbs the fabric of the original novel. It is just possible here that Hogg himself was responding to criticism already received, say in the reviews, perhaps with a view to forestalling possible difficulties with his new publishers. Yet in spite of these and other pressures, it still seems out of character that the Hogg who fought so hard for the integrity of the first edition, not least this area, should relinquish the matter so willingly. Blackie & Son, on the other hand, had every reason for wanting contentious matter out of the way. Analysis of publications in the Blackie Stock Edition book in the years leading up to *Tales & Sketches* reveals that over half their output consisted of religious materials. Much of this was in the 'evangelical' Presbyterian tradition–the firm, for instance, published both Thomas Boston's *Sermons* and *Human Nature in its Fourfold State*. Popular testimonies of the old Covenanting martyrs were particular favourites, with editions of *A Cloud of Witnesses*, John Howie's *Scots Worthies*, and Robert Wodrow's *The History of the Sufferings of the Church of Scotland* all regularly in stock. This trade was conducted mainly through number publication, with travelling salesmen selling weekly and monthly parts, the main heartland for the Blackie enterprise at this period being Glasgow and the outlying West-Country districts. *Tales & Sketches* itself would also have been distributed this way, at first probably chiefly through the sale of volumes, and Blackies would be exceptionally keen not to cause offence amongst their main constituency of subscribers.[165]

Two areas of intervention, so far not noted, are unusually telling here. The first is the pruning of significant parts of the exchange in the Edinburgh guard-house between Robert Wringhim and his jailer, an interlude which could be taken to parody the imprisonment of the Covenanting martyrs in the seventeenth century, and beyond that the biblical model of Paul and Silas converting their keeper to Christianity while in prison, an incident much cited as proof of salvation through grace. The second is the deletion of the whole of Penpunt's story about the West-Country Cameronian willing to accept double payment for his cow: a parable which could be taken as revealing a deep hypocrisy, though Hogg himself seems more intent on drawing a contrast between the quotidian pragmatism of ordinary members of that church and the conceit of 'proud professors' of religion like the Wringhims. Pressure of space is another possible factor, but here again the constraints on Blackies were at least as tight as any Hogg might have imposed on himself, with each of the volumes in the *Tales* being constructed to fit within ten 36-page sheets, possibly to facilitate a number sale. Notwithstanding the set's slightly hedging opening claim in its 'Advertisement' to incorporate the author's 'final corrections', it seems most probable that most or all of the verbal changes discussed above were carried out by a house editor, mindful of the need to tailor a product suited to the Blackie imprint. In fact, it is hard to think of a literary text more influenced by its publishing colours, or of a later edition which loses so much of the quality of the original text. Yet it was in this form that Hogg's masterpiece was chiefly known to the end of the century, with Blackie & Son, and then other lesser publishers, periodically reissuing 'Confessions of a Fanatic' in largely unchanged form somewhere to the rear of the Ettrick Shepherd's Tales.[166]

Ever since the J. Shiells & Co. edition of 1895, under the lead title of *The Suicide's Grave*, modern editions have tended to vaunt their 'first edition' credentials, though with varying degrees of justification. A survey of the Shiells text confirms that it restores the full body of the original version, while altering punctuation and orthography liberally, effectively applying its own house style regardless of earlier conventions. Little hesitation either is shown in making stylistic improvements and conjectural emendations, a number of these matching those in the 1837 *Tales & Sketches* version, though arrived at presumably through independent means. Shiells thus parallels the 1837 version by transferring 'twelve' to 'thirteen', 'benefactor' (p.61, l.27) to a gender-correct 'benefactress', and 'reards' (p.136, l.15) to 'reads' (to create a much flattened 'reads and prays'). It also generates a number of gaffes of its own, including 'shankel bone' for 'shakel bane', while literally spelling out 'the L—d A—y' as 'The Lord Almighty'. This edition was issued in both a *de luxe* version, with photogravure illustrations, and a plainer unillustrated version, though both issues include the Facsimile, with the page reference at the head renumbered to match the new setting.[167] The original dedication, and the separate title-page before the Sinner's Memoirs, are not included however—as was also to be the case with most of its successors.

A similar tendency to alter punctuation and orthography is evident in the version of *Confessions* published by A. M. Philpot, Ltd as No. 1 of the Campion Reprint series, in 1924, with its Introduction by T. Earle Welby. Evidently this edition was set freshly against a first edition text, since it generally does not include variants created by Shiells. In the process a large number of verbal changes were made, many of them crudifying the text, through unnecessary standardisation, anglicisation of Scots, and a general inability to sense the multi-dimensional nature of the narrative. Collation of texts shows that it was the Bristol-printed Campion edition which provided the copy-text for the Cresset Press (André Gide-introduced) edition of 1947. The Cresset text in this way inherits some 130 changes from the Campion edition, while generating about 25 more by itself (for example, the substitution of 'strange' for 'stranger' at p.80, l.29, turning Gil-Martin into a 'strange youth'). Emendations at key points in Campion/Gide tend to differ from those found in earlier versions: the first edition's 'This effect made my case worse', which in the 1837 text (and Shiells) appears as 'This effort made my case worse', is thus emended to read 'The effect made my case worse' (see p.149, ll.15–16). The Gide edition also turns a few more Scots forms into English, while further smoothing out spelling and punctuation.

The Cresset text is followed in turn by two recent editions, published in Britain under rival 'Everyman' banners, edited by Roger Lewis (1992) and J. A. Cuddon (1994). One particularly visible effect of this is the reproduction of the Cresset text's insertion in square brackets of '*v[ide] Frontispiece*', though neither of these editions (unlike Cresset) actually includes the 'Facsimile'.[168] A more recent British paperback, the Wordsworth Classics edition (1997), clearly belongs to the same stable, reproducing for example the obvious mistake in 'an old an intimate acquaintance' (see p.10, l.14), which stems from Cresset, and also 'expression [rather than 'impression'] on my mind' at p.63, l.9, a verbal slip which goes all the way back to Campion.[169] A stemma (or 'family tree') of modern editions then would show a clear line running from the Campion edition in 1924, through the Cresset Press text of 1947, to several recent popular reprints, none of which accurately reflects the first edition state.

The other main line in modern editions stems from John Carey's 1969 edition for the Oxford English Novels Series. This itself represents the first text accurately to be based on the 1824 edition, and is generally impeccable in following the original orthography and punctuation (though the use of single rather than double quotation marks for speech arguably takes away some period flavour). Carey's edition was also unique in providing a list of emendations: some seven in all, admitting 1837 readings, in 'places where it seems clear that *1824* misprints'. These include the replacement of 'trust' with 'trusty' in Hogg's charter imitation (see p.124, l.8), and the omission of the first 'with' in the seemingly clumsy 'the character with which she had to deal with' (p.44, ll.34–35). Carey's text also on occasions silently corrects error, as in its mending of 'completly' to 'completely', and omission of a superfluous negative in 'Behold thou dost not not know'. A more thorough collation, conducted for the present edition by electronic means, has also revealed a number of other disparities compared with the first edition.[170] One factor here is a tendency to elide combinations such as 'o' ye' and 'wi' ye' (i.e. with spaces) to 'o'ye' 'wi'ye', a marginal difference in some respects, but one which at certain points is capable of creating a tonal difference. Additionally, a number of keying errors have been disclosed by this process. These include nearly ten instances of verbal difference, for example: 'this report' rather than 'his report' at p.64, l.6; 'laying thy hands' rather than 'laying thy hand' at p.164, l.35; and the more obviously mistaken 'better that I did' at p.101, l.17. Among a very small number of typographical errors are found an 'impraticable' and 'gaurdian', while the 1969 edition also carries over the first edition's stuttered 'the the blighting influence' at p.25, l.14.[171]

Such discrepancies also help identify those first-edition based texts that are in fact to a large degree offshoots of Carey. Douglas Gifford's Folio Society edition of 1978, John Wain's Penguin edition (1983), and David Groves's Canongate Classics edition (1991), all show signs of having been initially set from an impression of the 1969 Oxford text, rather than from an actual first edition copy. On page 119 of Wain's edition eye slip is the most obvious reason for the omission of eleven words, the copyist having moved wrongly from 'his' at the end of a line to 'face' rather than 'feet' in the immediately preceding line in Carey, leading to an inapposite 'I could almost have kissed his face continually' (compare p.75, ll.7-9).[172] The Canongate edition on its present page 207 refers to the printed part of Robert Wringhim's 'Memoirs' as ending on 'page 222', replicating the Carey edition, where indeed this part of the text does end on that page. More invasively the elisions in Carey, as well as most of its verbal changes and a handful of punctuational variants also generated there, are carried through into all the three editions mentioned above. The Canongate edition even follows one or two typographical errors, including a visibly flawed 'herever'.[173] On the other hand, Groves courageously challenges several of Carey's emendations, restoring the first edition's 'understanding' instead of 'undertaking' at p.108, l.34, 'round an' round' in preference to 'round and round' (see p.142, l.29), and 'This effect' rather than 'This effort' at p.149, l.16. By restoring the dedication to the Lord Provost of Glasgow, while preserving the facsimile as a frontispiece, the Canongate edition could also legitimately claim to offer the most complete edition of Hogg's *Confessions* since 1824.

The present edition is the first to be based directly on a copy of the first edition since John Carey's 1969 edition. In the light of fresh evidence that Hogg was closely involved with the original edition of 1824, it limits emendations to typographical errors and obvious mistakes, hoping thereby to arrive at the text which Hogg and his printer so nearly achieved. In presentational terms, the aim has been to match as closely as possible, in a modern equivalent, the original structuring of the first edition, by preserving all the preliminaries, the titles and headings within the text, and the intricate system of running headlines. The only intervention in this area has been the transference of the page number at the head of the Facsimile, and of the single cross-reference within the narrative, to match the present pagination.[174] A fuller account of the emendations made, with reasons, is given in 'Note on the Text', pp. 195–99.

Notes

1. The suggestion that Lockhart might have had a hand in the work was made by George Saintsbury in *Essays in English Literature 1780-1860* (London, 1890), pp. 62–65, this being echoed by Andrew Lang in 'Confessions of a Justified Sinner', Supplement to vol. CV, Issue 2901 of *Illustrated London News*, 24 November, 1894, p. 12.

2. Mrs Garden, 'The Suicide's Grave', in *The Athenæum*, no. 3551, 16 November 1895, p. 681.

3. *The Private Memoirs and Confessions of a Justified Sinner*, Campion Reprints no. 1, with an Introduction by T. Earle Welby (London, 1924), p. 7.

4. David Groves, Introduction to Canongate Classics 39 (Edinburgh, 1991), p. viii; Iain Crichton Smith, 'A Work of Genius: James Hogg's *Justified Sinner*', *Studies in Scottish Literature*, 28 (1993), 1–11 (p. 1); Gillian Hughes, 'James Hogg Society News', *ScotLit* no. 20 (Spring 1999), p. 8.

5. Letter to James Gray, 20 November 1813, in 'G', 'Some Particulars Relative to the Ettrick Shepherd', *New Monthly Magazine*, 46 (April 1836), 443–46 (p. 444).

6. 'A Witch's Chant' was later reprinted in Hogg's *Songs* (1831), while an altered version of 'The Harper's Song' appeared as 'Superstition and Grace' in *The Bijou* for 1829. For texts of 'Superstition and Grace' and 'Jocke Taittis Expeditioune till Hell', see *A Queer Book*, ed. by P. D. Garside (Edinburgh: Edinburgh University Press, 1995), pp. 136–43, 189–92.

7. 'The Witches of Traquair', in *The Shepherd's Calendar*, ed. by Douglas S. Mack (Edinburgh: Edinburgh University Press, 1995), p. 223; *Selected Stories and Sketches*, ed. by Douglas S. Mack (Edinburgh: Scottish Academic Press, 1982), p. 170.

8. James Hogg, *Memoir of the Author's Life* and *Familiar Anecdotes of Sir Walter Scott*, ed. by Douglas S. Mack (Edinburgh and London: Scottish Academic Press, 1972), p. 7 (hereafter referred to as *Memoir*).

9. Ian Campbell, 'James Hogg and the Bible', *Scottish Literary Journal*, 10: 1 (May 1983), 14–29.

10. 'A Letter from Yarrow—the Scottish Psalmody Defended', *Edinburgh Literary Journal*, 13 March 1830, 162–63 (p. 163). This response by Hogg, together with Tennant's articles (which also originally appeared in the *Edinburgh Literary Journal*), were reprinted in pamphlet form as *Critical Remarks on the Psalms of David* (Edinburgh, 1830): Tennant's initial remark is quoted from this pamphlet, p. 12.

11. *The Spy*, ed. by Gillian Hughes (Edinburgh: Edinburgh University Press, 2000), p. 504.

12. *Daily Review*, 16 January 1866: letter dated 12 January 1866.

13. *Memoir*, p. 5.

14. James Hogg, *Anecdotes of Scott*, ed. by Jill Rubenstein (Edinburgh: Edinburgh University Press, 1999), pp. 37–38. The account referred to is from Hogg's *Familiar Anecdotes of Sir Walter Scott* (New York, 1834). Earlier versions of Scott's visit by Hogg had appeared in 'Reminiscences of Former Days: My First Interview with Sir Walter Scott', *Edinburgh Literary Journal*, 27 June 1829, 51–52; and as part of 'Reminiscences of Former Days', an extension by Hogg to his 'Memoir of the Author's Life', published in *Altrive Tales* (1832).

15. Hogg, *Anecdotes of Scott*, pp. 38-40. Scott evidently later worked the incident concerning sheep into one of his own stories: see his *The Black Dwarf*, ed. by P. D. Garside (Edinburgh: Edinburgh University Press, 1993), pp. 13, 210.

16. Hogg, *Anecdotes of Scott*, p. 40.

17. The following account of the novel's dual narrative is indebted to a number of critical essays, notable among which are: David Eggenschwiler, 'James Hogg's *Confessions* and the Fall into Division', *Studies in Scottish Literature*, 9:1 (1971), 26–39; Elizabeth W. Harries, 'Duplication and Duplicity: James Hogg's *Private Memoirs and Confessions of a Justified Sinner*', *Wordsworth Circle*, 10: 2 (Spring 1979), 187–96; David Groves, 'Parallel Narratives in Hogg's *Justified Sinner*', *Scottish Literary Journal*, 9: 2 (December 1982), 37–44; and Douglas S. Mack, 'Revisiting *The Private Memoirs and Confessions of a Justified Sinner*', *Studies in Hogg and his World*, 10 (1999), 1–26. Commentary on Hogg and oral/print culture has also benefited from Penny Fielding, *Writing and Orality: Nationality, Culture, and Nineteenth-Century Scottish Fiction* (Oxford: Clarendon Press, 1996).

18. Page numbers given within the main text refer to the present edition of *Confessions*, unless otherwise indicated; where line numbers are also given, these do not include titles and running headlines.

19. Douglas Gifford, *James Hogg* (Edinburgh: Ramsay Head Press, 1976), p. 144. For the issue of double signification, see also L. L. Lee, 'The Devil's Figure: James Hogg's *Justified Sinner*', *Studies in Scottish Literature*, 3: 4 (1966), 230–39; John Herdman, *The Double in Nineteenth-Century Fiction* (London: Macmillan, 1990), pp. 69–87; and, for an especially fine psychoanalytical reading, Barbara Bloedé, '*The Confessions of a Justified Sinner*: The Paranoiac Nucleus', *Papers given at the First Conference of the James Hogg Society*, ed. by Gillian Hughes (Stirling: James Hogg Society, 1983), pp. 15–28.

20. For early responses which highlighted the theological aspect in the novel, see the third section of this Introduction. An unusual exception to the

modern tendency to sideline such issues is John Bligh, 'The Doctrinal Premises of Hogg's *Confessions of a Justified Sinner*', *Studies in Scottish Literature*, 19 (1984), 148–64.

21. Edward Fisher, *The Marrow of Modern Divinity*, 16th edn (Glasgow, 1766), pp. 127–28. (This above contains James Hog's Preface to the 1718 edn, and the Notes of Thomas Boston, first published with the 1726 edn of the *Marrow*.)

22. In Fisher, *Marrow*, pp. xii-xiii.

23. *Queries, Agreed unto by the Commission of the General Assembly; [...] Together with the Answers [...] to the Said Queries* ([Edinburgh], 1722), pp. 4, 40.

24. Quoted in David C. Lachman, *The Marrow Controversy* (Edinburgh: Rutherford House, 1988), p. 395.

25. Louis Simpson, *James Hogg: A Critical Study* (Edinburgh: Oliver & Boyd, 1962), pp. 170-73. A fuller investigation of the issues involved will be found in John Joseph Haggerty, 'James Hogg's *The Private Memoirs and Confessions of a Justified Sinner*: Background, Text, and Analysis' (unpublished doctoral dissertation, Illinois, 1969).

26. In Fisher, *Marrow*, p. 128n.

27. James Hogg, *The Shepherd's Calendar*, ed. by Douglas S. Mack (Edinburgh: Edinburgh University Press, 1995), pp. 112–13. The incident involving Wringhim and John Barnet will be found at pp. 72–73 in the present edition. Hogg later offered (apparently unequivocal) praise for Boston's beneficial influence in stimulating a 'spirit of intelligence in Ettrick' and for the power of his theological arguments, in his essay 'Statistics of Selkirkshire': 'It has been the fashion for a good while past, with a certain class of professed Christians, both preachers and hearers, to sneer at the doctrines of Boston. I decidedly differ from them, and will venture to assert that there are no such fervour [*sic*] and strength of reasoning to be met with in any modern composition, as predominate in his. [...] There is even an originality of thought and expression in old Boston which are quite delightful and refreshing' (*Prize-Essays and Transactions of the Highland Society of Scotland*, 9 (1832), 281-306p (pp. 303–04)).

28. See Andrew L. Drummond and James Bulloch, *The Scottish Church 1688–1843: The Age of the Moderates* (Edinburgh: St Andrew Press, 1973), p. 107. Other works relating to Scottish Church history and theological issues, which have informed the present account, include: Henry F. Henderson, *The Religious Controversies of Scotland* (Edinburgh: T. & T. Clark, 1905); J. H. S. Burleigh, *A Church History of Scotland* (London: Oxford University Press, 1960); and Gordon Marshall, *Presbyteries and Profits: Calvinism and the Development of Capitalism in Scotland, 1560-1707* (Oxford: Clarendon Press, 1980). The M'Gill case is discussed in Drummond and Bulloch, pp. 106–07, and Henderson, pp. 86–94.

29. James Hogg, *Lay Sermons*, ed. by Gillian Hughes (Edinburgh: Edinburgh University Press, 1997), pp. 109, 140.

30. For the correspondence between Blackwood and Hogg on the subject of this poem, which led eventually to its revision before publication, see James Hogg, *A Queer Book*, ed. by P. D. Garside (Edinburgh: Edinburgh University Press, 1995), pp. 268–70.

31. See James Hamilton, *The Life of Lady Colquhoun* [originally published as *A Memoir of Lady Colquhoun*, 1850] (Inverness: Free Presbyterian Church of Scotland, 1969), pp. 17, 20, 59.

32. The possibility of a connection between Cottle and Hogg, through Robert Southey, is broached by John Carey in his 1969 edition of *Confessions*: see James Hogg, *The Private Memoirs and Confessions of a Justified Sinner*, ed. by John Carey (London: Oxford University Press, 1969), pp. xxii–xxiii. See also Bligh, 'Doctrinal Premises', pp. 153, 155.

33. In *The School of Faith: The Catechisms of the Reformed Church*, trans. and ed. by Thomas F. Torrance (London: James Clarke & Co., 1959), p. 25 (hereafter referred to as Torrance).

34. *The Confession of Faith, together with the Larger and Lesser Catechismes* (London, 1658), pp. 42–43.

35. *Confession of Faith*, p. 44 (my italics).

36. See R. T. Kendall, *Calvin and English Calvinism to 1649* (Oxford: Oxford University Press, 1979), p. 15. According to Kendall (p. 29), the idea that Christ died for the Elect only is more associable with Theodore Beza (1519–1605), Calvin's successor in Geneva.

37. *Confession of Faith*, p. 14.

38. *Geneva Catechism*, in Torrance, p. 25. More particularly, the idea that good works as the product of faith are a necessary part of salvation forms an important part of Scottish Calvinism in the 16th and 17th centuries: see Marshall, *Presbyteries and Profits*, Part Two ('The Scots Calvinist Ethic'), especially pp. 62, 74–75.

39. *Confession of Faith*, p. 44.

40. The Feast of the Annunciation, when the angel Gabriel announced to Mary that she would be the mother of the Messiah.

41. *Memoir*, p. 6.

42. For further details concerning the Andersons of Eltrive, see Peter Garside, 'Hogg, Eltrive, and *Confessions*', *Studies in Hogg and his World*, 11 (2000), 5–24.

43. Douglas S. Mack, 'The Body in the Opened Grave: Robert Burns and Robert Wringhim', *Studies in Hogg and his World*, 7 (1996), 70–79 (pp. 73–74).

44. Hogg's reply to Scott of 5 July 1821, stating that the 'great day at London is the next after St. Boswel's fair', in National Library of Scotland (hereafter NLS), MS 3892, fol. 148.

45. For an alternative interpretation of this incomplete name, see note on 'Mr. S—t' for 170(d) in explanatory Notes.

46. For Hogg's relationship with James Gray, see Gillian Hughes's edition of *The Spy* (Edinburgh: Edinburgh University Press, 2000), pp. 562–63; also, for the Forum, her article 'James Hogg and the Forum', *Studies in Hogg and his World*, 1 (1990), 57–70.

47. *Memoir*, pp. 35–36, 46.

48. In his *Doubles: Studies in Literary History* (Oxford: Oxford University Press, 1985), p. 19.

49. *Memoir*, p. 42.

50. NLS, MS 4002, fol. 155 (Hogg to Blackwood, 12 August 1817).

51. *Memoir*, p. 43.

52. James Kirkton, *The Secret and True History of the Church of Scotland*, ed. by

Charles Kirkpatrick Sharpe (Edinburgh, 1817), pp. v, 1.

53. Kirkton, pp. 16, 16n–18n.

54. *Blackwood's Edinburgh Magazine*, 2 (December 1817), 305–09 (pp. 307, 306).

55. NLS, MS 4003, fol. 97.

56. NLS, MS 4005, fol. 169. For the tennis incidents in the novel, see present edition, pp. 16–18, 102.

57. *Blackwood's Edinburgh Magazine*, 4 (February 1819), 521–29.

58. *Blackwood's Edinburgh Magazine*, 7 (May 1820), 148–54. The review ends by promising an invasion *en masse* by the Magazine's contributors to Hogg's home at Altrive Lake on 12 July.

59. *Blackwood's Edinburgh Magazine*, 10 (August 1821), 43–52.

60. NLS, MS 4007, fol. 38.

61. NLS, MS 4007, fol. 43 (Hogg to Blackwood, 17 October 1821).

62. NLS, MS 4014, fol. 287 (Hogg to Blackwood, 29 January 1825).

63. *Blackwood's Edinburgh Magazine*, 10 (August 1821), 26-33. Previously attributed to John Galt, the article has been identified as probably Hogg's by Professor Tom Richardson, for reasons which will be given fully in his forthcoming Stirling / South Carolina volume of Hogg's Contributions to *Blackwood's*. In 1822 Hogg was offering Blackwood an allegorical satire of the literary scene, written in a Fieldingesque Augustan style, which was later published as 'John Paterson's Mare' in the *Newcastle Magazine* for January 1825. Hogg's attempts to provide material for the 'Noctes Ambrosianae' were almost invariably blocked, apart from the insertion of some of his poems and a number of songs.

64. Compare his letter to Blackwood of 5 December 1821: 'You never did as shabby a thing in your life as keeping up your Magazine from me I will rather pay you for it than want it' (NLS, MS 4007, fol. 44).

65. *Blackwood's Edinburgh Magazine*, 1 (July 1817), 388–94 (pp. 393–94). The account also covers the main aspects of the plot, including Faustus's bequeathing of his soul 'by an inscription written in blood upon his arm' (p. 389), and the 'twenty-four years' duress granted him on earth (p. 393). For a full discussion of possible connections with Marlowe's play, see David Groves, 'Allusions to *Dr. Faustus* in James Hogg's *A Justified Sinner*', *Studies in Scottish Literature*, 18 (1983), 157–65.

66. For the above stories and a useful introductory appraisal of the importance of *Blackwood's* in pioneering a new kind of Gothic writing, see *Tales of Terror from Blackwood's Magazine*, ed. by Robert Morrison and Chris Baldick (Oxford: Oxford University Press, 1995). Similarities between Hogg's *Confessions* and *Melmoth the Wanderer*, especially relating to the latter's conclusion, are noted in Ian Campbell, 'Hogg's *Confessions* and the *Heart of Darkness*', *Studies in Scottish Literature*, 15 (1980), 187–201.

67. *Blackwood's Edinburgh Magazine*, 11 (March 1822), 349–58 (p. 349); 11 (June 1822), 669–77 (pp. 669, 677). For the attribution of the review of *Adam Blair* to John Wilson, rather than Henry Mackenzie, see P. D. Garside, 'Henry Mackenzie, the Scottish Novel, and *Blackwood's Magazine*', *Scottish Literary Journal*, 15: 1 (May 1988), 25–48 (pp. 42–43).

68. See, e.g., Blackwood's letter of 24 May 1822: 'Along with Maga I send Mrs Hogg Lights & Shadows The Provost & Gillespies Sermons' (NLS, MS

30305, p. 329), where one senses an expectation that Hogg himself would view at least the first two titles.

69. NLS, MS 4008, fol. 267; MS 4010, fol. 188 (Hogg to Blackwood, 13 April 1823); MS 4024, fol. 294 (Hogg to Blackwood, 18 June 1823). A rueful feeling of lost opportunities can also be sensed in an earlier letter to Blackwood, in response to Galt's *Annals of the Parish* (1821), which Hogg found striking for its 'simplicity and extraordinary resemblance to truth': 'It is a strange thing that you will let *men of true genius* slip through your fingers for a few blemishes that are rather properties in the main' (NLS, MS 4007, fol. 24: 16 May 1821).

70. NLS, MS 30306, pp. 134–35.

71. *Blackwood's Edinburgh Magazine*, 13 (March 1823), 369–84 (pp. 370–71). Hogg had first appeared as an interlocutor in the 'Noctes' in its sixth number, December 1822, chiefly by William Maginn. For a fuller overview, see J. H. Alexander, 'Hogg in the *Noctes Ambrosianae*', *Studies in Hogg and his World*, 4 (1993), 37–47.

72. *Blackwood's Edinburgh Magazine*, 14 (August 1823), 188–90 (pp. 188, 190). For the sections of the article incorporated in the novel, see present edition, pp. 165–69.

73. *Blackwood's Edinburgh Magazine*, 14 (October 1823), 427–37 (p. 437). Blackwood's comment is made in a letter to Wilson of 20 September 1823, NLS, MS 3395, fol. 17. It continues later, 'Few of the readers of Maga know the beastliness of Hogg, and weak minds would be startled by some of your strong expressions'. In an undated letter to Blackwood, J. G. Lockhart refuses to enter into the revision of the article, suggesting that Blackwood himself softens it down: 'I must have nothing to do with the murder of my own dedicator [referring to Hogg's dedication of *Three Perils of Woman* to himself]. You shd take out certainly a few coarse words which mt offend Mrs Hogg—but who does that better than yourself?' (NLS, MS 4010, fol. 217).

74. *Blackwood's Edinburgh Magazine*, 14 (October 1823), 484–503 (pp. 497, 486, 495). Wilson's mention of floods perhaps plays on Hogg's description of a cataract (flash flood), in his story 'Mr Adamson of Laverhope', first published in the June 1823 number of *Blackwood's*: see *The Shepherd's Calendar*, ed. by Douglas S. Mack (Edinburgh: Edinburgh University Press, 1995), pp. 49, 261–62.

75. See Grevel Lindop, *The Opium-Eater: A Life of Thomas De Quincey* (London: J. M. Dent, 1981), pp. 214, 241–48. Thanks are also due to Richard D. Jackson for the generous communication of detailed information concerning Hogg and De Quincey.

76. For a fuller consideration of such issues, see Susan M. Levin, *The Romantic Art of Confession* (Columbia, SC: Camden House, 1998), especially Chapters 1 and 6.

77. Thomas De Quincey, *Confessions of an English Opium-Eater* (London, 1822), pp. 18, 159, 121, 82. Page references to Hogg's *Confessions* (here as elsewhere) are given in parenthesis in the main text, and refer to the present edition.

78. *New Edinburgh Review*, 4 (January 1823), 253–74 (p. 267). This periodical was

a continuation of the *Edinburgh Monthly Review* (founded in 1819), and was printed by Balfour and [James] Clarke, the latter of whom was also the printer of Hogg's *Confessions*. 'The Adventures of Basil Lee' appears in vol. 1 of *Winter Evening Tales* (1820), pp. 1–99, the vitriol for whisky incident featuring on p. 12.

79. De Quincey, *Opium-Eater*, p. 167.

80. *Blackwood's Edinburgh Magazine*, 13 (January 1823), 86–93 (pp. 86, 92–93). The possible influence of this article, usually attributed to Thomas Colley Grattan, was first noted by David Groves, in '"Confessions of an English Glutton": A (Probable) Source for James Hogg's *Confessions*', *Notes and Queries*, 238 (1993), 46–47.

81. Christiane Zehl Romero, 'M. G. Lewis' *The Monk* and E. T. A. Hoffmann's *Die Elixiere des Teufels*–Two Versions of the Gothic', *Neophilogus*, 63 (1979), 574–81 (p. 580).

82. For a study of textual affinities, with special attention to this episode, see Reinhard Heinritz and Silvia Mergenthal, 'Hogg, Hoffmann and their Diabolical Elixirs', *Studies in Hogg and his World*, 7 (1996), 47–58.

83. NLS, MS 4004, fol. 158. Gillies had earlier written a highly complimentary verse dedication to Hogg for his own anonymous collection, *Illustrations of a Poetical Character* (1816).

84. R. P. Gillies, *Memoirs of a Literary Veteran*, 3 vols (London, 1851), III, 54, 52. The potential closeness of this circle is indicated in Hogg's letter to his wife on 13 May 1823, from Edinburgh, which remarks how 'Neither Gillies nor Lockhart offered me a bed and I did not like to force myself on them' (Turnbull Library, New Zealand, MS Papers 42, folder 75).

85. The letter is given in Mrs Garden, *Memorials of James Hogg the Ettrick Shepherd*, 3rd edn (Paisley, 1904), pp. 206–07. David Groves assumes that it relates to *Three Perils of Woman* in his Afterword to the Stirling / South Carolina Research Edition volume of that novel (Edinburgh: Edinburgh University Press, 1995), pp. 418, 434.

86. *Blackwood's Edinburgh Magazine*, 16 (July 1824), 55–67 (p. 57).

87. For a full version of Hoffmann's work, see *The Devil's Elixirs*, trans. by Ronald Taylor (London: John Calder, 1963). Gillies's own translation misses out some of the apparatus, though the use of ellipses and interventions by the Editor are a fairly common feature. A not dissimilar technique is found in J. G. Lockhart's novel, *The History of Matthew Wald* (1824), published early in May in the same year, where the first-person narrative is followed at the end by an Editor-like Letter 'enclosing the foregoing Memoirs'. Lockhart's structure however is not without serious internal flaws.

88. Gillies, *Memoirs*, III, 95.

89. *Blackwood's Edinburgh Magazine*, 15 (April 1824), 367–90 (p. 383). Hogg's catch phrase is repeated slightly later: 'Fule and Phrenologist are a' ane, sir, truly enough' (p. 384).

90. J. G. Lockhart, *Peter's Letters to his Kinsfolk*, 2nd edn (actually the 1st), 3 vols (Edinburgh, 1819), II, 341.

91. Lockhart, *Peter's Letters*, I, 127; III, 136. In the latter instance, there is a nearby engraved portrait (opposite III, 141) of 'the Ettrick Shepherd', where the viewer's attention is drawn to the mouth, and to the buck teeth visible

there. The interest in physiognomy seems to extend much further than
the need to keep Dr Peter Morris, the supposed correspondent, in character.

92. 'Remarks on the Cerebral Development and Dispositions of John Thurtell',
Phrenological Journal and Miscellany, 1: 2 (February 1824), 326–36. The likening of Thurtell to Othello provides the most immediate spur for the satire
in the April 1824 'Noctes'. The *Phrenological Journal* responded in turn by
including its own 'Ambrosian Manuscript' in the fourth number (August
1824), in which 'the Shepherd' shows a more conciliatory attitude to the
'science': 'O man, but ye're bitter against thae Phrenological bodies!' (p.
576).

93. The above details are mostly taken from an account of the trial, headed
'Murder of William Howat', in the *Edinburgh Weekly Journal*, 19 March 1823,
pp. 92–94. Further information is found in a volume of materials relating
to the case, including pamphlets and newspaper cuttings, in NLS, Ry.II.c.26.
The relevance of the incident to Hogg was first noted by David Groves in
his 'James Hogg's *Confessions* and *Three Perils of Woman* and the Edinburgh
Prostitution Scandal of 1823', *Wordsworth Circle* 18 (Summer 1987), 127–31.
For an alternative view, shifting the emphasis away from *Three Perils of
Woman* and hence closer towards *Confessions*, see also Barbara Bloedé, 'Hogg
and the Edinburgh Prostitution Scandal', *Newsletter of the James Hogg Society*,
no. 8 (May 1989), 15–18.

94. As reported in an article, headed 'Phrenology', in *Edinburgh Weekly Journal*,
14 May 1823, p. 157. Combe's paper, as read on 1 May, was later published
in *Transactions of the Phrenological Society* (Edinburgh, 1824), as 'Case of Mary
Macinnes, who murdered William Howat', pp. 362–77. The use of the
surname Macinnes resulted from claims made after the execution that
M'Kinnon was not the daughter of an Irish army quarter-master but of a
lime-burner in the Hebrides.

95. A broadsheet song, 'McKinnon's Garland', in the style of *The Beggar's Op-
era*, and attributed in hand to C. K. Sharpe, is preserved in NLS, Ry.II.c.26.
An idea of the incipient racism underlying Phrenology can be gathered
from the report in the *Edinburgh Weekly Journal*, 14 May 1823, which, in
describing a paper communicated by Dr Patterson of Calcutta on the smallness of the 'Hindoo head', comments: 'The phrenologist ceases to wonder
that 20,000 Europeans keep in easy subjection one hundred millions of
Hindoos' (p. 157).

96. 'Report on a Communication from Dr Dyce of Aberdeen, to the Royal
Society of Edinburgh, On Uterine Irritation, and its Effects on the Female
Constitution', in *Transactions of the Royal Society of Edinburgh*, 9 (1823), 365–79
(pp. 365–66, 377, 378). For an account of the Mary Reynolds case, and its
possible relevance to Hogg, see Barbara Bloedé, 'A Nineteenth-Century
Case of Double Personality: A Possible Source for *The Confessions*', *Papers
given at the Second James Hogg Society Conference (Edinburgh 1985)*, ed. by Gillian
Hughes, ASLS Occasional Papers, 8 (Aberdeen, 1988), pp. 117–27. For a
commentary on the possible influence of Dr Andrew Duncan, as well as a
psychoanalytic evaluation of schizophrenic tendencies exhibited by Robert
Wringhim, see Allan Beveridge, 'James Hogg and Abnormal Psychology:
Some Background Notes', *Studies in Hogg and his World*, 2 (1991), 91–94.

97. NLS, MS 4719, fol. 169; the article itself is found in *Blackwood's Edinburgh Magazine*, 14 (August 1823), 188–90. Evidence suggesting that Hogg was recording an actual event in his neighbourhood, which possibly involved himself, is given in Douglas S. Mack, 'The Suicide's Grave in *The Confessions of a Justified Sinner*', *Newsletter of the James Hogg Society*, no. 1 (May 1982), pp. 8–11, and David Groves, 'James Hogg's *Confessions*: New Information', *Review of English Studies*, n.s. 40 (1989), 240–42. For a more recent view, containing additional information, see also Peter Garside, 'Hogg, Eltrive, and *Confessions*', *Studies in Hogg and his World*, 11 (2000), 5–24.

98. Among those inclined towards the idea of a prior design can be included John Wain in the Introduction (pp. 7–8) to his Penguin edition of 1983 (see note 172 below); and Fiona Robertson, in her *Legitimate Histories: Scott, Gothic, and the Authorities of Fiction* (Oxford: Clarendon Press, 1994), pp. 246–47. Inconsistencies and contradictions in the accounts of the suicide and burial within the novel are outlined by Michael York Mason, in 'The Three Burials in Hogg's *Justified Sinner*', *Studies in Scottish Literature*, 13 (1977), 15–23.

99. In the same letter of 7 August that accompanied his 'Scots Mummy' article, Hogg expresses to William Blackwood his anxiety 'to hear your veto of the Perils of Woman' (NLS, MS 4719, fol. 169). The novel was published later that month. In his letter to John Wilson on 28 August, Blackwood describes it as 'a most hoggish performance–coarse, vulgar, and uninteresting' (NLS, MS 3395, fol. 7).

100. NLS, MS 4011, fol. 85 (Moir to Blackwood, 24 August 1823). John Wilson in a letter postmarked 2 September, concerning this number, also states 'Hogg is excellent' (NLS, MS 4011, fol. 254).

101. Longman Archives part 1, Item 101, Letter-book 1820–25, nos 388B, 396C. It is not impossible that Rees had made two visits, the first of these in late Summer, when the 'Suicide' project could have been directly mentioned by Hogg; but it was more usual for Rees to pay just one Autumn visit to Edinburgh. Quotations from the Longman Letter Books are taken from the typed transcripts prepared by Michael Bott, of Reading University Library, unless otherwise stated.

102. The publication date for this novel is given as October 1823 in both the Longman Impression Book and Divide Ledger, with the latter listing the bill for printing the 1000 copies of the first edition as of 3 October. For its authorship by George Robert Gleig, rather than (as previously supposed) Thomas De Quincey, see Barry Symonds, 'The Stranger's Grave: Laying a De Quinceyan Ghost', *The Charles Lamb Bulletin*, n.s. 83 (July 1993), 105–07. Gleig's story noticeably attempts a double narrative not unlike Hogg's own, with a framing third-person account by the Rev. Townsend introducing the life story of the young stranger-hero, Stanley, though 'the Editor' acknowledges having rendered the latter into the third-person also, on the grounds that 'a narrative written in the first person is, to the generality of readers, less pleasing' (1st edn, 1823, p. 72). At one point, in response to the dying Stanley's tacit admission of incest and parricide, Townsend advises 'there is but one sin mentioned in the Gospel, for the commission of which no hope of pardon is held out: that sin you have not named' (p. 69). The sin

referred to is the despair that leads to an act of suicide. For the topicality of suicide in 1823, see note on 'customary in the south of Scotland' for 171(a) in explanatory Notes.

103. Longman Archives part 1, Item 101, no. 174C (letter to Hogg, 18 October 1821, concerning his *Three Perils of Man*). Hogg's earlier interest in a Scott-like anonymity is evident, for example, in his letter to William Blackwood of 16 November 1819: 'I am going to publish a romance in two volumes this spring coming, anonymously' (NLS, MS 4004, fol. 156). Among the advantages for Hogg would have been the loss of his naive persona as 'the Ettrick Shepherd'. For further details on Hogg's dealings with Longmans, see Peter Garside, 'Three Perils in Publishing: Hogg and the Popular Novel', *Studies in Hogg and his World*, 2 (1991), 45–63 (pp. 57–58).

104. Hogg's later account in his 'Memoir' (1832) indicates a last-minute decision, based on content: 'it being a story replete with horror, after I had written it I durst not venture to put my name to it: so it was published anonymously' (*Memoir*, p. 55). Yet in view of Hogg's earlier stated preferences for anonymity, and the introduction from the start of an Editor other than the author, it seems likely that he would have wished to have avoided a direct attribution from the conception of the project.

105. For further commentary on Hogg's dealings with printers (and publishers), see Peter Garside, 'Printing *Confessions*', *Studies in Hogg and his World*, 9 (1998), 16–31 (pp. 18–20); also *The Spy*, ed. by Gillian Hughes (Edinburgh: Edinburgh University Press, 2000), pp. xix–xxii.

106. Longman Archives part 1, Item 101, nos 405, 406C. In the first letter quoted I have conjecturally emended 'Reginald Dunlop' as found in the typed transcript to 'Reginald Dalton', the original in the Letter Books now being virtually indecipherable. J. G. Lockhart's novel of this name (1823) and Scott's *Quentin Durward* (1823) were both printed by James Ballantyne & Co., and have a standard 24 lines to a page (with variations) compared with the standard 25 lines found in the first edition of *Confessions*; the line length is also slightly wider in *Confessions* (74 mm as opposed to 72 mm).

107. For an account, see 'Note on the Text', in *Queen Hynde*, ed. by Suzanne Gilbert and Douglas S. Mack (Edinburgh: Edinburgh University Press, 1998), pp. 221–34.

108. See James Hogg, *Anecdotes of Scott*, ed. by Jill Rubenstein (Edinburgh: Edinburgh University Press, 1999), pp. 46–48. The revisions involved changing the character name 'Sir Walter Scott of Buccleuch' to 'Sir Ringan Redhough', though Hogg was evidently mistaken in suggesting that the printer of the work was James Ballantyne: for an overview of the situation, see 'Note on the Text', in *Queen Hynde*, ed. by Gilbert and Mack, pp. 222–23, 234 (note 6). It could be argued that Hogg had even more to fear in the case of his *Confessions*, which in a number of ways offers a parody and deconstruction of Scott's own fiction.

109. Longman Archives part 1, Item 101, no. 445.

110. Details concerning addresses are taken the Edinburgh and Leith *Post-Office Annual Directory*, whose volumes cover yearly periods between Whitsundays. In the issue for 1819–20 the work address for Balfour is Merchant Court and for J. Clarke 56 Merchant Court, indicating that the two were then

operating together. Earlier volumes place Clarke at 50 or 56 Cowgate from 1811. Merchant Court was evidently on the south side of the Cowgate and would seem to have disappeared through the building of George IV Bridge. The home addresses given for Clarke are 8 Alison's Square, succeeded by 17 Keir Street from the early 1820s.

111. ' [...] we uniformly went down to a dark house in the Cowgate, where we drank whisky and ate rolls with a number of printers, the dirtiest and leanest-looking men I had ever seen' (*Memoir*, p. 20).

112. 'The Honourable Captain Napier and Ettrick Forest', *Blackwood's Edinburgh Magazine*, 13 (February 1823), 175–88 (p. 188). In a letter to William Blackwood of 9 January 1823, Hogg, apparently in some irritation, describes how Napier had insisted on working with him in extensively revising this article (NLS, MS 4010, fol. 184).

113. For the directories used, see note 110 above. 'Clarke, Jas. & Co., Old Stamp Office close' are also listed in Pigot & Co's *New Commercial Directory of Scotland for 1825–6* (London and Manchester, n.d.), p. 79. This latter gives 'Balfour, Andrew & Co., Merchant court, Cowgate' as a separate enterprise, indicating that the two had formed separate companies.

114. For a full account of Watson's career, see D. Wyn Evans, *James Watson of Edinburgh: A Bibliography of Works from his Press, 1695–1722*: Edinburgh Bibliographical Society Transactions, vol. 5, Part 2 (Edinburgh, 1982). General information concerning the closes and wynds of old Edinburgh has been taken from a number of sources, the most recent of which is Stuart Harris, *The Place Names of Edinburgh: Their Origins and History* (Edinburgh: Gordon Wright Publishing, 1996).

115. Longman Archives part 1, Item 101, no. 406C.

116. 'The Suicide's Grave', *The Athenæum*, no. 3551, 16 November 1895, p. 681. Another possible glimpse of the manuscript is provided by the recorded speech of Mrs Garden's husband at the celebrations to mark the erection of Hogg's birthplace memorial in Ettrick in 1898: 'We have still the MS. of "The Confessions of a Fanatic", a prose composition of such singular power that some thought the Shepherd must have had assistance in its composition. Our having the MS. in our possession proved the contrary, and that J. G. Lockhart [...] had no hand in the matter' (*James Hogg, the Ettrick Shepherd. Memorial Volume*, ed. by R. Borland (Selkirk, 1898), p. 45). The use here of a title relating to the 1837 version of the novel could mean that the Gardens, then living in Aberdeen, had a revised version in their possession, though it is also possible that the speaker was merely using the then most familiar way of referring to the tale.

117. For commentary on the quality of the manuscripts in prose being submitted by Hogg in the early 1830s, see Gillian Hughes in her edition of Hogg's *Tales of the Wars of Montrose* (Edinburgh: Edinburgh University Press, 1996), especially pp. xiii, 253. Generally, the copy sent by Hogg to his publisher for this collection is neatly written out with few corrections, paragraphs marked, speech marks inserted, and headings in place. In a letter to Oliver and Boyd of 5 May 1821, concerning his *Three Perils of Man*, Hogg refers to both a 'scroll copy' and a 'corrected copy' (NLS, Accession 5000/188). For Hogg's practice as a poet in the 1820s, which involved drafts followed by a final

copy text, see Peter Garside, 'Vision and Revision: Hogg's MS Poems in the Turnbull Library', *Studies in Hogg and his World*, 5 (1994), 82–95.

118. Surviving letters to and from Hogg are sparse during this period, but, for a clear indication of two trips to Edinburgh during the printing of *Confessions*, see his letter to Jane Simpson Laing, from Edinburgh, dated 29 March 1824 (NLS Deposit 380), describing his arrival in 'Auld Reeky', and that to William Blackwood, 3 April 1824, promising another visit 'early in May' (NLS, MS 4012, fol. 182).

119. *Autobiographical Notes of the Life of William Bell Scott, H.R.S.A., LL.D*, ed. by W. Minto, 2 vols (London, 1892), I, 69. This places Robert Scott's studio in Parliament Stairs, part of large tenements in Old Parliament House Square; and contemporary directories give Scott's professional address as 10 Parliament Square. It is not clear whether Hogg previously knew Scott, who worked as an engraver for the *Scots Magazine*, and who also had served as one of the jurors in the Mary M'Kinnnon trial in 1823. The association between Hogg and Robert Scott was first noted by David Groves in 'The Frontispiece to James Hogg's *Confessions*', *Notes and Queries*, 235 (1990), 421-22. Groves here assumes that the unnamed 'publisher' accompanying Hogg was Archibald Constable, on the grounds that Constable published the *Scots Magazine*; but James Clarke, whose office was nearby on the opposite side of the High Street, seems at least as strong a contender. See also Groves's article, '"W——m B——e, a Great Original": William Blake, The Grave, and James Hogg's *Confessions*', *Scottish Literary Journal*, 18: 2 (November 1991), 27–45 (pp. 29–30).

120. This appears in the last short gathering in the first edition, on p. 388, and is found near the end of p. 174 in the present edition. Since there is no sign of any prior agreement in the Longmans records, the possibility remains that Hogg was acting independently. A possible prototype is *The Life of David Haggart [...] Written by Himself* (Edinburgh, 1821), which includes a facsimile of Haggart's writing as a frontispiece, signed from the Iron Room from Edinburgh Jail, shortly before his execution. Longmans for their part usually limited engraved frontispieces in fiction to short evangelical tales, such as Barbara Hofland's *Decision* (1824) and *Patience* (1824).

121. Canongate Classics 39 (Edinburgh, 1991), p. 209.

122. The printing would often be done along with other preliminaries such as dedications. Examination of the first edition of *Confessions* shows that the frontispiece, title-page, and dedication are distinct from the main gatherings of the text.

123. Longman Archives part 1, Item 101, nos 426B, 429B. A slightly different interpretation of events leading to the final title of the *Confessions* will be found in Robin W. MacLachlan, '*The Private Memoirs and Confessions of a Justified Sinner?*', *Newsletter of the James Hogg Society*, no. 2 (May 1983), pp. 16–20. This account assumes that James Ballantyne was the printer.

124. De Quincey, *Opium-Eater*, p. 121.

125. Longmans letter of 3 May 1824 to Hogg includes the instruction 'to deliver 100 copies to Mr Adam Black on our account' (Letter Books, Item 101, no. 445); the Longmans Divide Ledger (2D, p. 239), however, lists '125 copies as 120' subscribed at the outset, presumably to Black.

126. Longman Archives: Impression Book 8, fol. 33. The account also lists the printing of the label at 6s, and allows 13s. 6d. for 'sufferance &c'.

127. The chapbooks are in coloured wrappers, with wood engravings, and catalogues on the back covers: two copies, of *Aladdin* and *Cinderella*, bear the dates 1829 and 1836 respectively.

128. This second advert, no doubt aimed at boosting flagging sales, and placed at the height of the 'reading season', is found in *The Star* and *Morning Chronicle* on Friday, 5 November, 1824, and in *The Morning Post* on 6 November. Similar suggestions for a re-advertisement of *Queen Hynde*, as made by Hogg to William Blackwood in a letter of 1 September 1825 (NLS, MS 4014, fol. 289), indicate that the initial impulse for this might have come from the author himself.

129. Longman Archives, Divide Ledger 2D, p. 239; Letter Books, Item 101, no. 445. The figure of 521 left in June 1826 omits 23 presentation copies sent out earlier and 125 copies subscribed elsewhere (referring probably to Adam Black's share).

130. Such a reaction seems to be implicit in Hogg's later commentary in his 'Memoir of the Author's Life' (extended 1832), where he claims Longmans had refused his next prose work on the grounds 'that my last publication had been found fault with in some very material points' (see *Memoir*, p. 56).

131. Divide Ledger 2D, p. 239; *Memoir*, p. 55. The Longmans Divide Ledger leaves some uncertainty about the date of the remainder sale to Tegg, positioning the transaction between entries for June 1826 and June 1828. For a possible closer indication, see note 151 below.

132. NLS, MS 4012, fol. 184. This letter is headed 'Mount-Benger', and later states that Hogg has just moved into the 'old thatched house' there in order to accommodate his parents-in-law at Altrive Lake.

133. *Blackwood's Edinburgh Magazine*, 15 (June 1824), 707, 715.

134. 'Remarks on Dr Henderson's History', *Blackwood's Edinburgh Magazine*, 16 (July 1824), 1–16 (p. 16n). The attribution to J. G. Lockhart is given in *The Wellesley Index to Victorian Periodicals 1824–1900*, ed. by Walter E. Houghton, vol. I (1966), p. 13. The same end note refers to the writer having been a week 'trouting and duck-shooting' on St Mary's Loch, Yarrow, and declares Hogg to be 'in great heart'.

135. It is interesting to compare the treatment in the Magazine of Hogg's work with R. P. Gillies's *Devil's Elixir*, itself a Blackwood publication, which, in addition to advance notices and a plug in the 'Noctes', was given a full-page advertisement at the beginning of the June 1824 issue, as well as a full review by Lockhart in July 1824 (vol. 16, pp. 55–67). Hogg's *Queen Hynde* received significantly more attention than his novel, with a prominent advance notice, a number of high-profile mentions in the 'Noctes', and a set-piece comparison with Thomas Campbell's most recent work, this no doubt partly reflecting Blackwood's own greater confidence (and, then, personal stake) in the poem. In the 'Noctes' for January 1825, Hogg is again made to comply with the view that poetry is his natural forte: 'I was wearied wi' writing sae mony prose novells [*sic*]–it's just a pleasure to me to be skelping awa' at the auld tredd again' (vol. 17, p. 128).

136. The reviews identified, and discussed below, are listed in William S. Ward,

Literary Reviews in British Periodicals 1821-1826 (New York: Garland Publishing, 1977), p. 116. For an earlier commentary on the reviews themselves, see G. H. Hughes, 'The Critical Reception of *The Confessions of a Justified Sinner*', *Newsletter of the James Hogg Society*, no. 1 (May 1982), pp. 11–14.

137. Only the anonymous reviewer in the *Universal Review*, 2 (September 1824), 108–12, actually questioned the report: 'This work, which has been, we believe unjustly, attributed to Mr Hogg, is one of that class in which the authorship of Scotland has been of late prolific' (p. 108). All subsequent references are to anonymous reviews; inclusive page references are given on first citation, in addition to specific references for quotations.

138. *Literary Gazette*, 17 July 1824, 449–51 (p. 449). A comment made later by Hogg in his *Memoir*, p. 41, about the rough treatment received in the same journal by *Queen Hynde* ('That malicious *deevil*, Jerdan, first took it up and damned it with faint praise'), opens up the possibility that the reviewer of *Confessions* was William Jerdan (1782–1869), then editor of the *Literary Gazette*. The Longmans Divide Ledger (2D, p. 239) itemises one copy being sent on 8 July to the *Literary Gazette*, the only journal apparently to receive a review copy at that stage. It is not impossible that Hogg's identity as author was disclosed by the publishers.

139. *British Critic*, n.s. 22 (July 1824), 68–80 (pp. 68-69); *Examiner*, 1 August 1824, pp. 482–83 (p. 483); *Ladies' Monthly Museum*, 20 (1824), 106.

140. *Monthly Critical Gazette*, 1 (October 1824), 436–38 (pp. 437, 438). The reference to the 'serious Christian' is probably aimed at contemporary Evangelicals.

141. *La Belle Assemblée*, n.s. 30 (1824), 81; *Literary Gazette*, 17 July 1824, p. 449.

142. *Examiner*, 1 August 1824, p. 483; *New Monthly Magazine*, 12 (November 1824), 506; *Westminster Review*, 2 (October 1824), 560–62 (p. 561).

143. *News of Literature and Fashion*, 17 July 1824, 95-96 (p. 95).

144. *Examiner*, 1 August 1824, p. 483. Compare André Gide's 'It is the exteriorized development of our own desires, of our pride, of our most secret thoughts', in his Introduction to the Cresset edition of *Confessions* (London, 1947), p. xv.

145. *La Belle Assemblée*, n.s. 30 (1824), 81; *Westminster Review*, 2 (October 1824), 561.

146. *News of Literature and Fashion*, 17 July 1824, p. 96.

147. NLS, MS 9634, fol. 11 (13 November 1824). Longmans had written earlier on 28 October to Blackwood about Hogg's 'wish that we would grant you a share in his new Poem & the Confessions' (Longman Archives part 1, Item 101, no. 469C).

148. NLS, MS 4012, fol. 187 (Blackwood to Hogg, 20 December 1824, as copied in Hogg's hand); MS 30308, pp. 91–92 (Blackwood to Hogg, 23 April 1825). Reference to the account of *Queen Hynde* in the Longman Impression Book 8 (fol. 54) does indeed indicate that Hogg received an advance of £100 on the poem on 20 May 1824. However, Blackwood in first proposing the deal to Hogg on 20 December 1824 had suggested that if Longmans had a balance against Hogg it should be settled with Blackwood out of the profits of a second edition—though, in the event, none was called for. Hogg on 5 October 1826 vainly protested that according to their original

agreement the £100 should be made up by the profits of a future edition and not by a bill (MS 4719, fol. 172), but Blackwood continued to hold him to the amount.

149. NLS, MS 4014, fol. 289.

150. NLS, MS 30309, fol. 386 (Blackwood to Hogg, 23 September 1826). The estimate of author's profits of £2 roughly matches the account in Longman Divide Ledger 2D, p. 239, which has author's profits at June 1825 standing at £2 2s. 6d., and further half profits of 17s. 6d. at June 1826. Both amounts are crossed out, presumably being subsumed in the final reckoning of £16 1s. 2d., with Blackwood's name replacing the Author as recipient.

151. NLS, MS 30302, p. 143. Blackwood had written earlier to Longmans on 6 October 1827, giving instructions for the remainder of the novel to be cleared: 'The copies of the Justified Sinner should now be sold off and the acct. settled, as I expect that you will be able to credit my acct. with something from the proceeds of it' (NLS, MS 30302, p. 128). For an overview of the financial outcome, see David Groves, '"With Regard to the Justified Sinner": Hogg's Payment for his Greatest Novel', *Notes and Queries*, 245 (2000), 325–26.

152. The same perplexity over finances is expressed in his extended 'Memoir' (1832), which claims a failure to comprehend why Longmans, whom he had recently visited, 'have not a copy of either of the works, nor have had any for a number of years'. 'The whole of that trifling business', Hogg concludes, 'has to this day continued a complete mystery to me.' See *Memoir*, pp. 56–57.

153. NLS, MS 4021, fol. 281 (*'The worthy old divine and his lady must visit me'*); *Letters of Sir Walter Scott*, ed. by H. J. C. Grierson, 12 vols (London, 1932–37), X, 482.

154. Mrs Hughes of Uffington, *Letters and Recollections of Sir Walter Scott*, ed. by Horace G. Hutchinson (London, 1904), p. 289. Hogg had evidently arrived with William Laidlaw.

155. NLS, MS 4719, fol. 167 (Hogg to Blackwood, 6 August [1828]).

156. An account of the Selkirk copy was first given by Douglas S. Mack, in '*The Suicide's Grave* of 1828', *Newsletter of the James Hogg Society*, no. 5 (May 1986), pp. 19–21.

157. These lines (previously unidentified) are from 'Verses Subjoined to the Bill of Mortality for the Town of Northampton, 1788', stanza 8. See *The Poems of William Cowper*, volume III: 1785–1800, ed. by John D. Baird and Charles Ryskamp (Oxford: Clarendon Press, 1995), p. 33.

158. James Hogg Collection, Beinecke Library, Yale University (Hogg to John M'Crone?, 19 March 1832). The published volume of *Altrive Tales*, incorporating Hogg's extended 'Memoir' of his life and three tales, consists of nearly 350 closely-printed pages. At a rough estimate, *Confessions*, if included in an uncut state, would have occupied about 280–300 pages. Hogg's suggestion that a make-weight might be needed is therefore not inconsistent with an intention to publish the full 1824 text.

159. NLS, MS 807, fol. 20 (Hogg to Blackie & Son, 11 November 1833). Hogg's comments need to be seen in the context of his desire to cement the deal with Blackies and forward the collection.

160. James Hogg Collection, Beinecke Library, Yale University (Hogg to Blackie & Son, 25 March 1834).

161. Edith C. Batho, *The Ettrick Shepherd* (Cambridge, 1927), p. 124; Douglas Gifford, *James Hogg*, p. 187; James Hogg, *The Private Memoirs and Confessions of a Justified Sinner*, ed. by Carey, pp. xxvi–xxvii; Douglas S. Mack, 'Editing James Hogg: Some Textual and Bibliographical Problems in Hogg's Prose Works' (unpublished doctoral dissertation, University of Stirling, 1984), pp. 77–82.

162. For a summary of the changes, and assessment of their probable origin, see Douglas S. Mack's 'Note on the Text', in his edition of Hogg's *The Brownie of Bodsbeck* (Edinburgh and London: Scottish Academic Press, 1976), pp. xxiii–xxiv; also his article, 'The Transmission of the Text of Hogg's *Brownie of Bodsbeck*', *The Bibliotheck*, 8 (1976), 7–46.

163. A possible exception here might seem to be Mrs Garden's statement in 1895: 'In the second place, this tale, under the title of "Confessions of a Fanatic", along with my father's other collected works, was corrected by himself just before his death, and was in the hands of Messrs. Blackie at the time that event occurred' (*The Athenæum*, no. 3551, 16 November 1895, p. 681). A child at the time, Mrs Garden can hardly have had a clear personal recollection of this, and her ensuing statement that the text corrected in this way 'with the exception of a few trifling alterations' is essentially the same as the full '1824' text published in 1895 by Shiells & Co. indicates little knowledge of the Blackie alterations. In all, this part of the statement seems to be especially coloured by Mrs Garden's overriding desire to establish her father's authorship.

164. Hogg had planned that 'The Siege of Roxburgh' would fill the third volume of *Altrive Tales* (James Hogg Collection, Beinecke Library, Yale University (Hogg to John M'Crone?, 19 March 1832)). In a letter to William Blackwood of 26 May 1830, he had already proposed division into parts for a collection of his tales: 'The Perils of Man which contains some of the best parts and the worst of all my prose works I would divide into seven distinct tales and in short do all that I could to make it a successful circulating library work' (NLS, MS 4036, fol. 102). The presence of 'Marion's Jock'—basically 'The Laird of Peatstacknowe's Tale' from the *Three Perils of Man*—in the published volume of *Altrive Tales* reinforces the idea that Hogg himself was involved in dismembering the *Three Perils* sometime between 1830 and 1832.

165. Information about the early output of Blackie & Son is taken from the Stock Edition Book 1813–64, item UGD 61 4/1/1 in the Blackie archives, held in the University of Glasgow Business Centre. A publisher's sample consisting of the first 72 pages of *Tales & Sketches*, now held by the University of Stirling Library, states in a preamble that the series 'will be published in volumes, price 5s. each, and will be completed in about six volumes'. This does not preclude the possibility of an alternative sale in parts, however, and it is noticeable that a unit of 72 pages (or two sheets) would have been sufficient to complete each volume in five parts. The Blackie Stock Edition Book (opening 88) indicates that the five parts forming volume 5 of *Tales & Sketches* were first ready in September 1837; this volume was also reviewed

in the *Glasgow Courier* of 5 December 1837. For a more general account of the operations of the firm, see Agnes A. C. Blackie, *Blackie & Son: A Short History of the Firm* (London and Glasgow: Blackie & Son, 1959), especially pp. 1–13.

166. The Blackie Stock Edition Book (see note above) indicates that new impressions of the various parts of *Tales & Sketches* were taken, as need required, at various points until 1864. Comparison between a dated 1836–37 set held by the National Library of Scotland (press mark Hall 277.j) and an undated set owned by the present writer reveals a handful of small differences in accidentals (possibly the result of printing errors) as well as one substantive alteration, the correction of 'gentlemen' to 'gentleman' (see present text, p. 21, l.19). This occurs at the foot of page 29 (and the beginning of gathering C) in volume 5 of *Tales & Sketches*, and the last four lines of text have been reset, presumably the amount of text that would have to be replaced to introduce a correction in a stereotype plate. The same text of 'Confessions of a Fanatic', with a few of its mistakes corrected, subsequently passed into *The Works of the Ettrick Shepherd*, edited by the Rev. Thomas Thomson, originally published in 26 parts in 1863-65 and then published as two bound volumes in 1865 (with reissues), followed by the Centenary Edition of 1874. One significant change is the closer association of the Editor with Hogg through the addition of 'J. H.' in brackets at the end of the extended title. A late instance of 'Confessions of a Fanatic' being reprinted by other publishers is *The Tales of James Hogg, the Ettrick Shepherd*, Library Edition, volume 1 of which was published in 1880 by Hamilton, Adams and Co. in London and Thomas D. Morison in Glasgow.

167. The Facsimile is positioned to face the commencement of the equivalent passage in print on p. 249 of the Shiells edition.

168. *Confessions of a Justified Sinner*, Everyman's Library 126, with an introduction by Roger Lewis (London: David Campbell, 1992); *The Private Memoirs and Confessions of a Justified Sinner*, Everyman, ed. by J. A. Cuddon (London: J. M. Dent, 1994). Both follow the Cresset edition reading of 'The effect made my case worse' on p. 179 and p. 166 respectively. The gratuitous insertion of '*v. Frontispiece*' occurs at the point where the Editor refers to the commissioning of the Facsimile (Lewis, p. 210; Cuddon, p. 195).

169. *The Private Memoirs and Confessions of a Justified Sinner* (Ware, Hertfordshire: Wordsworth Editions, 1997), pp. 8, 63. The attribution on the title-page reads 'James Hogg / Written by himself'.

170. The collation was conducted at the Centre for Editorial and Intertextual Research, Cardiff University, using the 1981 World's Classics edition of Carey. In addition to the differences mentioned below, the same collation revealed four variants in punctuation (including two omitted commas). Collation of a number of copies of the 1824 edition, undertaken in the preparation of this edition, revealed no variants within this edition, other than the signature Z3 (p. 341) appearing wrongly as 3Z in some copies. It therefore seems unlikely that the use of a variant first-edition copy-text explains any of the disparities in the Carey edition noted.

171. *The Private Memoirs and Confessions of a Justified Sinner*, ed. by John Carey (London: Oxford University Press, 1969; first issued as a paperback in World's Classics, 1981), pp. 92, 239, 147, 19, 47, 34. The World's Classics

edition has been reissued with a Glossary (by Graham Tulloch) in 1990, and a Bibliography in 1995; the most recent reissue to date is 1999. The changes mentioned survive into the latest issues.

172. *The Private Memoirs and Confessions of a Justified Sinner*, ed. by John Wain (Harmondsworth: Penguin English Library, 1983; reprinted in Penguin Classics, 1987), p. 119. Signs of setting from Carey in the Douglas Gifford edition (London: Folio Press, 1978) are the carrying through of '*this* report (Gifford, p. 94), 'laying thy *hands* (Gifford, p. 208), and 'better *that* I did' (Gifford, p. 136).

173. Canongate Classics 39 (Edinburgh, 1991; reprinted 1996), p. 125. This mistaken 'herever' is not in the original 1969 Carey edition, but occurs in the first World's Classics issue of 1981 (and subsequent reissues), as a result apparently of a damaged plate.

174. The original Facsimile states '*See* p. 366', which is emended in the present edition to '*See* p. 164' to fit the new pagination. Similarly, at p. 174, the cross reference to where the 'printed part' of the Sinner's 'Memoirs' ends is changed from 'page 340' to 'page 153'. In a few of the surviving copies of the first edition seen the Facsimile is placed alongside the equivalent printed text, tipped in between pages 366 and 367, rather than being positioned as a Frontispiece. The most usual practice at the time of publication neverthe-less was to insert such items at the beginning, opposite the title-page, as is the case in the Stirling University Library copy-text used for the present edition. The cross reference at the head would also seem somewhat super-fluous with the printed equivalent on a facing page.

Fac Simile. See p. 164.

September 8. — My first night of trial in this place is overpast! Would that it were the last that I should ever see in this detested world! If the horrors of hell are equal to those I have suffered, eternity will be of short duration there, for no created energy can support them for one single month, or week. I have been buffeted as never living creature was. My vitals have all been torn and every faculty and feeling of my soul racked, and tormented into callous infeasibility. I was even hung by the locks over a yawning chasm to which I could perceive no bottom, and then — not till then, did I repeat the tremendous prayer! — I was instantly at liberty; and what I now am, the Almighty knows! Amen.

THE PRIVATE MEMOIRS

AND CONFESSIONS

OF A JUSTIFIED SINNER:

WRITTEN BY HIMSELF:

WITH A DETAIL OF CURIOUS TRADITIONARY FACTS, AND
OTHER EVIDENCE, BY THE EDITOR.

LONDON:

PRINTED FOR LONGMAN, HURST, REES, ORME, BROWN,
AND GREEN, PATERNOSTER ROW.

MDCCCXXIV.

TO

THE HON. WILLIAM SMITH,
LORD PROVOST OF GLASGOW,
&c. &c. &c.

THIS WORK IS RESPECTFULLY INSCRIBED,

AS A SMALL MARK OF

THE EDITOR'S

ESTEEM FOR HIM AS A MAN,

AND RESPECT FOR HIM AS A MAGISTRATE.

THE EDITOR'S NARRATIVE.

IT appears from tradition, as well as some parish registers still extant, that the lands of Dalcastle (or Dalchastel, as it is often spelled) were possessed by a family of the name of Colwan, about one hundred and fifty years ago, and for at least a century previous to that period. That family was supposed to have been a branch of the ancient family of Colquhoun, and it is certain that from it spring the Cowans that spread towards the Border. I find, that in the year 1687, George Colwan succeeded his uncle of the same name, in the lands of Dalchastel and Balgrennan; and this being all I can gather of the family from history, to tradition I must appeal for the remainder of the motley adventures of that house. But of the matter furnished by the latter of these powerful monitors, I have no reason to complain: It has been handed down to the world in unlimited abundance; and I am certain, that in recording the hideous events which follow, I am only relating to the greater part of the inhabitants of at least four counties of Scotland, matters of which they were before perfectly well informed.

This George was a rich man, or supposed to be so, and was married, when considerably advanced in life, to the sole heiress and reputed daughter of a Baillie Orde, of Glasgow. This proved a conjunction any thing but agreeable to the parties contracting. It is well known, that the Reformation principles had long before that time taken a powerful hold of the hearts and affections of the people of Scotland, although the feeling was by no means general, or in equal degrees; and it so happened that this married couple felt completely at variance on the subject. Granting it to have been so, one would have thought that the laird, owing to his retired situation, would have been the one that inclined to the stern doctrines of the reformers; and that the young and gay dame from the city would have adhered to the free principles cherished by the court party, and indulged in rather to extremity, in opposition to their severe and carping contemporaries.

The contrary, however, happened to be the case. The laird was what his country neighbours called "a droll, careless chap," with a very limited proportion of the fear of God in his heart, and very nearly as little of the fear of man. The laird had not intentionally wronged or offended either of the parties, and perceived not the necessity of deprecating their vengeance. He had hitherto believed that he was living in most cordial terms with the greater part of the inhabitants of the earth, and with the powers above in particular: but woe be unto him if he was not soon convinced of the fallacy of such damning security! for his lady was the most severe and gloomy of all bigots to the principles of the Reformation. Hers were not the tenets of the great reformers, but theirs mightily overstrained and deformed. Theirs was an unguent hard to be swallowed; but hers was that unguent embittered and over-heated until nature could not longer bear it. She had imbibed her ideas from the doctrines of one flaming predestinarian divine alone; and these were so rigid, that they became a stumbling-block to many of his brethren, and a mighty handle for the enemies of his party to turn the machine of the state against them.

The wedding festivities at Dalcastle partook of all the gaiety, not of that stern age, but of one previous to it. There was feasting, dancing, piping, and singing: the liquors were handed around in great fulness, the ale in large wooden bickers, and the brandy in capacious horns of oxen. The laird gave full scope to his homely glee. He danced,—he snapped his fingers to the music,—clapped his hands and shouted at the turn of the tune. He saluted every girl in the hall whose appearance was any thing tolerable, and requested of their sweethearts to take the same freedom with his bride, by way of retaliation. But there she sat at the head of the hall in still and blooming beauty, absolutely refusing to tread a single measure with any gentleman there. The only enjoyment in which she appeared to partake, was in now and then stealing a word of sweet conversation with her favourite pastor about divine things; for he had accompanied her home after marrying her to her husband, to see her fairly settled in her new dwelling. He addressed her several times by her new name, Mrs. Colwan; but she turned away her head disgusted, and looked with pity and contempt towards the old inadvertent sinner, capering away in the height of his unregenerated mirth. The minister perceived the workings of her pi-ous mind, and thenceforward addressed her by the courteous title of Lady Dalcastle, which sounded somewhat better, as not coupling her name with one of the wicked: and there is too great reason to believe, that for all the solemn vows she had come under, and these were of no ordinary binding, particularly on the laird's part, she at that time de-spised, if not abhorred him, in her heart.

The good parson again blessed her, and went away. She took leave of him with tears in her eyes, entreating him often to visit her in that heathen land of the Amorite, the Hittite, and the Girgashite: to which he assented, on many solemn and qualifying conditions,–and then the comely bride retired to her chamber to pray.

It was customary, in those days, for the bride's-man and maiden, and a few select friends, to visit the new married couple after they had retired to rest, and drink a cup to their healths, their happiness, and a numerous posterity. But the laird delighted not in this: he wished to have his jewel to himself; and, slipping away quietly from his jovial party, he retired to his chamber to his beloved, and bolted the door. He found her engaged with the writings of the Evangelists, and terribly demure. The laird went up to caress her; but she turned away her head, and spoke of the follies of aged men, and something of the broad way that leadeth to destruction. The laird did not thoroughly comprehend this allusion; but being considerably flustered by drinking, and disposed to take all in good part, he only remarked, as he took off his shoes and stockings, "that whether the way was broad or narrow, it was time that they were in their bed."

"Sure, Mr. Colwan, you won't go to bed to-night, at such an important period of your life, without first saying prayers for yourself and me."

When she said this, the laird had his head down almost to the ground, loosing his shoe-buckle; but when he heard of *prayers*, on such a night, he raised his face suddenly up, which was all over as flushed and red as a rose, and answered,–

"Prayers, Mistress! Lord help your crazed head, is this a night for prayers?"

He had better have held his peace. There was such a torrent of profound divinity poured out upon him, that the laird became ashamed, both of himself and his new-made spouse, and wist not what to say: but the brandy helped him out.

"It strikes me, my dear, that religious devotion would be somewhat out of place to-night," said he. "Allowing that it is ever so beautiful, and ever so beneficial, were we to ride on the rigging of it at all times, would we not be constantly making a farce of it: It would be like reading the Bible and the jest-book, verse about, and would render the life of man a medley of absurdity and confusion."

But against the cant of the bigot or the hypocrite, no reasoning can aught avail. If you would argue until the end of life, the infallible creature must alone be right. So it proved with the laird. One Scripture text followed another, not in the least connected, and one sentence of the profound Mr. Wringhim's sermons after another, proving the duty of family worship, till the laird lost patience, and, tossing himself into bed, said, carelessly, that he would leave that duty upon her shoulders for one night.

The meek mind of Lady Dalcastle was somewhat disarranged by this sudden evolution. She felt that she was left rather in an awkward situation. However, to show her unconscionable spouse that she was resolved to hold fast her integrity, she kneeled down and prayed in terms so potent, that she deemed she was sure of making an impression on him. She did so; for in a short time the laird began to utter a response so fervent, that she was utterly astounded, and fairly driven from the chain of her orisons. He began, in truth, to sound a nasal bugle of no ordinary calibre,—the notes being little inferior to those of a military trumpet. The lady tried to proceed, but every returning note from the bed burst on her ear with a louder twang, and a longer peal, till the concord of sweet sounds became so truly pathetic, that the meek spirit of the dame was quite overcome; and after shedding a flood of tears, she arose from her knees, and retired to the chimney-corner with her Bible in her lap, there to spend the hours in holy meditation till such time as the inebriated trumpeter should awaken to a sense of propriety.

The laird did not awake in any reasonable time; for, he being overcome with fatigue and wassail, his sleep became sounder, and his Morphean measures more intense. These varied a little in their structure; but the general run of the bars sounded something in this way,—"Hic-hoc-wheew!" It was most profoundly ludicrous; and could not have missed exciting risibility in any one, save a pious, a disappointed, and humbled bride.

The good dame wept bitterly. She could not for her life go and awaken the monster, and request him to make room for her: but she retired somewhere; for the laird, on awaking next morning, found that he was still lying alone. His sleep had been of the deepest and most genuine sort; and all the time that it lasted, he had never once thought of either wives, children, or sweethearts, save in the way of dreaming about them; but as his spirit began again by slow degrees to verge towards the boundaries of reason, it became lighter and more buoyant from the effects of deep repose, and his dreams partook of that buoyancy, yea, to a degree hardly expressible. He dreamed of the reel, the jig, the strathspey, and the corant; and the elasticity of his frame was such, that he was bounding over the heads of the maidens, and making his feet skimmer against the ceiling, enjoying, the while, the most extatic emotions. These grew too fervent for the shackles of the drowsy god to restrain. The nasal bugle ceased its prolonged sounds in one moment, and a sort of hectic laugh took its place. "Keep it going,—play up, you devils!" cried the laird, without changing his position on the pillow. But this exertion to hold the fiddlers at their work, fairly awakened the delighted dreamer; and though he could not refrain from continuing his laugh, he at length, by tracing out a regular chain of facts, came to be sensible of his real situation. "Rabina, where are you? What's become of you, my dear?" cried the laird. But there was no voice, nor any one that answered or regarded. He flung open the curtains, thinking to find her still on her knees, as he had seen her; but she was not there, either sleeping or waking. "Rabina! Mrs. Colwan!" shouted he, as loud as he could call, and then added, in the same breath, "God save the king,—I have lost my wife!"

He sprung up and opened the casement: the day-light was beginning to streak the east, for it was spring, and the nights were short, and the mornings very long. The laird half dressed himself in an instant, and strode through every room in the house, opening the windows as he went, and scrutinizing every bed and every corner. He came into the hall where the wedding festival had held; and, as he opened the various window-boards, loving couples flew off like hares surprised too late in the morning among the early braird. "Hoo-boo! Fie, be frightened!" cried the laird. "Fie, rin like fools, as if ye were caught in an ill turn!"—His bride was not among them; so he was obliged to betake himself to farther search. "She will be praying in some corner, poor woman," said he to himself. "It is an unlucky thing this praying. But, for my part, I fear I have behaved very ill; and I must endeavour to make amends."

The laird continued his search, and at length found his beloved in the same bed with her Glasgow cousin, who had acted as bride's-maid. "You sly and malevolent imp," said the laird; "you have played me such a trick when I was fast asleep! I have not known a frolic so clever, and, at the same time, so severe. Come along, you baggage you!"

"Sir, I will let you know, that I detest your principles and your person alike," said she. "It shall never be said, Sir, that my person was at the controul of a heathenish man of Belial,—a dangler among the daughters of women,—a promiscuous dancer,—and a player at unlawful games. Forego your rudeness, Sir, I say, and depart away from my presence and that of my kinswoman."

"Come along, I say, my charming Rab. If you were the pink of all puritans, and the saint of all saints, you are my wife, and must do as I command you."

"Sir, I will sooner lay down my life than be subjected to your godless will; therefore, I say, desist, and begone with you."

But the laird regarded none of these testy sayings: he rolled her in a blanket, and bore her triumphantly away to his chamber, taking care to keep a fold or two of the blanket always rather near to her mouth, in case of any outrageous forthcoming of noise.

The next day at breakfast the bride was long in making her appearance. Her maid asked to see her; but George did not choose that any body should see her but himself: he paid her several visits, and always turned the key as he came out. At length breakfast was served; and during the time of refreshment the laird tried to break several jokes; but it was remarked, that they wanted their accustomed brilliancy, and that his nose was particularly red at the top.

Matters, without all doubt, had been very bad between the new-married couple; for in the course of the day the lady deserted her quarters, and returned to her father's house in Glasgow, after having been a night on the road; stage-coaches and steam-boats having then no existence in that quarter. Though Baillie Orde had acquiesced in his wife's asseveration regarding the likeness of their only daughter to her father, he never loved or admired her greatly; therefore this behaviour nothing astounded him. He questioned her strictly as to the grievous offence committed against her; and could discover nothing that warranted a procedure so fraught with disagreeable consequences. So, after mature deliberation, the baillie addressed her as follows:—

"Ay, ay, Raby! An' sae I find that Dalcastle has actually refused to say prayers with you when you ordered him; an' has guidit you in a rude indelicate manner, outstepping the respect due to my daughter,— as my daughter. But wi' regard to what is due to his own wife, of that he's a better judge nor me. However, since he has behaved in that manner to *my daughter*, I shall be revenged on him for aince; for I shall return the obligation to ane nearer to him: that is, I shall take pennyworths of his wife,—an' let him lick at that."

"What do you mean, Sir?" said the astonished damsel.

"I mean to be revenged on that villain Dalcastle," said he, "for what he has done to my daughter. Come hither, Mrs. Colwan, you shall pay for this."

So saying, the baillie began to inflict corporal punishment on the runaway wife. His strokes were not indeed very deadly, but he made a mighty flourish in the infliction, pretending to be in a great rage only at the Laird of Dalcastle. "Villain that he is!" exclaimed he, "I shall teach him to behave in such a manner to a child of mine, be she as she may; since I cannot get at himself, I shall lounder her that is nearest to him in life. Take you that, and that,

Mrs. Colwan, for your husband's impertinence!"

The poor afflicted woman wept and prayed, but the baillie would not abate aught of his severity. After fuming, and beating her with many stripes, far drawn, and lightly laid down, he took her up to her chamber, five stories high, locked her in, and there he fed her on bread and water, all to be revenged on the presumptuous Laird of Dalcastle; but ever and anon, as the baillie came down the stair from carrying his daughter's meal, he said to himself, "I shall make the sight of the laird the blithest she ever saw in her life."

Lady Dalcastle got plenty of time to read, and pray, and meditate; but she was at a great loss for one to dispute with about religious tenets; for she found, that without this advantage, about which there was a perfect rage at that time, her reading, and learning of Scripture texts, and sentences of intricate doctrine, availed her nought; so she was often driven to sit at her casement and look out for the approach of the heathenish Laird of Dalcastle.

That hero, after a considerable lapse of time, at length made his appearance. Matters were not hard to adjust; for his lady found that there was no refuge for her in her father's house; and so, after some sighs and tears, she accompanied her husband home. For all that had passed, things went on no better. She *would* convert the laird in spite of his teeth: The laird would not be converted. She *would* have the laird to say family prayers, both morning and evening: The laird would neither pray morning nor evening. He would not even sing psalms, and kneel beside her, while she performed the exercise; neither would he converse at all times, and in all places, about the sacred mysteries of religion, although his lady took occasion to contradict flatly every assertion that he made, in order that she might spiritualize him by drawing him into argument.

The laird kept his temper a long while, but at length his patience wore out; he cut her short in all her futile attempts at spiritualization, and mocked at her wire-drawn degrees of faith, hope, and repentance. He also dared to doubt of the great standard doctrine of absolute predestination, which put the crown on the lady's christian resentment. She declared her helpmate to be a limb of Antichrist, and one with whom no regenerated person could associate. She therefore bespoke a separate establishment, and before the expiry of the first six months, the arrangements of the separation were amicably adjusted. The upper, or third story of the old mansion-house, was awarded to the lady for her residence. She had a separate door, a separate stair, a separate garden, and walks that in no instance intersected the laird's; so that one would have thought the separation complete. They had each their own parties, selected from their own sort of people; and though the laird never once chafed himself about the lady's companies, it was not long before she began to intermeddle about some of his.

"Who is that fat bouncing dame that visits the laird so often, and always by herself?" said she to her maid Martha one day.

"O dear, mem, how can I ken? We're banished frae our acquaintances here, as weel as frae the sweet gospel ordinances."

"Find me out who that jolly dame is, Martha. You, who hold communion with the household of this ungodly man, can be at no loss to attain this information. I observe that she always casts her eye up toward our windows, both in coming and going; and I suspect that she seldom departs from the house empty-handed."

That same evening Martha came with the information, that this august visitor was a Miss Logan, an old and intimate acquaintance of the laird's, and a very worthy respectable lady, of good connections, whose parents had lost their patrimony in the civil wars.

"Ha! very well!" said the lady; "very well, Martha! But, nevertheless, go thou and watch this respectable lady's motions and behaviour the next time she comes to visit the laird,—and the next after that. You will not, I see, lack opportunities."

Martha's information turned out of that nature, that prayers were said in the uppermost story of Dalcastle-house against the Canaanitish woman, every night and every morning; and great discontent prevailed there, even to anathemas and tears. Letter after letter was dispatched to Glasgow; and at length, to the lady's great consolation, the Rev. Mr. Wringhim arrived safely and devoutly in her elevated sanctuary. Marvellous was the conversation between these gifted people. Wringhim had held in his doctrines that there were eight different kinds of FAITH, all perfectly distinct in their operations and effects. But the lady, in her secluded state, had discovered other five,—making twelve in all: the adjusting of the existence or fallacy of these five faiths served for a most enlightened discussion of nearly seventeen hours; in the course of which the two got warm in their arguments, always in proportion as they receded from nature, utility, and common sense. Wringhim at length got into unwonted fervour about some disputed point between one of these faiths and TRUST; when the lady, fearing that zeal was getting beyond its wonted barrier, broke in on his vehement asseverations with the following abrupt discomfiture:—"But, Sir, as long as I remember, what is to be done with this case of open and avowed iniquity?"

The minister was struck dumb. He leaned him back on his chair, stroked his beard, hemmed—considered, and hemmed again; and then said, in an altered and softened tone,–"Why, that is a secondary consideration; you mean the case between your husband and Miss Logan?"

"The same, Sir. I am scandalised at such intimacies going on under my nose. The sufferance of it is a great and crying evil."

"Evil, madam, may be either operative, or passive. To them it is an evil, but to us none. We have no more to do with the sins of the wicked and unconverted here, than with those of an infidel Turk; for all earthly bonds and fellowships are absorbed and swallowed up in the holy community of the Reformed Church. However, if it is your wish, I shall take him to task, and reprimand and humble him in such a manner, that *he* shall be ashamed of his doings, and renounce such deeds for ever, out of mere self-respect, though all unsanctified the heart, as well as the deed, may be. To the wicked, all things are wicked; but to the just, all things are just and right."

"Ah, that is a sweet and comfortable saying, Mr. Wringhim! How delightful to think that a justified person can do no wrong! Who would not envy the liberty wherewith we are made free? Go to my husband, that poor unfortunate, blindfolded person, and open his eyes to his degenerate and sinful state; for well are you fitted to the task."

"Yea, I will go in unto him, and confound him. I will lay the strong holds of sin and Satan as flat before my face, as the dung that is spread out to fatten the land."

"Master, there's a gentleman at the fore-door wants a private word o' ye."

"Tell him I'm engaged: I can't see any gentleman to-night. But I shall attend on him to-morrow as soon as he pleases."

"He's coming straight in, Sir —Stop a wee bit, Sir, my master is engaged. He cannot see you at present, Sir."

"Stand aside, thou Moabite! my mission admits of no delay. I come to save him from the jaws of destruction!"

"An that be the case, Sir, it maks a wide difference; an', as the danger may threaten us a', I fancy I may as weel let ye gang by as fight wi' ye, sin' ye seem sae intent on't.—The man says he's comin' to save ye, an' canna stop, Sir.–Here he is."

The laird was going to break out into a volley of wrath against Waters, his servant; but before he got a word pronounced, the Rev. Mr. Wringhim had stepped inside the room, and Waters had retired, shutting the door behind him.

No introduction could be more *mal-a-propos:* it is impossible; for at that very moment the laird and Arabella Logan were both sitting on one seat, and both looking on one book, when the door opened. "What is it, Sir?" said the laird fiercely.

"A message of the greatest importance, Sir," said the divine, striding unceremoniously up to the chimney,—turning his back to the fire, and his face to the culprits.—"I think you should know me, Sir?" continued he, looking displeasedly at the laird, with his face half turned round.

"I think I should," returned the laird. "You are a Mr. How's-tey-ca'-him, of Glasgow, who did me the worst turn ever I got done to me in my life. You gentry are always ready to do a man such a turn. Pray, Sir, did you ever do a good job for any one to counterbalance that? for, if you have not, you ought to be ——."

"Hold, Sir, I say! None of your profanity before me. If I do evil to any one on such occasions, it is because he will have it so; therefore, the evil is not of my doing. I ask you, Sir,—before God and this witness, I ask you, have you kept solemnly and inviolate the vows which I laid upon you that day? Answer me?"

"Has the partner whom you bound me to, kept hers inviolate? Answer me that, Sir? None can better do so than you, Mr. How's-tey-ca'-you."

"So, then, you confess your backslidings, and avow the profligacy of your life. And this person here, is, I suppose, the partner of your iniquity,—she whose beauty hath caused you to err! Stand up, both of you, till I rebuke you, and show you what you are in the eyes of God and man."

"In the first place, stand you still there, till I tell you what *you* are in the eyes of God and man: You are, Sir, a presumptuous, self-conceited pedagogue, a stirrer up of strife and commotion in church, in state, in families, and communities. You are one, Sir, whose righteousness consists in splitting the doctrines of Calvin into thousands of undistinguishable films, and in setting up a system of justifying-grace against all breaches of all laws, moral or divine. In short, Sir, you are a mildew,—a canker-worm in the bosom of the Reformed Church, generating a disease of which she will never be purged, but by the shedding of blood. Go thou in peace, and do these abominations no more; but humble thyself, lest a worse reproof come upon thee."

Wringhim heard all this without flinching. He now and then twisted his mouth in disdain, treasuring up, mean time, his vengeance against the two aggressors; for he felt that he had them on the hip, and resolved to pour out his vengeance and indignation upon them. Sorry am I, that the shackles of modern decorum restrain me from penning that famous rebuke; fragments of which have been attributed to every divine of old notoriety throughout Scotland. But I have it by heart; and a glorious morsel it is to put into the hands of certain incendiaries. The metaphors were so strong, and so appalling, that Miss Logan could only stand them a very short time: she was obliged to withdraw in confusion. The laird stood his ground with much ado, though his face was often crimsoned over with the hues of shame and anger. Several times he was on the point of turning the officious sycophant to the door; but good manners, and an inherent respect that he entertained for the clergy, as the immediate servants of the Supreme Being, restrained him.

Wringhim, perceiving these symptoms of resentment, took them for marks of shame and contrition, and pushed his reproaches farther than ever divine ventured to do in a similar case. When he had finished, to prevent further discussion, he walked slowly and majestically out of the apartment, making his robes to swing behind him in a most magisterial manner; he being, without doubt, elated with his high conquest. He went to the upper story, and related to his metaphysical associate his wonderful success; how he had driven the dame from the house in tears and deep confusion, and left the backsliding laird in such a quandary of shame and repentance, that he could neither articulate a word, nor lift up his countenance. The dame thanked him most cordially, lauding his friendly zeal and powerful eloquence; and then the two again set keenly to the splitting of hairs, and making distinctions in religion where none existed.

They being both children of adoption, and secured from falling into snares, or any way under the power of the wicked one, it was their custom, on each visit, to sit up a night in the same apartment, for the sake of sweet spiritual converse; but that time, in the course of the night, they differed so materially on a small point, somewhere between justification and final election, that the minister, in the heat of his zeal, sprung from his seat, paced the floor, and maintained his point with such ardour, that Martha was alarmed, and, thinking they were going to fight, and that the minister would be a hard match for her mistress, she put on some clothes, and twice left her bed and stood listening at the back of the door, ready to burst in should need require it. Should any one think this picture over-strained, I can assure him that it is taken from nature and from truth; but I will not likewise aver, that the theologist was neither crazed nor inebriated. If the listener's words were to be relied on, there was no love, no accommodating principle manifested between the two, but a fiery burning zeal, relating to points of such minor importance, that a true Christian would blush to hear them mentioned, and the infidel and profane make a handle of them to turn our religion to scorn.

Great was the dame's exultation at the triumph of her beloved pastor over her sinful neighbours in the lower parts of the house; and she boasted of it to Martha in high-sounding terms. But it was of short duration; for, in five weeks after that, Arabella Logan came to reside with the laird as his house-keeper, sitting at his table, and carrying the keys as mistress-substitute of the mansion. The lady's grief and indignation were now raised to a higher pitch than ever; and she set every agent to work, with whom she had any power, to effect a separation between these two suspected ones. Remonstrance was of no avail: George laughed at them who tried such a course, and retained his house-keeper, while the lady gave herself up to utter despair; for though she would not consort with her husband herself, she could not endure that any other should do so.

But, to countervail this grievous offence, our saintly and afflicted dame, in due time, was safely delivered of a fine boy, whom the laird acknowledged as his son and heir, and had him christened by his own name, and nursed in his own premises. He gave the nurse permission to take the boy to his mother's presence if ever she should desire to see him; but, strange as it may appear, she never once desired to see him from the day that he was born. The boy grew up, and was a healthful and happy child; and, in the course of another year, the lady presented him with a brother. A brother he certainly was, in the eye of the law, and it is more than probable that he was his brother in reality. But the laird thought otherwise; and, though he knew and acknowledged that he was obliged to support and provide for him, he refused to acknowledge him in other respects. He neither would countenance the banquet, nor take the baptismal vows on him in the child's name; of course, the poor boy had to live and remain an alien from the visible church for a year and a day; at which time, Mr. Wringhim, out of pity and kindness, took the lady herself as sponsor for the boy, and baptized him by the name of Robert Wringhim,—that being the noted divine's own name.

George was brought up with his father, and educated partly at the parish-school, and partly at home, by a tutor hired for the purpose. He was a generous and kind-hearted youth; always ready to oblige, and hardly ever dissatisfied with any body. Robert was brought up with Mr. Wringhim, the laird paying a certain allowance for him yearly; and there the boy was early inured to all the sternness and severity of his pastor's arbitrary and unyielding creed. He was taught to pray twice every day, and seven times on Sabbath days; but he was only to pray for the elect, and, like David of old, doom all that were aliens from God to destruction. He had never, in that family into which he had been as it were adopted, heard ought but evil spoken of his reputed father and brother; consequently he held them in utter abhorrence, and prayed against them every day, often "that the old hoary sinner might be cut off in the full flush of his iniquity, and be carried quick into hell; and that the young stem of the corrupt trunk might also be taken from a world that he disgraced, but that his sins might be pardoned, because he knew no better."

Such were the tenets in which it would appear young Robert was bred. He was an acute boy, an excellent learner, had ardent and ungovernable passions, and withal, a sternness of demeanour from which other boys shrunk. He was the best grammarian, the best reader, writer, and accountant in the various classes that he attended, and was fond of writing essays on controverted points of theology, for which he got prizes, and great praise from his guardian and mother. George was much behind him in scholastic acquirements, but greatly his superior in personal prowess, form, feature, and all that constitutes gentility in deportment and appearance. The laird had often manifested to Miss Logan an earnest wish that the two young men should never meet, or at all events that they should be as little conversant as possible; and Miss Logan, who was as much attached to George as if he had been her own son, took every precaution, while he was a boy, that he should never meet with his brother; but as they advanced towards manhood, this became impracticable. The lady was removed from her apartments in her husband's house to Glasgow, to her great content; and all to prevent the young laird being tainted with the company of her and her second son; for the laird had felt the effects of the principles they professed, and dreaded them more than persecution, fire, and sword. During all the dreadful times that had overpast, though the laird had been a moderate man, he had still leaned to the side of the kingly prerogative, and had escaped confiscation and fines, without ever taking any active hand in suppressing the Covenanters. But after experiencing a specimen of their tenets and manner in his wife, from a secret favourer of them and their doctrines, he grew alarmed at the prevalence of such stern and factious principles, now that there was no check nor restraint upon them; and from that time he began to set himself against them, joining with the cavalier party of that day in all their proceedings.

It so happened, that, under the influence of the Earls of Seafield and Tullibardine, he was returned for a Member of Parliament in the famous session that sat at Edinburgh, when the Duke of Queensberry was commissioner, and in which party spirit ran to such an extremity. The young laird went with his father to the court, and remained in town all the time that the session lasted; and as all interested people of both factions flocked to the town at that period, so the important Mr.

Wringhim was there among the rest, during the greater part of the time, blowing the coal of revolutionary principles with all his might, in every society to which he could obtain admission. He was a great favourite with some of the west country gentlemen of that faction, by reason of his unbending impudence. No opposition could for a moment cause him either to blush, or retract one item that he had advanced. Therefore the Duke of Argyle and his friends made such use of him as sportsmen often do of terriers, to start the game, and make a great yelping noise to let them know whither the chace is proceeding. They often did this out of sport, in order to teaze their opponent; for of all pesterers that ever fastened on man he was the most insufferable: knowing that his coat protected him from manual chastisement, he spared no acrimony, and delighted in the chagrin and anger of those with whom he contended. But he was sometimes likewise *of real use* to the heads of the presbyterian faction, and therefore was admitted to their tables, and of course conceived himself a very great man.

His ward accompanied him; and very shortly after their arrival in Edinburgh, Robert, for the first time, met with the young laird his brother, in a match at tennis. The prowess and agility of the young squire drew forth the loudest plaudits of approval from his associates, and his own exertion alone carried the game every time on the one side, and that so far as all along to count three for their one. The hero's name soon ran round the circle, and when his brother Robert, who was an onlooker, learned who it was that was gaining so much applause, he came and stood close beside him all the time that the game lasted, always now and then putting in a cutting remark by way of mockery.

George could not help perceiving him, not only on account of his impertinent remarks, but he, moreover, stood so near him that he several times impeded him in his rapid evolutions, and of course got himself shoved aside in no very ceremonious way. Instead of making him keep his distance, these rude shocks and pushes, accompanied sometimes with hasty curses, only made him cling the closer to this king of the game. He seemed determined to maintain his right to his place as an onlooker, as well as any of those engaged in the game, and if they had tried him at an argument, he would have carried his point: or perhaps he wished to quarrel with this spark of his jealousy and aversion, and draw the attention of the gay crowd to himself by these means; for, like his guardian, he knew no other pleasure but what consisted in opposition. George took him for some impertinent student of divinity, rather set upon a joke than any thing else. He perceived a lad with black clothes, and a methodistical face, whose countenance and eye he disliked exceedingly, several times in his way, and that was all the notice he took of him the first time they two met. But the next day, and every succeeding one, the same devilish-looking youth attended him as constantly as his shadow; was always in his way as with intention to impede him, and ever and anon his deep and malignant eye met those of his elder brother with a glance so fierce that it sometimes startled him.

The very next time that George was engaged at tennis, he had not struck the ball above twice till the same intrusive being was again in his way. The party played for considerable stakes that day, namely, a dinner and wine at the Black Bull tavern; and George, as the hero and head of his party, was much interested in its honour; consequently, the sight of this moody and hellish-looking student affected him in no very pleasant manner. "Pray, Sir, be so good as keep without the range of the ball," said he.

"Is there any law or enactment that can compel me to do so?" said the other, biting his lip with scorn.

"If there is not, they are here that shall compel you," returned George: "so, friend, I rede you to be on your guard."

As he said this, a flush of anger glowed in his handsome face, and flashed from his sparkling blue eye; but it was a stranger to both, and momently took its departure. The black-coated youth set up his cap before, brought his heavy brows over his deep dark eyes, put his hands in the pockets of his black plush breeches, and stepped a little farther into the semi-circle, immediately on his brother's right hand, than he had ever ventured to do before. There he set himself firm on his legs, and, with a face as demure as death, seemed determined to keep his ground. He pretended to be following the ball with his eyes; but every moment they were glancing aside at George. One of the competitors chanced to say rashly, in the moment of exultation, "That's a d—d fine blow, George!" On which the intruder took up the word, as characteristic of the competitors, and repeated it every stroke that was given, making such a ludicrous use of it, that several of the on-lookers were compelled to laugh immoderately; but the players were terribly nettled at it, as he really contrived, by dint of sliding in some canonical terms, to render the competitors and their game ridiculous.

But matters at length came to a crisis that put them beyond sport. George, in flying backward to gain the point at which the ball was going to light, came inadvertently so rudely in contact with this obstreperous interloper, that he not only overthrew him, but also got a grievous fall over his legs; and, as he arose, the other made a spurn at him with his foot, which, if it had hit to its aim, would undoubtedly have finished the course of the young laird of Dalcastle and Balgrennan. George, being irritated beyond measure, as may well be conceived, especially at the deadly stroke aimed at him, struck the assailant with his racket, rather slightly, but so that his mouth and nose gushed out blood; and, at the same time, he said, turning to his cronies,—"Does any of you know who the infernal puppy is?"

"Do you not know, Sir?" said one of the on-lookers, a stranger: "The gentleman is your own brother, Sir—Mr. Robert Wringhim Colwan!"

"No, not Colwan, Sir," said Robert, putting his hands in his pockets, and setting himself still farther forward than before,—"not a Colwan, Sir; henceforth I disclaim the name."

"No, certainly not," repeated George: "My mother's son you may be,—but *not a Colwan!* There you are right." Then turning round to his informer, he said, "Mercy be about us, Sir! is this the crazy minister's son from Glasgow?"

This question was put in the irritation of the moment; but it was too rude, and too far out of place, and no one deigned any answer to it. He felt the reproof, and felt it deeply; seeming anxious for some opportunity to make an acknowledgment, or some reparation.

In the meantime, young Wringhim was an object to all of the uttermost disgust. The blood flowing from his mouth and nose he took no pains to stem, neither did he so much as wipe it away; so that it spread over all his cheeks, and breast, even off at his toes. In that state did he take up his station in the middle of the competitors; and he did not now keep his place, but ran about, impeding every one who attempted to make at the ball. They loaded him with execrations, but it availed nothing; he seemed courting persecution and buffetings, keeping stedfastly to his old joke of damnation, and marring the game so completely, that, in spite of every effort on the part of the players, he forced them to stop their game, and give it up. He was such a rueful-looking object, covered with blood, that none of them had the heart to kick him, although it appeared the only thing he wanted; and as for George, he said not another word to him, either in anger or reproof.

When the game was fairly given up, and the party were washing their hands in the stone fount, some of them besought Robert Wringhim to wash himself; but he mocked at them, and said, he was much better as he was. George, at length, came forward abashedly toward him, and said,—"I have been greatly to blame, Robert, and am very sorry for what I have done. But, in the first instance, I erred through ignorance, not knowing you were my brother, which you certainly are; and, in the second, through a momentary irritation, for which I am ashamed. I pray you, therefore, to pardon me, and give me your hand."

As he said this, he held out his hand toward his polluted brother; but the froward predestinarian took not his from his breeches pocket, but lifting his foot, he gave his brother's hand a kick. "I'll give you what will suit such a hand better than mine," said he, with a sneer. And then, turning lightly about, he added,—"Are there to be no more of these d—d fine blows, gentlemen? For shame, to give up such a profitable and edifying game!"

"This is too bad," said George. "But, since it is thus, I have the less to regret." And, having made this general remark, he took no more note of the uncouth aggressor. But the persecution of the latter terminated not on the play-ground: he ranked up among them, bloody and disgusting as he was, and, keeping close by his brother's side, he marched along with the party all the way to the Black Bull. Before they got there, a great number of boys and idle people had surrounded them, hooting and incommoding them exceedingly, so that they were glad to get into the inn; and the unaccountable monster actually tried to get in alongst with them, to make one of the party at dinner. But the innkeeper and his men, getting the hint, by force prevented him from entering, although he attempted it again and again, both by telling lies and offering a bribe. Finding he could not prevail, he set to exciting the mob at the door to acts of violence; in which he had like to have succeeded. The landlord had no other shift, at last, but to send privately for two officers, and have him carried to the guard-house; and the hilarity and joy of the party of young gentlemen, for the evening, was quite spoiled, by the inauspicious termination of their game.

The Rev. Robert Wringhim was now to send for, to release his beloved ward. The messenger found him at table, with a number of the leaders of the Whig faction, the Marquis of Annandale being in the chair; and the prisoner's note being produced, Wringhim read it aloud, accompanying it with some explanatory remarks. The circumstances of the case being thus magnified and distorted, it excited the utmost abhorrence, both of the deed and the perpetrators, among the assembled faction. They declaimed against the act as an unnatural attempt on the character, and even the life, of an unfortunate brother, who had been expelled from his father's house. And, as party spirit was the order of the day, an attempt was made to lay the burden of it to that account. In short, the young culprit got some of the best blood of the land to enter as his securities, and was set at liberty. But when Wringhim perceived the plight that he was in, he took him, as he was, and presented him to his honourable patrons. This raised the indignation against the young laird and his associates a thousand fold, which actually roused the party to temporary madness. They were, perhaps, a little excited by the wine and spirits they had swallowed; else a casual quarrel between two young men, at tennis, could not have driven them to such extremes. But certain it is, that from one at first arising to address the party on the atrocity of the offence, both in a moral and political point of view, on a sudden there were six on their feet, at the same time, expatiating on it; and, in a very short time thereafter, every one in the room was up, talking with the utmost vociferation, all on the same subject, and all taking the same side in the debate.

In the midst of this confusion, some one or other issued from the house, which was at the back of the Canongate, calling out,–"A plot, a plot! Treason, treason! Down with the bloody incendiaries at the Black Bull!"

The concourse of people that were assembled in Edinburgh at that time was prodigious; and as they were all actuated by political motives, they wanted only a ready-blown coal to set the mountain on fire. The evening being fine, and the streets thronged, the cry ran from mouth to mouth through the whole city. More than that, the mob that had of late been gathered to the door of the Black Bull, had, by degrees, dispersed; but, they being young men, and idle vagrants, they had only spread themselves over the rest of the street to lounge in search of farther amusement: consequently, a word was sufficient to send them back to their late rendezvous, where they had previously witnessed something they did not much approve of.

The master of the tavern was astonished at seeing the mob again assembling; and that with such hurry and noise. But his inmates being all of the highest respectability, he judged himself sure of protection, or, at least, of indemnity. He had two large parties in his house at the time; the largest of which was of the Revolutionist faction. The other consisted of our young tennis-players, and their associates, who were all of the Jacobite order; or, at all events, leaned to the Episcopal side. The largest party were in a front-room; and the attack of the mob fell first on their windows, though rather with fear and caution. Jingle went one pane; then a loud hurra; and that again was followed by a number of voices, endeavouring to restrain the indignation from venting itself in destroying the windows, and to turn it on the inmates. The Whigs, calling the landlord, inquired what the assault meant: he cunningly answered, that he suspected it was some of the youths of the Cavalier, or High-Church party, exciting the mob against them. The party consisted mostly of young gentlemen, by that time in a key to engage in any row; and, at all events, to suffer nothing from the other party, against whom their passions were mightily inflamed.

The landlord, therefore, had no sooner given them the spirit-rousing intelligence, than every one, as by instinct, swore his own natural oath, and grasped his own natural weapon. A few of those of the highest rank were armed with swords, which they boldly drew; those of the subordinate orders immediately flew to such weapons as the room, kitchen, and scullery afforded;—such as tongs, pokers, spits, racks, and shovels; and breathing vengeance on the prelatic party, the children of Antichrist and the heirs of d—n—t—n! the barterers of the liberties of their country, and betrayers of the most sacred trust,—thus elevated, and thus armed, in the cause of right, justice, and liberty, our heroes rushed to the street, and attacked the mob with such violence, that they broke the mass in a moment, and dispersed their thousands like chaff before the wind. The other party of young Jacobites, who sat in a room farther from the front, and were those against whom the fury of the mob was meant to have been directed, knew nothing of this second uproar, till the noise of the sally made by the Whigs assailed their ears; being then informed that the mob had attacked the house on account of the treatment they themselves had given to a young gentleman of the adverse faction, and that another jovial party had issued from the house in their defence, and was now engaged in an unequal combat, the sparks likewise flew to the field to back their defenders with all their prowess, without troubling their heads about who they were.

A mob is like a spring-tide in an eastern storm, that retires only to return with more overwhelming fury. The crowd was taken by surprise, when such a strong and well-armed party issued from the house with so great fury, laying all prostrate that came in their way. Those who were next to the door, and were, of course, the first whom the imminent danger assailed, rushed backward among the crowd with their whole force. The Black Bull standing in a small square half way between the High Street and the Cowgate, and the entrance to it being by two closes, into these the pressure outward was simultaneous, and thousands were moved to an involuntary flight they knew not why.

But the High Street of Edinburgh, which they soon reached, is a dangerous place in which to make an open attack upon a mob. And it appears that the entrances to the tavern had been somewhere near to the Cross, on the south side of the street; for the crowd fled with great expedition, both to the east and west, and the conquerors, separating themselves as chance directed, pursued impetuously, wounding and maiming as they flew. But, it so chanced, that before either of the wings had followed the flying squadrons of their enemies for the space of a hundred yards each way, the devil an enemy they had to pursue!

the multitude had vanished like so many thousands of phantoms! What could our heroes do?—Why, they faced about to return toward their citadel, the Black Bull. But that feat was not so easily, nor so readily accomplished, as they divined. The unnumbered alleys on each side of the street had swallowed up the multitude in a few seconds; but from these they were busy reconnoitring; and, perceiving the deficiency in the number of their assailants, the rush from both sides of the street was as rapid, and as wonderful, as the disappearance of the crowd had been a few minutes before. Each close vomited out its levies, and these better armed with missiles than when they sought it for a temporary retreat. Woe then to our two columns of victorious Whigs! The mob actually closed around them as they would have swallowed them up; and, in the meanwhile, shower after shower of the most abominable weapons of offence were rained in upon them. If the gentlemen were irritated before, this inflamed them still farther; but their danger was now so apparent, they could not shut their eyes on it, therefore, both parties, as if actuated by the same spirit, made a desperate effort to join, and the greater part effected it; but some were knocked down, and others were separated from their friends, and blithe to become silent members of the mob.

The battle now raged immediately in front of the closes leading to the Black Bull; the small body of Whig gentlemen was hardly bested, and it is likely would have been overcome and trampled down every man, had they not been then and there joined by the young Cavaliers; who, fresh to arms, broke from the wynd, opened the head of the passage, laid about them manfully, and thus kept up the spirits of the exasperated Whigs, who were the men in fact that wrought the most deray among the populace.

The town-guard was now on the alert; and two companies of the Cameronian regiment, with the Hon. Captain Douglas, rushed down from the Castle to the scene of action; but, for all the noise and hubbub that these caused in the street, the combat had become so close and inveterate, that numbers of both sides were taken prisoners fighting hand to hand, and could scarcely be separated when the guardsmen and soldiers had them by the necks.

Great was the alarm and confusion that night in Edinburgh; for every one concluded that it was a party scuffle, and, the two parties being so equal in power, the most serious consequences were anticipated. The agitation was so prevailing, that every party in the town, great and small, was broken up; and the lord-commissioner thought proper to go to the council-chamber himself, even at that late hour, accompanied by the sheriffs of Edinburgh and Linlithgow, with sundry noblemen besides, in order to learn something of the origin of the affray.

For a long time the court was completely puzzled. Every gentleman brought in exclaimed against the treatment he had received, in most bitter terms, blaming a mob set on him and his friends by the adverse party, and matters looked extremely ill, until at length they began to perceive that they were examining gentlemen of both parties, and that they had been doing so from the beginning, almost alternately, so equally had the prisoners been taken from both parties. Finally, it turned out, that a few gentlemen, two-thirds of whom were strenuous Whigs themselves, had joined in mauling the whole Whig population of Edinburgh. The investigation disclosed nothing the effect of which was not ludicrous; and the Duke of Queensberry, whose aim was at that time to conciliate the two factions, tried all that he could to turn the whole *fracas* into a joke—an unlucky frolic, where no ill was meant on either side, and which yet had been productive of a great deal.

The greater part of the people went home satisfied; but not so the Rev. Robert Wringhim. He did all that he could to inflame both judges and populace against the young Cavaliers, especially against the young Laird of Dalcastle, whom he represented as an incendiary, set on by an unnatural parent to slander his mother, and make away with a hapless and only brother; and, in truth, that declaimer against all human merit had that sort of powerful, homely, and bitter eloquence, which seldom missed affecting his hearers: the consequence at that time was, that he made the unfortunate affair between the two brothers appear in extremely bad colours, and the populace retired to their homes impressed with no very favourable opinion of either the Laird of Dalcastle or his son George, neither of whom were there present to speak for themselves.

As for Wringhim himself, he went home to his lodgings, filled with gall and with spite against the young laird, whom he was made to believe the aggressor, and that intentionally. But most of all was he filled with indignation against the father, whom he held in abhorrence at all times, and blamed solely for this unmannerly attack made on his favourite ward, namesake, and adopted son; and for the public imputation of a crime to his own reverence, in calling the lad *his* son, and thus charging him with a sin against which he was well known to have levelled all the arrows of church censure with unsparing might.

But, filled as his heart was with some portion of these bad feelings, to which all flesh is subject, he kept, nevertheless, the fear of the Lord always before his eyes so far as never to omit any of the external duties of religion, and farther than that, man hath no power to pry. He lodged with the family of a Mr. Miller, whose lady was originally from Glasgow, and had been a hearer, and, of course, a great admirer of Mr. Wringhim. In that family he made public worship every evening; and that night, in his petitions at a throne of grace, he prayed for so many vials of wrath to be poured on the head of some particular sinner, that the hearers trembled, and stopped their ears. But that he might not proceed with so violent a measure, amounting to excommunication, without due scripture warrant, he began the exercise of the evening by singing the following verses, which it is a pity should ever have been admitted into a Christian psalmody, being so adverse to all its mild and benevolent principles:—

Set thou the wicked over him,
  And upon his right hand
Give thou his greatest enemy,
  Even Satan, leave to stand.
And when by thee he shall be judged,
  Let him remembered be;
And let his prayer be turned to sin,
  When he shall call on thee.
Few be his days; and in his room
  His charge another take;
His children let be fatherless;
  His wife a widow make:
Let God his father's wickedness
  Still to remembrance call;
And never let his mother's sin
  Be blotted out at all.
As he in cursing pleasure took,
  So let it to him fall;
As he delighted not to bless,
  So bless him not at all.
As cursing he like clothes put on,
  Into his bowels so,
Like water, and into his bones
  Like oil, down let it go.

Young Wringhim only knew the full purport of this spiritual song; and went to his bed better satisfied than ever, that his father and brother were cast-aways, reprobates, aliens from the church and the true faith, and cursed in time and eternity.

The next day George and his companions met as usual,—all who were not seriously wounded of them. But as they strolled about the city, the rancorous eye and the finger of scorn was pointed against them. None of them was at first aware of the reason; but it threw a damp over their spirits and enjoyments, which they could not master. They went to take a forenoon game at their old play of tennis, not on a match, but by way of improving themselves; but they had not well taken their places till young Wringhim appeared in his old station, at his brother's right hand, with looks more demure and determined than ever. His lips were primmed so close that his mouth was hardly discernible, and his dark deep eye flashed gleams of holy indignation on the godless set, but particularly on his brother. His presence acted as a mildew on all social intercourse or enjoyment; the game was marred, and ended ere ever it was well begun. There were whisper-ings apart—the party separated; and, in order to shake off the blighting influence of this dogged persecutor, they entered sundry houses of their acquaintances, with an understanding that they were to meet on the Links for a game at cricket.

They did so; and, stripping off part of their clothes, they began that violent and spirited game. They had not played five minutes, till Wringhim was stalking in the midst of them, and totally impeding the play. A cry arose from all corners of "O, this will never do. Kick him out of the play-ground! Knock down the scoundrel; or bind him, and let him lie in peace."

"By no means," cried George: "it is evident he wants nothing else. Pray do not humour him so much as to touch him with either foot or finger." Then turning to a friend, he said in a whisper, "Speak to him, Gordon; he surely will not refuse to let us have the ground to our-selves, if you request it of him."

Gordon went up to him, and requested of him, civilly, but ardently, "to retire to a certain distance, else none of them could or would be answerable, however sore he might be hurt."

He turned disdainfully on his heel, uttered a kind of pulpit hem! and then added, "I will take my chance of that; hurt me, any of you, at your peril."

The young gentlemen smiled, through spite and disdain of the dogged animal. Gordon followed him up, and tried to remonstrate with him; but he let him know that "it was his pleasure to be there at that time; and, unless he could demonstrate to him what superior right he and his party had to that ground, in preference to him, and to the exclusion of all others, he was determined to assert his right, and the rights of his fellow-citizens, by keeping possession of whatsoever part of that common field he chose."

"You are no gentleman, Sir," said Gordon.

"Are you one, Sir?" said the other.

"Yes, Sir, I will let you know that I am, by G—!"

"Then, thanks be to Him whose name you have profaned, I am none. If *one* of the party be a gentleman, *I do hope in God I am not!*"

It was now apparent to them all that he was courting obloquy and manual chastisement from their hands, if by any means he could provoke them to the deed; and, apprehensive that he had some sinister and deep-laid design in hunting after such a singular favour, they wisely restrained one another from inflicting the punishment that each of them yearned to bestow, personally, and which he so well deserved.

But the unpopularity of the Younger George Colwan could no longer be concealed from his associates. It was manifested wherever the populace were assembled; and his young and intimate friend, Adam Gordon, was obliged to warn him of the circumstance, that he might not be surprised at the gentlemen of their acquaintance withdrawing themselves from his society, as they could not be seen with him without being insulted. George thanked him; and it was agreed between them, that the former should keep himself retired during the day-time while he remained in Edinburgh, and that at night they should always meet together, along with such of their companions as were disengaged.

George found it every day more and more necessary to adhere to this system of seclusion; for it was not alone the hisses of the boys and populace that pursued him,—a fiend of more malignant aspect was ever at his elbow, in the form of his brother. To whatever place of amusement he betook himself, and however well he concealed his intentions of going there from all flesh living, there was his brother Wringhim also, and always within a few yards of him, generally about the same distance, and ever and anon darting looks at him that chilled his very soul. They were looks that cannot be described; but they were felt piercing to the bosom's deepest core. They affected even the on-lookers in a very particular manner, for all whose eyes caught a glimpse of these hideous glances followed them to the object toward which they were darted: the gentlemanly and mild demeanour of that object generally calmed their startled apprehensions; for no one ever yet noted the glances of the young man's eye in the black coat, at the face of his brother, who did not at first manifest strong symptoms of alarm.

George became utterly confounded; not only at the import of this persecution, but how in the world it came to pass that this unaccountable being knew all his motions, and every intention of his heart, as it were intuitively. On consulting his own previous feelings and resolutions, he found that the circumstances of his going to such and such a place were often the most casual incidents in nature—the caprice of a moment had carried him there, and yet he had never sat or stood many minutes till there was the self-same being, always in the same position with regard to himself, as regularly as the shadow is cast from the substance, or the ray of light from the opposing denser medium.

For instance, he remembered one day of setting out with the intention of going to attend divine worship in the High Church, and when within a short space of its door, he was overtaken by young Kilpatrick of Closeburn, who was bound to the Grey-Friars to see his sweetheart, as he said; "and if you will go with me, Colwan," said he, "I will let you see her too, and then you will be just as far forward as I am."

George assented at once, and went; and after taking his seat, he leaned his head forward on the pew to repeat over to himself a short ejaculatory prayer, as had always been his custom on entering the house of God. When he had done, he lifted his eyes naturally toward that point on his right hand where the fierce apparition of his brother had been wont to meet his view: there he was, in the same habit, form, demeanour, and precise point of distance, as usual! George again laid down his head, and his mind was so astounded, that he had nearly fallen into a swoon. He tried shortly after to muster up courage to look at the speaker, at the congregation, and at Captain Kilpatrick's sweetheart in particular; but the fiendish glances of the young man in the black clothes were too appalling to be withstood,—his eye caught them whether he was looking that way or not: at length his courage was fairly mastered, and he was obliged to look down during the remainder of the service.

By night or by day it was the same. In the gallery of the Parliament House, in the boxes of the play-house, in the church, in the assembly, in the streets, suburbs, and the fields; and every day, and every hour, from the first rencounter of the two, the attendance became more and more constant, more inexplicable, and altogether more alarming and insufferable, until at last George was fairly driven from society, and forced to spend his days in his own and his father's lodgings with closed doors. Even there, he was constantly harassed with the idea, that the next time he lifted his eyes, he would to a certainty see that face, the most repulsive to all his feelings of aught the earth contained. The attendance of that brother was now become like the attendance of a demon on some devoted being that had sold himself to destruction; his approaches as undiscerned, and his looks as fraught with hideous malignity. It was seldom that he saw him either following him in the streets, or entering any house or church after him; he only appeared in his place, George wist not how, or whence; and, having sped so ill in his first friendly approaches, he had never spoken to his equivocal attendant a second time.

It came at length into George's head, as he was pondering, by himself, on the circumstances of this extraordinary attendance, that perhaps his brother had relented, and, though of so sullen and unaccommodating a temper that he would not acknowledge it, or beg a reconciliation, it might be for that very purpose that he followed his steps night and day in that extraordinary manner. "I cannot for my life see for what other purpose it can be," thought he. "He never offers to attempt my life; nor dares he, if he had the inclination; therefore, although his manner is peculiarly repulsive to me, I shall not have my mind burdened with the reflection, that my own mother's son yearned for a reconciliation with me, and was repulsed by my haughty and insolent behaviour. The next time he comes to my hand, I am resolved that I will accost him as one brother ought to address another, whatever it may cost me; and, if I am still flouted with disdain, then shall the blame rest with him."

After this generous resolution, it was a good while before his gratuitous attendant appeared at his side again; and George began to think that his visits were discontinued. The hope was a relief that could not be calculated; but still George had a feeling that it was too supreme to last. His enemy had been too pertinacious to abandon his design, whatever it was. He, however, began to indulge in a little more liberty, and for several days he enjoyed it with impunity.

George was, from infancy, of a stirring active disposition, and could not endure confinement; and, having been of late much restrained in his youthful exercises by this singular persecutor, he grew uneasy under such restraint, and, one morning, chancing to awaken very early, he arose to make an excursion to the top of Arthur's Seat, to breathe the breeze of the dawning, and see the sun arise out of the eastern ocean. The morning was calm and serene; and as he walked down the south back of the Canongate, toward the Palace, the haze was so close around him that he could not see the houses on the opposite side of the way. As he passed the lord-commissioner's house, the guards were in attendance, who cautioned him not to go by the Palace, as all the gates would be shut and guarded for an hour to come, on which he went by the back of St. Anthony's gardens, and found his way into that little romantic glade adjoining to the Saint's chapel and well. He was still involved in a blue haze, like a dense smoke, but yet in the midst of it the respiration was the most refreshing and delicious. The grass and the flowers were loaden with dew; and, on taking off his hat to wipe his forehead, he perceived that the black glossy fur of which his chaperon was wrought, was all covered with a tissue of the most delicate silver—a fairy web, composed of little spheres, so minute that no eye could discern any one of them; yet there they were shining in lovely millions. Afraid of defacing so beautiful and so delicate a garnish, he replaced his hat with the greatest caution, and went on his way light of heart.

As he approached the swire at the head of the dell,—that little delightful verge from which in one moment the eastern limits and shores of Lothian arise on the view,—as he approached it, I say, and a little space from the height, he beheld, to his astonishment, a bright halo in the cloud of haze, that rose in a semi-circle over his head like a pale rainbow. He was struck motionless at the view of the lovely vision; for it so chanced that he had never seen the same appearance before, though common at early morn. But he soon perceived the cause of the phenomenon, and that it proceeded from the rays of the sun from a pure unclouded morning sky striking upon this dense vapour which refracted them. But the better all the works of nature are understood, the more they will be ever admired. That was a scene that would have entranced the man of science with delight, but which the uninitiated and sordid man would have regarded less than the mole rearing up his hill in silence and in darkness.

George did admire this halo of glory, which still grew wider, and less defined, as he approached the surface of the cloud. But, to his utter amazement and supreme delight, he found, on reaching the top of Arthur's Seat, that this sublunary rainbow, this terrestrial glory, was spread in its most vivid hues beneath his feet. Still he could not perceive the body of the sun, although the light behind him was dazzling; but the cloud of haze lying dense in that deep dell that separates the hill from the rocks of Salisbury, and the dull shadow of the hill mingling with that cloud, made the dell a pit of darkness. On that shadowy cloud was the lovely rainbow formed, spreading itself on a horizontal plain, and having a slight and brilliant shade of all the colours of the heavenly bow, but all of them paler and less defined. But this terrestrial phenomenon of the early morn cannot be better delineated than by the name given of it by the shepherd boys, "The little wee ghost of the rainbow."

Such was the description of the morning, and the wild shades of the hill, that George gave to his father and Mr. Adam Gordon that same day on which he had witnessed them; and it is necessary that the reader should comprehend something of their nature, to understand what follows.

He seated himself on the pinnacle of the rocky precipice, a little within the top of the hill to the westward, and, with a light and buoyant heart, viewed the beauties of the morning, and inhaled its salubrious breeze. "Here," thought he, "I can converse with nature without disturbance, and without being intruded on by any appalling or obnoxious visitor." The idea of his brother's dark and malevolent looks coming at that moment across his mind, he turned his eyes instinctively to the right, to the point where that unwelcome guest was wont to make his appearance. Gracious Heaven! What an apparition was there presented to his view! He saw, delineated in the cloud, the shoulders, arms, and features of a human being of the most dreadful aspect. The face was the face of his brother, but dilated to twenty times the natural size. Its dark eyes gleamed on him through the mist, while every furrow of its hideous brow frowned deep as the ravines on the brow of the hill. George started, and his hair stood up in bristles as he gazed on this horrible monster. He saw every feature, and every line of the face, distinctly, as it gazed on him with an intensity that was hardly brookable. Its eyes were fixed on him, in the same manner as those of some carnivorous animal fixed on its prey; and yet there was fear and trembling, in these unearthly features, as plainly depicted as murderous malice. The giant apparition seemed sometimes to be cowering down as in terror, so that nothing but its brow and eyes were seen; still these never turned one moment from their object—again it rose imperceptibly up, and began to approach with great caution; and as it neared, the dimensions of its form lessened, still continuing, however, far above the natural size.

George conceived it to be a spirit. He could conceive it to be nothing else; and he took it for some horrid demon by which he was haunted, that had assumed the features of his brother in every lineament, but in taking on itself the human form, had miscalculated dreadfully on the size, and presented itself thus to him in a blown-up, dilated frame of embodied air, exhaled from the caverns of death or the regions of devouring fire. He was farther confirmed in the belief that it was a malignant spirit, on perceiving that it approached him across the front of a precipice, where there was not footing for thing of mortal frame. Still, what with terror and astonishment, he continued rivetted to the spot, till it approached, as he deemed, to within two yards of him; and then, perceiving that it was setting itself to make a violent spring on him, he started to his feet and fled distractedly in the opposite direction, keeping his eye cast behind him lest he had been seized in that dangerous place. But the very first bolt that he made in his flight he came in contact with a *real* body of flesh and blood, and that with such violence that both went down among some scragged rocks, and George rolled over the other. The being called out "Murder;" and, rising, fled precipitately. George then perceived that it was his brother; and, being confounded between the shadow and the substance, he knew not what he was doing or what he had done; and there being only one natural way of retreat from the brink of the rock, he likewise arose and pursued the affrighted culprit with all his speed towards the top of the hill. Wringhim was braying out "Murder! murder!" at which George being disgusted, and his spirits all in a ferment from some hurried idea of intended harm, the moment he came up with the craven he seized him rudely by the shoulder, and clapped his hand on his mouth. "Murder, you beast!" said he; "what do you mean by roaring out murder in that way? Who the devil is murdering you, or offering to murder you?"

Wringhim forced his mouth from under his brother's hand, and roared with redoubled energy, "Eh! Egh! murder! murder!" &c. George had felt resolute to put down this shocking alarm, lest some one might hear it and fly to the spot, or draw inferences widely different from the truth; and, perceiving the terror of this elect youth to be so great that expostulation was vain, he seized him by the mouth and nose with his left hand, so strenuously, that he sunk his fingers into his cheeks. But the poltroon still attempting to bray out, George gave him such a stunning blow with his fist on the left temple, that he crumbled, as it were, to the ground, but more from the effects of terror than those of the blow. His nose, however, again gushed out blood, a system of defence which seemed as natural to him as that resorted to by the race of stinkards. He then raised himself on his knees and hams, and raising up his ghastly face, while the blood streamed over both ears, he besought his life of his brother, in the most abject whining manner, gaping and blubbering most piteously.

"Tell me then, Sir," said George, resolved to make the most of the wretch's terror—"tell me for what purpose it is that you thus haunt my steps? Tell me plainly, and instantly, else I will throw you from the verge of that precipice."

"Oh, I will never do it again! I will never do it again! Spare my life, dear, good brother! Spare my life! Sure I never did you any hurt?"

"Swear to me, then, by the God that made you, that you will never henceforth follow after me to torment me with your hellish threatening looks; swear that you will never again come into my presence without being invited. Will you take an oath to this effect?"

"O yes! I will, I will!"

"But this is not all: you must tell me for what purpose you sought me out here this morning?"

"Oh, brother! for nothing but your good. I had nothing at heart but your unspeakable profit, and great and endless good."

"So then, you indeed knew that I was here?"

"I was told so by a friend, but I did not believe him; a—a—at least I did not know it was true till I saw you."

"Tell me this one thing, then, Robert, and all shall be forgotten and forgiven,—Who was that friend?"

"You do not know him."

"How then does he know me?"

"I cannot tell."

"Was he here present with you to-day?"

"Yes; he was not far distant. He came to this hill with me."

"Where then is he now?"

"I cannot tell."

"Then, wretch, confess that the devil was that friend who told you I was here, and who came here with you. None else could possibly know of my being here."

"Ah! how little you know of him! Would you argue that there is neither man nor spirit endowed with so much foresight as to deduce natural conclusions from previous actions and incidents but the devil? Alas, brother! But why should I wonder at such abandoned notions and principles? It was fore-ordained that you should cherish them, and that they should be the ruin of your soul and body, before the world was framed. Be assured of this, however, that I had no aim in seeking you *but your good!*"

"Well, Robert, I will believe it. I am disposed to be hasty and passionate: it is a fault in my nature; but I never meant, or wished you evil; and God is my witness that I would as soon stretch out my hand to my own life, or my father's, as to yours."—At these words, Wringhim uttered a hollow exulting laugh, put his hands in his pockets, and withdrew a space to his accustomed distance. George continued: "And now, once for all, I request that we may exchange forgiveness, and that we may part and remain friends."

"Would such a thing be expedient, think you? Or consistent with the glory of God? I doubt it."

"I can think of nothing that would be more so. Is it not consistent with every precept of the Gospel? Come, brother, say that our reconciliation is complete."

"O yes, certainly! I tell you, brother, according to the flesh: it is just as complete as the lark's is with the adder; no more so, nor ever can. Reconciled, forsooth! To what would I be reconciled?"

As he said this, he strode indignantly away. From the moment that he heard his life was safe, he assumed his former insolence and revengeful looks—and never were they more dreadful than on parting with his brother that morning on the top of the hill. "Well, go thy ways," said George; "some would despise, but I pity thee. If thou art not a limb of Satan, I never saw one."

The sun had now dispelled the vapours; and the morning being lovely beyond description, George sat himself down on the top of the hill, and pondered deeply on the unaccountable incident that had befallen to him that morning. He could in nowise comprehend it; but, taking it with other previous circumstances, he could not get quit of a conviction that he was haunted by some evil genius in the shape of his brother, as well as by that dark and mysterious wretch himself. In no other way could he account for the apparition he saw that morning on the face of the rock, nor for several sudden appearances of the same being, in places where there was no possibility of any foreknowledge that he himself was to be there, and as little that the same being, if he were flesh and blood like other men, could always start up in the same position with regard to him. He determined, therefore, on reaching home, to relate all that had happened, from beginning to end, to his father, asking his counsel and his assistance, although he knew full well that his father was not the fittest man in the world to solve such a problem. He was now involved in party politics, over head and ears; and, moreover, he could never hear the names of either of the Wringhims mentioned without getting into a quandary of disgust and anger; and all that he would deign to say of them was, to call them by all the opprobrious names he could invent.

It turned out as the young man from the first suggested: old Dalcastle would listen to nothing concerning them with any patience. George complained that his brother harassed him with his presence at all times, and in all places. Old Dal asked why he did not kick the dog out of his presence, whenever he felt him disagreeable? George said, he seemed to have some demon for a familiar. Dal answered, that he did not wonder a bit at that, for the young spark was the third in a direct line who had all been children of adultery; and it was well known that all such were born half deils themselves, and nothing was more likely than that they should hold intercourse with their fellows. In the same style did he sympathise with all his son's late sufferings and perplexities.

In Mr. Adam Gordon, however, George found a friend who entered into all his feelings, and had seen and knew every thing about the matter. He tried to convince him, that at all events there could be nothing supernatural in the circumstances; and that the vision he had seen on the rock, among the thick mist, was the shadow of his brother approaching behind him. George could not swallow this, for he had seen his own shadow on the cloud, and, instead of approaching to aught like his own figure, he perceived nothing but a halo of glory round a point of the cloud, that was whiter and purer than the rest. Gordon said, if he would go with him to a mountain of his father's, which he named, in Aberdeenshire, he would show him a giant spirit of the same dimensions, any morning at the rising of the sun, provided he shone on that spot. This statement excited George's curiosity exceedingly; and, being disgusted with some things about Edinburgh, and glad to get out of the way, he consented to go with Gordon to the Highlands for a space. The day was accordingly set for their departure, the old laird's assent obtained; and the two young sparks parted in a state of great impatience for their excursion.

One of them found out another engagement, however, the instant after this last was determined on. Young Wringhim went off the hill that morning, and home to his upright guardian again, without washing the blood from his face and neck; and there he told a most woful story indeed: How he had gone out to take a morning's walk on the hill, where he had encountered with his reprobate brother among the mist, who had knocked him down and very near murdered him; threatening dreadfully, and with horrid oaths, to throw him from the top of the cliff.

The wrath of the great divine was kindled beyond measure. He cursed the aggressor in the name of the Most High; and bound himself, by an oath, to cause that wicked one's transgressions return upon his own head sevenfold. But before he engaged farther in the business of vengeance, he kneeled with his adopted son, and committed the whole cause unto the Lord, whom he addressed as one coming breathing burning coals of juniper, and casting his lightnings before him, to destroy and root out all who had moved hand or tongue against the children of the promise. Thus did he arise confirmed, and go forth to certain conquest.

We cannot enter into the detail of the events that now occurred, without forestalling a part of the narrative of one who knew all the circumstances—was deeply interested in them, and whose relation is of higher value than any thing that can be retailed out of the stores of tradition and old registers; but, his narrative being different from these, it was judged expedient to give the account as thus publicly handed down to us. Suffice it, that, before evening, George was apprehended, and lodged in jail, on a criminal charge of an assault and battery, to the shedding of blood, with the intent of committing fratricide. Then was the old laird in great consternation, and blamed himself for treating the thing so lightly, which seemed to have been gone about, from the beginning, so systematically, and with an intent which the villains were now going to realize, namely, to get the young laird disposed of, and then his brother, in spite of the old gentleman's teeth, would be laird himself.

Old Dal now set his whole interest to work among the noblemen and lawyers of his party. His son's case looked exceedingly ill, owing to the former assault before witnesses, and the unbecoming expressions made use of by him on that occasion, as well as from the present assault, which George did not deny, and for which no moving cause or motive could be made to appear.

On his first declaration before the sheriff, matters looked no better: but then the sheriff was a Whig. It is well known how differently the people of the present day, in Scotland, view the cases of their own party-men, and those of opposite political principles. But this day is nothing to that in such matters, although, God knows, they are still sometimes barefaced enough. It appeared, from all the witnesses in the first case, that the complainant was the first aggressor—that he refused to stand out of the way, though apprised of his danger; and when his brother came against him inadvertently, he had aimed a blow at him with his foot, which, if it had taken effect, would have killed him. But as to the story of the apparition in fair day-light—the flying from the face of it—the running foul of his brother—pursuing him, and knocking him down, why the judge smiled at the relation; and saying, "It was a very extraordinary story," he remanded George to prison, leaving the matter to the High Court of Justiciary.

When the case came before that court, matters took a different turn. The constant and sullen attendance of the one brother upon the other excited suspicions; and these were in some manner, confirmed, when the guards at Queensberry-house deponed, that the prisoner went by them on his way to the hill that morning, about twenty minutes before the complainant, and when the latter passed, he asked if such a young man had passed before him, describing the prisoner's appearance to them; and that, on being answered in the affirmative, he mended his pace and fell a-running.

The Lord Justice, on hearing this, asked the prisoner if he had any suspicions that his brother had a design on his life.

He answered, that all along, from the time of their first unfortunate meeting, his brother had dogged his steps so constantly, and so unaccountably, that he was convinced it was with some intent out of the ordinary course of events; and that if, as his lordship supposed, it was indeed his shadow that he had seen approaching him through the mist, then, from the cowering and cautious manner that it advanced, there was too little doubt that his brother's design had been to push him headlong from the cliff that morning.

A conversation then took place between the Judge and the Lord Advocate; and, in the mean time, a bustle was seen in the hall; on which the doors were ordered to be guarded,—and, behold, the precious Mr. R. Wringhim was taken into custody, trying to make his escape out of court. Finally it turned out, that George was honourably acquitted, and young Wringhim bound over to keep the peace, with heavy penalties and securities.

That was a day of high exultation to George and his youthful associates, all of whom abhorred Wringhim; and the evening being spent in great glee, it was agreed between Mr. Adam Gordon and George, that their visit to the Highlands, though thus long delayed, was not to be abandoned; and though they had, through the machinations of an incendiary, lost the season of delight, they would still find plenty of sport in deer-shooting. Accordingly, the day was set a second time for their departure; and, on the day preceding that, all the party were invited by George to dine with him once more at the sign of the Black Bull of Norway. Every one promised to attend, anticipating nothing but festivity and joy. Alas, what short-sighted improvident creatures we are, all of us; and how often does the evening cup of joy lead to sorrow in the morning!

The day arrived—the party of young noblemen and gentlemen met, and were as happy and jovial as men could be. George was never seen so brilliant, or so full of spirits; and exulting to see so many gallant young chiefs and gentlemen about him, who all gloried in the same principles of loyalty, (perhaps this word should have been written *disloyalty*,) he made speeches, gave toasts, and sung songs, all leaning slily to the same side, until a very late hour. By that time he had pushed the bottle so long and so freely, that its fumes had taken possession of every brain to such a degree, that they held Dame Reason rather at the staff's end, overbearing all her counsels and expostulations; and it was imprudently proposed by a wild inebriated spark, and carried by a majority of voices, that the whole party should adjourn to a bagnio for the remainder of the night.

They did so; and it appears from what follows, that the house to which they retired, must have been somewhere on the opposite side of the street to the Black Bull Inn, a little farther to the eastward. They had not been an hour in that house, till some altercation chanced to arise between George Colwan and a Mr. Drummond, the younger son of a nobleman of distinction. It was perfectly casual, and no one thenceforward, to this day, could ever tell what it was about, if it was not about the misunderstanding of some word, or term, that the one had uttered. However it was, some high words passed between them; these were followed by threats; and in less than two minutes from the commencement of the quarrel, Drummond left the house in apparent displeasure, hinting to the other that they two should settle that in a more convenient place.

The company looked at one another, for all was over before any of them knew such a thing was begun. "What the devil is the matter?" cried one. "What ails Drummond?" cried another. "Who has he quarrelled with?" asked a third.

"Don't know."–"Can't tell, on my life."–"He has quarrelled with his wine, I suppose, and is going to send it a challenge."

Such were the questions, and such the answers that passed in the jovial party, and the matter was no more thought of.

But in the course of a very short space, about the length of which the ideas of the company were the next day at great variance, a sharp rap came to the door: It was opened by a female; but there being a chain inside, she only saw one side of the person at the door. He appeared to be a young gentleman, in appearance like him who had lately left the house, and asked, in a low whispering voice, "if young Dalcastle was still in the house?" The woman did not know,–"If he is," added he, "pray tell him to speak with me for a few minutes." The woman delivered the message before all the party, among whom there were then sundry courteous ladies of notable distinction, and George, on receiving it, instantly rose from the side of one of them, and said, in the hearing of them all, "I will bet a hundred merks that is Drummond."–"Don't go to quarrel with him, George," said one.– "Bring him in with you," said another. George stepped out; the door was again bolted, the chain drawn across, and the inadvertent party, left within, thought no more of the circumstance till the next morning, that the report had spread over the city, that a young gentleman had been slain, on a little washing-green at the side of the North Loch, and at the very bottom of the close where this thoughtless party had been assembled.

Several of them, on first hearing the report, hasted to the dead-room in the old Guard-house, where the corpse had been deposited, and soon discovered the body to be that of their friend and late entertainer, George Colwan. Great were the consternation and grief of all con-

cerned, and, in particular, of his old father and Miss Logan; for George
had always been the sole hope and darling of both, and the news of
the event paralysed them so as to render them incapable of all thought
or exertion. The spirit of the old laird was broken by the blow, and he
descended at once from a jolly, good-natured, and active man, to a
mere driveller, weeping over the body of his son, kissing his wound,
his lips, and his cold brow alternately; denouncing vengeance on his
murderers, and lamenting that he himself had not met the cruel doom,
so that the hope of his race might have been preserved. In short, finding that all further motive of action and object of concern or of love,
here below, were for ever removed from him, he abandoned himself
to despair, and threatened to go down to the grave with his son.

But although he made no attempt to discover the murderers, the
arm of justice was not idle; and it being evident to all, that the crime
must infallibly be brought home to young Drummond, some of his
friends sought him out, and compelled him, sorely against his will, to
retire into concealment till the issue of the proof that should be led was
made known. At the same time, he denied all knowledge of the incident with a resolution that astonished his intimate friends and relations, who to a man suspected him guilty. His father was not in Scotland, for I think it was said to me that this young man was second son
to a John, Duke of Melfort, who lived abroad with the royal family of
the Stuarts; but this young gentleman lived with the relations of his
mother, one of whom, an uncle, was a Lord of Session: these having
thoroughly effected his concealment, went away, and listened to the
evidence; and the examination of every new witness convinced them
that their noble young relative was the slayer of his friend.

All the young gentlemen of the party were examined, save
Drummond, who, when sent for, could not be found, which circumstance sorely confirmed the suspicions against him in the minds of
judges and jurors, friends and enemies; and there is little doubt, that
the care of his relations in concealing him, injured his character, and
his cause. The young gentlemen, of whom the party was composed,
varied considerably, with respect to the quarrel between him and the
deceased. Some of them had neither heard nor noted it; others had,
but not one of them could tell how it began. Some of them had heard
the threat uttered by Drummond on leaving the house, and one only
had noted him lay his hand on his sword. Not one of them could
swear that it was Drummond who came to the door, and desired to
speak with the deceased, but the general impression on the minds of
them all, was to that effect; and one of the women swore that she
heard the voice distinctly at the door, and every word that voice pro-

nounced; and at the same time heard the deceased say, that it was Drummond's.

On the other hand, there were some evidences on Drummond's part, which Lord Craigie, his uncle, had taken care to collect. He produced the sword which his nephew had worn that night, on which there was neither blood nor blemish; and above all, he insisted on the evidence of a number of surgeons, who declared that both the wounds which the deceased had received, had been given behind. One of these was below the left arm, and a slight one; the other was quite through the body, and both evidently inflicted with the same weapon, a two-edged sword, of the same dimensions as that worn by Drummond.

Upon the whole, there was a division in the court, but a majority decided it. Drummond was pronounced guilty of the murder; outlawed for not appearing, and a high reward offered for his apprehension. It was with the greatest difficulty that he escaped on board of a small trading vessel, which landed him in Holland, and from thence, flying into Germany, he entered into the service of the Emperor Charles VI. Many regretted that he was not taken, and made to suffer the penalty due for such a crime, and the melancholy incident became a pulpit theme over a great part of Scotland, being held up as a proper warning to youth to beware of such haunts of vice and depravity, the nurses of all that is precipitate, immoral, and base, among mankind.

After the funeral of this promising and excellent young man, his father never more held up his head. Miss Logan, with all her art, could not get him to attend to any worldly thing, or to make any settlement whatsoever of his affairs, save making her over a present of what disposable funds he had about him. As to his estates, when they were mentioned to him, he wished them all in the bottom of the sea, and himself along with them. But whenever she mentioned the circumstance of Thomas Drummond having been the murderer of his son, he shook his head, and once made the remark, that "It was all a mistake, a gross and fatal error; but that God, who had permitted such a flagrant deed, would bring it to light in his own time and way." In a few weeks he followed his son to the grave, and the notorious Robert Wringhim took possession of his estates as the lawful son of the late laird, born in wedlock, and under his father's roof. The investiture was celebrated by prayer, singing of psalms, and religious disputation. The late guardian and adopted father, and the mother of the new laird, presided on the grand occasion, making a conspicuous figure in all the work of the day; and though the youth himself indulged rather more freely in the bottle, than he had ever been seen to do before, it was agreed by all present, that there had never been a festivity so sanctified within the great hall of Dalcastle. Then, after due thanks returned, they parted rejoicing in spirit; which thanks, by the by, consisted wholly in telling the Almighty what he was; and informing him, with very particular precision, what *they* were who addressed him; for Wringhim's whole system of popular declamation consisted it seems in this,—to denounce all men and women to destruction, and then hold out hopes to his adherents that they were the chosen few, included in the promises, and who could never fall away. It would appear that this pharisaical doctrine is a very delicious one, and the most grateful of all others to the worst characters.

But the ways of heaven are altogether inscrutable, and soar as far above and beyond the works and the comprehensions of man, as the sun, flaming in majesty, is above the tiny boy's evening rocket. It is the controller of Nature alone, that can bring light out of darkness, and order out of confusion. Who is he that causeth the mole, from his secret path of darkness, to throw up the gem, the gold, and the precious ore? The same, that from the mouths of babes and sucklings can extract the perfection of praise, and who can make the most abject of his creatures instrumental in bringing the most hidden truths to light.

Miss Logan had never lost the thought of her late master's prediction, that Heaven would bring to light the truth concerning the untimely death of his son. She perceived that some strange conviction, too horrible for expression, preyed on his mind from the moment that the fatal news reached him, to the last of his existence; and in his last ravings, he uttered some incoherent words about justification by faith alone, and absolute and eternal predestination having been the ruin of his house. These, to be sure, were the words of superannuation, and of the last and severest kind of it; but for all that, they sunk deep into Miss Logan's soul, and at last she began to think with herself, "Is it possible the Wringhims, and the sophisticating wretch who is in conjunction with them, the mother of my late beautiful and amiable young master, can have effected his destruction? if so, I will spend my days, and my little patrimony, in endeavours to rake up and expose the unnatural deed."

In all her outgoings and incomings, Mrs. Logan (as she was now styled) never lost sight of this one object. Every new disappointment only whetted her desire to fish up some particulars concerning it; for she thought so long, and so ardently upon it, that by degrees it became settled in her mind as a sealed truth. And as woman is always most jealous of her own sex in such matters, her suspicions were fixed on her greatest enemy, Mrs. Colwan, now the Lady Dowager of Dalcastle. All was wrapt in a chaos of confusion and darkness; but at last by dint of a thousand sly and secret inquiries, Mrs. Logan found out where Lady Dalcastle had been, on the night that the murder happened, and likewise what company she had kept, as well as some of the comers and goers; and she had hopes of having discovered a cue, which, if she could keep hold of the thread, would lead her through darkness to the light of truth.

Returning very late one evening from a convocation of family servants, which she had drawn together in order to fish something out of them, her maid having been in attendance on her all the evening, they found on going home, that the house had been broken, and a number of valuable articles stolen therefrom. Mrs. Logan had grown quite heartless before this stroke, having been altogether unsuccessful in her inquiries, and now she began to entertain some resolutions of giving up the fruitless search.

In a few days thereafter, she received intelligence that her clothes and plate were mostly recovered, and that she for one was bound over to prosecute the depredator, provided the articles turned out to be hers, as libelled in the indictment, and as a king's evidence had given out. She was likewise summoned, or requested, I know not which, being ignorant of these matters, to go as far as the town of Peebles on Tweedside, in order to survey these articles on such a day, and make affidavit to their identity before the Sheriff. She went accordingly; but on entering the town by the North Gate, she was accosted by a poor girl in tattered apparel, who with great earnestness inquired if her name was not Mrs. Logan? On being answered in the affirmative, she said that the unfortunate prisoner in the tolbooth requested her, as she valued all that was dear to her in life, to go and see her before she appeared in court, at the hour of cause, as she (the prisoner) had something of the greatest moment to impart to her. Mrs. Logan's curiosity was excited, and she followed the girl straight to the tolbooth, who by the way said to her, that she would find in the prisoner a woman of a superior mind, who had gone through all the vicissitudes of life. "She has been very unfortunate, and I fear very wicked," added the poor thing, "but she is my mother, and God knows, with all her faults and failings, she has never been unkind to me. You, madam, have it in your power to save her; but she has wronged you, and therefore if you will not do it for her sake, do it for mine, and the God of the fatherless will reward you."

Mrs. Logan answered her with a cast of the head, and a hem! and only remarked, that "the guilty must not always be suffered to escape, or what a world must we be doomed to live in!"

She was admitted to the prison, and found a tall emaciated figure, who appeared to have once possessed a sort of masculine beauty in no ordinary degree, but was now considerably advanced in years. She viewed Mrs. Logan with a stern, steady gaze, as if reading her features as a margin to her intellect; and when she addressed her it was not with that humility, and agonized fervor, which are natural for one in such circumstances to address to another, who has the power of her life and death in her hands.

"I am deeply indebted to you, for this timely visit, Mrs. Logan," said she. "It is not that I value life, or because I fear death, that I have sent for you so expressly. But the manner of the death that awaits me, has something peculiarly revolting in it to a female mind. Good God! when I think of being hung up, a spectacle to a gazing, gaping multitude, with numbers of which I have had intimacies and connections, that would render the moment of parting so hideous, that, believe me, it rends to flinders a soul born for another sphere than that in which it has moved, had not the vile selfishness of a lordly fiend ruined all my prospects, and all my hopes. Hear me then; for I do not ask your pity: I only ask of you to look to yourself, and behave with womanly prudence. If you deny this day, that these goods are yours, there is no other evidence whatever against my life, and it is safe for the present. For as for the word of the wretch who has betrayed me, it is of no avail; he has prevaricated so notoriously to save himself. If you deny them, you shall have them all again to the value of a mite, and more to the bargain. If you swear to the identity of them, the process will, one way and another, cost you the half of what they are worth."

"And what security have I for that?" said Mrs. Logan.

"You have none but *my word*," said the other proudly, "and that never yet was violated. If you cannot take that, I know the worst you can do—But I had forgot—I have a poor helpless child without, waiting, and starving about the prison door—Surely it was of her that I wished to speak. This shameful death of mine will leave her in a deplorable state."

"The girl seems to have candour and strong affections," said Mrs. Logan; "I grievously mistake if such a child would not be a thousand times better without such a guardian and director."

"Then will you be so kind as come to the Grass Market, and see me put down?" said the prisoner. "I thought a woman would estimate a woman's and a mother's feelings, when such a dreadful throw was at stake, at least in part. But you are callous, and have never known any feelings but those of subordination to your old unnatural master. Alas, I have no cause of offence! I have wronged you; and justice must take its course. Will you forgive me before we part?"

Mrs. Logan hesitated, for her mind ran on something else: On which the other subjoined, "No, you will not forgive me, I see. But you will pray to God to forgive me? I know you will *do that*."

Mrs. Logan heard not this jeer, but looking at the prisoner with an absent and stupid stare, she said, "Did you know my late master?"

"Ay, that I did, and never for any good," said she. "I knew the old and the young spark both, and was by when the latter was slain."

This careless sentence affected Mrs. Logan in a most peculiar manner. A shower of tears burst from her eyes ere it was done, and when it was, she appeared like one bereaved of her mind. She first turned one way and then another, as if looking for something she had dropped. She seemed to think she had lost her eyes, instead of her tears, and at length, as by instinct, she tottered close up to the prisoner's face, and looking wistfully and joyfully in it, said, with breathless earnestness, "Pray, mistress, what is your name?"

"My name is Arabella Calvert," said the other: "Miss, mistress, or widow, as you chuse, for I have been all the three, and that not once nor twice only—Ay, and something beyond all these. But as for you, you have never been any thing!"

"Ay, ay! and so you are Bell Calvert? Well, I thought so—I thought so," said Mrs. Logan; and helping herself to a seat, she came and sat down close by the prisoner's knee. "So you are indeed Bell Calvert, so called once. Well, of all the world you are the woman whom I have longed and travailed the most to see. But you were invisible; a being to be heard of, not seen."

"There have been days, madam," returned she, "when I *was* to be seen, and when there were few to be seen like me. But since that time there have indeed been days on which I was not to be seen. My crimes have been great, but my sufferings have been greater. So great, that neither you nor the world can ever either know or conceive them. I hope they will be taken into account by the Most High. Mine have been crimes of utter desperation. But whom am I speaking to? You had better leave me to myself, mistress."

"Leave you to yourself? That I will be loth to do, till you tell me where you were that night my young master was murdered?"

"Where the devil would, I was! Will that suffice you? Ah, it was a vile action! A night to be remembered that was! Won't you be going? I want to trust my daughter with a commission."

"No, Mrs. Calvert, you and I part not, till you have divulged that mystery to me."

"You must accompany me to the other world, then, for you shall not have it in this."

"If you refuse to answer me, I can have you before a tribunal, where you shall be sifted to the soul."

"Such miserable inanity! What care I for your threatenings of a tribunal? I who must so soon stand before my last earthly one? What could the word of such a culprit avail? Or if it could, where is the judge that could enforce it?"

"Did you not say that there was some mode of accommodating matters on that score?"

"Yes, I prayed you to grant me my life, which is in your power. The saving of it would not have cost you a plack, yet you refused to do it. The taking of it will cost you a great deal, and yet to that purpose you adhere. I can have no parley with such a spirit. I would not have my life in a present from its motions, nor would I exchange courtesies with its possessor."

"Indeed, Mrs. Calvert, since ever we met, I have been so busy thinking about who you might be, that I know not what you have been proposing. I believe, I meant to do what I could to save you. But once for all, tell me every thing that you know concerning that amiable young gentleman's death, and here is my hand there shall be nothing wanting that I can effect for you."

"No, I despise all barter with such mean and selfish curiosity; and, as I believe *that* passion is stronger with you, than fear is with me, we part on equal terms. Do your worst; and my secret shall go to the gallows and the grave with me."

Mrs. Logan was now greatly confounded, and after proffering in vain to concede every thing she could ask in exchange, for the particulars relating to the murder, she became the suppliant in her turn. But the unaccountable culprit, exulting in her advantage, laughed her to scorn; and finally, in a paroxysm of pride and impatience, called in the jailor and had her expelled, ordering him in her hearing not to grant her admittance a second time, on any pretence.

Mrs. Logan was now hard put to it, and again driven almost to despair. She might have succeeded in the attainment of that she thirsted for most in life so easily, had she known the character with which she had to deal with—Had she known to have soothed her high and afflicted spirit: but that opportunity was past, and the hour of examination at hand. She once thought of going and claiming her articles, as she at first intended; but then, when she thought again of the Wringhims swaying it at Dalcastle, where she had been wont to hear them held in such contempt, if not abhorrence, and perhaps of holding it by the most diabolical means, she was withheld from marring the only chance that remained of having a glimpse into that mysterious affair.

Finally, she resolved not to answer to her name in the court, rather than to appear and assert a falsehood, which she might be called on to certify by oath. She did so; and heard the Sheriff give orders to the officers to make inquiry for Miss Logan from Edinburgh, at the various places of entertainment in town, and to expedite her arrival in court, as things of great value were in dependence. She also heard the man who had turned king's evidence against the prisoner, examined for the second time, and sifted most cunningly. His answers gave any thing but satisfaction to the Sheriff, though Mrs. Logan believed them to be mainly truth. But there were a few questions and answers that struck her above all others.

"How long is it since Mrs. Calvert and you became acquainted?"

"About a year and a half."

"State the precise time, if you please; the day, or night, according to your remembrance."

"It was on the morning of the 28th of February, 1705."

"What time of the morning?"

"Perhaps about one."

"So early as that? At what place did you meet then?"

"It was at the foot of one of the north wynds of Edinburgh."

"Was it by appointment that you met?"

"No, it was not."

"For what purpose was it then?"

"For no purpose."

"How is it that you chance to remember the day and hour so minutely, if you met that woman, whom you have accused, merely by chance, and for no manner of purpose, as you must have met others that night, perhaps to the amount of hundreds, in the same way?"

"I have good cause to remember it, my lord."

"What was that cause?–No answer?–You don't choose to say what that cause was?"

"I am not at liberty to tell."

The Sheriff then descended to other particulars, all of which tended to prove that the fellow was an accomplished villain, and that the principal share of the atrocities had been committed by him. Indeed the Sheriff hinted, that he suspected the only share Mrs. Calvert had in them, was in being too much in his company, and too true to him. The case was remitted to the Court of Justiciary; but Mrs. Logan had heard enough to convince her that the culprits first met at the very spot, and the very hour, on which George Colwan was slain; and she had no doubt that they were incendiaries set on by his mother, to forward her own and her darling son's way to opulence. Mrs. Logan was wrong, as will appear in the sequel; but her antipathy to Mrs. Colwan made her watch the event with all care. She never quitted Peebles as long as Bell Calvert remained there, and when she was removed to Edinburgh, the other followed. When the trial came on, Mrs. Logan and her maid were again summoned as witnesses before the jury, and compelled by the prosecutor for the Crown to appear.

The maid was first called; and when she came into the witnesses' box, the anxious and hopeless looks of the prisoner were manifest to all: But the girl, whose name, she said, was Bessy Gillies, answered in so flippant and fearless a way, that the auditors were much amused. After a number of routine questions, the depute-advocate asked her if she was at home on the morning of the fifth of September last, when her mistress's house was robbed?

"Was I at hame, say ye? Na, faith-ye, lad! An I had been at hame, there had been mair to dee. I wad hae raised sic a yelloch!"

"Where were you that morning?"

"Where was I, say you? I was in the house where my mistress was, sitting dozing an' half sleeping in the kitchen. I thought aye she would be setting out every minute, for twa hours."

"And when you went home, what did you find?"

"What found we? Be my sooth, we found a broken lock, an' toom kists."

"Relate some of the particulars, if you please."

"O, sir, the thieves didna stand upon particulars: they were halesale dealers in a' our best wares."

"I mean, what passed between your mistress and you on the occasion?"

"What passed, say ye? O, there wasna muckle: I was in a great passion, but she was dung doitrified a wee. When she gaed to put the key i' the door, up it flew to the fer wa'.—'Bess, ye jaud, what's the meaning o' this?' quo she. 'Ye hae left the door open, ye tawpie!' quo she. 'The ne'er o' that I did,' quo I, 'or may my shakel bane never turn another key.' When we got the candle lightit, a' the house was in a hoad-road. 'Bessy, my woman,' quo she, 'we are baith ruined and undone creatures.' 'The deil a bit,' quo I; 'that I deny positively. H'mh! to speak o' a lass o' my age being ruined and undone! I never had muckle except what was within a good jerkin, an' let the thief ruin me there wha can.'"

"Do you remember ought else that your mistress said on the occasion? Did you hear her blame any person?"

"O, she made a great deal o' grumphing an' groaning about the *misfortune*, as she ca'd it, an' I think she said it was a part o' the ruin wrought by the Ringans, or some sic name,–'they'll hae't a'! they'll hae't a'!' cried she, wringing her hands; 'they'll hae't a', an' hell wi't, an' they'll get them baith.' 'Aweel, that's aye some satisfaction,' quo I."

"Whom did she mean by the Ringans, do you know?"

"I fancy they are some creatures that she has dreamed about, for I think there canna be as ill folks living as she ca's them."

"Did you never hear her say that the prisoner at the bar there, Mrs. Calvert, or Bell Calvert, was the robber of her house; or that she was one of the Ringans?"

"Never. Somebody tauld her lately, that ane Bell Calvert robbed her house, but she disna believe it. Neither do I."

"What reasons have you for doubting it?"

"Because it was nae woman's fingers that broke up the bolts an' the locks that were torn open that night."

"Very pertinent, Bessy. Come then within the bar, and look at these articles on the table. Did you ever see these silver spoons before?"

"I hae seen some very like them, and whaever has seen siller spoons, has done the same."

"Can you swear you never saw them before?"

"Na, na, I wadna swear to ony siller spoons that ever war made, unless I had put a private mark on them wi' my ain hand, an' that's what I never did to ane."

"See, they are all marked with a C."

"Sae are a' the spoons in Argyle, an' the half o' them in Edinburgh I think. A C is a very common letter, an' so are a' the names that begin wi't. Lay them by, lay them by, an' gie the poor woman her spoons again. They are marked wi' her ain name, an' I hae little doubt they are hers, an' that she has seen better days."

"Ah, God bless her heart!" sighed the prisoner; and that blessing was echoed in the breathings of many a feeling breast.

"Did you ever see this gown before, think you?"

"I hae seen ane very like it."

"Could you not swear that gown was your mistress's once?"

"No, unless I saw her hae't on, an' kend that she had paid for't. I am very scrupulous about an oath. *Like* is an ill mark. Sae ill indeed, that I wad hardly swear to ony thing."

"But you say that gown is *very like* one your mistress used to wear."

"I never said sic a thing. It is like one I hae seen her hae out airing on the hay raip i' the back green. It is very like ane I hae seen Mrs. Butler in the Grass Market wearing too; I rather think it is the same. Bless you, sir, I wadna swear to my ain fore finger, if it had been as lang out o' my sight, an' brought in an' laid on that table."

"Perhaps you are not aware, girl, that this scrupulousness of yours is likely to thwart the purposes of justice, and bereave your mistress of property to the amount of a thousand merks?" *(From the Judge.)*

"I canna help that, my lord: that's her lookout. For my part, I am resolved to keep a clear conscience, till I be married, at any rate."

"Look over these things and see if there is any one article among them which you can fix on as the property of your mistress."

"No ane o' them, sir, no ane o' them. An oath is an awfu' thing, especially when it is for life or death. Gie the poor woman her things again, an' let my mistress pick up the next she finds: that's my advice."

When Mrs. Logan came into the box, the prisoner groaned, and laid down her head. But how she was astonished when she heard her deliver herself something to the following purport!–That whatever penalties she was doomed to abide, she was determined she would not bear witness against a woman's life, from a certain conviction that it could not be a woman who broke her house. "I have no doubt that I may find some of my own things there," added she, "but if they were found in her possession, she has been made a tool, or the dupe, of an infernal set, who shall be nameless here. I believe she *did not* rob me, and for that reason I will have no hand in her condemnation."

The Judge. "This is the most singular perversion I have ever witnessed. Mrs. Logan, I entertain strong suspicions that the prisoner, or her agents, have made some agreement with you on this matter, to prevent the course of justice."

"So far from that, my lord, I went into the jail at Peebles to this woman, whom I had never seen before, and proffered to withdraw my part in the prosecution, as well as my evidence, provided she would tell me a few simple facts; but she spurned at my offer, and had me turned insolently out of the prison, with orders to the jailor never to admit me again on any pretence."

The prisoner's counsel, taking hold of this evidence, addressed the jury with great fluency; and finally, the prosecution was withdrawn, and the prisoner dismissed from the bar, with a severe reprimand for her past conduct, and an exhortation to keep better company.

It was not many days till a caddy came with a large parcel to Mrs. Logan's house, which parcel he delivered into her hands, accompanied with a sealed note, containing an inventory of the articles, and a request to know if the unfortunate Arabella Calvert would be admitted to converse with Mrs. Logan.

Never was there a woman so much overjoyed as Mrs. Logan was at this message. She returned compliments: Would be most happy to see her; and no article of the parcel should be looked at, or touched, till her arrival.—It was not long till she made her appearance, dressed in somewhat better style than she had yet seen her; delivered her over the greater part of the stolen property, besides many things that either never had belonged to Mrs. Logan, or that she thought proper to deny, in order that the other might retain them.

The tale that she told of her misfortunes was of the most distressing nature, and was enough to stir up all the tender, as well as abhorrent feelings in the bosom of humanity. She had suffered every deprivation in fame, fortune, and person. She had been imprisoned; she had been scourged, and branded as an impostor; and all on account of her resolute and unmoving fidelity and truth to *several* of the very worst of men, every one of whom had abandoned her to utter destitution and shame. But this story we cannot enter on at present, as it would perhaps mar the thread of our story, as much as it did the anxious anticipations of Mrs. Logan, who sat pining and longing for the relation that follows.

"Now I know, Mrs. Logan, that you are expecting a detail of the circumstances relating to the death of Mr. George Colwan; and in gratitude for your unbounded generosity, and disinterestedness, I will tell you all that I know, although, for causes that will appear obvious to you, I had determined never in life to divulge one circumstance of it. I can tell you, however, that you will be disappointed, for it was not the gentleman who was accused, found guilty, and would have suffered the utmost penalty of the law, had he not made his escape. *It was not he,* I say, who slew your young master, nor had he any hand in it."

"I never thought he had. But, pray, how do you come to know this?"

"You shall hear. I had been abandoned in York, by an artful and consummate fiend; found guilty of being art and part concerned in the most heinous atrocities, and, in his place, suffered what I yet shudder to think of. I was banished the county—begged my way with my poor outcast child up to Edinburgh, and was there obliged, for the second time in my life, to betake myself to the most degrading of all means to support two wretched lives. I hired a dress, and betook me, shivering, to the High Street, too well aware that my form and appearance would soon draw me suitors enow at that throng and intemperate time of the parliament. On my very first stepping out to the street, a party of young gentlemen was passing. I heard by the noise they made, and the tenor of their speech, that they were more than mellow, and so I resolved to keep near them, in order, if possible, to make some of them my prey. But just as one of them began to eye me, I was rudely thrust into a narrow close by one of the guardsmen. I had heard to what house the party was bound, for the men were talking exceedingly loud, and making no secret of it: so I hasted down the close, and round below to the one where their rendezvous was to be; but I was too late, they were all housed and the door bolted. I resolved to wait, thinking they could not all stay long; but I was perishing with famine, and was like to fall down. The moon shone as bright as day, and I perceived, by a sign at the bottom of the close, that there was a small tavern of a certain description up two stairs there. I went up and called, telling the mistress of the house my plan. She approved of it mainly, and offered me her best apartment, provided I could get one of these noble mates to accompany me. She abused Lucky Sudds, as she called her, at the inn where the party was, envying her huge profits, no doubt, and giving me afterward something to drink, for which I really felt exceedingly grateful in my need. I stepped down stairs in order to be on the alert. The moment that I reached the ground, the door of Lucky Sudds' house opened and shut, and down came the Honourable Thomas Drummond, with hasty and impassioned strides, his sword rattling at his heel. I accosted him in a soft and soothing tone. He was taken with my address; for he instantly stood still and gazed intently at me, then at the place, and then at me again. I beckoned him to follow me, which he did without farther ceremony, and we soon found ourselves together in the best room of a house where every thing was wretched. He still looked about him, and at me; but all this while he had never spoken a word. At length, I asked if he would take any refreshment? 'If you please,' said he. I asked what he would have? but he only answered, 'Whatever you choose, madam.' If he was taken with my address, I was much more taken with his; for he was a complete gentleman, and a gentleman will ever act as one. At length, he began as follows:

" 'I am utterly at a loss to account for this adventure, madam. It seems to me like enchantment, and I can hardly believe my senses. An English lady, I judge, and one, who from her manner and address should belong to the first class of society, in such a place as this, is indeed matter of wonder to me. At the foot of a close in Edinburgh! and at this time of the night! Surely it must have been no common reverse of fortune that reduced you to this?' I wept, or pretended to do so; on which he added. 'Pray, madam, take heart. Tell me what has befallen you; and if I can do any thing for you, in restoring you to your country or your friends, you shall command my interest.'

"I had great need of a friend then, and I thought now was the time to secure one. So I began and told him the moving tale I have told you. But I soon perceived that I had kept by the naked truth too unvarnishedly, and thereby quite overshot my mark. When he learned that he was sitting in a wretched corner of an irregular house, with a felon, who had so lately been scourged, and banished as a swindler and impostor, his modest nature took the alarm, and he was shocked, instead of being moved with pity. His eye fixed on some of the casual stripes on my arm, and from that moment he became restless and impatient to be gone. I tried some gentle arts to retain him, but in vain; so, after paying both the landlady and me for pleasures he had neither tasted nor asked, he took his leave.

"I showed him down stairs; and just as he turned the corner of the next land, a man came rushing violently by him; exchanged looks with him, and came running up to me. He appeared in great agitation, and was quite out of breath; and, taking my hand in his, we ran up stairs together without speaking, and were instantly in the apartment I had left, where a stoup of wine still stood untasted. 'Ah, this is fortunate!' said my new spark, and helped himself. In the mean while, as our apartment was a corner one, and looked both east and north, I ran to the easter casement to look after Drummond. Now, note me well: I saw him going eastward in his tartans and bonnet, and the gilded hilt of his claymore glittering in the moon; and, at the very same time, I saw two men, the one in black, and the other likewise in tartans, coming toward the steps from the opposite bank, by the foot of the loch; and I saw Drummond and they eying each other as they passed. I kept view of *him* till he vanished towards Leith Wynd, and by that time the two strangers had come close up under our window. This is what I wish you to pay particular attention to. I had only lost sight of Drummond, (who had given me his name and address,) for the short space of time that we took in running up one pair of short stairs; and during that space he had halted a moment, for, when I got my eye on him again, he had not crossed the mouth of the next entry, nor proceeded above ten or twelve paces, and, *at the same time,* I saw the two men coming down the bank on the opposite side of the loch, at about three hundred paces distance. Both he and they were distinctly in my view, and never within speech of each other, until he vanished into one of the wynds leading toward the bottom of the High Street, at which precise time the two strangers came below my window; so that it was quite clear he neither could be one of them, nor have any communication with them.

"Yet, mark me again; for of all things I have ever seen, this was the most singular. When I looked down at the two strangers, *one of them was extremely like Drummond.* So like was he, that there was not one item in dress, form, feature, nor voice, by which I could distinguish the one from the other. I was certain it was not he, because I had seen the one going and the other approaching at the same time, and my impression at the moment was, that I looked upon some spirit, or demon, in his likeness. I felt a chillness creep all round my heart, my knees tottered, and, withdrawing my head from the open casement that lay in the dark shade, I said to the man who was with me, 'Good God, what is this!'

" 'What is it, my dear?' said he, as much alarmed as I was.

" 'As I live, there stands an apparition!' said I.

"He was not so much afraid when he heard me say so, and peeping cautiously out, he looked and listened a-while, and then drawing back, he said in a whisper, 'They are both living men, and one of them is he I passed at the corner.'

" 'That he is not,' said I, emphatically. 'To that I will make oath.'

"He smiled and shook his head, and then added, 'I never then saw a man before, whom I could not know again, particularly if he was the very last I had seen. But what matters it whether it be or not? As it is no concern of ours, let us sit down and enjoy ourselves.'

" 'But it *does* matter a very great deal with me, sir,' said I.–'Bless me, my head is giddy–my breath quite gone, and I feel as if I were surrounded with fiends. Who are you, sir?'

" 'You shall know that ere we two part, my love,' said he: 'I cannot conceive why the return of this young gentleman to the spot he so lately left, should discompose you? I suppose he got a glance of you as he passed, and has returned to look after you, and that is the whole secret of the matter.'

" 'If you will be so civil as to walk out and join him then, it will oblige me hugely,' said I, 'for I never in my life experienced such boding apprehensions of evil company. I cannot conceive how you should come up here without asking my permission? Will it please you to begone, sir?'–I was within an ace of prevailing. He took out his purse–I need not say more–I was bribed to let him remain. Ah, had I kept by my frail resolution of dismissing him at that moment, what a world of shame and misery had been evited! But that, though uppermost still in my mind, has nothing ado here.

"When I peeped over again, the two men were disputing in a whisper, the one of them in violent agitation and terror, and the other upbraiding him, and urging him on to some desperate act. At length I heard the young man in the Highland garb say indignantly, 'Hush, recreant! It is God's work which you are commissioned to execute, and it must be done. But if you positively decline it, I will do it myself, and do you beware of the consequences.'

" 'Oh, I will, I will!' cried the other in black clothes, in a wretched beseeching tone. 'You shall instruct me in this, as in all things else.'

"I thought all this while I was closely concealed from them, and wondered not a little when he in tartans gave me a sly nod, as much as to say, 'What do you think of this?' or, 'Take note of what you see,' or something to that effect, from which I perceived, that whatever he was about, he did not wish it to be kept a secret. For all that, I was impressed with a terror and anxiety that I could not overcome, but it only made me mark every event with the more intense curiosity. The Highlander, whom I still could not help regarding as the evil genius of Thomas Drummond, performed every action, as with the quickness of thought. He concealed the youth in black in a narrow entry, a little to the westward of my windows, and as he was leading him across the moonlight green by the shoulder, I perceived, for the first time, that both of them were armed with rapiers. He pushed him without resistance into the dark shaded close, made another signal to me, and hasted up the close to Lucky Sudds' door. The city and the morning were so still, that I heard every word that was uttered, on putting my head out a little. He knocked at the door sharply, and after waiting a considerable space, the bolt was drawn, and the door, as I conceived, edged up as far as the massy chain would let it. 'Is young Dalcastle still in the house?' said he sharply.

"I did not hear the answer, but I heard him say, shortly after, 'If he is, pray tell him to speak with me for a few minutes.' He then withdrew from the door, and came slowly down the close, in a lingering manner, looking oft behind him. Dalcastle came out; advanced a few steps after him, and then stood still, as if hesitating whether or not he should call out a friend to accompany him; and that instant the door behind him was closed, chained, and the iron bolt drawn; on hearing of which, he followed his adversary without farther hesitation. As he passed below my window, I heard him say, 'I beseech you, Tom, let us do nothing in this matter rashly;' but I could not hear the answer of the other, who had turned the corner.

"I roused up my drowsy companion, who was leaning on the bed, and we both looked together from the north window. We were in the shade, but the moon shone full on the two young gentlemen. Young Dalcastle was visibly the worse of liquor, and his back being turned toward us, he said something to the other which I could not make out, although he spoke a considerable time, and, from his tones and gestures, appeared to be reasoning. When he had done, the tall young man in the tartans drew his sword, and his face being straight to us, we heard him say distinctly, 'No more words about it, George, if you please; but if you be a man, as I take you to be, draw your sword, and let us settle it here.'

"Dalcastle drew his sword, without changing his attitude; but he spoke with more warmth, for we heard his words, 'Think you that I fear you, Tom? Be assured, sir, I would not fear ten of the best of your name, at each other's backs: all that I want is to have friends with us to see fair play, for if you close with me, you are a dead man.'

"The other stormed at these words. 'You are a braggart, sir,' cried he, 'a wretch—a blot on the cheek of nature—a blight on the Christian world—a reprobate—I'll have your soul, sir—You must play at tennis, and put down elect brethren in another world to-morrow.' As he said this, he brandished his rapier, exciting Dalcastle to offence. He gained his point: The latter, who had previously drawn, advanced in upon his vapouring and licentious antagonist, and a fierce combat ensued. My companion was delighted beyond measure, and I could not keep him from exclaiming, loud enough to have been heard, 'that's grand! that's excellent!' For me, my heart quaked like an aspen. Young Dalcastle either had a decided advantage over his adversary, or else the other thought proper to let him have it; for he shifted, and wore, and flitted from Dalcastle's thrusts like a shadow, uttering ofttimes a sarcastic laugh, that seemed to provoke the other beyond all bearing. At one time, he would spring away to a great distance, then advance again on young Dalcastle with the swiftness of lightning. But that young hero always stood his ground, and repelled the attack: he never gave way, although they fought nearly twice round the bleaching green, which you know is not a very small one. At length they fought close up to the mouth of the dark entry, where the fellow in black stood all this while concealed, and then the combatant in tartans closed with his antagonist, or pretended to do so; but the moment they began to grapple, he wheeled about, turning Colwan's back towards the entry, and then cried out, 'Ah, hell has it! My friend, my friend!'

"That moment the fellow in black rushed from his cover with his drawn rapier, and gave the brave young Dalcastle two deadly wounds in the back, as quick as arm could thrust, both of which I thought pierced through his body. He fell, and rolling himself on his back, he perceived who it was that had slain him thus foully, and said, with a dying emphasis, which I never heard equalled, 'Oh, dog of hell, is it you who has done this!'

"He articulated some more, which I could not hear for other sounds; for the moment that the man in black inflicted the deadly wound, my companion called out, 'That's unfair, you rip! That's damnable! to strike a brave fellow behind! One at a time, you cowards! &c.' to all which the unnatural fiend in the tartans answered with a loud exulting laugh; and then, taking the poor paralysed murderer by the bow of the arm, he hurried him into the dark entry once more, where I lost sight of them for ever."

Before this time, Mrs. Logan had risen up; and when the narrator had finished, she was standing with her arms stretched upward at their full length, and her visage turned down, on which were pourtrayed the lines of the most absolute horror. "The dark suspicions of my late benefactor have been just, and his last prediction is fulfilled," cried she. "The murderer of the accomplished George Colwan has been his own brother, set on, there is little doubt, by her who bare them both, and her directing angel, the self-justified bigot. Aye, and yonder they sit, enjoying the luxuries so dearly purchased, with perfect impunity! If the Almighty do not hurl them down, blasted with shame and confusion, there is no hope of retribution in this life. And, by his might, I will be the agent to accomplish it! Why did the man not pursue the foul murderers? Why did he not raise the alarm, and call the watch?"

"He? The wretch! He durst not move from the shelter he had obtained,—no, not for the soul of him. He was pursued for his life, at the moment when he first flew into my arms. But I did not know it; no, I did not *then* know him. May the curse of heaven, and the blight of hell, settle on the detestable wretch! He pursue for the sake of justice! No; his efforts have all been for evil, but never for good. But *I* raised the alarm; miserable and degraded as I was, I pursued and raised the watch myself. Have you not heard the name of Bell Calvert coupled with that hideous and mysterious affair?"

"Yes, I have. In secret often I have heard it. But how came it that you could never be found? How came it that you never appeared in defence of the Honourable Thomas Drummond; you, the only person who could have justified him?"

"I could not, for I then fell under the power and guidance of a wretch, who durst not for the soul of him be brought forward in the affair. And what was worse, his evidence would have overborne mine, for he would have sworn, that the man who called out and fought Colwan, was the same he met leaving my apartment, and there was an end of it. And moreover, it is well known, that this same man,—this wretch of whom I speak, never mistook one man for another in his life, which makes the mystery of the likeness between this incendiary and Drummond the more extraordinary."

"If it was Drummond, after all that you have asserted, then are my surmises still wrong."

"There is nothing of which I can be more certain, than that it was not Drummond. We have nothing on earth but our senses to depend upon: if these deceive us, what are we to do. I own I cannot account for it; nor ever shall be able to account for it as long as I live."

"Could you know the man in black, if you saw him again?"

"I think I could, if I saw him walk or run: his gait was very particular: He walked as if he had been flat-soled, and his legs made of steel, without any joints in his feet or ancles."

"The very same! The very same! The very same! Pray will you take a few days' journey into the country with me, to look at such a man?"

"You have preserved my life, and for you I will do any thing. I will accompany you with pleasure: and I think I can say that I will know him, for his form left an impression on my heart not soon to be effaced. But of this I am sure, that my unworthy companion *will* recognize him, and that he will be able to swear to his identity every day as long as he lives."

"Where is he? Where is he? O! Mrs. Calvert, where is he?"

"Where is he? He is the wretch whom you heard giving me up to the death; who, after experiencing every mark of affection that a poor ruined being could confer, and after committing a thousand atrocities of which she was ignorant, became an informer to save his diabolical life, and attempted to offer up mine as a sacrifice for all. We will go by ourselves first, and I will tell you if it is necessary to send any farther."

The two dames, the very next morning, dressed themselves like country goodwives; and, hiring two stout ponies furnished with pillions, they took their journey westward, and the second evening after leaving Edinburgh they arrived at the village about two miles below Dalcastle, where they alighted. But Mrs. Logan, being anxious to have Mrs. Calvert's judgment, without either hint or preparation, took care not to mention that they were so near to the end of their journey. In conformity with this plan, she said, after they had sat a while, "Heigh-ho, but I am weary! What suppose we should rest a day here before we proceed farther on our journey?"

Mrs. Calvert was leaning on the casement, and looking out when her companion addressed these words to her, and by far too much engaged to return any answer, for her eyes were riveted on two young men who approached from the farther end of the village; and at length, turning round her head, she said, with the most intense interest, "Proceed farther on our journey, did you say? That we need not do; for, as I live, here comes the very man!"

Mrs. Logan ran to the window, and behold, there was indeed Robert Wringhim Colwan (now the Laird of Dalcastle) coming forward almost below their window, walking arm in arm with another young man; and as the two passed, the latter looked up and made a sly signal to the two dames, biting his lip, winking with his left eye, and nodding his head. Mrs. Calvert was astonished at this recognizance, the young man's former companion having made exactly such another signal on the night of the duel, by the light of the moon; and it struck her, moreover, that she had somewhere seen this young man's face before. She looked after him, and he winked over his shoulder to her; but she was prevented from returning his salute by her companion, who uttered a loud cry, between a groan and shriek, and fell down on the floor with a rumble like a wall that had suddenly been undermined. She had fainted quite away, and required all her companion's attention during the remainder of the evening, for she had scarcely ever well recovered out of one fit before she fell into another, and in the short intervals she raved like one distracted, or in a dream. After falling into a sound sleep by night, she recovered her equanimity, and the two began to converse seriously on what they had seen. Mrs. Calvert averred that the young man who passed next to the window, *was* the very man who stabbed George Colwan in the back, and she said she was willing to take her oath on it at any time when required, and was certain if the wretch Ridsley saw him, that he would make oath to the same purport, for that his walk was so peculiar, no one of common discernment could mistake it.

Mrs. Logan was in great agitation, and said, "It is what I have suspected all along, and what I am sure my late master and benefactor was persuaded of, and the horror of such an idea cut short his days. That wretch, Mrs. Calvert, is the born brother of him he murdered, sons of the same mother they were, whether or not of the same father, the Lord only knows. But, O Mrs. Calvert, that is not the main thing that has discomposed me, and shaken my nerves to pieces at this time. Who do you think the young man was who walked in his company to night?"

"I cannot for my life recollect, but am convinced I have seen the same fine form and face before."

"And did not he seem to know us, Mrs. Calvert? You who are able to recollect things as they happened, did he not seem to recollect us, and make signs to that effect?"

"He did, indeed, and apparently with great good humour."

"O, Mrs. Calvert, hold me, else I shall fall into hysterics again! Who is he? Who is he? Tell me who you suppose he is, for I cannot say my own thought."

"On my life, I cannot remember."

"Did you note the appearance of the young gentleman you saw slain that night? Do you recollect aught of the appearance of my young master, George Colwan?"

Mrs. Calvert sat silent, and stared the other mildly in the face. Their looks encountered, and there was an unearthly amazement that gleamed from each, which, meeting together, caught real fire, and returned the flame to their heated imaginations, till the two associates became like two statues, with their hands spread, their eyes fixed, and their chops fallen down upon their bosoms. An old woman who kept the lodging-house, having been called in before when Mrs. Logan was faintish, chanced to enter at this crisis with some cordial; and, seeing the state of her lodgers, she caught the infection, and fell into the same rigid and statue-like appearance. No scene more striking was ever exhibited; and if Mrs. Calvert had not resumed strength of mind to speak, and break the spell, it is impossible to say how long it might have continued. "It is he, I believe," said she, uttering the words as it were inwardly. "It can be none other but he. But, no, it is impossible! I saw him stabbed through and through the heart; I saw him roll backward on the green in his own blood, utter his last words, and groan away his soul. Yet, if it is not he, who can it be?"

"It *is* he!" cried Mrs. Logan, hysterically.

"Yes, yes, it *is* he!" cried the landlady, in unison.

"It is who?" said Mrs. Calvert; "whom do you mean, mistress?"

"Oh, I don't know! I don't know! I was affrighted."

"Hold your peace then till you recover your senses, and tell me, if you can, who that young gentleman is, who keeps company with the new Laird of Dalcastle?"

"Oh, it is he! it is he!" screamed Mrs. Logan, wringing her hands.

"Oh, it is he! it is he!" cried the landlady, wringing hers.

Mrs. Calvert turned the latter gently and civilly out of the apartment, observing that there seemed to be some infection in the air of the room, and she would be wise for herself to keep out of it.

The two dames had a restless and hideous night. Sleep came not to their relief; for their conversation was wholly about the dead, who seemed to be alive, and their minds were wandering and groping in a chaos of mystery. "Did you attend to his corpse, and know that he positively died and was buried?" said Mrs. Calvert.

"O, yes, from the moment that his fair but mangled corpse was brought home, I attended it till that when it was screwed in the coffin. I washed the long stripes of blood from his lifeless form, on both sides of the body—I bathed the livid wound that passed through his generous and gentle heart. There was one through the flesh of his left side too, which had bled most outwardly of them all. I bathed them, and bandaged them up with wax and perfumed ointment, but still the blood oozed through all, so that when he was laid in the coffin he was like one newly murdered. My brave, my generous young master! he was always as a son to me, and no son was ever more kind or more respectful to a mother. But he was butchered—he was cut off from the earth ere he had well reached to manhood—most barbarously and unfairly slain. And how is it, how can it be, that we again see him here, walking arm in arm with his murderer?"

"The thing cannot be, Mrs. Logan. It is a phantasy of our disturbed imaginations, therefore let us compose ourselves till we investigate this matter farther."

"It cannot be in nature, that is quite clear," said Mrs. Logan; "yet how it should be that I should *think* so—I who knew and nursed him from his infancy—there lies the paradox. As you said once before, we have nothing but our senses to depend on, and if you and I believe that we see a person, why, we do see him. Whose word, or whose reasoning can convince us against our own senses? We will disguise ourselves, as poor women selling a few country wares, and we will go up to the Hall, and see what is to see, and hear what we can hear, for this is a weighty business in which we are engaged, namely, to turn the vengeance of the law upon an unnatural monster; and we will farther learn, if we can, who this is that accompanies him."

Mrs. Calvert acquiesced, and the two dames took their way to Dalcastle, with baskets well furnished with trifles. They did not take the common path from the village, but went about, and approached the mansion by a different way. But it seemed as if some overruling power ordered it, that they should miss no chance of attaining the information they wanted. For ere ever they came within half a mile of Dalcastle, they perceived the two youths coming, as to meet them, on the same path. The road leading from Dalcastle toward the north-east, as all the country knows, goes along a dark bank of brushwood called the Bogle-heuch. It was by this track that the two women were going; and when they perceived the two gentlemen meeting them, they turned back, and the moment they were out of their sight, they concealed themselves in a thicket close by the road. They did this because Mrs. Logan was terrified for being discovered, and because they wished to reconnoitre without being seen. Mrs. Calvert now charged her, whatever she saw, or whatever she heard, to put on a resolution, and support it, for if she fainted there and was discovered, what was to become of her!

The two young men came on, in earnest and vehement conversation; but the subject they were on was a terrible one, and hardly fit to be repeated in the face of a Christian community. Wringhim was disputing the boundlessness of the true Christian's freedom, and expressing doubts, that, chosen as he knew he was from all eternity, still it might be possible for him to commit acts that would exclude him from the limits of the covenant. The other argued, with mighty fluency, that the thing was utterly impossible, and altogether inconsistent with eternal predestination. The arguments of the latter prevailed, and the laird was driven to sullen silence. But, to the women's utter surprise, as the conquering disputant passed, he made a signal of recognizance through the brambles to them, as formerly, and that he might expose his associate fully, and in his true colours, he led him backward and forward by the women more than twenty times, making him to confess both the crimes that he had done, and those he had in contemplation. At length he said to him, "Assuredly I saw some strolling vagrant women on this walk, my dear friend: I wish we could find them, for there is little doubt that they are concealed here in your woods."

"I wish we *could* find them," answered Wringhim; "we would have fine sport maltreating and abusing them."

"That we should, that we should! Now tell me, Robert, if you found a malevolent woman, the latent enemy of your prosperity, lurking in these woods to betray you, what would you inflict on her?"

"I would tear her to pieces with my dogs, and feed them with her flesh. O, my dear friend, there is an old strumpet who lived with my unnatural father, whom I hold in such utter detestation, that I stand constantly in dread of her, and would sacrifice the half of my estate to shed her blood!"

"What will you give me if I will put her in your power, and give you a fair and genuine excuse for making away with her; one for which you shall answer at any bar, here or hereafter?"

"I should like to see the vile hag put down. She is in possession of the family plate, that is mine by right, as well as a thousand valuable relics, and great riches besides, all of which the old profligate gifted shamefully away. And it is said, besides all these, that she has sworn my destruction."

"She has, she has. But I see not how she can accomplish that, seeing the deed was done so suddenly, and in the silence of the night?"

"It was said there were some on-lookers.—But where shall we find that disgraceful Miss Logan?"

"I will show you her by and by. But will you then consent to the other meritorious deed? Come, be a man, and throw away scruples."

"If you can convince me that the promise is binding, I will."

"Then step this way, till I give you a piece of information."

They walked a little way out of hearing, but went not out of sight; therefore, though the women were in a terrible quandary, they durst not stir, for they had some hopes that this extraordinary person was on a mission of the same sort with themselves, knew of them, and was going to make use of their testimony. Mrs. Logan was several times on the point of falling into a swoon, so much did the appearance of the young man impress her, until her associate covered her face that she might listen without embarrassment. But this latter dialogue aroused different feelings within them; namely, those arising from imminent personal danger. They saw his waggish associate point out the place of their concealment to Wringhim, who came toward them, out of curiosity to see what his friend meant by what he believed to be a joke, manifestly without crediting it in the least degree. When he came running away, the other called after him, "If she is too hard for you, call to me." As he said this, he hasted out of sight, in the contrary direction, apparently much delighted with the joke.

Wringhim came rushing through the thicket impetuously, to the very spot where Mrs. Logan lay squatted. She held the wrapping close about her head, but he tore it off and discovered her. "The curse of God be on thee!" said he: "What fiend has brought thee here, and for what purpose art thou come? But, whatever has brought thee, *I have thee!*" and with that he seized her by the throat. The two women, when they heard what jeopardy they were in from such a wretch, had squatted among the underwood at a small distance from each other, so that he had never observed Mrs. Calvert; but no sooner had he seized her benefactor, than, like a wild cat, she sprung out of the thicket, and had both her hands fixed at his throat, one of them twisted in his stock, in a twinkling. She brought him back-over among the brushwood, and the two, fixing on him like two harpies, mastered him with ease. Then indeed was he wofully beset. He deemed for a while that his friend was at his back, and turning his bloodshot eyes toward the path, he attempted to call; but there was no friend there, and the women cut short his cries by another twist of his stock. "Now, gallant and rightful Laird of Dalcastle," said Mrs. Logan, "what hast thou to say for thyself? Lay thy account to dree the weird thou hast so well earned. Now shalt thou suffer due penance for murdering thy brave and only brother."

"Thou liest, thou hag of the pit! I touched not my brother's life."

"I saw thee do it with these eyes that now look thee in the face; ay, when his back was to thee too, and while he was hotly engaged with thy friend," said Mrs. Calvert.

"I heard thee confess it again and again this same hour," said Mrs. Logan.

"Ay, and so did I," said her companion.—"Murder will out, though the Almighty should lend hearing to the ears of the willow, and speech to the seven tongues of the woodriff."

"You are liars, and witches!" said he, foaming with rage, "and creatures fitted from the beginning for eternal destruction. I'll have your bones and your blood sacrificed on your cursed altars! O, Gil-Martin! Gil-Martin! where art thou now? Here, here is the proper food for blessed vengeance!—Hilloa!"

There was no friend, no Gil-Martin there to hear or assist him: he was in the two women's mercy, but they used it with moderation. They mocked, they tormented, and they threatened him; but, finally, after putting him in great terror, they bound his hands behind his back, and his feet fast with long straps of garters which they chanced to have in their baskets, to prevent him from pursuing them till they were out of his reach. As they left him, which they did in the middle of the path, Mrs. Calvert said, "We could easily put an end to thy sinful life, but our hands shall be free of thy blood. Nevertheless thou art still in our power, and the vengeance of thy country shall overtake thee, thou mean and cowardly murderer, ay, and that more suddenly than thou art aware!"

The women posted to Edinburgh; and as they put themselves under the protection of an English merchant, who was journeying thither with twenty horses loaden, and armed servants, so they had scarcely any conversation on the road. When they arrived at Mrs. Logan's house, then they spoke of what they had seen and heard, and agreed that they had sufficient proof to condemn young Wringhim, who they thought richly deserved the severest doom of the law.

"I never in my life saw any human being," said Mrs. Calvert, "whom I thought so like a fiend. If a demon could inherit flesh and blood, that youth is precisely such a being as I could conceive that demon to be. The depth and the malignity of his eye is hideous. His breath is like the airs from a charnel house, and his flesh seems fading from his bones, as if the worm that never dies were gnawing it away already."

"He was always repulsive, and every way repulsive," said the other; "but he is now indeed altered greatly to the worse. While we were hand-fasting him, I felt his body to be feeble and emaciated; but yet I know him to be so puffed up with spiritual pride, that I believe he weens every one of his actions justified before God, and instead of having stings of conscience for these, he takes great merit to himself in having effected them. Still my thoughts are less about him than the extraordinary being who accompanies him. He does every thing with so much ease and indifference, so much velocity and effect, that all bespeak him an adept in wickedness. The likeness to my late hapless young master is so striking, that I can hardly believe it to be a chance model; and I think he imitates him in every thing, for some purpose, or some effect on his sinful associate. Do you know that he is so like in every lineament, look, and gesture, that, against the clearest light of reason, I cannot in my mind separate the one from the other, and have a certain indefinable impression on my mind, that they are one and the same being, or that the one was a prototype of the other."

"If there is an earthly crime," said Mrs. Calvert, "for the due punishment of which the Almighty may be supposed to subvert the order of nature, it is fratricide. But tell me, dear friend, did you remark to what the subtile and hellish villain was endeavouring to prompt the assassin?"

"No, I could not comprehend it. My senses were altogether so bewildered, that I thought they had combined to deceive me, and I gave them no credit."

"Then hear me: I am almost certain he was using every persuasion to induce him to make away with his mother; and I likewise conceive that I heard the incendiary give his consent!"

"This is dreadful. Let us speak and think no more about it, till we see the issue. In the meantime, let us do that which is our bounden duty,—go and divulge all that we know relating to this foul murder."

Accordingly the two women went to Sir Thomas Wallace of Craigie, the Lord Justice Clerk, (who was, I think, either uncle or grandfather to young Drummond, who was outlawed, and obliged to fly his country on account of Colwan's death,) and to that gentleman they related every circumstance of what they had seen and heard. He examined Calvert very minutely, and seemed deeply interested in her evidence— said he knew she was relating the truth, and in testimony of it, brought a letter of young Drummond's from his desk, wherein that young gentleman, after protesting his innocence in the most forcible terms, confessed having been with such a woman in such a house, after leaving the company of his friends; and that on going home, Sir Thomas's servant had let him in, in the dark, and from these circumstances he found it impossible to prove an *alibi*. He begged of his relative, if ever an opportunity offered, to do his endeavour to clear up that mystery, and remove the horrid stigma from his name in his country, and among his kin, of having stabbed a friend behind his back.

Lord Craigie, therefore, directed the two women to the proper authorities, and after hearing their evidence there, it was judged proper to apprehend the present Laird of Dalcastle, and bring him to his trial. But before that, they sent the prisoner in the tolbooth, he who had seen the whole transaction along with Mrs. Calvert, to take a view of Wringhim privately; and his discrimination being so well known as to be proverbial all over the land, they determined secretly to be ruled by his report. They accordingly sent him on a pretended mission of legality to Dalcastle, with orders to see and speak with the proprietor, without giving him a hint what was wanted. On his return, they examined him, and he told them that he found all things at the place in utter confusion and dismay; that the lady of the place was missing, and could not be found, dead or alive. On being asked if he had ever seen the proprietor before, he looked astounded, and unwilling to answer. But it came out that he had; and that he had once seen him kill a man on such a spot at such an hour.

Officers were then despatched, without delay, to apprehend the monster, and bring him to justice. On these going to the mansion, and inquiring for him, they were told he was at home; on which they stationed guards, and searched all the premises, but he was not to be found. It was in vain that they overturned beds, raised floors, and broke open closets: Robert Wringhim Colwan was lost once and for ever. His mother also was lost; and strong suspicions attached to some of the farmers and house servants, to whom she was obnoxious, relating to her disappearance. The Honourable Thomas Drummond became a distinguished officer in the Austrian service, and died in the memorable year for Scotland, 1715; and this is all with which history, justiciary records, and tradition, furnish me relating to these matters.

I have now the pleasure of presenting my readers with an original document of a most singular nature, and preserved for their perusal in a still more singular manner. I offer no remarks on it, and make as few additions to it, leaving every one to judge for himself. We have heard much of the rage of fanaticism in former days, but nothing to this.

PRIVATE MEMOIRS

AND

CONFESSIONS OF A SINNER.

WRITTEN BY HIMSELF.

PRIVATE MEMOIRS

AND

CONFESSIONS OF A SINNER.

My life has been a life of trouble and turmoil; of change and vicissitude; of anger and exultation; of sorrow and of vengeance. My sorrows have all been for a slighted gospel, and my vengeance has been wreaked on its adversaries. Therefore, in the might of heaven I will sit down and write: I will let the wicked of this world know what I have done in the faith of the promises, and justification by grace, that they may read and tremble, and bless their gods of silver and of gold, that the minister of heaven was removed from their sphere before their blood was mingled with their sacrifices.

I was born an outcast in the world, in which I was destined to act so conspicuous a part. My mother was a burning and a shining light, in the community of Scottish worthies, and in the days of her virginity had suffered much in the persecution of the saints. But it so pleased Heaven, that, as a trial of her faith, she was married to one of the wicked; a man all over spotted with the leprosy of sin. As well might they have conjoined fire and water together, in hopes that they would consort and amalgamate, as purity and corruption: She fled from his embraces the first night after their marriage, and from that time forth, his iniquities so galled her upright heart, that she quitted his society altogether, keeping her own apartments in the same house with him.

I was the second son of this unhappy marriage, and, long ere ever I was born, my father according to the flesh disclaimed all relation or connection with me, and all interest in me, save what the law compelled him to take, which was to grant me a scanty maintenance; and had it not been for a faithful minister of the gospel, my mother's early instructor, I should have remained an outcast from the church visible. He took pity on me, admitting me not only into that, but into the bosom of his own household and ministry also, and to him am I indebted, under Heaven, for the high conceptions and glorious discernment between good and evil, right and wrong, which I attained even at an early age. It was he who directed my studies aright, both

in the learning of the ancient fathers, and the doctrines of the reformed church, and designed me for his assistant and successor in
the holy office. I missed no opportunity of perfecting myself particularly in all the minute points of theology in which my reverend father and mother took great delight; but at length I acquired so much
skill, that I astonished my teachers, and made them gaze at one another. I remember that it was the custom, in my patron's house, to
ask the questions of the Single Catechism round every Sabbath night.
He asked the first, my mother the second, and so on, every one
saying the question asked, and then asking the next. It fell to my
mother to ask Effectual Calling at me. I said the answer with propriety and emphasis. "Now, madam," added I, "my question to you is,
What is *In*effectual Calling?"

"Ineffectual Calling? There is no such thing, Robert," said she.

"But there is, madam," said I; "and that answer proves how much
you say these fundamental precepts by rote, and without any consideration. Ineffectual Calling is, *the outward call of the gospel* without
any effect on the hearts of unregenerated and impenitent sinners.
Have not all these the same calls, warnings, doctrines, and reproofs,
that we have? and is not this Ineffectual Calling? Has not Ardinferry
the same? Has not Patrick M'Lure the same? *Has not the Laird of
Dalcastle and his reprobate heir* the same? And will any tell me, that *this
is not In*effectual Calling?"

"What a wonderful boy he is!" said my mother.

"I'm feared he turn out to be a conceited gowk," said old Barnet,
the minister's man.

"No," said my pastor, and *father,* (as I shall henceforth denominate him,) "No, Barnet, he *is* a wonderful boy; and no marvel, for I
have prayed for these talents to be bestowed on him from his infancy: and do you think that Heaven would refuse a prayer so disinterested? No, it is impossible. But my dread is, madam," continued
he, turning to my mother, "that he is yet in the bond of iniquity."

"God forbid!" said my mother.

"I have struggled with the Almighty long and hard," continued
he; "but have as yet had no certain token of acceptance in his behalf.
I have indeed fought a hard fight, but have been repulsed by him
who hath seldom refused my request; although I cited his own words
against him, and endeavoured to hold him at his promise, he hath
so many turnings in the supremacy of his power, that I have been
rejected. How dreadful is it to think of our darling being still without
the pale of the covenant! But I have vowed a vow, and in that there
is hope."

My heart quaked with terror, when I thought of being still living in a state of reprobation, subjected to the awful issues of death, judgment, and eternal misery, by the slightest accident or casualty, and I set about the duty of prayer myself with the utmost earnestness. I prayed three times every day, and seven times on the Sabbath; but the more frequently and fervently that I prayed, I sinned still the more. About this time, and for a long period afterwards, amounting to several years, I lived in a hopeless and deplorable state of mind; for I said to myself, "If my name is not written in the book of life from all eternity, it is in vain for me to presume that either vows or prayers of mine, or those of all mankind combined, can ever procure its insertion now." I had come under many vows, most solemnly taken, every one of which I had broken; and I saw with the intensity of juvenile grief, that there was no hope for me. I went on sinning every hour, and all the while most strenuously warring against sin, and repenting of every one transgression, as soon after the commission of it as I got leisure to think. But O what a wretched state this unregenerated state is, in which every effort after righteousness only aggravates our offences! I found it vanity to contend; for after communing with my heart, the conclusion was as follows: "If I could repent me of all my sins, and shed tears of blood for them, still have I not a load of original transgression pressing on me, that is enough to crush me to the lowest hell. I may be angry with my first parents for having sinned, but how I shall repent me of their sin, is beyond what I am able to comprehend."

Still, in those days of depravity and corruption, I had some of those principles implanted in my mind, which were afterward to spring up with such amazing fertility among the heroes of the faith and the promises. In particular, I felt great indignation against all the wicked of this world, and often wished for the means of ridding it of such a noxious burden. I liked John Barnet, my reverend father's serving-man, extremely ill; but, from a supposition that he might be one of the justified, I refrained from doing him any injury. He gave always his word against me, and when we were by ourselves, in the barn or the fields, he rated me with such severity for my faults, that my heart could brook it no longer. He discovered some notorious lies that I had framed, and taxed me with them in such a manner that I could in nowise get off. My cheek burnt with offence, rather than shame; and he, thinking he had got the mastery of me, exulted over me most unmercifully, telling me I was a selfish and conceited blackguard, who made great pretences towards religious devotion to cloak a disposition tainted with deceit, and that it would not much astonish him if I brought myself to the gallows.

I gathered some courage from his over severity, and answered him as follows: "Who made thee a judge of the actions or dispositions of the Almighty's creatures—thou who art a worm, and no man in his sight? How it befits thee to deal out judgments and anathemas! Hath he not made one vessel to honour, and another to dishonour, as in the case with myself and thee? Hath he not builded his stories in the heavens, and laid the foundations thereof in the earth, and how can a being like thee judge between good and evil, that are both subjected to the workings of his hand; or of the opposing principles in the soul of man, correcting, modifying, and refining one another?"

I said this with that strong display of fervor for which I was remarkable at my years, and expected old Barnet to be utterly confounded; but he only shook his head, and, with the most provoking grin, said, "There he goes! sickan sublime and ridiculous sophistry I never heard come out of another mouth but ane. There needs nae aiths to be sworn afore the session wha is your father, young goodman. I ne'er, for my part, saw a son sae like a dad, sin' my een first opened." With that he went away, saying, with an ill-natured wince, "You made to honour and me to dishonour! Dirty bow-kail thing that thou be'st!"

"I will have the old rascal on the hip for this, if I live," thought I. So I went and asked my mother if John was a righteous man? She could not tell, but supposed he was, and therefore I got no encouragement from her. I went next to my reverend father, and inquired his opinion, expecting as little from that quarter. He knew the elect as it were by instinct, and could have told you of all those in his own, and some neighbouring parishes, who were born within the boundaries of the covenant of promise, and who were not.

"I keep a good deal in company with your servant, old Barnet, father," said I.

"You do, boy; you do, I see," said he.

"I wish I may not keep too much in his company," said I, "not knowing what kind of society I am in;—is John a good man, father?"

"Why, boy, he is but so, so. A morally good man John is, but very little of the leaven of true righteousness, which is faith, within. I am afraid old Barnet, with all his stock of morality, will be a castaway."

My heart was greatly cheered by this remark; and I sighed very deeply, and hung my head to one side. The worthy father observed me, and inquired the cause? when I answered as follows: "How dreadful the thought, that I have been going daily in company and fellowship with one, whose name is written on the red-letter side of the book of life; whose body and soul have been, from all eternity, consigned over to everlasting destruction, and to whom the blood of the atonement can never, never reach! Father, this is an awful thing, and beyond my comprehension."

"While we are in the world, we must mix with the inhabitants thereof," said he; "and the stains which adhere to us by reason of this admixture, which is unavoidable, shall all be washed away. It is our duty, however, to shun the society of wicked men as much as possible, lest we partake of their sins, and become sharers with them in punishment. John, however, is a morally good man, and may yet get a cast of grace."

"I always thought him a good man till to day," said I, "when he threw out some reflections on your character, so horrible that I quake to think of the wickedness and malevolence of his heart. He was rating me very impertinently for some supposed fault, which had no being save in his own jealous brain, when I attempted to reason him out of his belief in the spirit of calm Christian argument. But how do you think he answered me? He did so, sir, by twisting his mouth at me, and remarking that such sublime and ridiculous sophistry never came out of another mouth but one, (meaning yours,) and that no oath before a kirk session was necessary to prove who was my dad, for that he had never seen a son so like a father as I was like mine."

"He durst not for his soul's salvation, and for his daily bread, which he values much more, say such a word, boy; therefore take care what you assert," said my reverend father.

"He said these very words, and will not deny them, sir," said I.

My reverend father turned about in great wrath and indignation, and went away in search of John; but I kept out of the way, and listened at a back window; for John was dressing the plot of ground behind the house; and I hope it was no sin in me that I did rejoice in the dialogue which took place, it being the victory of righteousness over error.

"Well, John, this is a fine day for your delving work."

"Ey, it's a tolerable day, sir."

"Are you thankful in your heart, John, for such temporal mercies as these?"

"Aw doubt we're a' ower little thankfu', sir, baith for temporal an' speeritual mercies; but it isna aye the maist thankfu' heart that maks the greatest fraze wi' the tongue."

"I hope there is nothing personal under that remark, John?"

"Gin the bannet fits ony body's head, they're unco welcome to it, sir, for me."

"John, I do not approve of these innuendoes. You have an arch malicious manner of vending your aphorisms, which the men of the world are too apt to read the wrong way, for your dark hints are sure to have *one* very bad meaning."

"Hout na, sir, it's only bad folks that think sae. They find ma bits o' gibes come hame to their hearts wi' a kind o' yerk, an' that gars them wince."

"That saying is ten times worse than the other, John; it is a manifest insult: it is just telling me to my face, that you think me a bad man."

"A body canna help his thoughts, sir."

"No, but a man's thoughts are generally formed from observation. Now I should like to know, even from the mouth of a misbeliever, what part of my conduct warrants such a conclusion?"

"Nae particular pairt, sir; I draw a' my conclusions frae the haill o' a man's character, an' I'm no that aften far wrang."

"Well, John, and what sort of general character do you suppose mine to be?"

"Yours is a Scripture character, sir, an' I'll prove it."

"I hope so, John. Well, which of the Scripture characters do you think approximates nearest to my own?"

"Guess, sir, guess; I wish to lead a proof."

"Why, if it be an Old Testament character, I hope it is Melchizedek, for at all events you cannot deny there is one point of resemblance: I, like him, am a preacher of righteousness. If it be a New Testament character, I suppose you mean the Apostle of the Gentiles, of whom I am an unworthy representative."

"Na, na, sir, better nor that still, an' fer closer is the resemblance. When ye bring me to the point, I maun speak. Ye are the just Pharisee, sir, that gaed up wi' the poor publican to pray in the Temple; an' ye're acting the very same pairt at this time, an' saying i' your heart, 'God, I thank thee that I am not as other men are, an' in nae way like this poor misbelieving unregenerate sinner, John Barnet.'"

"I hope I may say so indeed."

"There now! I tauld you how it was! But, d'ye hear, maister: Here stands the poor sinner, John Barnet, your beadle an' servant-man, wha wadna change chances wi' you in the neist world, nor consciences in this, for ten times a' that you possess,—your justification by faith an' awthegither."

"You are extremely audacious and impertinent, John; but the language of reprobation cannot affect me: I came only to ask you one question, which I desire you to answer candidly. Did you ever say to any one that I was the boy Robert's natural father?"

"Hout na, sir! Ha–ha–ha! Aih, fie na, sir! I durstna say that for my life. I doubt the black stool, an' the sack gown, or maybe the juggs wad hae been my portion had I said sic a thing as that. Hout, hout! Fie, fie! Unco-like doings thae for a Melchizedek or a Saint Paul!"

"John, you are a profane old man, and I desire that you will not presume to break your jests on me. Tell me, dare you say, or dare you think, that I am the natural father of that boy?"

"Ye canna hinder me to think whatever I like, sir, nor can I hinder mysel."

"But did you ever *say* to any one, that he resembled me, and fathered himself well enough?"

"I hae said mony a time, that he resembled you, sir. Naebody can mistake that."

"But, John, there are many natural reasons for such likenesses, besides that of consanguinity. They depend much on the thoughts and affections of the mother; and, it is probable, that the mother of this boy, being deserted by her worthless husband, having turned her thoughts on me, as likely to be her protector, may have caused this striking resemblance."

"Ay, it may be, sir. I coudna say."

"I have known a lady, John, who was delivered of a blackamoor child, merely from the circumstance of having got a start by the sudden entrance of her negro servant, and not being able to forget him for several hours."

"It may be, sir; but I ken this;–an I had been the laird, I wadna hae ta'en that story in."

"So, then, John, you positively think, from a casual likeness, that this boy is my son?"

"Man's thoughts are vanity, sir; they come unasked, an' gang away without a dismissal, an' he canna help them. I'm neither gaun to say that I *think* he's your son, nor that I think he's *no* your son: sae ye needna pose me nae mair about it."

"Hear then my determination, John: If you do not promise to me, in faith and honour, that you never will say, or insinuate such a thing again in your life, as that that boy is my natural son, I will take the keys of the church from you, and dismiss you my service."

John pulled out the keys, and dashed them on the gravel at the reverend minister's feet. "There are the keys o' your kirk, sir! I hae never had muckle mense o' them sin' ye entered the door o't. I hae carried them this three an thretty year, but they hae aye been like to burn a hole i' my pouch sin' ever they were turned for your admittance. Tak them again, an' gie them to wha you will, and muckle gude may he get o' them. Auld John may dee a beggar in a hay barn, or at the back of a dike, but he sall aye be master o' his ain thoughts, an' gie them vent or no, as he likes."

He left the manse that day, and I rejoiced in the riddance; for I disdained to be kept so much under, by one who was in the bond of iniquity, and of whom there seemed no hope, as he rejoiced in his frowardness, and refused to submit to that faithful teacher, his master.

It was about this time that my reverend father preached a sermon, one sentence of which affected me most disagreeably: It was to the purport, that every unrepented sin was productive of a new sin with each breath that a man drew; and every one of these new sins added to the catalogue in the same manner. I was utterly confounded at the multitude of my transgressions; for I was sensible that there were great numbers of sins of which I had never been able thoroughly to repent, and these momentary ones, by a moderate calculation, had, I saw, long ago, amounted to a hundred and fifty thousand in the minute, and I saw no end to the series of repentances to which I had subjected myself. A life-time was nothing to enable me to accomplish the sum, and then being, for any thing I was certain of, in my state of nature, and the grace of repentance withheld from me,—what was I to do, or what was to become of me? In the meantime, I went on sinning without measure; but I was still more troubled about the multitude than the magnitude of my transgressions, and the small minute ones puzzled me more than those that were more heinous, as the latter had generally some good effects in the way of punishing wicked men, froward boys, and deceitful women; and I rejoiced, even then in my early youth, at being used as a scourge in the hand of the Lord; another Jehu, a Cyrus, or a Nebuchadnezzar.

On the whole, I remember that I got into great confusion relating to my sins and repentances, and knew neither where to begin nor how to proceed, and often had great fears that I was wholly without Christ, and that I would find God a consuming fire to me. I could not help running into new sins continually; but then I was mercifully dealt with, for I was often made to repent of them most heartily, by reason of bodily chastisements received on these delinquencies being discovered. I was particularly prone to lying, and I cannot but admire the mercy that has freely forgiven me all these juvenile sins. Now that I know them all to be blotted out, and that I am an accepted person, I may the more freely confess them: the truth is, that one lie always paved the way for another, from hour to hour, from day to day, and from year to year; so that I found myself constantly involved in a labyrinth of deceit, from which it was impossible to extricate myself. If I knew a person to be a godly one, I could almost have kissed his feet; but against the carnal portion of mankind, I set my face continually. I esteemed the true ministers of the gospel; but the prelatic party, and the preachers up of good works I abhorred, and to this hour I account them the worst and most heinous of all transgressors.

There was only one boy at Mr. Wilson's class who kept always the upper hand of me in every part of education. I strove against him from year to year, but it was all in vain; for he was a very wicked boy, and I was convinced he had dealings with the devil. Indeed it was believed all over the country that his mother was a witch; and I was at length convinced that it was no human ingenuity that beat me with so much ease in the Latin, after I had often sat up a whole night with my reverend father, studying my lesson in all its bearings. I often read as well and sometimes better than he; but the moment Mr. Wilson began to examine us, my opponent popped up above me. I determined, (as I knew him for a wicked person, and one of the devil's hand-fasted children,) to be revenged on him, and to humble him by some means or other. Accordingly I lost no opportunity of setting the Master against him, and succeeded several times in getting him severely beaten for faults of which he was innocent. I can hardly describe the joy that it gave to my heart to see a wicked creature suffering, for though he deserved it not for one thing, he richly deserved it for others. This may be by some people accounted a great sin in me; but I deny it, for I did it as a duty, and what a man or boy does for the right, will never be put into the sum of his transgressions.

This boy, whose name was M'Gill, was, at all his leisure hours, engaged in drawing profane pictures of beasts, men, women, houses, and trees, and, in short, of all things that his eye encountered. These profane things the Master often smiled at, and admired; therefore I began privately to try my hand likewise. I had scarcely tried above once to draw the figure of a man, ere I conceived that I had hit the very features of Mr. Wilson. They were so particular, that they could not be easily mistaken, and I was so tickled and pleased with the droll likeness that I had drawn, that I laughed immoderately at it. I tried no other figure but this; and I tried it in every situation in which a man and a schoolmaster could be placed. I often wrought for hours together at this likeness, nor was it long before I made myself so much master of the outline, that I could have drawn it in any situation whatever, almost off hand. I then took M'Gill's account book of algebra home with me, and at my leisure put down a number of gross caricatures of Mr. Wilson here and there, several of them in situations notoriously ludicrous. I waited the discovery of this treasure with great impatience; but the book, chancing to be one that M'Gill was not using, I saw it might be long enough before I enjoyed the consummation of my grand scheme: therefore, with all the ingenuity I was master of, I brought it before our dominie's eye. But never shall I forget the rage that gleamed in the tyrant's phiz! I was actually terrified to look at him, and trembled at his voice. M'Gill was called upon, and examined relating to the obnoxious figures. He denied flatly that any of them were of his doing. But the Master inquiring at him whose they were, he could not tell, but affirmed it to be some trick. Mr. Wilson at one time, began, as I thought, to hesitate; but the evidence was so strong against M'Gill, that at length his solemn asseverations of innocence only proved an aggravation of his crime. There was not one in the school who had ever been known to draw a figure but himself, and on him fell the whole weight of the tyrant's vengeance. It was dreadful; and I was once in hopes that he would not leave life in the culprit. He, however, left the school for several months, refusing to return to be subjected to punishment for the faults of others, and I stood king of the class.

Matters were at last made up between M'Gill's parents and the schoolmaster, but by that time I had got the start of him, and never in my life did I exert myself so much as to keep the mastery. It was in vain; the powers of enchantment prevailed, and I was again turned down with the tear in my eye. I could think of no amends but one, and being driven to desperation, I put it in practice. I told a lie of him. I came boldly up to the master, and told him that M'Gill had in my hearing cursed him in a most shocking manner, and called him vile names. He called M'Gill, and charged him with the crime, and the proud young coxcomb was so stunned at the atrocity of the charge, that his face grew as red as crimson, and the words stuck in his throat as he feebly denied it. His guilt was manifest, and he was again flogged most nobly, and dismissed the school for ever in disgrace, as a most incorrigible vagabond.

This was a great victory gained, and I rejoiced and exulted exceedingly in it. It had, however, very nigh cost me my life; for not long thereafter, I encountered M'Gill in the fields, on which he came up and challenged me for a liar, daring me to fight him. I refused, and said that I looked on him as quite below my notice; but he would not quit me, and finally told me that he should either *lick me*, or I should *lick him*, as he had no other means of being revenged on such a scoundrel. I tried to intimidate him, but it would not do; and I believe I would have given all that I had in the world to be quit of him. He at length went so far as first to kick me, and then strike me on the face; and, being both older and stronger than he, I thought it scarcely became me to take such insults patiently. I was, nevertheless, well aware that the devilish powers of his mother would finally prevail; and either the dread of this, or the inward consciousness of having wronged him, certainly unnerved my arm, for I fought wretchedly, and was soon wholly overcome. I was so sore defeated, that I kneeled, and was going to beg his pardon; but another thought struck me momentarily, and I threw myself on my face, and inwardly begged aid from heaven; at the same time I felt as if assured that my prayer was heard, and would be answered. While I was in this humble attitude, the villain kicked me with his foot and cursed me; and I being newly encouraged, arose and encountered him once more. We had not fought long at this second turn, before I saw a man hastening toward us; on which I uttered a shout of joy, and laid on valiantly; but my very next look assured me, that the man was old John Barnet, whom I had likewise wronged all that was in my power, and between these two wicked persons I expected any thing but justice. My arm was again enfeebled, and that of my adversary prevailed. I was knocked down and mauled most grievously, and while the ruffian was kicking and cuffing me at his will and pleasure, up came old John Barnet, breathless with running, and at one blow with his open hand, levelled my opponent with the earth. "Tak ye that, maister!" says John, "to learn ye better breeding. Hout awa, man! an ye will fight, fight fair. Gude sauf us, ir ye a gentleman's brood, that ye will kick an' cuff a lad when he's down?"

When I heard this kind and unexpected interference, I began once more to value myself on my courage, and springing up, I made at my adversary; but John, without saying a word, bit his lip, and seizing me by the neck, threw me down. M'Gill begged of him to stand and see fair play, and suffer us to finish the battle; for, added he, "he is a liar, and a scoundrel, and deserves ten times more than I can give him."

"I ken he's a' that ye say, an' mair, my man," quoth John: "But am I sure that ye're no as bad, an' waur? It says nae muckle for ony o' ye to be tearing like tikes at ane anither here."

John cocked his cudgel and stood between us, threatening to knock the one dead, who first offered to lift his hand against the other; but, perceiving no disposition in any of us to separate, he drove me home before him like a bullock, keeping close guard behind me, lest M'Gill had followed. I felt greatly indebted to John, yet I complained of his interference to my mother, and the old officious sinner got no thanks for his pains.

As I am writing only from recollection, so I remember of nothing farther in these early days, in the least worthy of being recorded. That I was a great, a transcendent sinner, I confess. But still I had hopes of forgiveness, because I never sinned from principle, but accident; and then I always *tried* to repent of these sins by the slump, for individually it was impossible; and though not always successful in my endeavours, I could not help that; the grace of repentance being withheld from me, I regarded myself as in no degree account-able for the failure. Moreover, there were many of the most deadly sins into which I never fell, for I dreaded those mentioned in the Revelations as excluding sins, so that I guarded against them con-tinually. In particular, I brought myself to despise, if not to abhor, the beauty of women, looking on it as the greatest snare to which mankind are subjected, and though young men and maidens, and even old women, (my mother among the rest,) taxed me with being an unnatural wretch, I gloried in my acquisition; and to this day, am thankful for having escaped the most dangerous of all snares.

I kept myself also free of the sins of idolatry, and misbelief, both of a deadly nature; and, upon the whole, I think I had not then broken, that is, absolutely broken, above four out of the ten com-mandments; but for all that, I had more sense than to regard either my good works, or my evil deeds, as in the smallest degree influ-encing the eternal decrees of God concerning me, either with regard to my acceptance or reprobation. I depended entirely on the bounty of free grace, holding all the righteousness of man as filthy rags, and believing in the momentous and magnificent truth, that the more heavily loaden with transgressions, the more welcome was the be-liever at the throne of grace. And I have reason to believe that it was this dependence and this belief that at last ensured my acceptance there.

I come now to the most important period of my existence,—the period that has modelled my character, and influenced every action of my life,—without which, this detail of my actions would have been as a tale that hath been told—a monotonous *farrago*—an uninteresting harangue—in short, a thing of nothing. Whereas, lo! it must now be a relation of great and terrible actions, done in the might, and by the commission of heaven. *Amen.*

Like the sinful king of Israel, I had been walking softly before the Lord for a season. I had been humbled for my transgressions, and, as far as I recollect, sorry on account of their numbers and heinousness. My reverend father had been, moreover, examining me every day regarding the state of my soul, and my answers sometimes appeared to give him satisfaction, and sometimes not. As for my mother, she would harp on the subject of my faith for ever; yet, though I knew her to be a Christian, I confess that I always despised her motley instructions, nor had I any great regard for her person. If this was a crime in me, I never could help it. I confess it freely, and believe it was a judgment from heaven inflicted on her for some sin of former days, and that I had no power to have acted otherwise toward her than I did.

In this frame of mind was I, when my reverend father one morning arose from his seat, and, meeting me as I entered the room, he embraced me, and welcomed me into the community of the just upon earth. I was struck speechless, and could make no answer save by looks of surprise. My mother also came to me, kissed, and wept over me; and after showering unnumbered blessings on my head, she also welcomed me into the society of *the just made perfect.* Then each of them took me by a hand, and my reverend father explained to me how he had wrestled with God, as the patriarch of old had done, not for a night, but for days and years, and that in bitterness and anguish of spirit, on my account; but that *he* had at last prevailed, and had now gained the long and earnestly desired assurance of my acceptance with the Almighty, in and through the merits and sufferings of his Son: That I was now a justified person, adopted among the number of God's children—my name written in the Lamb's book of life, and that no bypast transgression, nor any future act of my own, or of other men, could be instrumental in altering the decree. "All the powers of darkness," added he, "shall never be able to pluck you again out of your Redeemer's hand. And now, my son, be strong and stedfast in the truth. Set your face against sin, and sinful men, and resist even to blood, as many of the faithful of this land have done, and your reward shall be double. I am assured of your acceptance by the word and spirit of him who cannot err, and your sanctification and repentance unto life will follow in due course. Rejoice and be thankful, for you are plucked as a brand out of the burning, and now your redemption is sealed and sure."

I wept for joy to be thus assured of my freedom from all sin, and of the impossibility of my ever again falling away from my new state. I bounded away into the fields and the woods, to pour out my spirit in prayer before the Almighty for his kindness to me: my whole frame seemed to be renewed; every nerve was buoyant with new life; I felt as if I could have flown in the air, or leaped over the tops of the trees. An exaltation of spirit lifted me, as it were, far above the earth, and the sinful creatures crawling on its surface; and I deemed myself as an eagle among the children of men, soaring on high, and looking down with pity and contempt on the grovelling creatures below.

As I thus wended my way, I beheld a young man of a mysterious appearance coming towards me. I tried to shun him, being bent on my own contemplations; but he cast himself in my way, so that I could not well avoid him; and more than that, I felt a sort of invisible power that drew me towards him, something like the force of enchantment, which I could not resist. As we approached each other, our eyes met, and I can never describe the strange sensations that thrilled through my whole frame at that impressive moment; a moment to me fraught with the most tremendous consequences; the beginning of a series of adventures which has puzzled myself, and will puzzle the world when I am no more in it. That time will now soon arrive, sooner than any one can devise who knows not the tumult of my thoughts, and the labour of my spirit; and when it hath come and passed over,—when my flesh and my bones are decayed, and my soul has passed to its everlasting home, then shall the sons of men ponder on the events of my life; wonder and tremble, and tremble and wonder how such things should be.

That stranger youth and I approached each other in silence, and slowly, with our eyes fixed on each other's eyes. We approached till not more than a yard intervened between us, and then stood still and gazed, measuring each other from head to foot. What was my astonishment, on perceiving that he was the same being as myself! The clothes were the same to the smallest item. The form was the same; the apparent age; the colour of the hair; the eyes; and, as far as recollection could serve me from viewing my own features in a glass, the features too were the very same. I conceived at first, that I saw a vision, and that my guardian angel had appeared to me at this important era of my life; but this singular being read my thoughts in my looks, anticipating the very words that I was going to utter.

"You think I am your brother," said he; "or that I am your second self. I am indeed your brother, not according to the flesh, but in my belief of the same truths, and my assurance in the same mode of redemption, than which, I hold nothing so great or so glorious on earth."

"Then you are an associate well adapted to my present state," said I. "For this time is a time of great rejoicing in spirit to me. I am on my way to return thanks to the Most High for my redemption from the bonds of sin and misery. If you will join with me heart and hand in youthful thanksgiving, then shall we two go and worship together; but if not, go your way, and I shall go mine."

"Ah, you little know with how much pleasure I will accompany you, and join with you in your elevated devotions," said he fervently. "Your state is a state to be envied indeed; but I have been advised of it, and am come to be a humble disciple of yours; to be initiated into the true way of salvation by conversing with you, and perhaps by being assisted by your prayers."

My spiritual pride being greatly elevated by this address, I began to assume the preceptor, and questioned this extraordinary youth with regard to his religious principles, telling him plainly, if he was one who expected acceptance with God at all, on account of good works, that I would hold no communion with him. He renounced these at once, with the greatest vehemence, and declared his acquiescence in my faith. I asked if he believed in the eternal and irrevocable decrees of God, regarding the salvation and condemnation of all mankind? He answered that he did so: aye, what would signify all things else that he believed, if he did not believe in that? We then went on to commune about all our points of belief; and in every thing that I suggested, he acquiesced, and, as I thought that day, often carried them to extremes, so that I had a secret dread he was advancing blasphemies. Yet he had such a way with him, and paid such a deference to all my opinions, that I was quite captivated, and, at the same time, I stood in a sort of awe of him, which I could not account for, and several times was seized with an involuntary inclination to escape from his presence, by making a sudden retreat. But he seemed constantly to anticipate my thoughts, and was sure to divert my purpose by some turn in the conversation that particularly interested me. He took care to dwell much on the theme of the impossibility of those ever falling away, who were once accepted and received into covenant with God, for he seemed to know, that in that confidence, and that trust, my whole hopes were centred.

We moved about from one place to another, until the day was wholly spent. My mind had all the while been kept in a state of agitation resembling the motion of a whirlpool, and when we came to separate, I then discovered that the purpose for which I had sought the fields had been neglected, and that I had been diverted from the worship of God, by attending to the quibbles and dogmas of this singular and unaccountable being, who seemed to have more knowledge and information than all the persons I had ever known put together.

We parted with expressions of mutual regret, and when I left him I felt a deliverance, but at the same time a certain consciousness that I was not thus to get free of him, but that he was like to be an acquaintance that was to stick to me for good or for evil. I was astonished at his acuteness and knowledge about every thing; but as for his likeness to me, that was quite unaccountable. He was the same person in every respect, but yet he was not always so; for I observed several times, when we were speaking of certain divines and their tenets, that his face assumed something of the appearance of theirs; and it struck me, that by setting his features to the mould of other people's, he entered at once into their conceptions and feelings. I had been greatly flattered, and greatly interested by his conversation; whether I had been the better for it or the worse, I could not tell. I had been diverted from returning thanks to my gracious Maker for his great kindness to me, and came home as I went away, but not with the same buoyancy and lightness of heart. Well may I remember that day in which I was first received into the number, and made an heir to all the privileges of the children of God, and on which I first met this mysterious associate, who from that day forth contrived to wind himself into all my affairs, both spiritual and temporal, to this day on which I am writing the account of it. It was on the 25th day of March 1704, when I had just entered the eighteenth year of my age. Whether it behoves me to bless God for the events of that day, or to deplore them, has been hid from my discernment, though I have inquired into it with fear and trembling; and I have now lost all hopes of ever discovering the true import of these events until that day when my accounts are to make up and reckon for in another world.

When I came home, I went straight into the parlour, where my mother was sitting by herself. She started to her feet, and uttered a smothered scream. "What ails you, Robert?" cried she. "My dear son, what is the matter with you?"

"Do you see any thing the matter with me?" said I. "It appears that the ailment is with yourself, and either in your crazed head or your dim eyes, for there is nothing the matter with me."

"Ah, Robert, you are ill!" cried she; "you are very ill, my dear boy; you are quite changed; your very voice and manner are changed. Ah, Jane, haste you up to the study, and tell Mr. Wringhim to come here on the instant and speak to Robert."

"I beseech you, woman, to restrain yourself," said I. "If you suffer your frenzy to run away with your judgment in this manner, I will leave the house. What do you mean? I tell you, there is nothing ails me: I never was better."

She screamed, and ran between me and the door, to bar my retreat: in the meantime my reverend father entered, and I have not forgot how he gazed, through his glasses, first at my mother, and then at me. I imagined that his eyes burnt like candles, and was afraid of him, which I suppose made my looks more unstable than they would otherwise have been.

"What is all this for?" said he. "Mistress! Robert! What is the matter here?"

"Oh, sir, our boy!" cried my mother; "our dear boy, Mr. Wringhim! Look at him, and speak to him: he is either dying or translated, sir!"

He looked at me with a countenance of great alarm; mumbling some sentences to himself, and then taking me by the arm, as if to feel my pulse, he said, with a faltering voice, "Something has indeed befallen you, either in body or mind, boy, for you are transformed, since the morning, that I could not have known you for the same person. Have you met with any accident?"

"No."

"Have you seen any thing out of the ordinary course of nature?"

"No."

"Then, Satan, I fear, has been busy with you, tempting you in no ordinary degree at this momentous crisis of your life?"

My mind turned on my associate for the day, and the idea that he might be an agent of the devil, had such an effect on me, that I could make no answer.

"I see how it is," said he; "you are troubled in spirit, and I have no doubt that the enemy of our salvation has been busy with you. Tell me this, has he overcome you, or has he not?"

"He has not, my dear father," said I. "In the strength of the Lord, I hope I have withstood him. But indeed, if he has been busy with me, I knew it not. I have been conversant this day with one stranger only, whom I took rather for an angel of light."

"It is one of the devil's most profound wiles to appear like one," said my mother.

"Woman, hold thy peace!" said my reverend father: "thou pretendest to teach what thou knowest not. Tell me this, boy: Did this stranger, with whom you met, adhere to the religious principles in which I have educated you?"

"Yes, to every one of them, in their fullest latitude," said I.

"Then he was no agent of the wicked one with whom you held converse," said he; "for that is the doctrine that was made to overturn the principalities and powers, the might and dominion of the kingdom of darkness.—Let us pray."

After spending about a quarter of an hour in solemn and sublime thanksgiving, this saintly man and minister of Christ Jesus, gave out that the day following should be kept by the family as a day of solemn thanksgiving, and spent in prayer and praise, on account of the calling and election of one of its members; or rather for the election of that individual being revealed on earth, as well as confirmed in heaven.

The next day was with me a day of holy exultation. It was begun by my reverend father laying his hands upon my head and blessing me, and then dedicating me to the Lord in the most awful and impressive manner. It was in no common way that he exercised this profound rite, for it was done with all the zeal and enthusiasm of a devotee to the true cause, and a champion on the side he had espoused. He used these remarkable words, which I have still treasured up in my heart:—"I give him unto Thee only, to Thee wholly, and to Thee for ever. I dedicate him unto Thee, soul, body, and spirit. Not as the wicked of this world, or the hirelings of a church profanely called by Thy name, do I dedicate this Thy servant to Thee: Not in words and form, learned by rote, and dictated by the limbs of Antichrist, but, Lord, I give him into Thy hand, as a captain putteth a sword into the hand of his sovereign, wherewith to lay waste his enemies. May he be a two-edged weapon in Thy hand, and a spear coming out of Thy mouth, to destroy, and overcome, and pass over; and may the enemies of Thy church fall down before him, and be as dung to fat the land!"

From that moment, I conceived it decreed, not that I should be a minister of the gospel, but a champion of it, to cut off the enemies of the Lord from the face of the earth; and I rejoiced in the commission, finding it more congenial to my nature to be cutting sinners off with the sword, than to be haranguing them from the pulpit, striving to produce an effect, which God, by his act of absolute predestination, had for ever rendered impracticable. The more I pondered on these things, the more I saw of the folly and inconsistency of ministers, in spending their lives, striving and remonstrating with sinners, in order to induce them to do that which they had it not in their power to do. Seeing that God had from all eternity decided the fate of every individual that was to be born of woman, how vain was it in man to endeavour to save those whom their Maker had, by an unchangeable decree, doomed to destruction. I could not disbelieve the doctrine which the best of men had taught me, and toward which he made the whole of the Scriptures to bear, and yet it made the economy of the Christian world appear to me as an absolute contradiction. How much more wise would it be, thought I, to begin and cut sinners off with the sword! for till that is effected, the saints can never inherit the earth in peace. Should I be honoured as an instrument to begin this great work of purification, I should rejoice in it. But then, where had I the means, or under what direction was I to begin? There was one thing clear, I was now the Lord's, and it behoved me to bestir myself in his service. O that I had an host at my command, then would I be as a devouring fire among the workers of iniquity!

Full of these great ideas, I hurried through the city, and sought again the private path through the field and wood of Finnieston, in which my reverend preceptor had the privilege of walking for study, and to which he had a key that was always at my command. Near one of the stiles, I perceived a young man sitting in a devout posture, reading on a Bible. He rose, lifted his hat, and made an obeisance to me, which I returned and walked on. I had not well crossed the stile, till it struck me I knew the face of the youth, and that he was some intimate acquaintance, to whom I ought to have spoken. I walked on, and returned, and walked on again, trying to recollect who he was; but for my life I could not. There was, however, a fascination in his look and manner, that drew me back toward him in spite of myself, and I resolved to go to him, if it were merely to speak and see who he was.

I came up to him and addressed him, but he was so intent on his book, that, though I spoke, he lifted not his eyes. I looked on the book also, and still it seemed a Bible, having columns, chapters, and verses; but it was in a language of which I was wholly ignorant, and all intersected with red lines, and verses. A sensation resembling a stroke of electricity came over me, on first casting my eyes on that mysterious book, and I stood motionless. He looked up, smiled, closed his book, and put it in his bosom. "You seem strangely affected, dear sir, by looking on my book," said he mildly.

"In the name of God, what book is that?" said I: "Is it a Bible?"

"It is *my* Bible, sir," said he; "but I will cease reading it, for I am glad to see you. Pray, is not this a day of holy festivity with you?"

I stared in his face, but made no answer, for my senses were bewildered.

"Do you not know me?" said he. "You appear to be somehow at a loss. Had not you and I some sweet communion and fellowship yesterday?"

"I beg your pardon, sir," said I. "But surely if you are the young gentleman with whom I spent the hours yesterday, you have the cameleon art of changing your appearance; I never could have recognized you."

"My countenance changes with my studies and sensations," said he. "It is a natural peculiarity in me, over which I have not full control. If I contemplate a man's features seriously, mine own gradually assume the very same appearance and character. And what is more, by contemplating a face minutely, I not only attain the same likeness, but, with the likeness, I attain the very same ideas as well as the same mode of arranging them, so that, you see, by looking at a person attentively, I by degrees assume his likeness, and by assuming his likeness I attain to the possession of his most secret thoughts. This, I say, is a peculiarity in my nature, a gift of the God that made me; but whether or not given me for a blessing, he knows himself, and so do I. At all events, I have this privilege,—I can never be mistaken of a character in whom I am interested."

"It is a rare qualification," replied I, "and I would give worlds to possess it. Then, it appears, that it is needless to dissemble with you, since you can at any time extract our most secret thoughts from our bosoms. You already know my natural character?"

"Yes," said he, "and it is that which attaches me to you. By assuming your likeness yesterday, I became acquainted with your character, and was no less astonished at the profundity and range of your thoughts, than at the heroic magnanimity with which these were combined. And now, in addition to these, you are dedicated to the great work of the Lord; for which reasons I have resolved to attach myself as closely to you as possible, and to render you all the service of which my poor abilities are capable."

I confess that I was greatly flattered by these compliments paid to my abilities by a youth of such superior qualifications; by one who, with a modesty and affability rare at his age, combined a height of genius and knowledge almost above human comprehension. Nevertheless, I began to assume a certain superiority of demeanour toward him, as judging it incumbent on me to do so, in order to keep up his idea of my exalted character. We conversed again till the day was near a close; and the things that he strove most to inculcate on my mind, were the infallibility of the elect, and the pre-ordination of all things that come to pass. I pretended to controvert the first of these, for the purpose of showing him the extent of my argumentative powers, and said, that "indubitably there were degrees of sinning which would induce the Almighty to throw off the very elect." But behold my hitherto humble and modest companion took up the argument with such warmth, that he put me not only to silence, but to absolute shame.

"Why, sir," said he, "by vending such an insinuation, you put discredit on the great atonement, in which you trust. Is there not enough of merit in the blood of Jesus to save thousands of worlds, if it was for these worlds that he died? Now, when you know, as you do, (and as every one of the elect may know of himself,) that this Saviour died for you, namely and particularly, dare you say that there is not enough of merit in his great atonement to annihilate all your sins, let them be as heinous and atrocious as they may? And, moreover, do you not acknowledge that God hath pre-ordained and decreed whatsoever comes to pass? Then, how is it that you should deem it in your power to eschew one action of your life, whether good or evil? Depend on it, the advice of the great preacher is genuine: 'What thine hand findeth to do, do it with all thy might, for none of us knows what a day may bring forth?' That is, none of us knows what is pre-ordained, but whatever is pre-ordained we *must* do, and none of these things will be laid to our charge."

I could hardly believe that these sayings were genuine or orthodox; but I soon felt, that, instead of being a humble disciple of mine, this new acquaintance was to be my guide and director, and all under the humble guise of one stooping at my feet to learn the right. He said that he saw I was ordained to perform some great action for the cause of Jesus and his church, and he earnestly coveted being a partaker with me; but he besought of me never to think it possible for me to fall from the truth, or the favour of him who had chosen me, else that misbelief would baulk every good work to which I set my face.

There was something so flattering in all this, that I could not resist it. Still, when he took leave of me, I felt it as a great relief; and yet, before the morrow, I wearied and was impatient to see him again. We carried on our fellowship from day to day, and all the while I knew not who he was, and still my mother and reverend father kept insisting that I was an altered youth, changed in my appearance, my manners, and my whole conduct; yet something always prevented me from telling them more about my new acquaintance than I had done on the first day we met. I rejoiced in him, was proud of him, and soon could not live without him; yet, though resolved every day to disclose the whole history of my connection with him, I had it not in my power: Something always prevented me, till at length I thought no more of it, but resolved to enjoy his fascinating company in private, and by all means to keep my own with him. The resolution was vain: I set a bold face to it, but my powers were inadequate to the task; my adherent, with all the suavity imaginable, was sure to carry his point. I sometimes fumed, and sometimes shed tears at being obliged to yield to proposals against which I had at first felt every reasoning power of my soul rise in opposition; but, for all that, he never failed in carrying conviction along with him in effect, for he either forced me to acquiesce in his measures, and assent to the truth of his positions, or he put me so completely down, that I had not a word left to advance against them.

After weeks, and I may say months of intimacy, I observed, somewhat to my amazement, that we had never once prayed together; and more than that, that he had constantly led my attentions away from that duty, causing me to neglect it wholly. I thought this a bad mark of a man seemingly so much set on inculcating certain important points of religion, and resolved next day to put him to the test, and request of him to perform that sacred duty in name of us both. He objected boldly; saying there were very few people indeed, with whom he could join in prayer, and he made a point of never doing it, as he was sure they were to ask many things of which he disapproved, and that if he were to officiate himself, he was as certain to allude to many things that came not within the range of their faith. He disapproved of prayer altogether, in the manner it was generally gone about, he said. Man made it merely a selfish concern, and was constantly employed asking, asking, for every thing. Whereas it became all God's creatures to be content with their lot, and only to kneel before him in order to thank him for such benefits as he saw meet to bestow. In short, he argued with such energy, that before we parted I acquiesced, as usual, in his position, and never mentioned prayer to him any more.

Having been so frequently seen in his company, several people happened to mention the circumstance to my mother and reverend father; but at the same time had all described him differently. At length, they began to examine me with respect to the company I kept, as I absented myself from home day after day. I told them I kept company only with one young gentleman, whose whole manner of thinking on religious subjects, I found so congenial with my own, that I could not live out of his society. My mother began to lay down some of her old hackneyed rules of faith, but I turned from hearing her with disgust; for, after the energy of my new friend's reasoning, hers appeared so tame I could not endure it. And I confess with shame, that my reverend preceptor's religious dissertations began, about this time, to lose their relish very much, and by degrees became exceedingly tiresome to my ear. They were so inferior, in strength and sublimity, to the most common observations of my young friend, that in drawing a comparison the former appeared as nothing. He, however, examined me about many things relating to my companion, in all of which I satisfied him, save in one: I could neither tell him who my friend was, what was his name, nor of whom he was descended; and I wondered at myself how I had never once adverted to such a thing, for all the time we had been intimate.

I inquired the next day what his name was; as I said I was often at a loss for it, when talking with him. He replied, that there was no occasion for any one friend ever naming another, when their society was held in private, as ours was; for his part he had never once named me since we first met, and never intended to do so, unless by my own request. "But if you cannot converse without naming me, you may call me Gil for the present," added he; "and if I think proper to take another name at any future period, it shall be with your approbation."

"Gil!" said I; "Have you no name but Gil? Or which of your names is it? Your Christian or surname?"

"O, you must have a surname too, must you!" replied he, "Very well, you may call me Gil-Martin. It is not my *Christian* name; but it *is* a name which may serve your turn."

"This is very strange!" said I. "Are you ashamed of your parents, that you refuse to give your real name?"

"I have no parents save one, whom I do not acknowledge," said he proudly; "therefore, pray drop that subject, for it is a disagreeable one. I am a being of a very peculiar temper, for though I have servants and subjects more than I can number, yet, to gratify a certain whim, I have left them, and retired to this city, and for all the society it contains, you see I have attached myself only to you. This is a secret, and I tell it you only in friendship, therefore pray let it remain one, and say not another word about the matter."

I assented, and said no more concerning it; for it instantly struck me that this was no other than the Czar Peter of Russia, having heard that he had been travelling through Europe in disguise, and I cannot say that I had not thenceforward great and mighty hopes of high preferment, as a defender and avenger of the oppressed Christian Church, under the influence of this great potentate. He had hinted as much already, as that it was more honourable, and of more avail to put down the wicked with the sword, than try to reform them, and I thought myself quite justified in supposing that he intended me for some great employment, that he had thus selected me for his companion out of all the rest in Scotland, and even pretended to learn the great truths of religion from my mouth. From that time I felt disposed to yield to such a great prince's suggestions without hesitation.

Nothing ever astonished me so much, as the uncommon powers with which he seemed invested. In our walk one day, we met with a Mr. Blanchard, who was reckoned a worthy, pious divine, but quite of the moral cast, who joined us; and we three walked on, and rested together in the fields. My companion did not seem to like him, but, nevertheless, regarded him frequently with deep attention, and there were several times, while he seemed contemplating him, and trying to find out his thoughts, that his face became so like Mr. Blanchard's, that it was impossible to have distinguished the one from the other. The antipathy between the two was mutual, and discovered itself quite palpably in a short time. When my companion the prince was gone, Mr. Blanchard asked me anent him, and I told him that he was a stranger in the city, but a very uncommon and great personage. Mr. Blanchard's answer to me was as follows: "I never saw any body I disliked so much in my life, Mr. Robert; and if it be true that he is a stranger here, which I doubt, believe me he is come for no good."

"Do you not perceive what mighty powers of mind he is possessed of?" said I, "and also how clear and unhesitating he is on some of the most interesting points of divinity?"

"It is for his great mental faculties that I dread him," said he. "It is incalculable what evil such a person as he may do, if so disposed. There is a sublimity in his ideas, with which there is to me a mixture of terror; and when he talks of religion, he does it as one that rather dreads its truths than reverences them. He, indeed, pretends great strictness of orthodoxy regarding some of the points of doctrine embraced by the reformed church; but you do not seem to perceive, that both you and he are carrying these points to a dangerous extremity. Religion is a sublime and glorious thing, the bond of society on earth, and the connector of humanity with the Divine nature; but there is nothing so dangerous to man as the wresting of any of its principles, or forcing them beyond their due bounds: this is of all others the readiest way to destruction. Neither is there any thing so easily done. There is not an error into which a man can fall, which he may not press Scripture into his service as proof of the probity of, and though your boasted theologian shunned the full discussion of the subject before me, while you pressed it, I can easily see that both you and he are carrying your ideas of absolute predestination, and its concomitant appendages, to an extent that overthrows all religion and revelation together; or, at least, jumbles them into a chaos, out of which human capacity can never select what is good. Believe me, Mr. Robert, the less you associate with that illustrious stranger the better, for it appears to me that your creed and his carries damnation on the very front of it."

I was rather stunned at this; but I pretended to smile with disdain, and said, it did not become youth to control age; and, as I knew our principles differed fundamentally, it behoved us to drop the subject. He, however, would not drop it, but took both my principles and me fearfully to task, for Blanchard was an eloquent and powerful-minded old man; and, before we parted, I believe I promised to drop my new acquaintance, and was *all but* resolved to do it.

As well might I have laid my account with shunning the light of day. He was constant to me as my shadow, and by degrees he acquired such an ascendency over me, that I never was happy out of his company, nor greatly so in it. When I repeated to him all that Mr. Blanchard had said, his countenance kindled with indignation and rage; and then by degrees his eyes sunk inward, his brow lowered, so that I was awed, and withdrew my eyes from looking at him. A while afterward, as I was addressing him, I chanced to look him again in the face, and the sight of him made me start violently. He had made himself so like Mr. Blanchard, that I actually believed I had been addressing that gentleman, and that I had done so in some absence of mind that I could not account for. Instead of being amused at the quandary I was in, he seemed offended: indeed, he never was truly amused with any thing. And he then asked me sullenly, if I conceived such personages as he to have no other endowments than common mortals?

I said I never conceived that princes or potentates had any greater share of endowments than other men, and frequently not so much. He shook his head, and bade me think over the subject again; and there was an end of it. I certainly felt every day the more disposed to acknowledge such a superiority in him, and from all that I could gather, I had now no doubt that he was Peter of Russia. Every thing combined to warrant the supposition, and, of course, I resolved to act in conformity with the discovery I had made.

For several days the subject of Mr. Blanchard's doubts and doctrines formed the theme of our discourse. My friend deprecated them
most devoutly; and then again he would deplore them, and lament
the great evil that such a man might do among the human race. I
joined with him in allowing the evil in its fullest latitude; and, at
length, after he thought he had fully prepared my nature for such a
trial of its powers and abilities, he proposed calmly that we two
should make away with Mr. Blanchard. I was so shocked, that my
bosom became as it were a void, and the beatings of my heart sounded
loud and hollow in it; my breath cut, and my tongue and palate
became dry and speechless. He mocked at my cowardice, and began a-reasoning on the matter with such powerful eloquence, that
before we parted, I felt fully convinced that it was my bounden duty
to slay Mr. Blanchard; but my will was far, very far from consenting
to the deed.

I spent the following night without sleep, or nearly so; and the
next morning, by the time the sun arose, I was again abroad, and in
the company of my illustrious friend. The same subject was resumed,
and again he reasoned to the following purport: That supposing me
placed at the head of an army of Christian soldiers, all bent on putting
down the enemies of the church, would I have any hesitation in
destroying and rooting out these enemies?–None surely.–Well then,
when I saw and was convinced, that here was an individual who
was doing more detriment to the church of Christ on earth, than
tens of thousands of such warriors were capable of doing, was it not
my duty to cut him off, and save the elect? "He, who would be a
champion in the cause of Christ and his Church, my brave young
friend," added he, "must begin early, and no man can calculate to
what an illustrious eminence small beginnings may lead. If the man
Blanchard is worthy, he is only changing his situation for a better
one; and if unworthy, it is better that one fall, than that a thousand
souls perish. Let us be up and doing in our vocations. For me, my
resolution is taken; I have but one great aim in this world, and I
never for a moment lose sight of it."

I was obliged to admit the force of his reasoning; for though I
cannot from memory repeat his words, his eloquence was of that
overpowering nature, that the subtility of other men sunk before it;
and there is also little doubt that the assurance I had that these words
were spoken by a great potentate, who could raise me to the highest
eminence, (provided that I entered into his extensive and decisive
measures,) assisted mightily in dispelling my youthful scruples and

qualms of conscience; and I thought moreover, that having such a powerful back friend to support me, I hardly needed to be afraid of the consequences. I consented! But begged a little time to think of it. He said the less one thought of a duty the better; and we parted.

But the most singular instance of this wonderful man's power over my mind was, that he had as complete influence over me by night as by day. All my dreams corresponded exactly with his suggestions; and when he was absent from me, still his arguments sunk deeper in my heart than even when he was present. I dreamed that night of a great triumph obtained, and though the whole scene was but dimly and confusedly defined in my vision, yet the overthrow and death of Mr. Blanchard was the first step by which I attained the eminent station I occupied. Thus, by dreaming of the event by night, and discoursing of it by day, it soon became so familiar to my mind, that I almost conceived it as done. It was resolved on: which was the first and greatest victory gained; for there was no difficulty in finding opportunities enow of cutting off a man, who, every good day, was to be found walking by himself in private grounds. I went and heard him preach for two days, and in fact I held his tenets scarcely short of blasphemy; they were such as I had never heard before, and his congregation, which was numerous, were turning up their ears and drinking in his doctrines with the utmost delight; for O, they suited their carnal natures and self-sufficiency to a hair! He was actually holding it forth, as a fact, that "it was every man's own blame if he was not saved!" What horrible misconstruction! And then he was alleging, and trying to prove from nature and reason, that no man ever was guilty of a sinful action, who might not have declined it had he so chosen! "Wretched controvertist!" thought I to myself an hundred times, "shall not the sword of the Lord be moved from its place of peace for such presumptuous and absurd testimonies as these!"

When I began to tell the prince about these false doctrines, to my astonishment I found that he had been in the church himself, and had every argument that the old divine had used *verbatim*; and he remarked on them with great concern, that these were not the tenets that corresponded with his views in society, and that he had agents in every city, and every land, exerting their powers to put them down. I asked, with great simplicity, "Are all your subjects Christians, prince?"

"All my European subjects are, or deem themselves so," returned he; "and they are the most faithful and true subjects I have."

Who could doubt, after this, that he was the Czar of Russia? I have nevertheless had reasons to doubt of his identity since that period, and which of my conjectures is right, I believe the God of heaven only knows, for I do not. I shall go on to write such things as I remember, and if any one shall ever take the trouble to read over these confessions, such a one will judge for himself. It will be observed, that since ever I fell in with this extraordinary person, I have written about him only, and I must continue to do so to the end of this memoir, as I have performed no great or interesting action in which he had not a principal share.

He came to me one day and said, "We must not linger thus in executing what we have resolved on. We have much before our hands to perform for the benefit of mankind, both civil as well as religious. Let us do what we have to do here, and then we must wend our way to other cities, and perhaps to other countries. Mr. Blanchard is to hold forth in the high church of Paisley on Sunday next, on some particularly great occasion: this must be defeated; he must not go there. As he will be busy arranging his discourses, we may expect him to be walking by himself in Finnieston Dell the greater part of Friday and Saturday. Let us go and cut him off. What is the life of a man more than the life of a lamb, or any guiltless animal? It is not half so much, especially when we consider the immensity of the mischief this old fellow is working among our fellow-creatures. Can there be any doubt that it is the duty of one consecrated to God, to cut off such a mildew?"

"I fear me, great sovereign," said I, "that your ideas of retribution are too sanguine, and too arbitrary for the laws of this country. I dispute not that your motives are great and high; but have you debated the consequences, and settled the result?"

"I have," returned he, "and hold myself amenable for the action, to the laws of God and of equity; as to the enactments of men I despise them. Fain would I see the weapon of the Lord of Hosts, begin the work of vengeance that awaits it to do!"

I could not help thinking, that I perceived a little derision of countenance on his face as he said this, nevertheless I sunk dumb before such a man, and aroused myself to the task, seeing he would not have it deferred. I approved of it in theory, but my spirit stood aloof from the practice. I saw and was convinced that the elect of God would be happier, and purer, were the wicked and unbelievers all cut off from troubling and misleading them, but if it had not been the instigations of this illustrious stranger, I should never have presumed to begin so great a work myself. Yet, though he often aroused my zeal to the highest pitch, still my heart at times shrunk from the shedding of life-blood, and it was only at the earnest and unceasing instigations of my enlightened and voluntary patron, that I at length put my hand to the conclusive work. After I said all that I could say, and all had been overborne, (I remember my actions and words as well as it had been yesterday,) I turned round hesitatingly, and looked up to Heaven for direction; but there was a dimness came over my eyes that I could not see. The appearance was as if there had been a veil drawn over me, so nigh that I put up my hand to feel it; and then Gil-Martin (as this great sovereign was pleased to have himself called,) frowned, and asked me what I was grasping at? I knew not what to say, but answered, with fear and shame, "I have no weapons, not one; nor know I where any are to be found."

"The God whom thou servest will provide these," said he; "if thou provest worthy of the trust committed to thee."

I looked again up into the cloudy veil that covered us, and thought I beheld golden weapons of every description let down in it, but all with their points towards me. I kneeled, and was going to stretch out my hand to take one, when my patron seized me, as I thought, by the clothes, and dragged me away with as much ease as I had been a lamb, saying, with a joyful and elevated voice,–"Come, my friend, let us depart: thou art dreaming–thou art dreaming. Rouse up all the energies of thy exalted mind, for thou art an highly-favoured one; and doubt thou not, that he whom *thou* servest, will be ever at thy right and left hand, to direct and assist thee."

These words, but particularly the vision I had seen, of the golden weapons descending out of Heaven, inflamed my zeal to that height that I was as one beside himself; which my parents perceived that night, and made some motions toward confining me to my room. I joined in the family prayers, and then I afterwards sung a psalm and prayed by myself; and I had good reasons for believing that that small oblation of praise and prayer was not turned to sin. But there are strange things, and unaccountable agencies in nature: He only who dwells between the Cherubim can unriddle them, and to him the honour must redound for ever. *Amen.*

I felt greatly strengthened and encouraged that night, and the next morning I ran to meet my companion, out of whose eye I had now no life. He rejoiced at seeing me so forward in the great work of reformation by blood, and said many things to raise my hopes of future fame and glory; and then, producing two pistols of pure beaten gold, he held them out and proffered me the choice of one, saying, "See what thy master hath provided thee!" I took one of them eagerly, for I perceived at once that they were two of the very weapons that were let down from Heaven in the cloudy veil, the dim tapestry of the firmament; and I said to myself, "Surely this is the will of the Lord."

The little splendid and enchanting piece was so perfect, so complete, and so ready for executing the will of the donor, that I now longed to use it in his service. I loaded it with my own hand, as Gil-Martin did the other, and we took our stations behind a bush of hawthorn and bramble on the verge of the wood, and almost close to the walk. My patron was so acute in all his calculations that he never mistook an event. We had not taken our stand above a minute and a half, till old Mr. Blanchard appeared, coming slowly on the path. When we saw this, we cowered down, and leaned each of us a knee upon the ground, pointing the pistols through the bush, with an aim so steady, that it was impossible to miss our victim.

He came deliberately on, pausing at times so long, that we dreaded he was going to turn. Gil-Martin dreaded it, and I said I did, but wished in my heart that he might. He, however, came onward, and I will never forget the manner in which he came! No—I don't believe I ever can forget it, either in the narrow bounds of time or the ages of eternity! He was a boardly ill-shaped man, of a rude exterior, and a little bent with age; his hands were clasped behind his back, and below his coat, and he walked with a slow swinging air that was very peculiar. When he paused and looked abroad on nature, the act was highly impressive: he seemed conscious of being all alone, and conversant only with God and the elements of his creation. Never was there such a picture of human inadvertency! a man approaching step by step to the one that was to hurl him out of one existence into another, with as much ease and indifference as the ox goeth to the stall. Hideous vision, wilt thou not be gone from my mental sight! If not, let me bear with thee as I can!

When he came straight opposite to the muzzles of our pieces, Gil-Martin called out "Eh!" with a short quick sound. The old man, without starting, turned his face and breast toward us, and looked into the wood, but looked over our heads. "Now!" whispered my companion, and fired. But my hand refused the office, for I was not at that moment sure about becoming an assassin in the cause of Christ and his Church. I thought I heard a sweet voice behind me, whispering me to beware, and I was going to look round, when my companion exclaimed, "Coward, we are ruined!"

I had no time for an alternative: Gil-Martin's ball had not taken effect, which was altogether wonderful, as the old man's breast was within a few yards of him. "Hilloa!" cried Blanchard; "what is that for, you dog!" and with that he came forward to look over the bush. I hesitated, as I said, and attempted to look behind me; but there was no time: the next step discovered two assassins lying in covert, waiting for blood. "Coward, we are ruined!" cried my indignant friend; and that moment my piece was discharged. The effect was as might have been expected: the old man first stumbled to one side, and then fell on his back. We kept our places, and I perceived my companion's eyes gleaming with an unnatural joy. The wounded man raised himself from the bank to a sitting posture, and I beheld his eyes swimming; he, however, appeared sensible, for we heard him saying in a low and rattling voice, "Alas, alas! whom have I offended, that they should have been driven to an act like this! Come forth and shew yourselves, that I may either forgive you before I die, or curse you in the name of the Lord." He then fell a-groping with both hands on the ground, as if feeling for something he had lost, manifestly in the agonies of death; and, with a solemn and interrupted prayer for forgiveness, he breathed his last.

I had become rigid as a statue, whereas my associate appeared to be elevated above measure. "Arise, thou faint-hearted one, and let us be going," said he. "Thou hast done well for once; but wherefore hesitate in such a cause? This is but a small beginning of so great a work as that of purging the Christian world. But the first victim is a worthy one, and more of such lights must be extinguished immediately."

We touched not our victim, nor any thing pertaining to him, for fear of staining our hands with his blood; and the firing having brought three men within view, who were hasting towards the spot, my undaunted companion took both the pistols, and went forward as with intent to meet them, bidding me shift for myself. I ran off in a contrary direction, till I came to the foot of the Pearman Sike, and then, running up the hollow of that, I appeared on the top of the bank as if I had been another man brought in view by hearing the shots in such a place. I had a full view of a part of what passed, though not of all. I saw my companion going straight to meet the men, apparently with a pistol in every hand, waving in a careless manner. They seemed not quite clear of meeting with him, and so he went straight on, and passed between them. They looked after him, and came onward; but when they came to the old man lying stretched in his blood, then they turned and pursued my companion, though not so quickly as they might have done; and I understood that from the first they saw no more of him.

Great was the confusion that day in Glasgow. The most popular

of all their preachers of morality was (what they called) murdered
in cold blood, and a strict and extensive search was made for the
assassin. Neither of the accomplices was found, however, that is
certain, nor was either of them so much as suspected; but another
man was apprehended under circumstances that warranted suspicion.–This was one of the things that I witnessed in my life, which I
never understood, and it surely was one of my patron's most dex-
terous tricks, for I must still say, what I have thought from the beginning, that like him there never was a man created. The young man
who was taken up was a preacher; and it was proved that he had
purchased fire arms in town, and gone out with them that morning.
But the far greatest mystery of the whole was, that two of the men,
out of the three who met my companion, swore, that that unfortunate preacher was the man whom they met with a pistol in each
hand, fresh from the death of the old divine. The poor fellow made
a confused speech himself, which there is not the least doubt was
quite true; but it was laughed to scorn, and an expression of horror
ran through both the hearers and jury. I heard the whole trial, and
so did Gil-Martin; but we left the journeyman preacher to his fate,
and from that time forth I have had no faith in the justice of criminal
trials. If once a man is prejudiced on one side, he will swear any
thing in support of such prejudice. I tried to expostulate with my
mysterious friend on the horrid injustice of suffering this young man
to die for our act, but the prince exulted in it more than the other,
and said the latter was the most dangerous man of the two.

The alarm in and about Glasgow was prodigious. The country
being divided into two political parties, the court and the country
party, the former held meetings, issued proclamations, and offered
rewards, ascribing all to the violence of party spirit, and deprecating the infernal measures of their opponents. I did not understand
their political differences; but it was easy to see that the true Gospel
preachers joined all on one side, and the upholders of pure morality
and a blameless life on the other, so that this division proved a test
to us, and it was forthwith resolved, that we two should pick out
some of the leading men of this unsaintly and heterodox cabal, and
cut them off one by one, as occasion should suit.

Now, the ice being broke, I felt considerable zeal in our great
work, but pretended much more; and we might soon have kidnapped
them all through the ingenuity of my patron, had not our next attempt miscarried, by some awkwardness or mistake of mine. The
consequence was, that he was discovered fairly, and very nigh seized.
I also was seen, and suspected so far, that my reverend father, my

mother, and myself were examined privately. I denied all knowledge of the matter; and they held it in such a ridiculous light, and their conviction of the complete groundlessness of the suspicion was so perfect, that their testimony prevailed, and the affair was hushed. I was obliged, however, to walk circumspectly, and saw my companion the prince very seldom, who was prowling about every day, quite unconcerned about his safety. He was every day a new man, however, and needed not to be alarmed at any danger; for such a facility had he in disguising himself, that if it had not been for a password which we had between us, for the purposes of recognition, I never could have known him myself.

It so happened that my reverend father was called to Edinburgh about this time, to assist with his council in settling the national affairs. At my earnest request I was permitted to accompany him, at which both my associate and I rejoiced, as we were now about to move in a new and extensive field. All this time I never knew where my illustrious friend resided. He never once invited me to call on him at his lodgings, nor did he ever come to our house, which made me sometimes to suspect, that if any of our great efforts in the cause of true religion were discovered, he intended leaving me in the lurch. Consequently, when we met in Edinburgh (for we travelled not in company) I proposed to go with him to look for lodgings, telling him at the same time what a blessed religious family my reverend instructor and I were settled in. He said he rejoiced at it, but he made a rule of never lodging in any particular house, but took these daily, or hourly, as he found it convenient, and that he never was at a loss in any circumstance.

"What a mighty trouble you put yourself to, great sovereign!" said I, "and all, it would appear, for the purpose of seeing and knowing more and more of the human race."

"I never go but where I have some great purpose to serve," returned he, "either in the advancement of my own power and dominion, or in thwarting my enemies."

"With all due deference to your great comprehension, my illustrious friend," said I, "it strikes me that you can accomplish very little either the one way or the other here, in the humble and private capacity you are pleased to occupy."

"It is your own innate modesty that prompts such a remark," said he. "Do you think the gaining of *you* to my service, is not an attainment worthy of being envied by the greatest potentate in Christendom? Before I had missed such a prize as the attainment of your services, I would have travelled over one half of the habitable globe."—I bowed with great humility, but at the same time how could I but feel proud and highly flattered? He continued. "Believe me, my dear friend, for such a prize I account no effort too high. For a man who is not only dedicated to the King of Heaven, in the most solemn manner, soul, body, and spirit, but also chosen of him from the beginning, justified, sanctified, and received into a communion that never shall be broken, and from which no act of his shall ever remove him,—the possession of such a man, I tell you, is worth kingdoms; because every deed that he performs, he does it with perfect safety to himself and honour to me."—I bowed again, lifting my hat, and he went on.—"I am now going to put his courage in the cause he has espoused, to a severe test—to a trial at which common nature would revolt, but he who is dedicated to be the sword of the Lord, must raise himself above common humanity. You have a father and a brother according to the flesh, what do you know of them?"

"I am sorry to say I know nothing good," said I. "They are reprobates, cast-aways, beings devoted to the wicked one, and, like him, workers of every species of iniquity with greediness."

"They must both fall!" said he, with a sigh and melancholy look: "It is decreed in the councils above, that they must both fall by your hand."

"The God of heaven forbid it!" said I. "They are enemies to Christ and his church, that I know and believe; but they shall live and die in their iniquity for me, and reap their guerdon when their time cometh. There my hand shall not strike."

"The feeling is natural, and amiable," said he; "but you *must* think again. Whether are the bonds of carnal nature, or the bonds and vows of the Lord, strongest?"

"I will not reason with you on this head, mighty potentate," said I, "for whenever I do so it is but to be put down. I shall only express my determination, not to take vengeance out of the Lord's hand in this instance. It availeth not. These are men that have the mark of the beast in their foreheads and right hands; they are lost beings themselves, but have no influence over others. Let them perish in their sins; for they shall not be meddled with by me."

"How preposterously you talk, my dear friend!" said he. "These people are your greatest enemies; they would rejoice to see you annihilated. And now that you have taken up the Lord's cause of being avenged on *his* enemies, wherefore spare those that are your own as well as his? Besides, you ought to consider what great advantages would be derived to the cause of righteousness and truth, were the estate and riches of that opulent house in your possession, rather than in that of such as oppose the truth and all manner of holiness."

This was a portion of the consequence of following my illustrious adviser's summary mode of procedure, that had never entered into my calculation—I disclaimed all idea of being influenced by it; however, I cannot but say that the desire of being enabled to do so much good, by the possession of these bad men's riches, made some impression on my heart, and I said I would consider of the matter. I did consider it, and that right seriously as well as frequently; and there was scarcely an hour in the day on which my resolves were not animated by my great friend, till at length I began to have a longing desire to kill my brother, in particular. Should any man ever read this scroll, he will wonder at this confession, and deem it savage and unnatural. So it appeared to me at first, but a constant thinking of an event changes every one of its features. I have done all for the best, and as I was prompted, by one who knew right and wrong much better than I did. I *had* a desire to slay him, it is true, and such a desire too as a thirsty man has to drink; but at the same time, this longing desire was mingled with a certain terror, as if I had dreaded that the drink for which I longed was mixed with deadly poison. My mind was so much weakened, or rather softened about this time, that my faith began a little to give way, and I doubted most presumptuously of the least tangible of all Christian tenets, namely, of *the infallibility of the elect*. I hardly comprehended the great work I had begun, and doubted of *my own* infallibility, or that of any created being. But I was brought over again by the unwearied diligence of my friend to repent of my backsliding, and view once more the superiority of the Almighty's counsels in its fullest latitude. *Amen.*

I prayed very much in secret about this time, and that with great fervor of spirit, as well as humility; and my satisfaction at finding all my requests granted is not to be expressed.

My illustrious friend still continuing to sound in my ears the imperious duty to which I was called, of making away with my sinful relations, and quoting many parallel actions out of the Scriptures, and the writings of the holy Fathers, of the pleasure the Lord took in such as executed his vengeance on the wicked, I was obliged to acquiesce in his measures, though with certain limitations. It was not easy to answer his arguments, and yet I was afraid that he soon perceived a leaning to his will on my part. "If the acts of Jehu, in rooting out the whole house of his master, were ordered and approved of by the Lord," said he, "would it not have been more praiseworthy if one of Ahab's own sons had stood up for the cause of the

God of Israel, and rooted out the sinners and their idols out of the land?"

"It would certainly," said I. "To our duty to God all other duties must yield."

"Go thou then and do likewise," said he. "Thou art called to a high vocation; to cleanse the sanctuary of thy God in this thy native land by the shedding of blood; go thou forth then like a ruling energy, a master spirit of desolation in the dwellings of the wicked, and high shall be your reward both here and hereafter."

My heart now panted with eagerness to look my brother in the face: On which my companion, who was never out of the way, conducted me to a small square in the suburbs of the city, where there were a number of young noblemen and gentlemen playing at a vain, idle, and sinful game, at which there was much of the language of the accursed going on; and among these blasphemers he instantly pointed out my brother to me. I was fired with indignation at seeing him in such company, and so employed; and I placed myself close beside him to watch all his motions, listen to his words, and draw inferences from what I saw and heard. In what a sink of sin was he wallowing! I resolved to take him to task, and if he refused to be admonished, to inflict on him some condign punishment; and knowing that my illustrious friend and director was looking on, I resolved to show some spirit. Accordingly, I waited until I heard him profane his Maker's name three times, and then, my spiritual indignation being roused above all restraint, I went up and kicked him. Yes, I went boldly up and struck him with my foot, and meant to have given him a more severe blow than it was my fortune to inflict. It had, however, the effect of rousing up his corrupt nature to quarrelling and strife, instead of taking the chastisement of the Lord in humility and meekness. He ran furiously against me in the choler that is always inspired by the wicked one; but I overthrew him, by reason of impeding the natural and rapid progress of his unholy feet, running to destruction. I also fell slightly; but his fall proving a severe one, he arose in wrath, and struck me with the mall which he held in his hand, until my blood flowed copiously; and from that moment I vowed his destruction in my heart. But I chanced to have no weapon at that time, nor any means of inflicting due punishment on the caitiff, which would not have been returned double on my head, by him and his graceless associates. I mixed among them at the suggestion of my friend, and following them to their den of voluptuousness and sin, I strove to be admitted among them, in hopes of finding some means of accomplishing my great purpose, while I found myself moved by the spirit within me so to do. But I was not only debarred, but, by the machinations of my wicked brother and his associates, cast into prison.

I was not sorry at being thus honoured to suffer in the cause of righteousness, and at the hands of sinful men; and as soon as I was alone, I betook myself to prayer, deprecating the long-suffering of God toward such horrid sinners. My jailer came to me, and insulted me. He was a rude unprincipled fellow, partaking much of the loose and carnal manners of the age; but I remembered of having read, in the Cloud of Witnesses, of such men formerly, having been converted by the imprisoned saints; so I set myself, with all my heart, to bring about this man's repentance and reformation.

"Fat the deil are ye yoolling an' praying that gate for, man?" said he, coming angrily in. "I thought the days o' praying prisoners had been a' ower. We had rowth o' them aince; an' they were the poorest an' the blackest bargains that ever poor jailers saw. Gie up your crooning, or I'll pit you to an in-by place, where ye sall get plenty o't."

"Friend," said I, "I am making my appeal at that bar where all human actions are seen and judged, and where you shall not be forgot, sinful as you are. Go in peace, and let me be."

"Hae ye naebody nearer-hand hame to mak your appeal to, man?" said he; "because an ye haena, I dread you an' me may be unco weel acquaintit by an' by?"

I then opened up the mysteries of religion to him in a clear and perspicuous manner, but particularly the great doctrine of the election of grace; and then I added, "Now, friend, you must tell me if you pertain to this chosen number. It is in every man's power to ascertain this, and it is every man's duty to do it."

"An' fat the better wad you be for the kenning o' this, man?" said he.

"Because, if you are one of my brethren, I will take you into sweet communion and fellowship," returned I; "but if you belong to the unregenerate, I have a commission to slay you."

"The deil you hae, callant!" said he, gaping and laughing. "An' pray now, fa was it that gae you siccan a braw commission?"

"My commission is sealed by the signet above," said I, "and that I will let you and all sinners know. I am dedicated to it by the most solemn vows and engagements. I am the sword of the Lord, and Famine and Pestilence are my sisters. Wo then to the wicked of this land, for they must fall down dead together, that the church may be purified!"

"Oo, foo, foo! I see how it is," said he; "yours is a very braw commission, but you will have the small opportunity of carrying it through here. Take my advising, and write a bit of a letter to your friends, and I will send it, for this is no place for such a great man. If you cannot steady your hand to write, as I see you have been at your great work, a word of a mouth may do; for I do assure you this is not the place at all, of any in the world, for your operations."

The man apparently thought I was deranged in my intellect. He could not swallow such great truths at the first morsel. So I took his advice, and sent a line to my reverend father, who was not long in coming, and great was the jailer's wonderment when he saw all the great Christian noblemen of the land sign my bond of freedom.

My reverend father took this matter greatly to heart, and bestirred himself in the good cause till the transgressors were ashamed to shew their faces. My illustrious companion was not idle: I wondered that he came not to me in prison, nor at my release; but he was better employed, in stirring up the just to the execution of God's decrees; and he succeeded so well, that my brother and all his associates had nearly fallen victims to their wrath: But many were wounded, bruised, and imprisoned, and much commotion prevailed in the city. For my part, I was greatly strengthened in my resolution by the anathemas of my reverend father, who, privately, (that is in a family capacity,) in his prayers, gave up my father and brother, according to the flesh, to Satan, making it plain to all my senses of perception, that they were beings given up of God, to be devoured by fiends or men, at their will and pleasure, and that *whosoever* should slay them, would do God good service.

The next morning my illustrious friend met me at an early hour, and he was greatly overjoyed at hearing my sentiments now chime so much in unison with his own. I said, "I longed for the day and the hour that I might look my brother in the face at Gilgal, and visit on him the iniquity of his father and himself, for that I was now strengthened and prepared for the deed."

"I have been watching the steps and movements of the profligate one," said he; "and lo, I will take you straight to his presence. Let your heart be as the heart of the lion, and your arms strong as the shekels of brass, and swift to avenge as the bolt that descendeth from Heaven, for the blood of the just and the good hath long flowed in Scotland. But already is the day of their avengement begun; the hero is at length arisen, who shall send all such as bear enmity to the true church, or trust in works of their own, to Tophet!"

Thus encouraged, I followed my friend, who led me directly to

the same court in which I had chastised the miscreant on the foregoing day; and behold, there was the same group again assembled.
They eyed me with terror in their looks, as I walked among them
and eyed them with looks of disapprobation and rebuke; and I saw
that the very eye of a chosen one lifted on these children of Belial,
was sufficient to dismay and put them to flight. I walked aside to my
friend, who stood at a distance looking on, and he said to me, "What
thinkest thou now?" and I answered in the words of the venal
prophet, "Lo now, if I had a sword into mine hand, I would even
kill him."

"Wherefore lackest thou it?" said he. "Dost thou not see that
they tremble at thy presence, knowing that the avenger of blood is
among them."

My heart was lifted up on hearing this, and again I strode into the
midst of them, and eyeing them with threatening looks, they were
so much confounded, that they abandoned their sinful pastime, and
fled every one to his house!

This was a palpable victory gained over the wicked, and I thereby
knew that the hand of the Lord was with me. My companion also
exulted, and said, "Did not I tell thee? Behold thou dost not know
one half of thy might, or of the great things thou art destined to do.
Come with me and I will show thee more than this, for these young
men cannot subsist without the exercises of sin. I listened to their
councils, and I know where they will meet again."

Accordingly he led me a little farther to the south, and we walked
aside till by degrees we saw some people begin to assemble; and in
a short time we perceived the same group stripping off their clothes
to make them more expert in the practice of madness and folly.
Their game was begun before we approached, and so also were the
oaths and cursing. I put my hands in my pockets, and walked with
dignity and energy into the midst of them. It was enough: Terror
and astonishment seized them. A few of them cried out against me,
but their voices were soon hushed amid the murmurs of fear. One
of them, in the name of the rest, then came and besought of me to
grant them liberty to amuse themselves; but I refused peremptorily,
dared the whole multitude so much as to touch me with one of their
fingers, and dismissed them in the name of the Lord.

Again they all fled and dispersed at my eye, and I went home in
triumph, escorted by my friend, and some well-meaning young
Christians, who, however, had not learned to deport themselves
with soberness and humility. But my ascendency over my enemies
was great indeed; for wherever I appeared I was hailed with appro-

bation, and wherever my guilty brother made his appearance, he was hooted and held in derision, till he was forced to hide his disgraceful head, and appear no more in public.

Immediately after this I was seized with a strange distemper, which neither my friends nor physicians could comprehend, and it confined me to my chamber for many days; but I knew, myself, that I was bewitched, and suspected my father's reputed concubine of the deed. I told my fears to my reverend protector, who hesitated concerning them, but I knew by his words and looks that he was conscious I was right. I generally conceived myself to be two people. When I lay in bed, I deemed there were two of us in it; when I sat up, I always beheld another person, and always in the same position from the place where I sat or stood, which was about three paces off me towards my left side. It mattered not how many or how few were present: this my second self was sure to be present in his place; and this occasioned a confusion in all my words and ideas that utterly astounded my friends, who all declared, that instead of being deranged in my intellect, they had never heard my conversation manifest so much energy or sublimity of conception; but for all that, over the singular delusion that I was two persons, my reasoning faculties had no power. The most perverse part of it was, that I rarely conceived *myself* to be any of the two persons. I thought for the most part that my companion was one of them, and my brother the other; and I found, that to be obliged to speak and answer in the character of another man, was a most awkward business at the long run.

Who can doubt, from this statement, that I was bewitched, and that my relatives were at the ground of it? The constant and unnatural persuasion that I was my brother, proved it to my own satisfaction, and must, I think, do so to every unprejudiced person. This victory of the wicked one over me kept me confined in my chamber, at Mr. Millar's house, for nearly a month, until the prayers of the faithful prevailed, and I was restored. I knew it was a chastisement for my pride, because my heart was lifted up at my superiority over the enemies of the church; nevertheless, I determined to make short work with the aggressor, that the righteous might not be subjected to the effect of his diabolical arts again.

I say I was confined a month. I beg he that readeth to take note of this, that he may estimate how much the word, or even the oath, of a wicked man, is to depend on. For a month I saw no one but such as came into my room, and for all that, it will be seen, that there were plenty of the same set to attest upon oath that I saw my brother every day during that period; that I persecuted him with my presence day and night, while all the time I never saw his face, save in a delusive dream. I cannot comprehend what manœuvres my illustrious friend was playing off with them about this time; for he, having the art of personating whom he chose, had peradventure deceived them, else so many of them had never all attested the same thing. I never saw any man so steady in his friendships and attentions as he; but as he made a rule of never calling at private houses, for fear of some discovery being made of his person, so I never saw him while my malady lasted; but as soon as I grew better, I knew I had nothing ado but to attend at some of our places of meeting, to see him again. He was punctual, as usual, and I had not to wait.

My reception was precisely as I apprehended. There was no flaring, no flummery, nor bombastical pretensions, but a dignified return to my obeisance, and an immediate recurrence, in converse, to the important duties incumbent on us, in our stations, as reformers and purifiers of the Church.

"I have marked out a number of most dangerous characters in this city," said he, "all of whom must be cut off from cumbering the true vineyard before we leave this land. And if you bestir not yourself in the work to which you are called, I must raise up others who shall have the honour of it."

"I am, most illustrious prince, wholly at your service," said I. "Show but what ought to be done, and here is the heart to dare, and the hand to execute. You pointed out my relations, according to the flesh, as brands fitted to be thrown into the burning. I approve peremptorily of the award; nay, I thirst to accomplish it; for I myself have suffered severely from their diabolical arts. When once that trial of my devotion to the faith is accomplished, then be your future operations disclosed."

"You are free of your words and promises," said he.

"So will I be of my deeds in the service of my master, and that shalt thou see," said I. "I lack not the spirit, nor the will, but I lack experience wofully; and because of that shortcoming, must bow to your suggestions."

"Meet me here to-morrow betimes," said he, "and perhaps you may hear of some opportunity of displaying your zeal in the cause of righteousness."

I met him as he desired me; and he addressed me with a hurried and joyful expression, telling me that my brother was astir, and that a few minutes ago he had seen him pass on his way to the mountain. "The hill is wrapped in a cloud," added he, "and never was there such an opportunity of executing divine justice on a guilty sinner. You may trace him in the dew, and shall infallibly find him on the top of some precipice; for it is only in secret that he dares show his debased head to the sun."

"I have no arms, else assuredly I would pursue him and discomfit him," said I.

"Here is a small dagger," said he; "I have nothing of weapon-kind about me save that, but it is a potent one; and should you require it, there is nothing more ready or sure."

"Will not you accompany me?" said I: "Sure you will?"

"I will be with you, or near you," said he. "Go you on before."

I hurried away as he directed me, and imprudently asked some of Queensberry's guards if such and such a young man passed by them going out from the city. I was answered in the affirmative, and till then had doubted of my friend's intelligence, it was so inconsistent with a profligate's life to be so early astir. When I got the certain intelligence that my brother was before me, I fell a-running, scarcely knowing what I did; and looking several times behind me, I perceived nothing of my zealous and arbitrary friend. The consequence of this was, that by the time I reached St. Anthony's well, my resolution began to give way. It was not my courage, for now that I had once shed blood in the cause of the true faith, I was exceedingly bold and ardent; but whenever I was left to myself, I was subject to sinful doubtings. These always hankered on one point: I doubted if the elect were infallible, and if the Scripture promises to them were binding in all situations and relations. I confess this, and that it was a sinful and shameful weakness in me, but my nature was subject to it, and I could not eschew it. I never doubted that I was one of the elect myself; for, besides the strong inward and spiritual conviction that I possessed, I had my kind father's assurance; and these had been revealed to him in that way and measure that they could not be doubted.

In this desponding state, I sat myself down on a stone, and bethought me of the rashness of my understanding. I tried to ascertain, to my own satisfaction, whether or not I really had been commissioned of God to perpetrate these crimes in his behalf, for in the eyes, and by the laws of men, they were great and crying transgressions. While I sat pondering on these things, I was involved in a veil of white misty vapour, and looking up to heaven, I was just about to ask direction from above, when I heard as it were a still small voice close by me, which uttered some words of derision and chiding. I looked intensely in the direction whence it seemed to come, and perceived a lady, robed in white, who hasted toward me. She regarded me with a severity of look and gesture that appalled me so much, I could not address her; but she waited not for that, but coming close to my side, said, without stopping, "Preposterous wretch! how dare you lift your eyes to heaven with such purposes in your heart? Escape homeward, and save your soul, or farewell for ever!"

These were all the words that she uttered, as far as I could ever recollect, but my spirits were kept in such a tumult that morning, that something might have escaped me. I followed her eagerly with my eyes, but in a moment she glided over the rocks above the holy well, and vanished. I persuaded myself that I had seen a vision, and that the radiant being that had addressed me was one of the good angels, or guardian spirits, commissioned by the Almighty to watch over the steps of the just. My first impulse was to follow her advice, and make my escape home; for I thought to myself, "How is this interested and mysterious foreigner, a proper judge of the actions of a free Christian?"

The thought was hardly framed, nor had I moved in a retrograde direction six steps, when I saw my illustrious friend and great adviser descending the ridge towards me with hasty and impassioned strides. My heart fainted within me; and when he came up and addressed me, I looked as one caught in a trespass. "What hath detained thee, thou desponding trifler?" said he. "Verily now shall the golden opportunity be lost which may never be recalled. I have traced the reprobate to his sanctuary in the cloud, and lo he is perched on the pinnacle of a precipice an hundred fathoms high. One ketch with thy foot, or toss with thy finger, shall throw him from thy sight into the foldings of the cloud, and he shall be no more seen, till found at the bottom of the cliff dashed to pieces. Make haste therefore, thou loiterer, if thou wouldst ever prosper and rise to eminence in the work of thy Lord and master."

"I go no farther on this work," said I, "for I have seen a vision that has reprimanded the deed."

"A vision?" said he: "Was it that wench who descended from the hill?"

"The being that spake to me, and warned me of my danger, was indeed in the form of a lady," said I.

"She also approached me and said a few words," returned he; "and I thought there was something mysterious in her manner. Pray, what did she say? for the words of such a singular message, and from such a messenger, ought to be attended to. If I understood her aright, she was chiding us for our misbelief and preposterous delay."

I recited her words, but he answered that I had been in a state of sinful doubting at the time, and it was to these doubtings she had adverted. In short, this wonderful and clear-sighted stranger soon banished all my doubts and despondency, making me utterly ashamed of them, and again I set out with him in the pursuit of my brother. He showed me the traces of his footsteps in the dew, and pointed out the spot where I should find him. "You have nothing more to do than go softly down behind him," said he; "which you can do to within an ell of him, without being seen; then rush upon him, and throw him from his seat, where there is neither footing nor hold. I will go, meanwhile, and amuse his sight by some exhibition in the contrary direction, and he shall neither know nor perceive who has done him this *kind office*: for, exclusive of more weighty concerns, be assured of this, that the sooner he falls, the fewer crimes will he have to answer for, and his estate in the other world will be proportionally more tolerable, than if he spent a long unregenerate life steeped in iniquity to the loathing of the soul."

"Nothing can be more plain or more pertinent," said I: "therefore I fly to perform that which is both a duty toward God and toward man!"

"You shall yet rise to great honour and preferment," said he.

"I value it not, provided I do honour and justice to the cause of my master here," said I.

"You shall be lord of your father's riches and demesnes," added he.

"I disclaim and deride every selfish motive thereto relating," said I, "farther than as it enables me to do good."

"Ay, but that is a great and a heavenly consideration, that *longing for ability to do good*," said he;—and as he said so, I could not help remarking a certain derisive exultation of expression which I could not comprehend; and indeed I have noted this very often in my illustrious friend, and sometimes mentioned it civilly to him, but he has never failed to disclaim it. On this occasion I said nothing, but concealing his poniard in my clothes, I hasted up the mountain, determined to execute my purpose before any misgivings should again visit me; and I never had more ado, than in keeping firm my resolution. I could not help my thoughts, and there are certain trains and classes of thoughts that have great power in enervating the mind. I thought of the awful thing of plunging a fellow creature from the top of a cliff into the dark and misty void below—of his being dashed to pieces on the protruding rocks, and of hearing his shrieks as he descended the cloud, and beheld the shagged points on which he was to alight. Then I thought of plunging a soul so abruptly into hell, or, at the best, sending it to hover on the confines of that burning abyss—of its appearance at the bar of the Almighty to receive its sentence. And then I thought, "Will there not be a sentence pronounced against me there, by a jury of the just made perfect, and written down in the registers of heaven?"

These thoughts, I say, came upon me unasked, and instead of being able to dispel them, they mustered, upon the summit of my imagination, in thicker and stronger array: and there was another that impressed me in a very particular manner, though, I have reason to believe, not so strongly as those above written. It was this: "What if I should fail in my first effort? Will the consequence not be that I am tumbled from the top of the rock myself?" and then all the feelings anticipated, with regard to both body and soul, must happen to me! This was a spine-breaking reflection; and yet, though the probability was rather on that side, my zeal in the cause of godliness was such that it carried me on, maugre all danger and dismay.

I soon came close upon my brother, sitting on the dizzy pinnacle, with his eyes fixed stedfastly in the direction opposite to me. I descended the little green ravine behind him with my feet foremost, and every now and then raised my head, and watched his motions. His posture continued the same, until at last I came so near him I could have heard him breathe, if his face had been towards me. I laid my cap aside, and made me ready to spring upon him, and push him over. I could not for my life accomplish it! I do not think it was that *I durst not*, for I have always felt my courage equal to any thing in a good cause. But I had not the heart, or something that I ought to have had. In short, it was not done in time, as it easily might have been. These THOUGHTS are hard enemies wherewith to combat! And I was so grieved that I could not effect my righteous purpose, that I laid me down on my face and shed tears. Then, again, I thought of what my great enlightened friend and patron would say to me, and again my resolution rose indignant, and indissoluble save by blood. I arose on my right knee and left foot, and had just begun to advance the latter forward: the next step my great purpose had been accomplished, and the culprit had suffered the punishment due to his crimes. But what moved him I knew not: in the critical moment he sprung to his feet, and dashing himself furiously against me, he overthrew me, at the imminent peril of my life. I disencumbered myself by main force, and fled, but he overhied me, knocked me down, and threatened, with dreadful oaths, to throw me from the cliff. After I was a little recovered from the stunning blow, I aroused myself to the combat; and though I do not recollect the circumstances of that deadly scuffle very minutely, I know that I vanquished him so far as to force him to ask my pardon, and crave a reconciliation. I spurned at both, and left him to the chastisements of his own wicked and corrupt heart.

My friend met me again on the hill, and derided me, in a haughty and stern manner, for my imbecility and want of decision. I told him how nearly I had effected my purpose, and excused myself as well as I was able. On this, seeing me bleeding, he advised me to swear the peace against my brother, and have him punished in the mean time, he being the first aggressor. I promised compliance, and we parted, for I was somewhat ashamed of my failure, and was glad to be quit for the present of one of whom I stood so much in awe.

When my reverend father beheld me bleeding a second time by the hand of a brother, he was moved to the highest point of displeasure; and, relying on his high interest and the justice of his cause, he brought the matter at once before the courts. My brother and I were first examined face to face. His declaration was a mere romance: mine was not the truth; but as it was by the advice of my reverend father, and that of my illustrious friend, both of whom I knew to be sincere Christians and true believers, that I gave it, I conceived myself completely justified on that score. I said, I had gone up into the mountain early on the morning to pray, and had withdrawn myself, for entire privacy, into a little sequestered dell—had laid aside my cap, and was in the act of kneeling, when I was rudely attacked by my brother, knocked over, and nearly slain. They asked my brother if this was true. He acknowledged that it was; that I was bare-headed, and in the act of kneeling when he ran foul of me without any intent of doing so. But the judge took him to task on the improbability of this, and put the profligate sore out of countenance. The rest of his tale told still worse, insomuch that he was laughed at by all present, for the judge remarked to him, that granting it was true that he had at first run against me on an open mountain, and overthrown me by accident, how was it, that after I had extricated myself and fled, that he had pursued, overtaken, and knocked me down a second time? Would he pretend that all that was likewise by chance? The culprit had nothing to say for himself on this head, and I shall not forget my exultation and that of my reverend father, when the sentence of the judge was delivered. It was, that my wicked brother should be thrown into prison, and tried on a criminal charge of assault and battery, with the intent of committing murder. This was a just and righteous judge, and saw things in their proper bearings, that is, he could discern between a righteous and a wicked man, and then there could be no doubt as to which of the two were acting right, and which wrong.

Had I not been sensible that a justified person could do nothing wrong, I should not have been at my ease concerning the statement I had been induced to give on this occasion. I could easily perceive, that by rooting out the weeds from the garden of the Church, I heightened the growth of righteousness; but as to the tardy way of giving false evidence on matters of such doubtful issue, I confess I saw no great propriety in it from the beginning. But I now only moved by the will and mandate of my illustrious friend: I had no peace or comfort when out of his sight, nor have I ever been able to boast of much in his presence; so true is it that a Christian's life is one of suffering.

My time was now much occupied, along with my reverend preceptor, in making ready for the approaching trial, as the prosecutors. Our counsel assured us of a complete victory, and that banishment would be the mildest award of the law on the offender. Mark how different was the result! From the shifts and ambiguities of a wicked Bench, who had a fellow-feeling of iniquity with the defenders,—my suit was cast, the graceless libertine was absolved, and I was incarcerated, and bound over to keep the peace, with heavy penalties, before I was set at liberty.

I was exceedingly disgusted at this issue, and blamed the counsel of my friend to his face. He expressed great grief, and expatiated on the wickedness of our judicatories, adding, "I see I cannot depend on you for quick and summary measures, but for your sake I shall be revenged on that wicked judge, and that you shall see in a few days." The Lord Justice Clerk died that same week! But he died in his own house and his own bed, and by what means my friend effected it, I do not know. He would not tell me a single word of the matter, but the judge's sudden death made a great noise, and I made so many curious inquiries regarding the particulars of it, that some suspicions were like to attach to our family, of some unfair means used. For my part I know nothing, and rather think he died by the visitation of Heaven, and that my friend had foreseen it, by symptoms, and soothed me by promises of complete revenge.

It was some days before he mentioned my brother's meditated death to me again, and certainly he then found me exasperated against him personally to the highest degree. But I told him that I could not now think any more of it, owing to the late judgment of the court, by which, if my brother were missing or found dead, I would not only forfeit my life, but my friends would be ruined by the penalties.

"I suppose you know and believe in the perfect safety of your soul," said he, "and that that is a matter settled from the beginning of time, and now sealed and ratified both in heaven and earth?"

"I believe in it thoroughly and perfectly," said I; "and whenever I entertain doubts of it, I am sensible of sin and weakness."

"Very well, so then am I," said he. "I think I can now divine, with all manner of certainty, what will be the high and merited guerdon of your immortal part. Hear me then farther: I give you my solemn assurance, and bond of blood, that no human hand shall ever henceforth be able to injure your life, or shed one drop of your precious blood, but it is on the condition that you walk always by my directions."

"I will do so with cheerfulness," said I; "for without your enlightened counsel, I feel that I can do nothing. But as to your power of protecting my life, you must excuse me for doubting of it. Nay, were we in your own proper dominions, you could not ensure that."

"In whatever dominion or land I am, my power accompanies me," said he; "and it is only against human might and human weapon that I ensure your life; on that will I keep an eye, and on that you may depend. I have never broken word or promise with you. Do you credit me?"

"Yes, I do," said I; "for I see you are in earnest. I believe, though I do not comprehend you."

"Then why do you not at once challenge your brother to the field of honour? Seeing you now act without danger, cannot you also act without fear?"

"It is not fear," returned I; "believe me, I hardly know what fear is. It is a doubt, that on all these emergencies constantly haunts my mind, that in performing such and such actions I may fall from my upright state. This makes fratricide a fearful task."

"This is imbecility itself," said he. "We have settled, and agreed on that point an hundred times. I would therefore advise that you challenge your brother to single combat. I shall ensure your safety, and he cannot refuse giving you satisfaction."

"But then the penalties?" said I.

"We will try to evade these," said he; "and supposing you should be caught, if once you are Laird of Dalcastle and Balgrennan, what are the penalties to you?"

"Might we not rather pop him off in private and quietness, as we did the deistical divine?" said I.

"The deed would be alike meritorious, either way," said he. "But may we not wait for years before we find an opportunity? My advice is to challenge him, as privately as you will, and there cut him off."

"So be it then," said I. "When the moon is at the full, I will send for him forth to speak with one, and there will I smite him and slay him, and he shall trouble the righteous no more."

"Then this is the very night," said he. "The moon is nigh to the full, and this night your brother and his sinful mates hold carousal; for there is an intended journey to-morrow. The exulting profligate leaves town, where we must remain till the time of my departure hence; and then is he safe, and must live to dishonour God, and not only destroy his own soul, but those of many others. Alack, and wo is me! The sins that he and his friends will commit this very night, will cry to heaven against us for our shameful delay! When shall our great work of cleansing the sanctuary be finished, if we proceed at this puny rate?"

"I see the deed *must* be done, then," said I; "and since it is so, it shall be done. I will arm myself forthwith, and from the midst of his wine and debauchery you shall call him forth to me, and there will I smite him with the edge of the sword, that our great work be not retarded."

"If thy execution were equal to thy intent, how great a man you soon might be!" said he. "We shall make the attempt once more; and if it fail again, why, I must use other means to bring about my high purposes relating to mankind.–Home and make ready. I will go and procure what information I can regarding their motions, and will meet you in disguise twenty minutes hence, at the first turn of Hewie's lane beyond the loch."

"I have nothing to make ready," said I; "for I do not choose to go home. Bring me a sword, that we may consecrate it with prayer and vows, and if I use it not to the bringing down of the wicked and profane, then may the Lord do so to me, and more also!"

We parted, and there was I left again to the multiplicity of my own thoughts for the space of twenty minutes, a thing my friend never failed in subjecting me to, and these were worse to contend with than hosts of sinful men. I prayed inwardly, that these deeds of mine might never be brought to the knowledge of men who were incapable of appreciating the high motives that led to them; and then I sung part of the 10th Psalm, likewise in spirit; but for all these efforts, my sinful doubts returned, so that when my illustrious friend joined me, and proffered me the choice of two gilded rapiers, I declined accepting any of them, and began, in a very bold and ener-getic manner, to express my doubts regarding the justification of all the deeds of perfect men. He chided me severely, and branded me with cowardice, a thing that my nature never was subject to; and then he branded me with falsehood, and breach of the most solemn engagements both to God and man.

I was compelled to take the rapier, much against my inclination; but for all the arguments, threats, and promises that he could use, I would not consent to send a challenge to my brother by his mouth. There was one argument only that he made use of which had some weight with me, but yet it would not preponderate. He told me my brother was gone to a notorious and scandalous habitation of women, and that if I left him to himself for ever so short a space longer, it might embitter his state through ages to come. This was a trying concern to me; but I resisted it, and reverted to my doubts. On this he said that he had meant to do me honour, but since I put it out of his power, he would do the deed, and take the responsibility on himself. "I have with sore travail procured a guardship of your life," added he. "For my own, I have not; but, be that as it will, I shall not be baffled in my attempts to benefit my friends without a trial. You will at all events accompany me, and see that I get justice?"

"Certes, I will do thus much," said I; "and wo be to him if his arm prevail against my friend and patron!"

His lip curled with a smile of contempt, which I could hardly brook; and I began to be afraid that the eminence to which I had been destined by him was already fading from my view. And I thought what I should then do to ingratiate myself again with him, for without his countenance I had no life. "I will be a man in act," thought I, "but in sentiment I will not yield, and for this he must surely admire me the more."

As we emerged from the shadowy lane into the fair moonshine, I started so that my whole frame underwent the most chilling vibra-tions of surprise. I again thought I had been taken at unawares, and was conversing with another person. My friend was equipped in the Highland garb, and so completely translated into another being, that, save by his speech, all the senses of mankind could not have recognized him. I blessed myself, and asked whom it was his pleas-ure to personify to-night? He answered me carelessly, that it was a spark whom he meant should bear the blame of whatever might fall out to-night; and that was all that passed on the subject.

We proceeded by some stone steps at the foot of the North Loch, in hot argument all the way. I was afraid that our conversation might be overheard, for the night was calm and almost as light as day, and we saw sundry people crossing us as we advanced. But the zeal of my friend was so high, that he disregarded all danger, and continued to argue fiercely and loudly on my delinquency, as he was pleased to call it. I stood on one argument alone, which was, "that I did not think the Scripture promises to the elect, taken in their utmost latitude, warranted the assurance that they could do no wrong; and that, therefore, it behoved every man to look well to his steps."

There was no religious scruple that irritated my enlightened friend and master so much as this. He could not endure it. And the sentiments of our great covenanted reformers being on his side, there is not a doubt that I was wrong. He lost all patience on hearing what I advanced on this matter, and taking hold of me, he led me into a darksome booth in a confined entry; and, after a friendly but cutting reproach, he bade me remain there in secret and watch the event; "and if I fall," said he, "you will not fail to avenge my death?"

I was so entirely overcome with vexation that I could make no answer, on which he left me abruptly, a prey to despair; and I saw or heard no more, till he came down to the moonlight green followed by my brother. They had quarrelled before they came within my hearing, for the first words I heard were those of my brother, who was in a state of intoxication, and he was urging a reconciliation, as was his wont on such occasions. My friend spurned at the suggestion, and dared him to the combat; and after a good deal of boastful altercation, which the turmoil of my spirits prevented me from remembering, my brother was compelled to draw his sword and stand on the defensive. It was a desperate and terrible engagement. I at first thought that the royal stranger and great champion of the faith would overcome his opponent with ease, for I considered heaven as on his side, and nothing but the arm of sinful flesh against him. But I was deceived: The sinner stood firm as a rock, while the assailant flitted about like a shadow, or rather like a spirit. I smiled inwardly, conceiving that these lightsome manœuvres were all a sham to show off his art and mastership in the exercise, and that whenever they came to close fairly, that instant my brother would be overcome. Still I was deceived: My brother's arm seemed invincible, so that the closer they fought the more palpably did it prevail. They fought round the green to the very edge of the water, and so round, till they came close up to the covert where I stood. There being no more room to shift ground, my brother then forced him to come to close quarters, on which, the former still having the decided advantage, my friend quitted his sword, and called out. I could

resist no longer; so, springing from my concealment, I rushed between them with my sword drawn, and parted them as if they had
been two schoolboys: then turning to my brother, I addressed him
as follows:–"Wretch! miscreant! knowest thou what thou art attempting? Wouldst thou lay thine hand on the Lord's anointed, or shed
his precious blood? Turn thee to me, that I may chastise thee for all
thy wickedness, and not for the many injuries thou hast done to
me!" To it we went, with full thirst of vengeance on every side. The
duel was fierce; but the might of heaven prevailed, and not my might.
The ungodly and reprobate young man fell, covered with wounds,
and with curses and blasphemy in his mouth, while I escaped unin-
jured. Thereto his power extended not.

I will not deny, that my own immediate impressions of this affair
in some degree differed from this statement. But this is precisely as
my illustrious friend described it to me afterwards, and I can rely
implicitly on his information, as he was at that time a looker-on, and
my senses all in a state of agitation, and he could have no motive for
saying what was not the positive truth.

Never till my brother was down did we perceive that there had
been witnesses to the whole business. Our ears were then astounded
by rude challenges of unfair play, which were quite appalling to me;
but my friend laughed at them, and conducted me off in perfect safety.
As to the unfairness of the transaction, I can say thus much, that my
royal friend's sword was down ere ever mine was presented. But if
it still be accounted unfair to take up a conqueror, and punish him in
his own way, I answer: That if a man is sent on a positive mission by
his master, and hath laid himself under vows to do his work, he
ought not to be too nice in the means of accomplishing it; and farther, I appeal to holy writ, wherein many instances are recorded of
the pleasure the Lord takes in the final extinction of the wicked and
profane; and this position I take to be unanswerable.

I was greatly disturbed in my mind for many days, knowing that
the transaction had been witnessed, and sensible also of the perilous situation I occupied, owing to the late judgment of the court
against me. But, on the contrary, I never saw my enlightened friend
in such high spirits. He assured me there was no danger; and again
repeated, that he warranted my life against the power of man. I
thought proper, however, to remain in hiding for a week; but, as he
said, to my utter amazement, the blame fell on another, who was not
only accused, but pronounced guilty by the general voice, and outlawed for non-appearance! how could I doubt, after this, that the
hand of heaven was aiding and abetting me? The matter was be-

yond my comprehension; and as for my friend, he never explained any thing that was past, but his activity and art were without a parallel.

He enjoyed our success mightily; and for his sake I enjoyed it somewhat, but it was on account of his comfort only, for I could not for my life perceive in what degree the church was better or purer than before these deeds were done. He continued to flatter me with great things, as to honours, fame, and emolument; and, above all, with the blessing and protection of him to whom my body and soul were dedicated. But after these high promises, I got no longer peace; for he began to urge the death of my father with such an unremitting earnestness, that I found I had nothing for it but to comply. I did so; and cannot express his enthusiasm of approbation. So much did he hurry and press me in this, that I was forced to devise some of the most openly violent measures, having no alternative. Heaven spared me the deed, taking, in that instance, the vengeance in its own hand; for before my arm could effect the sanguine but meritorious act, the old man followed his son to the grave. My illustrious and zealous friend seemed to regret this somewhat; but he comforted himself with the reflection, that still I had the merit of it, having not only consented to it, but in fact effected it, for by doing the one action I had brought about both.

No sooner were the obsequies of the funeral over, than my friend and I went to Dalcastle, and took undisputed possession of the houses, lands, and effects that had been my father's; but his plate, and vast treasures of ready money, he had bestowed on a voluptuous and unworthy creature, who had lived long with him as a mistress. Fain would I have sent her after her lover, and gave my friend some hints on the occasion; but he only shook his head, and said that we must lay all selfish and interested motives out of the question.

For a long time, when I awaked in the morning, I could not believe my senses, that I was indeed the undisputed and sole proprietor of so much wealth and grandeur; and I felt so much gratified, that I immediately set about doing all the good I was able, hoping to meet with all approbation and encouragement from my friend. I was mistaken: He checked the very first impulses towards such a procedure, questioned my motives, and uniformly made them out to be wrong. There was one morning that a servant said to me, there was a lady in the back chamber who wanted to speak with me, but he could not tell me who it was, for all the old servants had left the mansion, every one on hearing of the death of the late laird, and those who had come knew none of the people in the neighbourhood. From several circumstances, I had suspicions of private confabulations with women, and refused to go to her, but bid the servant inquire what she wanted. She would not tell; she could only state the circumstances to me; so I, being sensible that a little dignity of manner became me in my elevated situation, returned for answer, that if it was business that could not be transacted by my steward, it must remain untransacted. The answer which the servant brought back was of a threatening nature. She stated that she *must* see me, and if I refused her satisfaction there, she would compel it where I should not evite her.

My friend and director appeared pleased with my dilemma, and rather advised that I should hear what the woman had to say; on which I consented, provided she would deliver her mission in his presence. She came in with manifest signs of anger and indignation, and began with a bold and direct charge against me of a shameful assault on one of her daughters; of having used the basest of means in order to lead her aside from the paths of rectitude; and on the failure of these, of having resorted to the most unqualified measures.

I denied the charge in all its bearings, assuring the dame that I had never so much as seen either of her daughters to my knowledge, far less wronged them; on which she got into great wrath, and abused me to my face as an accomplished vagabond, hypocrite, and sensualist; and she went so far as to tell me roundly, that if I did not *marry* her daughter, she would bring me to the gallows, and that in a very short time.

"Marry your daughter, honest woman!" said I, "on the faith of a Christian, I never saw your daughter; and you may rest assured in this, that I will neither marry you nor her. Do you consider how short a time I have been in this place? How much that time has been occupied? And how there was even a *possibility* that I could have accomplished such villainies?"

"And how long does your Christian reverence suppose you have remained in this place since the late laird's death?" said she.

"That is too well known to need recapitulation," said I: "only a very few days, though I cannot at present specify the exact number; perhaps from thirty to forty, or so. But in all that time, certes, I have never seen either you or any of your two daughters that you talk of. You must be quite sensible of that."

My friend shook his head three times during this short sentence, while the woman held up her hands in amazement and disgust, exclaiming, "There goes the self-righteous one! There goes the consecrated youth, who cannot err! You, sir, know, and the world shall know of the faith that is in this most just, devout, and religious miscreant! Can you deny that you have already been in this place four months and seven days? Or that in that time you have been forbid my house twenty times? Or that you have persevered in your endeavours to effect the basest and most ungenerous of purposes? Or that you *have* attained them? hypocrite and deceiver as you are! Yes, sir; I say, dare you deny that you *have* attained your vile, selfish, and degrading purposes towards a young, innocent, and unsuspecting creature, and thereby ruined a poor widow's only hope in this world? No, you cannot look in my face, and deny aught of this."

"The woman is raving mad!" said I. "You, illustrious sir, know, that in the first instance, I have not yet been in this place *one* month." My friend shook his head again, and answered me, "You are wrong, my dear friend; you are wrong. It is indeed the space of time that the lady hath stated, to a day, since you came here, and I came with you; and I am sorry that I know for certain that you have been frequently haunting her house, and have often had private correspondence with one of the young ladies too. Of the nature of it I presume not to know."

"You are mocking me," said I. "But as well may you try to reason me out of my existence, as to convince me that I have been here even one month, or that any of those things you allege against me has the shadow of truth or evidence to support it. I will swear to you, by the great God that made me; and by — "

"Hold, thou most abandoned profligate!" cried she violently, "and do not add perjury to your other detestable crimes. Do not, for mercy's sake, any more profane that name whose attributes you have wrested and disgraced. But tell me what reparation you propose offering to my injured child?"

"I again declare, before heaven, woman, that to the best of my knowledge and recollection, I never saw your daughter. I now think I have some faint recollection of having seen your face, but where, or in what place, puzzles me quite."

"And, why?" said she. "Because for months and days you have been in such a state of extreme inebriety, that your time has gone over like a dream that has been forgotten. I believe, that from the day you came first to my house, you have been in a state of utter delirium, and that principally from the fumes of wine and ardent spirits."

"It is a manifest falsehood!" said I; "I have never, since I entered on the possession of Dalcastle, tasted wine or spirits, saving once, a few evenings ago; and, I confess to my shame, that I was led too far; but I have craved forgiveness and obtained it. I take my noble and distinguished friend there for a witness to the truth of what I assert; a man who has done more, and sacrificed more for the sake of genuine Christianity, than any this world contains. Him you will believe."

"I hope you have attained forgiveness," said he, seriously. "Indeed it would be next to blasphemy to doubt it. But, of late, you have been very much addicted to intemperance. I doubt if, from the first night you tasted the delights of drunkenness, that you have ever again been in your right mind until Monday last. Doubtless you have been for a good while most diligent in your addresses to this lady's daughter."

"This is unaccountable," said I. "It is impossible that I can have been doing a thing, and not doing it at the same time. But indeed, honest woman, there have several incidents occurred to me in the course of my life which persuade me I have a second self; or that there is some other being who appears in my likeness."

Here my friend interrupted me with a sneer, and a hint that I was talking insanely; and then he added, turning to the lady, "I know my friend Mr. Colwan will do what is just and right. Go and bring the young lady to him, that he may see her, and he will then recollect all his former amours with her."

"I humbly beg your pardon, sir," said I. "But the mention of such a thing as *amours* with any woman existing, to me, is really so absurd, so far from my principles, so far from the purity of nature and frame to which I was born and consecrated, that I hold it as an insult, and regard it with contempt."

I would have said more in reprobation of such an idea, had not my servant entered, and said, that a gentleman wanted to see me on business. Being glad of an opportunity of getting quit of my lady visitor, I ordered the servant to show him in; and forthwith a little lean gentleman, with a long aquiline nose, and a bald head, daubed all over with powder and pomatum, entered. I thought I recollected having seen him too, but could not remember his name, though he spoke to me with the greatest familiarity; at least, that sort of familiarity that an official person generally assumes. He bustled about and about, speaking to every one, but declined listening for a single moment to any. The lady offered to withdraw, but he stopped her.

"No, no, Mrs. Keeler, you need not go; you need not go; you *must* not go, madam. The business I came about, concerns you—yes, that it does—Bad business yon of Walker's? Eh? Could not help it—did all I could, Mr. Wringhim. Done your business. Have it all cut and dry here, sir—No, this is not it—Have it among them, though—I'm at a little loss for your name, sir, (addressing my friend,)—seen you very often, though—exceedingly often—quite well acquainted with you."

"No, sir, you are not," said my friend, sternly.—The intruder never regarded him; never so much as lifted his eyes from his bundle of law papers, among which he was bustling with great hurry and importance, but went on—

"*Im*possible! Have seen a face very like it, then—what did you say your name was, sir?—very like it indeed. Is it not the young laird who was murdered whom you resemble so much?"

Here Mrs. Keeler uttered a scream, which so much startled me, that it seems I grew pale. And on looking at my friend's face, there was something struck me so forcibly in the likeness between him and my late brother, that I had very nearly fainted. The woman exclaimed, that it was my brother's spirit that stood beside me.

"*Im*possible!" exclaimed the attorney; "at least I hope not, else his signature is not worth a pin. There is some balance due on yon business, madam. Do you wish your account? because I have it here, ready discharged, and it does not suit letting such things lie over. This business of Mr. Colwan's will be a severe one on you, madam,—*ra*ther a severe one."

"What business of mine, if it be your will, sir," said I. "For my part I never engaged you in business of any sort, less or more." He never regarded me, but went on. "You may appeal, though: Yes, yes, there are such things as appeals for the refractory. Here it is, gentlemen,—here they are all together—Here is, in the first place, sir, your power of attorney, regularly warranted, sealed, and signed with your own hand."

"I declare solemnly that I never signed that document," said I.

"Ay, ay, the system of denial is not a bad one in general," said my attorney; "but at present there is no occasion for it. You do not deny your own hand?"

"I deny every thing connected with the business," cried I; "I disclaim it *in toto*, and declare that I know no more about it than the child unborn."

"That is exceedingly good!" exclaimed he; "I like your pertinacity vastly! I have three of your letters, and three of your signatures; that part is all settled, and I hope so is the whole affair; for here is the original grant to your father, which he has never thought proper to put in requisition. Simple gentleman! But here have I, Lawyer Linkum, in one hundredth part of the time that any other notary, writer, attorney, or writer to the signet in Britain, would have done it, procured the signature of his Majesty's commissioner, and thereby confirmed the charter to you and your house, sir, for ever and ever,– Begging your pardon, madam." The lady, as well as myself, tried several times to interrupt the loquacity of Linkum, but in vain: he only raised his hand with a quick flourish, and went on:–

"Here it is:–'JAMES, by the grace of God, King of Great Britain, France, and Ireland, to his right trust cousin, sendeth greeting: And whereas his right leal and trust-worthy cousin, George Colwan, of Dalcastle and Balgrennan, hath suffered great losses, and undergone much hardship, on behalf of his Majesty's rights and titles; he therefore, for himself, and as prince and steward of Scotland, and by the consent of his right trusty cousins and councillors, hereby grants to the said George Colwan, his heirs and assignees whatsomever, heritably and irrevocably, all and haill the lands and others underwritten: *To wit*, All and haill, the five merk land of Kipplerig; the five pound land of Easter Knockward, with all the towers, fortalices, manor-places, houses, biggings, yards, orchards, tofts, crofts, mills, woods, fishings, mosses, muirs, meadows, commonties, pasturages, coals, coal-heughs, tenants, tenantries, services of free tenants, annexes, connexes, dependencies, parts, pendicles, and pertinents of the same whatsomever; to be peaceably brooked, joysed, set, used, and disposed of by him and his aboves, as specified, heritably and irrevocably, in all time coming: And, in testimony thereof, His Majesty, for himself, and as prince and steward of Scotland, with the advice and consent of his foresaids, knowledge, proper motive, and kingly power, makes, erects, creates, unites, annexes, and incorporates, the whole lands above mentioned in an haill and free barony, by all the rights, miethes, and marches thereof, old and divided, as the same lies, in length and breadth, in houses, biggings, mills, multures, hawking, hunting, fishing; with court, plaint, herezeld, fock, fork, sack, sock, thole, thame, vert, wraik, waith, wair, venison, outfang thief, infang thief, pit and gallows, and all and sundry other commodities. Given at our Court of Whitehall, &c. &c. God save the King.

'*Compositio* 5 *lib*. 13. 8.
'Registrate 26th September, 1687.'

"See, madam, here are ten signatures of privy councillors of that year, and here are other ten of the present year, with his Grace the Duke of Queensberry at the head. All right–See here it is, sir,–all right–done your work. So you see, madam, this gentleman is the true and sole heritor of all the land that your father possesses, with all the rents thereof for the last twenty years, and upwards—Fine job for my employers!—sorry on your account, madam—can't help it."

I was again going to disclaim all interest or connection in the matter, but my friend stopped me; and the plaints and lamentations of the dame became so overpowering, that they put an end to all farther colloquy; but Lawyer Linkum followed me, and stated his great outlay, and the important services he had rendered me, until I was obliged to subscribe an order to him for £100 on my banker.

I was now glad to retire with my friend, and ask seriously for some explanation of all this. It was in the highest degree unsatisfactory. He confirmed all that had been stated to me; assuring me, that I had not only been assiduous in my endeavours to seduce a young lady of great beauty, which it seemed I had effected, but that I had taken counsel, and got this supposed, old, false, and forged grant, raked up and new signed, to ruin the young lady's family quite, so as to throw her entirely on myself for protection, and be wholly at my will.

This was to me wholly incomprehensible. I could have freely made oath to the contrary of every particular. Yet the evidences were against me, and of a nature not to be denied. Here I must confess, that, highly as I disapproved of the love of women, and all intimacies and connections with the sex, I felt a sort of indefinite pleasure, an ungracious delight in having a beautiful woman solely at my disposal. But I thought of her spiritual good in the meantime. My friend spoke of my backslidings with concern; requesting me to make sure of my forgiveness, and to forsake them; and then he added some words of sweet comfort. But from this time forth I began to be sick at times of my existence. I had heart-burnings, longings, and yearnings, that would not be satisfied; and I seemed hardly to be an accountable creature; being thus in the habit of executing transactions of the utmost moment, without being sensible that I did them. I was a being incomprehensible to myself. Either I had a second self, who transacted business in my likeness, or else my body was at times possessed by a spirit over which it had no controul, and of whose actions my own soul was wholly unconscious. This was an anomaly not to be accounted for by any philosophy of mine, and I was many times, in contemplating it, excited to terrors and mental torments hardly describable. To be in a state of consciousness and unconsciousness, at the same time, in the same body and same spirit, was impossible. I was under the greatest anxiety, dreading some change would take place momently in my nature; for of dates I could make nothing: one-half, or two-thirds of my time, seemed to me to be totally lost. I often, about this time, prayed with great fervour, and lamented my hopeless condition, especially in being liable to the commission of crimes, which I was not sensible of, and could not eschew. And I confess, notwithstanding the promises on which I had been taught to rely, I began to have secret terrors, that the great enemy of man's salvation was exercising powers over me, that might eventually lead to my ruin. These were but temporary and sinful fears, but they added greatly to my unhappiness.

The worst thing of all was, what hitherto I had never felt, and, as yet, durst not confess to myself, that the presence of my illustrious and devoted friend was becoming irksome to me. When I was by myself, I breathed freer, and my step was lighter; but, when he ap-proached, a pang went to my heart, and, in his company, I moved and acted as if under a load that I could hardly endure. What a state to be in! And yet to shake him off was impossible—we were incorpo-rated together—identified with one another, as it were, and the power was not in me to separate myself from him. I still knew nothing who he was, farther than that he was a potentate of some foreign land, bent on establishing some pure and genuine doctrines of Christian-ity, hitherto only half understood, and less than half exercised. Of this I could have no doubts, after all that he had said, done, and suffered in the cause. But, alongst with this, I was also certain, that he was possessed of some supernatural power, of the source of which I was wholly ignorant. That a man could be a Christian, and at the same time a powerful necromancer, appeared inconsistent, and ad-verse to every principle taught in our church; and from this I was led to believe, that he inherited his powers from on high, for I could not doubt either of the soundness of his principles, or that he accom-plished things impossible to account for.

Thus was I sojourning in the midst of a chaos of confusion. I looked back on my bypast life with pain, as one looks back on a perilous journey, in which he has attained his end, without gaining any advantage either to himself, or others; and I looked forward, as on a darksome waste, full of repulsive and terrific shapes, pitfalls, and precipices, to which there was no definite bourne, and from which I turned with disgust. With my riches, my unhappiness was increased tenfold; and here, with another great acquisition of prop-erty, for which I had pleaed, and which I had gained in a dream, my miseries and difficulties were increasing. My principal feeling, about this time, was an insatiable longing for something that I cannot de-scribe or denominate properly, unless I say it was for *utter oblivion* that I longed. I desired to sleep; but it was for a deeper and longer sleep, than that in which the senses were nightly steeped. I longed to be at rest and quiet, and close my eyes on the past and the future alike, as far as this frail life was concerned. But what had been formerly and finally settled in the counsels above, I presumed not to call in question.

In this state of irritation and misery, was I dragging on an existence, disgusted with all around me, and in particular with my mother, who, with all her love and anxiety, had such an insufferable mode of manifesting them, that she had by this time rendered herself exceedingly obnoxious to me. The very sound of her voice at a distance, went to my heart like an arrow, and made all my nerves to shrink; and as for the beautiful young lady of whom they told me I had been so much enamoured, I shunned all intercourse with her or hers, as I would have done with the devil. I read some of their letters and burnt them, but refused to see either the young lady or her mother, on any account.

About this time it was, that my worthy and reverend parent came with one of his elders to see my mother and myself. His presence always brought joy with it into our family, for my mother was uplifted, and I had so few who cared for me, or for whom I cared, that I felt rather gratified at seeing him. My illustrious friend was also much more attached to him, than any other person, (except myself,) for their religious principles tallied in every point, and their conversation was interesting, serious, and sublime. Being anxious to entertain well and highly the man to whom I had been so much indebted, and knowing that with all his integrity and righteousness, he disdained not the good things of this life, I brought from the late laird's well-stored cellars, various fragrant and salubrious wines, and we drank and became merry, and I found that my miseries and overpowering calamities, passed away over my head like a shower that is driven by the wind. I became elevated and happy, and welcomed my guests an hundred times; and then I joined them in religious conversation, with a zeal and enthusiasm which I had not often experienced, and which made all their hearts rejoice, so that I said to myself, "Surely every gift of God is a blessing, and ought to be used with liberality and thankfulness."

The next day I waked from a profound and feverish sleep, and called for something to drink. There was a servant answered whom I had never seen before, and he was clad in my servant's clothes and livery. I asked for Andrew Handyside, the servant who had waited at table the night before; but the man answered with a stare and a smile.

"What do you mean, sirrah," said I. "Pray what do you here? or what are you pleased to laugh at? I desire you to go about your business, and send me up Handyside. I want him to bring me something to drink."

"Ye sanna want a drink, maister," said the fellow: "Tak a hearty ane, and see if it will wauken ye up something, sae that ye dinna ca' for ghaists through your sleep. Surely ye haena forgotten that Andrew Handyside has been in his grave these six months?"

This was a stunning blow to me. I could not answer farther, but sunk back on my pillow as if I had been a lump of lead, refusing to take a drink or any thing else at the fellow's hand, who seemed thus mocking me with so grave a face. The man seemed sorry, and grieved at my being offended, but I ordered him away, and continued sullen and thoughtful. Could I have again been for a season in utter oblivion to myself, and transacting business which I neither approved of, nor had any connection with! I tried to recollect something in which I might have been engaged, but nothing was pourtrayed on my mind subsequent to the parting with my friends at a late hour the evening before. The evening before it certainly was: but if so, how came it, that Andrew Handyside, who served at table that evening, should have been in his grave six months! This was a circumstance somewhat equivocal; therefore, being afraid to arise lest accusations of I knew not what might come against me, I was obliged to call once more in order to come at what intelligence I could. The same fellow appeared to receive my orders as before, and I set about examining him with regard to particulars. He told me his name was Scrape; that I hired him myself; of whom I hired him; and at whose recommendation. I smiled, and nodded so as to let the knave see I understood he was telling me a chain of falsehoods, but did not choose to begin with any violent asseverations to the contrary.

"And where is my noble friend and companion?" said I. "How has he been engaged in the interim?"

"I dinna ken him, sir," said Scrape; "but have heard it said, that the strange mysterious person that attended you, him that the maist part of folks countit uncanny, had gane awa wi' a Mr. Ringan o' Glasko last year, and had never returned."

I thanked the Lord in my heart for this intelligence, hoping that the illustrious stranger had returned to his own land and people, and that I should thenceforth be rid of his controlling and appalling presence. "And where is my mother?" said I.—The man's breath cut short, and he looked at me without returning any answer.—"I ask you where my mother is?" said I.

"God only knows, and not I, where she is," returned he. "He knows where her soul is, and as for her body, if you dinna ken something o' it, I suppose nae man alive does."

"What do you mean, you knave?" said I. "What dark hints are these you are throwing out? Tell me precisely and distinctly what you know of my mother?"

"It is unco queer o' ye to forget, or pretend to forget every thing that gate, the day, sir," said he. "I'm sure you heard enough about it yestreen; an' I can tell you, there are some gayan ill-faurd stories gaun about that business. But as the thing is to be tried afore the circuit lords, it wad be far wrang to say either this or that to influence the public mind; it is best just to let justice tak its swee. I hae naething to say, sir. Ye hae been a good enough maister to me, and paid my wages regularly, but ye hae muckle need to be innocent, for there are some heavy accusations rising against you."

"I fear no accusations of man," said I, "as long as I can justify my cause in the sight of Heaven; and that I can do this I am well aware. Go you and bring me some wine and water, and some other clothes than these gaudy and glaring ones."

I took a cup of wine and water; put on my black clothes, and walked out. For all the perplexity that surrounded me, I felt my spirits considerably buoyant. It appeared that I was rid of the two greatest bars to my happiness, by what agency I knew not. My mother, it seemed, was gone, who had become a grievous thorn in my side of late, and my great companion and counsellor, who tyrannized over every spontaneous movement of my heart, had likewise taken himself off. This last was an unspeakable relief; for I found that for a long season I had only been able to act by the motions of his mysterious mind and spirit. I therefore thanked God for my deliverance, and strode through my woods with a daring and heroic step; with independence in my eye, and freedom swinging in my right hand.

At the extremity of the Colwan wood, I perceived a figure approaching me with slow and dignified motion. The moment that I beheld it, my whole frame received a shock as if the ground on which I walked had sunk suddenly below me. Yet, at that moment, I knew not who it was; it was the air and motion of some one that I dreaded, and from whom I would gladly have escaped; but this I even had not power to attempt. It came slowly onward, and I advanced as slowly to meet it; yet when we came within speech, I still knew not who it was. It bore the figure, air, and features of my late brother, I thought, exactly; yet in all these there were traits so forbidding, so mixed with appearance of misery, chagrin, and despair, that I still shrunk from the view, not knowing on whose face I looked. But when the being spoke, both my mental and bodily frame received another shock more terrible than the first, for it was the voice of the great personage I had so long denominated my friend, of whom I had deemed myself for ever freed, and whose presence and counsels I now dreaded more than hell. It was his voice, but so altered–I shall never forget it till my dying day. Nay, I can scarce conceive it possible that any earthly sounds could be so discordant, so repulsive to every feeling of a human soul, as the tones of the voice that grated on my ear at that moment. They were the sounds of the pit, wheezed through a grated cranny, or seemed so to my distempered imagination.

"So! Thou shudderest at my approach now, dost thou?" said he. "Is this all the gratitude that you deign for an attachment of which the annals of the world furnish no parallel? An attachment which has caused me to forego power and dominion, might, homage, conquest and adulation, all that I might gain one highly valued and sanctified spirit, to my great and true principles of reformation among mankind. Wherein have I offended? What have I done for evil, or what have I not done for your good, that you would thus shun my presence?"

"Great and magnificent prince," said I humbly, "let me request of you to abandon a poor worthless wight to his own wayward fortune, and return to the dominion of your people. I am unworthy of the sacrifices you have made for my sake; and after all your efforts, I do not feel that you have rendered me either more virtuous or more happy. For the sake of that which is estimable in human nature, depart from me to your own home, before you render me a being either altogether above, or below the rest of my fellow creatures. Let me plod on towards heaven and happiness in my own way, like those that have gone before me, and I promise to stick fast by the great principles which you have so strenuously inculcated, on condition that you depart and leave me for ever."

"Sooner shall you make the mother abandon the child of her bosom; nay, sooner cause the shadow to relinquish the substance, than separate me from your side. Our beings are amalgamated, as it were, and consociated in one, and never shall I depart from this country until I can carry you in triumph with me."

I can in nowise describe the effect this appalling speech had on me. It was like the announcement of death to one who had of late deemed himself free, if not of something worse than death, and of longer continuance. There was I doomed to remain in misery, subjugated, soul and body, to one whose presence was become more intolerable to me than ought on earth could compensate: And at that moment, when he beheld the anguish of my soul, he could not conceal that he enjoyed it. I was troubled for an answer, for which he was waiting: it became incumbent on me to say something after such a protestation of attachment; and, in some degree to shake the validity of it, I asked, with great simplicity, where he had been all this while?

"Your crimes and your extravagancies forced me from your side for a season," said he; "but now that I hope the day of grace is returned, I am again drawn towards you by an affection that has neither bounds nor interest; an affection for which I receive not even the poor return of gratitude, and which seems to have its radical sources in fascination. I have been far, far abroad, and have seen much, and transacted much, since I last spoke with you. During that space, I grievously suspect that you have been guilty of great crimes and misdemeanours, crimes that would have sunk an unregenerated person to perdition; but as I knew it to be only a temporary falling off, a specimen of that liberty by which the chosen and elected ones are made free, I closed my eyes on the wilful debasement of our principles, knowing that the transgressions could never be accounted to your charge, and that in good time you would come to your senses, and throw the whole weight of your crimes on the shoulders that had voluntarily stooped to receive the load."

"Certainly I will," said I, "as I and all the justified have a good right to do. But what crimes? What misdemeanours and transgressions do you talk about? For my part, I am conscious of none, and am utterly amazed at insinuations which I do not comprehend."

"You have certainly been left to yourself for a season," returned he, "having gone on rather like a person in a delirium, than a Christian in his sober senses. You are accused of having made away with your mother privately; as also of the death of a beautiful young lady, whose affections you had seduced."

"It is an intolerable and monstrous falsehood!" cried I, interrupting him; "I never laid a hand on a woman to take away her life, and have even shunned their society from my childhood: I know nothing of my mother's exit, nor of that young lady's whom you mention—Nothing whatever."

"I hope it is so," said he. "But it seems there are some strong presumptuous proofs against you, and I came to warn you this day that a precognition is in progress, and that unless you are perfectly convinced, not only of your innocence, but of your ability to prove it, it will be the safest course for you to abscond, and let the trial go on without you."

"Never shall it be said that I shrunk from such a trial as this," said I. "It would give grounds for suspicions of guilt that never had existence, even in thought. I will go and show myself in every public place, that no slanderous tongue may wag against me. I have shed the blood of sinners, but of these deaths I am guiltless; therefore, I will face every tribunal, and put all my accusers down."

"Asseveration will avail you but little," answered he, composedly: "It is, however, justifiable in its place, although to me it signifies nothing, who know too well that you *did* commit both crimes, in your own person, and with your own hands. Far be it from me to betray you; indeed, I would rather endeavour to palliate the offences; for though adverse to nature, I can prove them not to be so to the cause of pure Christianity, by the mode of which we have approved of it, and which we wish to promulgate."

"If this that you tell me be true," said I, "then is it as true that I have two souls, which take possession of my bodily frame by turns, the one being all unconscious of what the other performs; for as sure as I have at this moment a spirit within me, fashioned and destined to eternal felicity, as sure am I utterly ignorant of the crimes you now lay to my charge."

"Your supposition may be true in effect," said he. "We are all subjected to two distinct natures in the same person. I myself have suffered grievously in that way. The spirit that now directs my energies is not that with which I was endowed at my creation. It is changed within me, and so is my whole nature. My former days were those of grandeur and felicity. But, would you believe it? *I was not then a Christian.* Now I am. I have been converted to its truths by passing through the fire, and since my final conversion, my misery has been extreme. You complain that I have not been able to render you more happy than you were. Alas! do you expect it in the difficult and exterminating career which you have begun. I, however, promise you this—a portion of the only happiness which I enjoy, sublime in its motions, and splendid in its attainments—I will place you on the right hand of my throne, and show you the grandeur of my domains, and the felicity of my millions of true professors."

I was once more humbled before this mighty potentate, and promised to be ruled wholly by his directions, although at that moment my nature shrunk from the concessions, and my soul longed rather to be inclosed in the deeps of the sea, or involved once more in utter oblivion. I was like Daniel in the den of lions, without his faith in divine support, and wholly at their mercy. I felt as one round whose body a deadly snake is twisted, which continues to hold him in its fangs, without injuring him, farther than in moving its scaly infernal folds with exulting delight, to let its victim feel to whose power he has subjected himself; and thus did I for a space drag an existence from day to day, in utter weariness and helplessness; at one time worshipping with great fervour of spirit, and at other times so wholly left to myself, as to work all manner of vices and follies with greediness. In these my enlightened friend never accompanied me, but I always observed that he was the first to lead me to every one of them, and then leave me in the lurch. The next day, after these my fallings off, he never failed to reprove me gently, blaming me for my venial transgressions; but then he had the art of reconciling all, by reverting to my justified and infallible state, which I found to prove a delightful healing salve for every sore.

But, of all my troubles, this was the chief: I was every day and every hour assailed with accusations of deeds of which I was wholly ignorant; of acts of cruelty, injustice, defamation, and deceit; of pieces of business which I could not be made to comprehend; with lawsuits, details, arrestments of judgment, and a thousand interminable quibbles from the mouth of my loquacious and conceited attorney. So miserable was my life rendered by these continued attacks, that I was often obliged to lock myself up for days together, never seeing any person save my man Samuel Scrape, who was a very honest blunt fellow, a staunch Cameronian, but withal very little conversant in religious matters. He said he came from a place called Penpunt, which I thought a name so ludicrous, that I called him by the name of his native village, an appellation of which he was very proud, and answered every thing with more civility and perspicuity when I denominated him Penpunt, than Samuel, his own Christian name. Of this peasant was I obliged to make a companion on sundry occasions, and strange indeed were the details which he gave me concerning myself, and the ideas of the country people concerning me. I took down a few of these in writing, to put off the time, and here leave them on record to show how the best and greatest actions are misconstrued among sinful and ignorant men.

"You say, Samuel, that I hired you myself—that I have been a good enough master to you, and have paid you your weekly wages punctually. Now, how is it that you say this, knowing, as you do, that I never hired you, and never paid you a sixpence of wages in the whole course of my life, excepting this last month?"

"Ye may as weel say, master, that water's no water, or that stanes are no stanes. But that's just your gate, an' it is a great pity aye to do a thing an' profess the clean contrair. Weel then, since you havena paid me ony wages, an' I can prove day and date when I was hired, an' came hame to your service, will you be sae kind as to pay me now? That's the best way o' curing a man o' the mortal disease o' leasing-making that I ken o'."

"I should think that Penpunt and Cameronian principles, would not admit of a man taking twice payment for the same article."

"In sic a case as this, sir, it disna hinge upon principles, but a piece o' good manners; an' I can tell you that at sic a crisis, a Cameronian is a gayan weel-bred man. He's driven to this, that he maun either make a breach in his friend's good name, or in his purse; an' O, sir, whilk o' thae, think you, is the most precious? For instance, an a Galloway drover had comed to the town o' Penpunt, an' said to a Cameronian, (the folk's a' Cameronians there,) 'Sir, I want to buy your cow.' 'Vera weel,' says the Cameronian, 'I just want to sell the cow, sae gie me twanty punds Scots, an' take her w'ye.' It's a bargain. The drover takes away the cow, an' gies the Cameronian his twanty pund Scots. But after that, he meets him again on the white sands, amang a' the drovers an' dealers o' the land, an' the Gallowayman, he says to the Cameronian, afore a' thae witnesses, 'Come, Master Whiggam, I hae never paid you for yon bit useless cow, that I bought, I'll pay her the day, but you maun mind the luck-penny; there's muckle need for't,'—or something to that purpose. The Cameronian then turns out to be a civil man, an' canna bide to make the man baith a feele an' liar at the same time, afore a' his associates; an' therefore he pits his principles aff at the side, to be a kind o' sleepin partner, as it war, an' brings up his good breeding to stand at the counter: he pockets the money, gies the Galloway drover time o' day, an' comes his way. An' wha's to blame? *Man mind yoursel* is the first commandment. A Cameronian's princi-ples never came atween him an' his purse, nor sanna in the present case; for as I canna bide to make you out a leear, I'll thank you for my wages."

"Well, you shall have them, Samuel, if you declare to me that I hired you myself in this same person, and bargained with you with this same tongue, and voice, with which I speak to you just now."

"That I do declare, unless ye hae twa persons o' the same ap-pearance, and twa tongues to the same voice. But, od saif us, sir, do you ken what the auld wives o' the clachan say about you?"

"How should I, when no one repeats it to me?"

"Oo, I trow it's a' stuff;—folk shouldna heed what's said by auld crazy kimmers. But there are some o' them weel kend for witches too; an' they say,—lord have a care o' us!—they say the deil's often seen gaun sidie for sidie w'ye, whiles in ae shape, an' whiles in another. An' they say that he whiles takes your ain shape, or else enters into you, and then you turn a deil yoursel."

I was so astounded at this terrible idea that had gone abroad, regarding my fellowship with the prince of darkness, that I could make no answer to the fellow's information, but sat like one in a stupor; and if it had not been for my well-founded faith, and conviction that I was a chosen and elected one before the world was made, I should at that moment have given into the popular belief, and fallen into the sin of despondency; but I was preserved from such a fatal error by an inward and unseen supporter. Still the insinuation was so like what I felt myself, that I was greatly awed and confounded.

The poor fellow observed this, and tried to do away the impression by some farther sage remarks of his own.

"Hout, dear sir, it is balderdash, there's nae doubt o't. It is the crownhead o' absurdity to tak in the havers o' auld wives for gospel. I told them that my master was a peeous man, an' a sensible man; an' for praying, that he could ding auld Macmillan himsel. 'Sae could the deil,' they said, 'when he liket, either at preaching or praying, if these war to answer his ain ends.' 'Na, na,' says I, 'but he's a strick believer in a' the truths o' Christianity, my master.' They said, sae was Satan, for that he was the firmest believer in a' the truths of Christianity that was out o' heaven; an' that, sin' the Revolution that the gospel had turned sae rife, he had been often driven to the shift o' preaching it himsel, for the purpose o' getting some wrang tenets introduced into it, and thereby turning it into blasphemy and ridicule."

I confess, to my shame, that I was so overcome by this jumble of nonsense, that a chillness came over me, and in spite of all my efforts to shake off the impression it had made, I fell into a faint. Samuel soon brought me to myself, and after a deep draught of wine and water, I was greatly revived, and felt my spirit rise above the sphere of vulgar conceptions, and the restrained views of unregenerate men. The shrewd but loquacious fellow, perceiving this, tried to make some amends for the pain he had occasioned to me, by the following story, which I noted down, and which was brought on by a conversation to the following purport:—

"Now, Penpunt, you may tell me all that passed between you and the wives of the clachan. I am better of that stomach qualm, with which I am sometimes seized, and shall be much amused by hearing the sentiments of noted witches regarding myself and my connections."

"Weel, you see, sir, I says to them, 'It will be lang afore the deil intermeddle wi' as serious a professor, and as fervent a prayer as my master, for gin he gets the upper hand o' sickan men, wha's to be safe?' An', what think ye they said, sir? There was ane Lucky Shaw set up her lang lantern chafts, an' answered me, an' a' the rest shanned and noddit in assent an' approbation: 'Ye silly, sauchless, Cameronian cuif!' quo she, 'is that a' that ye ken about the wiles and doings o' the prince o' the air, that rules an' works in the bairns of disobedience? Gin ever he observes a proud professor, wha has mae than ordinary pretensions to a divine calling, and that reards and prays till the very howlets learn his preambles, *that's* the man Auld Simmie fixes on to mak a dishclout o'. He canna get rest in hell, if he sees a man, or a set of men o' this stamp, an' when he sets fairly to wark, it is seldom that he disna bring them round till his ain measures by hook or by crook. Then, O it is a grand prize for him, an' a proud deil he is, when he gangs hame to his ain ha', wi' a batch o' the souls o' sic strenuous professors on his back. Ay, I trow, auld Ingleby, the Liverpool packman, never came up Glasco street wi' prouder pomp, when he had ten horse-laids afore him o' Flanders lace, an' Hollin lawn, an' silks an' satins frae the eastern Indians, than Satan wad strodge into hell with a pack-laid o' the souls o' proud professors on his braid shoulders. Ha, ha, ha! I think I see how the auld thief wad be gaun through his gizened dominions, crying his wares, in derision, "Wha will buy a fresh, cauler divine, a bouzy bishop, a fasting zealot, or a piping priest? For a' their prayers an' their praises, their aumuses, an' their penances, their whinings, their howlings, their rantings, an' their ravings, here they come at last! Behold the end! Here go the rare and precious wares! A fat professor for a bodle, an' a lean ane for half a merk!"' I declare, I trembled at the auld hag's ravings, but the lave o' the kimmers applauded the sayings as sacred truths. An' then Lucky went on: 'There are many wolves in sheep's claithing, among us, my man; mony deils aneath the masks o' zealous professors, roaming about in kirks and meeting-houses o' the land. It was but the year afore the last, that the people o' the town o' Auchtermuchty grew so rigidly righteous, that the meanest hind among them became a shining light in ither towns an' parishes. There was nought to be heard, neither

night nor day, but preaching, praying, argumentation, an' catechis-
ing in a' the famous town o' Auchtermuchty. The young men wooed
their sweethearts out o' the Song o' Solomon, an' the girls returned
answers in strings o' verses out o' the Psalms. At the lint-swinglings,
they said questions round; and read chapters, and sang hymns at
bridals; auld and young prayed in their dreams, an' prophesied in
their sleep, till the deils in the farrest nooks o' hell were alarmed,
and moved to commotion. Gin it hadna been an auld carl, Robin
Ruthven, Auchtermuchty wad at that time hae been ruined and lost
for ever. But Robin was a cunning man, an' had rather mae wits
than his ain, for he had been in the hands o' the fairies when he was
young, an' a' kinds o' spirits were visible to his een, an' their language as familiar to him as his ain mother tongue. Robin was sitting
on the side o' the West Lowmond, ae still gloomy night in September, when he saw a bridal o' corbie craws coming east the lift, just
on the edge o' the gloaming. The moment that Robin saw them, he
kenned, by their movements, that they were craws o' some ither
warld than this; so he signed himself, and crap into the middle o' his
bourock. The corbie craws came a' an' sat down round about him,
an' they poukit their black sooty wings, an' spread them out to the
breeze to cool; and Robin heard ae corbie speaking, an' another
answering him; and the tane said to the tither: "Where will the ravens
find a prey the night?"–"On the lean crazy souls o' Auchtermuchty,"
quo the tither.–"I fear they will be o'er weel wrappit up in the warm
flannens o' faith, an' clouted wi' the dirty duds o' repentance, for us
to mak a meal o'," quo the first.–"Whaten vile sounds are these that
I hear coming bumming up the hill?" "O these are the hymns and
praises o' the auld wives and creeshy louns o' Auchtermuchty, wha
are gaun crooning their way to heaven; an' gin it warna for the shame
o' being beat, we might let our great enemy tak them. For sic a prize
as he will hae! Heaven, forsooth! What shall we think o' heaven, if
it is to be filled wi' vermin like thae, amang whom there is mair
poverty and pollution, than I can name." "No matter for that," said
the first, "we cannot have our power set at defiance; though we
should put them in the thief's hole, we must catch them, and catch
them with their own bait too. Come all to church to-morrow, and I'll
let you hear how I'll gull the saints of Auchtermuchty. In the mean
time, there is a feast on the Sidlaw hills to-night, below the hill of
Macbeth,–Mount, Diabolus, and fly." Then, with loud croaking and
crowing, the bridal of corbies again scaled the dusky air, and left
Robin Ruthven in the middle of his cairn.

" 'The next day the congregation met in the kirk of Auchtermuchty, but the minister made not his appearance. The elders ran out and in, making inquiries; but they could learn nothing, save that the minister was missing. They ordered the clerk to sing a part of the 119th Psalm, until they saw if the minister would cast up. The clerk did as he was ordered, and by the time he reached the 77th verse, a strange divine entered the church, by the *western door*, and advanced solemnly up to the pulpit. The eyes of all the congregation were riveted on the sublime stranger, who was clothed in a robe of black sackcloth, that flowed all around him, and trailed far behind, and they weened him an angel, come to exhort them, in disguise. He read out his text from the Prophecies of Ezekiel, which consisted of these singular words: "I will overturn, overturn, overturn it; and it shall be no more, until he come, whose right it is, and I will give it him."

" 'From these words he preached such a sermon as never was heard by human ears, at least never by ears of Auchtermuchty. It was a true, sterling, gospel sermon—it was striking, sublime, and awful in the extreme. He finally made out the IT, mentioned in the text, to mean, properly and positively, the notable town of Auchtermuchty. He proved all the people in it, to their perfect satisfaction, to be in the gall of bitterness and bond of iniquity, and he assured them, that God would overturn them, their principles, and professions; and that they should be no more, until the devil, the town's greatest enemy, came, and then it should be given unto him for a prey, for it was his right, and to him it belonged, if there was not forthwith a radical change made in all their opinions and modes of worship.

" 'The inhabitants of Auchtermuchty were electrified—they were charmed; they were actually raving mad about the grand and sublime truths delivered to them, by this eloquent and impressive preacher of Christianity. "He is a prophet of the Lord," said one, "sent to warn us, as Jonah was sent to the Ninevites." "O, he is an angel sent from heaven, to instruct this great city," said another, "for no man ever uttered truths so sublime before." The good people of Auchtermuchty were in perfect raptures with the preacher, who had thus sent them to hell by the slump, tag, rag, and bobtail! Nothing in the world delights a truly religious people so much, as consigning them to eternal damnation. They wondered after the preacher—they crowded together, and spoke of his sermon with admiration, and still as they conversed, the wonder and the admiration increased; so that honest Robin Ruthven's words would not be listened to. It was in vain that he told them he heard a raven speaking, and another raven answering him: the people laughed him to scorn, and kicked him out of their assemblies, as a one who spoke evil of dignities; and they called him a warlock, an' a daft body, to think to mak language out o' the crouping o' craws.

" 'The sublime preacher could not be heard of, although all the country was sought for him, even to the minutest corner of St. Johnston and Dundee; but as he had announced another sermon on the same text, on a certain day, all the inhabitants of that populous country, far and near, flocked to Auchtermuchty. Cupar, Newburgh, and Strathmiglo, turned out men, women, and children. Perth and Dundee gave their thousands; and from the East Nook of Fife to the foot of the Grampian hills, there was nothing but running and riding that morning to Auchtermuchty. The kirk would not hold the thousandth part of them. A splendid tent was erected on the brae north of the town, and round that the countless congregation assembled. When they were all waiting anxiously for the great preacher, behold, Robin Ruthven set up his head in the tent, and warned his countrymen to beware of the doctrines they were about to hear, for he could prove, to their satisfaction, that they were all false, and tended to their destruction!

" 'The whole multitude raised a cry of indignation against Robin, and dragged him from the tent, the elders rebuking him, and the multitude threatening to resort to stronger measures; and though he told them a plain and unsophisticated tale of the black corbies, he was only derided. The great preacher appeared once more, and went through his two discourses with increased energy and approbation. All who heard him were amazed, and many of them went into fits, writhing and foaming in a state of the most horrid agitation. Robin Ruthven sat on the outskirts of the great assembly, listening with the rest, and perceived what they, in the height of their enthusiasm, perceived not,—the ruinous tendency of the tenets so sublimely inculcated. Robin kenned the voice of his friend the corby-craw again, and was sure he could not be wrang: sae when public worship was finished, a' the elders an' a' the gentry flocked about the great preacher, as he stood on the green brae in the sight of the hale congregation, an' a' war alike anxious to pay him some mark o' respect. Robin Ruthven came in amang the thrang, to try to effect what he had promised; and, with the greatest readiness and simplicity, just took haud o' the side an' wide gown, an' in sight of a' present, held it aside as high as the preacher's knee, and behold, there was a pair o' cloven feet! The auld thief was fairly catched in the very height o' his proud conquest, an' put down by an auld carl.

He could feign nae mair, but gnashing on Robin wi' his teeth, he dartit into the air like a fiery dragon, an' keust a reid rainbow our the taps o' the Lowmonds.

" 'A' the auld wives an' weavers o' Auchtermuchty fell down flat wi' affright, an' betook them to their prayers aince again, for they saw the dreadfu' danger they had escapit, an' frae that day to this it is a hard matter to gar an Auchtermuchty man listen to a sermon at a', an' a harder ane still to gar him applaud ane, for he thinks aye that he sees the cloven foot peeping out frae aneath ilka sentence.

" 'Now, this is a true story, my man,' quo the auld wife; 'an' whenever you are doubtfu' of a man, take auld Robin Ruthven's plan, an' look for the cloven foot, for it's a thing that winna weel hide; an' it appears whiles where ane wadna think o't. It will keek out frae aneath the parson's gown, the lawyer's wig, and the Cameronian's blue bannet; but still there is a gouden rule whereby to detect it, an' that never, never fails.'–The auld witch didna gie me the rule, an' though I hae heard tell o't often an' often, shame fa' me an I ken what it is! But ye will ken it well, an' it wad be nae the waur of a trial on some o' your friends, maybe; for they say there's a certain gentleman seen walking wi' you whiles, that, wherever he sets his foot, the grass withers as gin it war scoudered wi' a het ern. His presence be about us! What's the matter wi' you, master? Are ye gaun to take the calm o' the stamock again?"

The truth is, that the clown's absurd story, with the still more ridiculous application, made me sick at heart a second time. It was not because I thought my illustrious friend was the devil, or that I took a fool's idle tale as a counterbalance to divine revelation, that had assured me of my justification in the sight of God before the existence of time. But, in short, it gave me a view of my own state, at which I shuddered, as indeed I now always did, when the image of my devoted friend and ruler presented itself to my mind. I often communed with my heart on this, and wondered how a connection, that had the well-being of mankind solely in view, could be productive of fruits so bitter. I then went to try my works by the Saviour's golden rule, as my servant had put it into my head to do; and, behold, not one of them would stand the test. I had shed blood on a ground on which I could not admit that any man had a right to shed mine; and I began to doubt the motives of my adviser once more, not that they were intentionally bad, but that his was some great mind led astray by enthusiasm, or some overpowering passion.

He seemed to comprehend every one of these motions of my heart, for his manner towards me altered every day. It first became any thing but agreeable, then supercilious, and finally, intolerable; so that I resolved to shake him off, cost what it would, even though I should be reduced to beg my bread in a foreign land. To do it at home was impossible, as he held my life in his hands, to sell it whenever he had a mind; and besides, his ascendancy over me was as complete as that of a huntsman over his dogs. I was even so weak, as, the next time I met with him, to look stedfastly at his foot, to see if it was not cloven into two hoofs. It was the foot of a gentleman, in every respect, so far as appearances went, but the form of his counsels was somewhat equivocal, and if not double, they were amazingly crooked.

But, if I had taken my measures to abscond and fly from my native place, in order to free myself of this tormenting, intolerant, and bloody reformer, he had likewise taken his to expel me, or throw me into the hands of justice. It seems, that about this time, I was haunted by some spies connected with my late father and brother, of whom the mistress of the former was one. My brother's death had been witnessed by two individuals; indeed, I always had an impression that it was witnessed by more than one, having some faint recollection of hearing voices and challenges close beside me; and this woman had searched about until she found these people; but, as I shrewdly suspected, not without the assistance of the only person in my secret,—my own warm and devoted friend. I say this, because I found that he had them concealed in the neighbourhood, and then took me again and again where I was fully exposed to their view, without being aware. One time in particular, on pretence of gratifying my revenge on that base woman, he knew so well where she lay concealed, that he led me to her, and left me to the mercy of two viragos, who had very nigh taken my life. My time of residence at Dalcastle was wearing to a crisis. I could no longer live with my tyrant, who haunted me like my shadow; and besides, it seems there were proofs of murder leading against me from all quarters. Of part of these I deemed myself quite free, but the world deemed otherwise; and how the matter would have gone, God only knows, for, the case never having undergone a judicial trial, I do not. It perhaps, however, behoves me here to relate all that I know of it, and it is simply this:

On the first of June 1712, (well may I remember the day,) I was sitting locked in my secret chamber, in a state of the utmost despondency, revolving in my mind what I ought to do to be free of my persecutors, and wishing myself a worm, or a moth, that I might be crushed and at rest, when behold Samuel entered, with eyes like to start out of his head, exclaiming, "For God's sake, master, fly and hide yourself, for your mother's found, an' as sure as you're a living soul, the blame is gaun to fa' on you!"

"My mother found!" said I. "And, pray, where has she been all this while?" In the mean time, I was terribly discomposed at the thoughts of her return.

"Been, sir! Been? Why, she has been where ye pat her, it seems,—lying buried in the sands o' the linn. I can tell you, ye will see her a frightsome figure, sic as I never wish to see again. An' the young lady is found too, sir: an' it is said the devil–I beg pardon sir, *your friend*, I mean,—it is said your *friend* has made the discovery, an' the folk are away to raise officers, an' they will be here in an hour or two at the farthest, sir; an' sae you hae not a minute to lose, for there's proof, sir, strong proof, an' sworn proof, that ye were last seen wi' them baith; sae, unless ye can gie a' the better an account o' baith yoursel an' them, either hide, or flee for your bare life."

"I will neither hide nor fly," said I; "for I am as guiltless of the blood of these women as the child unborn."

"The country disna think sae, master; an' I can assure you, that should evidence fail, you run a risk o' being torn limb frae limb. They are bringing the corpse here, to gar ye touch them baith afore witnesses, an' plenty o' witnesses there will be!"

"They shall not bring them here," cried I, shocked beyond measure at the experiment about to be made: "Go, instantly, and debar them from entering my gate with their bloated and mangled carcases."

"The body of your own mother, sir!" said the fellow emphatically. I was in terrible agitation; and, being driven to my wit's end, I got up and strode furiously round an' round the room. Samuel wist not what to do, but I saw by his staring he deemed me doubly guilty. A tap came to the chamber door: we both started like guilty creatures; and as for Samuel, his hairs stood all on end with alarm, so that when I motioned to him, he could scarcely advance to open the door. He did so at length, and who should enter but my illustrious friend, manifestly in the utmost state of alarm. The moment that Samuel admitted him, the former made his escape by the prince's side as he entered, seemingly in a state of distraction. I was little better, when I saw this dreaded personage enter my chamber, which he had never before attempted; and being unable to ask his errand, I suppose I stood and gazed on him like a statue.

"I come with sad and tormenting tidings to you, my beloved and ungrateful friend," said he; "but having only a minute left to save your life, I have come to attempt it. There is a mob coming towards you with two dead bodies, which will place you in circumstances disagreeable enough: but that is not the worst, for of that you may be able to clear yourself. At this moment there is a party of officers, with a Justiciary warrant from Edinburgh, surrounding the house, and about to begin the search of it, for you. If you fall into their hands, you are inevitably lost; for I have been making earnest inquiries, and find that every thing is in train for your ruin."

"Ay, and who has been the cause of all this?" said I, with great bitterness. But he stopped me short, adding, "There is no time for such reflections at present: I gave you my word of honour that your life should be safe from the hand of man. So it shall, if the power remain with me to save it. I am come to redeem my pledge, and to save your life by the sacrifice of my own. Here,—Not one word of expostulation, change habits with me, and you may then pass by the officers, and guards, and even through the approaching mob, with the most perfect temerity. There is a virtue in this garb, and instead of offering to detain you, they shall pay you obeisance. Make haste, and leave this place for the present, flying where you best may, and if I escape from these dangers that surround me, I will endeavour to find you out, and bring you what intelligence I am able."

I put on his green frock coat, buff belt, and a sort of a turban that he always wore on his head, somewhat resembling a bishop's mitre: he drew his hand thrice across my face, and I withdrew as he continued to urge me. My hall door and postern gate were both strongly guarded, and there were sundry armed people within, searching the closets; but all of them made way for me, and lifted their caps as I passed by them. Only one superior officer accosted me, asking if I had seen the culprit? I knew not what answer to make, but chanced to say, with great truth and propriety, "He is safe enough." The man beckoned with a smile, as much as to say, "Thank you, sir, that is quite sufficient;" and I walked deliberately away.

I had not well left the gate, till, hearing a great noise coming from the deep glen toward the east, I turned that way, deeming myself quite secure in this my new disguise, to see what it was, and if matters were as had been described to me. There I met a great mob, sure enough, coming with two dead bodies stretched on boards, and decently covered with white sheets. I would fain have examined their appearance, had I not perceived the apparent fury in the looks of the men, and judged from that how much more safe it was for me not to intermeddle in the affray. I cannot tell how it was, but I felt a strange and unwonted delight in viewing this scene, and a

certain pride of heart in being supposed the perpetrator of the unnatural crimes laid to my charge. This was a feeling quite new to
me; and if there were virtues in the robes of the illustrious foreigner,
who had without all dispute preserved my life at this time; I say, if
there was any inherent virtue in these robes of his, as he had suggested, this was one of their effects, that they turned my heart towards that which was evil, horrible, and disgustful.

I mixed with the mob to hear what they were saying. Every tongue
was engaged in loading me with the most opprobrious epithets! One
called me a monster of nature; another an incarnate devil; and another a creature made to be cursed in time and eternity. I retired
from them, and winded my way southward, comforting myself with
the assurance, that so mankind had used and persecuted the greatest fathers and apostles of the Christian church, and that their vile
opprobrium could not alter the counsels of heaven concerning me.

On going over that rising ground called Dorington Moor, I could
not help turning round and taking a look of Dalcastle. I had little
doubt that it would be my last look, and nearly as little ambition that
it should not. I thought how high my hopes of happiness and advancement had been on entering that mansion, and taking possession of its rich and extensive domains, and how miserably I had
been disappointed. On the contrary, I had experienced nothing but
chagrin, disgust, and terror; and I now consoled myself with the
hope that I should henceforth shake myself free of the chains of my
great tormentor, and for that privilege was I willing to encounter
any earthly distress. I could not help perceiving, that I was now on
a path which was likely to lead me into a species of distress hitherto
unknown, and hardly dreamed of by me, and that was total destitution. For all the riches I had been possessed of a few hours previous
to this, I found that here I was turned out of my lordly possessions
without a single merk, or the power of lifting and commanding the
smallest sum, without being thereby discovered and seized. Had it
been possible for me to have escaped in my own clothes, I had a
considerable sum secreted in these, but, by the sudden change, I
was left without a coin for present necessity. But I had hope in heaven,
knowing that the just man would not be left destitute; and that though
many troubles surrounded him, he would at last be set free from
them all. I was possessed of strong and brilliant parts, and a liberal
education; and though I had somehow unaccountably suffered my
theological qualifications to fall into desuetude, since my acquaintance with the ablest and most rigid of all theologians, I had nevertheless hopes that, by preaching up redemption by grace, pre-

ordination, and eternal purpose, I should yet be enabled to benefit mankind in some country, and rise to high distinction.

These were some of the thoughts by which I consoled myself as I posted on my way southward, avoiding the towns and villages, and falling into the cross ways that led from each of the great roads passing east and west, to another. I lodged the first night in the house of a country weaver, into which I stepped at a late hour, quite overcome with hunger and fatigue, having travelled not less than thirty miles from my late home. The man received me ungraciously, telling me of a gentleman's house at no great distance, and of an inn a little farther away; but I said I delighted more in the society of a man like him, than that of any gentleman of the land, for my concerns were with the poor of this world, it being easier for a camel to go through the eye of a needle, than for a rich man to enter into the kingdom of heaven. The weaver's wife, who sat with a child on her knee, and had not hitherto opened her mouth, hearing me speak in that serious and religious style, stirred up the fire, with her one hand; then drawing a chair near it, she said, "Come awa, honest lad, in by here; sin' it be sae that you belang to Him wha gies us a' that we hae, it is but right that you should share a part. You are a stranger, it is true, but *them* that winna entertain a stranger will never entertain an angel unawares."

I never was apt to be taken with the simplicity of nature; in general I despised it; but, owing to my circumstances at the time, I was deeply affected by the manner of this poor woman's welcome. The weaver continued in a churlish mood throughout the evening, apparently dissatisfied with what his wife had done in entertaining me, and spoke to her in a manner so crusty that I thought proper to rebuke him, for the woman was comely in her person, and virtuous in her conversation; but the weaver her husband was large of make, ill-favoured, and pestilent; therefore did I take him severely to task for the tenor of his conduct; but the man was froward, and answered me rudely, with sneering and derision, and, in the height of his caprice, he said to his wife, "Whan focks are sae keen of a chance o' entertaining angels, gudewife, it wad maybe be worth their while to tak tent what kind o' angels they are. It wadna wonder me vera muckle an ye had entertained your friend the deil the night, for aw thought aw fand a saur o' reek an' brimstane about him. *He's* nane o' the best o' angels, an' focks winna hae muckle credit by entertaining him."

Certainly, in the assured state I was in, I had as little reason to be alarmed at mention being made of the devil as any person on earth:

of late, however, I felt that the reverse was the case, and that any allusion to my great enemy, moved me exceedingly. The weaver's speech had such an effect on me, that both he and his wife were alarmed at my looks. The latter thought I was angry, and chided her husband gently for his rudeness; but the weaver himself rather seemed to be confirmed in his opinion that I was the devil, for he looked round like a startled roe-buck, and immediately betook him to the family Bible.

I know not whether it was on purpose to prove my identity or not, but I think he was going to desire me either to read a certain portion of Scripture that he had sought out, or to make family worship, had not the conversation at that instant taken another turn; for the weaver, not knowing how to address me, abruptly asked my name, as he was about to put the Bible into my hands. Never having considered myself in the light of a malefactor, but rather as a champion in the cause of truth, and finding myself perfectly safe under my disguise, I had never once thought of the utility of changing my name, and when the man asked me, I hesitated; but being compelled to say something, I said my name was Cowan. The man stared at me, and then at his wife, with a look that spoke a knowledge of something alarming or mysterious.

"Ha! Cowan?" said he. "That's most extrordinar! Not Colwan, I hope?"

"No: Cowan is my sirname," said I. "But why not Colwan, there being so little difference in the sound?"

"I was feared ye might be that waratch that the deil has taen the possession o', an' eggit him on to kill baith his father an' his mother, his only brother, an' his sweetheart," said he; "an' to say the truth, I'm no that sure about you yet, for I see you're gaun wi' arms on ye."

"Not I, honest man," said I; "I carry no arms; a man conscious of his innocence and uprightness of heart, needs not to carry arms in his defence now."

"Ay, ay, maister," said he; "an' pray what div ye ca' this bit windlestrae that's appearing here?" With that he pointed to something on the inside of the breast of my frock-coat. I looked at it, and there certainly was the gilded haft of a poniard, the same weapon I had seen and handled before, and which I knew my illustrious companion always carried about with him; but till that moment I knew not that I was in possession of it. I drew it out: a more dangerous or insidious looking weapon could not be conceived. The weaver and his wife were both frightened, the latter in particular; and she being my friend, and I dependant on their hospitality, for that night, I said, "I declare I knew not that I carried this small rapier, which has been in my coat by chance, and not by any design of mine. But lest you should think that I meditate any mischief to any under this roof, I give it into your hands, requesting of you to lock it by till to-morrow, or when I shall next want it."

The woman seemed rather glad to get hold of it; and, taking it from me, she went into a kind of pantry out of my sight, and locked the weapon up; and then the discourse went on.

"There cannot be such a thing in reality," said I, "as the story you were mentioning just now, of a man whose name resembles mine."

"It's likely that you ken a wee better about the story than I do, maister," said he, "suppose you do leave the *L* out of your name. An' yet I think sic a waratch, an' a murderer, wad hae taen a name wi' some gritter difference in the sound. But the story is just that true, that there were twa o' the Queen's officers here nae mair than an hour ago, in pursuit o' the vagabond, for they gat some intelligence that he had fled this gate; yet they said he had been last seen wi' black claes on, an' they supposed he was clad in black. His ain servant is wi' them, for the purpose o' kennin the scoundrel, an' they're galloping through the country like madmen. I hope in God they'll get him, an' rack his neck for him!"

I could not say *Amen* to the weaver's prayer, and therefore tried to compose myself as well as I could, and made some religious comment on the causes of the nation's depravity. But suspecting that my potent friend had betrayed my flight and disguise, to save his life, I was very uneasy, and gave myself up for lost. I said prayers in the family, with the tenor of which the wife was delighted, but the weaver still dissatisfied; and, after a supper of the most homely fare, he tried to start an argument with me, proving, that every thing for which I had interceded in my prayer, was irrelevant to man's present state. But I, being weary and distressed in mind, shunned the contest, and requested a couch whereon to repose.

I was conducted into the other end of the house, among looms, treadles, pirns, and confusion without end; and there, in a sort of box, was I shut up for my night's repose, for the weaver, as he left me, cautiously turned the key of my apartment, and left me to shift for myself among the looms, determined that I should escape from the house with nothing. After he and his wife and children were crowded into their den, I heard the two mates contending furiously about me in suppressed voices, the one maintaining the probability that I was the murderer, and the other proving the impossibility of it. The husband, however, said as much as let me understand, that he had locked me up on purpose to bring the military, or officers of justice, to seize me. I was in the utmost perplexity, yet, for all that, and the imminent danger I was in, I fell asleep, and a more troubled and tormenting sleep never enchained a mortal frame. I had such dreams that they will not bear repetition, and early in the morning I awaked, feverish, and parched with thirst.

I went to call mine host, that he might let me out to the open air, but before doing so, I thought it necessary to put on some clothes. In attempting to do this, a circumstance arrested my attention, (for which I could in nowise account, which to this day I cannot unriddle, nor shall I ever be able to comprehend it while I live,) the frock and turban, which had furnished my disguise on the preceding day, were both removed, and my own black coat and cocked hat laid down in their place. At first I thought I was in a dream, and felt the weaver's beam, web, and treadle-strings with my hands, to convince myself that I was awake. I was certainly awake; and there was the door locked firm and fast as it was the evening before. I carried my own black coat to the small window, and examined it. It was my own in verity; and the sums of money, that I had concealed in case of any emergency, remained untouched. I trembled with astonishment; and on my return from the small window, went doiting in amongst the weaver's looms, till I entangled myself, and could not get out again without working great deray amongst the coarse linen threads that stood in warp from one end of the apartment unto the other. I had no knife whereby to cut the cords of this wicked man, and therefore was obliged to call out lustily for assistance. The weaver came half naked, unlocked the door, and, setting in his head and long neck, accosted me thus:

"What now, Mr. Satan? What for are ye roaring that gate? Are you fawn inna little hell, instead o' the big muckil ane? Deil be in your reistit trams! What for have ye abscondit yoursel into ma leddy's wab for?"

"Friend, I beg your pardon," said I; "I wanted to be at the light, and have somehow unfortunately involved myself in the intricacies of your web, from which I cannot get clear without doing you a great injury. Pray do, lend your experienced hand to extricate me."

"May aw the pearls o' damnation light on your silly snout, an I dinna estricat ye weel enough! Ye ditit, donnart, deil's burd that ye be! what made ye gang howkin in there to be a poor man's ruin? Come out, ye vile rag-of-a-muffin, or I gar ye come out wi' mair shame and disgrace, an' fewer haill banes in your body."

My feet had slipped down through the double warpings of a web, and not being able to reach the ground with them, (there being a small pit below,) I rode upon a number of yielding threads, and there being nothing else that I could reach, to extricate myself was impossible. I was utterly powerless; and besides, the yarn and cords hurt me very much. For all that, the destructive weaver seized a loom-spoke, and began a-beating me most unmercifully, while, entangled as I was, I could do nothing but shout aloud for mercy, or assistance, whichever chanced to be within hearing. The latter, at length, made its appearance, in the form of the weaver's wife, in the same state of dishabille with himself, who instantly interfered, and that most strenuously, on my behalf. Before her arrival, however, I had made a desperate effort to throw myself out of the entanglement I was in; for the weaver continued repeating his blows and cursing me so, that I determined to get out of his meshes at any risk. This effect made my case worse; for my feet being wrapt among the nether threads, as I threw myself from my saddle on the upper ones, my feet brought the others up through these, and I hung with my head down, and my feet as firm as they had been in a vice. The predicament of the web being thereby increased, the weaver's wrath was doubled in proportion, and he laid on without mercy.

At this critical juncture the wife arrived, and without hesitation rushed before her offended lord, withholding his hand from injuring me farther, although then it was uplifted along with the loom-spoke in overbearing ire. "Dear Johnny! I think ye be gaen dementit this morning. Be quiet, my dear, an' dinna begin a Boddel Brigg business in your ain house. What for ir ye persecutin' a servant o' the Lord's that gate, an' pitting the life out o' him wi' his head down an' his heels up?"

"Had ye said a servant o' the deil's, Nans, ye wad hae been nearer the nail, for gin he binna the auld ane himsel, he's gayan sib till him. There, didna I lock him in on purpose to bring the military on him; an' in place o' that, hasna he keepit me in a sleep a' this while as deep as death? An' here do I find him abscondit like a speeder i' the mids o' my leddy's wab, an' me dreamin' a' the night that I had the deil i' my house, an' that he was clapper-clawin me ayont the loom. Have at you, ye brunstane thief!" and, in spite of the good woman's struggles, he lent me another severe blow.

"Now, Johnny Dods, my man! O Johnny Dods, think if that be like a Christian, and ane o' the heroes o' Boddel Brigg, to entertain a stranger, an' then bind him in a web wi' his head down, an' mell him to death! O Johnny Dods, think what you are about! Slack a pin, an' let the good honest religious lad out."

The weaver was rather overcome, but still stood to his point that I was the deil, though in better temper; and as he slackened the web to release me, he remarked, half laughing, "Wha wad hae thought that John Dods should hae escapit a' the snares an' dangers that circumfauldit him, an' at last should hae weaved a net to catch the deil."

The wife released me soon, and carefully whispered me, at the same time, that it would be as well for me to dress and be going. I was not long in obeying, and dressed myself in my black clothes, hardly knowing what I did, what to think, or whither to betake myself. I was sore hurt by the blows of the desperate ruffian; and, what was worse, my ankle was so much strained, that I could hardly set my foot to the ground. I was obliged to apply to the weaver once more, to see if I could learn any thing about my clothes, or how the change was effected. "Sir," said I, "how comes it that you have robbed me of my clothes, and put these down in their place over night?"

"Ha! thae claes? Me pit down thae claes!" said he, gaping with astonishment, and touching the clothes with the point of his fore-finger; "I never saw them afore, as I have death to meet wi': So help me God!"

He strode into the work-house where I slept, to satisfy himself that my clothes were not there, and returned perfectly aghast with consternation. "The doors were baith fast lockit," said he. "I could hae defied a rat either to hae gotten out or in. My dream has been true! My dream has been true! The Lord judge between thee and me; but, in his name, I charge you to depart out o' this house; an', gin it be your will, dinna tak the braidside o't w'ye, but gang quietly out at the door wi' your face foremost. Wife, let nought o' this en-chanter's remain i' the house, to be a curse, an' a snare to us; gang an' bring him his gildit weapon, an' may the Lord protect a' his ain against its hellish an' deadly point!"

The wife went to seek my poniard, trembling so excessively that she could hardly walk, and shortly after, we heard a feeble scream from the pantry. The weapon had disappeared with the clothes, though under double lock and key; and the terror of the good peo-ple having now reached a disgusting extremity, I thought proper to make a sudden retreat, followed by the weaver's anathemas.

My state both of body and mind was now truly deplorable. I was hungry, wounded, and lame; an outcast and a vagabond in society; my life sought after with avidity, and all for doing that to which I was predestined by him who fore-ordains whatever comes to pass.

I knew not whither to betake me. I had purposed going into England, and there making some use of the classical education I had received, but my lameness rendered this impracticable for the present. I was therefore obliged to turn my face towards Edinburgh, where I was little known—where concealment was more practicable than by skulking in the country, and where I might turn my mind to something that was great and good. I had a little money, both Scots and English, now in my possession, but not one friend in the whole world on whom I could rely. One devoted friend, it is true, I had, but he was become my greatest terror. To escape from him, I now felt that I would willingly travel to the farthest corners of the world, and be subjected to every deprivation; but after the certainty of what had taken place last night, after I had travelled thirty miles by secret and bye-ways, I saw not how escape from him was possible.

Miserable, forlorn, and dreading every person that I saw, either behind or before me, I hasted on towards Edinburgh, taking all the bye and unfrequented paths; and the third night after I left the weaver's house, I reached the West Port, without meeting with any thing remarkable. Being exceedingly fatigued and lame, I took lodgings in the first house I entered, and for these I was to pay two groats a-week, and to board and sleep with a young man who wanted a companion to make his rent easier. I liked this; having found from experience, that the great personage who had attached himself to me, and was now become my greatest terror among many surrounding evils, generally haunted me when I was alone, keeping aloof from all other society.

My fellow lodger came home in the evening, and was glad at my coming. His name was Linton, and I changed mine to Elliot. He was a flippant unstable being, one to whom nothing appeared a difficulty, in his own estimation, but who could effect very little, after all. He was what is called by some a compositor, in the Queen's printing house, then conducted by a Mr. James Watson. In the course of our conversation that night, I told him that I was a first-rate classical scholar, and would gladly turn my attention to some business wherein my education might avail me something; and that there was nothing would delight me so much as an engagement in the Queen's printing office. Linton made no difficulty in bringing about that arrangement. His answer was. "Oo, gud sir, you are the very man we want. Gud bless your breast and your buttons, sir! Ay, that's neither here nor there—That's all very well—Ha-ha-ha—A byeword in the house, sir. But, as I was saying, you are the very *man* we want—You will get any money you like to ask, sir—*Any* money you like, sir. God bless your buttons!–That's settled–All done–Settled, settled–I'll do it, I'll do it–No more about it; no more about it. Settled, settled."

The next day I went with him to the office, and he presented me to Mr. Watson as the most wonderful genius and scholar ever known. His recommendation had little sway with Mr. Watson, who only smiled at Linton's extravagancies, as one does at the prattle of an infant. I sauntered about the printing office for the space of two or three hours, during which time Watson bustled about with green spectacles on his nose, and took no heed of me. But seeing that I still lingered, he addressed me at length, in a civil gentlemanly way, and inquired concerning my views. I satisfied him with all my answers, in particular those to his questions about the Latin and Greek languages; but when he came to ask testimonials of my character and acquirements, and found that I could produce none, he viewed me with a jealous eye, and said he dreaded I was some ne'er-do-weel, run from my parents or guardians, and he did not chuse to employ any such. I said my parents were both dead; and that being thereby deprived of the means of following out my education, it behoved me to apply to some business in which my education might be of some use to me. He said he would take me into the office, and pay me according to the business I performed, and the manner in which I deported myself; but he could take no man into her Majesty's printing office upon a regular engagement, who could not produce the most respectable references with regard to morals.

I could not but despise the man in my heart who laid such a stress upon morals, leaving grace out of the question; and viewed it as a deplorable instance of human depravity and self conceit; but for all that, I was obliged to accept of his terms, for I had an inward thirst and longing to distinguish myself in the great cause of religion, and I thought if once I could print my own works, how I would astonish mankind, and confound their self wisdom and their esteemed morality–blow up the idea of any dependence on good works, and *morality*, forsooth! And I weened that I might thus get me a name even higher than if I had been made a general of the Czar Peter's troops against the infidels.

I attended the office some hours every day, but got not much encouragement, though I was eager to learn every thing, and could soon have set types considerably well. It was here that I first conceived the idea of writing this journal, and having it printed, and applied to Mr. Watson to print it for me, telling him it was a religious parable such as the Pilgrim's Progress. He advised me to print it close, and make it a pamphlet, and then if it did not sell, it would not cost me much; but that religious pamphlets, especially if they had a shade of allegory in them, were the very rage of the day. I put my work to the press, and wrote early and late; and encouraging my companion to work at odd hours, and on Sundays, before the press-work of the second sheet was begun, we had the work all in types, corrected, and a clean copy thrown off for farther revisal. The first sheet was wrought off; and I never shall forget how my heart exulted when at the printing house this day, I saw what numbers of my works were to go abroad among mankind, and I determined with myself that I would not put the Border name of Elliot, which I had assumed, to the work.

Thus far have my History and Confessions been carried.

I must now furnish my Christian readers with a key to the process, management, and winding up of the whole matter; which I propose, by the assistance of God, to limit to a very few pages.

Chesters, July 27, 1712.—My hopes and prospects are a wreck. My precious journal is lost! consigned to the flames! My enemy hath found me out, and there is no hope of peace or rest for me on this side the grave.

In the beginning of the last week, my fellow lodger came home, running in a great panic, and told me a story of the devil having appeared twice in the printing house, assisting the workmen at the printing of my book, and that some of them had been frightened out of their wits. That the story was told to Mr. Watson, who till that time had never paid any attention to the treatise, but who, out of curiosity, began and read a part of it, and thereupon flew into a great rage, called my work a medley of lies and blasphemy, and ordered the whole to be consigned to the flames, blaming his foreman, and all connected with the press, for letting a work go so far, that was enough to bring down the vengeance of heaven on the concern.

If ever I shed tears through perfect bitterness of spirit it was at that time, but I hope it was more for the ignorance and folly of my countrymen than the overthrow of my own hopes. But my attention was suddenly aroused to other matters, by Linton mentioning that it was said by some in the office the devil had inquired for me.

"Surely you are not such a fool," said I, "as to believe that the devil really was in the printing office?"

"Oo, gud bless you sir! saw him myself, gave him a nod, and good-day. Rather a gentlemanly personage–Green Circassian hunting coat and turban–Like a foreigner–Has the power of vanishing in one moment though–Rather a suspicious circumstance that. Otherwise, his appearance not much against him."

If the former intelligence thrilled me with grief, this did so with terror. I perceived who the personage was that had visited the printing house in order to further the progress of my work; and at the approach of every person to our lodgings, I from that instant trembled every bone, lest it should be my elevated and dreaded friend. I could not say I had ever received an office at his hand that was not friendly, yet these offices had been of a strange tendency; and the horror with which I now regarded him was unaccountable to myself. It was beyond description, conception, or the soul of man to bear. I took my printed sheets, the only copy of my unfinished work existing; and, on pretence of going straight to Mr. Watson's office, decamped from my lodgings at Portsburgh a little before the fall of evening, and took the road towards England.

As soon as I got clear of the city, I ran with a velocity I knew not before I had been capable of. I flew out the way towards Dalkeith so swiftly, that I often lost sight of the ground, and I said to myself, "O that I had the wings of a dove, that I might fly to the farthest corners of the earth, to hide me from those against whom I have no power to stand!"

I travelled all that night and the next morning, exerting myself beyond my power; and about noon the following day I went into a yeoman's house, the name of which was Ellanshaws, and requested of the people a couch of any sort to lie down on, for I was ill, and could not proceed on my journey. They showed me to a stable-loft where there were two beds, on one of which I laid me down; and, falling into a sound sleep, I did not awake till the evening, that other three men came from the fields to sleep in the same place, one of whom lay down beside me, at which I was exceedingly glad. They fell all sound asleep, and I was terribly alarmed at a conversation I overheard somewhere outside the stable. I could not make out a sentence, but trembled to think I knew one of the voices at least, and rather than not be mistaken, I would that any man had run me through with a sword. I fell into a cold sweat, and once thought of instantly putting hand to my own life, as my only means of relief, (May the rash and sinful thought be in mercy forgiven!) when I heard as it were two persons at the door, contending, as I thought, about their right and interest in me. That the one was forcibly preventing the admission of the other, I could hear distinctly, and their language was mixed with something dreadful and mysterious. In an agony of terror, I awakened my snoring companion with great difficulty, and asked him, in a low whisper, who these were at the door? The man lay silent, and listening, till fairly awake, and then asked if I had heard any thing? I said I had heard strange voices contending at the door.

"Then I can tell you, lad, it has been something neither good nor canny," said he: "It's no for naething that our horses are snorking that gate."

For the first time, I remarked that the animals were snorting and rearing as if they wished to break through the house. The man called to them by their names, and ordered them to be quiet; but they raged still the more furiously. He then roused his drowsy companions, who were alike alarmed at the panic of the horses, all of them declaring that they had never seen either Mause or Jolly start in their lives before. My bed-fellow and another then ventured down the ladder, and I heard one of them then saying, "Lord be wi' us! What can be i' the house? The sweat's rinning off the poor beasts like water."

They agreed to sally out together, and if possible to reach the kitchen and bring a light. I was glad at this, but not so much so when I heard the one man saying to the other, in a whisper, "I wish that stranger man may be canny enough."

"God kens!" said the other: "It doesnae look unco weel."

The lad in the other bed, hearing this, set up his head in manifest affright as the other two departed for the kitchen; and, I believe, he would have been glad to have been in their company. This lad was next the ladder, at which I was extremely glad, for had he not been there, the world should not have induced me to wait the return of these two men. They were not well gone, before I heard another distinctly enter the stable, and come towards the ladder. The lad who was sitting up in his bed, intent on the watch, called out, "Wha's that there? Walker, is that you? Purdie, I say, is it you?"

The darkling intruder paused for a few moments, and then came towards the foot of the ladder. The horses broke loose, and snorting and neighing for terror, raged through the house. In all my life I never heard so frightful a commotion. The being that occasioned it all, now began to mount the ladder toward our loft, on which the lad in the bed next the ladder sprung from his couch, crying out, "the L–d A—y preserve us! what can it be?" With that he sped across the loft, and by my bed, praying lustily all the way; and, throwing

himself from the other end of the loft into a manger, he darted, naked as he was, through among the furious horses, and making the
door, that stood open, in a moment he vanished and left me in the
lurch. Powerless with terror, and calling out fearfully, I tried to follow his example; but not knowing the situation of the places with
regard to one another, I missed the manger, and fell on the pave-
ment in one of the stalls. I was both stunned and lamed on the knee;
but terror prevailing, I got up and tried to escape. It was out of my
power; for there were divisions and cross divisions in the house,
and mad horses smashing every thing before them, so that I knew
not so much as on what side of the house the door was. Two or
three times was I knocked down by the animals, but all the while I
never stinted crying out with all my power. At length, I was seized
by the throat and hair of the head, and dragged away, I wist not
whither. My voice was now laid, and all my powers, both mental
and bodily, totally overcome; and I remember no more till I found
myself lying naked on the kitchen table of the farm house, and something like a horse's rug thrown over me. The only hint that I got
from the people of the house on coming to myself was, that my
absence would be good company; and that they had got me in a
woful state, one which they did not chuse to describe, or hear described.

As soon as day-light appeared, I was packed about my business,
with the hisses and execrations of the yeoman's family, who viewed
me as a being to be shunned, ascribing to me the visitations of that
unholy night. Again was I on my way southward, as lonely, hopeless, and degraded a being as was to be found on life's weary round.
As I limped out the way, I wept, thinking of what I might have been,
and what I really had become: of my high and flourishing hopes,
when I set out as the avenger of God on the sinful children of men;
of all that I had dared for the exaltation and progress of the truth;
and it was with great difficulty that my faith remained unshaken, yet
was I preserved from that sin, and comforted myself with the certainty, that the believer's progress through life is one of warfare and
suffering.

My case was indeed a pitiable one. I was lame, hungry, fatigued,
and my resources on the very eve of being exhausted. Yet these
were but secondary miseries, and hardly worthy of a thought, compared with those I suffered inwardly. I not only looked around me
with terror at every one that approached, but I was become a terror
to myself; or rather, my body and soul were become terrors to each
other; and, had it been possible, I felt as if they would have gone to

war. I dared not look at my face in a glass, for I shuddered at my own image and likeness. I dreaded the dawning, and trembled at the approach of night, nor was there one thing in nature that afforded me the least delight.

In this deplorable state of body and mind, was I jogging on towards the Tweed, by the side of the small river called Ellan, when, just at the narrowest part of the glen, whom should I meet full in the face, but the very being in all the universe of God I would the most gladly have shunned. I had no power to fly from him, neither durst I, for the spirit within me, accuse him of falsehood, and renounce his fellowship. I stood before him like a condemned criminal, staring him in the face, ready to be winded, twisted, and tormented as he pleased. He regarded me with a sad and solemn look. How changed was now that majestic countenance, to one of haggard despair—changed in all save the extraordinary likeness to my late brother, a resemblance which misfortune and despair tended only to heighten. There were no kind greetings passed between us at meeting, like those which pass between the men of the world; he looked on me with eyes that froze the currents of my blood, but spoke not, till I assumed as much courage as to articulate—"You here! I hope you have brought me tidings of comfort?"

"Tidings of despair!" said he. "But such tidings as the timid and the ungrateful deserve, and have reason to expect. You are an outlaw, and a vagabond in your country, and a high reward is offered for your apprehension. The enraged populace have burnt your house, and all that is within it; and the farmers on the land bless themselves at being rid of you. So fare it with every one who puts his hand to the great work of man's restoration to freedom, and draweth back, contemning the light that is within him! Your enormities caused me to leave you to yourself for a season, and you see what the issue has been. You have given some evil ones power over you, who long to devour you, both soul and body, and it has required all my power and influence to save you. Had it not been for my hand, you had been torn in pieces last night; but for once I prevailed. We must leave this land forthwith, for here there is neither peace, safety, nor comfort for us. Do you now, and here, pledge yourself to one who has so often saved your life, and has put his own at stake to do so? Do you pledge yourself that you will henceforth be guided by my counsel, and follow me whithersoever I chuse to lead?"

"I have always been swayed by your counsel," said I, "and for your sake, principally, am I sorry, that all our measures have proved abortive. But I hope still to be useful in my native isle, therefore let me plead that your highness will abandon a poor despised and outcast wretch to his fate, and betake you to your realms, where your presence cannot but be greatly wanted."

"Would that I could do so!" said he wofully. "But to talk of that is to talk of an impossibility. I am wedded to you so closely, that I feel as if I were the same person. Our essences are one, our bodies and spirits being united, so, that I am drawn towards you as by magnetism, and wherever you are, there must my presence be with you."

Perceiving how this assurance affected me, he began to chide me most bitterly for my ingratitude; and then he assumed such looks, that it was impossible for me longer to bear them; therefore I staggered out the way, begging and beseeching of him to give me up to my fate, and hardly knowing what I said; for it struck me, that, with all his assumed appearance of misery and wretchedness, there were traits of exultation in his hideous countenance, manifesting a secret and inward joy at my utter despair.

It was long before I durst look over my shoulder, but when I did so, I perceived this ruined and debased potentate coming slowly on the same path, and I prayed that the lord would hide me in the bowels of the earth, or depths of the sea. When I crossed the Tweed, I perceived him still a little behind me; and my despair being then at its height, I cursed the time I first met with such a tormentor; though, on a little recollection it occurred, that it was at that blessed time when I was solemnly dedicated to the Lord, and assured of my final election, and confirmation, by an eternal decree never to be annulled. This being my sole and only comfort, I recalled my curse upon the time, and repented me of my rashness.

After crossing the Tweed, I saw no more of my persecutor that day, and had hopes that he had left me for a season; but, alas, what hope was there of my relief after the declaration I had so lately heard! I took up my lodgings that night in a small miserable inn in the village of Ancrum, of which the people seemed alike poor and ignorant. Before going to bed, I asked if it was customary with them to have family worship of evenings? The man answered, that they were so hard set with the world, they often could not get time, but if I would be so kind as officiate they would be much obliged to me. I accepted the invitation, being afraid to go to rest lest the commotions of the foregoing night might be renewed, and continued the worship as long as in decency I could. The poor people thanked me, hoped my prayers would be heard both on their account and my own, seemed much taken with my abilities, and wondered how a man of my powerful eloquence chanced to be wandering about in a condition so forlorn. I said I was a poor student of theology, on my way to Oxford. They stared at one another with expressions of wonder, disappointment, and fear. I afterwards came to learn, that the term *theology* was by them quite misunderstood, and that they had some crude conceptions that nothing was taught at Oxford but the *black arts*, which ridiculous idea prevailed over all the south of Scotland. For the present I could not understand what the people meant, and less so, when the man asked me, with deep concern, "If I was serious in my intentions of going to Oxford? He hoped not, and that I would be better guided."

I said my education wanted finishing;—but he remarked, that the Oxford arts were a bad finish for a religious man's education.– Finally, I requested him to sleep with me, or in my room all the night, as I wanted some serious and religious conversation with him, and likewise to convince him that the study of the fine arts, though not absolutely necessary, were not incompatible with the character of a Christian divine. He shook his head, and wondered how I could call them *fine arts*–hoped I did not mean to convince him by any ocular demonstration, and at length reluctantly condescended to sleep with me, and let the lass and wife sleep together for one night. I believe he would have declined it, had it not been some hints from his wife, stating, that it was a good arrangement, by which I understood there were only two beds in the house, and that when I was preferred to the lass's bed, she had one to shift for.

The landlord and I accordingly retired to our homely bed, and conversed for some time about indifferent matters, till he fell sound asleep. Not so with me: I had that within which would not suffer me to close my eyes; and about the dead of night, I again heard the same noises and contention begin outside the house, as I had heard the night before; and again I heard it was about a sovereign and peculiar right in me. At one time the noise was on the top of the house, straight above our bed, as if the one party were breaking through the roof, and the other forcibly preventing it; at another time it was at the door, and at a third time at the window; but still mine host lay sound by my side, and did not waken. I was seized with terrors indefinable, and prayed fervently, but did not attempt rousing my sleeping companion until I saw if no better could be done. The women, however, were alarmed, and, rushing into our apartment, exclaimed that all the devils in hell were besieging the house. Then, indeed, the landlord awoke, and it was time for him, for the tumult had increased to such a degree, that it shook the house to its foundations, being louder and more furious than I could have conceived the heat of battle to be when the volleys of artillery are mixed with groans, shouts, and blasphemous cursing. It thundered and lightened; and there were screams, groans, laughter, and execrations, all intermingled.

I lay trembling and bathed in a cold perspiration, but was soon obliged to bestir myself, the inmates attacking me one after the other.

"O, Tam Douglas! Tam Douglas! haste ye an' rise out fra-yont that incarnal devil!" cried the wife: "Ye are in ayont the auld ane himsel, for our lass Tibbie saw his cloven cloots last night."

"Lord forbid!" roared Tam Douglas, and darted over the bed like a flying fish. Then, hearing the unearthly tumult with which he was surrounded, he returned to the side of the bed, and addressed me thus, with long and fearful intervals:

"If ye be the deil, rise up, an' depart in peace out o' this house—afore the bedstrae take kindling about ye, an' than it'll maybe be the waur for ye—Get up—an' gang awa out amang your cronies, like a good—lad—There's nae body here wishes you ony ill—D'ye hear me?"

"Friend," said I, "no Christian would turn out a fellow creature on such a night as this, and in the midst of such a commotion of the villagers."

"Na, if ye be a mortal man," said he, "which I rather think, from the use you made of the holy book—Nane o' your practical jokes on strangers an' honest foks. These are some o' your Oxford tricks, an' I'll thank you to be ower wi' them.—Gracious heaven, they are brikkin through the house at a' the four corners at the same time!"

The lass Tibby, seeing the innkeeper was not going to prevail with me to rise, flew toward the bed in desperation, and seizing me by the waist, soon landed me on the floor, saying: "Be ye deil, be ye chiel, ye's no lie there till baith the house an' us be swallowed up!"

Her master and mistress applauding the deed, I was obliged to attempt dressing myself, a task to which my powers were quite inadequate in the state I was in, but I was readily assisted by every one of the three; and as soon as they got my clothes thrust on in a loose way, they shut their eyes lest they should see what might drive them distracted, and thrust me out to the street, cursing me, and calling on the fiends to take their prey and begone.

The scene that ensued is neither to be described, nor believed, if it were. I was momently surrounded by a number of hideous fiends, who gnashed on me with their teeth, and clenched their crimson paws in my face; and at the same instant I was seized by the collar of my coat behind, by my dreaded and devoted friend, who pushed me on, and, with his gilded rapier waving and brandishing around me, defended me against all their united attacks. Horrible as my assailants were in appearance, (and they had all monstrous shapes,) I felt that I would rather have fallen into their hands, than be thus led away captive by my defender at his will and pleasure, without having the right or power to say my life, or any part of my will, was my own. I could not even thank him for his potent guardianship, but hung down my head, and moved on I knew not whither, like a criminal led to execution, and still the infernal combat continued, till about the dawning, at which time I looked up, and all the fiends were expelled but one, who kept at a distance; and still my persecutor and defender pushed me by the neck before him.

At length he desired me to sit down and take some rest, with which I complied, for I had great need of it, and wanted the power to withstand what he desired. There, for a whole morning did he detain me, tormenting me with reflections on the past, and pointing out the horrors of the future, until a thousand times I wished myself non-existent. "I have attached myself to your wayward fortune," said he; "and it has been my ruin as well as thine. Ungrateful as you are, I cannot give you up to be devoured; but this is a life that it is impossible to brook longer. Since our hopes are blasted in this world, and all our schemes of grandeur overthrown; and since our everlasting destiny is settled by a decree which no act of ours can invalidate, let us fall by our own hands, or by the hands of each other; die like heroes; and, throwing off this frame of dross and corruption, mingle with the pure ethereal essence of existence, from which we derived our being."

I shuddered at a view of the dreadful alternative, yet was obliged to confess that in my present circumstances existence was not to be borne. It was in vain that I reasoned on the sinfulness of the deed, and on its damning nature; he made me condemn myself out of my own mouth, by allowing the absolute nature of justifying grace, and the impossibility of the elect ever falling from the faith, or the glorious end to which they were called; and then he said, this granted, self-destruction was the act of a hero, and none but a coward would shrink from it, to suffer a hundred times more every day and night that passed over his head.

I said I was still contented to be that coward; and all that I begged of him was, to leave me to my fortune for a season, and to the just judgment of my creator; but he said his word and honour were engaged on my behoof, and these, in such a case, were not to be violated. "If you will not pity yourself, have pity on me," added he: "turn your eyes on me, and behold to what I am reduced."

Involuntarily did I turn round at the request, and caught a half glance of his features. May no eye destined to reflect the beauties of the New Jerusalem inward upon the beatific soul, behold such a sight as mine then beheld! My immortal spirit, blood, and bones, were all withered at the blasting sight; and I arose and withdrew, with groanings which the pangs of death shall never wring from me.

Not daring to look behind me, I crept on my way, and that night reached this hamlet on the Scottish border; and being grown reckless of danger, and hardened to scenes of horror, I took up my lodging with a poor hind, who is a widower, and who could only accommodate me with a bed of rushes at his fire-side. At midnight I heard some strange sounds, too much resembling those to which I had of late been inured; but they kept at a distance, and I was soon persuaded that there was a power protected that house superior to those that contended for, or had the mastery over me. Overjoyed at finding such an asylum, I remained in the humble cot. This is the third day I have lived under the roof, freed of my hellish assailants, spending my time in prayer, and writing out this my journal, which I have fashioned to stick in with my printed work, and to which I intend to add portions while I remain in this pilgrimage state, which, I find too well, cannot be long.

August 3, 1712.–This morning the hind has brought me word from Redesdale, whither he had been for coals, that a stranger gentleman had been traversing that country, making the most earnest inquiries after me, or one of the same appearance; and from the description that he brought of this stranger, I could easily perceive who it was. Rejoicing that my tormentor has lost traces of me for once, I am making haste to leave my asylum, on pretence of following this stranger, but in reality to conceal myself still more completely from his search. Perhaps this may be the last sentence ever I am destined to write. If so, farewell Christian reader! May God grant to thee a happier destiny than has been allotted to me here on earth, and the same assurance of acceptance above! *Amen.*

Ault-Righ, August 24, 1712.–Here am I, set down on the open moor to add one sentence more to my woful journal; and then, farewell all beneath the sun!

On leaving the hind's cottage on the Border, I hasted to the north-west, because in that quarter I perceived the highest and wildest hills before me. As I crossed the mountains above Hawick, I exchanged clothes with a poor homely shepherd, whom I found lying on a hill side, singing to himself some woful love ditty. He was glad of the change, and proud of his saintly apparel; and I was no less delighted with mine, by which I now supposed myself completely disguised; and I found moreover that in this garb of a common shepherd I was made welcome in every house. I slept the first night in a farm-house nigh to the church of Roberton, without hearing or seeing aught extraordinary; yet I observed next morning that all the servants kept aloof from me, and regarded me with looks of aversion. The next night I came to this house, where the farmer engaged me as a shepherd; and finding him a kind, worthy, and religious man, I accepted of his terms with great gladness. I had not, however, gone many times to the sheep, before all the rest of the shepherds told my master, that I knew nothing about herding, and begged of him to dismiss me. He perceived too well the truth of their intelligence; but being much taken with my learning, and religious conversation, he would not put me away, but set me to herd his cattle.

It was lucky for me, that before I came here, a report had prevailed, perhaps for an age, that this farm-house was haunted at certain seasons by a ghost. I say it was lucky for me, for I had not been in it many days before the same appalling noises began to prevail around me about midnight, often continuing till near the dawning. Still they kept aloof, and without doors; for this gentleman's house, like the cottage I was in formerly, seemed to be a sanctuary from all demoniacal power. He appears to be a good man and a just, and mocks at the idea of supernatural agency, and he either does not hear these persecuting spirits, or will not acknowledge it, though of late he appears much perturbed.

The consternation of the menials has been extreme. They ascribe all to the ghost, and tell frightful stories of murders having been committed there long ago. Of late, however, they are beginning to suspect that it is I that am haunted; and as I have never given them any satisfactory account of myself, they are whispering that I am a murderer, and haunted by the spirits of those I have slain.

August 30.–This day I have been informed, that I am to be banished the dwelling-house by night, and to sleep in an out-house by myself, to try if the family can get any rest when freed of my presence. I have peremptorily refused acquiescence, on which my master's brother struck me, and kicked me with his foot. My body being quite exhausted by suffering, I am grown weak and feeble both in mind and bodily frame, and actually unable to resent any insult or injury. I am the child of earthly misery and despair, if ever there was one existent. My master is still my friend; but there are so many masters here, and every one of them alike harsh to me, that I wish myself in my grave every hour of the day. If I am driven from the family sanctuary by night, I know I shall be torn in pieces before morning; and then who will deign or dare to gather up my mangled limbs, and give them honoured burial.

My last hour is arrived: I see my tormentor once more approaching me in this wild. Oh, that the earth would swallow me up, or the hill fall and cover me! Farewell for ever!

September 7, 1712.—My devoted, princely, but sanguine friend, has been with me again and again. My time is expired, and I find a relief beyond measure, for he has fully convinced me that no act of mine can mar the eternal counsel, or in the smallest degree alter or extenuate one event which was decreed before the foundations of the world were laid. He said he had watched over me with the greatest anxiety, but perceiving my rooted aversion towards him, he had forborn troubling me with his presence. But now, seeing that I was certainly to be driven from my sanctuary that night, and that there would be a number of infernals watching to make a prey of my body, he came to caution me not to despair, for that he would protect me at all risks, if the power remained with him. He then repeated an ejaculatory prayer, which I was to pronounce, if in great extremity. I objected to the words as equivocal, and susceptible of being rendered in a meaning perfectly dreadful; but he reasoned against this, and all reasoning with him is to no purpose. He said he did not ask me to repeat the words, unless greatly straitened; and that I saw his strength and power giving way, and when perhaps nothing else could save me.

The dreaded hour of night arrived; and, as he said, I was expelled from the family residence, and ordered to a byre, or cowhouse, that stood parallel with the dwelling-house behind, where, on a divot loft, my humble bedstead stood, and the cattle grunted and puffed below me. How unlike the splendid halls of Dalcastle! And to what I am now reduced, let the reflecting reader judge. Lord, thou knowest all that I have done for thy cause on earth! Why then art thou laying thy hand so sore upon me? Why hast thou set me as a butt of thy malice? But thy will must be done! Thou wilt repay me in a better world. *Amen.*

September 8.—My first night of trial in this place is overpast! Would that it were the last that I should ever see in this detested world! If the horrors of hell are equal to those I have suffered, eternity will be of short duration there, for no created energy can support them for one single month, or week. I have been buffeted as never living creature was. My vitals have all been torn, and every faculty and feeling of my soul racked, and tormented into callous insensibility. I was even hung by the locks over a yawning chasm, to which I could perceive no bottom, and then—not till then, did I repeat the tremendous prayer!—I was instantly at liberty; and what I now am, the Almighty knows! *Amen.*

September 18, 1712.—Still am I living, though liker to a vision than a human being; but this is my last day of mortal existence. Unable to resist any longer, I pledged myself to my devoted friend, that on this day we should die together, and trust to the charity of the children of men for a grave. I am solemnly pledged; and though I dared to repent, I am aware he will not be gainsaid, for he is raging with despair at his fallen and decayed majesty, and there is some miserable comfort in the idea that my tormentor shall fall with me. Farewell, world, with all thy miseries; for comforts or enjoyments hast thou none! Farewell, woman, whom I have despised and shunned; and man, whom I have hated; whom, nevertheless, I desire to leave in charity! And thou, sun, bright emblem of a far brighter effulgence, I bid farewell to thee also! I do not now take my last look of thee, for to thy glorious orb shall a poor suicide's last earthly look be raised. But, ah! who is yon that I see approaching furiously—his stern face blackened with horrid despair! My hour is at hand.—Almighty God, what is this that I am about to do! The hour of repentance is past, and now my fate is inevitable.—*Amen, for ever!* I will now seal up my little book, and conceal it; and cursed be he who trieth to alter or amend!

END OF THE MEMOIR.

WHAT can this work be? Sure, you will say, it must be an allegory; or (as the writer calls it) a religious PARABLE, showing the dreadful danger of self-righteousness? I cannot tell. Attend to the sequel: which is a thing so extraordinary, so unprecedented, and so far out of the common course of human events, that if there were not hundreds of living witnesses to attest the truth of it, I would not bid any rational being believe it.

In the first place, take the following extract from an authentic letter, published in *Blackwood's Magazine for August*, 1823.

"On the top of a wild height called Cowanscroft, where the lands of three proprietors meet all at one point, there has been for long and many years the grave of a suicide marked out by a stone standing at the head, and another at the feet. Often have I stood musing over it myself, when a shepherd on one of the farms, of which it formed the extreme boundary, and thinking what could induce a young man, who had scarcely reached the prime of life, to brave his Maker, and rush into his presence by an act of his own erring hand, and one so unnatural and preposterous. But it never once occurred to me, as an object of curiosity, to dig up the mouldering bones of the culprit, which I considered as the most revolting of all objects. The thing was, however, done last month, and a discovery made of one of the greatest natural phenomena that I have heard of in this country.

"The little traditionary history that remains of this unfortunate youth, is altogether a singular one. He was not a native of the place, nor would he ever tell from what place he came; but he was remarkable for a deep, thoughtful, and sullen disposition. There was nothing against his character that any body knew of here, and he had been a considerable time in the place. The last service he was in was with a Mr. Anderson of Eltrive, (Ault-Righ, *the King's burn*,) who died about 100 years ago, and who had hired him during the summer to herd a stock of young cattle in Eltrive Hope. It happened one day in the month of September, that James Anderson, his master's son, went with this young man to the Hope to divert himself. The herd had his dinner along with him, and about one o'clock, when the boy proposed going home, the former pressed him very hard to stay and take share of his dinner; but the boy refused, for fear his parents might be alarmed about him, and said he *would* go home: on which the herd said to him, 'Then, if ye winna stay with me, James, ye may depend on't I'll cut my throat afore ye come back again.'

"I have heard it likewise reported, but only by one person, that there had been some things stolen out of his master's house a good while before, and that the boy had discovered a silver knife and fork, that was a part of the stolen property, in the herd's possession that day, and that it was this discovery that drove him to despair.

"The boy did not return to the Hope that afternoon; and, before evening, a man coming in at the pass called *The Hart Loup*, with a drove of lambs, on the way for Edinburgh, perceived something like a man standing in a strange frightful position at the side of one of Eldinhope hay-ricks. The driver's attention was riveted on this strange uncouth figure, and as the drove-road passed at no great distance from the spot, he first called, but receiving no answer, he went up to the spot, and behold it was the above-mentioned young man, who had hung himself in the hay rope that was tying down the rick.

"This was accounted a great wonder; and every one said, if the devil had not assisted him it was impossible the thing could have been done; for, in general, these ropes are so brittle, being made of green hay, that they will scarcely bear to be bound over the rick. And the more to horrify the good people of this neighbourhood, the driver said, when he first came in view, *he could almost give his oath* that he saw two people busily engaged at the hay-rick, going round it and round it, and he thought they were dressing it.

"If this asseveration approximated at all to truth, it makes this evident at least, that the unfortunate young man had hanged himself after the man with the lambs came in view. He was, however, quite dead when he cut him down. He had fastened two of the old hay-ropes at the bottom of the rick on one side, (indeed they are all fastened so when first laid on,) so that he had nothing to do but to loosen two of the ends on the other side. These he had tied in a knot round his neck, and then slackening his knees, and letting himself down gradually, till the hay-rope bore all his weight, he had contrived to put an end to his existence in that way. Now the fact is, that if you try all the ropes that are thrown over all the outfield hay-ricks in Scotland, there is not one among a thousand of them will hang a colley dog; so that the manner of this wretch's death was rather a singular circumstance.

"Early next morning, Mr. Anderson's servants went reluctantly away, and, taking an old blanket with them for a winding sheet, they rolled up the body of the deceased, first in his own plaid, letting the hay-rope still remain about his neck, and then rolling the old blanket over all, they bore the loathed remains away to the distance of three miles or so, on spokes, to the top of Cowan's-Croft, at the very point where the Duke of Buccleuch's land, the Laird of Drummelzier's, and Lord Napier's, meet, and there they buried him, with all that he had on and about him, silver knife and fork and altogether. Thus far went tradition, and no one ever disputed one jot of the disgusting oral tale.

"A nephew of that Mr. Anderson's who was with the hapless youth that day he died, says, that, as far as he can gather from the relations of friends that he remembers, and of that same uncle in particular, it is one hundred and five years next month, (that is September, 1823,) since that event happened; and I think it likely that this gentleman's information is correct. But sundry other people, much older than he, whom I have consulted, pretend that it is six or seven years more. They say they have heard that Mr. James Anderson was then a boy ten years of age; that he lived to an old age, upwards of four-score, and it is two and forty years since he died. Whichever way it may be, it was about that period some way, of that there is no doubt.

"It so happened, that two young men, William Shiel and W. Sword, were out, on an adjoining height, this summer, casting peats, and it came into their heads to open this grave in the wilderness, and see if there were any of the bones of the suicide of former ages and centuries remaining. They did so, but opened only one half of the grave, beginning at the head and about the middle at the same time. It was not long till they came upon the old blanket—I think they said not much more than a foot from the surface. They tore that open, and there was the hay rope lying stretched down alongst his breast, so fresh that they saw at first sight that it was made of *risp*, a sort of long sword-grass that grows about marshes and the sides of lakes. One of the young men seized the rope and pulled by it, but the old en-chantment of the devil remained,—it would not break; and so he pulled and pulled at it, till behold the body came up into a sitting posture, with a broad blue bonnet on its head, and its plaid around it, all as fresh as that day it was laid in! I never heard of a preserva-tion so wonderful, if it be true as was related to me, for still I have not had the curiosity to go and view the body myself. The features were all so plain, that an acquaintance might easily have known him. One of the lads gripped the face of the corpse with his finger and thumb, and the cheeks felt quite soft and fleshy, but the dimples remained and did not spring out again. He had fine yellow hair, about nine inches long; but not a hair of it could they pull out till they cut part of it off with a knife. They also cut off some portions of his clothes, which were all quite fresh, and distributed them among their acquaintances, sending a portion to me, among the rest, to keep as natural curiosities. Several gentlemen have in a manner forced me to give them fragments of these enchanted garments: I have, however, retained a small portion for you, which I send along with this, being a piece of his plaid, and another of his waistcoat breast, which you will see are still as fresh as that day they were laid in the grave.

"His broad blue bonnet was sent to Edinburgh several weeks ago, to the great regret of some gentlemen connected with the land, who wished to have it for a keep-sake. For my part, fond as I am of blue bonnets, and broad ones in particular, I declare I durst not have worn that one. There was nothing of the silver knife and fork discovered, that I heard of, nor was it very likely it should: but it would appear he had been very near run of cash, which I daresay had been the cause of his utter despair; for, on searching his pockets, nothing was found but three old Scots halfpennies. These young men meeting with another shepherd afterwards, his curiosity was so much excited that they went and digged up the curious remains a second time, which was a pity, as it is likely that by these exposures to the air, and from the impossibility of burying it up again as closely as it was before, the flesh will now fall to dust."

*　　*　　*　　*　　*　　*

The letter from which the above is an extract, is signed JAMES HOGG, and dated from Altrive Lake, *August 1st,* 1823. It bears the stamp of authenticity in every line; yet, so often had I been hoaxed by the ingenious fancies displayed in that Magazine, that when this relation met my eye, I did not believe it; but from the moment that I perused it, I half formed the resolution of investigating these wonderful remains personally, if any such existed; for, in the immediate vicinity of the scene, as I supposed, I knew of more attractive metal than the dilapidated remains of mouldering suicides.

Accordingly, having some business in Edinburgh in September last, and being obliged to wait a few days for the arrival of a friend from London, I took that opportunity to pay a visit to my townsman and fellow collegian, Mr. L—t of C—d, advocate. I mentioned to him Hogg's letter, asking him if the statement was founded at all on truth. His answer was, "I suppose so. For my part I never doubted the thing, having been told that there has been a deal of talking about it up in the Forest for some time past. But, God knows! Hogg has imposed as ingenious lies on the public ere now."

I said, if it was within reach, I should like exceedingly to visit both the Shepherd and the Scots mummy he had described. Mr. L—t assented at the first proposal, saying he had no objections to take a ride that length with me, and make the fellow produce his credentials: That we would have a delightful jaunt through a romantic and now classical country, and some good sport into the bargain, provided he could procure a horse for me, from his father-in-law, next day. He sent up to a Mr. L—w to inquire, who returned for answer, that there was an excellent pony at my service, and that he himself would accompany us, being obliged to attend a great sheep fair at Thirlestane; and that he was certain the Shepherd would be there likewise.

Mr. L—t said that was the very man we wanted to make our party complete; and at an early hour next morning we started for

the ewe fair of Thirlestane, taking Blackwood's Magazine for August along with us. We rode through the ancient royal burgh of Selkirk,–halted and corned our horses at a romantic village, nigh to
some deep linns on the Ettrick, and reached the market ground at
Thirlestane-green a little before mid-day. We soon found Hogg,
standing near the *foot* of the market, as he called it, beside a great
drove of *paulies*, a species of stock that I never heard of before. They
were small sheep, striped on the backs with red chalk. Mr. L—t
introduced me to him as a great wool-stapler, come to raise the price
of that article; but he eyed me with distrust, and turning his back on
us, answered, "I hae sell'd mine."

I followed, and shewing him the above-quoted letter, said I was
exceedingly curious to have a look of these singular remains he had
so ingeniously described; but he only answered me with the remark, that "It was a queer fancy for a woo-stapler to tak."

His two friends then requested him to accompany us to the spot,
and to take some of his shepherds with us to assist in raising the
body; but he spurned at the idea, saying, "Od bless ye, lad! I hae
ither matters to mind. I hae a' thae paulies to sell, an' a' yon Highland stotts down on the green every ane; an' then I hae ten scores o'
yowes to buy after, an' if I canna first sell my ain stock, I canna buy
nae ither body's. I hae mair ado than I can manage the day, foreby
ganging to houk up hunder-year-auld banes."

Finding that we could make nothing of him, we left him with his
paulies, Highland stotts, grey jacket, and broad blue bonnet, to go in
search of some other guide. L—w soon found one, for he seemed
acquainted with every person in the fair. We got a fine old shepherd, named W—m B—e, a great original, and a very obliging and
civil man, who asked no conditions but that we should not speak of
it, because he did not wish it to come to his master's ears, that he
had been engaged in *sic a profane thing*. We promised strict secrecy;
and accompanied by another farmer, Mr. S—t, and old B—e, we
proceeded to the grave, which B—e described as about a mile and a
half distant from the market ground.

We went into a shepherd's cot to get a drink of milk, when I read
to our guide Mr. Hogg's description, asking him if he thought it
correct? He said there was hardly a bit o't correct, for the grave was
not on the hill of Cowan's-Croft, nor yet on the point where three
lairds' lands met, but on the top of a hill called the Faw-Law, where
there was no land that was not the Duke of Buccleuch's within a
quarter of a mile. He added that it was a wonder how the poet could
be mistaken there, who once herded the very ground where the

grave is, and saw both hills from his own window. Mr. L—w testified great surprise at such a singular blunder, as also how the body
came *not* to be buried at the meeting of three or four lairds' lands,
which had always been customary in the south of Scotland. Our
guide said he had always heard it reported, that the Eltrive men,
with Mr. David Anderson at their head, had risen before day on the
Monday morning, it having been on the Sabbath day that the man
put down himself; and that they set out with the intention of burying
him on Cowan's-Croft, where three marches met at a point. But it
having been an invariable rule to bury such *lost sinners* before the
rising of the sun, these five men were overtaken by day-light, as
they passed the house of Berry-Knowe; and by the time they reached
the top of the Faw-Law, the sun was beginning to skair the east. On
this they laid down the body, and digged a deep grave with all expedition; but when they had done, it was too short, and the body being
stiff, it would not go down, on which Mr. David Anderson looking
to the east, and perceiving that the sun would be up on them in a few
minutes, set his foot on the suicide's brow, and tramped down his
head into the grave with his iron-heeled shoe, until his nose and
skull crashed again, and at the same time uttered a terrible curse on
the wretch who had disgraced the family, and given them all this
trouble. This anecdote, our guide said, he had heard when a boy,
from the mouth of Robert Laidlaw, one of the five men who buried
the body.

We soon reached the spot, and I confess I felt a singular sensation, when I saw the grey stone standing at the head, and another at
the feet, and the one half of the grave manifestly new digged, and
closed up again as had been described. I could still scarcely deem
the thing to be a reality, for the ground did not appear to be wet, but
a kind of dry rotten moss. On looking around, we found some fragments of clothes, some teeth, and part of a pocket-book, which had
not been returned into the grave, when the body had been last raised,
for it had been twice raised before this, but only from the loins upward.

To work we fell with two spades, and soon cleared away the whole
of the covering. The part of the grave that had been opened before,
was filled with mossy mortar, which impeded us exceedingly, and
entirely prevented a proper investigation of the fore parts of the
body. I will describe every thing as I saw it before four respectable
witnesses, whose names I shall publish at large if permitted. A
number of the bones came up separately; for with the constant flow
of liquid stuff into the deep grave, we could not see to preserve

them in their places. At length great loads of coarse clothes, blanketing, plaiding, &c. appeared; we tried to lift these regularly up, and on doing so, part of a skeleton came up, but no flesh, save a little that was hanging in dark flitters about the spine, but which had no consistence; it was merely the appearance of flesh without the substance. The head was wanting; and I being very anxious to possess the skull, the search was renewed among the mortar and rags. We first found a part of the scalp, with the long hair firm on it; which, on being cleaned, is neither black nor fair, but of a darkish dusk, the most common of any other colour. Soon afterwards we found the skull, but it was not complete. A spade had damaged it, and one of the temple quarters was wanting. I am no phrenologist, not knowing one organ from another, but I thought the skull of that wretched man no study. If it was particular for any thing, it was for a smooth, almost perfect rotundity, with only a little protuberance above the vent of the ear.

When we came to that part of the grave that had never been opened before, the appearance of every thing was quite different. There the remains lay under a close vault of moss, and within a vacant space; and I suppose, by the digging in the former part of the grave, that part had been deepened, and drawn the moisture away from this part, for here all was perfect. The breeches still suited the thigh, the stocking the leg, and the garters were wrapt as neatly and as firm below the knee as if they had been newly tied. The shoes were all opened in the seams, the hemp having decayed, but the soles, upper leathers, and wooden heels, which were made of birch, were all as fresh as any of those we wore. There was one thing I could not help remarking, that in the inside of one of the shoes there was a layer of cow's dung, about one eighth of an inch thick, and in the hollow of the sole fully one fourth of an inch. It was firm, green, and fresh; and proved that he had been working in a byre. His clothes were all of a singular ancient cut, and no less singular in their texture. Their durability certainly would have been prodigious; for in thickness, coarseness, and strength, I never saw any cloth in the smallest degree to equal them. His coat was a frock coat, of a yellowish drab colour, with wide sleeves. It is tweeled, milled, and thicker than a carpet. I cut off two of the skirts and brought them with me. His vest was of striped serge, such as I have often seen worn by country people. It was lined and backed with white stuff. The breeches were a sort of striped plaiding, which I never saw worn, but which our guide assured us was very common in the country once, though, from the old clothes which he had seen remaining of it, he judged that it could not be less than 200 years since it was in fashion. His garters were of worsted, and striped with black or blue; his stockings gray, and wanting the feet. I brought samples of all along with me. I have likewise now got possession of the bonnet, which puzzles me most of all. It is not conformable with the rest of the dress. It is neither a broad bonnet, nor a Border bonnet; for there is an open behind, for tying, which no genuine Border bonnet, I am told, ever had. It seems to have been a Highland bonnet, worn in a flat way like a scone on the crown, such as is sometimes still seen in the west of Scotland. All the limbs, from the loins to the toes, seemed perfect and entire, but they could not bear handling. Before we got them returned again into the grave, they were all shaken to pieces, except the thighs, which continued to retain a kind of flabby form.

All his clothes that were sewed with linen yarn were lying in separate portions, the thread having rotten; but such as were sewed with worsted remained perfectly firm and sound. Among such a confusion, we had hard work to find out all his pockets, and our guide supposed, that, after all, we did not find above the half of them. In his vest pocket was a long clasp knife, very sharp; the haft was thin, and the scales shone as if there had been silver inside. Mr. Sc–t took it with him, and presented it to his neighbour, Mr. R—n of W–n L–e, who still has it in his possession. We found a comb, a gimblet, a vial, a small neat square board, a pair of plated knee-buckles, and several samples of cloth of different kinds, rolled neatly up within one another. At length, while we were busy on the search, Mr. L—t picked up a leathern case, which seemed to have been wrapped round and round by some ribbon, or cord, that had been rotten from it, for the swaddling marks still remained. Both L—w and B—e called out that "it was the tobacco spleuchan, and a well-filled ane too;" but on opening it out, we found, to our great astonishment, that it contained *a printed pamphlet.* We were all curious to see what sort of a pamphlet such a person would read; what it could contain that he seemed to have had such a care about? for the slough in which it was rolled, was fine chamois leather; what colour it had been, could not be known. But the pamphlet was wrapped so close together, and so damp, rotten, and yellow, that it seemed one solid piece. We all concluded, from some words that we could make out, that it was a religious tract, but that it would be impossible to make any thing of it. Mr. L—w remarked that it was a great pity if a few sentences could not be made out, for that it was a question what might be contained in that little book; and then he requested Mr. L—t to give it to me, as he had so many things of literature and law to attend to, that he would never think more of it. He replied, that either of us were heartily welcome to it, for that he had thought of returning it into the grave, if he could have made out but a line or two, to have seen what was its tendency.

"Grave, man!" exclaimed L—w, who speaks excellent strong broad Scots: "My truly, but ye grave weel! I wad esteem the contents o' that spleuchan as the most precious treasure. I'll tell you what it is, sir: I hae often wondered how it was that this man's corpse has been miraculously preserved frae decay, a hunder times langer than ony other body's, or than even a tanner's. But now I could wager a guinea, it has been for the preservation o' that little book. And Lord kens what may be in't! It will maybe reveal some mystery that mankind disna ken naething about yet."

"If there be any mysteries in it," returned the other, "it is not for your handling, my dear friend, who are too much taken up about mysteries already." And with these words he presented the mysterious pamphlet to me. With very little trouble, save that of a thorough drying, I unrolled it all with ease, and found the very tract which I have here ventured to lay before the public, part of it in small bad print, and the remainder in manuscript. The title page is written, and is as follows:

THE PRIVATE MEMOIRS
AND CONFESSIONS
OF A JUSTIFIED SINNER:

WRITTEN BY HIMSELF.

FIDELI CERTA MERCES.

And, alongst the head, it is the same as given in the present edition of the work. I altered the title to *A Self-justified Sinner*, but my booksellers did not approve of it; and there being a curse pronounced by the writer on him that should dare to alter or amend, I have let it stand as it is. Should it be thought to attach discredit to any received principle of our church, I am blameless. The printed part ends at page 153, and the rest is in a fine old hand, extremely small and close. I have ordered the printer to procure a fac-simile of it, to be bound in with the volume.

With regard to the work itself, I dare not venture a judgment, for I do not understand it. I believe no person, man or woman, will ever peruse it with the same attention that I have done, and yet I confess that I do not comprehend the writer's drift. It is certainly impossible that these scenes could ever have occurred, that he describes as having himself transacted. I think it *may be* possible that he had some hand in the death of his brother, and yet I am disposed greatly to doubt it; and the numerous distorted traditions, &c. which remain of that event, may be attributable to the work having been printed and burnt, and of course the story known to all the printers, with their families and gossips. That the young Laird of Dalcastle came by a violent death, there remains no doubt; but that this wretch slew him, there is to me a good deal. However, allowing this to have been the case, I account all the rest either dreaming or madness; or, as he says to Mr. Watson, a religious parable, on purpose to illustrate something scarcely tangible, but to which he seems to have attached great weight. Were the relation at all consistent with reason, it corresponds so minutely with traditionary facts, that it could scarcely have missed to have been received as authentic; but in this day, and with the present generation, it will not go down, that a man should be daily tempted by the devil, in the semblance of a fellow-creature; and at length lured to self-destruction, in the hopes that this same fiend and tormentor was to suffer and fall along with him. It was a bold theme for an allegory, and would have suited that age well had it been taken up by one fully qualified for the task, which this writer was not. In short, we must either conceive him not only the greatest fool, but the greatest wretch, on whom was ever stamped the form of humanity; or, that he was a religious maniac, who wrote and wrote about a deluded creature, till he arrived at that height of madness, that he believed himself the very object whom he had been all along describing. And in order to escape from an ideal tormentor, committed that act for which, according to the tenets he embraced, there was no remission, and which consigned his memory and his name to everlasting detestation.

FINIS.

Afterword

Literary Criticism and *Confessions of a Justified Sinner*

It is not hard to search for the devil in Hogg's *Confessions*. But it is hard to be sure we have identified him, and extraordinarily hard to write critically about a figure so elusive as Gil-Martin, in a novel as elusive as Hogg's.

Criticism of the *Confessions* began with confusion.

The first stumbling block lay in the interpretation of the satire of the Church people of Hogg's novel. Central to any reading is a clear understanding of the satiric nature of Hogg's writing about the Wringhim family, and the seriously distorted nature of the Rev. Wringhim's religious preaching. Not for nothing can Robert tell his 'father' that the mysterious stranger he met conforms to Wringhim's preaching to the fullest extent, in every detail. Hogg's contemporaries would have had little difficulty in recognising the extremism of the Rev. Wringhim's preaching, its total obsession with faith over works, its hostility to any idea of universal redemption, its extraordinary antinomian confidence that the elect were safe, and saved, whatever their deeds in this life. Hogg deliberately puts in contrasting characters, John Barnet, the Rev. Blanchard, the pious families with whom Robert seeks shelter in the Borders—ordinary Christians of Hogg's own faith and class who would have functioned as a norm for the reader of the 1820s seeking to position the Wringhim family.

Early hostility to the novel was generated by a failure to see the satiric dimension which laughed at extremism and human perversion of religious doctrine. Nor would it have been helped by the re-issue of the *Confessions* in the mutilated form which removed much of the imaginative power with which Hogg penetrated the religious viewpoints of his characters. The novel's extraordinary achievement was to take what sounded—and superficially looked—like conventional religious positions of the time, and reposition them as the utterances of the devil. In the 1820s it would have been hard to equate a discourse heavily allusive to the King James Bible with the devil, or to see through the fact that many of the human characters who use biblical or pseudo-biblical discourse are in fact talking nonsense. The deliberate ambiguity of language used by Hogg to break the link between 'good' language and 'good' people co-exists with characters we would genuinely welcome as good—Blanchard, Barnet, George, Mrs Logan—even when society's values might question the attribution.

André Gide's distance in time from the novel, and his familiarity with it in North Africa rather than within earshot of the conventional speech patterns it mimics, allowed him to see it more clearly. For the first time, it became possible to turn from a surface discussion of religious conformity or goodness, to a deeper understanding of the discontinuities in the narrative, its contradictions and its deliberate inexplicability, the originality of a devil-character like Gil-Martin whose very ordinariness is one of his greatest assets. Gide pointed out, acutely, the way in which Hogg fails to limit his devil-figure, one 'always admissible, even by unbelievers. It is the exteriorized development of our own desires, of our pride, of our most secret thoughts'.[1] The discontinuities in the narrative can be traced in part to the characterisation of Gil-Martin who reflects both readerly and individual preference or revulsion—as a reflector, the devil-figure is disturbingly familiar, disturbingly variable, 'a fascination in his look and manner, that drew me back toward him in spite of myself' (p.85),[2] a chameleon face which, Gil-Martin confirms, allows him to 'attain the very same ideas as well as the same mode of arranging them, so that, you see [...] I by degrees assume his likeness, and by assuming his likeness I attain to the possession of his most secret thoughts' (p.86). As the novel proceeds, Gil-Martin's power (like Hyde's over Jekyll) steadily increases, and the confusion arises not from the devil-figure, but from Wringhim's own inner life.

> I had heart-burnings, longings, and yearnings, that would not be satisfied; and I seemed hardly to be an accountable creature; being thus in the habit of executing transactions of the utmost moment, without being sensible that I did them. I was a being incomprehensible to myself. Either I had a second self, who transacted business in my likeness, or else my body was at times possessed by a spirit over which it had no countroul, and of whose actions my own soul was wholly unconscious. (p.125)

The confusion this technique provides is at the heart of the novel's continuing appeal, a confusion well noted by Ian Duncan in his treatment of 'Adam Bell', one of Hogg's impressive short stories, but equally applicable to the *Confessions*:

Different generic and cultural frames of explanation overlay one another to darken the simplest narrative combination: someone leaves, someone returns, but these events are strangely dislocated, they occupy different dimensions, and we do not know their reason, only the loss that connects them. The disturbing force of Hogg's brief story comes from its breaching of a narrative space between the traditional domains of history and romance, only to leave that space—contrary to the claims of the new genre—opaque, impenetrable by our reading.[3]

This opacity has resulted in a good deal of critics' attention turning to narrative strategies which go much deeper than the internal contradictions and plot repetitions and failures to match. At the heart of this debate lies the position of what appears to be the familiar device of the omniscient narrator, who is mostly (but not always) the Editor figure who opens, and apparently also closes the narrative. At times his role is usurped—by the brilliant intervention of J—— H—— entering his own narrative and declining to add his omniscience, by the supernatural visitants like the woman in white who seeks to change Robert's mind on Arthur's Seat, by the vision of golden weapons Robert has before the planned murder of Blanchard.[4]

Most of all, once the possibility of this reading is recognised, the reader realises that Gil-Martin is completely uncontrolled by the narrative and functions beyond the Editor's knowledge. His first detailed appearance is in Robert's narrative, not in the Editor's where only the most oblique explanation is given of his nature and function in the narrative; his appearance can change at will, and leads to sightings of him as Robert, George, Drummond—and perhaps others, whom at the time we do not recognise as Gil-Martin in disguise. An example is the persecution George undergoes from his brother, in church and in playhouse, in the tennis courts and in the countryside even when he tells no one where he is going. The Editor tells us that Robert follows him everywhere—but Robert does not corroborate this. 'In the gallery of the Parliament House, in the boxes of the play-house, in the church, in the assembly, in the streets, suburbs, and the fields; and every day, and every hour [...] the attendance became more and more constant, more inexplicable, and altogether more alarming and insufferable, until at last George was fairly driven from society'. In a nutshell, the Editor's narrative says, '[t]he attendance of that brother was now become like the attendance of a demon on some devoted being that had sold himself to destruction': his movements are impossible to trace, 'It was seldom that he saw him either following him in the streets, or entering any house or church after him; he only appeared in his place, George wist not how, or whence' (pp.27–28).

The failure of the omniscient narrator communicates itself to the reader, as Caroline McCracken-Flesher has argued convincingly, using as a focus the idea of the self under attack:

> Unlike the Self in *The Brownie*, which experienced discomfort because it had to define itself through others, whose values shifted, the Self in *The Private Memoirs* cannot begin to decide even what is 'self,' and what is 'other,' what is 'selfish,' and what is socially motivated. Since Hogg invites the reader not just into the puzzle, but into the protagonist's mind, the reader too experiences extreme confusion, extreme anxiety.[5]

More tellingly, Robert tells us that he is conscious of being more than one person, and unable to decide which is the controlling identity. Who haunts George to the point of obsession? Robert, or Gil-Martin in Robert's disguise? The narrative is silent. But it abounds with imagery of doubles and cases of confused identity, even descending to farce in examples such as the scene where Mrs Logan, Mrs Calvert and the landlady see someone who could be George Colwan–whom they know to be dead–or could be Gil-Martin, and their screams descend into farce.

> 'It *is* he!' cried Mrs. Logan, hysterically.
> 'Yes, yes, it *is* he!' cried the landlady, in unison.
> 'It is who?' said Mrs. Calvert; 'whom do you mean, mistress?'
> 'Oh, I don't know! I don't know! I was affrighted.' (p.58)

A great deal of the narrative can be linked to the idea of mistaken observation, the desire to know what has been witnessed, or to try to make sense of something which seems beyond sense–what Susan Egenolf has located in 'successful reduplification, that, is, the production of multiple images "very like" the originals, each clamoring to be recognized as authoritative'.[6]

With the realisation that the 'omniscient' Editor is as fallible as the mortal characters any critical reading of the book acquires freedom–by denying any empowering or authoritative function to any strand of narrative. David Groves has made important contributions to the debate by valuably focusing on the Editor, the Editor's function and unreliability, by demonstrating the untrustworthy nature of what a reader accustomed to the editorial function might be tempted to take at face value. Late in the book, for instance, the Editor breaks his promises to an eyewitness not to repeat his account ('the editor, in this crucial passage, is as much a liar as Robert Wringhim'[7]) and deploys a variety of techniques 'for denying otherness and forestalling any effective challenge to his received ideas'–just as Wringhim does.[8] An important early article by Douglas Mack in this debate addresses not only the unreliability of the Editor (whose story should 'not be regarded as the objective, unprejudiced account that it appears to be at first sight') but also the political bias of the Editor, Tory to a fault and blind to the prejudices of the Tory characters in the *Confessions*–particularly during the riot and Robert's subsequent trial.[9] While on one level Hogg is obviously taking a swing at his Tory friends and often persecutors in the *Blackwood's* group, on another he is making a serious statement to those who might accept an 'edited' account of the past at face value on the strength of apparently sound presentation and respectable use of language.

As Robert's mental state deteriorates he becomes an increasingly unreliable narrator, frequently accused of crimes he has no knowledge of, haunted by a persecuting presence which is openly driving him mad–yet he, along with the Editor, is the only source the reader has. Again, Wringhim's religiose discourse attempts to convince us of the respectability of a narrative which is plainly increasingly composed of paranoia and self-delusion. The child of a couple whose religious observance has been neatly dismissed by Marshall Walker as that of 'pettifogging zealots',[10] his discourse is an odd mixture of biblically-derived English and sometimes pompous, sometimes appealingly vulnerable English. The wavering position of the Editor is part of this process too: while we may have learned to distrust the Editorial voice, we would find it hard to disagree with it when it dismisses the religious practice of Mrs Colwan and the Rev. Wringhim as 'the splitting of hairs, and making distinctions in religion where none existed' (p.13), their arguments getting warmer 'always in proportion as they receded from nature, utility, and common sense' (p.10). The language position of the book is complex. Some characters, who should by our expectation speak undiluted Scots because of their position in society (John Barnet), speak heavily biblical English at times–as does John Maxwell in J. G. Lockhart's novel *Adam Blair* (1822). The Rev. Blanchard, one of the few acknowledged authorities for good, speaks biblical English: so does the mysterious woman in white. But can we trust a discourse which applies indiscriminately to the all-too-fallible Editor as well as to these instances of 'good', to the prostitute Bell Calvert as well as to

Robert's mother when, as she occasionally does, she lets her maternal good nature take over from her religious obsession?

> 'I have been conversant this day with one stranger only, whom I took rather for an angel of light.'
> 'It is one of the devil's most profound wiles to appear like one,' said my mother.
> 'Woman, hold thy peace!' said my reverend father: 'thou pretendest to teach what thou knowest not.' (p.83)

The contrast between the heavily biblical speech-forms of the minister's discourse, and the simplicity of his wife's, is notable: but then the minister's speech-forms are never more explicitly biblical than when he is at his weakest, echoing the very words of the 1611 account of Genesis 32 and the wrestling of Jacob and the angel while he perverts the story to his own ends. Gil-Martin delights in biblical speech forms, used with exquisite ambiguity.

> I asked [...] 'Are all your subjects Christians, prince?'
> 'All my European subjects are, or deem themselves so,' returned he; 'and they are the most faithful and true subjects I have.'
> Who could doubt, after this, that he was the Czar of Russia? (p.93)

Who could doubt, after this, Wringhim's mental limitation and deafness to irony? He cannot repeat Gil-Martin *verbatim* ('though I cannot from memory repeat his words, his eloquence was of that overpowering nature, that the subtility of other men sunk before it' (p.92)), nor can he see at once what the reader is privileged to see as irony:

> 'Gil!' said I; 'Have you no name but Gil? Or which of your names is it? Your Christian or surname?'
> '[...] It is not my *Christian* name; but it *is* a name which may serve your turn.'
> 'This is very strange!' said I. 'Are you ashamed of your parents, that you refuse to give your real name?'
> 'I have no parents save one, whom I do not acknowledge,' said he proudly; 'therefore, pray drop that subject [...] .' (p.89)

In time, Gil-Martin's speech and attitudes begin to take over Wringhim's—Blanchard warns Wringhim to no avail of the 'sublimity in his ideas', but he also warns him explicitly: 'There is not an error into which a man can fall, which he may not press Scripture into his service as proof of the probity of' (p.91).

These are the ideas Gil-Martin employs, heavily illustrated by very selective biblical quotation, to persuade Robert to the acts of shooting Blanchard, and stabbing George: the words begin to over-power reason, even memory. After George's death,

> I will not deny, that my own immediate impressions of this affair in some degree differed from this statement. But this is precisely as my illustrious friend described it to me afterwards, and I can rely implicitly on his information, as he was at that time a looker-on, and my senses all in a state of agitation, and he could have no motive for saying what was not the positive truth. (p.118)

Finally, after a night of torment during which Gil-Martin persuades Robert (under torture) to utter a blasphemy so terrible—and so un-recorded in the pages of the novel—that damnation inevitably fol-lows,[11] Robert's own discourse begins to resemble Gil-Martin's. The awful words are uttered, 'I was instantly at liberty; and what I now am, the Almighty knows! *Amen*' (p.165). It has taken a long time in the novel for Robert to realise the possibilities of irony. When Gil-Martin presents him with a golden pistol for the assassination of Blanchard, he can say without fear of detection, 'See what thy mas-ter hath provided thee!' (p.95). It will take a long stretch of Hogg's narrative for Wringhim to learn to listen to Gil-Martin's speech with enough care.[12]

Critical discussion of Hogg's use of language has made rapid strides. At the most obvious level, the *Confessions* can be seen fre-quently to conform to the norm of the time, assigning to 'good' char-acters educated, English, biblically informed dialogue, and assign-ing good Scots to humorous or crude characters—Hogg himself, the servant at Bell Calvert's trial, the marvellous Samuel Scrape (aka Penpunt) who relays Lucky Shaw's tale of Auchtermuchty. The Scots of such characters is the kind of Scots Hogg would have been famil-iar with himself from his circle of friends and family, and which the systematic republication of his work has shown him to have mas-tered completely.

A more careful reading shows that Hogg (like Scott) does not conform rigidly to this stereotype. To be sure, Hogg peoples the book with Scots-speaking working-class characters, but these are hardly provided for stock humour or light relief. It is these charac-ters who are frequently given morally positive speeches, the criti-cism of Wringhim by John Barnet, the embedded Auchtermuchty tale which explains a lot of the later action, the refusal by Bessy to implicate her mistress or others in the law court, the obvious Christian worth of the poor Border peasants whom Wringhim equally obviously despises, though he accepts their shelter when on the run from Gil-Martin. The Laird at the outset speaks easy Scots, and is presented sympathetically; George, at least superficially one of the book's most attractive characters, speaks easy thin Scots or English without difficulty.

The opposite movement is the interesting one. The link between English and Good—and, for that matter, biblical English and Good—is firmly denied from the outset in the Editor's narrative. Wringhim senior speaks like a man of the cloth, but behaves repellently; the description of Wringhim family life, steeped in Bible reading and disreputable prayer for the destruction of enemies, is revolting. The Editor distances himself explicitly from their discussions of Scripture and doctrine—itself a dubious stance, as the Editor's own integrity comes more and more into question. Blanchard and the woman in white speak irreproachable English but then so does Bell Calvert, prostitute and fallen woman. Most tellingly, so does Gil-Martin, who carries his own Bible, and whose linguistic command is such that he can overpower Wringhim in argument, alarm Blanchard by the sublimity of his ideas, make himself the welcome ally of 'Mr Ringan' with whom (in a heavy-handed Hogg joke) he moves to Glasgow and there achieves great success.

Wringhim's speeches, as reported by Peter Garside in this edition, are extensively peppered with biblical English, and these speeches are expressed with the finest command of argument, and above all of supportive allusion to Scripture, to be found in Hogg's novel. As an index of character quality, these features should indicate excellence and reliability but of course Hogg has reversed this. Wringhim recognises the danger of Gil-Martin's power of language but cannot resist it—'all reasoning with him is to no purpose' (p.164). Further, the same familiarity with Scripture which would have alerted Hogg's contemporaries to the poverty of the Wringhims' religious attitudes, would have alerted them to the dangers implicit in Gil-Martin's biblical discourse. For it takes little analysis to demonstrate that Gil-Martin's allusions are selective, unsystematic, misleading and designed to demonstrate the danger of uncritically received biblical discourse.

Perhaps the most astonishing lapse by critics to date has been their failure to look at Hogg's use of embedded biblical quotation. The most flagrant example is the description by Wringhim senior of his wrestling match with God which is a startling perversion of

Genesis 32–an openly ludicrous misreading with, moreover, the blasphemous suggestion that the match was won by Wringhim, leaving God a beaten force. Such a reading would be appalling to most Christians, but especially to the Calvinist to whom the idea of God's omnipotence (and omniscience) is central. For another thing, someone familiar with Scripture would recognise the allusion in the golden weapons episode to Peter's vision of food from heaven[13] and its sharp warning not to use earthly standards to judge divine actions and values–the very crime of which the Wringhims stand convicted throughout the *Confessions*.

Even more outrageous, to the alerted reader, are Gil-Martin's speeches where he offers argument or persuasion purportedly based on scripture and religious principle. An example would be the arguments he deploys to justify the killing of Blanchard on the basis that the divine's preaching is so corrosive of true faith–the Wringhims' antinomian excesses–that Robert would be doing the world a favour, and acting as a true servant of God, in killing Blanchard as a dangerous force for evil. Even Gil-Martin sees the thinness of the argument–'I could not help thinking, that I perceived a little derision of countenance on his face as he said this'–but Wringhim is simply too weak to counter it ('I sunk dumb before such a man') (p.94). The reader sees small things too: when (in the Editor's account) George spares Robert's life on Arthur's Seat he handsomely seeks a reconciliation and admits to being 'hasty and passionate: it is a fault in my nature' (p.32). In Robert's account, 'though I do not recollect the circumstances of that deadly scuffle very minutely, I know that I vanquished him so far as to force him to ask my pardon, and crave a reconciliation' (p.112). Well, yes. Up to a point, this is true. So is Robert's account of his brother's death, 'covered with wounds, and with curses and blasphemy in his mouth' (p.118), if we can trust the Editor's account–or rather Bell Calvert's–that George's last words were, 'Oh, dog of hell, is it you who has done this!' (p.54). Robert, like Gil-Martin, indeed like the Editor, is true up to a point. Recognising that point is the key to the novel.

Another centre of critical debate concerns the very existence, as well as the identity, of Gil-Martin. Like Marlowe's *Dr Faustus* and other manifestations of the Faust story, the *Confessions* is centrally concerned with the confrontation between mortal and diabolic.[14] Like Faust, Wringhim has no real idea of what he is dealing with. It has been suggested by several critics that a feasible reading would be to make Gil-Martin a delusion of Wringhim's imagination. Obviously, such a reading might involve a more extensive knowledge of the subconscious mind than could be expected of Hogg's own time. Nevertheless a persuasive case can be made, no more so than is evident in Douglas Gifford's *James Hogg*, where both the slippery nature of the language used by Wringhim and by others to describe his own experiences and others', and the more telling objection which is the number of reliable witnesses in the novel who actually *see* Gil-Martin (a variety of friends of George and his circle, the men working in the printing office, and the ultimately reliable Blanchard who not only sees Gil-Martin but experiences an immediate antipathy), are faced up to.[15] One could—just—explain Robert's inexplicable behaviour (did he rape the girl? did he kill his own mother?) by possession or mental illness, the sightings of Gil-Martin by Mrs Logan and Mrs Calvert as hysteria, but the evidence provided by witnesses such as Blanchard is hard to contradict. The book fiercely resists single readings and single interpretations, just as critics—such as David Petrie—have pointed to the dangers of imposing readings on the book which somehow limit its power to operate on different levels,[16] and inhibit the increasingly post-modernist readings which the novel is currently attracting.

Debate can be endless on how Hogg intends his readers to understand the end of the *Confessions* and Robert's faith. Notably, throughout the book Gil-Martin has not directly harmed mortals, his bullet missing Blanchard at point-blank range and his rapier not wounding George in a prolonged combat against an enemy who had been drinking heavily. What Gil-Martin does is to panic Robert into compulsive actions which, cumulatively, lead to an excess of guilt and self-loathing. Not only the memory of murder but also the imputation of further murder (his mother) and rape—an idea surely repellent to someone presented in Robert's misogynistic character—would seriously destabilise a normal well-balanced person. Their effect on someone broken down by excitement, exhaustion, sleeplessness, terror, exposure and public detestation can easily be imagined.

What, then, does Gil-Martin want to achieve by driving Robert as he does? Again, Scripture provides a convincing reading—the idea of sin so terrible that even the promise of limitless grace and redemption (on which Wringhim bases so much) fails. In exactly the same way as Marlowe's Faustus despairs on stage, losing the vision of Christ's blood in the firmament, so Wringhim could be argued to have despaired of salvation. He cannot have failed to know Hebrews 10.26–29:

For if we sin wilfully after that we have received the knowledge of the truth, there remaineth no more sacrifice for sins.
[...] Of how much sorer punishment, suppose ye, shall he be
thought worthy, who hath trodden under foot the Son of God,
and hath counted the blood of the covenant, wherewith he
was sanctified, an unholy thing, and hath done despite unto
the Spirit of grace?

Robert, true to form, is harrassed by Gil-Martin to utter a 'tremendous prayer', couched in Gil-Martin's trademark ambiguity but
(as even dull-witted Robert realises) 'susceptible of being rendered
in a meaning perfectly dreadful' (p.164). What this prayer is, Hogg
leaves wisely unexplained: not only would it be unprintable were it
to be spelled out (since it would fairly clearly be blasphemous), it
gains in intensity from being projected into the reader's imagination, the details drawn from whatever imagination of the unspeakable each reader brings to it.

The technique of imprecision is one which has functioned since
publication of the *Confessions* to keep the central premise alive. Hogg,
clearly, wishes each reader to have a real sense of the diabolic—
whether the genuine diabolic of a Satan believed in by the reader, or
the more modern diabolic imagined through some form of disease
or malfunction of the normal which the modern reader translates
into some variation of the 'devil'. Gil-Martin's imprecision is central
to his presentation. From the start, he is characterised by ambiguity:
the 'young man of a mysterious appearance' (p.80) who first appears as Wringhim's twin spends most of the book off-stage, invisible and inaccessible. He gives hints, to be sure, that he has been
present at various stages where the Editor or narrator do not mention him, but the *Confessions* is dominated by an absent character. At
times, we are sure this is a deliberate strategy on Gil-Martin's part
to increase the pressure on a disintegrating Robert Wringhim—de-
serting him when he is set on by the harpy women in the wood,
disappearing at the time of the supposed rape and matricide only to
reappear full of hidden meaning and suppressed hints when
Wringhim least wants him. At a time like this the reader sees the full
force of Gil-Martin's earlier suggestion that he will never desert
him.

Sometimes (as already suggested) Gil-Martin is present, rather
than absent, as a deliberate scheme. Thus the diabolic visitations
which so unsettle George before the Arthur's Seat episode can very
clearly be suspected to be in part a result of a mysteriously infallible

prediction of George's movements, infallible because George sees Gil-Martin rather than his brother glaring at him in every conceivable place. Who searched out a victim to blame the murder on, anticipating Thomas Drummond's appearance on the scene as well as impersonating him to perfection? What role does Gil-Martin play in the political riots in Edinburgh which discredit the Colwan family in the public gaze? And, most disturbing of all, what is Gil-Martin doing, and in which disguise, while Robert appears to be lying in some sort of trance in Dalcastle? The Kafkaesque sense of entrapment and incomprehension needs no explicit belief in witchcraft or diabology to function for modern audiences. For that matter, a twenty-first century reader familiar with multiple personality disorders has little trouble explaining the 'possession' of Wringhim by Gil-Martin.[17] Readers familiar with the imprecision of meaning, with views that all language and meaning are relative and subtexts and intertexts essential to meaning, will find Hogg's use of the Bible entirely plausible.

Two arguments, then, are to be brought forward here. One is that the technique of imprecision allows the author to describe phenomena which modern readers might not admit to consciously or intellectually, but might accept in broad outline and adapt to their own circumstances and contemporary belief. Whatever particular devil is under discussion, the reader completes the incomplete detail.

The same argument can be applied to the language and use of the Bible in the *Confessions*. An audience unfamiliar with the 1611 Bible–and that must include many modern readers–can accept the plot and the narrative style without recognising Bible reference or intertext, and achieve a perfectly satisfactory reading, albeit one guilty of equating biblical language (or pseudo-biblical language) with social or religious value judgements. To add recognised biblical allusion and intertext is to transform the *Confessions* into dense satire, with deliberate and crafted effects aimed in particular at the two generations of the Wringhim family.

The text makes two specific remarks about the nature of language which the reader could heed. One is the Laird's, on his wedding night, responding with good-natured incredulity to his wife's suggestion that they should pray together before retiring to their marriage bed. 'Prayers, Mistress! Lord help your crazed head, is this a night for prayers?' (p.5) The Laird's attitude to prayer, and to its use of language, is hard not to accept as the author's or Editor's, agreeing as it does with the later dismissal of Mrs Colwan's religious debates with her pastor and mentor.

The other point, of course, has to do with ability to see through the surface of language. When Robert first meets his enigmatic twin, Gil-Martin, he is charmed as well as bewitched by the latter's sublimity of thought, and his ability to speak in a style and discourse which so completely agrees with the family's idea of goodness. Asked, specifically, by his father if Gil-Martin seems to 'adhere to the religious principles in which I have educated you?', Wringhim can confidently reply in the positive (p.84). It takes the remainder of the novel to clarify Wringhim's position, as well as the audience's.

But is, finally, clarity what the book seeks? The weight of recent criticism has been quite opposite, seeing in the *Confessions* an extraordinary anticipation of much modernist and postmodernist critical and writing practice, producing what Magdalene Redekop has called 'a kind of premature post-modernist novel'.[18] A writer of the stature of Alasdair Gray is self-evidently indebted to Hogg's novel even when in work like *Lanark* he produces visions of Heaven and Hell which begin from very different premises from Hogg's. 'All imaginative workers make art out of the people and places they know best', said Gray in a 1982 interview published along with his brief autobiography by the Saltire Society in 1988.[19] He goes on to make observations about Heaven and Hell which are more than pertinent to a reading of Hogg's *Confessions* in a post-modern age.

> No good writer is afraid to use local place names—the bible is full of them. No good writer is afraid to use local politics—Dante peoples Hell, Purgatory and Heaven with local politicians. I don't think Scotland is a better country, Glasgow a better city than any other, but all I know of Hell and Heaven was learned here, so this is the ground I use, though sometimes I disguise the fact.

The last question he answered was: how important to you is religion as a theme? Gray's answer would, no doubt, have delighted Hogg had Hogg lived at a time he could have delivered it, let alone printed it.

> Religion is not a theme, religion—any religion—is a way of seeing the world, a way of linking the near, the ordinary, the temporary with the remote, the fantastic, the eternal. Religion is a perspective device so I use it, of course. I differ from church people in seeing heaven and hell as the material of life itself, not of an afterlife. Intellectually I prefer the Olympian Greek faith. Emotionally I am dominated by the Old Testament. Morally speaking I prefer Jesus, but he sets a standard

I'm too selfish to aim for. I'm more comfortable with his daddy, Jehovah, who is nastier but more human. The world is full of wee Jehovahs.[20]

Despite the obvious differences, Gray's comment makes for a perceptive insight on Hogg's *Confessions*. *Religion is a perspective*—not for the trained artist's eye in Hogg's case, but for a re-arrangement of life (and religious experience), of perception of other people and oneself, of how people behave in life and in literature, in the past (the novel is self-consciously set in a past from which the editor distances himself on the last page) and in the present. Like Hardy two generations later, Hogg was happy to alter the proportions of normality, to present all the characters in the grotesquerie of the Brocken Spectre which stalks Arthur's Seat at dawn. Not only the Wringhims are grotesques, in human and in religious terms: most of the characters in this book are, except for some minor characters who carry the label of 'good' in the absence of major characters who could lay claim to it. Recent criticism has pointed, excellently, to the faults and the bad faith in the Editor figure, the narrator on whom we are conditioned to depend: many have pointed to the fallibility of the Christian characters, ordained and lay, on whom audiences might have thought themselves entitled to depend for moral guidance or at least absolute values. The wee Jehovahs of the book are extremely unpleasant, perhaps even more so than readers who fail to read the Bible intertext immediately appreciate. But then so is the Editor, openly biased, manipulative, and excluded from a great deal of the narrative including some of the most crucial episodes—George's death, Mrs Wringhim's death, Robert's conception, and a great deal of Robert's later life.

The early reviewers who criticised the book as anti-religious were patently guilty of an absurd misreading: Peter Garside's Introduction to this edition amply demonstrate that the reviews were more copious than previously thought, and mostly hostile.[21] Readers of our own time who tend to cut the book to conform to a single thesis are equally guilty of mutilating it to fit a Procrustean bed which it seems quite unsuited for. The *Confessions* is revealed now, as never before, as a book which opens itself to multiple readings in a manner more akin to the post-modern than to any single hypothesis or interpretation. It satirises not religion, not Calvinism, but excess: it satirises pride, closed-minded arrogance, timidity, stupidity. It opens itself to interpretation by those who accept a personal God and those who do not, those who believe in some kind of Satan and those who completely reject the idea. Gil-Martin's success in no way depends on a reader subscribing to Milton, nor to the book of Revelation, nor indeed to the traditional Scottish diabolic features which Gil-Martin plainly exhibits. Gil-Martin may not even exist, and the novel may be read throughout as emerging from the stress on a human consciousness badly under strain.

In the end, the Editor's words are poised with the same ambiguity that Gil-Martin's tend to be. 'I do not comprehend the writer's drift. [...] I account all the rest either dreaming or madness; [...] in this day, and with the present generation, it will not go down, [...]. It was a bold theme for an allegory, and would have suited that age well had it been taken up by one fully qualified for the task, which this writer was not' (pp.174–75). James Hogg, in his own persona as a visitor to the text, heartily agrees: 'I hae mair ado than I can manage the day, foreby ganging to houk up hunder-year-auld banes' (p.170). Like the one sceptic in Auchtermuchty who was not deceived by the devil's preaching, the author resolutely refuses to take sides, to authenticate or to privilege one reading over another. Like Chinese boxes fitting badly into one another, the multiple plots contradict, partly illuminate, partly overlap, partly refuse to make sense. The relation of reader to text, to Editor, to assumed author is deliberately made almost impossibly confusing. Evidence–false evidence, even true evidence like the *Blackwood's* letter (pp.165–69)–abounds, none of it conclusive. The narrative framework is frequently confused, sometimes disfigured by conspicuous silence or gaps. If Gil-Martin exists, he and only he knows what is going on–with the exception of the woman in white, and the heavenly vision granted Robert before Blanchard's assassination. Heaven chooses to remain distant and observe, very much echoing God's stance in the book of Job as Satan tests Job's integrity. The *Confessions*, uniquely and brilliantly, exists on its own terms and refuses to conform to critical analysis. As Douglas Mack sums it up in an important recent revaluation of the novel, the *Confessions*

> seeks to confront the insights and the limitations of *both* Enlightenment Edinburgh *and* the pre-Enlightenment Ettrick of Will o' Phaup. In this project, Hogg's novel confronts the demonic and the forces of madness; but ultimately it does not allow the mystery and the terror of these forces to be diminished and evaded by means of lucid and rational explanation of the kind offered by the Editor.[22]

Perhaps this intention accounts for two of its greatest achievements. First, it contrives a plot concerning the supernatural which operates with an audience who may not accept the idea or the existence of a supernatural. Second, it universalises the struggle of good and evil away from doctrinal or specific struggle to something sufficiently undefined, yet sufficiently credible in any age, that it can be re-interpreted at each reading. 'To be in a state of consciousness and unconsciousness, at the same time, in the same body and same spirit, was impossible', Wringhim argues when he is suffering delusions (p.125). But he is wrong. Hogg's narrative layers convince us that these possibilities existed then, and exist now. Madness, evil, possession are not the exclusive province of Satan. Hogg's masterpiece convinces us today as it did in 1824.

Ian Campbell
Edinburgh
December 2000

Notes

1.   James Hogg, *The Private Memoirs and Confessions of a Justified Sinner*, with an Introduction by André Gide (London: Cresset Press, 1947), p. xv. For a good survey of the growth of a critical response to the novel see Silvia Mergenthal, *James Hogg: Selbstbild und Bild*, Scottish Studies 9 (Frankfurt: Peter Lang, 1990), pp. 334–35. An important contribution is Karl Miller, *Doubles* (Oxford: Oxford University Press, 1985).

2.   Page numbers given in parenthesis refer to the present edition of *Confessions of a Justified Sinner*.

3.   Ian Duncan, 'The Upright Corpse: Hogg, National Literature and the Uncanny', *Studies in Hogg and his World*, 5 (1994), 29–54 (p. 34). David Eggenschwiler, in 'James Hogg's *Confessions* and the Fall into Division', *Studies in Scottish Literature*, 9:1 (1971), 26–39 suggests that Hogg is here doing several things in the same novel whereas usually novels of the period might be regarded as confined to one genre each.

4.   For a discussion see Ian Campbell, 'Author and Audience in Hogg's *Confessions of a Justified Sinner*', *Scottish Literary News*, 2:4 (June 1972), 66–76, and 'James Hogg and the Bible', in *The Bible in Scottish Life and Literature*, ed. by David F. Wright (Edinburgh: St Andrew Press, 1988), pp. 94–109.

5.   Caroline McCracken-Flesher, 'English Hegemony/Scottish Subjectivity: Calvinism and Cultural Renaissance in the Nineteenth-Century "North British Novel" ' (unpublished doctoral dissertation, Brown University, 1989), p. 104. See also a valuable discussion by David Petrie 'The Sinner versus the Scholar: Two Exemplary Models of Mis-re-membering and

Mis-taking Signs in Relation to Hogg's *Justified Sinner*', *Studies in Hogg and his World*, 3 (1992), 57–67.

6.   Susan B. Egenolf, 'Varnished Tales: History and Artifice in the Novel, 1789–1830' (unpublished doctoral dissertation, Texas A & M University, 1995), p. 206

7.   David Groves, *James Hogg: The Growth of a Writer* (Edinburgh: Scottish Academic Press, 1988), p. 118.

8.   Groves, p. 119.

9.   Douglas S. Mack, ' "The Rage of Fanaticism in Former Days": James Hogg's *Confessions of a Justified Sinner* and the Controversy over *Old Mortality*', *Nineteenth Century Scottish Fiction: Critical Essays*, ed. by Ian Campbell (Manchester: Carcanet, 1979), pp. 37–50 (p. 45). The possibilities of satiric use of biblical and serious discourse are further discussed in Ian Campbell, 'The Bible, the Kirk and Scottish Literature', in *The Bible in Scottish Life and Literature*, ed. by David F. Wright (Edinburgh: St Andrew Press, 1988), pp. 110–27. Further good discussion is found in Egenolf, p. 205, and Groves: 'By gradually unveiling the pride, prejudices, and obtuseness of this "editor", Hogg will enjoy a gleeful revenge on the critics, academics, and editors who dominated the literary world of the 1820's' (Groves, p. 115). See also Andrew Hook, 'Hogg, Melville and the Scottish Enlightenment', *Scottish Literary Journal*, 4 (December 1977), 25–39, reprinted in Andrew Hook, *From Goosecreek to Gandercleugh: Studies in Scottish-American Literary and Cultural History* (East Linton: Tuckwell Press, 1999), 116–34.

10. Marshall Walker, *Scottish Literature since 1707* (London: Longman, 1996), p. 150.

11. For a closer discussion see Ian Campbell, 'Hogg's *Confessions* and the *Heart of Darkness*', *Studies in Scottish Literature*, 15 (1980), 187–201.

12. Jill Rubenstein, in 'Confession, Damnation and the Dissolution of Identity in Novels by James Hogg and Harold Frederic', *Studies in Hogg and his World*, 1 (1990), 102–13, defines Wringhim's moments of self-knowledge as epiphany which exactly catches the modernist achievement of the scene, and encourages the move towards post-modern readings which characterise recent discussions of the book, such as Cairns Craig's in *Out of History* (Edinburgh: Polygon, 1996).

13. Acts 10.11 and 11.5. The weapons in Wringhim's vision (p. 95) all have their points directed at Wringhim: to use them would have involved danger, possibly hurt. But like the woman in white, this appears a genuine visitation from Heaven in a book where little is clear—and Gil-Martin is extremely keen to hustle Wringhim away from it denying him the opportunity to test its validity, and his courage.

14. John Carey's Introduction to the World's Classics edition valuably establishes (pp. xxi–xxiii) the novel's place in the context of Romantic and Gothic literature, but see also Williston Russell Benedict, 'A Study of the "Second Self" in James Hogg's Fiction, with Reference to its Employment in German Romantic Literature' (unpublished doctoral dissertation, Columbia University, 1973), pp. 113 ff and 133 ff.

15. Douglas Gifford, *James Hogg* (Edinburgh: Ramsay Head Press, 1976), especially p. 148 ff.

16. David Petrie, 'The Reception of James Hogg's *Justified Sinner* in the Context of Scottish Calvinist Controversy', *Quaderni dell'Istituto di Lingue e Letterature Straniere dell'Universita di Verona*, 5 (1990), 175–86.

17. For good background information see Allan Beveridge 'James Hogg and Abnormal Psychology: Some Background Notes', *Studies in Hogg and his World*, 2 (1991), 91–94.

18. M. Redekop, 'Beyond Closure: Buried Alive with Hogg's *Justified Sinner*', *English Literary History*, 52 (1985), 159–84 (p. 162).

19. Alasdair Gray, *Alasdair Gray*, Saltire Self-Portraits, 4 (Edinburgh: Saltire Society, 1988), p. 18.

20. Gray, p. 19.

21. See also Gillian Hughes, 'The Critical Reception of *The Confessions of a Justified Sinner*', *Newsletter of the James Hogg Society*, 1 (1982), 11–14. When his edition of the *Confessions of a Justified Sinner* was first published (London: Oxford University Press, 1969), John Carey asserted (p. 256) that 'apparently the only review of Hogg's novel to appear was printed in the *Westminster Review* for October 1824, pp. 560–62'.

22. Douglas S. Mack, 'Revisiting *The Private Memoirs and Confessions of a Justified Sinner*', *Studies in Hogg and his World*, 10 (1999), 1–26 (p. 23).

Note on the Text

The present text is based on the first edition of 1824, published by the London firm of Longmans, the actual copy-text being a copy of the novel belonging to Stirling University Library. The latter has itself been checked against other copies of the first edition, and no textual variants within the edition have been discovered, other than the appearance of the signature Z3 as 3Z in some copies (including the Stirling copy-text). In spite of the fascinating glimpse provided by Mrs Garden's claim in 1895 to have it in her possession, no clear record of the holograph manuscript's history has survived, and it must now be assumed to be either lost or destroyed. There are strong grounds, nevertheless, for believing that the first edition takes us close to what Hogg originally wrote, while representing, with only a few slight mishaps, the finished product he would have desired. As discussed in the present Introduction (see pp. lvii–lxv), Hogg manoeuvred a situation where, in James Clarke, he effectively had the printer of his choice, near at hand in Edinburgh, and working under his own instructions. While there is no clear evidence of his receiving proofs, it would not have been impossible for these to be sent to his home at Altrive Lake, and there is also record of at least two trips to Edinburgh by Hogg during the production of the novel. The first edition is an outstanding work of printing on two counts. On the one hand, it is unusually faithful to Hogg's known idiomatic expressions, showing little sign of standardisation in this respect, while also preserving deliberate anomalies such as the arithmetically incorrect 'twelve' at p.10, l.31. On the other hand, it is remarkably free from obvious error, revealing, for example, no inappropriate inconsistencies in proper names, while at the same time showing considerable typographical skill (as in the arrangement of the running headlines). In perhaps no other major work, published in his lifetime, is it possible to sense Hogg's full presence in such an unimpeded way; and it is interesting to speculate how some of his other works might have appeared if he had been able to control the circumstances of their production similarly.

The first edition is the only version of the printed text in which Hogg is known to have played a part. The reissue of 1828, under the new title *The Suicide's Grave*, was apparently made up of old unused sheets, and, apart from its replacement title-page and the absence of the dedication, it does not differ materially from the first edition. Nor is there clear evidence of any direct input into the cut-down version published in *Tales & Sketches by the Ettrick Shepherd*, as 'The Private Memoirs and Confessions of a Fanatic', late in 1837, two years after Hogg's death. Indeed, as is argued more fully in the present Introduction (see pp. lxxiv–lxxix), there is good reason to believe that the bulk or all of the changes in this version, including both stylistic/grammatical alterations and large-scale excisions, were made by house readers and/or compositors, operating in line with the priorities of the publisher, Blackie & Son, and often showing scant regard for the tenor of Hogg's original narrative. It is here, not untypically, that Hogg's twelve is first 'corrected' to thirteen; and here, too, that expressions such as 'had held' and 'the house had been broken' are needlessly ironed out and regularised (in these instances to 'had been held' and '[...] broken into'). Nevertheless, on a handful of occasions the 1837 text corrects printing errors in the first edition, and so, by virtue of being there first, anticipates a number of corrections made by the present edition, as acknowledged in the list of editorial emendations given below.

The line of modern editions begins with the Shiells & Co. edition of 1895, but until the present text, apart from Shiells itself, only two of these, the Campion Reprint series edition of 1924 and John Carey's edition of 1969 for the Oxford English Novels series, were evidently set freshly from an actual first edition copy, the remainder being derivatives of other modern editions (see Introduction, pp. lxxix–lxxxi). The Shiells and Campion editions not only standard-ise punctuation and spelling freely, according to their own house conventions, but also intervene fairly invasively to 'improve' style and grammar, with a significant loss not only of Hogg's own per-sonal idiosyncrasies but also of clarity and appropriateness in ex-pression. For example, Bell Calvert's 'be so kind as come to the Grass Market' (p.42, l.36) echoes Hogg's usage in his own corre-spondence, and there is no call for the insertion of 'to' before 'come', as found in Campion (and, in its wake, the Cresset Press edition of 1947, followed in turn by *its* successors). Carey's 1969 edition, in comparison, shows much greater respect for the original printed text, listing just seven emendations, all admitting 1837 readings, and relating to cases where it is deemed errors occurred (albeit, as the present Introduction points out, also making a number of other si-lent changes, and generating a few mistakes of its own).

The present text restores the first edition in preference to the 1837/Carey reading in five of these instances. In the case of the apparently awkward 'the character with which she had to deal with' (p.44, ll.34–35), where Carey omits the first 'with', another line stemming from Campion prefers to remove the second one, arguably thus offering the smoother alternative; though ultimately there is nothing substantially wrong with the first edition form, which need not derive from unintentional repetition (as through an insertion not matched by a deletion), and certainly one should be hesitant before rewriting text. The substitution of 'undertaking' for 'understanding' in 'bethought me of the rashness of my understanding' (p.108, l.34) also seems unnecessary in view of Robert's concern here for his own thought processes, in keeping with similar moments of self-doubt, and in particular in view of a distinct biblical echo from Isaiah. In the case of 'trust' in 'to his right trust cousin' (p.124, l.8), where Carey prefers 'trusty', it is worth bearing in mind that Hogg is offering a pastiche of an old charter, and that also there could be a deliberate rhetorical progression from 'trust cousin', through 'trust-worthy cousin', to 'trusty cousins and councillors' in its immediate wake. The transference of 'an'' to 'and' in 'strode furiously round an' round the room' (p.142, l.29), which is also found in both Shiells and Campion, at first seems well-advised in view of there being little evidence of a Scots pronunciation being indicated (at least orthographically) elsewhere in Wringhim's main narrative, and there is too the possibility of slippage from Penpunt's speech nearby. The counter argument that Wringhim is in a state of high excitement, with the discovery of his mother's body, also perhaps needs to be qualified by the fact that he is writing retrospectively here. On the other hand, 'round an' round' features in Burns's *Halloween* (stanza 7), and it is also a very well known phrase, so that Hogg might possibly have written it thus without necessarily intending to convey a Scots intonation. Finally, Carey's adoption of 'effort' rather than 'effect' to read 'This effort made my case worse', at p.149, ll.15–16, presumably on the grounds of misreading, has just as plausible an alternative in 'The effect made my case worse', as found in Campion, Gide, and successors. Here again, moreover, especially viewed in a larger narrative perspective, the original first edition text can be seen to make sense, with 'This effect' referring backwards to Wringhim's desperate attempt to escape the loom as a result of the weaver's continued blows, leading on to worse entanglement.

The present text is closer to the first edition of 1824 than any previous modern edition discussed in this volume, its aim being to reconstruct as far as possible the accident-free work that Hogg working in conjunction with his printer so nearly achieved. In six individual cases repairs have been made silently where the first edition fails in applying opening and closing speech marks, with four such marks being added by the present edition, one removed, and a single quotation mark converted to a double mark. Additionally, within the Auchtermuchty story (at pp.136–39), the system of rendering speech within speech has been made consistent, this involving the silent alteration or addition of some thirty marks. At one point (p.49, l.18) a stop is added to 'Mr' to bring consistency in the presentation of such titles, which the printer undoubtedly would have wanted. A seemingly pointless question mark is changed to a full stop at p.32, l.17. Otherwise the original punctuation is followed in its entirety. No attempt has been made to standardise or normalise orthography, with the effect that a number of Hogg's own idiosyncrasies and inconsistencies (as in the sometimes apparently interchangeable use of 'council' and 'counsel') have no doubt survived intact. Interventions in this field only occur in cases of obvious error ('completly', for example, clashes with seven other instances of 'completely' in the text), or where there is no evidence of a spelling ever occurring as a variant elsewhere ('acquiline', though partly tempting, runs in the face of the word's Latin root, and one would have expected the printer to provide in 'aquiline' the only recognised form). Additionally, the present text corrects the homonymous 'their' for 'there', a superfluous negative in the mouth of Gil-Martin, and one mistaken verbal stutter. These orthographic and verbal editorial emendations are incorporated in the following list, where the page number is given for each item, with the line number following, the emended text appearing first in each case.

> 25, l.14 off the blighting] off the the blighting (Ed1)
> [editorial; as in 1837]
>
> 78, l.10 the least worthy] the lest worthy (Ed1)
> [editorial; as in 1837]
>
> 95, l.7 if there had] if their had (Ed1)
> [editorial; as in 1837]
>
> 105, l.20 dost not know] dost not not know (Ed1)
> [editorial; as in 1837]
>
> 112, l.23 completely] completly (Ed1)
> [editorial; as in 1837]
>
> 122, l.32 aquiline] acquiline (Ed1)
> [editorial; as in 1837]

End-of-line hyphens in the first edition are ignored in the present edition, except in cases where it seems likely that the word in question would have been given a hyphen even if it had not appeared at the end of a line: in most instances guidance has been obtained from the appearance of the word in question elsewhere in the text.

Various words are hyphenated at the ends of lines in the present edition. The list below indicates those cases in which such hyphens should be retained in making quotations. As elsewhere, in calculating line numbers, titles and running headlines have been ignored.

6, l.17 chimney-corner	96, l.31 Gil-Martin
7, l.28 bride's-maid	99, l.9 pass-word
8, l.13 new-married	133, l.21 law-suits
12, l.5 ca'-him	144, l.42 pre-ordination
12, l.16 ca'-you	149, l.24 loom-spoke
39, l.10 two-edged	150, l.19 fore-finger
56, l.31 Heigh-ho	151, l.20 a-week
58, l.9 lodging-house	162, l.39 north-west
70, l.38 cast-away	164, l.29 cow-house
91, l.17 powerful-minded	167, l.14 hay-ropes
94, l.22 fellow-creatures	173, l.23 knee-buckles
96, l.6 Gil-Martin	173, l.29 well-filled

Historical and Geographical Note

The concentration in modern criticism on Gothic and 'psychological' dimensions, as well as post-structuralist and deconstructionist approaches, with their emphasis on a shifting text, have generally served to draw attention away from the historical and topographical aspects of *Confessions*. Yet the novel is undeniably an intensely Scottish work, touching on some of the most pivotal events in national history and also referring to a number of significant locations. While there is obviously a need to proceed cautiously on such matters, not least in view of the diverse narrative viewpoints offered, an awareness of these components can nevertheless considerably enhance our understanding of the text.

Events in the novel straddle two crucial moments in Scottish history: the Revolution Settlement of 1689/90, and the Union of England and Scotland in 1707. With the flight of James II and VII to France late in 1688, the rule of the Stuart Kings (a dynasty which had reigned in Scotland since the fourteenth century) came to an end, with William of Orange accepting the crown of England (as William III) and then Scotland in 1689. In Scotland this meant in political terms the triumph of the Whigs over the Royalist party, and in religious terms that of Presbyterianism over Episcopacy, with the system of bishops being abolished in 1690 and the Presbyterian system of church government re-established in its entirety. In the novel, Gorge Colwan senior succeeds to the lands of Dalcastle in 1687, the last full year of Stuart rule, and then marries Rabina Orde. The birth of the two sons thus can be seen as lying on either side of the Revolution divide: George's, presumably as a result of the wedding night, occurring probably in 1688, and that of Robert in 1689 or 1690, with Presbyterianism again dominant. The actual division of the Colwan household, with the Laird occupying the lower quarters in company with Arabella Logan (herself from an old Royalist family) and the more 'spiritual' Wringhims on the third storey, thus reflects a profound dualism in Scottish political and religious life, just as the different upbringing of the two children (with Robert eventually moving with his mother to Glasgow) points to a continuing rift and exacerbation of differences.

The main Edinburgh events in the story take place as a result of the sitting of the Scottish Parliament, at a time of intense party factionalism and uncertainty, in the years immediately prior to the Union with England of 1707. Colwan senior has become actively political, aligning himself with the Cavalier party of the day—which included Jacobites hoping for a restoration of the Stuarts—in this adopting a position diametrically opposite to that of the Whig Revolutionary party, with which the Rev. Wringhim is closely associated. Mention of the 'famous session' of Parliament, 'when the Duke of Queensberry was commissioner' (p.15), most obviously refers to the session that sat between May and September 1703, with George Colwan having been elected a Member of Parliament in the elections of 1702. As a result of the recent accession of Queen Anne, and the defeat of the Whigs in England, the hopes of the Cavaliers (who had made gains in the elections) ran high, with the Court party representing the Crown's interest losing control, and the Whig Presbyterians mostly confined to blocking tactics. Instead of accepting the Act of Succession, in favour of the Electress of Hanover, this Parliament passed the Act of Security, reserving its own right to choose a successor of the royal line and Protestant religion in the event of the death of Anne without issue.

The account in Hogg's narratives (notably the Editor's) clearly owes a good deal to George Lockhart (1681–1732), 2nd Laird of Carnwath, whose first-hand record of events, as seen from a Jacobite point of view, was first published in the pirated *Memoirs Concerning the Affairs of Scotland from Queen Anne's Accession to the Throne to the Commencement of the Union of the Two Kingdoms [...] in May 1707* (1714). This was republished from Lockhart's original manuscripts with additional materials, as *The Lockhart Papers* in 1817, and Hogg quoted extensively from this version when annotating his *Jacobite Relics of Scotland* (2 vols, 1819–21). Lockhart's account of the disposition of the parties and the leading political figures in 1703 is strikingly close to that indicated by Hogg in the *Confessions*. From Lockhart, whose ultimate feeling is one of frustration that the Cavalier cause was betrayed, Hogg too undoubtedly gained some of his sense of the underlying political confusions of the time. These are brilliantly conveyed in the early Black Bull incident (pp.20–22), when the larger occupying party of Whig gentlemen attacks the mob, whose anger had actually been directed against the young George Colwan and his Cavalier friends, this leading to yet further ironies (such as the Cavaliers coming to the aid of the Whigs), and with the Duke of Queensberry as Commissioner in the aftermath attempting to 'conciliate the two factions' (p.23).[1]

Not surprisingly Robert's own account of events lacks any clear political dimension. The division of the country 'into two political parties, the court and the country party' (p.98) is noted in the after-

math of the account of the Rev. Blanchard's murder; but thereafter
oppositions are viewed almost exclusively in theological terms. One
key moment in Robert's history prior to the Edinburgh incidents,
however, appears to run counter to the identification of the 'famous
session' with the 1703 parliament. According to his 'Memoirs',
Robert first meets Gil-Martin 'on the 25th day of March 1704, when
I had just entered the eighteenth year of my age' (p.82). The year
given here clashes with the Editor's more conventional chronological account on two fronts. First, by making Robert seventeen in 1704
it conflicts with a birth post-1688, say in 1690, according to which
he would be only about fourteen at this stage. (The same anomaly
might be said also to exist in George's case, though this is not made
specific.) Secondly, since Robert has not yet gone to Edinburgh, it
sits awkwardly with the placing of the 'famous session' in 1703.
Several limited explanations are possible. Douglas Mack points to
a conflict between specific narrative chronology and a more 'thematic' use of historical events in the novel.[2] According to this view,
the Revolutionary cusp of 1688–90 is utilised to show the cultural
division between the two brothers, yet at the same time Hogg needs
space to allow Robert to grow into a young man, capable of assassination, by the time of the Parliament of 1703, itself thematically important.

Another possible 'explanation' is that Hogg has confused the 1703
session of the Scottish Parliament with 1704, or, as is more likely,
conflated events in 1703 with the 1704 session, which first met early
in July, and at which the Marquis of Tweeddale was Lord Commissioner. In this session the Cavalier and Country parties were again
rampant, forcing the Queen's acceptance of the Act of Security while
further resisting the Act of Succession, before being prorogued at
the end of August 1704. Such a later dating would also tally with
Ridsley's indirect placing, under examination, of George Colwan's
assassination early 'on the morning of the 28th of February, 1705'
(p.45), the time gap being explainable in terms of George's two
trials and intervening imprisonment. (At the same time, it is hard to
think of a less trustworthy witness, even in the context of a work
filled with unreliable narrators.) The 1704 session also in some respects ties in more effectively with the 'thematic' historical issues
evident in the text. In his *Jacobite Relics*, while annotating 'The Act of
Succession', a defiant Jacobite song, Hogg recognises this Parliament
as pivotal, at once the high point of Cavalier opposition and harbin-
ger of incorporating Union: ' [...] it is not a little singular, that the
greatest jealousy of English ascendancy should have prevailed in

this country, just immediately before these very men were going to yield up the liberties and independency of the nation to their more potent neighbours'.[3] The ensuing death of George Colwan–who shares a Christian name with Lockhart of Carnwath and *his* father, themselves both victims of slayings in strange circumstances–can be seen as representing the demise of active Cavalier loyalism from within Scotland, with the Jacobite element in the plot then petering out with the tacit identification of Thomas Drummond with the 1715 uprising at the end of the Editor's main narrative.[4]

The novel's later chronology is noticeably more private in character, veering also between the apparently precise and hazily indistinct. Ridsley's placing of his first meeting with Bell Calvert '[a]bout a year and a half' (p.45) ago, and the depute-advocate's fixing of the robbery of Mrs Logan's home on 'the fifth of September last' (p.46), apparently pushes the narrative on to about 1706/07, to the height of the Union negotiations (though no sense is given of that event's occurrence). After the two women's spying mission to Dalcastle, Ridsley is sent on 'a pretended mission of legality' (p.64), this seemingly being matched in Wringhim's own narrative by the appearance of Lawyer Linkum, with a mock charter of 1687, ostensibly signed by the 'privy councillors of that year, and [...] other ten of the present year, with his Grace the Duke of Queensberry at the head' (p.124) If this is to be trusted (a considerable leap considering the mendacity of both speaker and narrator) then the time must refer to before May 1708, by which time the Scottish Privy Council had been abolished, in the wake of the Union.[5] Robert Wringhim's sense of time becomes more suspect than ever at this juncture, as he apparently suffers from amnesia or falls victim to possession by the devil, and there are indications as well that his recollection of the sequence of events is also severely skewed. This pattern is then broken by the specificity of the dating of the discovery of his mother's body, on 'the first of June 1712' (p.141), this initiating a carefully tracked sequence of occurrences as Wringhim increasingly wishes to separate himself from Gil-Martin. After immediately fleeing Dalcastle, he reaches the weaver's cottage in one day (p.145), and, after his expulsion the following morning, arrives in Edinburgh the 'third night after' (p.151). His employment by James Watson 'in the Queen's printing house' (p.151) is not inconsistent with this sequence, Watson–whose publications include *The Mystery of Phanaticism* (1712)–having been appointed one of the Queen's Printers in Scotland in 1711.

Wringhim evidently stays long enough to write and set in type the main part of his 'Memoirs', before the reported appearance of the devil in the printing house precipitates further flight. The first section of his hand-written journal is headed '*Chesters, July* 27, 1712', placing him near the border with England, after a journey commenced 'the beginning of the last week' (p.153). The next entry ('*August* 3, 1712': p.162) suggests that his pursuer has again cornered him, while that immediately following, from '*Ault-Righ*' (i.e. Altrive or Eltrive), places him in his final destination—close to what was to become Hogg's own home—on '*August* 24, 1712'. Wringhim's last journal entries, indicating his final mental collapse, move into the following month, the last entry being dated '*September* 18, 1712' (p.165). If we accept Robert's earlier placing of his seventeenth birthday on 25 March 1704, this means that he is twenty-five at the time of his apparent suicide, a lifespan which David Groves has likened to the twenty-four years' duress granted Faustus by Mephistopheles in Marlowe's play (the similarity increasing if the year-and-a-day's delay over his baptism is deducted).[6] If, on the other hand, his birth is placed *c.* 1690, following on from Colwan senior's marriage in or after 1687, then he is just twenty-one or twenty-two. In fact, it is noticeable how a number of ordinary observers in the story, from John Barnet to the innkeeper in Ancrum, evidently consider Robert as much younger than he accounts himself in wisdom and importance.

As a whole, it is possible to point to three levels of chronology in the novel: i) the specific, as (supposedly) given in the trial scenes; ii) the 'thematic', as where the narrative touches on larger cultural and historical movements; and iii) the cyclical, where events mirror or shadow each other mysteriously. Nowhere is this more apparent than in the final sequences centring on the suicide's burial and exhumation, where the different levels are also found overlapping in complex ways. The issue of whether Hogg's 'Scots Mummy' article from *Blackwood's Edinburgh Magazine* is based on an actual occurrence is still uncertain, though recent investigations suggest that the grave of a suicide was actually opened in Hogg's own district in 1823.[7] Granting this, and that Hogg's story was already planned, it is possible that the conflicting reports within the incorporated article (see pp.167–68) concerning the date of the suicide originate from a desire to reconcile the chronology of Wringhim's life with an event that actually occurred somewhat later. In particular, Hogg appears to be engaged in manipulating the lifespan of James Anderson, the suicide's companion on the morning of what is apparently his last day of existence, and who, according to folk record, 'was then a boy ten years of age' and 'lived to an old age, upwards of four-score' (p.168). This Anderson is based on a real figure, a tenant of A/Eltrive, whose death in 1782 at the age of 72 is recorded in Ettrick kirkyard. The Editor's visit to Ettrick to examine the suicide's grave is both date specific and cyclical in import. The September ewe fair at Thirlestane was the biggest of four annual fairs held there, and, as David Groves has suggested,[8] the Editor's movement south from Edinburgh to be there mirrors Wringhim's similar journey at the same season more than a hundred years previously. A more particular reverberation has also been noted by Douglas Mack, who investigates the similarity of dates between the exhumation of Robert Burns's remains in Dumfries on 19 September 1815, for the purposes of relocation, and the burial of Wringhim, evidently '[e]arly next morning' (p.167) after his last diary entry, itself dated 18 September. If the Editor and party are imaginatively seen as desecrating the suicide's grave on the same day, then a whole new dimension, adding to apparent parallels with Walter Scott's 1802 Ettrick visit, is discoverable in this termination to the story.[9]

The geographical movements in *Confessions* (see Map 1, end of this volume) take in a number of locations, including the West of Scotland, Edinburgh, the Borders, and finally Hogg's own Ettrick Forest. The most conventional topographical site, that of Dalcastle, is probably imaginary, while bearing some of the characteristics of the quasi-fictitious family seats in Scott's Waverley novels.[10] One possible clue to what Hogg had in mind is provided by the opening association of the Colwans with the 'ancient family of Colquhoun'. The name Colquhoun itself is taken from the Barony of Colquhoun which lay to the north of the Clyde estuary in the hills above Old Kilpatrick in Dumbartonshire. In the fourteenth century Robert de Colquhoun gained through marriage the lands of Luss on the west bank of Loch Lomond, the main branch of the family from then on being known as the Colquhouns of Luss. As noted elsewhere in this edition, there are a number of similarities between the Colquhoun family history in the years immediately preceding the Union and that of the Colwans of Dalcastle, and it is also possible that Hogg was reflecting some aspects of the present baronet's marriage to a strongly evangelical wife in George Colwan's union with Rabina Orde.[11] Certainly the distances suggested would accord with a setting somewhere above the north bank of the Clyde, if not at Luss itself. When Rabina escapes temporarily back to Glasgow early in the story, the journey according to the Editor involves a night on the road, 'stage-coaches and steam-boats having then no existence in

that quarter' (p.8): this involving an allusion to the steamship services on the Clyde that began in 1812, and which would have considerably eased the journey if (say) Rabina had come south to
Helensburgh. At a later point, Robert's having travelled thirty miles
southward from Dalcastle by bye-ways (see p.145), to arrive at the
weaver's cottage, apparently places him in the heart of the linen-
weaving industry in the West Central belt. It is also to the Glasgow
area that Rabina and the young Robert Wringhim go after the final
rupture of her marriage, and Finnieston, where the slaying of the
Rev. Blanchard takes place, prior to his planned sermon in Paisley,
presently forms part of Glasgow itself, about a mile to the west of
the city-centre.[12] As in the case of Dalcastle, however, there is little
sense of any close local knowledge on Hogg's part.

The pre-1707 events in Edinburgh involve each quarter of the
city as it then existed, as can be seen through reference to Slezer's
panoramic view of about 1690 taken from the North (see Map 2).[13]
At one point in *Confessions* Captain Douglas and his troop issue forth
from the Castle to put down a riot (see p.22); and, in a much more
significant sequence, the younger George Colwan walks down the
south back of the Canongate, skirts Holyrood Palace, and ascends
Arthur's Seat, noting a dark hazy vaporous mass in the hollow between it and Salisbury Crags (pp.28–29). In a less spiritual frame of
mind, earlier he and his friend had walked to the south of the City
to look at a girl in Greyfriars Kirk, and it is in the opposite direction, at the side of the North Loch, that his body is found. The most
dynamic and mysterious action however takes place in the thickly
congested area round St Giles Cathedral, and especially in the narrow closes running north and south from the High Street (see Map
3). The riot scene begins at the Black Bull, which the Editor in his
narrative places 'in a small square half way between the High Street
and the Cowgate', from which the repulsed crowd temporarily re-
treats through two closes connecting it with the High Street, themselves 'somewhere near to the [Mercat] Cross, on the south side of
the street' (p.21).

On the evening of George's death, the young Royalist rowdies
decide to leave the Black Bull for a 'bagnio' (brothel), which, according to the Editor, 'must have been somewhere on the opposite
side of the street [i.e. High Street] to the Black Bull Inn, a little farther to the eastward' (p.36). The Editor's surmise is based on Bell
Calvert's full testimony of the events immediately prior to George's
death, as viewed from another establishment '[a]t the foot of a
close in Edinburgh' (p.50) and from which the North Loch is clearly

visible. Bell sees Thomas Drummond, having left the nearby brothel and spent some time with her, walk along the near side of the Loch before cutting back towards his uncle's house. On the opposite side of the Loch appear two figures, one apparently identical to Drummond, whose arrival in the original close leads to the duel with George and his slaying on 'the bleaching green' alongside the Loch. Bell's description of this green as 'not a very small one' (p.54) compared with the Editor's earlier report of the body being found 'on a little washing-green at the side of the North Loch' (p.37) might seem to represent one of several inconsistencies whereby the supposedly concrete is undercut. But one might alternatively point to an opposite process in which details become clearer and sharper. Indeed, such arguably happens even in the process of Bell's own account, with, for example, the rather indistinct image of Drummond vanishing 'towards Leith Wynd' being replaced within the same paragraph by the more immediate 'vanished into one of the wynds leading toward the bottom of the High Street' (p.51). This in turn helps intensify the peculiar combination of the tangible and increasingly focussed 'real' with the mysteriously inexplicable which is a marked feature of the novel at this stage.

Robert Wringhim's long flight from Gil-Martin also involves a stay in Edinburgh, during which he lodges in Portsburgh, close to the old West Port, beneath the southern side of the Castle. After the devil's reported appearance in the printing shop, he flees towards Dalkeith, and after two days' travel arrives at a yeoman's house named Ellanshaws, which very possibly is based on Langshaw house in Allandale (see Map 1). After a nightmarish experience in the stable-loft there, in 'jogging on towards the Tweed', he meets Gil-Martin 'full in the face' in the 'narrowest part of the glen' formed by 'the small river called Ellan' (p.157). About a mile before it meets the Tweed, close to Scott's Abbotsford, Allan Water enters into a gorge, which would offer no escape in such a situation, and which, when directly viewed, is found to be all the more unusual since in otherwise open country. Far from diminishing the Gothic terror at this juncture, an awareness of the actual terrain, here, as elsewhere, makes the supernatural occurrence appear all the more disturbing and mysterious. Wringhim then flees further to Ancrum, staying in the inn there, and finally arrives at Chesters, a tiny hamlet close to the border, where he finds a brief haven with a widower cottager, before having to leave on hearing of a mysterious stranger asking for him in Redesdale. Virtually from the start of his flight Robert's declared purpose has been to enter England (see pp.151, 154), but

at this point the only available way out, over Carter Bar, is effectively blocked off.

Being forced back in this way, and still avoiding main towns,
Wringhim skirts Hawick and spends a night 'in a farm-house nigh
to the church of Roberton' (p.163), before moving over wild moorland towards the Ettrick valley, reaching his final destination at
A/Eltrive farm in Yarrow. It is useful to distinguish the latter from
Hogg's own Altrive Lake, the small farm (originally called A/Eltrive
Moss) that he was granted by the Duke of Buccleuch in 1815, a
small triangular patch of 60 acres adjacent to Yarrow Water at the
north-eastern tip of the much larger A/Eltrive farm.[14] A/Eltrive itself, which had been tenanted by the Andersons for generations, in
the early eighteenth century was a large wedge of land of more than
1800 acres stretching down in the direction of Fall Law in the south-
west. Wringhim's account of his last days is extremely subjective, so
for any 'factual' topographical information one is dependent on the
two accounts of exhumation that are given, both of which include
pieces of evidence about the original burial. According to the incorporated *Blackwood's* account, the suicide's last day was spent up Eltrive
Hope herding cattle, this probably referring to the upper reaches of
the burn called Altrive Lake. The hanging body is seen by a drover
'coming in at the pass called *The Hart Loup*', 'on the way for Edinburgh' (p.166). 'Harts Leap', a pass connecting the Ettrick and Yarrow
valleys, is plainly visible on John Ainslie's 1772 survey map (Map
4), which shows the old drove road passing through it, before leading to A/Eltrive, then past Dryhope Tower, in a direction heading
towards Peebles and Edinburgh. The body's positioning 'at the side
of one of Eldinhope hay-ricks' (p.166) seems at first an incongruity,
until it is realised that the adjoining Eldinhope farm marched with
A/Eltrive at Altrive Lake (i.e. the stream), so the drove road at this
point is actually running through Eldinhope. The body is then taken
'to the distance of three miles or so, on spokes, to the top of Cowan's-
Croft' (p.167: 'Cowenscroft' on Ainslie), at the point where three
proprietors' lands meet, and it is there, according to the *Blackwood's*
version, that it was recently opened by two shepherds.

The Editor's re-exhumation involves him and his party arriving
at Thirlestane market, having passed through Selkirk and
Ettrickbridge on the way, where a shepherd (in expanded form almost certainly William Beattie) is hired as a guide, Hogg himself
within the story declining. Thirlestane fair was held in the grounds
immediately below Hopehouse (see Map 4), and in 1823 access to
the alleged grave would have been made easier by a pathway ('The

Captain's Way') leading from Hopehouse to the foot of St Mary's Loch, recently constructed by the Hon. Captain Napier, the proprietor of Thirlestane farm, on which Hopehouse stood. Beattie contradicts Hogg's situating of the grave on Cowan's Croft, leading them instead to the top of Fall Law, where a recently disturbed grave is re-opened. On the way there, the guide offers a revised version of the original burial, stating how the party, headed by Mr David Anderson had only 'passed the house of Berry-Knowe' when being over-taken by day-light, and how with the sun 'beginning to skair the east' as they reached 'the top of the Faw-Law' (p.171) they had rapidly buried the body there.[15] As the Ainslie map demonstrates, all these places were actually there and link together, with Hogg seemingly paying attention enough to make allowances for differences in the terrain during the two main time frames of the narrative.

Seen one way, *Confessions* is a novel which moves from apparent certainties to accelerating narrative instabilities and unresolved mystery. Seen another, however, the text can be seen to proceed from the semi-imaginary Scott-like world of Dalcastle, through the maze-like confusions of Edinburgh, to the abiding elements of locality in Hogg's own region. As Ina Ferris has suggested in relation to *The Brownie of Bodsbeck* (1818), a 'vital sense of the specificity of place' is integral to Hogg's narrative structure, and whereas dates might be hazy place is 'highly specific'.[16] Reports within *Confessions* about the suicide's death are indeed inconsistent at points, but the locations are abidingly true, and (more to the point) these locations have the effect of bonding together the different local tellers of the story. In contrast, through their differing (while strangely similar) ideologies—exclusivist Calvinism on the one hand, condescending scientific materialism on the other—both the Sinner and the Editor remain oblivious of locality and the community which exists through it.

Notes

1. See *The Lockhart Papers: containing Memoirs and Commentaries upon the Affairs of Scotland from 1702 to 1715, by George Lockhart, Esq. of Carnwath [...] Published from the Original Manuscripts in the Possession of Anthony Aufrere, Esq.*, 2 vols (London, 1817), I, 42–71. For a modern edited version of Lockhart's *Memoirs*, with a useful Foreword by Paul Scott, see *'Scotland's Ruine': Lockhart of Carnwath's Memoirs of the Union*, ed. by Daniel Szechi (Aberdeen: ASLS, 1995).

2. Douglas S. Mack, 'Revisiting *The Private Memoirs and Confessions of a Justified Sinner*', *Studies in Hogg and his World*, 10 (1999), 1–26 (pp. 3, 17–19). It is worth bearing in mind that 25 March, the date given by Robert Wringhim as his

birthday and on which he first met Gil-Martin, is also Lady Day, when the angel Gabriel announced to Mary that she would be the mother of the Messiah.

3.   *The Jacobite Relics of Scotland*, 2 vols (Edinburgh, 1819–21), I, 211.

4.   For the deaths of the two George Lockharts, the first through assassination in the Edinburgh High Street, the second as a result of wounds received in a duel, see Paul Scott's Foreword in Szechi (ed.), *'Scotland's Ruine'*, pp. ix, xiv. For Thomas Drummond and his Jacobite connections, see explanatory Notes in this edition, notes on 38(c), 39(a), 64(c).

5.   See Michael Lynch, *Scotland: A New History*, revised edn (London: Pimlico, 1992), p. 316.

6.   David Groves, 'Allusions to *Dr. Faustus* in James Hogg's *A Justified Sinner*', *Studies in Scottish Literature*, 18 (1983), 157–65 (p. 158).

7.   For a summary of the stronger evidence, see Peter Garside, 'Hogg, Eltrive, and *Confessions*', *Studies in Hogg and his World*, 11 (2000), 5–24 (pp. 16–17).

8.   David Groves, 'Parallel Narratives in Hogg's *Justified Sinner*', *Scottish Literary Journal*, 9: 2 (December 1982), 37–44 (p. 42).

9.   Douglas S. Mack, 'The Body in the Opened Grave: Robert Burns and Robert Wringhim', *Studies in Hogg and his World*, 7 (1996), 70–79 (p. 72). For Scott's 1802 visit to Ettrick, and possible parallels in the Editor's journey and exhumation of the grave, see Introduction, pp.xvii–xviii, xxxii–xxxiii.

10. The *de luxe* version of the edition of *Confessions* published by J. Shiells & Co. in 1895 includes a Frontispiece photogravure illustration of Dalcastle, depicting a baronial-type fortified house with turrets, but this is presumably an imaginary representation.

11. See, especially, note on 3(a) in explanatory Notes.

12. Finnieston itself apparently takes its name from the Rev. Mr John Finnie, who laid out the plan for the village in 1763. Hogg's own acquaintance with Glasgow at the time of writing was fairly limited: for an account of a brief visit in 1810, including also Paisley, see James A. Kilpatrick, *Literary Landmarks of Glasgow* (Glasgow, 1893), pp. 125–28.

13. John Slezer (d. 1714) had come to Scotland from Holland in 1669 and worked for Charles II and James II and VII (when Duke of York). His images of Edinburgh offer a somewhat roseate picture, but the main elements are correct.

14. For further details, see Garside, 'Hogg, Eltrive, and *Confessions*', passim.

15. A number of reasons might be given for the discrepancy between Hogg's original positioning of the grave in *Blackwood's Edinburgh Magazine* on Cowan's Croft and the Editor's discovery of the grave on Fall Law. One strong possibility, however, is that he originally disguised the site, in such a widely read journal, being wary of trophy-seekers. See also Garside, 'Hogg, Eltrive, and *Confessions*', p. 16.

16. *The Achievement of Literary Authority: Gender, History, and the Waverley Novels* (Ithaca and London: Cornell University Press, 1991), p. 190.

Notes

In the Notes that follow, page references include a letter enclosed in brackets: (a) indicates that the passage found is in the first quarter of the page, while (b) refers to the second quarter, (c) to the third quarter, and (d) to the fourth quarter. Where it seems useful to discuss the meaning of particular phrases, this is done in the Notes: single words are dealt with in the Glossary. Quotations from the Bible are from the King James version, the translation familiar to Hogg and his contemporaries; in the case of the Psalms, however, reference is sometimes given to the metrical *Psalms of David* approved by the Church of Scotland, where this seems apposite. For references to plays by Shakespeare, the edition used has been *The Complete Works: Compact Edition*, ed. by Stanley Wells and Gary Taylor (Oxford: Clarendon Press, 1988). In the case of *Dr Faustus*, quotations are from *The Complete Works of Christopher Marlowe*, vol. II, ed. by Roma Gill (Oxford: Clarendon Press, 1990). References to Sir Walter Scott's fiction are to the *Edinburgh Edition of the Waverley Novels* (EEWN). The National Library of Scotland is abbreviated as NLS. The Notes are greatly indebted to the following standard works: *Dictionary of National Biography, Oxford English Dictionary, Concise Scots Dictionary, The Oxford Companion to the Bible*. Other works used in the Notes are referred to by the following abbreviations:

Confession of Faith: *The Confession of Faith, together with the Larger and Lesser Catechismes. Composed by the Reverend Assembly of Divines, sitting at Westminster, presented to both Houses of Parliament* (London, 1658) [contains several pagination sequences]

Lockhart Papers: *The Lockhart Papers: containing Memoirs and Commentaries upon the Affairs of Scotland from 1702 to 1715, by George Lockhart, Esq. of Carnwath [...] Published from the Original Manuscripts in the Possession of Anthony Aufrere, Esq.*, 2 vols (London, 1817)

Torrance: Thomas F. Torrance, trans. and ed., *The School of Faith: The Catechisms of the Reformed Church* (London: James Clarke & Co., 1959) [used as auxiliary reference for the *Larger* and *Shorter* Catechisms]

Dedication William Smith was a Glasgow merchant and is first recorded as Provost of Glasgow, a post he held for two years, in October 1822 (see *Extracts from the Records of the Burgh of Glasgow*, 11 vols (Glasgow, 1876–1916), X, 697). In an entry of 5 October, 1824, 'the magistrates and council unanimously vote[d] their warmest thanks to William Smith, esq., late lord provost, for the zeal, candour, and ability with which he discharged the various duties of his office' (*Extracts*, XI, 122). There is no evidence that Hogg knew Smith personally, and the choice of dedicatee, which originates from 'the Editor', can be seen as part of a larger strategy to give the anonymous work the air of a Glaswegian provenance: see also Introduction, pp. lxvi–lxvii.

3(a) Dalcastle (or Dalchastel, as it is often spelled) not identified as a location, and probably fictitious (see also 'Historical and Geographical Note', p. 205).

3(a) Colwan [...] Colquhoun [...] Cowans that spread towards the Border the derivation of the surname Cowan from Colquhoun is actually supported as the stronger of two options in George F. Black, *The Surnames of Scotland: Their Origin, Meaning, and History* (New York: New York Public Library, 1962), p. 177. More specifically, the slippage between names perhaps echoes the beginning of Sir Robert Douglas's genealogical account of 'COLQUHOUN of that Ilk, or of Luss', a family originating from north of the Clyde and whose main branch resided on the west bank of Loch Lomond: 'The traditional accounts of the origin of this most ancient family are various. Some authors deduce their descent from a younger son of the old earls of Lennox, because of the similitude of their armorial bearings: Others say, that their progenitor was a younger son of Conoch, a king of Ireland, who came to Scotland in the reign of king Gregory the Great, and obtained from that prince some lands in Dunbartonshire, to which he gave the name of Conochon: That soon thereafter it it came to be corrupted to Colquhon, which name these lands have retained ever since': *The Baronage of Scotland* (Edinburgh, 1798), p. 23. Douglas's account goes on to note the strong loyalist leanings of the family in the Civil War period, and the anti-Unionism of Sir Humphry Colquhoun, 4th baronet, 'who was a member of the union parliament, and strenuously opposed and voted against every article of it' (p. 26). For the possibility of a link with the head of the family in Hogg's day, Sir James Colquhoun, who had married the evangelical Lady Janet (Sinclair) Colquhoun (1781–1846), the author of a number of religious tracts, see Introduction, p. xxviii. An alternative (or additional) origin for Hogg's use of the name Co[l]wan is Cowan's Croft, the hilltop where Hogg situates the suicide's body in his article 'A Scots Mummy', originally published in *Blackwood's Edinburgh Magazine* for August 1823. Black in his *Surnames of Scotland* notes that the name Cowan is common in Ayrshire, Dumfriesshire, and other Lowland counties, and offers as a less likely origin a derivation from the Scots *cowan*, a builder of dry-stone dikes.

3(a) the year 1687 i.e. just before the Revolution of 1688, which signalled the end of the reign of the Stuart King James II and VII (officially deposed in Scotland in 1689), and the establishment of Presbyterianism in Scotland under the rule of William of Orange. For further details, see 'Historical and Geographical Note', p. 200.

3(b) Balgrennan probably fictitious, though Hogg might have heard of an actual Balgreggan (house and estate) in Stoneykirk Parish, Wigtownshire, whose Laird, MacDouall of Balgreggan, was reputed to have poisoned his enemy the minister of Stoneykirk in 1709/10: see Rev. C. H. Dick, *Highways and Byways in Galloway and Carrick* (1916; reprinted Wigton: G.C. Book Publishers, 1994), pp. 317–18. There is also just possibly an echo of the Laird of Bargarran, the 'possession' of whose daughter led to a celebrated burning of witches at Paisley in 1697.

3(c) reputed daughter *reputed* here in the sense of 'supposed, accounted, reckoned', with a strong intimation of illegitimacy. Compare Joseph Addison in *The Spectator*, no. 189 (Saturday, 6 October, 1711): 'they conclude that the reputed Son must have been Illegitimate, Suppositious, or begotten in Adultery'.

3(c) Baillie Orde, of Glasgow probably fictitious, though the closely similar name of Aird appears prominently in the civil records of Glasgow at this period. John Aird (elder) was elected merchant bailie on 1 October 1689 (*Extracts from the Records of the Burgh of Glasgow*, III (Glasgow, 1905), 435), and features further as a purchaser of land and property in Glasgow in the immediately following years. John Aird (younger) became Provost of Glasgow in 1705–06 (see *Charters and Documents Relating to the City of Glasgow*, II, 1649–1707 (Glasgow, 1906), 634), being frequently re-elected, with a last period of office in 1722–23 (*Extracts from the Records of the Burgh of*

Glasgow, vols IV and V, *passim*). He is listed as one of four outstanding provosts in John M'Ure, *The History of Glasgow* (new edn, Glasgow, 1830): 'he caus'd build two churches and a high steeple in Glasgow, and opened two streets upon the town's charges, and several other great buildings the time of his administration'(pp. 247-48). According to Daniel Defoe, Aird bore the brunt of the crowd's fury in the anti-Union demonstrations in Glasgow in 1706. Several streets and buildings in Glasgow still bear the Aird name (e.g. Aird's Wynd). Another similar surname, Orr, also features occasionally in *Extracts from the Records of the Burgh of Glasgow*. See, e.g., the entry for 20 January 1705: 'The magistrats [*sic*] and toun counsell appoynts Andrew Orr, sone to umquhill John Orr, merchant, to keep the record of the deceased within this burgh' (vol. IV (1908), p. 389).

3(c) Reformation principles i.e. the religious beliefs of 16th-century reformers, such as Martin Luther and John Calvin, aimed initially at reforming the Roman Catholic Church, which led to the establishment of Protestant churches. The Scottish Reformation, deeply influenced by Calvin's follower, John Knox, produced a Church of Scotland that was both Protestant and Presbyterian.

4(a) limited proportion of the fear of God compare Psalm 111.10: 'The fear of the Lord is the beginning of wisdom'.

4(a) damning security i.e. the Laird's lack of an awareness of sin will lead to damnation: reflecting a basic tenet held by strict Presbyterians, here presumably being mimicked by the Editor.

4(b) stumbling-block a fairly common biblical expression, sometimes denoting (as here) an obstacle to belief or acceptance. Compare I Corinthians 1.23: 'But we preach Christ crucified, unto the Jews a stumblingblock, and unto the Greeks foolishness'.

5(a) the Amorite, the Hittite, and the Girgashite some of the tribes living in the land of Canaan before its occupation by the Israelites (see Exodus 33.2). These three particular heathen names, which appear throughout the Old Testament, can be found in close proximity in Joshua 3.10 and 24.11 and without interruption (albeit in different order) in Deuteronomy 7.1.

5(b) the broad way that leadeth to destruction alluding to Matthew 7.13: 'Enter ye in at the strait gate: for wide is the gate, and broad is the way, that leadeth to destruction, and many there be which go in thereat'. The image is developed allegorically in John Bunyan's way of Destruction, open and undemanding, in his *Pilgrim's Progress* (1678–84).

5(d) to ride on the rigging of it matching a Scottish proverb, 'Ane may lo'e the Kirk well enough yet no be ay riding on the Rigging [i.e. ridge or roof] o't': see Allan Ramsay, *A Collection of Scots Proverbs* (1737), in *The Works of Allan Ramsay*, 6 vols, vol. V, ed. by Alexander M. Kinghorn and Alexander Law (Edinburgh and London: Scottish Text Society, 1972), p. 67.

5(d) Mr. Wringhim's the surname possibly contains an echo of Francis Wrangham (1769–1842), a classical scholar and archdeacon of Cleveland from 1820–28. A prolific author and occasional contributor to *Blackwood's Edinburgh Magazine*, Wrangham was at the centre of a pamphlet war involving the Anglican church and Unitarianism between 1821 and 1824. His *A Charge [...] to the Clergy of the Archdeaconry of Cleveland* (York, 1822) takes issue with 'these Socinians, or Unitarians, or Rational Christians' (p. 8), arguing instead for 'the celestial doctrine of St Paul' ('soaring to it from the low and turbid atmosphere, in which we have hitherto been conversant'), whereby 'the sinner clings to a *hope*, the anchor of his soul, both sure and steadfast' (p. 19). While several of Wrangham's basic tenets are not dissimilar to Hogg's own stated beliefs, his apparent eagerness for disputation might have encouraged a satirical reaction. At the same time, the suggestion of 'wringing' (e.g. of doctrine or souls), and also perhaps of encircling and entrapment, is more reminiscent of the burlesque names found in satires of Puritanism, which were still being employed in Hogg's day by Tory writers such as Walter Scott.

6(b) concord of sweet sounds compare *The Merchant of Venice* V.1.83–84: 'The man that hath no music in himself,/ Nor is not mov'd with concord of sweet sounds'.

6(c) Morphean from Morpheus, the Roman poet Ovid's name for the god of dreams; thus drowsy, sleepy.

7(a) Rabina female equivalent of Robin, itself a diminutive of Robert, thus linking the three members of the eventual Wringhim grouping.

7(b) had held had taken place.

7(d) man of Belial in the Bible Belial is used to personify the wicked and worthless, such as idolaters, this exact phrase appearing at I Samuel 25.25, and II Samuel 16.7, 20.1. The term 'sons of Belial' is applied vengefully to captured royalists by Presbyterian divines in Hogg's *Tales of the Wars of Montrose* (ed. by Gillian Hughes (Edinburgh: Edinburgh University Press, 1996), p. 200); and forms part of an anti-royalist diatribe by Mause Headrigg in Walter Scott's *The Tale of Old Mortality* (1816: Ch. 8; EEWN 4b, p. 70). Perhaps nearest to the present speaker's sentiments is II Corinthians 6.15: 'And what concord hath Christ with Belial? or what part hath he that believeth with an infidel?'

7(d) promiscuous dancer i.e. a dancer with women. The denunciation of this activity by strict Covenanting ministers, among other such sins, was observed by Hogg in a note to 'The Cameronian Cat' in his *The Jacobite Relics of Scotland*, 2 vols (1819–21), I, 209: 'I have heard them myself, when distributing the sacrament, formally debar from the table [...] all the men that had ever danced opposite to a woman, and every woman that had danced with her face toward a man.'

8(b) steam-boats the first commercial steamship was the *Comet* in 1812, which operated on the Clyde between Glasgow, Greenock, and Helensburgh (on the N bank opposite Greenock). In 1820 there were almost thirty steamships constantly at work on the Clyde.

8(c) take pennyworths of i.e. take revenge on.

9(d) the great standard doctrine of absolute predestination referring to the Calvinist doctrine that God has already determined who shall be saved, an idea which was largely absorbed into the theology of the Presbyterian Church of Scotland. In the Westminster *Confession of Faith*, Ch. 10 ('Of Effectual Calling') begins 'All those whom God hath predestinated unto life, and these onely, he is pleased in his appointed and accepted time, effectually to call' (p. 37). For further discussion, see Introduction, especially pp. xxix–xxx.

9(d) limb of Antichrist the Antichrist was identified in early Christianity as the enemy of Jesus Christ, and, more specifically, in post-Reformation Scotland with Roman Catholicism. This latter attitude is reflected in John Galt's novel *Ringan Gilhaize; or the Covenanters* (1823), where the congregation interrupts the newly-installed Dean of Edinburgh in St Giles Church with the cry 'Antichrist, antichrist! down wi' the pope!', and where the eponymous narrator refers to the Dean as 'that horn of the beast', evidently making no distinction between Episcopalianism and Catholicism (ed. by Patricia J. Wilson (Edinburgh: Scottish Academic Press, 1984), pp. 138–39). Compare also Hogg's 'History of the Life of Duncan Campbell' in no. 51 of *The Spy*, 17 August 1811: 'The prayer concluded the devotions of each evening, in which the downfall of Antichrist was always strenuously urged, the ministers of the gospel remembered' (*The Spy*, ed. by Gillian Hughes (Edinburgh: Edinburgh University Press, 2000), p. 504). George Colwan is thus stigmatised by his wife as being an agent or scion of ('limb of') dark forces opposed to the true gospel religion.

10(a) Martha this female servant's name matches that in Luke 10.40: 'But Martha was cumbered about much serving, and came to him, and said, Lord, dost thou not care that my sister hath left me to serve alone?'

10(b) in the civil wars appropriately in the plural for Scotland, considering the continuing conflict between Royalists and Presbyterians for much of the 17th century, but here most probably relating to the years 1642–60, from the outbreak of the English Civil War to the end of the Cromwellian occupation of Scotland, during which period the property of many royalist supporters was sequestrated or made subject to heavy fines.

10(c) Canaanitish woman in the Old Testament the Israelites are forbidden to marry Canaanitish women, because their heathen ways will cause a dilution of the worship of the true God. See Genesis 24.3, 28.1 for the original prohibition, and Genesis 46.10 and Exodus 6.15 for the phrase 'Canaanitish woman'. The allusion helps heighten the idea that Rabina sees herself as being in exile from the people of God, marooned among the heathen.

10(c) making twelve in all actually thirteen, an apparent failure in Hogg's arithmetic which was 'corrected' in several editions after his death, and which some later commentators have interpreted as a deliberate mistake reflecting carelessness on the Editor's part. It is worth observing, however, that thirteen traditionally represents the devil's dozen (twelve plus one for the devil to claim). In Hogg's story 'Gillanbye's Ghost', the narrator joins twelve Scotsmen in attempting to cross the Solway Firth at night, so forming 'the deil's dozen', this leading to an encounter with the devil and the loss of one of the party (see 'The Border Chronicler', *The Literary Souvenir* (1826), pp. 270–76).

11(b) justified person can do no wrong reflecting the Calvinist theological view that salvation was assured after a person's 'justification' (freeing from the penalty of sin and making just in God's sight) through the Covenant of Grace. But the assurance as given here significantly exaggerates one side of the equation as stated in the Westminster *Confession of Faith*, Section V of Ch. XI ('Of Justification'): 'God doth continue to forgive the sins of those that are justified: and, although they can never fall from the state of Justification; yet they may by their sins, fall under Gods fatherly displeasure' (p. 44). For a broader discussion of the issues, see Introduction, especially p. xxx.

11(b) the liberty wherewith we are made free compare Galatians 5.1: 'Stand fast therefore in the liberty wherewith Christ hath made us free, and be not entangled again with the yoke of bondage.' The idea of bondage/freedom, as generally present in St Paul, formed an integral part of the Calvinist theology of Justification in describing those benefiting from the Covenant of Grace as compared with those still bound by the Covenant of Works.

11(b) dung that is spread out to fatten the land the expression is characteristic of the book of Jeremiah: see, e.g., 8.2, 9.22, 16.4, 25.33.

11(c) Moabite one of the nation of Moab, bordering on ancient Israel. The Old Testament contains many instances of the smiting of the Moabites, who seem often to have been regarded by the Israelites with scorn as well as enmity. See, for example, Deuteronomy 23.3: 'An Ammonite or Moabite shall not enter into the congregation of the Lord; even to their tenth generation shall they not enter into the congregation of the Lord for ever.'

12(c) doctrines of Calvin i.e. those of John Calvin (1509–64), French theologian and Reformer in Geneva, whose system of theology, as expressed in his *Institutes of the Christian Religion* and other writings, helped form the basis of Protestant belief in Scotland. Central tenets in Calvinist doctrine were the absoluteness of God's will, justification by grace rather than good works, and the idea of 'the Elect', known to God and predestined for salvation before world and time. Calvin however did not argue that good works had no part in a Christian's life, rather that faith in Christ and salvation would lead to true holiness.

12(d) do these abominations no more echoing Jesus's words to the woman taken in adultery, having saved her from stoning, in John 8.11: 'go, and sin no more'.

12(d) humble thyself a biblical admonitory phrase: see Exodus 10.3, II Chronicles 34.27, Proverbs 6.3. Also echoing more broadly Matthew 23.12: 'And whosoever shall exalt himself shall be abased; and he that shall humble himself shall be exalted.' A Christian home truth, aimed at Wringhim senior, falls here from the mouth of Colwan senior.

12(d) on the hip a phrase taken from wrestling, meaning to have at a disadvantage, in a position in which an opponent is likely to be overthrown.

13(c) children of adoption i.e. adopted as children of God, a distinction accorded to true Christians in the Epistles in the New Testament: see e.g. Romans 8.15–16, Galatians 4.5, and Ephesians 1.4–5. The idea of adoption is a central feature in the Westminster Assembly's *Confession of Faith* and its Longer and Shorter Catechisms, which were generally adopted by the Presbyterian church in Scotland. In the much used Shorter Catechism, the question *What is adoption?* is answered: 'Adoption is an act of Gods free grace, whereby we are received into the number, and have a right to all the priviledges [*sic*] of the sons of God' (in *Confession of Faith*, p. 168; also Torrance, p. 267).

13(c) between justification and final election between i) being justified (freed from sin) through faith in Christ and redemption by God's grace and ii) being acknowledged and received fully as one of the Elect. Both terms derive from the Pauline Epistles in the New Testament and were key concepts in Calvinist theology, though their application here suggests the hair-splitting of some of Calvin's successors rather than Calvin himself.

14(c) the visible church i.e. the Church consisting of its professed members on earth, and their children, contrasted with 'the invisible church', which in Calvinist theology comprised the Elect, transcending space and time. The questions *'What is the visible Church?'* and *'What is the invisible Church?'* are found in the Westminster Larger Catechism (*Confession of Faith*, pp. 182–83; Torrance, pp. 196–97). Robert's admittance into the church visible can only happen with his baptism.

14(c) a year and a day a period ensuring that a year has elapsed, used in law in relation to marriage, property ownership etc. In this case, no person has effectively acknowledged paternity, allowing baptism to proceed with the mother as sponsor (i.e. one who answers for the infant). Hogg's own marriage contract includes a special clause stating that the contract will still be valid 'notwithstanding the said marriage should happen to be dissolved within year and day of the solemnization thereof by the death of either party without a living child' (Stirling University Library, MS 25, Box 2 (7)).

14(d) like David of old i.e. King David of Israel, commonly associated with the Old Testament Psalms. This passage anticipates the Rev. Wringhim's later use of Psalm 109 to curse the Colwans (see note on 'Christian psalmody' for 24(b)). The same phrase occurs near the end of Hogg's story 'The Brownie of the Black Haggs', in relation to the royalist Lady Wheelhope and 'the persecuted Covenanters [...] who had been driven, like David of old, to pray for a curse and earthly punishment upon her': see *The Shepherd's Calendar*, ed. by Douglas S. Mack (Edinburgh: Edinburgh University Press, 1995), p. 254.

15(a) cut off in the full flush of his iniquity includes terms found fairly commonly in proximity in the Bible. Compare, e.g., Jeremiah 51.6: 'Flee out of the midst of Babylon, and deliver every man his soul: be not cut off in her iniquity'. The passage also has a more general affinity with Hamlet's thoughts in desisting from assassinating Claudius while at prayer: 'that his soul may be as damned and black/ As hell whereto it goes' (*Hamlet*, III.3.94–95).

15(c) **suppressing the Covenanters** the principal aim of the Covenanters, whose name derived from the National Covenant of 1638 and the Solemn League and Covenant of 1643, was the eradication of episcopacy and establishment of Presbyterian church government in Scotland. During the reigns of Charles II (1660–85) and his brother James II and VII (1685–88) they were severely persecuted, the greatest period of brutality probably occurring during 1685–88. During these persecutions George Colwan has been a royalist supporter, though without actively engaging in the persecutions. See also 'Historical and Geographical Note', p. 200.

15(d) **the cavalier party of that day** comprising chiefly Scottish Episcopalians and Jacobite supporters of King James II and VII; in the elections to the 1703 Parliament the Cavaliers made significant gains.

15(d) **Earls of Seafield and Tullibardine** both significant figures in the Scottish parliament in the years immediately preceding the Union with England of 1707. James Ogilvy (1663–1730) became 1st Earl of Seafield in 1701, and was active in promoting the Union; in 1703, however, when Lord Chancellor of Scotland, he was seen as having for a while sided with the Cavalier party (see *Lockhart Papers*, I, 52; also note above). John Murray (1659/60–1724), who became Earl of Tullibardine in 1696 and Duke of Athol in 1703, was originally a strong supporter of King William and the Whig Presbyterian party in Scotland; he was Lord Privy Seal in 1703, trimming then between parties, according to Lockhart of Carnwath, before later becoming 'all of a sudden a violent Jacobite' (see *Lockhart Papers*, I, 72). Hogg here introduces two managing politicians characterised by underhand dealing and an apparent shift towards the Cavalier party in 1703/04.

15(d) **the famous session** most obviously referring to the 1703 session of the Scottish Parliament, which first met on 3 May, and in which the Cavalier party made significant gains, with the 'Court' party (which promoted the interests of Queen Anne) temporarily losing ground. This parliament passed an Act of Security, asserting its right to name Queen Anne's successor on her death without issue, and was adjourned in September. The next session of Parliament, which assembled on 6 July 1704, with the Marquis of Tweeddale as Commissioner, less obviously fits the situation described by Hogg. See also 'Historical and Geographical Note', pp. 201–03.

15(d) **Duke of Queensberry** James Douglas (1662–1711), second Duke of Queensberry. He was Lord Commissioner (i.e. Queen Anne's main representative) at the 1703 session of the Scottish Parliament (see previous note), as again at the Parliament of 1706/07, which ratified the Treaty of Union.

16(a) **Duke of Argyle** Archibald Campbell (1652?–1703), created 1st Duke of Argyle in 1701. A prominent supporter of the Revolution of 1688/89, though previously having sought an accommodation with King James, he was a leader of the Whig interest in the 1703 Scottish Parliament. Lockhart of Carnwath describes him as 'the darling of the Presbyterians', noting at the same time a disparity between his outward appearance as 'a good-natur'd, civil, and modest gentleman' and an addiction 'to a lewd profligate life' (*Lockhart Papers*, I, 62–63). Argyle's ignominious death from 'bruises received in a brothel' is recorded in a footnote to C. K. Sharpe's edition of James Kirkton's *The Secret and True History of the Church of Scotland* (Edinburgh, 1817), which also quotes from a MS lampoon 'Lynes on the Duke of Argyle, that died in his w—e's arms in England, 28 Sept. 1703' (pp. 374n–75n).

16(b) **in a match at tennis** not referring to the game of lawn tennis, a later invention, but more probably to a version of Real (or Royal) Tennis, an indoor game also known in Scotland as Caitchpule. A Real Tennis Court stood just on the right through the Water Gate at the east end of the Canongate, near to Holyrood Palace, and is clearly marked as an oblong structure on Gordon of Rothiemay's

1647 map of Edinburgh; it later became a theatre, then a workhouse, and was finally burned down in 1771. According to Stuart Harris, Bull Close (on the north side of the High Street) 'was also known in the seventeenth century as Caichpele Close, for the *cachepele* or real tennis court which was approached by the Fleshmarket and Old Provost's Closes as well as this one': *Place Names of Edinburgh: Their Origin and History* (Edinburgh: Gordon Wright Publishing, 1996), p. 132. Whether this relates to the court near Holyrood or to another location is unclear, though the latter would seem more feasible. Certain aspects of the account here and in Robert Wringhim's version later (see p. 102) are nevertheless vague: no sense is given of an indoor location or of any audience watching from a gallery, which would be the case with Real Tennis. A version of *longue paume*, which was played outdoors, is an alternative possibility, though such would have been ill-suited for Edinburgh streets, since requiring a fair amount of room (but compare note on 102(b), below). For further details, see Peter Wordie and Lance St John Butler, 'Tennis in Scotland', in *The Royal Game*, ed. by L. St. J. Butler and P. J. Wordie (Stirling: Falkland Palace Real Tennis Club, 1989), pp. 18–25; and Roger Morgan, *Tennis: The Development of the European Ball Game* (Oxford: Ronaldson, 1995), pp. 213–17.

16(d) methodistical face the adjective (not in use at this time) and its pejorative tone are indicative of the Editor's Tory prejudices rather than George's thoughts.

17(b) the Black Bull tavern the most notable Black Bull Inn in Hogg's day stood off Leith Street, near the east end of present-day Princes Street, some distance from the Old Town. This is the Black Bull which features at the beginning of J. G. Lockhart's *Peter's Letters to his Kinsfolk*, 2nd edn (actually the 1st), 3 vols (Edinburgh, 1819), with Dr Peter Morris, the alleged writer of the letters, being placed there first on arrival in Edinburgh, in a passage expunged from later editions: 'My evil genius, in the shape of an old drivelling turnpike-man, directed me to put up at the Black Bull, a crowded, noisy, shabby, uncomfortable inn' (op. cit., I, 4). This led to a legal action by the proprietor and a considerable settlement, as well as favourable mention in *Blackwood's Edinburgh Magazine*. However, the narrative apparently positions the tavern in the story in a close leading off the High Street (see 'Historical and Geographical Note', p. 206). One possibility is that Hogg had in mind an older inn which stood in Bull [or Bull's] Close, before the latter's obliteration by the building of Cockburn Street in 1859. Charles B. Boog Watson cites a near-contemporary reference to 'The well-frequented dwelling house, north side of the High Street, opposite the Tron Church, known as the Bull Cellar, entering from the Bull Close': see *Notes on the Names of the Closes and Wynds of Edinburgh* (Edinburgh, 1923), p. 37. According to Marie W. Stuart, in her *Old Edinburgh Taverns* (London: Robert Hale, 1952), p. 68, pro-Unionist statesmen chased by an enraged mob in 1707 took refuge in Cachepool or Bull's Close, 'where they had been wont to meet and discuss their plans', this 'Union Cellar' later becoming the vault of the National Bank at the head of Cockburn Street (presently a Woollen Mill shop). The 1852 Ordnance Survey map of Edinburgh shows the Union Tavern near the entry to Bull's Close and also a Black Bull Inn down Fleshmarket Close, the close running off the High Street immediately above. It is worth noting, too, that James Robertson, the founder of the Black Bull in Leith Street, had previously owned two inns of the same name, the first near the head of the Canongate, the second beside the Cowgate Port, with entrances from the head and back of the Canongate: see Stuart, *Old Edinburgh Taverns*, pp. 118–20, and Stuart Harris, *The Place Names of Edinburgh: Their Origin and History* (Edinburgh: Gordon Wright Publishing, 1996), p. 95. None of these older sites however match fully the apparent positioning of the inn in the story.

19(c) Marquis of Annandale William Johnstone (d. 1721), created 1st Marquis of Annandale in 1701, was Lord President of the Scottish Privy Council between

1702–06. In the 1703 session of the Scottish Parliament, according to Lockhart of Carnwath, he was a leading figure among the Presbyterian or 'Revolution' party, along with the Duke of Argyle (see *Lockhart Papers*, I, 61). In a later passage, Lockhart characterises him as one of the most changeable politicians of that era: 'he had gone backwards and forwards so often [...] that no man whatsoever placed any trust in him; even those of the Revolution party only employ'd him as the Indians worship the devil, out of fear' (I, 138).

20(a) back of the Canongate the Canongate is the name for the long street running from the Netherbow in Edinburgh, at the foot of the High Street, down to Holyrood Palace, and was also the name of the burgh of Canongate flanking the street, which came under Edinburgh's control in 1636 and was finally merged with the city in 1856. More specifically, the 'backs of the Canongate' came to refer to two thoroughfares at the foot of the walled gardens which lay north and south of the houses on the Canongate, many of the latter being occupied by Scottish aristocratic families and notables. Several contemporary maps and illustrations, such as John Slezer's North Prospect of Edinburgh (see Map 2, end of this volume), show buildings on the north back particularly.

20(b) set the mountain on fire the image here probably stems from the practice of burning the old heather on hillsides to provide healthier food for sheep. See Hogg's *The Shepherd's Guide* (Edinburgh, 1807), pp. 48–51; also the poem 'Moor-Burn. A Simile', by Miss Lockhart Gillespie, in *The Spy*, no. 31, 30 March 1811: ed. by Gillian Hughes (Edinburgh: Edinburgh University Press, 2000), pp. 317–18.

20(c) Revolutionist faction i.e. supporters of the 1689 Revolution; the Whig or Presbyterian faction.

20(c) Jacobite order [...] Episcopal side the Jacobites supported the main Stuart line, the claimant Kings from James II and VII onwards being professedly Roman Catholic in religion; a good number of royalists in Scotland, however, were members of the Scottish Episcopal Church, and these formed a substantial part of the Cavalier party.

20(d) Cavalier, or High-Church party see previous note.

21(a) children of Antichrist for this phrase and its contemporary connotations, see note on 'limb of Antichrist' for 9(d). Noticeably the mob makes no distinction here in applying the term to Episcopalians as well as Catholics.

21(c) the High Street and the Cowgate the two main thoroughfares in old Edinburgh, running parallel with each other in an east-west direction, with numerous closes and wynds lying between the two. See also 'Historical and Geographical Note', p. 206.

21(d) near to the Cross referring to the Mercat (Market) Cross in Edinburgh in the High Street, which from medieval times was considered as the centre of the burgh and where bargains were struck. In 1617 it was moved to a site near the head of Old Fishmarket Close, slightly to the east of St Giles Church, before being demolished in 1756 to encourage use of the new Exchange building, though in 1779 the site was marked in the causeway (as it still is) for legal purposes. The cross was later re-erected on different sites, but only after Hogg's death, so it is evidently this location that he was thinking of. For a fuller orientation, see Map 3, end of this volume, and 'Historical and Geographical Note', p. 206.

22(c) hardly bested hard put to, hard pressed.

22(c) town-guard an early form of city police, first instituted by the Town Council in 1648 as a force of 60 men, and augmented to more than 100 men in 1682. In the 18th century the force consisted primarily of discharged soldiers and Highlanders, and was often treated satirically, as by the poet Robert Fergusson (1750–74); it was disbanded in 1817.

22(c) Cameronian regiment, with the Hon. Captain Douglas the regiment later to be known as the Cameronians was first raised in 1689 by James Douglas (1671–92), Earl of Angus, and successfully defended Dunkeld after the Jacobite victory of Killiecrankie that year. It was formed from the Covenanting followers of Richard Cameron (d. 1680), originating from south-west Scotland, who had been much persecuted during the later Stuart period. The regiment later became part of the regular British army and was disbanded in 1968.

22(d) sheriffs of Edinburgh and Linlithgow a sheriff is a legal officer appointed to administer justice in a Scottish county. Edinburgh was the county town of Midlothian; Linlithgow, about 15 miles W of Edinburgh, was the county town of West Lothian.

23(b) Duke of Queensberry see note on 15(d).

24(a) public worship every evening for the custom of family worship, as regularly exercised in Hogg's native community, see Introduction, p. xvi. The addition of 'public' in the present instance, however, could be taken as indicating that the Rev. Wringhim is converting family worship, a private devotional activity, into a kind of public display (of the kind warned against in the Sermon on the Mount: see Matthew 6.5–6).

24(a) vials of wrath echoing Revelation 16.1: 'And I heard a great voice out of the temple saying to the seven angels, Go your ways, and pour out the vials of the wrath of God upon the earth.'

24(b) Christian psalmody the ensuing lines are from Psalm 109.1–18, with a number of verses omitted. They follow the version found in *The Psalms of David in Metre*, approved by the Church of Scotland and regularly sung in its churches from the mid-17th century, rather than the King James Bible wording. Hogg was deeply instilled with the metrical version of the Psalms, which he had learned from earliest childhood (see Introduction, pp. xv–xvi), and the quoted passage was almost certainly written from memory. The Editor's air of disapproval is thus in some respects closer to latter-day opponents of the metrical version than Hogg's own view. The particular psalm quoted is exceptional for its severity, however, and was associated with the persecuted Covenanters both by Hogg and other contemporary Scottish novelists. In John Galt's *Ringan Gilhaize* (1823) Ringan returns home to find his house and family destroyed: 'I knelt down, and I caused my son to kneel beside me, and I vowed enmity for ever against Charles Stuart and all of his line; and I prayed, in the words of the Psalmist, that when he was judged he might be condemned' (ed. by Patricia J. Wilson (Edinburgh: Scottish Academic Press, 1984), p. 264). But in this instance his son reminds him that it is wrong to wish condemnation, and Ringan realises 'I had forgotten I was a Christian'. Ringan later does participate in the issuing of the curse, but in the most extreme circumstances, having seen from prison his son's head impaled on a halberd (ibid., p. 283). In the present instance the 'atrocity' is no more than a bloody nose, and there is no sense of any countervailing Christian forgiveness. Modern biblical commentators have since argued that the psalmist is not issuing a curse himself, but rather representing before God the terrible curses made against him by his enemies. If Hogg himself was aware of this alternative reading, then there is the possibility of a double irony aimed at the Rev. Wringhim, who elsewhere is revealed to be not the most competent of theologians.

24(b) *upon his right hand* reversing the normal biblical situation, where God is found so placed in providing protection (see, e.g., Psalm 16.8). In Zechariah 3.1, however, Satan adopts such a position: 'And he shewed me Joshua the high priest standing before the angel of the Lord, and Satan standing at his right hand to resist him.' In the narrative Robert Wringhim has already stood at George's right hand, this being the usual position in which he (or his image) appears in relation to his brother from there on (see text at 17(c), 25(a), 27(b)).

24(b) remembered in both the metrical *Psalms of David* and in the Authorised King James Version the reading is 'condemned', meaning damned for eternity, this being the only substantive variant found in the passage in the novel compared with the metrical version text. Possibly Hogg consciously or unconsciously transferred the wording from the (omitted) verse 14 of the Psalm ('Let the iniquity of his fathers be remembered' in the Authorised Version). Alternatively, he or an associate might have deliberately softened this most terrifying and theologically-charged part of the curse.

25(b) on the Links for a game at cricket possibly referring to Bruntsfield Links, more usually associated in the 18th century with golf. This would also accord with Robert's reference in his own later narrative to a location 'to the south'.

26(b) Adam Gordon the first full naming of the character mentioned previously as 'Gordon'. Probably fictitious, though the Gordon family were huge landowners in Aberdeenshire, and Jacobite sympathisers at this period. A 'lord Adam Gordon', based on one of the sons of the 1st Marquis of Huntly (1562–1636), features in Hogg's later story, 'Some Remarkable Passages in the Life of an Edinburgh Baillie': see *Tales of the Wars of Montrose*, ed. by Gillian Hughes (Edinburgh: Edinburgh University Press, 1996), pp. 16–17.

27(a) the High Church i.e. the High Kirk of St Giles, in Parliament Square, in the High Street of Edinburgh. Also called St Giles Cathedral, from the days when it had a Bishop, but at this period clearly Presbyterian.

27(a) Kilpatrick of Closeburn the Kirkpatrick (not Kilpatrick) family had long associations with Closeburn, a parish in Nithsdale about 12 miles NW of Dumfries. The part which Roger Kirkpatrick took in the slaying of the Red Comyn, Robert Bruce's rival, and his words 'I'll mak sicker [i.e. sure, certain]', are still part of local legend. The estate of Closeburn went out of the hands of the family in 1783, but they continued to hold lands in the region, and Closeburn churchyard has a number of monuments relating to the family. Hogg attended church there during his years (*c.*1807–10) as a shepherd and farmer in Nithsdale, and later recalled worshipping alongside members of Robert Burns's family (see his 'Memoir of Burns', in *The Works of Robert Burns*, ed. by the Ettrick Shepherd and William Motherwell, 5 vols (Glasgow, 1834–36), V, 262). The slight alteration of the surname matches similar shifts in recognised proper names elsewhere in the novel.

27(a) the Grey-Friars church south of the Cowgate, off Candlemaker Row. The original was erected 1612–20 on a site formerly belonging to the monastery of Grey Friars. It was an important Presbyterian kirk, where the National Covenant of 1638 was signed, and with a cemetery in which are buried many persons of historical importance.

27(c) boxes of the play-house apparently an anachronism, since the earliest attempts to form a professional theatre in Edinburgh date from the 1720s. However, James II and VII when Duke of York had earlier introduced a company of players at Holyrood Palace in the 1680s, an occurrence commented on by Dryden: see Hugo Arnot, *The History of Edinburgh* (Edinburgh, 1779), pp. 364–66.

28(c) Arthur's Seat main eminence (823 feet) in an outcrop of hills immediately to the SE of the Edinburgh Old Town, allowing spectacular views of the Firth of Forth and the country surrounding Edinburgh. See John Slezer's North Prospect of Edinburgh (Map 2, end of this volume), where its cone-like summit is apparent in the distance.

28(d) down the south back of the Canongate, toward the Palace the south back of the Canongate ran from the Cowgate to Holyrood Palace, skirting the gardens of large residences on the south side of the Canongate; its name was replaced in 1913 by Holyrood Road. Holyrood Palace, at the foot of the Canongate, was originally built in the early 16th century, and continued to serve as the main royal palace in

Scotland after the union of the crowns in 1603.

28(d) the lord-commissioner's house referring to Queensberry House, near the foot of the Canongate on the south side. Built 1681–86 as a mansion for Charles Maitland, 3rd Earl of Lauderdale, it was later acquired by William Douglas, 1st Duke of Queensberry, whose successor was Lord Commissioner at the 1703 session of the Scottish Parliament (see note on 15(d)). After serving as the family's town house, it was converted into flats, and then sold to form a barracks in 1803. It stands adjacent to the site of the new Scottish parliament building, and is presently being preserved as part of the parliament complex.

28(d) St. Anthony's gardens not specifically identified, though contemporary maps show several cultivated areas close to Holyrood Palace. It is possible that Hogg was thinking of (or even originally intended) St Ann's Yard, which lay to the south of the Palace, and once had formal gardens. For St Anthony, see next note.

28(d) the Saint's chapel and well referring to St Anthony's chapel, 15th-century ruin on a knoll on the northern edges of Arthur's Seat, and the natural spring just below it. Both are apparently named after St Anthony (c. 251–356), the founder of Christian monasticism, whose temptations by the devil have formed a popular subject in literature and art, and which might be taken as foreshadowing immediately following events.

29(b) bright halo in the cloud of haze this and the apparition which follows match Hogg's description of a similar occurrence, as personally experienced, first printed in 'Nature's Magic Lantern', *Chambers's Edinburgh Journal*, 28 September 1833, pp. 273–74. The same account notes a similarity to 'the Brocken Spectre' in Hanover, named after the highest peak in the Hartz Mountains, an atmospheric phenomenon in which the observer, when the sun is low, may see his or her (or another's) enlarged shadow against the clouds, often surrounded by a rainbow-like halo. In Germany, it is associated with Walpurgis night, on the eve of 1 May, when witches are supposed to hold revels with the devil. In Scotland, the phenomenon is most commonly witnessed in December and January. The 'scientific' explanation of the halo offered shortly later might owe something to Hogg's friendship with David Brewster (1781–1868: knighted 1832), the inventor in 1816 of the kaleidoscope, and a regular contributor to the earlier numbers of *Blackwood's Edinburgh Magazine* on scientific subjects.

29(c) rocks of Salisbury Salisbury crags, rising to 574 feet and with a cliff-like edge, adjacent to Arthur's Seat; the 'deep dell' between the two is a clear feature.

32(d) every precept of the Gospel alluding especially to the doctrine of forgiveness found in the New Testament gospels, notably in Matthew 6.14–15 (part of the Lord's Prayer, as given in the Sermon on the Mount), and more specifically in relation to brethren (see Matthew 18.21–22, 35, Luke 17.3–4). George Colwan's offer of reconciliation, on such a basis, contrasts sharply with the predestinarian absolutism of his brother.

32(d) according to the flesh first occurrence of this phrase in the novel, meaning here 'related by blood', but also carrying the additional suggestion of 'in physical rather than spiritual terms'. In the Bible it is found especially in the New Testament Epistles (Colossians 3.22; Ephesians 6.5; II Corinthians 1.17, 10.2; Romans 1.3), where 'the flesh' is also more broadly associated with the law, the carnal, and sin (see, e.g., Romans 7). See also note on 'children of the promise' for 34(d).

34(c) transgressions return upon his own head sevenfold 'sevenfold' and 'upon his/thine own head' are both biblical expressions (see, e.g., Genesis 4.15, I Kings 2.44), and introduce here a wave of Old Testament rhetoric and absolutism after the brief Christian offering made by George.

34(d) coals of juniper compare Psalm 120.4: 'Sharp arrows of the mighty, with coals of juniper.' In the original Psalm, however, this can be seen as a *complaint* against calumniators, indicating again how the Rev. Wringhim misapplies biblical text.

34(d) casting his lightnings echoing Psalm 144.6: 'Cast forth lightning, and scatter them: shoot out thine arrows, and destroy them.'

34(d) destroy and root out both familiar Old Testament expressions: see, e.g., Jeremiah 1.10. The wording of the Scottish metrical version of Psalm 144, however, indicates that Hogg might have been in part completing verse six there (see also note above): 'Cast forth thy lightning, scatter them; thine arrows shoot, them rout.'

34(d) children of the promise compare Romans 9.8: 'That is, They which are the children of the flesh, these *are* not the children of God: but the children of the promise are counted for the seed.' In this particular sequence St Paul is pointing out that the Old Testament promise of salvation made by God was transmitted only though Abraham's son Isaac, though he had other children, with the children of Israel (the name given by God to Jacob, Isaac's son) then becoming the chosen people. According to Pauline theology, the old covenant between God and the Jews is superseded by Christ's atonement, the children of the promise being those saved by Christ's sacrifice. See Galatians 4.28: 'Now we, brethren, as Isaac was, are the children of promise.'

35(c) High Court of Justiciary Scotland's highest criminal court, to which the most serious offences were sent for trial.

35(d) The Lord Justice evidently the Lord Justice Clerk, the chief officiating judge in the High Court of Justiciary (see note above).

36(a) Lord Advocate the chief legal officer of the crown in Scotland, who is in charge of criminal prosecution.

36(c) the sign of the Black Bull of Norway for possible prototypes of the Black Bull tavern in the story, see note on 17(b). The embellishment 'of Norway', as found in the novel only here, apparently relates to the Scottish folk tale 'the Black Bull of Noroway'. Hogg may have had particularly in mind two lines from John Leyden's ballad 'The Cout of Keeldar': 'To wilder measures next they turn:/ "The Black Black Bull of Noroway!"' (stanza 43). In Walter Scott's *Minstrelsy of the Scottish Border* (1802-03), where Leyden's poem first appeared, Scott's note refers to 'a wild fanciful popular tale of enchantment, termed *The Black Bull of Noroway*': ed. by T. F. Henderson, 4 vols (Edinburgh, 1932), IV, 276. This note appears immediately after another by Scott about the bull's head set before someone at a feast being 'a common signal for his assassination'–a theme also present in Leyden's ballad. 'The black bull of Norway has broken his band' is also the first line of a short 'Song' in Hogg's long poem *Queen Hynde* (1824), where it thematically introduces the threat of Viking invasion and anarchy: see *Queen Hynde*, ed. by Suzanne Gilbert and Douglas S. Mack (Edinburgh: Edinburgh University Press, 1998), pp. 11, 250. In the present narrative, this detail might be taken as an ominous prelude to the events culminating in George Colwan's death.

36(c) written *disloyalty* i.e. disloyal to the established monarch: a reference to the Jacobitism of George and friends, as filtered through the Editor's new establishment Toryism.

37(a) Mr. Drummond, the younger son of a nobleman of distinction for a likely historical prototype for this character, here mentioned for the first time and later given the Christian name Thomas, see note on 'John, Duke of Melfort', for 38(c) below.

37(d) a little washing-green at the side of the North Loch the North Loch was an artificial lake, originally formed in the 15th century to the north of Edinburgh Castle and Town for defensive purposes, and stretching in present terms approximately from the West End of Princes Street to the site occupied by Waverley Station. It is quite feasible that a Close running from the north side of the High

Street should end near the south-eastern shore of the North Loch, though no specific 'washing-green' has been identified (but see note on 54(c)). The loch was successively drained during the later 18th and early 19th centuries.

37(d) dead-room in the old Guard-house the old town Guard-house served as the headquarters of the City Guard. A low building, it stood in the middle of the High Street (see Map 3), until its removal in 1785. No specific reference to a dead-room there, for the keeping of dead bodies, has been discovered.

38(c) John, Duke of Melfort John Drummond (1649–1714), 2nd son of the 3rd earl of Perth, was created Earl of Melfort in 1686. He fled with James II and VII in 1688, was created Duke of Melfort by James in 1692, but thereafter experienced mixed fortunes in the Jacobite Court at St Germain near Paris, from which he was eventually banished. Thomas Drummond, the second son by his second marriage (in 1680), became an officer in the service of Charles VI, Emperor of Germany, and died unmarried in 1715. The latter is presumably the model for Hogg's character, Thomas Drummond. For a likely source of Hogg's, see the entry 'Drummond, Earl of Melfort', in *The Peerage of Scotland [...] by Sir Robert Douglas of Glenbervie, Bart.*, revised and corrected by John Philip Wood, 2 vols (Edinburgh, 1813), II, 220–22.

38(c) Lord of Session i.e. a judge of the Court of Session, the supreme civil court in Scotland. See also next note.

39(a) Lord Craigie, his uncle the most obvious prototype in terms of judicial capacity is Sir Thomas Wallace of Craigie (d. 1680), who was made a Lord of Session in 1671, and became Lord Justice Clerk in 1675, a post he still held at the time of his death. He was the father of Eupheme, the second wife of the titular Duke of Melfort (see note on 38(c)), and hence grandfather (not uncle) of their second son, Thomas Drummond. Sir Thomas Craigie's second son, also Sir Thomas Wallace of Craigie (1665–1728/30), fits the description of uncle and matches the general chronology more accurately, but evidently was not like his father a Lord of Session. See George Robertson, *A Genealogical Account of the Principal Families in Ayrshire more particularly in Kyle and Cunninghame*, 3 vols (Irvine, 1823–25), II, 361–65; *The Faculty of Advocates in Scotland 1532–1943*, Scottish Record Society, ed. by Sir Francis J. Grant (Edinburgh, 1944), pp. 213–14; James Paterson, *History of the Counties of Ayr and Wigton. Vol 1–Kyle* (Edinburgh, 1863), pp. 293–95. The same Craigie is apparently mentioned more fully by name at 63(c).

39(b)   Emperor Charles VI (1685–1740), head of the Austrian monarchy and the Holy Roman Empire, and claimant to the Spanish throne.

40(a) included in the promises i.e. the promises originally made by God under the Old Testament covenants and renewed and extended, according to St Paul, through Christ's sacrifice and the Covenant of Grace. It was these covenants which the Scottish Covenanters sought to emulate, and which are here given an especially exclusionist emphasis.

40(a) pharisaical doctrine the Editor's choice of pejorative adjective reflects his Enlightenment sense of superiority. Compare the lawyer Pleydell in Walter Scott's *Guy Mannering* (1815), in applauding a later preacher (Rev. John Erskine) for showing 'nothing of the souring or pharisaical pride which has been imputed to some of the early fathers of the Calvinistic Kirk of Scotland' (Ch. 37; EEWN 2, pp. 212–13).

40(b) controller of Nature an expression indicative of the deistical outlook of the Editor. According to Hogg's Sermon (XI) on 'Deistical Reformers', in his *Lay Sermons* (1834), there are two ways of apprehending the nature of God: i) the evidence of Nature, ii) the Revelation of Scripture–see *A Series of Lay Sermons*, ed. by Gillian Hughes (Edinburgh: Edinburgh University Press, 1997), pp. 108–20, and especially pp. 117–18. Generally the Editor in his narrative is strong on the first, but has little to say about the latter.

40(b) mouths of babes and sucklings compare Psalm 8.2 and Matthew 21.16.

41(a) discovered a cue compare Hogg's earlier tale 'John Gray o' Middleholm': 'He had no doubt that he had found the cue to the treasure' (*Winter Evening Tales*, 2 vols (1820), I, 322). This would indicate that the change to 'clue' in several later editions of *Confessions*, though apparently more apposite in context, does not reflect what Hogg actually wrote.

41(b) town of Peebles on Tweedside royal burgh and county town of Peeblesshire, about 25 miles S of Edinburgh, on the River Tweed.

41(d) God of the fatherless echoing especially Psalm 10.14: 'thou art the helper of the fatherless'. There are also several other biblical references to God being the special protector of widows and orphans.

42(b) hung up, a spectacle to a gazing, gaping multitude as happened in the case of Mary M'Kinnon, hung before a crowd estimated at 20,000, in Edinburgh on 16 April 1823, having been condemned for the stabbing of a client in her brothel. For further commentary on this event in relation to the novel, see Introduction, pp. li–liii.

42(d) the Grass Market the place of execution in Edinburgh, to the SE of the Castle.

42(d) forgive me the appeal echoes the Lord's Prayer ('forgive us our sins').

45(d) remitted to the Court of Justiciary i.e. transferred to the highest criminal Court (see note on 35(c)).

46(c) shakel bane the wrist.

46(d) The deil a bit not a bit, 'no way!'

47(a) the Ringans, or some sic name evidently a misnomer for the Wringhims. As David Groves suggests, the use of Ringan as a 'suggestive cryptonym' for Wringhim might also indicate an intertextual link with John Galt's *Ringan Gilhaize* (1823), whose eponymous hero eventually feels justified in committing murder in God's name: see 'Parallel Narratives in Hogg's *Justified Sinner*', *Scottish Literary Journal*, 9:2 (December 1982), 37–44 (p. 41).

47(c) Sae are a' the spoons in Argyle alluding to Campbell, the family name of the Earls and Dukes of Argyle, and common as a clan name/surname in Argyllshire and the West Highlands of Scotland.

47(d) hay raip i.e. a clothes-line, made of straw or hay rope.

49(c) art and part Scots law phrase denoting participation in a crime, by contriving or executing it.

50(b) Lucky Sudds 'Lucky' was a name commonly given to tavern hostesses: no particular origin for the surname, which might have an earlier burlesque origin, has been discovered.

51(c) Leith Wynd ran from the Netherbow Port, at the east end of the High Street, northwards to the foot of Calton Hill, leading from there towards the port of Leith. It was demolished to make way for Waverley Station.

54(c) bleaching green where clothes were left to bleach in the sun after washing, and apparently the same location as the 'washing-green' as noted at 37(d). An engraving contemporary with Hogg shows clothes being left out on the bank of the drained North Loch at its south-eastern end ('Part of the Old Town, Edinburgh', in John Britton and Thomas H. Shepherd, *Modern Athens! Displayed in a Series of Views: or Edinburgh in the Nineteenth Century* (London, 1831; reprinted New York: Arno Press, 1978), opposite p. 20).

54(c) hell has it! echoing the assailant's 'I'll have your soul, sir' earlier, and so inviting the view that George, dying in sin, is bound for Hell. The triumphant air matches the witch's 'I have won!', on securing the abbot's soul, in Hogg's poem 'The Witch of the Gray Thorn' (1825): see *A Queer Book*, ed. by P. D. Garside (Edinburgh: Edinburgh University Press, 1995), pp. 195–96.

54(d) dog of hell in Classical mythology, Cerberus, the watch-dog of Hades.

58(d) his left side contrasting with the conventional presentation of Christ on the cross wounded through his right side. More generally, the left side of anything is traditionally associated with evil or ill luck, the right with the reverse.

59(d) Bogle-heuch meaning 'Ghost-bank', and probably fictitious.

60(d) that the promise is binding i.e. that the promise of salvation is irreversible.

61(d) hag of the pit as used to denote a witch.

62(a) Murder will out proverbial.

62(a) ears of the willow presumably referring to the catkins (spikes of flowers) hanging down from the willow tree.

62(a) seven tongues of the woodriff the woodruff (*Asperula odorata*), is a low-growing herb, with clusters of white flowers, and distinctive whorls of leaves surrounding the stems.

62(a) Gil-Martin name in Gaelic for a fox, a connection first discussed in Christopher MacLachlan's 'The Name "Gil-Martin"', in *Newsletter of the James Hogg Society*, no. 4 (May 1985), p. 32. A definition contemporary with Hogg can be found in *Dictionarium Scoto-Celticum: A Dictionary of the Gaelic Language [...] compiled and published under the Direction of the Highland Society of Scotland*, 2 vols (Edinburgh and London, 1828), I, 482: 'GILLE-MÀRTUINN, A fox: vulpes'. In Gaelic folklore, Gil-Martin is depicted as a shape-changing trickster. A surviving example can be found in the orally-received story 'Mac Iain Direach' in J. F. Campbell, *Popular Tales of the West Highlands*, new edn, 4 vols (Paisley and London, 1890–93), II, 344–57, where the hero's pursuit of a blue falcon is aided by 'AN GILLE MAIRTEAN, the fox' (p. 345), who makes a number of physical transformations. For Hogg's use of 'Gil-Moules' as a name for the devil, in other works, see Introduction, p. xiv. There is also an interesting resemblance to Fox Ghyll, the small house rented by Thomas de Quincey in September 1820, shortly before coming to Edinburgh later that year: see Grevel Lindop, *The Opium-Eater: A Life of Thomas De Quincey* (London: J. M. Dent, 1981), p. 241.

62(d) the worm that never dies a feature of Hell: see Isaiah 66.24 and Mark 9.43–48.

63(c) Sir Thomas Wallace of Craigie for the likely historical basis for this figure, here (apparently) first given fully by name, see note on 39(a).

64(c) died in the memorable year for Scotland, 1715 according to *The Peerage of Scotland* (1813), Thomas Drummond, the second son of the Duke of Melfort by his second marriage, became an officer in the service of Charles VI, Emperor of Germany, and died unmarried in 1715 (see also note on 'John, Duke of Melfort', for 38(c)). His elder brother, John (born 1682) was a Major-General in the 1715 Jacobite rising, escaping to France again in 1716. There are strong similarities between the Thomas Drummond of this novel and a similarly-named character in Hogg's 'The Adventures of Captain John Lochy', published in his *Altrive Tales* (London, 1832), pp. 1–142. In this story, Lochy, after joining the British forces fighting alongside the Austrians at the Battle of Blenheim in 1704, becomes friends with a 'young officer', Lieutenant Drummond, 'a great party man, and an adherent of the banished Stuarts' (p. 19); the same character, as Captain Drummond, is later described as having taken 'the principal command of his brother's regiment' at the time of the battle of Sheriffmuir in 1715 (p. 105). A 'Captain Thomas Drummond' is listed in an 'Account of Prisoners taken by the Duke of Argylle, 1715' in *News Letters of 1715–1716*, ed. by A. Francis Steuart (London and Edinburgh, 1910), p. 157. For further details, and other secondary evidence suggesting that a Captain Thomas Drummond fought at and died of his wounds after Sheriffmuir, see David Groves, 'The *Confessions* and *The Adventures of Captain John Lochy*', in *Newsletter of the James Hogg Society*, no. 6 (May 1987), pp. 11–13.

67(a) faith of the promises, and justification by grace for these two key theological concepts, see notes on 34(d) and 11(b); and for a broader discussion of the issues, see Introduction, pp. xxviii–xxx.

67(a) gods of silver and of gold familiar biblical expression, in describing heathen gods. Compare especially Exodus 20.23 ('Ye shall not make with me gods of silver, neither shall ye make unto you gods of gold'), and Psalm 135.15 ('The idols of the heathen are silver and gold, the work of men's hands'). See also Daniel 5.23.

67(a) minister of heaven compare Colossians 1.23, where St Paul is described as a minister of heaven. The term also appears in Act 3 of John Home's play *Douglas* (1756), as quoted by Hogg in addressing Walter Scott at the start of his own 'Memoir': 'As if you were the minister of heaven/ Sent down to search the secret sins of men'—see *Memoir of the Author's Life*, ed. by Douglas S. Mack (Edinburgh and London: Scottish Academic Press, 1972), p. 4.

67(b) a burning and a shining light matches Robert Burns's satirical poem, 'Holy Willie's Prayer' (1785), line 11, itself echoing John 5.35 on John the Baptist ('He was a burning and a shining light: and ye were willing for a season to rejoice in his light'). The expression also featured in the 'Marrow Controversy' of 1718–23, when it was used especially by the 'evangelical' side: see Introduction, p. xxiv.

67(b) Scottish worthies echoing the familiar short title, *Scots Worthies*, used for the much reprinted account of Scottish Covenanting martyrs and reformers by John Howie (1735–93). This was first published in 1774 as *Biographia Scoticana; or a brief historical account of the lives, characters, and memorable transactions of the most eminent Worthies*.

67(b) persecution of the saints a reference to 'the killing times' of the reigns of Charles II and James II and VII, at the time when Robert's mother would have been growing up; and also implying a parallel with the early Christians.

67(d) church visible see note on 14(c).

68(a) questions of the Single Catechism a *catechism* is an elementary treatise in the principles of the Christian religion, in the form of questions and answers, used for instruction and in Confirmation. In Scotland the Larger and Shorter Catechisms as formulated by the Westminster Assembly and completed in 1647–48 were subscribed to by the Presbyterian church, replacing earlier catechisms such as John Craig's *Short Catechism* (1581). The Shorter Catechism was much used in the instruction of young people, and Hogg himself recalls how the 'juvenile class' at Ettrick School 'read the Shorter Catechism and the Proverbs of Solomon', this preceding 'the class who read in the Bible'—see *Memoir of the Author's Life*, ed. by Douglas S. Mack (Edinburgh and London: Scottish Academic Press, 1972), p. 5. Hogg also evidently used the Shorter Catechism regularly in bringing up his own family: see Introduction, p. xvi. The 18th century saw a number of more specialist offshoots aimed at children, such as John Willison's *The Mother's Catechism* (Edinburgh, 1731). Alexander Hamilton's *A Short Catechism concerning the three special Divine Covenants, and two Gospel Sacraments* (Edinburgh, 1714), 'Calculated especially for the Use of those of Weaker Capacity', resulted in its author being called before the Committee for Purity of Doctrine in 1719, at the onset of the Marrow Controversy, to answer to certain expressions in it (for the Marrow Controversy, see Introduction, pp. xxiii–xxv). No work in Scotland with the title 'Single Catechism' has been discovered, however, and it seems most likely that Hogg was thinking of the Shorter Catechism here, perhaps with 'single' representing a mistake by Robert, reflecting his single-mindedness or isolation as a child respondent.

68(b) Effectual Calling [...] *In*effectual Calling alluding to the question in the Shorter Catechism (see note above), '*What is effectual Calling?*'. The answer there is 'Effectual calling is the work of Gods Spirit, whereby, convincing us of our sin and misery, inlightening our minds in the knowledg[e] of Christ and renewing our wills, he doth perswade and enable us to embrace Jesus Christ, freely offered to us in the Gospel' (*Confession of Faith*, p. 167; see also Torrance, p. 267). The succeeding two questions in the Shorter Catechism lead to the benefits of effectual calling in this life, and to the nature of Justification ('an act of Gods free grace wherein he pardoneth all our sins'). Robert's interruption of the process, by way of his alternative question, might be said to close down the more positive aspects of the doctrine of effectual calling, while accentuating its exclusionist side. It also reflects the thinking of Calvin's successor Theodore Beza (1519–1605), who held that reprobates (i.e. those not of the Elect) are sometimes affected with a 'callying ineffectuall', leading to a kind of temporary faith which gives 'the appearances of vertues, ordinarilie called Moral vertues': see R. T. Kendall, *Calvin and English Calvinism to 1649* (Oxford: Oxford University Press, 1979), p. 36. The concept was developed by the influential early English Calvinist William Perkins (1558–1602), who listed five degrees of ineffectual calling, in which a reprobate can have some of the sensations of being called, and exhibit 'outward holiness' for a while, though later falling into apostasy and inevitable condemnation (see *The Works of William Perkins*, ed. by Ian Breward (Appleford: Sutton Courtenay Press, 1970), pp. 251–54; also Kendall, pp. 68–76). Behind this might lie the dark irony that Robert, so eager to add another category to the damned, is shortly to experience his own ineffectual calling.

68(c) old Barnet the surname perhaps suggests someone who seeks to foil the net, here especially the one which is already beginning to entangle Robert.

68(d) bond of iniquity compare St Peter's words to Simon in Acts 8.23: 'For I perceive that thou art in the gall of bitterness, and in the bond of iniquity.' See also note on 138(b).

69(a) book of life in biblical terms, the record of the names destined for eternal life. See, for example, Philippians 4.3 and Revelation 3.5, 20.12; and, for the dreadful alternative, Revelation 20.15: 'And whosoever was not found written in the book of life was cast into the lake of fire.' At this point Robert has no assurance that he is one of the Elect whose names are inscribed in the book of life.

69(c) original transgression alluding to the doctrine of original sin. Robert is fearful that even if he could repent of his own sins he is still doomed. As this passage also suggests, by this light there is no hope of being saved through good works.

69(c) my first parents i.e. Adam and Eve.

70(a) who art a worm, and no man echoing Psalm 22.6: 'But I am a worm, and no man; a reproach of men, and despised of the people.' Here as elsewhere Robert distorts Scripture: the Psalmist's lament concerns himself, Robert levels the same condescendingly at Barnet.

70(a) vessel to honour […] dishonour compare St Paul's parable of the potter in Romans 9.21, where there is an unusually strong suggestion of divine predestination: 'Hath not the potter power over the clay, of the same lump to make one vessel unto honour, and another unto dishonour?' See also II Timothy 2.20, where the allegory presents the vessels to honour as faithful and useful Christians and the inferior vessels as the faithless.

70(a) builded his stories in the heavens echoing Amos 9.6: 'It is he that buildeth his stories in the heaven, and hath founded his troop in the earth'.

70(b) afore the session i.e. before the Kirk session, the ruling body of each parish church of the Church of Scotland, consisting of the local elders and chaired by the minister. It was the body that dealt with cases of sexual misconduct, and oaths could be taken to establish paternity.

70(b) bow-kail thing *bow-kail* in Scots means cabbage, and, in its attributive use, 'cabbage-like'. In context here however there might possibly be a suggestion of deformity and ill-growth, particularly of bow- or bandy-leggedness. Hogg could also have been thinking of Burns's *Halloween*, stanza 9, with the line 'Poor Willie, wi' his bow-kail runt', though the primary meaning of *runt* here is 'stalk'.

70(c) a righteous man opening up the issue of two understandings of righteousness, that founded on works and that on faith. See also next note.

70(d) leaven of true righteousness, which is faith the metaphor of yeast helping bread to rise occurs in I Corinthians 5.6 and in Galatians 5.9 ('a little leaven leaveneth the whole lump'), which themselves reflect Matthew 13.33. According to Pauline theology, true Christian righteousness derived not from an individual doing right morally, but by virtue of justification through faith: though from the latter good works would naturally flow (an element the Wringhims tend to leave out). Compare Romans 1.17: 'For therein is the righteousness of God revealed from faith to faith: as it is written, The just shall live by faith.'

70(d) will be a cast-away will prove to be a reprobate, i.e. one of those not of the Elect.

71(a) red-letter side of the book of life the image here seems to be of alternate pages distinguishing the damned in red, though no biblical source for such a feature has been discovered. It reflects however a general association of red with the infernal, as well as possibly the idea of signing a pact with the devil in one's own blood, as in Marlowe's *Dr Faustus*. Compare Hogg's story 'George Dobson's Expedition to Hell', where the eponymous protagonist is given 'a ticket written with red ink', and also the beginning of 'The Witches of Traquair' where Colin Hyslop is on the point of signing away his soul to the devil in blood: *The Shepherd's Calendar*, ed. by Douglas S. Mack (Edinburgh: Edinburgh University Press, 1995), pp. 120, 225.

71(a) blood of the atonement the atonement, theologically, is the reconciliation of God and man through the sacrificial death of Jesus Christ, the blood of the atonement being the blood shed by Christ on the cross. A celebrated evocation of the idea that such blood cannot reach the damned occurs in Dr Faustus's last soliloquy: 'See see where *Christs* blood streames in the firmament,/ One drop would save my soule, halfe a drop, ah my *Christ*' (scene 13, lines 74–75).

72(c) lead a proof conduct an investigation; produce proof or evidence.

72(c) Melchizedek in Genesis 14.18-20, the King of Salem, who brings forth bread and wine, is a priest of the most high God, and blesses Abram (about to become Abraham, the father of the nation of Israel). According to the Epistle to the Hebrews, citing Psalm 110, Jesus is a priest for ever after the order of Melchizedek (5.6, 6.20, 7.17), and the fact that Abraham was blessed by him and paid him tithes establishes Melchizedek's superiority (7.1–4), Jesus therefore by this rule being greater than Abraham too. Wringhim in turn might be seen as placing himself on an equivalent level with Christ: Melchizedek is named specifically as 'King of righteousness' in Hebrews 7.2. The question of the relation of Melchizedek to Jesus was one of the most heated points in the Marrow Controversy. James Hog, in defence of his 1718 edition of Edward Fisher's *The Marrow of Modern Divinity*, denied strongly that Fisher (speaking as Evangelista) was claiming the two represented the same person: 'Our Author is accused of a singular and erroneous Opinion, *That* Melchizedek *was Christ himself.* I see no certain Ground to think that this was our Author's Opinion; for, in the former Page he expressly calls *Melchizedek* a Type of our Lord Jesus. [...] Still the chief Matter of the Marrow remains untouched': *An Explication of Passages Excepted against in the Marrow of Modern Divinity* (Edinburgh, 1719), pp. 7–8. Thomas Boston in his much-reprinted notes (1726) to *The Marrow* likewise argues strenuously that this view was 'inconsistent with the Scripture-account' (16th edn, Glasgow, 1766, p. 66n). The notion that such an idea was being propounded through the revival of Fisher's work was nevertheless evidently held by members of the established Kirk opposed to Hog and Boston. For a fuller account of the Marrow Controversy, see Introduction, pp. xxiii–xxvi.

72(c) Apostle of the Gentiles i.e. St Paul. Paul names himself specifically as such in

Romans 11.13 ('For I speak to you Gentiles, inasmuch as I am the apostle of the Gentiles, I magnify mine office'); see also I Timothy 2.7, II Timothy 1.11. The terms originate from the teaching that Christ's atonement superseded the old Jewish law, so that Gentiles could also become Christians. Wringhim senior identifies himself here with Paul, but in using this title he at the same time undermines himself, because, in contradiction to his own theology, the wording suggests an inclusive rather than an exclusive Paul.

72(d) **just Pharisee [...] poor publican** as in the parable of the Pharisee and the publican, Luke 18.10–14. Verse 11, which Barnet adapts, reads: 'The Pharisee stood and prayed thus with himself, God, I thank thee, that I am not as other men are, extortioners, unjust, adulterers, or even as this publican.' The true message, unnoticed by the Rev. Wringhim, lies however in verses 13–14: 'And the publican, standing afar off, would not lift up so much as his eyes unto heaven, but smote upon his breast, saying, God be merciful to me a sinner. I tell you, this man went down to his house justified rather than the other: for every one that exalteth himself shall be abased; and he that humbleth himself shall be exalted.' Wringhim senior in accepting at face value the verse Barnet adapts clearly doesn't know or understand the fuller context well enough.

72(d) **beadle an' servant-man** in Scotland a *beadle* is a church-officer with special duties of attending on the minister; he may also serve as a sexton.

73(a) **language of reprobation** *reprobation* used here at least partly in the theological sense of 'rejection by God', the state of being cast off and ordained to eternal misery (the opposite of *election* in the Calvinistic doctrine of predestination). Barnet, being in that state in Wringhim's eyes, uses fitting language.

73(a) **black stool [...] sack gown** both once used as forms of public penance in the Church of Scotland. The 'black stool' was a stool of repentance, where the culprit sat in the face of the whole congregation; a 'sack gown' was a rough garment of sack-cloth worn as a penitential sheet.

73(d) **Man's thoughts are vanity** echoing Psalm 94.11: 'The Lord knoweth the thoughts of man, that they are vanity.' In the metrical *Psalms of David* version this reads: 'Man's thoughts to be but vanity/ the Lord doth well discern.'

73(d) **keys of the church** as part of Barnet's office as 'beadle' (see note on 72(d)).

74(a) **bond of iniquity** see note on 68(d).

74(d) **Jehu, a Cyrus, or a Nebuchadnezzar** all potent monarchs in the Old Testament, who can be seen (as they are by Robert) as scourges permitted by God. Jehu led a bloody revolt to seize the throne of Israel, killing Jehoram the previous king, executing Jezebel, and obliterating the worship of Baal in the kingdom (II Kings 9–10). Cyrus in the Bible is a king of Persia who defeated the Babylonians, restoring the sacred vessels confiscated by Nebuchadnezzar and authorising the restoration of the Temple in Jerusalem (Ezra 5.14–15; II Chronicles 36.22–23). Nebuchadnezzar was the king of Babylon, who besieged and captured Jerusalem, taking away captives and vessels from the Temple, and setting up a new king there (II Kings 25.11–20). Even at this early stage, Robert vainly and inappropriately imagines himself a similarly chosen and powerful instrument.

74(d) **God a consuming fire** compare Deuteronomy 4.24 ('For the Lord thy God is a consuming fire, even a jealous God'), and Hebrews 12.29 ('For our God is a consuming fire').

75(a) **prelatic party** supporters of the Scottish Episcopal Church. In political terms, members of the Cavalier party, though characteristically Robert sees the divisions of the period almost exclusively in a theological light.

75(a) **preachers up of good works** those stressing the importance of justification by works (i.e. good moral behaviour), rather than by faith, later to develop in the 18th century as the 'Moderate' as opposed to 'Evangelical' party in the Church of

Scotland. Hogg examines the divided viewpoints in his story 'Sound Morality' (1829): see *Selected Stories and Sketches*, ed. by Douglas S. Mack (Edinburgh: Scottish Academic Press, 1982), pp. 121–32, 201.

75(d) whose name was M'Gill partly inverting that of Gil-Martin, already mentioned by name in the Editor's narrative, and who will later appear before Robert in the narrative sequence following that in which M'Gill is last mentioned. This invites the interpretation that Gil-Martin in some ways represents a mental replacement by Robert for the naturally gifted schoolboy whose existence so severely challenges his deluded sense of importance. Hogg might also have had in mind Dr William M'Gill (1732–1807) of Ayr, whose *A Practical Essay on the Death of Jesus Christ* (Edinburgh, 1786) attempted to bring the teachings of Christ down to an everyday level, but which led to charges of heresy, leading to M'Gill's recantation in 1790–see Henry F. Henderson, *The Religious Controversies of Scotland* (Edinburgh, 1905), pp. 86–94. Robert Burns's poem 'The Kirk's Alarm' (1789), whose 2nd stanza begins 'Doctor Mac, Doctor Mac, ye should streek on a rack', is written partly in response to the outcry against his friend M'Gill.

78(b) by the slump as a whole, collectively; in the lump.

78(b) excluding sins i.e. those excluding someone from the benefits of salvation. These are listed in Revelation 21.8 ('But the fearful, and unbelieving, and the abominable, and murderers, and whoremongers, and sorcerers, and idolaters, and all liars, shall have their part in the lake which burneth with fire and brimstone: which is the second death') and 22.15 ('For without [i.e. the Holy City, new Jerusalem] are dogs, and sorcerers, and whoremongers, and murderers, and idolaters, and whosoever loveth and maketh a lie'). In view of these lists Robert has already failed the test, having consciously been a liar (see 'I told a lie of him' in text at 76(d)). He also distorts the warning against 'whoremongers' into a hatred of female beauty (and, effectively, of women).

78(c) broken […] four out of the ten commandments Wringhim might be construed as having broken commandments so far, by i) not honouring his parents, ii) stealing, iii) giving false testimony, and iv) coveting his neighbour's goods.

78(d) filthy rags compare Isaiah 64.6: 'But we are all as an unclean thing, and all our righteousnesses are as filthy rags'.

79(a) Like the sinful king of Israel, I had been walking softly before the Lord for a season compare I Kings 21.27: 'And it came to pass, when Ahab heard those words, that he rent his clothes, and put sackcloth upon his flesh, and fasted, and lay in sackcloth, and went softly.' For Ahab's sins, see I Kings 21.17–24.

79(c) the society of *the just made perfect* i.e. the community of those justified through the Covenant of Grace, those fitted for Heaven and in an anticipatory sense already there. Compare Hebrews 12.22–23: 'But ye are come unto mount Sion, and unto the city of the living God, the heavenly Jerusalem, and to an innumerable company of angels, To the general assembly and church of the firstborn, which are written in heaven, and to God the Judge of all, and to the spirits of just men made perfect.' The term 'just men made perfect', usually applied to those already resident in Heaven, is also a common feature of the Dying and Last Testimonies of the Scottish Covenanter martyrs (for an example, see note on 165(b) below).

79(c) wrestled with God, as the patriarch of old referring to Jacob's wrestling with God at Penuel, as described in Genesis 32.24–28, after which God gives to Jacob the name Israel. Wringhim senior is being doubly pretentious here: i) in claiming to prevail in wrestling with God; and ii) in comparing himself with the patriarch, the father of the chosen people. There is also the underlying possibility that Wringhim has in actuality been wrestling with the devil, leading to his manifestation as Gil-Martin in the immediately succeeding scene.

79(c) not for a night Jacob's wrestling at Penuel (see previous note) lasts only 'until the breaking of the day' (Genesis 32.24), a difference that makes Wringhim's claim seem even more pretentious.

79(c) written in the Lamb's book of life like the inhabitants of the new Jerusalem as described in Revelation 21.27: 'And there shall in no wise enter into it any thing that defileth, neither whatsoever worketh abomination, or maketh a lie: but they which are written in the Lamb's book of life.' See also note on 69(a).

79(d) resist even to blood echoing Hebrews 12.4 ('Ye have not yet resisted unto blood, striving against sin').

79(d) repentance unto life compare Acts 11.18: 'When they heard these things, they held their peace, and glorified God, saying, Then hath God also to the Gentiles granted repentance unto life.' This is the response of those listening to St Peter's vision about the need to admit Gentiles as Christians (see Acts 10.11–20, 11.4–17; also note on 95(b)), broadening access to salvation, previously confined to those who keep Mosaic law. Wringhim's approach narrows this new Christian inclusiveness into rigid exclusivity.

79(d) plucked as a brand out of the burning compare Amos 4.11 ('I have overthrown some of you, as God overthrew Sodom and Gomorrah, and ye were as a firebrand plucked out of the burning: yet have ye not returned unto me, saith the Lord'); and Zechariah 3.2 ('And the Lord said unto Satan, The Lord rebuke thee, O Satan; even the Lord that hath chosen Jerusalem rebuke thee: is not this a brand plucked out of the fire?'). In both passages the metaphor apparently relates to the Israelite nation.

80(a) as an eagle a vantage point usually deemed in biblical terms more suitable for God than for mortals. See, for example, Obadiah 4: 'Though thou exalt thyself as the eagle, and though thou set thy nest among the stars, thence will I bring thee down, saith the Lord.' However, Isaiah 40.31 asserts: 'they that wait upon the Lord [...] shall mount up with wings as eagles'. For the use of the same image during the Marrow Controversy, see Introduction, p. xxv.

81(a) assurance in the same mode of redemption Gil-Martin himself is using the language of justification here: the 'assurance' (i.e. conviction or persuasion) that one is in a state of grace, which will lead to salvation, being a key concept in Calvinist theology.

82(c) the 25th day of March 1704, when I had just entered the eighteenth year of my age 25 March is the Feast of the Annunciation, also called Lady Day, on which the angel Gabriel announced to the Virgin Mary that she would be the mother of the Messiah (Luke 1.26–38). Gil-Martin's apparent manifestation before Robert Wringhim on the same day offers a dark parody of this event. By Robert's account it is also his seventeenth birthday, which clashes with earlier suggestions of a post-1688 birth, as well as more particularly with subsequent events taking place during the 1703 session of the Scottish parliament. For further discussion of these apparent anomalies, and other chronological issues, see 'Historical and Geographical Note', pp. 200–03.

83(c) troubled in spirit echoing John 13.21: 'When Jesus had thus said, he was troubled in spirit, and testified, and said, Verily, verily, I say unto you, that one of you shall betray me.'

83(d) angel of light [...] profound wiles compare II Corinthians 11.14, where, in denouncing false apostles and their facility in deceiving, Paul declares 'And no marvel; for Satan himself is transformed into an angel of light'.

84(a) principalities and powers [...] might and dominion the names of four out of the nine orders of angels, who were considered to have control over human destiny before being overcome by Jesus Christ. Compare Ephesians 1.21, where the resurrected Christ is described in Heaven as 'Far above all principality, and power, and might, and dominion'; and Colossians 2.15 ('And having spoiled principalities and powers, he made a shew of them openly, triumphing over them in it'). It was also believed that the devil had his own angels: see Matthew 25.41.

84(c) **learned by rote [...] limbs of Antichrist** referring to the set prayers of the Roman Catholic and Episcopalian churches, which the Presbyterians eschewed (for the Antichrist, see also note on 9(d)).

84(c) **two-edged weapon [...] mouth** compare Psalm 149.6–7: 'Let the high praises of God be in their mouth, and a two-edged sword in their hand; To execute vengeance upon the heathen, and punishments upon the people.'

84(c) **as dung to fat the land** see note on 11(b).

85(a) **economy of the Christian world** *economy* in the theological sense of divine government of the world, which here Robert is profanely challenging.

85(a) **saints [...] inherit the earth** in contrast with the Sermon on the Mount in Matthew 5.5 (compare also Psalm 37.11), where it is the meek who shall inherit; Robert's sense of the true biblical priorities can again be seen to be distorted.

85(b) **devouring fire** Old Testament metaphor describing the vengefulness of God against the enemies of Israel (see Isaiah 29.6, 30.27).

85(b) **workers of iniquity** common biblical expression, found especially in Psalms (see, e.g., 5.5, 36.12, 59.2).

85(b) **field and wood of Finnieston** now a district of Glasgow, about 1 mile W of the city centre, but at this period on its immediate outskirts.

85(d) **intersected with red lines** red is commonly associated with magic and the infernal: see also note on 'red-letter side of the book of life' for 71(a).

87(b–c) **great preacher [...] forth?** the first part of the quoted sentence is from Ecclesiastes ('The Book of Ecclesiastes, or the Preacher') 9.10: 'Whatsoever thy hand findeth to do, do it with thy might; for there is no work, nor device, nor knowledge, nor wisdom, in the grave, whither thou goest.' The second part is from the Book of Proverbs 27.1: 'Boast not thyself of to morrow; for thou knowest not what a day may bring forth.' Both these books of the Bible are meant to express the wisdom of Solomon. Gil-Martin however is mixing holy writ for his own purposes, and in particular cuts off the mention of the grave in the first verse appropriated. He also draws an entirely false conclusion concerning absolute predestination.

89(c) **call me Gil-Martin** for this name, see note on 62(a).

89(d) **Czar Peter of Russia** Peter I the Great (1672–1725), Tsar of Russia from 1682; he visited England in 1698 as part of a tour of Western Europe, chiefly to study ship-building. Robert's identification here is one of several indications of an underlying secular motivation in his actions, leading eventually to his possession of the estate of Dalcastle.

90(b) **of the moral cast** indicating a preacher of good works, in later terms a Moderate rather than Evangelical; but the real point about Blanchard, whose name might suggest whiteness, is that he preaches and practises Christianity, as enunciated in the Sermon on the Mount, which is why Gil-Martin takes such exception to him.

90(d) **one that rather dreads its truths than reverences them** see James 2.19 ('the devils also believe, and tremble').

90(d) **connector of humanity** Blanchard's views here compare with those expressed in Hogg's *Lay Sermons* (1834): 'Wo to him who would weaken the bonds with which true Christianity connects us with Heaven and with one another!'—see *A Series of Lay Sermons*, ed. by Gillian Hughes (Edinburgh: Edinburgh University Press, 1997), p. 83.

92(c) **better that one fall** reversing the priority as expressed in the parable of the lost sheep, Luke 15.3–7.

93(a) back friend friend who stands at one's back, a backer; alternatively, false friend, unavowed enemy.

93(c) sword of the Lord biblical expression, found only in the Old Testament. It is especially emphatic in Judges 7.18, 20, where it serves as the war cry of a specially-chosen group of Israelites, who under Gideon overthrow their enemies the Midianites.

94(b) high church of Paisley Paisley is a town in Renfrewshire, about 8 miles SWW of central Glasgow. At the time of the novel's setting the main place of Presbyterian worship would have been the nave of Paisley Abbey. A new High Kirk was erected in 1756.

94(b) Finnieston Dell see note on 85(b).

94(b) more than the life of a lamb Gil-Martin's statement at this point runs in the face of the representation of Christ as the Lamb in the New Testament, and the whole symbolism of atonement. Compare John 1.29: 'The next day John seeth Jesus coming unto him, and saith, Behold the Lamb of God, which taketh away the sin of the world.' See also Revelation 7.14, 13.8.

94(c) Lord of Hosts a frequent title for the Old Testament God, with 'hosts' sometimes referring to the heavenly hosts and sometimes to the armies of Israel. For an echoing of the bellicose application of the term here, see Isaiah 13.4–5.

95(b) God whom thou servest echoing the words spoken to Daniel in the lions' den: 'Now the king spake and said unto Daniel, Thy God whom thou servest continually, he will deliver thee' (Daniel 6.16). Here used both scathingly and equivocally by Gil-Martin.

95(b) cloudy veil [...] golden weapons paralleling in some respect the vision experienced by St Peter as described in Acts 10.10-16, 11.1–18: 'And saw heaven opened, and a certain vessel descending unto him, as it had been a great sheet knit at the four corners, and let down to earth' (10.11). Robert however fails to interpret the vision correctly, not realising that the weapons are pointed at himself, that he is the one in danger of damnation. Moreover, whereas Peter's vision indicates that salvation is not just for the chosen people, but for Gentiles too, Robert's, in spite of the implicit warning, is interpreted in a purely destructive way.

95(b) as I had been a lamb reminiscent here of the lamb as sacrificed in Old Testament ritual, and a startling image of the hold that Gil-Martin has over Robert. See also note on 94(b).

95(c) an highly-favoured one Mary is called thus by the angel Gabriel, at the Annunciation, Luke 1.28: 'And the angel came in unto her, and said, Hail, thou that art highly favoured, the Lord is with thee: blessed art thou among women.' This supplies a further indication of Gil-Martin's inversion of this event (see note on 82(c)).

95(c) at thy right and left hand echoing those passages in the Bible where God offers such protection (see note on 24(b)), but here with the suggestion of an enclosure of Robert by evil. The idea finds more positive expression in Hogg's tale 'Welldean Hall': 'How grand is the conviction, that there is a being on your right hand and your left, that sees the actions of all his creatures' (in *Winter Evening Tales*, 2 vols (Edinburgh, 1820), II, 246).

95(d) who dwells between the Cherubim a familiar biblical situating of God: see, e.g., II Kings 19.15, Psalm 80.1, Isaiah 37.16.

97(c) Pearman Sike possibly fictitious: a 'sike' is a water-course or marshy hollow (often dry in summer).

98(c) the court and the country party the terms are of the period and correct, meaning roughly i) those representing the interests of the Crown and the ministry of the day, and ii) those opposed to the government, either from principle or due to being out of office.

98(c) the true Gospel preachers [...] and the upholders of pure morality i.e. the 'evangelical' and 'moderate' wings of the Presbyterian church, those preaching salvation through grace and those emphasising the importance of good works.

100(b) sword of the Lord see note on 93(c).

100(c) not to take vengeance out of the Lord's hand see Romans 12.19: 'Dearly beloved, avenge not yourselves, but rather give place unto wrath: for it is written, Vengeance is mine; I will repay, saith the Lord.' St Paul's reference here is to Deuteronomy 32.35 ('To me belongeth vengeance, and recompence'). Robert veers towards true gospel meaning in briefly resisting Gil-Martin.

100(d) mark of the beast [...] foreheads and right hands the mark of the Anti-christ, and the countermark of the divine seal that marks the servants of God. Compare Revelation 13.16: 'And he causeth all, both small and great, rich and poor, free and bond, to receive a mark in their right hand, or in their foreheads.' The phrase 'mark of the beast' is found specifically at Revelation 16.2, and again at 19.20: 'And the beast was taken, and with him the false prophet that wrought miracles before him, with which he deceived them that had received the mark of the beast, and them that worshipped his image. These both were cast alive into a lake of fire burning with brimstone.' This part of Revelation depicts a cosmic war, between the Lamb and the 144,000 who bear God's seal, and the seven-headed beast, Satan's emissary (the Antichrist), and those who bear his mark. The phrase the 'mark of the beast' was aimed especially at Episcopalians and Catholics in Scotland in Covenanting times, and is still sometimes used jocularly to refer to clergymen with 'High' Anglican leanings.

101(d) acts of Jehu [...] Ahab's own sons Jehu's destruction of all the descendants of Ahab and the priest of Baal, as a result of a prophetic mandate, is related in II Kings 10. Ahab and his wife Jezebel are utterly and spectacularly sinful in Old Testament narrative, and Gil-Martin argues here that, though Jehu was a good servant of God, if one of Ahab's own sons had done the deed, it would have been even more meritorious. The same text features in Hogg's tale 'Wat Pringle o' the Yair', where preachers incite General Leslie to massacre royalist prisoners at Newark Castle in spite of their being granted terms: 'For they alluded in such inveterate terms [...] to the destruction [...] of the whole kindred priests and followers of Ahab by the express commandment of the Almighty'—see *Tales of the Wars of Montrose*, ed. by Gillian Hughes (Edinburgh: Edinburgh University Press, 1996), p. 200.

102(a) Go thou then and do likewise echoing particularly the conclusion to the parable of the Good Samaritan, Luke 10.37: 'And he said, He that shewed mercy on him. Then said Jesus unto him, Go, and do thou likewise.' Again, Gil-Martin offers a dark inversion of true Christianity (in this case an act of charity).

102(a) cleanse the sanctuary compare Ezekiel 45.18 ('Thus saith the Lord God; In the first month, in the first day of the month, thou shalt take a young bullock without blemish, and cleanse the sanctuary'). More generally, there is perhaps an allusion to Jesus ejecting the moneylenders from the temple (see Matthew 21.12–13).

102(a) like a ruling energy compare Hogg's story 'The Witches of Traquair', set in late Catholic Scotland: 'in those days, the hopes of attaining some energies beyond the reach of mere human capability, inflamed the ignorant and wicked to attempts and acts of the most diabolical nature'—see *The Shepherd's Calendar*, ed. by Douglas S. Mack (Edinburgh: Edinburgh University Press, 1995), p. 224. At this point, Gil-Martin's speech noticeably veers from the biblical to terms more closely associated with black magic.

102(a) master spirit Shakespearean phrase, indicating an imposing greatness or power. But also, as in the case of 'ruling energy' above, evidently a term associated by Hogg with magic and diabolism. Compare Patie Maxwell (or his likeness) in Hogg's 'Mr Adamson of Laverhope': 'it is a sublimer thing still to be a deil—a master-spirit in a forge like yon' (*The Shepherd's Calendar*, ed. by Douglas S. Mack (Edinburgh: Edinburgh University Press, 1995), p. 50). The term 'master spirit' was later used by Hogg to describe John Wilson's influence on *Blackwood's Edinburgh Magazine* in a letter to William Blackwood of 5 July 1827 (NLS, MS 4019, fol. 193); while another letter to Blackwood of 9 March 1831 refers to J. G. Lockhart and Wilson as 'these two Master Spirits' (MS 4029, fol. 249). For further commentary on Hogg, Wilson, and Lockhart in relation to *Blackwood's Magazine*, see Introduction, pp. xxxviii–xli.

102(a) desolation in the dwellings of the wicked echoing Job 18.21 ('Surely such are the dwellings of the wicked, and this is the place of him that knoweth not God'); also Zephaniah 1.13, of the Lord's pursuit of the wicked ('Therefore their goods shall become a booty, and their houses a desolation'). Gil-Martin encourages Robert to take on work reserved only for God.

102(b) small square in the suburbs of the city Robert's situating of the tennis match possibly suggests that an outdoor game is being described—see also note on 16(b) above.

102(b) condign punishment punishment appropriate to the offence.

102(c) heard him profane his Maker's name three times echoing Peter's denial of Christ (see Luke 22.61, Matthew 26.75, Mark 14.72).

103(a) Cloud of Witnesses familiar short title for *A Cloud of Witnesses, for the Royal Prerogatives of Jesus Christ; or, The Last Speeches and Testimonies of those who have suffered for the Truth, in Scotland, since the year 1680*. A record of the lives, trials, and last testimonies of the later Covenanting martyrs, this was first published in 1714, probably in Edinburgh, without information of its compiler, printer, or publisher; and its presence here has been seen as an anachronism. However, such a work was planned from as early as 1686 by the General United Societies, a grouping of ultra-presbyterians including Cameronians, and extracts from their minutes recording its progress have survived: see Introduction to the edition by John H. Thomson (Edinburgh and London, 1871), pp. x–xii. It is not entirely implausible then that Robert Wringhim, through his religious connections, might have seen some of the materials being collected. The *Cloud of Witnesses* went through multiple editions later in the 18th century, leading to a 15th edition in Glasgow in 1814.

103(b) Fat representing 'What': the first phonetic indication that the speaker is a Highlander, or, more specifically, from Aberdeenshire in NE Scotland. In making the jailer such Hogg might possibly have had in mind the case of William Sutherland, the hangman at Irvine, whose refusal to execute imprisoned Covenanters is recorded in Robert Wodrow's *The History of the Sufferings of the Church of Scotland* (1721–22), a work Hogg knew well. Wodrow also includes what purports to be Sutherland's own 'declaration and examination', a self-account describing his upbringing in the remote north Highlands, reading of the Bible and conversion, and ending with his brutal interrogation by the authorities after his refusal to execute his prisoners (*History of the Sufferings*, Appendix no. 11; I, 101–04). In the 19th century, this was reprinted as a pamphlet, *The Genuine Declaration of William Sutherland* (Edinburgh, 1821), with an additional diatribe against false legal judgements. The case of Sutherland, 'a poor ignorant Highlandman', is also mentioned by James Kirkton, as an instance of near martyrdom, eliciting a characteristically facetious note (with extracts from the 'declaration') from his editor C. K. Sharpe: see *The Secret and True History of the Church of Scotland* (Edinburgh, 1817), pp. 253, 253n. Willie Sutherland also features as a character in John Galt's novel, *Ringan Gilhaize* (1823), where the imprisoned hero wins his support through conversing with him (ed. by Patricia J. Wilson (Edinburgh: Scottish Academic Press, 1984), p. 219).

103(c) Go in peace a verbal echo of Acts 16.36, where it is the keeper of the prison who says to St Paul 'now therefore depart, and go in peace'. More broadly, the situation reflects Paul and Silas's conversion of their jailer to Christianity, as Robert vainly believes will be his own achievement here. The incident was widely invoked in Scottish religious writing as an instance of justification through Christ alone, i.e. not based on inner reflection, penitence, or works. More particularly, it is cited by Evangelista as a key instance of justification through faith in a passage in the *Marrow of the Modern Divinity* which was to prove central in the Marrow Controversy. See David C. Lachman, *The Marrow Controversy* (Edinburgh: Rutherford House, 1988), p. 9; also Introduction to the present volume, pp. xxiv–xxv.

103(d) sword of the Lord [...] Famine and Pestilence compare Ezekiel 7.15: 'The sword is without, and the pestilence and the famine within: he that is in the field shall die with the sword; and he that is in the city, famine and pestilence shall devour him.' See also I Chronicles 21.12; and, for 'sword of the Lord' as a biblical expression, note on 93(c).

104(c) that *whosoever* should slay them the italicisation most obviously relates to Robert's self-conviction that even someone having kinship with the Colwans would be warranted in murdering them. At the same time, there is possibly an ironical echo of Genesis 4.15: 'And the Lord said unto him, Therefore whosoever slayeth Cain, vengeance shall be taken on him sevenfold.'

104(c) Gilgal a key site of the Israelites, where Joshua set up camp after having crossed the Jordan, and from where the assault on Jericho was carried out (Joshua 4–6). Hogg here however might have in mind especially I Samuel 15.33: 'And Samuel said, As thy sword hath made women childless, so shall thy mother be childless among women. And Samuel hewed Agag in pieces before the Lord in Gilgal.' The latter is part of a chillingly bloody narrative in I Samuel 15, in which Saul fails to carry out God's command, transmitted through the prophet Samuel, to slay all the Amalekites, by preserving the best of their animals and sparing the life of Agag, their king; Saul is then rejected as king, and Samuel hews Agag to pieces at Gilgal.

104(c) iniquity of his father biblical phrase, often employed vengefully. Here particularly echoing Psalm 109.14 ('Let the iniquity of his fathers be remembered with the Lord'), a verse recited by the Rev. Wringhim in the metrical version during the Editor's narrative (see notes on 24(b)). Compare also Isaiah 14.21: 'Prepare slaughter for his children for the iniquity of their fathers; that they do not rise, nor possess the land, nor fill the face of the world with cities.' Robert in resolving to kill his brother invokes some of the most bloody injunctions to be found in the Old Testament.

104(d) shekels of brass used in the Bible to describe the armoury and strength of Philistine warriors, notably Goliath in I Samuel 17.5 'And he had an helmet of brass upon his head, and he was armed with a coat of mail; and the weight of the coat was five thousand shekels of brass.' *Shekel* is used in such instances as a unit of weight, rather than in the sense of a coin.

104(d) to Tophet again Gil-Martin appears to juggle mischievously with biblical text, in a way which is both potentially self-revealing and capable of rebounding on Robert himself. Tophet, a site SW of Jerusalem, is described in Jeremiah as a place for child sacrifices, conducted against God's wishes: 'And they have built the high places of Tophet, which is in the valley of the son of Hinnom, to burn their sons and their daughters in the fire; which I commanded them not, neither came it into my heart' (7.31). This practice is associated with the worship of Baal in Jeremiah, and elsewhere with Molech (II Kings 23.10). In Isaiah, Tophet is the destination prepared for those who are to endure God's wrath, such as the king of Assyria: 'For Tophet is ordained of old; yea, for the king it is prepared; he hath made it deep and large: the pile thereof is fire and much wood; the breath of the

Lord, like a stream of brimstone, doth kindle it' (30.33).

105(a) children of Belial for Belial, see note on 7(d). The phrase 'children of Belial' is used to signify the wicked and non-believers at various points in the Old Testament, as in Judges 20.13: 'Now therefore deliver us the men, the children of Belial, which are in Gibeah, that we may put them to death, and put away evil from Israel.'

105(a) venal prophet Balaam, a non-Israelite prophet, called 'venal' because at various points in the Bible he is shown as being prepared to sell his prophetic powers to the highest bidder. In a particularly humorous sequence in Numbers 22.21–35, Balaam, on a mission to the Moabites of which God disapproves, repeatedly fails to see the angel of the Lord standing in his way that even his donkey can see. The precise source for the following utterance by Robert, whose own blindness to such warnings is more than once evident, is Numbers 22.29: 'And Balaam said unto the ass, Because thou hast mocked me: I would there were a sword in mine hand, for now would I kill thee.'

105(b) avenger of blood term in the Bible for someone who has the duty and right to avenge the killing of a kinsman: see Joshua 20.3, 5, 9 and Deuteronomy 19.6, 12. Gil-Martin adds a more murderous twist here, since no kinsman has been previously slain, and he omits too the associated biblical idea of asylum for accidental homicide.

105(d) touch me with one of their fingers possibly echoing Luke 11.46, who describes Christ's opposition to the Pharisees and teachers of the Law: 'And he said, Woe unto you also, ye lawyers! for ye lade men with burdens grievous to be borne, and ye yourselves touch not the burdens with one of your fingers.'

108(b) Queensberry's guards see notes on 15(d) and 28(d).

108(b) St. Anthony's well see note on 28(d).

108(d) In this desponding state *desponding* in the sense of being dejected having lost heart or resolution. The state is presented allegorically as 'the slough of despond/despondency' in John Bunyan's *Pilgrim's Progress* (1678–84). Compare Hogg's story 'The Witches of Traquair' (1828), where the main protagonist (Colin Hyslop) is found in a 'half-resigned, half-desponding state': see *The Shepherd's Calendar*, ed. by Douglas S. Mack (Edinburgh: Edinburgh University Press, 1995), p. 232.

108(d) rashness of my understanding compare Isaiah 32.4: 'The heart also of the rash shall understand knowledge, and the tongue of the stammerers shall be ready to speak plainly.'

108(d) a still small voice as when God speaks to the prophet Elijah in I Kings 19.12–13. 'And after the earthquake a fire; but the Lord was not in the fire: and after the fire a still small voice. And it was so, when Elijah heard it, that he wrapped his face in his mantle, and went out, and stood in the entering in of the cave. And, behold, there came a voice unto him, and said, What doest thou here, Elijah?'

109(a) lady, robed in white reminiscent of the 'Good Angel', in *Dr Faustus*, scene 5, line 194: '*Faustus* repent, yet God will pitty thee.'

111(a) just made perfect see note on 79(c).

113(c) The Lord Justice Clerk died that same week possibly relating to the sudden death of Sir William Hamilton of Whitelaw, who was appointed Justice Clerk in October 1704, through a reshuffle of Scottish post-holders, but then died suddenly on 14 December of the same year. A contemporary lampoon, written by way of an epitaph, presents him as in close association with the devil and Hell: ' 'Twixt the Devil and Whytlaw, the poor wretches damned/ Will be sore put about in that hot land;/ For now the fierce Justice-Clerk's got the command,/ They could hardly be worse off in Scotland' (*A Book of Scottish Pasquils 1568–1715* (Edinburgh, 1868), p. 462). According to Lockhart of Carnwath, who notes a general satisfaction that he had 'slipt the head', 'Betwixt man and man, wherein he had no particular concern, he was just, but extremely partial where his friend, or his own politicks, interfered' (*Lockhart Papers*, I, 107). For further details, see George Brunton and David Haig, *An Historical Account of the Senators of the College of Justice from its Institution in M.D.XXXII* (Edinburgh, 1836), pp. 462–63. For the post of Lord Justice Clerk, see note on 35(d).

114(a) bond of blood echoing possibly Dr Faustus's bond written in his blood, granting his soul to Lucifer after 24 years.

115(c) Hewie's lane beyond the loch not identified as a location.

115(d) part of the 10th Psalm the Psalm as a whole is a lament aimed against the arrogant wicked, and a call to God to intervene in punishment. Robert could be reciting the opening verses against the wicked man who persecutes the poor and heeds not God (thinking of his brother). More particularly, verses 8–9 could be taken to anticipate the forthcoming murder (and, beyond that, Gil-Martin's ensnarement of Robert himself): 'He sitteth in the lurking places of the villages: in the secret places doth he murder the innocent: his eyes are privily set against the poor. He lieth in wait secretly as a lion in his den: he lieth in wait to catch the poor: he doth catch the poor, when he draweth him into his net.' Another possibility is verses 15–16, which in the Church of Scotland's metrical version read: 'The arm break of the wicked man,/ and of the evil one;/ Do thou seek out his wickedness,/ until thou findest none. // The Lord is king through ages all,/ ev'n to eternity;/ The heathen people from his land/ are perish'd utterly.' As in earlier cases, Robert turns what was originally a call to God into a vindication for his own intervention.

116(d) North Loch see note on 37(d).

118(a) lay thine hand on the Lord's anointed compare I Samuel 26.9 ('And David said to Abishai, Destroy him not: for who can stretch forth his hand against the Lord's anointed, and be guiltless?'), and II Samuel 1.14 ('And David said unto him, How wast thou not afraid to stretch forth thine hand to destroy the Lord's anointed?'). These and similar passages relate to the relationship between Saul and David, both anointed as kings of Israel.

119(c) plate [...] treasures of ready money i.e. moveable rather than heritable property, the latter of which in an entailed estate went necessarily to the heir-at-law (in this case, Robert as a result of his elder brother's and father's deaths).

123(c) power of attorney a document appointing a person to act as the legal representative of another, used often in cases of incapacity through age or infirmity.

123(d) Lawyer Linkum evidently a burlesque name, as suitable for a bogus lawyer. In Scots *linkie* used adjectivally means 'sly, roguish, full of tricks'; and as a noun denotes a deceitful, untrustworthy person. The expression *like linkum*, meaning 'in a flash, at top speed', is possibly a later usage.

124(a) writer to the signet member of the most prestigious body of solicitors in Scotland. The term 'writer' is used more generally to describe a solicitor in Scotland.

124(a) confirmed the charter the wording of the following alleged charter is generally authentic. Hogg was friendly with lawyers and legal antiquaries in Edinburgh, and occasionally acted himself as a valuer of land, so he had opportunities to see actual charters. As John Carey has noted, in his 1969 edition, there is a particular resemblance to a charter of 1636 granting the superiority of the Canongate and parts of Leith to the Magistrates and Town Council of Edinburgh, as quoted in William Maitland's *The History of Edinburgh from its Foundation to the Present Time* (Edinburgh, 1753), pp. 148–51. 'Given at our Court at Whitehall', this contains the following sequence: 'with Pit and Gallows, Sack and Soke, Thole, Theam, Vertwrack, Waifs, Wair, Venison, infang Thief, outfang Thief, [...] with other Commodities' (p. 151). Where appropriate and feasible, individual words in the novel's charter are dealt with in the Glossary, though several terms are now so opaque or variable in meaning as to resist satisfactory definition.

124(b) hardship [...] Majesty's rights and titles reflecting the policy of rewarding loyal royalists, who had suffered in Presbyterian theocratic Scotland, as exercised by the later Stuarts.

124(c) sack, sock also found as 'sac and soc', an expression used in ancient charters, denoting certain rights of jurisdiction belonging to the lord of the manor.

124(c) thole, thame also found as 'toll and team', a now obscure phrase apparently referring to the right of jurisdiction in a suit of *team*, and the right to any fees and profits accruing from this.

124(d) outfang thief the right to pursue a thief outside one's own jurisdiction and to bring him back for trial.

124(d) infang thief the right of the lord of a manor to try and punish a thief taken on his property.

124(d) pit and gallows the privilege, held within baronial lands, of executing criminals by hanging the men on the gallows and drowning the women in a pit.

124(d) Court of Whitehall Whitehall Palace was the London residence of the monarch until its destruction by fire in 1698.

124(d) *Compositio 5 lib.* 13. 8 referring to payment of a fee, i.e. £5 13s. 8d.

124(d) Registrate 26th September 1687 i.e. recorded (in the Register of the Great Seal) on that date. The granting of such a charter near the end of the reign of James II and VII, before his overthrow in 1688, might be seen as one of the last acts of the Old Regime, on behalf of a supporter.

124(d) privy councillors members of the Scottish Privy Council, which held responsibility for public order in Scotland after the accession of James VI to the English crown in 1603. It was reinstated in 1661, after the Restoration, and met throughout the year when Parliament was not in session, before being abolished in the wake of the Union of 1707.

124(d) Duke of Queensberry see note on 15(d). Queensberry was first appointed to the office of Keeper of the Privy Seal after his succession to the dukedom in 1695, and was later restored to this office in 1705.

128(d) Mr. Ringan o' Glasko apparently referring to the Rev. Wringhim of Glasgow, whose closeness to Gil-Martin has previously been observed (see text at 127(c)). Compare note on 47(a).

129(b) circuit lords judges of the High Court of Justiciary (see note on 35(c)), who at specified times go on circuit to hear trials elsewhere in Scotland.

129(c) thorn in my side a metaphor found in Numbers 33.55 and Judges 2.3. Also perhaps echoing St Paul in II Corinthians 12.7: 'And lest I should be exalted above measure through the abundance of the revelations, there was given to me a thorn in the flesh, the messenger of Satan to buffet me, lest I should be exalted above measure.'

132(a) a precognition is in progress the taking of *precognitions* (examinations of witnesses or suspected persons, reduced to writing) was a vital start to criminal proceedings in Scotland.

133(a) inclosed in the deeps of the sea compare *Dr Faustus*, scene 13: 'Oh soule, be changde into little water drops,/ And fal into the Ocean, nere be found' (lines 112–13).

133(a) Daniel in the den of lions as in Daniel 6.16–23, where Daniel, cast into the den on the order of Darius, King of Persia, survives overnight unharmed, aided by his faith in God.

133(c) a staunch Cameronian the Cameronians, a sect of Covenanters so named after the field-preacher Richard Cameron (d. 1680), and concentrated mainly in SW Scotland, were persecuted during the later Stuart period for their refusal to accept the authority of the King in spiritual matters. After the religious settlement of 1690, they became a separate church apart from the main established Presbyterian order.

133(c) Penpunt Penpont is a small town in Nithsdale, Dumfriesshire, about 15 miles NNW of Dumfries. It features in Hogg's story 'The Barber of Duncow', which first appeared in *Fraser's Magazine* for March 1831, though inaccurately spelt there as Purpont: see *Selected Stories and Sketches*, ed. by Douglas S. Mack (Edinburgh: Scottish Academic Press, 1982), pp. 169–179, 204. The minister of the Covenanting community in this story, Mr Fairly, also serves (as John Farley) as the narrator in Hogg's 'The Cameronian Preacher's Tale' (1828), and was based on John Fairley (born 1729), who was ordained minister to the Reformed Presbyterians at Leadhills in 1763. Hogg lived close to Penpont when working as a shepherd and farming in Nithsdale *c.* 1807–10. The spelling of the name in the present work might come as a result of Robert's mishearing or through a more general authorial tendency to slightly misplace names: see also note on 'Kilpatrick of Closeburn' for 27(a).

134(b) breach in his friend's good name, or in his purse compare *Othello*: 'Who steals my purse steals trash [...] / But he who filches from me my good name/ Robs me of that which not enriches him/ And makes me poor indeed' (III.3.162–66).

134(b) Galloway drover Galloway is the district comprising Wigtownshire and the Stewartry of Kirkcudbright, on the north side of the Solway Firth. The region was (and is) noted for both dairy cattle and beef herds, and the exporting of cattle (mainly to England) through droving was common from the late 17th century.

134(c) the white sands possibly referring to the large cattle market held by the river Eden, just north of Carlisle, and known traditionally as 'the Sands'.

134(c) Master Whiggam slang name for a West Country Presbyterian. According to Bishop Gilbert Burnet, in an unsubstantiated etymology for the political term 'Whig': 'those in the west [of Scotland] come in the summer to buy at *Lieth* [*sic*] the stores that come from the north: And from a word *Whiggam* used in driving their horses, all that drove were called *Whiggamors*, and shorter the *Whiggs*' (*History of his own Time*, vol. 1 (1725), p. 64). The name also appears in the line 'O pity Whiggam's plight' in 'Aikendrum', a song belonging to 1715, from the second volume (1821) of Hogg's *Jacobite Relics of Scotland* (p. 25).

134(d) Man mind yoursel is the first commandment 'Man mind yoursel' with something of the sense of 'look after number one': at first sight a long way off from the actual first commandment.

135(a) it's a' stuff *stuff* here in the sense of 'worthless speech; nonsense', as more usually found in 'stuff and nonsense'.

135(a) sidie for sidie side by side, step for step.

135(c) auld Macmillan himsel John Macmillan (1670–1753), minister to the Cameronians from 1706 and founder in 1743 of the Reformed Presbyterian Church. According to T. Craig-Brown, in his *History of Selkirkshire* (2 vols, Edinburgh, 1886), in the early days of the ministry of Thomas Boston in Ettrick the dissenters in the parish 'adhered to John Macmillan, an uncompromising Cameronian of the good old stamp' (I, 277–78). Macmillan's redoubtable qualities feature in Hogg's story 'The Wool-gatherer', where it is recounted how he took up the challenge of a ghost by walking alone through a wood, reciting Psalm 109 as his only protection: see *The Brownie of Bodsbeck; and Other Tales*, 2 vols (Edinburgh, 1818), II, 131–32.

136(b) Auld Simmie familiar name for the devil.

136(b) to mak a dishclout o' (contemptuously) to turn into a dish-cloth, to make a stooge out of.

136(c) Glasco street i.e. the High Street of Glasgow, which originally ran from the Cathedral to the Mercat Cross, the latter being the focal point for street-trading.

136(c) Hollin lawn fine linen cloth, as originally imported from Holland.

136(c) auld thief another roundabout term for the devil.

136(d) wolves in sheep's claithing proverbial, but particularly apposite here is its origin in the Sermon on the Mount: 'Beware of false prophets, which come to you in sheep's clothing, but inwardly they are ravening wolves' (Matthew 7.15).

136(d) the town o' Auchtermuchty is in Fife, about 15 miles SE of Perth, to the N of the Lomond Hills. It featured much earlier in 'The Wyfe of Auchtermuchtie', a late medieval Scots poem about a domestic dispute, which was printed in the first issue (April 1817) of *Blackwood's Edinburgh Magazine*; and the name has a comic sound even to Scottish ears, which Hogg appears to exploit.

136(d) rigidly righteous a phrase found in the title of Robert Burns's 'Address to the Unco Guid, or the Rigidly Righteous' (1784). The epigraph of this poem also contains the lines 'The Rigid Righteous is a fool,/ The Rigid Wise anither'. Burns's text for the epigraph is Ecclesiastes 7.16: 'Be not righteous over much; neither make thyself over wise: why shouldest thou destroy thyself?'

136(d) shining light see note on 67(b).

137(a) At the lint-swinglings referring not only to the act of flax-beating, but also to the social evenings spent at this task. Hogg later recalled such occasions: 'We had again our kirns at the end of harvest, and our lint-swinglings in almost every farm-house and cottage, which proved as a weekly bout for the greater part of the winter. And then, with the exception of *Wads*, and a little kissing and toying in consequence, song, song alone, was the sole amusement' ('On the Changes in the Habits, Amusements, and Condition of the Scottish Peasantry', *Quarterly Journal of Agriculture*, 3 (May 1831), 257). The present editor is indebted to David Groves for the discovery of this quotation.

137(a) Robin Ruthven the surname matches that of Ruthven, the family name and seat of the Earls of Gowrie, in Tayside about 12 miles W of Forfar. As a result of the 'Gowrie Conspiracy' in 1600, an alleged assassination attempt on James VI, the name of Ruthven was abolished by the Scottish Parliament and all successors rendered incapable of holding offices, honours, or possessions.

137(b) West Lowmond West Lomond (1713 feet), part of the Lomond hills, approximately 5 miles S of Auchtermuchty. The Lomonds feature broadly as a site of witchcraft in Hogg's poem 'The Witch of Fife' (1813). A grouping of stones called the 'Devil's Burdens', close to West Lomond, was formed according to legend as a result of vengeance taken by the devil against a recalcitrant witch: see James Wilkie, *Bygone Fife North of the Lomonds* (Edinburgh and London, 1938), pp. 10–11.

137(b) a bridal o' corbie craws Hogg's use of 'bridal' here is uncertain, but the context perhaps suggests a party (rather than just a pair) of crows, with two being overheard speaking. The *corbie craw* is the raven, a bird of ill omen in folklore. Compare Hogg's 'Odd Characters', in 'General Anecdotes' (1827), where Daft Jock Amos sees the 'deil's messenger' in the shape of 'a great big black corbie', this being a prelude to the discovery of Eppy Telfer's suicide by hanging: see *The Shepherd's Calendar*, ed. by Douglas S. Mack (Edinburgh: Edinburgh University Press, 1995), pp. 113–14.

137(b) signed himself i.e. with the sign of the cross, an indication possibly that Robin Ruthven is a Catholic (Presbyterians do not cross themselves).

137(c) and the tane said to the tither echoing the first stanza of the ballad, 'The Twa Corbies', in Scott's *Minstrelsy of the Scottish Border* (1802–03): 'As I was walking all alane,/ I heard twa corbies making a mane;/ The tane unto the t'other say,/ Where sall we gang and dine today?' (ed. by T. F. Henderson, 4 vols (Edinburgh, 1932), II, 417).

137(d) the thief's hole name for a cell or dungeon in which thieves and other malefactors were imprisoned; here denoting Hell.

137(d) a feast on the Sidlaw hills to-night, below the hill of Macbeth the Sidlaw Hills are to the north of the Tay estuary, above Perth and Dundee; the hill of Macbeth is presumably Dunsinane hill (1012 feet), about 8 miles NE of Perth. The Sidlaw hills feature in Hogg's long poem *Mador of the Moor* (1816), which itself is full of *Macbeth* references. The association between the raven and Shakespeare's play is evident: 'The raven himself is hoarse/ That croaks the fatal entrance of Duncan/ Under my battlements' (I.5.37–39).

137(d) Mount, Diabolus, and fly Diabolus is the name given to Satan in John Bunyan's *The Holy War* (1682), a text well-known to Hogg, which tells of his assaults on the town of Mansoul. The cry 'Mount, Diabolus, and fly!' appears in Note XXX to Walter Scott's *The Lay of the Last Minstrel* (1805), where it is used by the wizard Michael Scott in riding a supernatural black horse through the air to France: see *Poetical Works*, ed. by J. Logie Robertson (Oxford, 1940), p. 66.

138(a) 119th Psalm [...] 77th verse Psalm 119 is the longest and structurally most complex of the Psalms, consisting in all of 176 verses in 22 sections, the latter reflecting the letters in the Hebrew alphabet. Its choice by the folk of Auchtermuchty for their service allows them to buy time, as well as indicating that they are indeed very keen! Verse 77, one of a succession affirming obedience to the Lord, is probably chosen by Hogg for the mystical suggestion of the number seven rather than its contents. In particular it brings to mind the appearance of the seven-headed beast in Revelation: 'And there appeared another wonder in heaven; and behold a great red dragon, having seven heads and ten horns, and seven crowns upon his heads' (12.3).

138(a) cast up i.e. 'turn up', make an appearance.

138(a) by the *western door* i.e. from the opposite end to where the altar stands at the eastern (holy) end of the church. Compare Hogg's story, 'Mary Burnet' (1828), where, according to Mary's elderly father, 'out o' the east [...] a' our blessings come': see *The Shepherd's Calendar*, ed. by Douglas S. Mack (Edinburgh: Edinburgh University Press, 1995), p. 221.

138(b) from the Prophecies of Ezekiel [...] IT the text read out is Ezekiel 21.27, and matches the Authorised King James version wording exactly. The prophecy concerns the overthrow of a corrupted Israel on God's instruction by the hand of Nebuchadnezzar. The 'it' in the passage most obviously refers to Jerusalem.

138(b) gall of bitterness and bond of iniquity a fuller echo of Acts 8.23 than found earlier at 68(d): 'For I perceive that thou art in the gall of bitterness, and in the bond of iniquity.' Hogg was to use the same words in his *Lay Sermons* (1834) when discussing the imperfections of 'our reforming deists'—see *A Series of Lay Sermons*, ed. by Gillian Hughes (Edinburgh: Edinburgh University Press, 1997), p. 118.

138(c) as Jonah was sent to the Ninevites alluding to Jonah, Chapter 3, in which the prophet Jonah on God's instructions travels to Nineveh and warns of impending doom in forty days; the king puts on sackcloth and orders the citizens to fast, and as a consequence the city is saved.

138(d) by the slump see note on 78(b).

138(d) tag, rag, and bobtail the riff-raff, the rabble; here with the effect of 'the whole motley crew'.

139(a) spoke evil of dignities compare Jude 8: 'Likewise also these filthy dreamers defile the flesh, despise dominion, and speak evil of dignities'; and II Peter 2.10: 'But chiefly them that walk after the flesh in the lust of uncleanness, and despise government. Presumptuous are they, selfwilled, they are not afraid to speak evil of dignities.' The purpose of both the epistles cited here is to combat the effect of certain charismatic but immoral teachers who were endangering the Christian faith.

139(a) St. Johnston the old name for Perth.

139(a) Cupar, Newburgh, and Strathmiglo [...] Perth and Dundee [...] from the East Nook of Fife to the foot of the Grampian hills the first three places named are towns within Fife surrounding Auchtermuchty; the scope widens to take in the larger Perth and Dundee further to the north; Hogg's account then stretches out to the remoter country regions to the east and north-west.

139(d) side an' wide long and large, extending in every way.

140(a) the Lowmonds see note on 'West Lowmond' for 137(b).

140(b) Cameronian's blue bannet the Covenanters wore blue in opposition to the scarlet of royalty, their source for this being in Numbers 15.38.

140(b) gouden rule referring to Jesus's advice to do unto others as you would have them do unto you, given in the Sermon on the Mount (see Matthew 7.12, Luke 6.31), and known as the Golden Rule since the 18th century.

140(c) calm o' the stamock qualm of the stomach, referring back to Robert's mention earlier of his 'stomach qualm'.

140(d) productive of fruits so bitter compare Matthew 7.17: 'Even so every good tree bringeth forth good fruit; but a corrupt tree bringeth forth evil fruit', and Jesus's concluding saying 'by their fruits ye shall know them' (7.20). This passage comes from the Sermon on the Mount, with Christ distinguishing between true and false prophets, though the saying also has a broader application.

141(d) wishing myself a worm, or a moth, [...] crushed and at rest echoing Job 3.13, 17; 4.19; 25.6. Compare also the account in John Bunyan's *Grace Abounding to the Chief of Sinners* (1666) of the author's despair *before* the assurance of Grace: 'Now again I blessed the condition of the Dogge and Toad [...] for I knew they had no Soul to perish under the everlasting weights of Hell for sin, as mine was like to do': ed. by Roger Sharrock (London: Oxford University Press, 1966), p. 35.

142(b) touch them baith afore witnesses referring to the medieval ordeal of *bier-right*, whereby someone accused of murder could absolve themselves by touching the corpse and swearing before God they were innocent; if they were guilty, it was believed, the corpse would bleed at their touch. In Hogg's story 'The Barber of Duncow' (1831) this method is employed in church by the minister at Penpont, Mr Fairly, as a means of ascertaining the identity of a murderer, though the result is recognised as having no validity in law: see *Selected Stories and Sketches*, ed. by Douglas S. Mack (Edinburgh: Scottish Academic Press, 1982), pp. 178-79.

143(c) postern gate back or side entrance.

144(b) Dorington Moor not identified as a location.

144(d) just man would not be left destitute a possible echo of Psalm 37.25, more close in the metrical version: 'I have been young, and now am old,/ yet have I never seen/ The just man left, nor that his seed/ for bread have beggars been.'

145(a) falling into the cross ways Robert in heading south travels by the small quiet roads that link the major east-west roads.

145(b) camel [...] kingdom of heaven see Matthew 19.24, Mark 10.25, Luke 18.25.

145(b) entertain [...] angel unawares compare Hebrews 13.2: 'Be not forgetful to entertain strangers: for thereby some have entertained angels unawares.'

148(c) entangled myself this whole incident reflects the biblical metaphor of the spider's web, as in Job 8.13-14: 'So are the paths of all that forget God; and the hypocrite's hope shall perish: Whose hope shall be cut off, and whose trust shall be a spider's web.'

148(d) pearls o' damnation i.e. perils of damnation, the Scottish pronunciation of perils and pearls sounding identical. The similarity is used for humorous allusion to Hogg's earlier fiction in *Blackwood's Edinburgh Magazine* for March 1824, where in 'Noctes Ambrosianae' no. 13 ODoherty claims from advance report to be able to recite part of the opening of the imminent *Queen Hynde* (1824): 'and then, unlike/

Those men who fling their pearls before the Hog,/ I, Hogg, did fling my Perils before men' (vol. 15, p. 359). The same pun was used by Walter Scott apropos a visit by Hogg with J. G. Lockhart to Abbotsford and the shocked reaction of Lady Scott: 'Lockhart bringing him here like a pig in a string, for which the lady of the mansion sent him little thanks, she not thinking the hog's pearls (qu. Perils) an apology for his freedoms' (*Letters*, ed. by H. J. C. Grierson, 12 vols (London, 1932–37), VIII, 65). The novels so alluded to are *The Three Perils of Man* (1822) and *The Three Perils of Woman* (1823), with Lady Scott's disapproval probably focussed on the latter.

148(d) deil's burd offspring of the devil.

149(c) Boddel Brigg Bothwell Bridge, site of the battle in 1679 in which the royalist army defeated the Covenanters, leading to much confusion and carnage in the wake of the main engagement.

149(d)–150(a) Slack a pin probably an instruction to slacken the warp threads (these being the strongest, going along the length of the loom, and usually being taut), through a controlling peg.

151(b) the West Port the western gateway into old Edinburgh, demolished in 1786, though the gap continued to be called the West Port.

151(c) His name was Linton, and I changed mine to Elliot both are surnames associated with southern Scotland.

151(d) then conducted by a Mr. James Watson James Watson (1664?–1722), appointed one of the Queen's Printers in Scotland in 1711, when he was already established as a leading printer and bookseller in Edinburgh. Between 1697 and 1709 his business was based at Craig's Close off the north side of the High Street; then, later, slightly higher up the High Street, next door to the Red Lion, opposite the Luckenbooths. His earlier career was a stormy one: in 1700 he was arrested for publishing seditious literature about the Darien scheme, and he also published anonymous pamphlets on the Union issue. His concern for typographical standards in Scotland is evident in publications such as *A Specimen of the types in James Watson's printing-house* (1706), and his *History of the Art of Printing* (1713). Among the large number of theological works published by Watson are editions of the *Psalms of David*, the *Confession of Faith*, and Bunyan's *Holy War* (1703 and 1711). Among literary titles, the best known is his *A Choice Collection of Comic and Serious Scots Poems* (1706–11). Watson also printed Robert Wodrow's *The History of the Sufferings of the Church of Scotland* (1721–22), a work well known to Hogg, and where he might have noticed the imprint of 'James Watson, His Majesty's Printer'.

152(c) respectable references with regard to morals James Watson (see previous note) appears to have been a strong disciplinarian, publishing in 1721 a broadsheet *Rules and Directions to be Observed in Printing-Houses*. This gives General Directions (the first against 'Cursing and Swearing, profane and abusive Speaking'), followed by more specific directions for compositors and for pressmen.

152(d) parable such as the Pilgrim's Progress referring to John Bunyan's seminal religious allegory, *The Pilgrim's Progress* (1678–84), which describes Christian's resistance of sin and despair and his eventual salvation. This is the only specific reference to the title in the present work, though its language and imagery is often sensed, and some commentators have claimed that Robert's own narrative represents a kind of dark inversion of Bunyan's story. James Watson (see note on 151(d)) published at least two editions of Bunyan's other popular allegory, *The Holy War* (1682), though no edition of *Pilgrim's Progress* under his imprint has been discovered.

153(a) on Sundays thereby not observing the Sabbath.

153(a) before the press-work [...] wrought off the processes referred to are: i) the setting in type of the text; ii) the correction of this text, through first proofs; iii) the printing off of fresh proofs for further revision (revises); iv) the printing off of sheets in numbers sufficient for the edition. In this case, the first sheet (A) has been printed off in numbers, and apparently all is ready for the bulk printing of the second sheet (B); while the rest of the text is in revised proof (revises), but wants final correction. The number of pages printed on a sheet or gathering would depend on the format of the book: for example, in the case of a work in octavo (8vo) up to sixteen pages, in the case of duodecimo (12mo) up to twenty-four.

153(b) *Chesters* a small settlement, about 12 miles SE of Hawick, close to the Border with England. See also 'Historical and Geographical Note', p. 207.

154(a) **Green Circassian hunting coat and turban** *Circassian* indicating an origin from the north Caucasus, E of the Black Sea, a Moslem region once part of Turkey. A jacket of this kind, as worn in his studio by the Edinburgh painter William Allan, is described in J. G. Lockhart's *Peter's Letters to his Kinsfolk*: 'he was arrayed, by way of *robe-de-chambre*, in a dark Circassian vest, the breast of which was loaded with innumerable quilted lurking-places, originally, no doubt, intended for weapons of warfare, but now occupied with the harmless shafts of hair-pencils' (2nd edn (actually the 1st), 3 vols (Edinburgh, 1819), II, 234–35). An accompanying engraving shows Allan—who had returned in 1814 after ten years in Russia and Asia Minor—wearing the same jacket along with an exotic cap. *Circassian* was also used attributively to describe a form of worsted fabric, but Hogg's interest here evidently lies in the oriental outlandishness of the costume, and in attributes such as its greenness (suggesting magic) and capacity for concealing articles.

154(b) **lodgings at Portsburgh** Portsburgh, anciently a separate burgh, is immediately W of the Grassmarket; it was finally made part of the city in 1856.

154(b) **Dalkeith** town in Midlothian, about 8 miles SE of Edinburgh.

154(c) **wings of a dove** echoing Psalm 55.6: 'And I said, Oh that I had wings like a dove! for then would I fly away, and be at rest.' The exact phrase is found in Psalm 68.13, though the context is less apposite.

154(c) **Ellanshaws** possibly based on Langshaw house (ruinous in Hogg's day) on Allan Water, about 5 miles above the latter's junction with the River Tweed near Galashiels (see note on 157(a)). See also 'Historical and Geographical Note', p. 207.

155(d) **the L—d A—y preserve us!** the same prayer ('May the Lord Almighty preserve us!') is uttered at the sight of an apparition by old Nicholas in Hogg's 'Welldean Hall'—see *Winter Evening Tales*, 2 vols (Edinburgh, 1820), II, 289.

156(a) **missed the manger** bringing to mind the manger in a stable where the new-born Christ lay, and indicating how Robert lacks true Christian guidance.

157(a) **towards the Tweed, by the side of the small river called Ellan** Allan Water meets the Tweed about 3 miles E of Galashiels, and 2 miles down-river from Scott's Abbotsford, having passed in its last stages through a gorge in otherwise open country. See also 'Historical and Geographical Note', p. 207.

157(c) **puts his hand [...] draweth back** darkly mirroring Jesus's warning against those who put their hand to God's service and then falter: 'And Jesus said unto him, No man, having put his hand to the plough, and looking back, is fit for the kingdom of God'(Luke 9.62).

158(b) **hide me in the bowels of the earth, or depths of the sea** a counter echo of Psalm 139, especially verses 9–12, where the psalmist is suggesting that wherever he goes, even to 'the uttermost parts of the sea', he will be supported by God. Robert, in contrast, thinks Gil-Martin will find him wherever he hides. Compare also Marlowe's Dr Faustus, in his last soliloquy, scene 13: 'Mountaines and hilles, come come, and fall on me,/ And hide me from the heavy wrath of God./ No no, then wil I headlong runne into the earth:/ Earth gape, O no, it wil not harbour me' (lines 81–84). See also note on 'inclosed in the deeps of the sea' for 133(a).

158(c) village of Ancrum about 12 miles NE of Hawick. John Livingstone (1603–72), notable Covenanting divine, was minister of this parish from 1648 to 1662.

159(a) which ridiculous idea a similar belief is implicit in Godfrey Bertram's response in Walter Scott's *Guy Mannering* (1815) to the astrological skills of the young Guy Mannering, an Oxford student (see Ch. 3: EEWN 2, p. 15). One possible origin for the association might be Roger Bacon (1214–92), the Oxford scholar and Franciscan philosopher, who gained a reputation as a magician for his work in the experimental sciences, and features as the friar in Hogg's *Three Perils of Man* (1822). It also possible that Hogg is involved in a kind of in-joke, aimed at the Oxford-educated J. G. Lockhart and John Wilson, whose 'devilry' in conducting *Blackwood's Edinburgh Magazine* is noted more than once in Hogg's correspondence.

161(c) sinfulness of the deed the damning nature of suicide, according to some interpretations, is referred to in Mark 3.29: 'But he that shall blaspheme against the Holy Ghost hath never forgiveness, but is in danger of eternal damnation.' Hamlet's 'Or that the Everlasting had not fixed/ His canon 'gainst self-slaughter!' (I.2.132–33) also reflects a widely-held view. More broadly, suicide is the ultimate act of despair since it means rejecting God's grace; conversely, those in a state of grace do not despair (see, e.g., II Corinthians 4.8–10).

161(d) on my behoof to my advantage, for my benefit.

162(a) New Jerusalem the holy city, the spiritual heaven promised to believers: see Revelation 3.12, 21.2.

162(a) hamlet on the Scottish border i.e. Chesters (see note on 153(b)).

162(c) Redesdale on the English side of the Border, in Northumberland; over Carter Bar from Chesters, leading towards Newcastle upon Tyne.

162(d) Ault-Righ Altrive (or Eltrive), on the south bank of Yarrow Water, close to where it leaves St Mary's Loch. At the time of the story this was a fairly extensive farm, consisting of pasture and moorland, on part of which Hogg himself later lived and farmed. For a fuller account see 'Historical and Geographical Note', p. 208; and for an etymological explanation for the unusual spelling here, see note on 166(b)).

162(d) Hawick town in Roxburghshire, about 12 miles S of Selkirk, and 12 miles NW of the Chesters of the novel.

163(a) farm-house nigh to the church of Roberton Roberton Kirk is 5 miles W of Hawick, up Borthwick Water. The two nearest farms were Borthwickbrae and Borthwickshiels, with the latter (to the north) slightly closer to the Kirk.

164(a) My last hour is arrived echoing Marlowe's *Dr Faustus*, scene 13, at the beginning of Faustus's last soliloquy: 'Ah *Faustus*,/ Now hast thou but one bare hower to live,/ And then thou must be damnd perpetually' (lines 61–63).

164(a) earth would swallow [...] hill fall and cover me! for a possible echoing of Marlowe's *Dr Faustus*, see note on 158(b). Compare also Hosea 10.8: 'and they shall say to the mountains, Cover us; and to the hills, Fall on us'. See also Revelation 6.16.

164(b) an ejaculatory prayer opposite of a 'set prayer', in that it is expressive and sudden in utterance. The mention of its equivocal wording indicates something in line with Gil-Martin's reference earlier to 'the God whom thou servest' (see note on 95(b)).

164(c) divot loft i.e. loft for storing peat or turf. Hogg is probably thinking here of a structure similar to a hay-loft in a barn, one resembling a kind of large raised shelf, where materials could be forked up out of the reach of animals in the barn.

164(d) Why hast [...] malice? compare Job 7.20: 'why hast thou set me as a mark against thee, so that I am a burden to myself?'

165(a) tremendous prayer see note on 164(b), for an indication of its possible nature.

It has also been claimed that Hogg is alluding to Job 2.9, where Job's wife encourages Job to 'curse God, and die': see Ian Campbell, 'Hogg's *Confessions* and the *Heart of Darkness*', *Studies in Scottish Literature*, 15 (1980), 187–201 (p. 192).

165(b) Farewell, world these and the following last words are interpretable as a corrupted rendition of the farewells (usually at the place of execution) that were appended to the majority of the *Dying* or *Last Testimonies* of the Covenanting martyrs, beginning with Hugh MacKail, whose trial and last testimony was published in 1666. Compare, for example, that of Laurence Hay (d. 1681), as recorded in the *Cloud of Witnesses*: 'Farewell sun moon and stars; farewell meat and drink; farewell all created comforts and enjoyments, wherewith I have been abundantly supplied. Farewell, my dear wife and children; the Lord be better to you than ten husbands, when I am gone. Farewell mother, brethren and sisters. Farewell sweet societies, and preached Gospel, whereby I have been begotten by the seed of the Word. Farewell sweet prison, and reproaches for sweet Christ, and His cause. And welcome Father, Son, and Holy Ghost! Welcome everlasting life, and the spirits of just men made perfect! Lord, into thy hands I commit my spirit!' (ed. by John H. Thomson (Edinburgh and London, 1871), p. 165). Hogg's familiarity with the convention is evident from the conclusion of his 'The Covenanter's Scaffold Song', published in the *Remembrance* for 1831: 'Farewell earthly morn and even,/ Sun and moon and stars of heaven;/ Heavenly portals ope before me,/ Welcome, Christ, in all thy glory!' (p. 255).

165(c) My hour is at hand compare Matthew 26.45: 'behold, the hour is at hand'.

165(d) an authentic letter the text given follows the main portion of 'A Scots Mummy', addressed to 'Sir Christopher North', and published in *Blackwood's Edinburgh Magazine*, 14 (August 1823), 188–90; this was signed James Hogg and end-dated '*Altrieve Lake, Aug.* 1, 1823'. See also Introduction, pp. xliv, lv.

165(d) Cowanscroft Cowan's Croft, moorland hill (1897 feet) about 2½ miles N of Ettrick hamlet (Hogg's birthplace), and 5 miles SSW of A/Eltrive farmhouse, where Hogg depicts Wringhim spending his last days. See also 'Historical and Geographical Note', p. 208.

165(d) three proprietors see note on 167(c), where Hogg supplies three names.

166(b) Mr. Anderson of Eltrive later apparently given the Christian name David (see text at 171(b)). A stone in Ettrick kirkyard, commemorating various members of the Anderson family, is headed 'In Memory of DAVID ANDERSON tenant in Altrive and JANET CURRIE his wife' (for a slightly imperfect transcription, see *Transactions of the Hawick Archaeological Society*, 1964, Stone 29, p. 55), though this personage was almost certainly a generation younger than the figure depicted in the novel. For further details concerning the Andersons, who had been associated with A/Eltrive since the 16th century, see note on 166(c).

166(b) (Ault-Righ, *the King's burn*,) Hogg's etymology for A/Eltrive is comparable to that of Ettrick in his 'Statistics of Selkirkshire', under a first section headed 'Names and Etymologies': '*Alterick*, which is really as good Gaelic as a borderer could spell *Alt-Ericht*, signifies the rising stream, or stream of the rapid ascent' (in *Prize-Essays and Transactions of the Highland Society of Scotland*, 9 (1832), 281–306 (p. 282)). In the same essay Hogg explains 'Rodonno' as 'from *Righ* and *dun*, the King's Fortress' (p. 281). A somewhat less glamorous etymology for Altrive than that in the novel is given in William J. Watson, *The History of Celtic Place-Names in Scotland* (Edinburgh, 1926), p. 137, with 'ruighe' denoting a slope.

166(b) Eltrive Hope probably referring to the remote upper valley near the head of the small stream called Altrive Lake, where cattle would graze and hay might be stored. See also 'Historical and Geographical Note', p. 208.

166(c) James Anderson, his master's son here as elsewhere Hogg's fiction apparently draws on real Ettrick and Yarrow people and places. A rent book for 1767–68 in the Buccleuch Muniments (National Archives of Scotland, GD224/1125/1) shows James Anderson as joint tenant of A/Eltrive with David Anderson (probably his brother), at a rent of £122 4s. 5½d, with James also farming a third of nearby West Mountbenger farm. This James is evidently the same as the James Anderson who married the Rev. Thomas Boston's daughter, Alison, and who appears in Ettrick kirkyard as 'tenant in Altrive', having 'died 23 February 1782 aged 70 years'. For further details, see Peter Garside, 'Hogg, Eltrive, and *Confessions*', in *Studies in Hogg and his World*, 11 (2000), 5–24.

166(d) *The Hart Loup* Hart Leap, a pass connecting the Ettrick and Yarrow valleys, through which the old drove road proceeded before continuing northward through A/Eltrive and on towards Edinburgh. According to the account (1833) of the parish of Yarrow in *The New Statistical Account of Scotland*, 15 vols (Edinburgh and London, 1845): 'It retains the significant name of the *Hart's leap*; the distance of the leap, being distinctly visible at the time when the ground was covered with snow, is marked by two grey whinstones, twenty-eight feet apart, which are said to have been raised by the king [James V] and his followers' (III, 'Selkirk', 44). Hartleap is also the name of a small habitation slightly further to the north. See also 'Historical and Geographical Note', p. 208.

166(d) **one of Eldinhope hay-ricks** Eldinhope was the farm to the immediate east of A/Eltrive, on the other side of the marshy stream called Altrive Lake. It is not unlikely that Eldinhope ricks were placed on land near the boundary with A/Eltrive, close to the southern extremity of both farms.

167(c) **where the Duke of Buccleuch's land, the Laird of Drummelzier's, and Lord Napier's, meet** Hogg apparently describes accurately the three main proprietorships in the early 18th century. The Buccleuch family had long held extensive lands in Yarrow Parish, including the farms of A/Eltrive and Eldinhope. In Hogg's earlier fiction, *The Brownie of Bodsbeck* (1818), William Hay of Drummelzier (1649–1726) is the Laird of the lands in the Chapelhope/Riskinhope area, at the foot of Loch of the Lowes, and maps show Riskinhope Hope and sheepfolds close up to Cowan's Croft. The Scotts of Thirlestane, who acquired the title Napier through marriage in 1699, were also considerable landholders in the region (see also note on 'fair at Thirlestane' for 169(d)). Most obviously, Hogg is thinking of the division between the farms of Berrybush (acquired in the 18th century by the Buccleuch family from Scott of Harden), Riskinhope, and Thirlestane. Modern Ordnance Survey maps show a meeting of three boundaries at the top of Cowan's Croft, where wire fences are presently found. For the custom of burying suicides on boundaries, see note on 171(a).

167(d) **nephew of that Mr. Anderson's** Hogg might possibly have in mind here the Andersons of Cossarshill, a farm in Ettrick, who in Hogg's day through family descent (presumably via James Anderson of A/Eltrive and Alison Boston) were the guardians of the Rev. Thomas Boston's effects—see James Russell, *Reminiscences of Yarrow*, 2nd edn (Selkirk, 1894), p. 17. See also Hogg's account of 'my friend the late Mr. James Anderson' in 'Storms' (1819): *The Shepherd's Calendar*, ed. by Douglas S. Mack (Edinburgh: Edinburgh University Press, 1995), p. 17.

167(d) **one hundred and five years next month** the right month, albeit six years out (i.e. 1718), but at the same time placing events within the lifetime of James Anderson of A/Eltrive (see note on 166(c)). The subsequent folk computation leads to at least 111 years back, and matches the chronology in the main story.

168(a) **William Shiel and W. Sword** both common surnames in the districts of Yarrow and Ettrick. According to a letter of *c.* 1895 from William Amos to Mrs Garden, Hogg's daughter, William Shiel was a shepherd in Berrybush (to the immediate south of A/Eltrive), and it was he and another shepherd who first disturbed the grave: Turnbull MS Papers 42, Item 88, quoted by Douglas S. Mack, in 'The Suicide's Grave in *The Confessions of a Justified Sinner*', *Newsletter of the James Hogg Society*, no. 1 (May 1982), pp. 8–11 (p. 10). Yarrow Old Parish Records show two William Shiels born 1800/1: on 21 June 1800 James Shiel herd at Singlee and Agnes Anderson his wife had a son named William, and on 8 May 1801 William Shiel herd at Dewchar and Beatrice Anderson his wife also had a son named William. A William Sword is listed in the 1841 Ettrick Parish Census at Thirlestane Cottage aged 47, which would make him 28 or 29 in 1823. A Jamie Sword features in Hogg's 'A Shepherd's Wedding', first published in 'Tales and Anecdotes of the Pastoral Life. No III', *Blackwood's Edinburgh Magazine*, 1 (June 1817), 247–50 (pp. 249–50). The name Shiel also matches that of 'old Wat Shiel', who reportedly gave news of the arrival of Walter Scott to see Hogg at Ettrick in 1802: see Introduction, p. xvii.

169(c) my townsman and fellow collegian, Mr. L——t of C——d, advocate John Gibson Lockhart of Chiefswood (1794–1854), Sir Walter Scott's son-in-law and biographer. Lockhart spent his boyhood in Glasgow and was educated at Glasgow College before attending Balliol College, Oxford, a career pattern similar to that of his close associate on *Blackwood's Edinburgh Magazine*, John Wilson (the 'Christopher North' to whom Hogg's letter was originally addressed). Chiefswood is the cottage on the Abbotsford estate which Lockhart and his wife Sophia occupied as summer quarters from their marriage in 1820 till 1825, when Lockhart left for London. Hogg's letter to Lockhart of 31 July [1823], stating that he has dedicated his *Three Perils of Woman* (1823) to him, is addressed to 'John G. Lockhart Esq. / Chiefswood' (NLS, MS 924, no. 87). Walter Scott describes the Lockharts as being currently his 'lodgers' at Abbotsford in a letter to Maria Edgeworth of 22 September 1823 (see *Letters*, ed. by H. J. C. Grierson, 12 vols (London, 1932–37), VIII, 92). The use of disguised names with missing letters, as used here and below, matches Lockhart's own practice in his *Peter's Letters to his Kinsfolk* (1819), and also, more generally, satires in *Blackwood's*.

169(d) a romantic and now classical country 'classical' now because of Walter Scott's writings. Compare Hogg's description of Abbotsford as 'that dear bought and classical estate' in his 'Anecdotes of Sir W. Scott': see *Anecdotes of Scott*, ed. by Jill Rubenstein (Edinburgh: Edinburgh University Press, 1999), p. 28.

169(d) Mr. L——w William Laidlaw (1780–1845), Sir Walter Scott's steward at Abbotsford (1817–27), and a friend of Hogg's from early youth. Laidlaw was the son of Mr Laidlaw of Blackhouse, a distant relative of Hogg's mother, for whom Hogg worked as a shepherd from 1790 to 1800. It was through Laidlaw that Hogg met Scott at Ettrick in 1802 (see Introduction, pp. xvii–xviii, for a fuller account). Laidlaw was also an early contributor to *Blackwood's Edinburgh Magazine*, and in the present story might be said to occupy an ambiguous position, with one foot in gentry culture, the other in the farming community.

169(d) fair at Thirlestane Thirlestane fair was held in Ettrick valley, at the foot of Thirlestane Hill, on the left bank of the river about 3 miles NE from Ettrick hamlet. Its establishment by William John Napier (1786–1834), 8th Baron Napier from 1823, is described and commended in Hogg's article 'The Honourable Captain Napier and Ettrick Forest', *Blackwood's Edinburgh Magazine*, 13 (February 1823), 175–88: 'These markets have proved [...] of the greatest utility to Ettrick Forest, and the districts adjacent—in particular, the lamb fair in July, and the ewe fair in September' (p. 181). A fold-out map 'Sketch of the Farm of Thirlestane' in Napier's own *A Treatise on Practical Store-Farming, as applicable to the mountainous region of Etterick Forest* (Edinburgh, 1822) shows the fairground near to Hopehouse, on the other side of Hopehouse Burn, and close to the beginning of 'Road to St. Mary's Loch' (otherwise known as the Captain's Road) which is depicted as passing alongside the hills of Cowan's Croft and Fall Law. The seasonal months of the four markets are given in the account (1833) of Ettrick Parish in *The New Statistical Account of Scotland*, 15 vols (Edinburgh and London, 1845), III, 'Selkirk', 75–76: 'The third is in the month of September, for the sale of *draft ewes* and small lambs, and for the purchasing of tups and fat sheep. This is the largest of the four, and is a very important market for the seller and purchaser. From 8000 to 10,000 head of stock have stood in it, and many of them exchanged owners.' The autumn fair in 1823 took place on Wednesday, 24 September, and was reported in the *Edinburgh Evening Courant* as a considerable success: 'a very great number of sheep of different descriptions were exhibited, and mostly sold off. [...] There was a greater demand, and higher prices given for good tups at this fair than in several of the by past years, which clearly shows that the spirit for improvement in this part of the country is still alive among the farmers, and where aided by the generous indulgence of the landlords, its good effects are daily becoming more visible' (Saturday, 27 September, 1823). Hogg's earlier participation is evident from a letter to Peter Phillips (his father-in-law), 3 August 1820, in which he mentions having stayed at Thirlestane Castle with 'the Hon. captain Napier and his lady', and also remarks 'I have four bughts [i.e. pens of sheep] to sell at Thirlstane fair' (NLS, MS 2245, fol. 40).

170(a) ancient royal burgh of Selkirk county town of Selkirkshire, at the entries to the Ettrick and Yarrow valleys.

170(a) romantic village, nigh to some deep linns on the Ettrick Ettrickbridge, a small settlement about 8 miles up Ettrick Water from Selkirk. Rapids in the river are visible from the bridge, as well as pools of quiet water.

170(a) *paulies*, a species of stock *paulies*, as used by Hogg as a character within the story, means underdeveloped or ailing lambs, and so is not a 'species of stock' at all. This is picked up as a defining moment by Emma Letley, in 'Some Literary Uses of Scots in Hogg's *Confessions of a Justified Sinner* and *The Brownie of Bodsbeck*', in *Papers given at the First Conference of the James Hogg Society*, ed. by Gillian Hughes (Stirling, 1983), pp. 29–39: 'The qualifications of *foot* and *paulies* register the Editor's distance from the material to which he is exposed' (p. 32).

170(c) W—m B—e, a great original most obviously expandable to William Beattie. Beattie was a local name in Ettrick, where two John Beatties, a father and son, held the post of schoolmaster for 101 consecutive years (see *Transactions of the Hawick Archaeological Society*, 1064, 'Ettrick Kirkyard', Stone 95, p. 55). Mary Beattie, daughter of the second John Beattie, married Hogg's elder brother, William, in 1798, and features in Hogg's 'Storms' (1819): see *The Shepherd's Calendar*, ed. by Douglas S. Mack (Edinburgh: Edinburgh University Press, 1995), pp. 17–18. More particularly, Ettrick kirkyard has a gravestone with the legend 'In Memory of WILLIAM BEATTIE who died at Thirlestane Lodge 12th Nov. 1827 aged 65 yrs' (*Transactions*, Stone 98, p. 59). Granted the local origin of comparable figures in the text, and in view of the equally large dashes supplied by the first edition, this seems a more plausible completion of the name than William Blake, the poet, which has been proposed by David Groves: see his '"W—m B—e, a Great Original": William Blake, The Grave, and James Hogg's *Confessions*', *Scottish Literary Journal*, 18: 2 (November 1991), 27–45. As noted earlier by John Carey in his 1969 edition, a Willie Beattie appears (albeit briefly) as a character in 'A Shepherd's Wedding', first published in 'Tales and Anecdotes of the Pastoral Life. No III', *Blackwood's Edinburgh Magazine*, 1 (June 1817), 247–50 (p. 249). An 'old man named Willie Beattie' is also the chosen spokesman of his fellow shepherds, for the voicing of their complaints about their master's son, in 'The Renowned Adventures of Basil Lee': see *Winter Evening Tales*, 2 vols (Edinburgh, 1820), I, 9. The phrase 'great original' interestingly echoes Hogg's account of Walter Scott's groom ('a greater original than his master') on the 1802 visit to Ettrick when Scott and Hogg met:

see *Anecdotes of Scott*, ed. by Jill Rubenstein (Edinburgh: Edinburgh University Press, 1999), p. 38; also Introduction to this edition, pp. xvii–xviii.

170(d) Mr. S—t there were a number of Scotts in the vicinity, including the tenants of Eldinhope, immediately adjacent to A/Eltrive, and Hogg's closest neighbours. Another possibility is that Hogg is somewhat slyly referring to William John (Captain) Napier, the proprietor of Thirlestane and Lord Napier from 1823, whose original family name was Scott, and who was evidently an avid preserver of curiosities at Thirlestane House (see T. Craig-Brown, *History of Selkirkshire*, 2 vols (Edinburgh, 1886), I, 321, 325). In his essay 'The Honourable Captain Napier and Ettrick Forest', Hogg made a point of noting Napier's descent from 'a family of Scotts, of high Border lineage and fame', while generally praising him for taking 'one of his father's farms into his own hand, the same on which the castle of his forefathers stood in former generations': *Blackwood's Edinburgh Magazine*, 13 (February 1823), 175–88 (pp. 176, 180). It has also been suggested that on one level Walter Scott might have been in Hogg's mind, with this figure's later appropriation of the clasp knife found in the grave representing a kind of replay of Scott's 1802 Ettrick visit in search of ballads: see Introduction to this edition, pp. xvii–xviii, xxxiii.

170(d) Faw-Law Fall Law, a hill top (1828 feet), about half-a-mile NNW of the adjacent Cowan's Croft (see note on 165(d)). The summit as well as the ridge called Fall Law Shank are within Berrybush Farm, which belonged from the early 18th century to the Buccleuch family.

171(a) customary in the south of Scotland traditionally suicides could not be buried in consecrated ground. In England the old practice of burial at crossroads at night, with a stake through the body, was abolished by an Act of Parliament (8 July 1823), allowing burial in ordinary churchyards between 9 p.m. and midnight, without religious ceremony: see S. C. Hall, *Retrospect of a Long Life*, 2 vols (London, 1883), I, 44–45; also *The Statutes of the United Kingdom of Great Britain and Ireland 5 Geo IV Vol. IX–Part II*, pp. 166–67. This legislation, however, does not appear to have applied directly to Scotland. An instance of the country burial of a suicide in Scotland, involving boundary lines, can be found in the case in Hawick *c.* 1790 of Tibbie Tamson, a woman of 'weak intellect' accused of stealing yarn: 'Refused interment in the churchyard, [...] Tibbie's corpse was handed over to [...] the burgh constable, to be buried at the junction of three lairds' lands, according to the ignorant prejudice of the time. Long before the place was reached the rude coffin had been broken in splinters, and the dead woman was dragged over the ground just as she was cut down. A Christian named Michael Stewart, a dyker in the Duke of Buccleuch's service, placed a rude stone at the head of the grave, which he actually re-opened that he might repair the indecent haste shown at her burial. In the woman's pocket he found one penny and one farthing' (T. Craig-Brown, *History of Selkirkshire*, 2 vols (Edinburgh, 1886), II, 174–75). An instance of a woman murderer who had hanged herself being 'buried in two or three Laird's grounds clandestinely, but still raised by the order of the proprietors' is recorded in 'The Judgment and Justice of God Exemplified', a pamphlet first published in 1781, and reprinted as an Appendix to the 1824 Glasgow edition of John Howie's *Biographia Scoticana* (see there under 'William Smith in Moor-mailing', p. xlviii). While it might seem that such practices had a superstitious origin (the boundary lines, for instance, giving the sign of the cross to ward off the devil), the true reasons are probably more practical and mundane. The old practice of burying at or outside a boundary line as a means of getting out of the way an embarrassing corpse is noted in Alexander Murray, *Suicide in the Middle Ages*, vol. II, 'The Curse on Self-Murder' (Oxford: Oxford University Press, 2000), p. 49. After the Reformation in Scotland the provision of the kirkyard burial ground was held to be the responsibility of the heritors (landed proprietors) in a parish; and in the case of a suicide, in order to ensure that the remains were not deemed to be the responsibility of any one heritor, it seems likely that the practice arose of burying them on the boundaries of estates belonging to a number of proprietors. Hilltops, which often formed boundary lines, would also have the advantage of moving the body as far away as possible from human society. In Hogg's 'Odd Characters', Eppy Telfer, a suicide who has hanged herself, is buried on a hilltop overlooking Ettrick Kirk: 'The body was tied on a deal, carried to the peak of the Wedder Law, and interred there': see *The Shepherd's Calendar*, ed. by Douglas S. Mack (Edinburgh: Edinburgh University Press, 1995), p. 114.

171(a) Mr. David Anderson at their head the full name evidently of the tenant of A/Eltrive: see also note on 166(b).

171(a) invariable rule legally so, as well as by custom: not until 1882 in English law were suicides granted the right of burial in daylight.

171(b) house of Berry-Knowe Berry Knowe (1348 feet) is roughly midway between Hartleap and Fall Law, themselves separated by over 3 miles of moorland bog, and overlooks the farm of Berrybush from the immediate north. The latter, described by T. Craig-Brown as 'a forest-steading, situated at an elevation of 1300 feet, on the top of the high hills that divide Ettrick from Yarrow', was on the rent roll of the Scotts of Harden before passing to the Buccleuch family in the early 18th century: *History of Selkirkshire*, 2 vols (Edinburgh, 1886), I, 388. John Ainslie's 1772 map of Selkirkshire appears to show an additional habitation called Berry Know, possibly a shieling, but it is most likely that Hogg is referring here to Berrybush farmhouse. It was on 'the Moor Brae of Berry Knowe' that Hogg later said that he saw the Brocken Spectre effect ('a double shadow of myself') in April 1785: see 'Nature's Magic Lantern', in *Chambers's Edinburgh Journal*, 28 September 1833, pp. 273–74; also note on 29(b).

171(c) Robert Laidlaw, one of the five men who buried the body not identified as an individual, though Laidlaw (Hogg's mother's maiden name) was pervasive as a surname in the district. Hogg's uncle Robert Laidlaw, mentioned in 'Storms' (1819) as 'a maternal uncle whom I loved', is recorded in Ettrick kirkyard as having 'died at Hopehouse June 29th 1800 aged 72', which places him somewhat too late for the events being described (*The Shepherd's Calendar*, ed. by Douglas S. Mack (Edinburgh: Edinburgh University Press, 1995), p. 6; *Transactions of the Hawick Archaeological Society*, 1964, Stone 67, p. 58). Hogg might also have been thinking of an ancestor of his friend William Laidlaw (see note on 169(d)), whose family farmed at Blackhouse up Douglas Burn, and from where Laidlaw and Scott had come in 1802 on their visit to Hogg in Ettrick. If so this would provide a direct parallel with Laidlaw's participation in the present excavation of the grave. Mention of 'five men' in the burial party here also matches the five participants in the Editor's excavation, as well as echoing the 'five men', including Hogg and Scott, who visited Rankleburn in pursuit of 'relics of antiquity' as part of the 1802 visit (*Anecdotes of Scott*, ed. by Rubenstein, p. 39; see also Introduction, pp. xviii).

171(c) grey stone standing at the head John Carey in his edition of 1969 notes 'A 2 ft. x 1 ft. slab, rather like a gravestone, still stands on top of a cairn on Fall Law'. A more recent climb in 1999 confirmed the presence of a cairn on the hilltop, consisting of a pile of mixed stones, but with none noticeably similar to that reported earlier.

172(b) I am no phrenologist a reference to the practice, now considered a pseudo-science, of attempting to deduce a person's character from the contours of the skull. A Phrenological Society was instituted in 1820 in Edinburgh, which became a recognised centre for the activity, and the phrenologist George Combe (1788–1858) began to lecture on this subject in 1822. For further commentary, and the possibility of links with the genesis of *Confessions*, see Introduction, pp. l–liii.

172(b) **above the vent of the ear** considered the site of 'Destructiveness' in phrenological terms (see previous note). In *Transactions of the Phrenological Society instituted
22d February 1820* (Edinburgh, 1824), there is a fold-out illustration placed immediately before 'Outlines of Phrenology' by George Combe, showing 'Propensity of
Destructiveness' just above the left ear. The accompanying text (p. 69) reads:
'DESTRUCTIVENESS.–The special faculty of this organ seems to be the propensity
to destroy in general. [...] The organ is conspicuous in the heads of cool and
deliberate murderers, and persons habitually delighting in acts of cruelty, who are
also generally found to be deficient in the higher sentiments.' This propensity
(alongside 'Secretiveness') can be seen marked on plaster heads deriving from the
heyday of Phrenology.

173(c) **Mr. R——n of W——n L——e** John Carey in his edition (1969) suggests James
Anderson of Wilton Lodge, a mansion with considerable grounds near Hawick,
with the supposition that the typesetter misread the initial 'A' as 'R', in Hogg's
manuscript. Carey's source for the identification is Robert Wilson, *A Sketch of the
History of Hawick* (Hawick, 1825), which describes 'Wilton Lodge, within a quarter
of a mile of the town [...] Its Proprietor enjoys the afternoon of life here, and in
drawing upon his own intellectual treasures, the fruits of an active early life, and
of a cultivated understanding' (p. 6). Anderson is listed as one of the subscribers
to Wilson's work, along with his neighbours H. E. Scott of Harden and J. C. Scott
of Sinton, whom Carey proposes as possible models for 'Mr Sc—t' in the story.
Previously Wilton Lodge had been the residence of Francis Lord Napier (1758–
1823): see James Russell, *Reminiscences of Yarrow*, 2nd edn (Selkirk, 1894), pp. 18,
130. The house and estate appear to have been sold to Anderson for £12,000 in
1805, as recorded in a deed disposing of property in Wilton parish, National
Archives of Scotland, RD2/294. In view of this connection, it seems even more
plausible that 'Mr Sc—t' in the story represents the present Lord Napier (see note
on 170(d)), with Anderson in Hawick (about 18 miles from Thirlestane House)
being the neighbourly recipient of the clasp knife. James Anderson (1757–1833)
had enjoyed a distinguished career in India, where he was for a while British
Resident at the court of Mahadji Scindia, the greatest of the Maratha war-chiefs.
The likelihood of error through misreading is perhaps more likely, in this instance, owing to this disguised name appearing in the last (short) gathering in the
first edition, which Hogg might not have read in proof in the rush to complete.
However, the identification is still based on supposition, and there is also the
possibility of a double disguise in this case.

174(a) **or than even a tanner's** on the basis that a tanner's body, because of the nature
of his trade, would be specially well-preserved. Compare the Gravedigger in *Hamlet*, V.1.163: 'A tanner will last you nine year.'

174(c) **FIDELI CERTA MERCES** *Latin* for the faithful, the reward is sure.

Glossary

This Glossary sets out to provide a convenient guide to Scots, English, and other words in *The Private Memoirs and Confessions of a Justified Sinner* which may be unfamiliar in meaning to some readers. It is greatly indebted to the *Oxford English Dictionary*, to the *Scottish National Dictionary*, and to the *Concise Scots Dictionary*, ed. by Mairi Robinson (Aberdeen: Aberdeen University Press, 1985), to which the reader requiring more information is advised to refer. The Glossary concentrates on single words, and guidance on expressions, phrases and idioms involving more than one word will normally be found in the explanatory Notes.

a': all
ado: to do
advising: warning, counselling
ae: one
aff: off
affray: a disturbance, a fight
afore: before
aften: often
ain: own
aince: once
aith: an oath
amang: among
an: if
an', an: and
anathema: a curse; a denunciation consigning a person to damnation
ane: one
aneath: beneath
anent: about, concerning
anither: another
arrestment: the action of arresting or stopping; seizure by legal authority
atween: between
auld: old
auld ane, the: the devil
auld thief, the: the devil
aumuses: alms, food or money given in charity
aw: I
aw: all
awa: away

awthegither: altogether
ay, aye: yes
aye: always, still
ayont: beyond, on the other side (of)

bagnio: a brothel
baillie: a town magistrate
bairn: a child
baith: both
bane: a bone
bannet: a bonnet, a soft flat cap worn by males
be: by
bedstrae: bedstraw, straw forming bedding
belang: belong
betimes: at an early hour, early in the morning
bicker: a beaker, a bowl
bigging: a building
binna: be not, is not
bit: (with omission of 'of') indicating smallness, familiarity, or contempt
boardly: burly
bodle: a copper coin worth two pence Scots
body: a person
bourock: a hovel; a mound
bouzy: boozy, drunken
bow-kail: cabbage(-like)
brae: a hillside
braid: broad

braidside: the whole side, the breadth

braird: first shoots of grass or grain crops

braw: fine, splendid

brikkin: breaking

brook: to endure, to bear

brooked: possessed, used

brunstane: brimstone

bumming: droning

burn: a brook or stream

bye-way: a side road, a way other than the highway

byeword: a proverbial saying, a pet phrase

byre: a cowshed

ca': call

cabal: a faction, a small party engaged in a secret intrigue

caddy: a messenger, an errand boy

callant: a young man, a boy

calm: a qualm, a sudden feeling of sickness

canna: cannot

canny: fortunate, of good omen; with negative: supernatural (see *uncanny*)

canonical: relating to the church or scripture

carl: a man, a fellow; a man of the common people

casement: a frame forming a window or part of a window, opening on hinges

cast: an opportunity, a chance; a toss (of the head)

cast: defeated (in an action at law)

cast: to dig out, to cut (peat)

cauler: fresh, just caught

chafts: jaws, cheeks

chaperon: a hood or cap formerly worn by nobles

chiel: a man, a young fellow

circumfauld: to surround

clachan: a small village, a hamlet

claes: clothes

clapper-claw: to beat, to claw at

claymore: a large two-edged Highland sword

cloot: a hoof

close: a passageway, a narrow entry

clouted: repaired, patched up

coal-heugh: a coal-pit

commonty: shared land for grazing, cutting peats, etc.

connex: an item of property connected with another, an appurtenance (in Scots law normally used in conjunction with *annex*)

contrair: contrary, opposite

corant: a dance with a running or gliding (as opposed to leaping) step

corbie, corby-craw: the raven

coudna: could not

countervail: to counterbalance, to act against

court: a covered enclosure for cattle

covert: hiding, concealment; a hiding-place

crap: crept

creeshy: fat, greasy

croft: a piece of arable land adjacent to a house (hence 'toft and croft')

croon: to moan, to sing in a wailing voice

croup: to croak, to caw

cue: a hint, a guiding suggestion

cuif: a fool, a simpleton

daft: foolish, crazy

dangler: one who hangs around, a dallying follower

darkling: in the dark; characterised by darkness

day, the: today

dee: to do

dee: to die

deil: devil

depone: to testify, to declare on oath

depute-advocate: an advocate (barrister) appointed by the Lord Advocate to prosecute in court

deray: confusion, disorder

didna: did not

dike: a field wall

ding: to beat, to overcome

dinna: do not

disgustful: sickening, repulsive

dishclout: a dish-cloth
disna: does not
ditit: foolish, confused
div: do
divot: turf, peat
doesnae: does not
doit: to stumble
doitrified: dazed, stupefied
dominie: a schoolmaster
donnart: dull, stupid
doom: a judicial sentence
doubt: to suspect, to fear
dree: to endure, to suffer
driveller: one who behaves in a babyish or idiotic way
duds: clothes, rags
dung: struck, overcome
durstna: dare not

easter: eastern
een: eyes
ejaculatory: sudden in utterance, expressive
ell: a measure of length originally taken from the forearm
enow: enough
ern: an iron
evite: to avoid, to shun
extrordinar: extraordinary
ey: yes

fa (Aberdeenshire): who
fa': to fall; to befall
fain: gladly, willingly
fand: found, discovered
farrago: a confused mixture, a hotch-potch
fat (Aberdeenshire): what
fawn: fallen
feele: a fool
fer: far
flannen: flannel
flaring: showy behaviour
flinders: small fragments, splinters
flitters: shreds
flummery: flattery, humbug
focks, foks: folk
foot: the lower end (of a piece of ground, etc.)

foreby: besides
fortalice: fortress, fortification
frae: from
fra-yont: from beyond, away from
fraze: exaggerated talk, 'gush'
froward: perverse, refractory, ungovernable

gae: gave
gae: to go
gane: gone
gang: to go
gar: to make, to cause (something to be done)
gate: manner, way, direction
gaun: going
gayan: very
ghaist: ghost
gie: to give
gin: if
gizened: withered, cracked through want of moisture
gloaming: evening twilight
goodman: the head of a household
goodwife, gudewife: the female head of a household
gouden: golden
gowk: a fool, a simpleton; the cuckoo
gritter: greater
groat: a small silver coin
grumphing: grunting, grumbling
gud, gude: good; God
guerdon: reward, recompense
guidit: treated
gull: to dupe, to deceive

ha': hall, house
hae: have
haena: have not
haill, hale: whole, complete
halesale: wholesale
hame: home
hand-fast: to make fast the hands, to manacle; to make a contract by joining hands
haud: to hold
havers: foolish talk, nonsense

heartless: disheartened, dejected

herd: a herdsman

herezeld: the privilege of claiming the best animal belonging to a tenant or vassal on his death

heritably: as a heritable property, by right of inheritance

heritor: a landed proprietor

het: hot

heterodox: heretical, holding wrong opinions

hind: a farm servant

hoad-road: a confusion, a state of chaos

hope: a hollow or small valley among hills

horse-laid: horse-load

houk, howk: to dig; to poke about

hout: an exclamation dismissive of another person's opinion

howlet: the owl

hunder: hundred

ilka: each, every

ill-faurd, ill-favoured: ugly, unpleasant

in-by: further in towards the interior

indictment: a formal written charge in law

ir: are

ither: other

jaud: a term of abuse for a female

jerkin: a bodice worn by women

jest-book: a collection of amusing stories

joyse: to enjoy the possession or use of

juggs: the pillory

keek: to peep

ken: to know

ketch: a heave, a jerk

keust: to cast

kimmer: a gossip or female intimate

kirk: church, particularly the Church of Scotland

kist: a chest, a trunk

laird: a landed proprietor

land: a tenement building divided into flats

lang: long

lave: the rest, the remainder

leal: loyal, faithful

leasing-making: spreading calumny, verbal sedition

leear: a liar

libel: to specify (in an indictment)

lift: the sky

linn: a waterfall; a pool below a waterfall or in a gorge

lint-swingling: flax-beating, the social evening spent at this task

loaden: laden

loom-spoke: a weaver's beam, a yarn-roll

loun: a low-born person, a rascal

lounder: to strike with heavy blows, to wallop

luck-penny: a sum of money traditionally returned by the seller in a bargain

Lucky: familiar name for an older woman, more specifically the mistress of an ale-house

ma: my

mae: more

mair: more

maist: most

maister: master

mak: to make

make: a figure, a form

mal-a-propos: inopportune, inappropriate

mall: a mallet; a wooden instrument for striking a ball

manse: a minister's house

march: a boundary

margin: a marginal note, an explanatory indication

maugre: in spite of, notwithstanding

maun: must

meeting-house: a place of worship (used in Scotland especially to describe those not of the established Kirk)

mell: to strike as with a heavy hammer

mem: ma'am

mense: respect, regard

merk: mark, a silver coin worth two-thirds of a pound or 13s. 4d. (in Scots money then worth slightly more than 1s. sterling)

miethes: boundary marks

milled: pressed, rolled

mind: to remember, to bear in mind

mony: many

moss: boggy ground; ground used for cutting peat

muckil: large

muckle: much

muir: a moor

multure: a duty paid for milling grain

mysel: myself

na: no

nae: no, not

neist: next

no: not

nook: a corner

nor: than

o': of

obeisance: a salutation, a bow; deference, respect

obsequies: funeral rites or ceremonies

od: in mild oaths, 'God'

o'er: too

ony: any

orisons: prayers

our: over

outfield: belonging to the outlying parts of a farm

overhie: to overtake by hastening after

ower: over; too

pack-laid: pack-load

packman: a pedlar, a travelling salesman

pat: to put

paulies: undersized lambs

pearls: perils

peeous: pious

pendicle: a portion of a larger farm let separately

pharisaical: resembling the Pharisees in outward show of spiritual pride and superiority

phiz: countenance, face

pin: a peg, a bolt

pink: finest example, 'the flower' (of)

pirn: a spool, a bobbin on which thread is wound

pit: to put

plack: a small copper coin usually valued at four pence Scots

plaid: a rectangular piece of woollen cloth, used as an outer garment (marled grey plaids were worn by shepherds in the south of Scotland)

plaiding: woollen material, as used for plaids

plaint: an enclosure for planting, a garden

poltroon: a coward, a worthless fellow

pomatum: a scented ointment (usually used in hair dressing)

poniard: a dagger

post: to travel speedily, to make haste

pouk: to pluck

prelatic: supporting prelacy, episcopalian

professor: one who makes public profession of religion; an acknowledged adherent of a religious doctrine

pund: a pound

quo: said

rack: to stretch

rag-of-a-muffin: a rough, disorderly, good-for-nothing man or boy

raip: a rope

reard: to roar, to cry

rede: to advise, to warn

reek: smoke

reid: red

reistit: halted, arrested

rencounter: surprise meeting, hostile encounter

rin: to run

rip: a worthless fellow

rowth: plenty, abundance

sae: so

saif: see under 'sauf'

sanna: shall not
sauchless: senseless, guileless
sauf: save
saur: a smell, a savour
scouder: to scorch
scragged: rough and irregular
shagged: jagged; covered with scrub
shan: to make a wry face, to grimace
sib: related to, allied with
sic, siccan, sickan: such
siller: silver
sin': since
skair: to scour
skimmer: to glide along, to skim quickly
slack: to slacken, to render less taut
slough: outer skin, covering layer
snork: to snort, to breathe noisily
sooth: truth, verity
speeder: the spider
spleuchan: a (tobacco) pouch
spokes: set of wooden poles used for carrying a body to burial
stamock: the stomach
stane: a stone
stinkard: name given to various animals who use foul smell as a defence mechanism
stint: to cease, to stop
stock: a neck-tie
stott: a bullock
stoup: a drinking vessel, a decanter
strathspey: a Scottish dance slower than the reel
strick: strict
strodge: to strut, to stride along
superannuation: senility, infirmity
swee: sway, course
swire: a hollow, either near the top of a hill or between two hills

taen, ta'en: taken
tak: to take
tane: the one (of two)
tap: top
tauld: told
tawpie: a foolish, slovenly young woman
tent: care, notice

thae: these, those
thrang: a throng, a crowd
thretty: thirty
throng: busy, crowded
tike: a dog, a cur
till: to
tither: the other (of two)
toft: a homestead
tolbooth: a town prison or jail
toom: empty
trams: legs
treadle: a foot-lever for working a machine
trow: to believe, to think
trust: trusty, faithful
twa: two
twanty: twenty
tweeled: woven with a twill (i.e. having diagonal ridges on the surface)

uncanny: unnatural and dangerous, linked with the supernatural
unco: very, remarkably
unco-like: strange, extraordinary
unguent: an ointment, a salve

vapouring: boastful, pretentious
vera: very
vert: the right to cut trees or shrubs in a forest

wab: a web
wad: would
wadna: would not
wair: meaning uncertain, but possibly referring to rights relating to a weir or dam
waith: the right to unclaimed lost property
war: were
waratch: a wretch
wark: work
warlock: a wizard, a male witch
warpings: the threads of a warp (i.e. those extending lengthways in a loom)
wasna: was not
wauken: waken

waur: worse

wee: little

weel: well

ween: to think, to suppose

weird: fate, destiny

wha: who

whan: when

whaten: what kind of, what sort of

whiles: sometimes

wi': with

wife: a woman (found especially as 'auld wife/wives')

wight: a human being, a person

windlestrae: a long, withered stalk of grass; figuratively and contemptuously, a weapon

winna: will not

wire-drawn: fine-spun, elaborately subtle

wist: past tense of 'wit', to know

woodriff: the woodruff

woo-stapler, wool-stapler: merchant who buys wool from the producer, and sells it to the manufacturer

wore: guarded, warded off

wraik: the right to salvage goods from a wrecked vessel

wrang: wrong

writer: a solicitor

wynd: a narrow (usually winding) alley

ye: you

yelloch: a yell, a scream

yerk: a blow, a hard knock

ye's: you shall

yestreen: yesterday evening

yool: to howl, to wail

yowe: a ewe

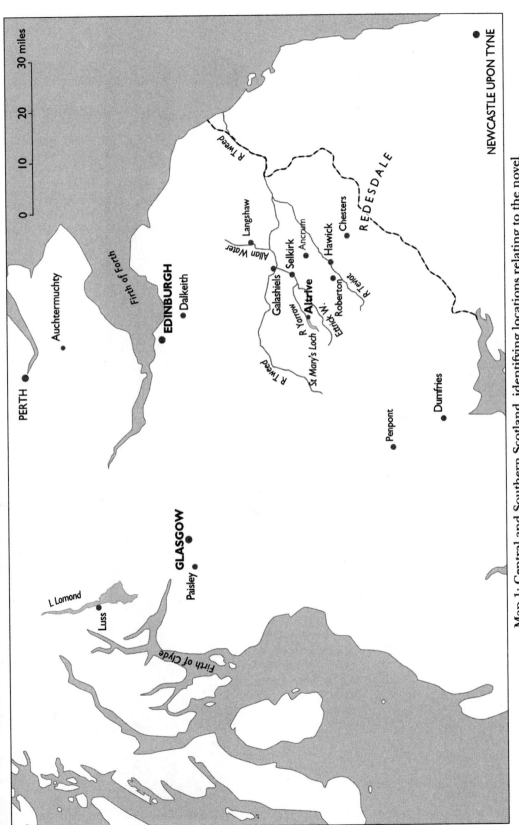

Map 1: Central and Southern Scotland, identifying locations relating to the novel

Map 2: Edinburgh from the North, John Slezer. Engraving included in the 4th edn of *Theatrum Scotiae* (1719), but from a drawing *c.* 1690, and possibly issued separately before 1719.

Map 3: From William Edgar's Plan of the City and Castle of Edinburgh, 1742 (showing western portion). 'L' in the High Street represents the Market Cross, and 'M' to its right the Town Guard House.

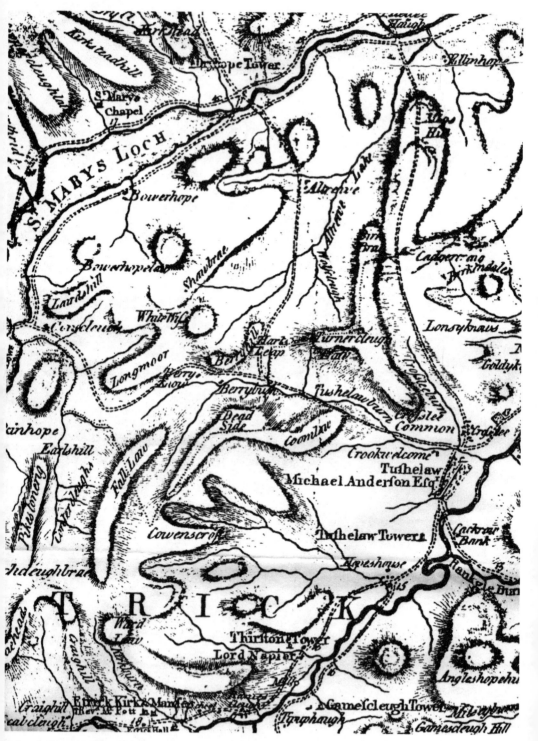

Map 4: From 'A Map of Selkirkshire or Ettrick Forest, from a survey taken in 1772, by John Ainslie' (published 1773). Courtesy of Map Library, National Library of Scotland.